NEWS FROM THE EMPIRE

Originally published in Spanish as *Noticias del Imperio* by Diana literaria, 1987
Copyright © Fernando del Paso, 1987
Translation copyright © Alfonso González & Stella T. Clark, 2009
First English translation, 2009

Library of Congress Cataloging-in-Publication Data

Paso, Fernando del, 1935-
[Noticias del Imperio. English]
 News from the Empire / Fernando del Paso ; translation by Alfonso Gonzalez and
Stella T. Clark.
   p. cm.
 ISBN 978-1-56478-533-6 (pbk. : alk. paper)
 1. Paso, Fernando del, 1935---Translation into English. I. González, Alfonso, 1938- II.
Clark, Stella T. III. Title.
 PQ7298.26.A76N6813 2009
 862'.64--dc22

                    2008048684

Partially funded by grants from the National Endowment for the Arts, a federal
agency; the Illinois Arts Council, a state agency; and by the University of Illinois
at Urbana-Champaign

La presente traducción fue realizada con apoyo del Programa de Apoyo a la Traducción
de Obras Mexicanas en Lenguas Extranjeras (PROTRAD).

This translation was carried out with the support of the Program to Support the Translation of Mexican Works into Foreign Languages (PROTRAD).

www.dalkeyarchive.com

Cover: design by Danielle Dutton; photo of Empress Charlotte shot in 1867 (Photo by
Hulton Archive/Getty Images)

Printed on permanent/durable acid-free paper and bound in the United States
of America

NEWS FROM THE EMPIRE
FERNANDO DEL PASO

translated by Alfonso González
& Stella T. Clark

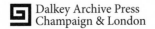 Dalkey Archive Press
Champaign & London

CONTENTS

I

BOUCHOUT CASTLE, 1927   1

II

MAY YOU FIND YOURSELF BETWEEN NAPOLEONS, 1861–62
1. Juárez and Mustachoo   17
2. From Last Night's Ball at the Tuileries   36
3. The King of Rome   48

III

BOUCHOUT CASTLE, 1927   57

IV

A MATTER FOR WOMEN, 1862–63
1. *Partant pour le Méxique*   72
2. The Archduke at Miramare   88
3. From the Correspondence—Incomplete—between Two Brothers   96

V

BOUCHOUT CASTLE, 1927   107

VI

"A PRETTY BOY THIS ARCHDUKE TURNED OUT TO BE," 1863
1. Brief Account of the Siege of Puebla   122
2. "That's Correct, Mr. President"   142
3. The City and Its Vendors   161

VII

BOUCHOUT CASTLE, 1927   177

VIII

"MUST I LEAVE MY GOLDEN CRIB FOREVER?" 1863–64
1. Cittadella Accepts the Throne of Tours   193
2. "Camarón, Camarón . . ."   217
3. From the Correspondence—Incomplete—between Two Brothers   226

IX

BOUCHOUT CASTLE, 1927   239

X

"MASSIMILIANO: NON TE FIDARE," 1864–65
1. From Miramare to Mexico   255
2. With Your Heart Pierced by an Arrow   273
3. Scenes of Daily Life: Mexican Nothingness   284

XI

BOUCHOUT CASTLE, 1927   308

XII

"WE'LL CALL HIM THE AUSTRIAN," 1865
1. "He's Like Jelly . . ."   324
2. "A Man of Letters"   340
3. The Emperor at Miravalle   350

XIII

BOUCHOUT CASTLE, 1927   361

XIV

AN EMPEROR WITHOUT AN EMPIRE, 1865–66
1. Court Chronicles   377
2. Seductions (I): "Not Even with a Thousand Hail Marys?"   398
3. From the Correspondence—Incomplete—between Two Brothers   410

XV

BOUCHOUT CASTLE, 1927   423

XVI

"BYE-BYE, MAMÁ CARLOTA," 1866
1. On the Road to Paradise and Oblivion   439
2. The Manatee of Florida   463
3. *Un Pericolo di Vita*   479

XVII
BOUCHOUT CASTLE, 1927   503

XVIII
QUERÉTARO, 1866–67
1. In the Mousetrap   518
2. *Cimex domesticus Queretari*   538
3. Seductions (II): "Hold It, Hope . . ."   554

XIX
BOUCHOUT CASTLE, 1927   562

XX
LAS CAMPANAS HILL, 1867
1. The Traitorous Friend and the Princess on Her Knees   578
2. Ballad of the Coup de Grâce   601
3. Saint Ursula's Black Eyes   612

XXI
BOUCHOUT CASTLE, 1927   631

XXII
"HISTORY WILL BE OUR JUDGE," 1872–1927
1. "What Are We Going to Do with You, Benito?"   649
2. The Last of the Mexicans   660
3. Ceremonial for the Execution of an Emperor   681

XXIII
BOUCHOUT CASTLE, 1927   692

Acknowledgments   707

For my wife,
Socorro

For my children,
Fernando
Alejandro
Adriana
Paulina

To the memory of my parents,
Fernando
Irene

In 1861 President Benito Juárez suspended payment on the foreign debt of Mexico. This suspension was the pretext that the then-Emperor of the French, Napoleon III, used to send an army of occupation to Mexico with the purpose of creating a monarchy there, at the helm of which would be a European Catholic monarch. An Austrian, Ferdinand Maximilian of Habsburg, was chosen. He arrived in Mexico in the middle of 1864 accompanied by his wife, Princess Charlotte of Belgium. This book is based on these historical facts, and on the story of the tragic end of this ephemeral Emperor and Empress of Mexico.

I
BOUCHOUT CASTLE
1927

"La imaginación, la loca de la casa . . ."
—attributed to Malebranche

I am Marie Charlotte of Belgium, Empress of Mexico and of America. I am Marie Charlotte Amélie, cousin of the Queen of England, Grand Magister of the Cross of Saint Charles, and Vicereine of the Lombardo-Veneto Provinces, which Austria's clemency and mercy has subsumed under the two-headed eagle of the House of Habsburg. I am Marie Charlotte Amélie Victoria, daughter of Leopold, Prince of Saxe-Coburg and King of Belgium, known as "The Nestor of Europe," and who would take me onto his lap, caress my chestnut tresses, and call me the little sylph of the Castle of Laeken. I am Marie Charlotte Amélie Victoria Clémentine, daughter of Louise Marie of Orléans, the saintly queen with the blue eyes and the Bourbon nose who died of consumption and of the sorrow caused by the exile and death of Louis Philippe, my grandfather, who, as the King of France, showered me with chestnuts and covered my face with kisses in the Tuileries Gardens. I am Marie Charlotte Amélie Victoria Clémentine Léopoldine, niece of Prince Joinville and cousin of the Count of Paris; I am sister of the Duke of Brabant, who became King of Belgium and colonized the Congo, and of the Count of Flanders in whose arms I learned to dance, at the age of ten, under the shade of flowering hawthorns. I am Charlotte Amélie, wife of Ferdinand Maximilian Joseph, Archduke of Austria, Prince of Hungary and Bohemia, Count of Habsburg, Prince of Lorraine, Emperor of Mexico and King of the World, who was born in the Imperial Palace of Schönbrunn, and who was the first descendant of the Catholic Monarchs Ferdinand and Isabella to cross the ocean and tread on American soil; who built a white palace for me with a view of the sea on the shores of

1

the Adriatic; who later took me to Mexico to live in a gray castle with a view of the valley and the snowcapped volcanoes and who, on a June morning, many years ago, was executed in the city of Querétaro. I am Charlotte Amélie, Regent of Anáhuac, Queen of Nicaragua, Baroness of Matto Grosso, and Princess of Chichén Itzá. I am Charlotte Amélie of Belgium, Empress of Mexico and America. I am eighty-six years old and for sixty years now I've quenched my lunatic thirst with water from Roman fountains.

Today the messenger arrived with news from the Empire. He came bearing memories and dreams on a caravel whose sails were swelled by a single, luminous gust of wind, teeming with parrots. He brought me a handful of sand from the Isle of Sacrifices, a pair of chamois gloves, and an enormous cask made of precious woods, brimming with hot and foaming chocolate in which I shall bathe every single day for the rest of my life, until my Bourbon-princess skin, my crazed octogenarian skin, my white, Alençon-and-Brussels lace skin, my skin snowy as the magnolias in the Gardens of Miramare, Maximilian, my skin cracked by the centuries and the storms and the fall of dynasties, until my white, Memling-angel skin, my Béguinage-bride skin, disintegrates, and I grow a new skin, dark and aromatic as the chocolate from Soconusco, fragrant as vanilla from Papantla, that will cover my whole body, Maximilian, from my dark brow to the tip of my bare, perfumed, Mexican Indian toes, the toes of a dark Madonna, of an Empress of America.

My dear Max, the messenger also brought me a locket with some hairs from your golden beard, your beard that flowed and fluttered like an enormous golden butterfly on your breast, with its gleaming Aztec Eagle, as you rode through the Apam plains in clouds of glory and dust, clad in your *charro* suit, a sterling-silver trimmed sombrero on your head. They say, Maximilian, that while your body was still warm and your plaster of paris death mask was still wet, those barbarians, those savages yanked out your whiskers and your locks to sell in pieces for a few piastres. Who would have thought, Maximilian, that you would suffer the same fate as your father, if indeed your father was that unfortunate Duke of Reichstadt whom nothing and no one could save from an early grave—not the muriatic acid baths, not the donkey's milk, not the love of your mother, the Archduchess Sophie? Barely a few seconds after he had died in the very same Schönbrunn Palace where you'd just been born, his golden ringlets were all shorn to become pious souvenirs for his people. He was spared, but you were not, Maximilian, from having his heart chopped up in little pieces and sold for a few coins. The messenger told me everything. He heard it from Tüdös, your loyal Hungarian chef, who followed you to the wall and extinguished the flames that had engulfed your waistcoat after the coup de grâce. The messenger brought me a cedar chest from Prince and Princess Salm-Salm, containing a zinc box that held a rosewood box where I found, Maximilian, a piece of your heart next to the bullet that ended your life and your empire, on Las Campanas Hill. All day I clutch that box in my hands so tightly that no one will ever take it from me. My ladies-in-waiting have to spoon-feed me because I never let go of it. Countess d'Hulst feeds me milk as though she were nursing a baby, as though I were still Papa Leopold's little angel, the tiny chestnut-haired Bonapartist, because I cannot let you go.

And that is the only reason, I swear to you, Maximilian, that they say I am mad. That is why they call me The Madwoman of Miramare, of Terveuren, of Bouchout. If they tell you that I was crazy when I left Mexico and that I was crazy when I crossed the ocean, locked up in my stateroom on the *Impératrice Eugénie* after ordering the captain to lower the French flag and to raise the Mexican Imperial tricolor; if they tell you that I never left my stateroom because I'd gone mad, and that I was mad not because they gave me potions in Yucatán nor because I knew that both Napoleon and the Pope would refuse to help us, would abandon us to our fate, to our miserable fate in Mexico, but that I was mad and desperate, lost because I was carrying a son who was not yours but Colonel Van der Smissen's in my womb; if they tell you all of those things, tell them it isn't true, that you always were, and always will be, the love of my life. Tell them that, if I am mad, it is from hunger and thirst, that I have been mad since that fateful day in the Palace of Saint-Cloud when the devil himself, Napoleon III, and his wife Eugenia de Montijo, offered me a glass of cold orangeade, and I knew—everybody knew—that it was poisoned, because it wasn't enough for them to betray us, they wanted to erase us from the face of the Earth, to poison us. And it wasn't only Little Napoleon and that Montijo woman who wanted to kill us, but also our closest friends, our own servants— you won't believe it Max—even Blasio. Beware of the indelible pencil he uses to write the letters that you dictate to him on the way to Cuernavaca, of his saliva, of the sulfurous water of the Cuautla Springs, of the pulque with champagne. Beware, Max, just as I've had to beware of everyone, even of Señora Neri del Barrio who rode along with me to the Trevi Fountain every morning in my black carriage because I made up my mind to drink only the water from the fountains of Rome, and only using the Murano glass that His Holiness Pius IX gave me when I paid him a surprise visit, without asking for an audience, while he ate his breakfast, and he realized that I was starving and dying of thirst. Would the Empress of Mexico like some grapes? Would she care for a buttered croissant? Maybe some milk, Doña Carlota, fresh from a nanny goat? But the only thing I wanted was to wet my fingers in that scalding and foamy liquid that I knew would burn and tan my skin, so I stuck my fingers in His Holiness's hot chocolate. I licked them, Max. I don't know what I would have done, if I hadn't gone to the market myself for the nuts and the oranges I would take to the Albergo di Roma. I chose them all myself; I wiped them clean with the black lace mantilla that Eugenia had given me; I scrutinized their shells and peels, I cracked them and peeled them; I devoured them with some roasted chestnuts that I bought on the Appian Way and I can't imagine how I would have managed without Madame Kuchacsevich and the cat, who tasted all my food before I ate it, or my chambermaid, Mathilde Doblinger, who procured a coal stove and brought me some chickens to the imperial suite so that I could eat only those eggs that I had seen lain with my own eyes.

In those days, Maximilian, when I was the little angel, the sylph of Laeken, who slid down the wooden banister of the palace stairs and played at keeping quiet forever in the gardens while my brother, the Count of Flanders, stood on his head and made faces at me to make me laugh, and my other brother, the Duke of Brabant, made up imaginary cities and told me about famous shipwrecks; in those days, when my father took me out to dinner, just the two of us, and when he crowned me with roses and showered me with presents, I used to visit my grandmother Marie Amélie every year, who lived in Claremont. Do you remember Max, that she told us not to go to Mexico because we would be murdered there? I met my cousins Queen Victoria and Prince Albert in Windsor Castle on one of those trips. In those days, my dear Max, when I was a chestnut-haired child and my bed was a white, warm, downy nest of snow in which my mother Louise Marie would moisten her lips, my cousin Victoria, who marveled that I could recite the name of every English king from Harold to her uncle William IV, rewarded my studiousness with a dollhouse. When it arrived in Brussels, my father Leopich, as I used to call him, summoned me to see it, seated me on his lap, caressed my forehead, and, as he had once done with his niece Victoria, Queen of England, urged me to keep my conscience as immaculate as I would keep my doll house, every night of every day. From that time forward, Maximilian, not a night goes by that I don't put my house and my conscience in order. I air out the livery of my miniature footmen and I forgive you for having cried in Madeira over the death of a girl-friend whom you loved more than me. I wash the thousand minuscule dishes of Sèvres china in a basin, and I forgive you for leaving me alone in my impe-rial bed in Puebla, under its tulle and brocade canopy, while you would lie on a field cot masturbating as you dreamed about the little Countess von Linden. I polish the miniature silver platters, I clean my Lilliputian guards' halberds, I wash the tiny clusters of tiny crystal grapes and I forgive you for making love to a gardener's wife in the shade of a bougainvillea in Borda Gardens. Later, I use a broom, small as a thumb, to sweep castle rugs the size of handkerchiefs. I dust the paintings and I empty a spittoon like a thimble, and the miniature ashtrays, and as I forgive all that you did, I forgive all of our enemies and I forgive Mexico.

How can I not forgive Mexico, Maximilian, when every single day I dust your crown, I polish the insignia of the Order of Guadalupe with ashes, I rub milk on my Biedemeyer piano keys, on which I play the Mexican Imperial Anthem every afternoon? Every day I go down the castle staircase and kneel at the banks of the moat to launder the Mexican Imperial Flag in its waters. I rinse it, I wring it out, and I hang it out to dry from the highest castle tower, and I iron it, Maximilian, I caress it, I fold it and put it away, vowing to take it out again on the morrow so that it may wave before all of Europe, from Ostend to the Carpathians, from Tyrol to Transylvania. And only after that's done, af-ter my house and my conscience are in order, do I undress and put on my mi-nuscule nightdress, say my tiny prayers, and retire to my grand miniature bed. Only then do I put your heart under a pillow the size of a pincushion embroi-dered with thistles, and listen to its beating, as I hear the roar of the cannons from the Citadel in Trieste and from the Rock of Gibraltar when they salute the *Novara,* and as I listen to the clackety-clack of the train from Veracruz to Loma Alta, and I hear the music of the *Domine Salvum fac Imperatorem.* Again, as I hear the gunshots from Querétaro, and I dream, I would like to dream, Maximilian, that we never left Miramare and Lacroma, that we never went to Mexico, that we stayed here, where we grew old, and raised many children and grandchildren, that you stayed here in your blue office decorated with anchors and astrolabes, writing poems about your future journeys on the yacht *Ondina* through the Greek Islands and along the coast of Turkey and dreaming about Leonardo's mechanical bird, and that I stayed behind forever adoring you and drinking the blue of the Adriatic with my eyes. But my own screams woke me up at that point, and I felt so ravenous, Max, you can't imagine, after centuries of only eating anguish and anxiety, and so parched, Max, after centuries of only drinking my own tears, that I devoured your heart and drank your blood. But your heart and blood, my dear, my cherished Max, had both been poisoned.

What a coincidence that the rain we ran into on the way from Paris to Trieste and from Trieste to Rome, Maximilian, had been as heavy as or even heavier than the rain on the night that we arrived in Córdoba. Do you remember that we rode in a government carriage because our imperial coach had lost a wheel on Chiquihuite Hill and we were mud-spattered from head to toe, thanking God that we had left the pestilent jungles of Veracruz behind, its vultures and yellow fever? Do you remember how, in one or two more days, from the foothills of Mount Popocatépetl, we were to behold the same vast transparent valley and city of a thousand palaces built of red lava from the volcanoes and the yellow sands of the swamps that Hernán Cortés and Baron von Humboldt had seen before us? It rained cats and dogs in Savoy and again, as my train and entourage crossed Mount Cenis, all the way through Maribor, Mantua, Reggio, and all those cities we passed through because of the cholera epidemic in Venice, where Italians and Garibaldi's Red Shirts greeted me with cheers and tears, and it rained when your friend, Admiral Tegetthoff, the same one who brought your body from Veracruz to Trieste on board the *Novara*, in a funeral chapel surmounted by an angel's wings, ordered the Austrian Fleet to parade before me in the same formation he had used in the Battle of Lissa that won him his fame. I sent a message to you in Mexico, Max, telling you that if *Plus Ultra* had been the motto and battle cry of your ancestors, it had to be yours as well and that, just as Charles V had pointed the way beyond the Pillars of Hercules, you would have to keep on going. "Thou shalt not abdicate," I told you, "Thou shalt not abdicate." That is the eleventh commandment that God etched with fire in the heart of those rulers to whom he granted the Divine Right, that unrenounceable right, to govern any nation. "Thou shalt not abdicate," I told you a thousand times when you were in Orizaba strolling with Bilimek, as he explained to you how to make soap with castor seeds, and when you played hide-and-seek with Dr. Basch and with General Castelnau in the coffee groves, and amid the white flowers of the manioc plant. I wrote you,

Maximilian. Tell me, did you get my letters? I told them to tell you, "Thou shalt not abdicate"—did they do it?—when you were at the Xonaca Plantation and when you returned to Mexico City, and when you went to Querétaro, yes, even if you have to eat cat and horse meat with your generals Mejía and Miramón, and with your Prince Salm-Salm who threw bread crumbs to your guards. And you, my dear Max, forever a hopeless case, who gave final instructions to Dr. Szänger on the embalming of your body, and dictated to Blasio the changes that you wanted to make in the *Court Ceremonial*, because you never believed that you would really be assassinated, Max, as indeed you were.

So that, during those journeys from Paris to Trieste and from Trieste to Rome, and back again to Trieste, until we arrived at Miramare, all I needed was to stretch out my cupped hands from the carriage to catch the only drink that I could be sure wasn't poisoned—rainwater—as I do now from the castle balconies. There, in the basin that overflows with crystal-clear water, a white dove is perching on its rim. When the messenger comes disguised as a white dove and he brings me the words of the song by Concha Méndez from Cuba, there, in my cupped hands as at the bottom of a patera, I see your face and I drink it sip by sip, your dead face, eyes shut and the weight of all the dust of all the time that's passed since the year of your execution on their lids. That was the same year the waltz of the "Blue Danube" was born. How I would love to have danced it with you. I see your dead face, your eyes staring wide, those black glass beads that they put in your empty sockets in Querétaro. Those glass eyes look at me from far away, from the foot of a hill covered with dirt and cacti. They look at me in wonder as though to ask why and how it is that so many things have happened that you never heard of before.

Did anyone tell you, Maximilian, that the telephone was invented? Or neon gas? And the automobile, Max? Did they tell you that your brother Franz Joseph, who regarded himself as the last ruler of the old school, only rode in a motor car once in his life? Did you know, Maximilian, that in your beloved Vienna, you can never again see the phaetons and the Daumont-style coaches, the chaises, and the landaus, not even those great stud horses, their manes and tails braided in gold, because the streets are crowded with automobiles, Max? Did you know all that? And that the phonograph was invented so that you and I could go on a picnic, just the two of us, with the "Blue Danube" playing in the background just for you and me on the banks of Chapultepec Lake, no musicians lurking in the treetops? So that we could dance under the golden, violet shade of the living, trembling arches of the Avenue of the Poets, with no orchestra hiding under the bridge of the lake, Maximilian? Did you know that nothing remains of the Dianabad, that Viennese ballroom where the "Blue Danube" was played for the first time? That it was destroyed by bombs just like the Palace of Saint-Cloud was, and that nothing remains of Mignard's Olympus, the ceiling mural in the Mars Ballroom where Napoleon and Eugénie offered me a glass of orangeade, the same ballroom where Cambacérès offered the Crown of France to Napoleon Bonaparte? And that all the furnishings and carpets, the colossal mantelpiece crowned by a Gobelin tapestry, are gone forever, leaving only ruins and memories? That nothing remains of the staircase at the foot of which Loulou—the little Imperial Prince—greeted me, wearing the decorations of the Mexican Eagle and of the Arab equestrian guards around his neck? And that only dust and lizards are left in place of the Saint-Cloud Pond and of the boats that the Emperor of Cochin China gave to Loulou?

When I remember all that, Maximilian, it seems unreal that all these years have gone by, that all those days we thought would never arrive have already come and gone. Because, did you know, Maximilian, every day comes—sooner or later—whether or not you believe in it or want it to happen? Every day comes, no matter how distant it may seem. The day you turn eighteen and go to your first ball, the day you marry and are happy. And when your last day comes, the day you die, all of your days become one. And then it turns out that you, that all of us, have always been dead. And—how it hurts me to tell you, Maximilian—it turns out that even when your sister-in-law Sisi was a child who danced in the squares of Bavaria as her father played the violin dressed in gypsy's clothes, she had already been stabbed by the stiletto that a madman plunged into the Empress Elisabeth's breast at the banks of Leman Lake fifty years later. And it turns out, how awful that you have to hear this, that even when your father, the Eaglet, was a child imagining the Battle of Austerlitz and the invasion of Mantua with such amazement while eating his truffled turkey and carrots, his mouth was already full of the blood that would drain away the life of the Duke of Reichstadt in a dark and icy chamber of the Schönbrunn Palace.

Yes, it's very sad, Maximilian, but I have to tell you that every day comes, believe it or not. Yes, the day came when my uncle Ton Ton, Prince Joinville, showed me the watercolors that he painted aboard the ship called *La Belle Poule*, that brought Napoleon the Great's remains back to France from the Isle of St. Helena. The day came when I gathered violets in the Tuileries Gardens and I threw myself into the arms of my grandfather, the Citizen King, he of the pear-shaped head and the black umbrella, to ask him what it felt like to be a king, and I asked my grandmother, Marie Amélie, how it felt to be a queen and to be married. At that time, Maximilian, I never thought that the day would come that I would be, first a wife, and then a wife and a sovereign. But the day came, Maximilian—every day comes sooner or later—on which I became your wife and I was crowned with a tiara of diamonds interwoven with orange blossoms, and wore my veil from Brussels, my brocade shoes from Ypres, my handkerchief from Ghent and the royal cloak on my shoulders from Bruges. And I married a prince, a sailor prince dressed as an admiral and decorated with the Golden Fleece. I married you, Maximilian, and with him, with you, I sailed up the Rhine and down the Danube to the Vienna Woods. I sailed on waltzes and in your arms and when I met your people, your bourgeois citizens in black and gray who waved to us with their hats, those Kärnten men in blue stockings and crimson waistcoats who waved at us with their handkerchiefs, and the Steiermark women with the multicolored skirts who threw carnations from the bridges, I never thought the day would come when I myself would rule such an Empire, so vast and magnificent but from which we only got the crumbs, because I went to Milan and to Venice with you, Maximilian, and you and I became the Viceroy and the Vicereine of a masked ball. And we returned to Miramare to molder in loneliness and love, and I never thought a day would come when they would offer you the throne of Mexico, when they would place an Empire at your feet greater and more splendid than Constantine's, more magnificent than the admirable Habsburgs, the House that God empowered to crush heresy in Hungary, Bohemia, Germany, and Flanders, and then the day when you accepted that Empire, when you and I swore to reign in a country of eighteen different climates and four hundred volcanoes and butterflies large as birds and birds small as bees, in a country, Maximilian, of smoldering hearts. But it came to pass, Maximilian, because every day comes sooner or later. You were Emperor and I was Empress. Crowned, we crossed the Atlantic and its foam bathed our royal purple, and in Martinique we were greeted by orchids and black dancers who cried "Long Live Emperor Perfumed Flower!" and we were greeted by fat, flying roaches, foul-smelling when we crushed them, and in Veracruz we were met by empty streets, by sand and yellow fever, by the north wind that knocked down the triumphal arches, and in Puebla we were greeted by cacti and angels, and in the Mexican Imperial Palace we were met by bedbugs and that first night you slept on a billiards table. Do you remember, Maximilian? And for you, I became Empress and I governed Mexico. For you I washed and kissed the feet of twelve old women and with my royal hands touched the ulcers of lepers, and I wiped the brows of the wounded and I held orphans on my lap. And for you, only for you, I seared my lips with the dust of the roads to Tlaxcala and I seared my eyes with the sun from Uxmal. For you, also, I pushed the Papal Nuncio out the palace window. Do you remember, Max? He flew away over the transparent valley like a vulture from the tropics, swollen with rotten communion wafers.

But, Maximilian, they gave us a throne of cacti, prickly with bayonets. They gave us a crown of thorns and shadows. They deceived us, Maximilian, and you deceived me. We were abandoned, Max, and I was abandoned by you. For sixty years, three hundred and sixty-five days a year, I have repeated the following to my mirror and to your portrait, in order to learn to believe it: We never went to Mexico, I never returned to Europe, your death never came, nor the day that I'm living through even now, as I am today. But for sixty times three hundred and sixty-five days the mirror and your portrait have repeated ad nauseam that I am mad, that I am old, that my heart is covered with scabs and that cancer is rotting my breasts. In the meantime, tell me, what have you been doing with your life all these years, while I've been dragging my imperial rags from palace to palace and from castle to castle, from Chapultepec to Miramare, from Miramare to Laeken, from Laeken to Terveuren, and from Terveuren to Bouchout? What have you done with yourself but hang on gallery walls, tall, blond, impassive, not a line marring your face, not a gray hair on your head, frozen at thirty-five, another Christ figure, forever young, forever beautiful, dressed in your finery and mounted on your steed Orispelo, those big Amozoc spurs on your feet? Tell me, Maximilian, what have you done with your life since you died in Querétaro like a hero and a dog, begging your executioners to aim at your chest, shouting "Long Live Mexico!"? What have you done except stand around in portraits in palaces and museums? Maximilian with his three brothers, Maximilian on the stern of the yacht *Fantasie*, Maximilian in the Hall of Seagulls at Miramare Castle, frozen at eighteen, at twenty-three, at twenty-six, and frozen also in my memories: my beloved Max in the Smyrna slave market, my dearest, beloved Max with his butterfly net at the banks of the Blanco River, my darling, adored, lazy Max, spending all morning in his robe and slippers sipping Rhine wines and nibbling on sherried ladyfingers. What have you done, tell me, but remain in the Capuchin Crypt, still and embalmed, stuffed with myrrh and spices and looking at the world through Saint Ursula's eyes, keeping as still as possible so that nothing else will happen to you, so that no one else will offend or defeat you, so that you'll never have to pay me thirty thousand florins to lie there with you, or to give twenty gold coins to your executioners to take your life? What have you done since that time but remain still, so that your beard will quietly grow back to cover the bloody coagulated medals that you bought at Las Campanas Hill? What have you done, Maximilian, while I've been growing older and madder each day? What have you accomplished, tell me, besides dying in Mexico?

The messenger also brought me a bar of silver from the Real del Monte mines. A spider monkey from San Luis. A violin from Tacámbaro. A sandalwood chest filled with jumping beans. He also brought me a sugar skull with your name spelled out on its brow. And he brought me a blank book and some red ink so that I can write the story of my life. But you'll have to help me, Max, because I'm becoming so forgetful and absentminded that some days I ask myself where I could have left my thoughts, where I've misplaced my memories, which drawer I put them in, on what trip I left them behind. If you could see me, wild with anxiety, as I look for these memories in your letters from Brazil where you wrote about how you walked through the jungle in a blue shirt, red boots, and a nightcap, your knapsack filled with flasks of glowing insects. You were so proud of your praying mantis collection, of bringing a tapir and a guatí to the Schönbrunn Zoo, of finding a whale skeleton on the shores of Itaparica, my poor Max. And I search for my memories in the letters that you wrote me from Querétaro, after you had fallen to the Juaristas and where you told me that you always thought Juárez would pardon you and where you said, how funny, Max, that when you arrived at Las Campanas Hill the door on your black coach got stuck and you had to crawl out the window; and you wrote me, how admirable, that you refused a blindfold, and you said, how pitiful, that your first coffin was so short that your feet stuck out, and how unjust, Max, that the doctor who embalmed you expressed such pleasure at his being able to wash his hands in the blood of an emperor. How funny, how pitiful, how sad, my poor Max, my poor Mambrú who went to war and died in battle, what a feat, what an injustice, what a pity that they had to embalm you twice. And how just that the Austrian fleet fired one hundred and one cannons to salute you as it left Mexican waters. What a pity that it snowed the day of your funeral, Max, how sad, how cold it was. And then I wish I could plunge my face in your letters and drown in the fragrance of mangos and vanilla, and choke on the stench of gunpowder and your spilled blood. But I can't do that, Max, because sometimes I can't even find those letters. I've searched for them under my bed, in the chest where I still keep—next to my kerchiefs and my shawls—the brown sugar cones and the spice breads that those Walloon peasants gave me on my wedding day. I've looked for them in the kitchen. I've sent divers to search in the moat at Bouchout, in the Bruges canals, and in Chapultepec Lake. I've had the Laeken garbage dumps searched, every room in the Mexican Imperial Palace, the cellars of the Teresitas Convent in Querétaro, in the *Novara's* bilges, and in the nests that storks build in the chimneys of Ghent when they fly in from Alsace. But I can't find the letters, Max, and I think at times that you never did write me and that now I will have to write your letters for you, every single day.

If you only knew, Max, how terrified I was the first time I saw all those blank pages, when I realized that if I couldn't find my memories that I would have to invent them. When I felt unsure as to what language to choose from all the many that I've learned and then forgotten. When I realized that I couldn't decide what tense to use because I'm so confused that at times I'm not sure if I was really Marie Charlotte of Belgium, if I'm still the Empress of Mexico, if perhaps some day I shall be the Empress of America; I'm so confused that I don't know where the truth of my dreams ends and the lies of my life begin. The other night I dreamed that Marshal Bazaine was a fat old woman who ate pistachios and spit the shells into her white-plumed, two-cornered hat. Another day I dreamed that I had borne a child who had the face of Benito Juárez. I also dreamed that General Santa Anna came to visit me and made me a gift of his leg. I dreamed that I was in the Alps, lying on a living carpet of forget-me-nots and blue gentians. I dreamed that I got up and climbed down the mountains and the sun became hotter and hotter; and I got to Mexico at noon and I kept walking and at night I came to a desert and I was freezing. My wild-duck feather coverlet had slipped off and the fire had died. I called my ladies-in-waiting and they didn't come. I called the guards and they didn't hear me. I called them again and Bazaine came into my bedroom to rape me with the baton that the French Marshal carried between his legs. If you could only see how strong I still am, Maximilian, despite my old age. I strangled him with my own hands and then I found a hearth with a glowing fire where I lit a torch and set fire to Marshal Bazaine's body and then to the whole wing of Terveuren Castle, which turned to ashes.

Everyone else has turned to ashes too, Maximilian. There are no witnesses to my life. If you don't help me, who else will, Max? Everyone's turn to die came. How sad and how happy I am to have to tell you this. Happy, yes, to know that the little imperial prince who received me on the staircase at Saint-Cloud perished in Zululand, on the banks of the Blood River, in an English uniform and mud-covered boots. Happy to know that his father, Little Napoleon, died in exile, his mustache drooping and his bladder full of stones, and that all his paramours are dead as well: the Gordon woman, la Castiglione, Miss Howard, la Belle Sabotière; and that his wife the Empress Eugénie died old and ugly, nearly blind, in wrinkled petticoats. It's right and proper that you have no idea, Maximilian, of how many people have died. The other afternoon as I sat embroidering flowers my ladies-in-waiting told me, in the middle of a rose, that your nephew Rudolf had died in Mayerling. The other day while I painted the Santa Anita Promenade with its water vendors and oak-coal peddlers from memory, I found out that Franz Joseph had died. The other afternoon, while I ate lunch, they told me that Leonardo Márquez was dead. And also Father Fischer, and that the Archduke Franz Ferdinand of Austria had been assassinated in Sarajevo. Benito Juárez died of angina pectoris. General Escobedo died. Concha Méndez died. The son that you conceived in Borda Gardens was executed at Vincennes, and his mother, Concepción Sedano, died as well. Baby died, the faithful dog that followed you to Querétaro, and Florian, your brother the Emperor's favorite horse. And the other day, as I looked out the window, I discovered that the century had died, as had the Austro-Hungarian Empire, and that a million men had perished in the Somme Valley.

And now, who among the living can say that he witnessed the birth of your father, Napoleon II, King of Rome? Who among them can say that he saw him ride the silver and mother-of-pearl carriage that my great-grandmother, Queen Caroline of Naples, had given him, the carriage drawn by two trained goats that wore the red ribbons of the Legion of Honor? Who saw you play with your brother Franz Joseph in the Aladdin Room in the Schönbrunn Palace? Who saw you meditate under the orange trees in the Hofburg and prance about on your sorrel horse with its braided tail in the Spanish Riding School of Vienna? And standing by Vesuvius's crater on the multicolored sulfur, on the orange, red, and verdigris-frosted rocks? Who saw you, who remembers you? Tell me, Maximilian, who can remember our triumphant entrance into Milan when I wore a rose-and-diamond tiara? Who remembers that in honor of the Viceroy and the Vicereine of the Lombard-Venetto Provinces they played the Austrian and Belgian National Anthems? Who, tell me, remembers the gold dalmatic that Archbishop Labastida wore when he greeted us at the door of San Hipólito Cathedral in Mexico City? Who, more than sixty years later, can say now that he remembers the forty-eight cathedral bells pealing enthusiastically to welcome the Emperor and the Empress of Mexico? Your mother the Archduchess Sophie, who plunged her face into the snow that crowned your coffin when you returned to Vienna as a mummy, has died. Your brother Karl Ludwig died and your nephew Otto died of a venereal disease. Colonel Platón Sánchez died, murdered by bandits. Your brother Karl Ludwig died, imprisoned for life in a castle and surrounded only by women since he liked to sleep with men. Our friend Colonel López died, foaming at the mouth. And now, who among the living saw you swim in the springs next to the hanging gardens of Chapultepec where Malinche bathed, and can say that he saw us gazing at Lakes Xaltocan and Chalco from the castle terraces, those lakes embroidered with water lilies, and looking out toward snowy peaks like angels' wings above the pure sky of Anáhuac? I dressed up, for the court painters, as a Lombard peasant and as a *china poblana*. In the Venice market I bought tangerines and muscatel grapes. In the Portal de Mercaderes in Mexico City I bought silk *rebozos*, Olinalá lacquers, chirimoyas, and poinsettias. I read the poems of King Netzahualcóyotl out loud and I learned the legend of the Our Lord of the Venom—the wooden Christ that had absorbed all the poison from a devout, dying woman, and then turned black—by heart in Porta Coeli Street. We kissed in the shade of the clematis-covered walls of the convent in the Island of Lacroma where Richard the Lionhearted was shipwrecked. On our wedding day the Royal English House and the British Navy toasted our happiness with wine and grog. At the Alcázar in Seville you breathed the sweet fragrance of amber and in the Chamber of Secrets in the Alhambra you heard the whispers of Philip II's children. They gave you a gigantic scolopendra in the Canaries and in Mexico a bronze culverin with Charles III's coat of arms that had been forged in Manila. We arrived in a gondola at the *Théâtre de L'Harmonie* where we were affronted by the presence of the Milanese aristocrats' servants. On board the *Elizabeth* we made love on a stormy night as

14

brooms and teacups and wine bottles danced about, crazily, over the waves. Wearing your serape from Saltillo on your shoulders, you shouted "Long Live Independence!" in Dolores while I stayed in Mexico City to govern, to sign decrees and to give soirees. Who among the living remembers us? Who saw me locked in the Miramare Gartenhaus, the windows screwed shut and the doors bolted down, as I ruminated on my madness and my despair? And who saw you, Maximilian, in your cell at the Teresitas Convent in Querétaro, sitting on your high porcelain chamber pot the entire day, with an endless case of diarrhea? Who remembers, Max, how graceful Colonel Van der Smissen looked leading the Belgian Volunteer Corps, how affectionate our little Prince Iturbide was, or how bloodthirsty Colonel Dupin was, how humble our little Mexican Indians as they crossed themselves in front of our portrait and filled my lap with dahlias, turquoise eggs, and scorpions made from vanilla pods? Who saw, who remembers how homely Benito Juárez was, how brave the triumphant French soldiers in Magenta and Solferino were? Who, tell me, who remembers how green that traitor López's eyes were? Only History and I do, Maximilian.

I remember Colonel López, beautiful as an angel of light as he rode at my side on the way to Córdoba and offered me orchid bouquets. History remembers how King Alexander and Queen Draga of Serbia were assassinated and how Benito Juárez's chest was scalded with boiling water and how the Library of Lovaina caught fire. I remember, Maximilian, because I watched from the windows of Bouchout Castle as the forts burned, down in Antwerp. I saw how General Prim was assassinated in Madrid and how Bazaine died in exile and poverty and how Bismarck proclaimed the German Empire in the Hall of Mirrors in Versailles and how the face of the Imperial Prince Louis Napoleon was devoured by jackals, and how Maria Vetsera, your nephew Rudolf's lover, had an eye pop out of its socket, and how Buena Vista Palace became a cigarette factory and how, Maximilian, your faithful cook Tüdös and your valet Grill dipped their handkerchiefs in your blood at the Las Campanas Hill, where you were executed. I, Marie Charlotte Amélie of Belgium, Countess of Maracaibo, Archduchess of the Gran Sertão, Princess of Mapimí, Maximilian, I who tasted canned pineapple, who traveled on the Orient Express, who spoke with Rasputin on the telephone, who danced the fox-trot, who saw a gringo steal the head of Pancho Villa, and Eugénie's coffin crossing Paris covered in violets, I who etched your name with my breath on the jasper vases that decked the staircase at Miramare, I who saw your dead face in the sacred wells of Yucatán where they once sacrificed virgin princesses, I, Maximilian, who every night of every year of the sixty years that I have lived in loneliness and silence have loved you secretly, Maximilian; I, who spend my life embroidering your initials on sheets, on handkerchiefs, on drapes, and on tablecloths—"Maximilian I, Emperor of Mexico and King of the World"—on napkins and on your shroud, on the roses on your pillows and on the skin of my lips . . . I, who from the top of the Acultzingo Mountains, where the rarefied air brightens the constellations and magnifies the stars, showed you the curvature of the sky and told you that there, in the Ship, and the Southern Cross, and on Arcturus and Centaur, the destinies of the greatest of your ancestors were written . . . Your ancestors like Charlemagne, founder of the Holy Roman Empire; Rudolf of Habsburg who crossed the Danube with an army on a bridge rigged of boats; Albert II, Prince of Peace; Charles V, in whose kingdom the sun never set; Maximilian I and Maria Theresa of Austria; Philip II, victor of the Battle at San Quentin and scourge of the Moors; of Leopold I, savior of Europe and victor over the Vizier Kara Mustapha; and Joseph II, the rebel dressed in purple from whom you learned the idea that your subjects might be allowed a little freedom . . . But I also told you that there too was written the destiny of a man who would be greater than all of them, the destiny of a man called Maximilian I, Emperor of Mexico. Who, tell me, who but me among the living can remember that sixty years ago I said good-bye to you under the scented orange trees at Ayotla and left you alone forever, on your horse Orispelo, dressed as a *charro* with your Admiral of the Austrian Fleet telescope. And who but History—after it left you lying there, bleeding to death at Las Campanas Hill, your waistcoat in flames, left you hanging upside down from the dome of the Chapel of San Andrés so that all the embalming liquids would drip out, so that they could embalm you anew in the hope that your skin, Maximilian, would stop turning blacker and blacker, and that your swollen mummy's flesh, my poor beloved Max, would keep from smelling even more foul—who but History can remember? Only History and I, Maximilian—both of us alive and out of our minds. But my own life is almost over.

II
MAY YOU FIND YOURSELF BETWEEN NAPOLEONS
1861–62

1. Juárez and Mustachoo

In the year of our Lord 1861, a sallow Indian named Benito Juárez governed Mexico. He had been orphaned at three, and at eleven had become a shepherd who climbed the trees by the Enchanted Lagoon to play his reed flute and talk to the birds and beasts in Zapotec, the only language he knew.

On the other side of the Atlantic, Napoleon III reigned in France. Some had given him the nickname "Mustachoo" because of his long, full, black, and pointed mustache, which he treated with Hungarian ointments; others called him the Little Napoleon to distinguish him from his famous uncle, Napoleon the Great—that is, Napoleon Bonaparte.

One day, Benito Pablo left the relatives who had taken him in. He abandoned his sheep, and the town of his birth, Guelatao—a word meaning "deep dark night" in his language—and walked twenty-six leagues to the city of Oaxaca, where he could find work as a servant in a wealthy home like his older sister had done; and most of all where he could get an education. Oaxaca, the capital of the state of the same name, was a city that could be described as "ultramontane," not only because it was located beyond the mountains, but also because of its sanctimoniousness and its submissiveness to Rome. There, Juárez learned Spanish, arithmetic and algebra, Latin, theology, and law. In time, not only in Oaxaca, but also in other cities, undergoing other exiles—whether he was stubbornly pursuing a goal or fulfilling a destiny sent by Heaven—he also learned to be a representative, then governor of his State, Minister of Justice, Secretary of the Interior, and, finally, President of the Republic.

Little Napoleon didn't manage to become Emperor of France until his third attempt. Nothing seemed to help: not Napoleon and Josephine's wedding ring, which, people say, he had used as a talisman during his first attempt; not the strip of bacon some say he fastened to his hat during his second attempt—so that an eaglet, a bird he had bought for a pound sterling at Gravesend soon after embarking down the Thames on the *Edinburgh Castle*—would always follow him and hover around him. No, none of these ploys helped Little Napoleon gain the power he sought on his arrival in France. It only took a few hours to foil his first foolhardy attempt in 1836, when he arrived at the city of Strasbourg and convinced the Fourth Cavalry Regiment to support him. Louis Napoleon was summarily dispatched on a ship bound for the United States. Four years later, in his second attempt, it took the police and the National Guard of Boulogne only a few hours to sow panic among his forty or fifty followers who—rumor had it—wore French military uniforms rented from a costume shop in London. They found Louis Napoleon shivering, not so much from fear but from the cold, soaked to the bone with algae hanging from his mustache. They captured and rescued him at the same time, plucking him from the freezing, unfriendly waters of the English Channel into which he had fallen when his lifeboat sank during his attempted escape. This time, King Louis Philippe sentenced him to life in prison at Fort Ham in the north of France, on the banks of the Somme River.

Always dressed in a black frockcoat and holding a cane, Don Benito Juárez read and reread the works of Rousseau and Benjamin Constant. Through these and other readings he formed his liberal ideas. He translated Tacitus from Latin into Spanish, a language he had learned to read, write, and speak all at once—as, in the best of cases, one would hope to learn a foreign language. He began to realize that those he'd called "his people," those he had sworn to enlighten and exalt and help to overcome their confusions, vices, and shortcomings, numbered many more than the handful he'd considered his responsibility, many more than the five million quiet and cunning, passive and melancholy Indians who, when Juárez was governor, would come down from the Ixtlán Mountains to leave their humble offerings at his doorstep: doves, fruit, corn, and oak charcoal from the hills of Pozuelos or Calvario. "His people" were also the others, all the ones who thought that Benito Juárez had taken on the entire nation in the same way that he would always don his black frockcoat: as though it was something that didn't fit him. Moreover, while his coat may have been tailored for him, the nation had not. It was simply too big for him—it spread out far beyond Oaxaca, and also far beyond the century in

18

which he'd been born. Along the lines of the old saying "You can't make a silk purse out of a sow's ear," his critics composed the following verse:

You put on a coat and tie
And think that's all you need to get by

Meanwhile, with all the time in the world to contemplate the falling leaves, to read *The Gallic Wars*, or to reflect proudly that many years before, Joan of Arc, the Maid of Orléans, had been held captive in that same prison, Louis Napoleon, Little Napoleon, who in his own way was, at that time, a sort of Saint-Simonian socialist, began worrying about poverty and injustice. So it was that he wrote, among other things, a small volume entitled *The Extinction of Pauperism* there. It was also there that, worried about his future, he asked the British government to intercede for him with Louis Philippe, the French King, promising never to return to Europe in exchange for his liberty. He would again board a ship that would take him to the American continent; he would become the Emperor of Nicaragua and he would realize one of his old dreams, to build an interoceanic canal from Punta Gigante to Punta Gorda that, in spite of the dunes, mosquitoes, and banana groves, would some day join and reconcile the waters of the Atlantic Ocean to those of the Pacific. Since the Great Napoleon had been able to marry a Creole woman from Martinique without tarnishing his image, Little Napoleon would choose a sultry, dark-eyed native girl for his Empress. From his imperial observation deck in the Solentiname Islands he would use his binoculars to watch the passing of the Manila galleons loaded with tea and fabrics from Shantung, aromatic woods and dozens of Chinese coolies destined to work in Havana's tobacco factories. But the British Prime Minister, Sir Robert Peel, never bothered to ask Louis Philippe for Louis Napoleon's freedom, and at no time did the pear-headed Citizen King think to grant him liberty on condition of exile. The king, carrying his black umbrella, dressed in a Parisian business suit—a four-buttoned maroon jacket, in galoshes to protect his shoes from the mud—spent his time cutting flowers in the Tuileries Gardens. He sent them, pressed between the pages of *Fabiola* or of a book of fairy tales, to his granddaughter Charlotte, the little Belgian princess. So Louis Napoleon, Napoleon III, had no other choice than to plot his escape from the Fort Ham dungeon. He donned a wig and a blue apron, and thus disguised as a worker named Badinguet, he walked out the door carrying a wooden plank on his shoulder. He went to live in London, where for several years, he rubbed shoulders with the English aristocracy in the clubs of Saint James, drank Amontillado sherry, and rode around Pall Mall with his blonde paramour, Miss Howard, in a carriage with the imperial Napoleonic eagle embossed on its doors.

Agatha, the saint who placed her two severed breasts on a platter, taught Benito Pablo, the child, the letter "A." Blandina the martyr, who died tangled in a net, trampled and gored by a bull, taught him the letter "B." Casiano of Inmola, who was stabbed to death by his own disciples with their iron pens, taught him the letter "C." And in spite of this, in spite of having learned his ABCs from *The Lives and Martyrdom of the Saints*, thanks to the patience and unselfish love of his teacher Salanueva, a layman who was virtually a friar, wearing the brown sackcloth of the Discalced Carmelites, Benito Juárez, as Minister of Justice, promulgated a law that bore his name ending the jurisdiction of ecclesiastical tribunals in civil matters, and reigniting the old quarrel between Church and State. Besides provoking bloody battles, it also caused the expulsion of six clergymen, among them the Bishop of Puebla, Pelagio Antonio de Labastida y Dávalos. The Angelopolitans—as the inhabitants of Puebla are called—accompanied their bishop, whimpering and sniveling all the while, a good stretch of the way toward his place of exile.

Also, despite Juárez being an outstanding student at the Seminary of Oaxaca—he'd wanted to be a priest before he decided to study law—and having sworn as Governor of Oaxaca to protect and defend the Holy Roman Catholic and Apostolic Church, in the name of God and the Holy Gospels, and to begin all decrees by invoking the name of Almighty God—Father, Son, and Holy Spirit as three persons in one godhead—and in spite of Salanueva's teachings which included the art of hand-binding Ripalda catechisms and respect and veneration for the Nazarene of the Via Crucis, who passed by his house every afternoon—in spite of this, Benito Juárez, in his role as president of the Republic, confiscated the assets of the Mexican Church, abolished all privileges of the clergy, and recognized all religions. Thanks to this, Mexican and European conservatives, and of course the Vatican and Pope Pius IX—that future creator of the concept of Papal Infallibility—considered Juárez a sort of Antichrist. Because he could not ride a horse nor fire a pistol and didn't aspire to a glorious military career, he was accused of being weak and cowardly. Because he wasn't white or of European extraction; because he wasn't Aryan or blond (the archetypal qualities of superior humanity according to the Count of Gobineau's *Essay on the Inequality of the Human Races*, published in Paris in 1853); because he wasn't even a middle-class half-breed, Juárez, the cunning Indian, was—in the opinion of the monarchs and leaders of the Old World— incapable of governing a country that in itself appeared to be ungovernable.

It's true that Thomas Corwin, the U.S. minister in Mexico, exaggerated when he wrote to William Seward, the U.S. Secretary of State, that in forty years Mexico had had thirty-six different forms of government. In reality there had only been one, with rare and sporadic exceptions: militarism. It's also true that Mr. Corwin's arithmetic was wrong when he asserted that in those same forty years Mexico had had sixty-three presidents. In reality, not only had there been fewer, but among this number there were several who had themselves been president over and over again, like a tertian fever for which the country had no cure. But, as Monsieur Masseras, editor in chief of the journal *L'Ère Nouvelle*, published in French in Mexico, wrote, the hapless nation was only hoping for one thing: a government of order, prosperity, and organization. Still, these three words, the journalist added, when applied to Mexico, a nation proverbially prone to revolutions and counter-revolutions, were likely to sound exceedingly ironic. For his part, Monsieur Charles Bordillon, a correspondent for the English daily *Times*, declared that the only moral law known to this nation—whose race was "deeply perverted"—was theft, in itself the primary objective of all political parties. And the illustrious Lord Palmerston shared these points of view. For him, the Mexican people were degenerate and corrupt to the core, without strength or courage. He assured Queen Victoria one day at Balmoral Castle that Mexico would be devoured by the Anglo-Saxon race, and that the natives would go the way of the redskins when the white man arrived in force.

Then, in addition to the criticism regarding the deficiencies of his race and the personal remarks about his individual flaws—"demagogue," "despot," "Jacobin," "traitor," and "red tyrant" were some of the adjectives his enemies hung on him—the President of Mexico had the added burden of being markedly ugly, this handicap being underscored, according to many who knew him, and among them Princess Salm-Salm, by a horrible and bloody scar that never, for some reason, showed up in his portraits. Margarita, his wife, was the daughter of the masters and protectors who had welcomed him when he arrived in the city asking for "Doctrine and Spanish." Every morning she knotted his black bow tie and blessed his white-as-dawn, impeccably starched shirtfronts. She would tell herself, and her children, "He is very ugly, but he is very good."

Yes, Little Napoleon was white, though not blond, and not particularly ugly, though he had the face of a melancholy parrot. Neither his German accent when speaking French, nor his Swiss education, nor his English manners ever dissuaded him from considering himself anything other than a Corsican by origin and a Frenchman by right, and by family tradition. In other words, he was a man who belonged to what he called the "Latin race," for whose destiny and future greatness—defying Anglo-Saxon voracity and ambition—he took responsibility not only in Europe but across the sea. Having transformed himself into the Emperor of France, he heard the name "Mexico" pealing in his ears like Sonoran silver. But a few years went by before he could follow his dream. And above all there were some intervening events—like those of 1848, the year of the revolution that someone called a decisive moment in history where history couldn't make up its mind, and the year in which the doctrine of human rights began stirring up several European countries, like France, Italy, Poland, and the nations under the Habsburg Empire. Among other things, radical students in Budapest demanded equal rights for all nationalities and the end of the uncompensated peasants. The rebel Johann Strauss the Younger took his orchestra to the barricades to play polkas and mazurkas while Johann Strauss the Older kept on playing them at the Hofburg and Schönbrunn Palaces. The radical Milanese snatched burning cigars from pedestrians on the streets as a protest against their Austrian dominators who besides having a monopoly on power also had one on tobacco. In Munich, students expelled the Irish dancer Lola Montez, mistress of the old King Louis I of Bavaria. Count Latour, the Austrian Minister of War, ended up disemboweled and hanged from a lamppost on the beautiful Platz Am Hof. The Prussian leftists clamored for the suppression of the Czech rebels. The farmer-leader Tancsics crossed the bridge that united Buda with Pest on the shoulders of the people and the students, and the poet Sándor Petőfi was assassinated and his body dumped into a mass grave. The German Karl Marx, who, in his periodical the *Neue Rheinische Zeitung*, encouraged an insurrection against the government of the King of Prussia, was soon to be accused of high treason. General Cavaignac repressed the June insurrection in the streets of Paris with unprecedented brutality. The powerful Austrian Chancellor, Metternich, disappeared, but before doing so he managed to have the semi-imbecile Emperor Ferdinand of Austria-Hungary abdicate in favor of his nephew Franz Joseph, older brother of the Archduke Ferdinand Maximilian. Following in the footsteps of the Irish who fled from their country due to the Great Potato Famine, Germans by the thousands immigrated to the United States. Hungary declared itself to be a republic and elected Kossuth as its president. And, just as in the time of the Sun King, the fecal content of the royal chamber pots—which also served as fertilizer for the roses, begonias, and wallflowers, and as fodder for the beetles in the royal dunghill—went flying out the windows of Versailles every morning, Louis Philippe's throne was soon tossed out of a Tuileries Palace window and later reduced to ashes in the Place de la Bastille.

After more than two months of humiliations, during which he was in turn imprisoned and expelled from several towns, cities, and ranches, the Honorable Benito Juárez was taken to the Fort of San Juan de Ulúa. Made out of *múcar* stone—a type of coral—on top of La Gallega reef at the entrance to the Mexican port of Veracruz, built in a tropical land where malaria and yellow fever were endemic, the fortress of San Juan de Ulúa, last stronghold of the Spaniards who abandoned it almost four years after the Mexicans had won their independence, had cost Spain many millions. So many, they say, that one day a certain King of Spain was asked what he was looking at through his telescope in the Escorial, near Madrid, and the King answered that he was trying to locate the Fort of San Juan de Ulúa: "It's cost the Spanish treasury so much," he said, "that we should at least be able to see it from here." Thirteen years after the withdrawal of the Spaniards, in October of 1838, the fortress surrendered under the bombardment of a French naval squadron under the command of Admiral Charles Baudin. Also in the expedition was Prince Joinville, son of Louis Philippe of France and uncle of Princess Charlotte of Belgium, who demanded in the name of the French government an indemnity of six hundred thousand pesos on behalf of French citizens residing in Mexican territory who complained of the gradual or sudden decrease of their capital due to the forced loans or legal thefts that Mexican authorities all too often decreed in order to finance their continual revolutions and the perpetual losses they suffered from embezzlers in their own offices. Due to the fact that there was a pastry cook in Tacubaya among the French plaintiffs, who claimed to have lost sixty thousand pesos in merchandise ten years earlier, consisting of éclairs, vol-au-vents, babas au rhum, and jellyrolls, this first armed conflict between Mexico and France was called the Pastry War. During the defense of the Port of Veracruz, a Mexican general lost his left leg. This was the same general—he had once been served dinner by Benito Juárez while the latter was still a servant in a wealthy home in Oaxaca—now responsible for the many mistreatments being suffered by the Indian President and his subsequent exile: Antonio López de Santa Anna, who had already been president of Mexico five times himself, and who after having his heroic leg buried with honors and parades, tears and a commemorative gravestone, volleys of gunfire and military fanfares, would be president a further six terms. Sometimes a hero, sometimes a traitor, sometimes both simultaneously, Santa Anna woke up a captain and went to bed a lieutenant colonel one day during the Mexican War of Independence. A general at twenty-seven and a national hero at thirty-five, Santa Anna was "decorated" by the arrow of an Indian during his first campaign in Texas, that Mexican province which so wanted to become an independent republic. Already a hero, Santa Anna became a bit more of one when he returned to the rebel province years later in order to take the Fort of El Alamo by force, winning a bloody triumph—"Remember the Alamo, remember Goliad!"—and having all his prisoners executed. He became a bit less of a hero, however, when, defeated by Sam Houston, after the battle of San Jacinto, he fled on horseback and then on foot, was captured and imprisoned, and, either out of fear, in order to obtain his liberty, or because it was simply a *fait accompli*, he recognized the existence of the Republic of Texas. After his leg was exhumed and dragged through the streets by the populace, he was still able to return to power and was president twice more in 1847, the year in which the North American expansionist invasion reached a point of no return, resulting in the cession of Mexican territory to the United States covering an area of over one million three hundred and fifty thousand square kilometers, including the provinces of New Mexico and Upper California. Added to Texas, this was equivalent to half the national territory. Santa Anna was a great traitor then, when, having left the government in the hands of an interim president so that he could lead his troops into battle, he was defeated by General Taylor in Sacramento, and finally took his leave of the United States, washing his hands of it, passing through enemy ranks unscathed, as though in his own backyard. It was said that Santa Anna had received huge sums of money from the North Americans following the defeat in order to influence the approval, in the Mexican Congress, of the Treaty of Guadalupe Hidalgo, which, besides ratifying the cession of the territory, reaffirmed the old bonds of friendship between

Mexico and the United States. Despite all this, Santa Anna returned to power a few years later and became Supreme Dictator and Serene Highness, and then, again, even more of a traitor, if that were possible, when he signed the Treaty of La Mesilla by which Mexico sold the United States another 100,000 square kilometers of borderland that included, among other things, the area called the *Minera de Arizona*, which produced native silver in large chunks weighing up to one hundred *arrobas* or about two hundred and fifty pounds, a land that a short time before, Raousset-Boulbon, a French filibuster, associated with the Swiss-Mexican firm Jecker de La Torre, had tried to conquer, and as a result of which campaign, and of having declared the independence of Sonora, he was executed next to the seashore.

Louis Philippe left France after he was dethroned and his throne defenestrated. The Little Napoleon returned, this time without the rasher of bacon in his hat and without an eaglet—though many had said that what hovered over him the first time was not an eaglet but a vulture—and before the end of the year, he was elected first a representative and then President of the Second Republic by six million Frenchmen. Nineteen years had passed since the son of Napoleon the Great and the Austrian Marie Louise had died at Schönbrunn Palace in Vienna. Eleven years had gone by since the day that the lancers with their tricolor plumes preceded the casket containing the remains of Napoleon the Great, taken to France by the Prince of Joinville, in its march to *Les Invalides*, followed by a white riderless horse, white like the battle mount of the Great Corsican, led by two grooms dressed in gold and green. The Bonaparte dynasty had seemed then to be dying out. But on the morning of December 2, 1851, the anniversary of the Battle of Austerlitz and of the coronation of Napoleon I, the skins on the drums of the National Guard were in shreds, the bells silenced, anti-Bonaparte newspapers and presses were shut down, and the houses and buildings, the kiosks and the triumphal arches of Paris were all covered with posters in which President Louis Napoleon announced the dissolution of the Assembly and the restoration of universal suffrage. This first act, the dissolution of the Assembly—a crime of high treason—completed when the last assemblymen who had fled the Palais Bourbon in order to seek refuge in the City Hall of Saint Germain were taken to prison flanked by two rows of *Chasseurs d'Afrique*—gave Louis Napoleon absolute executive power. The second, the restoration of universal suffrage, allowed him a few months later to convoke a national plebiscite in which he proposed the restoration of a hereditary imperial system, and the people backed him up with two million votes more—eight million in total—than he had gotten when elected president. With this coup d'état the Napoleonic dynasty was restored in the person of Napoleon III, who forgot from that moment on, or perhaps a few days before—in truth almost all of France forgot—that as president he had sworn respect to the Constitution and loyalty to the democratic Republic, one and indivisible. But, then, this same dynasty had originated out of another forgotten principle, after all: when he, the Great Napoleon, had founded it, when he'd proclaimed himself Emperor, and later when he divorced Josephine for not having given him an heir, in order to marry the Austrian Marie Louise—whose lips were a matter of great pride to the Habsburgs, because it proved her to be a "a true descendant of the Caesars"—he had forgotten that his own ascent to the throne had been the result of his rejection of the alleged divine right to rule of all the Bourbons who had governed France before him. "Another Napoleon, what a shame!" said the poet Charles Baudelaire, who tinted his hair green and strolled through the boulevards of Paris arm in arm with a black woman. Another French writer of that time, Victor Hugo—the very one who had nicknamed Louis Napoleon "The Little One"—would write in *Les Châtiments* about the boy who died with his head shattered by soldiers' bullets, one among the many other atrocities that followed the proclamation of the Second Empire. Though, perhaps, despite this, these particular atrocities numbered less than those that had occurred during the revolution of 1848: one or two of the charges by lancers against the hot-headed republicans coming out of the Café des Peuples shouting "Long Live the National Assembly!," for instance; or one or two of the point-blank executions of those Parisians who had dared to flaunt their subversive ideology by wearing red caps and ties; or one or two of the women crushed by rifle butts whose blood mixed with the rivers of milk pouring out of the ripped skins of a delivery wagon (used to improvise a barricade in the Rue Transonian: torn down three times by riflemen and as many times rebuilt). Or, finally, one or two counts, deputies, butchers, doctors, masons, and/or children who like Hugo's had had their heads shattered by bullets, and whose bodies were piled up in carts and taken out of Paris at dawn, the time when the ragpickers of Paris would come out of their burrows and shacks to dig in the dump sites. Once Paris was pacified by Napoleon III, however, the new Imperial Regime silenced the zealous Provençals and the rebellious mountaineers and sent ten thousand of the twenty-seven thousand arrested insurgents to Algeria, and a few hundred to Cayenne. These events were quickly forgotten by the French, who could attend the theater free of charge on the Emperor's birthday to see the cancan or *La Dame aux camélias;* be blinded by the reflection of the sun in the steel helmets of the Squadron of the One Hundred Guards on horseback (the commander of this squadron was famous for being able to make even the fiercest stallion drop to its knees merely by squeezing his legs around it); go to the Gare du Nord in early fall to watch the departure of Napoleon III's guests, riding a special train to Compiègne to hunt hares, wild hogs, pheasants, and partridges; admire the long lines of luxurious carriages, some of which were going to the "Bal Mabille," the immense dance hall with its walls covered in red damask and its five thousand lamps infinitely multiplied in the great sparkling gilt-framed Venetian mirrors; admire other carriages crowded with Sylphs and Queens of Hearts, Spanish Conquistadors in shiny armor, and Eves recently bathed in the honey rivers of Eden, all on their way to the masked balls given by the Emperor in the Tuileries; or watch, in the afternoons and long winter nights, the sleighs shaped as swans, pegasi, or dragons pulled by white horses crowned with feathered plumes and bells that plowed the snow-covered roads of the Bois de Boulogne, while the ladies wrapped in their sables and the gentlemen in their long cashmere scarves skated on the frozen lake under torchlight. It seems that all these spectacles compensated the French for the loss, not only of a republic, but also of some of its most sacred symbols: *La Marseillaise* was replaced by an old song that Queen Hortense, mother of Louis Napoleon, had set to music, *"Partant pour la Syrie,"* which told how the young and handsome Dunois—*le jeune et beau Dunois*—asked the Virgin Mary—*venait prier Marie*—when he left for Syria—*partant pour la Syrie*—to bless his undertaking—*de bénir ses exploits.*

There, in one of the dungeons of San Juan de Ulúa, called "the tubs" because they were located under sea level and water constantly oozed through the *múcar* stone walls only to evaporate almost instantly, the lawyer Benito Juárez spent eleven days in solitary confinement. Afterwards he boarded the liner *Avon,* whose passengers took up a collection to pay for his ticket to the first port of call, Havana, from which the Honorable Juárez then departed shortly afterwards for New Orleans, the old capital of Louisiana, where he met other liberal Mexicans including Melchor Ocampo, like him a disciple of Rousseau and Proudhon. Ocampo, whom Juárez so admired for his clarity of mind, would later become one of his closest collaborators. Juárez rolled tobacco to earn a living; Ocampo made clay pots and demijohns. Some of their other exiled countrymen worked as waiters, if they were lucky, or as dishwashers in some of the French restaurants. Standing, facing the ocean, contemplating the broad delta of the Mississippi, Juárez would wait for the ship that brought letters from his wife and friends. Margarita and the children had moved to the town of Etla, where they eked out a living from a small business. His friends asked him to be patient; sometimes they would send him money; some reproached him for having chosen the United States as his place of exile and swore to him that Santa Anna would soon fall from power, this time for good. With his back to the ocean, Juárez would follow the course of the Mississippi with his eyes, that river with forty tributaries, its origins far to the north in Minnesota, and think about an extraordinary coincidence: for the same amount of money—fifteen million dollars—in exchange for which Mexico had ceded the provinces of New Mexico and Upper California to the North Americans, Napoleon the Great had sold two million three hundred thousand square kilometers of the eastern basin of the Mississippi to the United States—that portion of the immense territory named *La Louisiane*, in honor of Louis XIV, the Sun King, which had still belonged to France in 1803. That's how the United States had grown: paying Napoleon six dollars and fifty-six cents and Mexico eleven dollars and fifty-three cents per square kilometer. But Juárez further calculated that if he included the Republic of Texas in his reckoning, for which Mexico hadn't received a single penny in indemnification, then the eleven and some dollars were reduced to only six. What a deal!

One evening, Juárez and his friends went to see a *troupe de minstrels* that was passing through New Orleans. It consisted of a group of white musicians, who, painted black, moved like blacks, and spoke and sang like blacks. And like blacks, they played the banjo and the *bones*, a castanet-like instrument made from two animal ribs. "I don't understand," said Juárez. "Yes, English is very hard to learn," said one of the Mexicans who didn't know what Juárez meant. The only one who always knew what Juárez meant was his friend Melchor Ocampo, who, on some of their wet Sunday afternoons together, strolling on the docks in shirtsleeves, displayed his erudition, which ranged from politics to botany. Ocampo, the politician, proposed the fulfillment of the Reform initiated during the first years of the country's independence as a remedy to Mexico's ills—when government troops had occupied land earmarked for the Philippines missions; a practice continued by President Gómez Farias, the first time without success, but with better luck the second, when he confiscated Church property in order to raise money for the struggle against the American invasion. Ocampo remembered and cited examples and historical antecedents that came into his mind at random, such as the nationalization of Church property decreed in Spain in 1835 by a liberal prime minister, the confiscation of Church property in Bohemia in the fifteenth century as a result of the Hussite Revolution, "Which, nevertheless," Ocampo used to say, "only benefited the rich—like the disentitlement after the French Revolution, or, better still, the measures adopted by the Austrian Emperor Joseph II, which only managed to move money from one of the Church's pockets to another . . . he auctioned off almost half the convents and monasteries, with the proceeds going straight to the parishes—which proves that if Joseph II didn't love his monks, he undoubtedly had little, if anything, against his priests." And Ocampo, the botanist, lover of rare plants—once seen kneeling and crying in front of some Yucatecan lilies he'd found growing wild at the Tejería train station and cultivator himself of many exotic species at his Michoacán ranch, named "Pomoca" (an anagram of his surname)—would propose a potion made out of Cupid's flower crushed in water as a cure for the Honorable Benito Juárez's diarrhea, and would tell him how the particular passion of Empress Josephine, the first wife of the first Napoleon, had been a flower of Mexican origin, the *dahlia excelsa*, which she had planted in the gardens of Malmaison and forbade anyone else in France to grow; and how after someone stole a few plants from her garden and they began appearing in other places, Josephine lost interest in it and banished it forever, not only from Malmaison, but also from her *corazón*. How about that, Your Honor? And please forgive the rhyme.

The French people, most of them, also forgave Napoleon III—the man who had promised a kingdom of peace—for his bellicose alliances, his imperialistic expeditions, and for his colonialist wars, which he began planning almost as soon as he moved into the Tuileries Palace, wanting all the while to restore France to its former glory and military prestige. Some of these undertakings were blessed by God or by luck, others were not. The flyswatter blow Dey Hussein, Governor of Algiers, gave to the French Consul as the Ottoman Empire was spreading through Northern Africa was the pretext the Emperor used to initiate the conquest of Algerian territory, and Little Napoleon took this campaign even farther when he decided to conquer the Kabylia desert tribes. The deaths of French missionaries at the hands of Indochinese natives provoked the deployment of a Franco-Spanish force to occupy Saigon and the three provinces of Annam. Russia's demand to exercise a Protectorate over the Turkish Orthodox Church and the subsequent invasion of the Principalities of the Danube by Russian troops reminded Napoleon that France had committed itself to the protection of all Christians who lived under Turkish rule. It also reminded Queen Victoria that the passageway to India for both her war and merchant ships was in serious danger, and so the English and French allied in combat against the Russian bear in the Crimean War, remembered not only for Florence Nightingale and for the disastrous suicidal charge of the English light cavalry in Balaclava, but also for the Battles of Alma, Inkerman, and Sebastopol. Less sonorous—though more colorful—were the names of the battles that took place during the campaign launched by Napoleon III after his having made a secret pact with Count Cavour, Prime Minister of Sardinia, to help a divided Italy free itself from its Austrian oppressors: Magenta and Solferino. Magenta was the name the Italians gave to a crimson-red mineral— fuchsine—discovered shortly before the battle, which soon ended with the surrender of the city of the same name. But the color "solferino," a reddish purple, only became fashionable in the boulevards of Paris after the triumph of the Franco-Piedmontese troops over the Austrians in the battle of the city of *that* name, which followed the battle of Magenta. Without a doubt, however, the color that impressed the Emperor most lay between the two shades of red that abounded in this brutal campaign—which didn't manage to unify Italy, but did cover both the Austrian and French flags with blood. During Louis Napoleon's promised reign of peace, the French also sent an expeditionary force to Syria—perhaps in order to justify the Imperial Anthem—and another one to China, this one to join the English in avenging the bad treatment accorded by the Chinese to some European delegates; and, once again, hand in hand, the English-French forces reduced the Summer Palace of Peking to ashes. But of all of these warmongering adventures, the one that most attracted and seduced, absorbed, and preoccupied Louis Napoleon was the French intervention in Mexico. His objective was to create an Empire in that remote, exotic country of the American continent. The fact that Mexico wasn't really functioning as a republic was evident from its civil war, which except for a few truces had lasted for forty years. The fact too that the Mexicans, like the French and most peoples of the world, loved royal pageantry was evident from three hundred years of viceroyalty, and also from the successes of his Most Serene Highness, General Antonio López de Santa Anna. This man was a grandiloquent speaker with a love of inflated rhetoric, a mercenary and a womanizer, a hardened gambler and a lover of protocol, tassels, and plumed tricorns, of titles and heraldry, of orders and medals, which he created and bestowed en masse. It was this Creole Napoleon—"May you find yourself between Napoleons—though they are all pretty small," Juárez used to say—who gambled with his office and power in the same way that he gambled with cards or his fighting cocks, who could take or leave the presidency, assuming power or abdicating whenever it was convenient, or when it was to his advantage for political or health reasons, as it were, or just because he'd had a whim, or to punish someone else, or because his friends or enemies would force him out, or because the people or their oppressors had demanded he resume his role, or because he'd had to leave his self-imposed exile in Manga del Clavo to do battle against a "foreign enemy who had dared desecrate the fatherland"—to use the words of the National Anthem created under his aegis—or because the people or their oppressors had gone looking for him in exile in his house in Turbaco where Simón Bolívar, the Liberator, had once lived, or in the Virgin Islands where Santa Anna grew tobacco and sugar cane and raised his fighting cocks, urging him to come back to punish the hand that had disturbed the august temple of the Constitution (to quote Santa Anna's own words) . . . It was this shoddy Napoleon, we were saying, who seemed to justify all the words and theories of the Viscount of Castlereagh, the British War Minister, at the turn of the century, when the Spanish colonies in America, some of them very close to independence, had already been targeted by England. Lord Castlereagh, although normally a man of action—he nearly killed Lord Canning, a Cabinet member like himself, with a pistol-shot, just a few years before he killed himself with a better aimed gash to his jugular—believed that instead of trying to reconquer these colonies by force, it would be better to impose monarchies in them and place European princes at their helms, princes who would favor the interests of the Old Continent. In this way they would give those countries, mired in atavistic ignorance, superstition, and alcoholism, the continuity of the old patriarchal regimes of pomp and circumstance—absolutist, but controlled by Europe, to whose rule they had been accustomed by Spain since the Conquest. Lord Canning had the same idea. According to Ralph Roeder, the historian, he would tear out a page of Genesis, fan himself with it, and in reference to Spanish America say, "I have given birth to a new world." These same ideas had been expressed from time to time by the Duke of Wellington, who asked the famous Fouché to send Fernando VII, the Desired One, to be king or emperor in an American country, since his abdication had cleared the way for Pepe Botella, the brother of the Great Napoleon, to govern Spain. Fernando VII was also desired as a monarch by the Caudillos, who in 1810 initiated the Independence of Mexico. An American ex-vice president, Aaron Burr, also aspired to be Emperor of Mexico. A short time later, an obscure Spanish *dieguino* friar, Joaquín Arenas, who arrived in Mexico chained and was executed on the way to Chapultepec, conspired to reestablish Spanish control of Mexico under a local monarchy. And there were even pro-monarchy Mexican presidents who advocated the installation of a foreign prince. Among them were Mariano Paredes and later Santa Anna himself, who asked for Europe's help, requesting that it send a man who would put an end to all the corruption and banditry, and who would collaborate in the redemption of a people whose cruelty, documented by conquistadors and travelers, could also be corroborated by the illustrious intellectuals and politicians of the time. The famous French parliamentarian and historian Émile Ollivier told, in his history *L'Empire liberal*, how the Mexican Emperor Iturbide had had three hundred prisoners shot in celebration of Good Friday. His compatriot the Count of Kératry, who arrived in Mexico with the French troops, related in his book *La contre-guérilla française au Mexique* (The French Counter-Guerrilla in Mexico), how, during the assault on the La Loma railroad campsite, the Juárez guerrillas found a baker busy at work, killed him with machetes, and then continued mixing the flour with his blood.

The Little Napoleon, Louis Napoleon, who had once dreamed of setting up an empire in Nicaragua, only had to climb a few degrees in latitude in order to find Mexico. France, protector of order and civilization, of freedom and the Catholic faith, was destined, under the reign of Napoleon the Great's nephew, to put a halt to the expansion of Anglo-Saxon power and of Protestantism on the American Continent, a continent consisting primarily of people that belonged to the Latin race, just like the French. And he would do it by creating a throne in Mexico and seating a European prince on it. Louis Napoleon had gotten the idea from the beautiful Eugenia, the Spanish Eugenia, daughter of the Count of Montijo and granddaughter of a dealer in Scotch whiskies who had emigrated to the Iberian peninsula. As a young woman, Eugenia had tried to commit suicide when the Duke of Alba, descendant of the sinister noble-man of the same name, scourge of God and of Spain, creator of the Tribunal of Blood in the Low Countries, chose to marry her sister, Paca, instead of her. However, Eugenia survived her attempted suicide and outlived her sister in order to achieve the exalted destiny waiting for her and which she began fulfilling the day that five hundred musicians played Meyerbeer's march, *Le Prophète*, in front of the Cathedral of Notre Dame in Paris, from which Eugenia emerged on the arm of the Emperor of the French people, dressed in a white silk dress with Alençon velvet, a bouquet of orange blossoms in her hands, and Queen Marie Louise's diamond tiara on her head. France and the world belonged to Eugenia, and if the golden crown cresting the carriage that had brought her to the cathedral—the same one in which Napoleon and Marie Louise had traveled on their wedding day—if that crown had tumbled to the ground on leaving the Tuileries, as it had the day Napoleon the Great got married, then that incredible, extraordinary coincidence could only be interpreted as an augury of happiness.

And Juárez, Juárez the Indian, gave Napoleon his best excuse. When Juárez returned to Mexico after traveling a long circuit—from New Orleans to Panama, then across the Darien Mountains to board a ship to Acapulco, on the Pacific—he served as Minister of Justice and Minister of State, and later was named President of the Supreme Court of Justice by President Juan Alvarez, who after resigning the presidency, left Ignacio Comonfort in power, nick-named the "Substitute President." Toward the end of 1857, Comonfort staged a coup d'état when he supported the Tacubaya Plan proclaimed by General Félix Zuloaga, who was unaware of the brand-new Constitution drafted that same year, and who reestablished all the old military and ecclesiastical privi-leges. Benito Juárez was arrested and freed a few weeks later on January 11, 1858. Without support and not wishing to remain in the presidency, Comonfort left Mexico. Two days before Comonfort's departure to that eternal safe heaven for Mexican liberals, the United States, Benito Juárez, who in his posi-tion of President of the Supreme Court, automatically became President of the Republic, took office in the city of Guanajuato and from there went to Guadalajara. General Zuloaga was elected Interim President by the conserva-tives, but resigned a year later, naming General Miguel Miramón as his suc-cessor, a twenty-eight-year-old often called the "Young Maccabee," who had, during the American Intervention in 1847, been one of the young cadets who defended the Military School Headquarters at Chapultepec Castle. Thus, for almost three years, Mexico had two governments. The conservatives governed in the capital. Juárez decided to install his government in the city of Veracruz, where he arrived after another one of those long detours that he seemed to prefer and that were a prelude to the ambulatory fate his government would have during the French intervention. He sailed from the Pacific port of Manzanillo to Panama, where he crossed the Darien Mountains, and then crossed the Atlantic again toward the Gulf of Mexico. With the Tacubaya Plan, another of the many bloody conflicts between liberals and conservatives began, the so-called War of Reform or Three-Year War. When the liberals finally won, it was a precarious triumph, a Pyrrhic victory, because the country was completely bankrupt. The treasury's coffers were empty and the farmlands abandoned and unproductive. Moreover, the nationalized lands of the church didn't yield what had been hoped, partly because the properties were immediately sold, and too cheaply, by their new owners, anxious to transform them into hard cash as soon as possible, and the treasure that had been stripped from the temples—the gold artifacts of worship, the valuable paintings, the silver candelabra, the jeweled reliquaries—had all ended up in the pockets, houses, and coffers of many military men and not a few civilians. In order to get out of this trouble, on July 17, 1861, the government of Benito Juárez decreed the suspension of payments on the interest of Mexico's foreign debt for a period of two years—an amount slightly over 82,000,000 pesos. The main creditors were England, Spain, and France. Mexico owed 69,000,000 pesos to the English, 9,500,000 to the Spaniards, and 2,800,000 pesos to the French.

To its 69,000,000 the English added several demands, among them the restitution of 660,000 pesos taken by force from the headquarters of the English delegation in Mexico by ex-President Miramón, and then 680,000 pesos, the value of a silver convoy, property of the Crown's English subjects, that had been confiscated in Laguna Seca by the liberal General Santos Degollado. The Juárez government had previously recognized its "national responsibility" for both cases, and agreed to pay the corresponding amounts, according to the Treaty of Wyke-Zamacona, but the Mexican Congress failed to approve these payments.

To their 9,500,000 pesos, the Spaniards added a demand for the indemnification of the murder of several Spanish citizens in the Mexican haciendas of San Vicente and Chiconcuaque. Ex-President Miramón had agreed to this demand in the treaty of Mont-Almonte.

To its 2,800,000 pesos, the French added the 15,000,000 of the so-called "Jecker Bonds." Jean-Baptiste Jecker was a Swiss banker who owned businesses in Mexico—where one of his brothers lived and prospered—and who, a few years earlier, had given a loan to the government of Miramón. The House of Jecker gave the young Mexican president 1,500,000 in cash and clothes for his troops, and in exchange Miramón's government issued bonds payable at the custom houses in the amount of 15,000,000 pesos, or 900% of the original loan.

"*Morny est dans l'affaire*," they used to say. Morny has his hand in the affair. And if in fact Morny did, his participation was almost a guarantee of success. Duke Auguste de Morny was a bastard twice over: he was the natural son that Hortense de Beauharnais had with Count Auguste Charles Flahault de la Billarderie, himself the bastard son of an excommunicated priest who was Grand Chamberlain for both Napoleon the Great and Prince Talleyrand. *Arbiter elegantiarum*, creator of fashions such as the hat, gloves, and monocle *à la Morny*, owner of beet-sugar mills in Clermont-Ferrand, lover and connoisseur of race horses, investor in the stock market—in short, Duke Morny was an immensely rich man: he kept live lions in his palace and monkeys in his bedrooms and living rooms, incorporating the *Hortensia* flower into his coat of arms—for which he was also called "Count Hortensia"—after the French name, Hortense, of his mother, whom he shared with the French Emperor, Louis Napoleon.

Thus, when Juárez refused to recognize the outrageous terms of the contract that bore his name, Jean-Baptiste Jecker went to Duke of Morny. Jecker promised Morny 5,000,000 pesos, and besides making Jecker a French citizen—in order to make the demand a properly French one—Morny promised that he would again pressure his half brother to intervene in Mexico.

As a start, Morny convinced Louis Napoleon to replace the Viscount de Gabriac, the French representative in Mexico, with his friend—and partner in the Jecker business—Count Charles Dubois de Saligny. Besides claiming to be the victim of an attempt on his life in Mexico, the count added other significant claims to the 17,800,000 pesos that the French were already demanding, including one for a shipment of French wines sent forty years before to Agustín de Iturbide. The ephemeral Mexican emperor had never paid for his wine, perhaps because—among other reasons—he'd been executed by the time the bill had arrived.

It hardly matters whether Napoleon knew about the deal between Morny and Jecker. For him, the objective of the intervention was never a matter of collecting a few millions more or less, but to fulfill what the poet Lamartine had described as "a sublime conception . . . as vast as the ocean . . . a grand enterprise that will turn out the honor of this century in Europe and the honor of France in Spanish America."

And he decided that the time to carry out that grandiose idea had come.

2. From Last Night's Ball at the Tuileries

It was snowing in Paris. It was snowing on the Pont d'Alma. It was snowing on the Rue Rivoli as Cleopatra went by, fresh from her champagne and donkey-milk bath.

"The Roman Senate salutes the Republic of Venice," said the Roman senator in his gleaming white toga to the Venetian nobleman in the cassock with the golden sleeves that hung almost to the floor.

"Oh, Venice, Venice! Nothing easier in this palace than to give one's regards to Venice, my dear Senator. You will find Venice, or at least the spirit of Venice, in every nook and cranny here. You'll find it most especially in the Emperor's desk, beneath the map of the new Paris."

This was the Paris where it was snowing: on its bridges, on its treetops, in the avenues where queens of Sheba were always riding by.

"I don't understand, Your Majesty."

"Don't gossipmongers say that the spirit of Venice wanders the corridors of the Tuileries?"

And this was the palace, the Tuileries, glowing in the snow that evening, its windows ablaze, where naiads, in aquamarine velvet masks, were coming in.

"Your Majesty . . . I wouldn't dare . . ."

"I am not a Majesty," said the Venetian nobleman, "Therefore, I can allow myself to make statements, which—coming as they are from a foreigner in this land—aren't necessarily lies or fabrications. I beg you then, not to address me as Your Majesty. Don't you find it an extraordinary coincidence that we've both come as senators?"

The Roman senator bowed his head. He had no traces of snow in his hair.

"Would you allow me a timely observation?" he asked. "Judging by the width of your sleeves, your robe is more a doge's than a senator's."

"Please, my dear Prince, don't be so demanding. I didn't arrive here on the yacht *Il Bucentoro*. Not even in a humble gondola. Regard me as your equal."

"Many centuries separate Rome from Venice."

"But only some hundred leagues of the same Italian land where both you and I, or rather, your people and mine, live."

"Your Majesty . . ."

And some snow filtered in onto the Empress's Staircase every time a gladiator or a Greek goddess walked in.

"Dispense with that title once and for all and I promise you not to say 'Your Highness' or 'my dear Ambassador' to you. At least until such time as we remove our masks."

"The Senator is very clever . . ."

"*Signor Procurante.* That is my title," said the Venetian nobleman with a bow. His sleeves touched the floor; had it been snowing inside the Tuileries, they would have collected some nearly melted flakes.

"Do I then have the pleasure of meeting one of Voltaire's august contemporaries?"

"To a certain extent, yes. I am a child of the Enlightenment and an admirer of those rulers who gave their all for their subjects, but without their subjects' help. Joseph II, Frederick the Great—such a Francophile and a friend of Voltaire himself . . . but perhaps I erred in mentioning Frederick the Great, who, I would imagine, is an unwelcome reminder to your people . . ."

"If Your Majesty can speak as a Frenchman, I shall speak as a German: past quarrels belong in the past. Joseph II and Frederick the Great were both great rulers of the German people."

"Are you calling me a Frenchman?"

That figure in the enormous caftan-like garment had to be a Persian hunter. He was accompanied by a salamander.

"Anyway, it's all relative. For example," continued the Venetian nobleman from behind a mask that resembled a bird's beak, "French culture belongs to the whole world. Napoleon I, a Corsican, belonged to France, and I . . ."

"You?"

37

"My dear Senator, as a cosmopolitan man I belong to Europe, and am committed to the struggle for man's freedom and dignity on our entire continent. But we will only reach that goal when peace prevails. And we shall attain peace when . . ."

The Venetian nobleman glanced distractedly toward Ariadne, in a crown of gold and stars, accompanied by a Bacchus who wore earrings, a necklace, and garlands of purple and green grape clusters. The muscular, half-nude lackey who followed was no doubt the constellation Hercules on his knees.

"But you were saying . . ."

"Oh, yes—as a Venetian I fight for the liberation of Venice . . . Doesn't that seem the most natural course?"

"And does the *Signor Procurante* not think that it's equally natural for Venice's masters to refuse to give it up?"

"Masters? Hm. You know that there's an offer in the works, and that its acceptance will contribute greatly to the expansion of the House of Austria . . ."

"The throne of Mexico, Your Majesty, could contribute greatly to enhance your reputation . . . that is, if the gamble is successful. If not . . ."

"Please don't call it a gamble. It's a very serious enterprise."

"But it would in no way increase the actual power of the House of Austria, nor expand its territories . . ."

Everyone was represented, as were all the centuries: young philosophers in Doric tunics and white chlamyses; Henry VII as portrayed by the Holbein school; pike-bearing lansquenets from *Il Sacco di Roma*. The Duchess of Urbino as painted by Piero della Francesca.

The Venetian nobleman scratched his head.

"Wide sleeves aren't exclusive to ancient Venetian doges," he said. "Magicians such as Merlin wear them too. I can't turn myself into a hound or a hare as he could, but I might have more than one trick up said sleeves. I can't promise you that the Roman Empire will ever reach from the Hibernian Ocean to Rocky Arabia again . . . I've always loved those old names: *Arabia Petraea*, *Arabia Felix* . . . But, I ask myself, wouldn't the heirs of the Holy Roman Empire, founded by Charlemagne, want to expand their kingdoms east of the Danube?"

Six of the windows in the enormous and high-vaulted Salon of the Marshals at the Tuileries looked out into the Carousel Plaza, and one into the garden. One could see, through them, that it was still snowing in Paris.

"To expand the Austrian Empire east of the Danube? Now that we've withdrawn our troops from our principalities, so that they can unite and form Romania? I dare say, Your Majesty, that this offer of yours comes too late."

It was snowing in Paris. It snowed on L'Avenue Montaigne. On the mass graves at Montmartre Cemetery. It snowed on the ramparts of Clignancourt Gate, on the poverty-stricken slums, and on the fur of the Punjab tigers and the Afghan leopards at the Paris Zoo.

"My dear Senator, the fact that the Sultan of Turkey has expressed . . . when was this? . . . well, several weeks ago . . . his approval of the unification of Moldavia and Wallachia means absolutely nothing. Romania isn't a nation yet. It's only a name. To become a true nation, the temporary protection of one or two world powers is, shall we say, helpful. Nothing is carved in stone on the map of Europe."

And it had also snowed on the enormous headdress, made with quetzal feathers, of the Aztec princess, hiding her face behind a jade mask.

"It is clear," said the Roman senator, "that the spirit of Mexico roams the Tuileries."

"On my word, this is only another extraordinary coincidence. I'm not acquainted with this lady, who has been so felicitously daring."

Tristran of Lyoness and Lancelot of the Lake were exchanging swords and kissing a hundred times. They both appeared to be men, but they could just as well have been women.

"An Aztec princess out during a snowstorm—isn't it amusing, Senator?"

"Yes, very humorous. And absurd. As absurd, if I may say so, as a golden carriage in the middle of the tropics. I'm afraid, Your Majesty, that to place a European prince on the Mexican throne will require rather a lot of cannon-fire—and it will take even more to keep him there."

"No, I don't think that it will be all that difficult an undertaking. The Mexican people have lost all their old grandeur. Have you read Prescott, the American historian? I think he's the one who compared Mexico to Egypt and to Greece: conquered races, my dear Prince, who share nothing with their ancestors."

"Mexico has been a republic for many years."

"Mexico has been a disaster for many years. And consider this: if France itself has not proven sufficiently mature to be a republic, how can Mexico be one? How can those poor Spanish-American nations, always in the midst of revolutions, become republics? You've mentioned a golden carriage in the tropics, so let me ask you: what does Your Highness have to say about Brazil, a nation that's had more than a quarter-century of peace and prosperity under the reign of Pedro II? Railroads, highways, and new industry: that is Brazil. Yes, a royal coach in the middle of the tropics, but a coach with smokestacks, my dear Prince, a steam-powered coach that moves on steel rails, like progress, which, in turn, either takes great leaps forward or can hardly be called progress. Take Suez. We started to dig the canal with shovels and buckets and we now have developed incredible technology, thanks to the genius of De Lesseps. Not to mention the fact that we've turned it into a source of immense wealth for the French. Everyone in Paris—barbers, masons, and butchers alike—has stock in the Canal. And we'll follow it up with a canal in Nicaragua, or Panama, perhaps . . ."

The Venetian nobleman dreamed on. He focused on Diana, wearing a fur turban, with a quiver on her shoulder, making her way inside, two lackeys following behind her with a deer carcass, ready for roasting. A Queen Bee flapped her gossamer wings, surrounded by midgets dressed as drones who danced and buzzed.

"But Mexico is a far more violent nation than Brazil. An emperor could suffer the same fate there as William Walker did in Central America, or Raousset-Boulbon in Mexico itself."

"Yes, it is curious that Walker and Boulbon both started out by invading Sonora and that they were both executed . . . But, for God's sake, my dear Senator, there is no real comparison. Permit me to remind you that Walker was an adventurer, a pirate. We will be sending a prince of royal blood who will have material support from the European powers at his disposal, and the French army behind him."

"Walker relied on the United States to help him conquer Nicaragua."

"We will count on the support of the Confederacy."

"My position as a Roman senator will allow me to ask *Signore Procurante* if the rumors are true, that Texas and Louisiana will be deeded to France if it recognizes the Confederacy."

There was a notable absence of the Harlequins that had abounded at the balls held during the austere years of Louis Philippe's reign. The security guards were disguised exclusively as unadorned dominoes: Louis Napoleon wanted to avoid being assassinated during a masked ball, as King Gustav of Sweden had been.

"Rumor, Senator, is correct. Yes, I confess that I would like to correct some of France's historical missteps, for which my illustrious ancestor was in large part responsible . . . Louisiana, for example . . . To think that Bonaparte said at the time that in Louisiana he had given England a rival at sea that would soon overtake its proud navy. If we could go back in time, Senator, I would convince Napoleon to follow Colbert's advice always to maintain France's presence in Louisiana and Santo Domingo. I think that if we had recognized L'Ouverture's government we would not have lost Haiti. Don't you agree? And after the defeat on the Nile, my uncle should have insisted on the reconquest of our dominion in India . . . But you see, Clive secured the English presence in that nation, and now it's one of the pillars of the British Empire . . . But if you will allow me, I shall return to the topic of Raousset-Boulbon. He was a different matter entirely . . ."

"Because he was French?"

"Because he was a European. Because he predicted that the power of the United States would grow so rapidly that in ten years not a cannon would be fired in Europe without their permission . . . of course he was exaggerating, but you see my point. Besides, de Tocqueville had already stated something similar, more than thirty years earlier. He predicted, you will remember, that the United States and Russia were both destined to rule their halves of the world . . . But we can't allow Tocqueville and Raousset to become prophets, now can we?"

"I presume that we will all be thanking France and England for defeating the Russians in the Crimea."

"And the Confederates, my dear Senator, for the shots fired on Fort Sumter, which have turned the United States into the Disunited States. It's a pity, really, that your people didn't participate in the Crimean War . . . But we accomplished our goal of stopping the Russians at their own borders. Although I ask myself sometimes if it wouldn't have been better to divide Turkey up amongst ourselves instead of supporting it . . . Austria, as I told Archduke Maximilian, could have expanded its territory with Albania and Herzegovina . . ."

But there was a lady passing now who was dressed as a tree, and from whose arms hung many red velvet apples. Two or three macaroni from the late eighteenth century, in long, prodigiously curly wigs and tiny slippers with enormous, snow-spattered golden buckles, were nearby, gargling with champagne.

"How much longer, Your Majesty?"

The Venetian nobleman remarked that the macaroni's wigs reminded him of those the first Hohenzollern king wore to hide his hump. He added:

"How much longer what . . . ?"

"How much longer will they continue to be the 'Disunited States'? The North has greater access to important resources than the South."

"But the South has a more powerful army."

"The North is capable of increasing its troops threefold in a relatively short time."

"My dear Senator. The North is fighting for *Uncle Tom's Cabin* and the South for an economic structure and a way of life that it will not part with easily. Remember that there are three million slaves there."

"The enemy within one's own home."

"We could provide them with an escape valve by stimulating the migration of slaves to the Mexican Empire . . . There's an American, a man named Corwin, who has very interesting ideas on the matter . . ."

"But if the Confederates have gone to war to protect slavery, I doubt they'll let go of their slaves . . ."

"I'm referring to a controlled migration . . ."

There were also two or three Spanish conquistadors wearing steel masks. And the Arnolfinis were there, followed by a lackey who held up a concave mirror to their faces. Or was it convex?

"If the Senator would only look at it as a transaction rather than a surrender," the Venetian nobleman continued, "we could use words like 'compensation.' The Mexican Empire will recognize the Confederacy, and the latter, in turn, will reimburse the Empire with human resources . . ."

"Would Mexico be purchasing slaves, then?"

And there were some Lombards, wearing linen tunics bordered in heavy, dark fur.

"We would buy their freedom. We will turn Mexico into a new Liberia. You know, the Empress, who is always so interested in history, was fascinated when I told her that the word Liberia comes from "Liberty," and that its capital, Monrovia, is named after President Monroe—just like the Monroe Doctrine, which is giving us so much trouble—who created that nation so that American slaves could live free there . . . But, what happened? Only a few went, and they enslaved the poor locals . . . It was a failure . . . No, we don't want Mexico to end up as the slave nation that Walker wanted to make of Nicaragua. From the moment they set foot on Mexican land, the slaves will be freed."

"*Signor Procurante*, I don't believe that such a migration will improve the Latin race."

And to avoid damage to the carpets and the parquet floors in the Tuileries, the Greek courtesans had removed their golden sandals with cleats on the soles spelling out the words "Follow me" in reverse, so that they could be read properly in the dirt or dust of roads and streets. Or, in the case of this evening, on the snow—because it was still snowing in Paris.

"Mexico has enormous uninhabited territories. We shall distribute the slaves strategically. Moreover, when we say that this project has the objective of protecting the Latin character of Spanish-America, we aren't talking about protecting a particular race. It's not a matter of skin color but of protecting Latin culture and tradition. We could also argue that European culture and tradition belong just as much to the millions of Indians on that continent."

The Venetian nobleman led the Roman senator by the arm away from the orchestra.

"Juárez," he continued "is nourished by the spirit of Rousseau, as we are, and not by the political philosophy of the Aztecs or the Incas, if such a thing ever existed."

"It doesn't seem to be Rousseau's spirit that inspires Mexican monarchists like Gutiérrez Estrada . . ."

"Oh, please don't mention that madman to me. Did you know that just hearing his name makes the Empress shiver? She says that he reminds her of Philip II. Or Torquemada. But don't fret. Gutiérrez Estrada will remain quietly at Marescotti Palace. He can't live without kissing the Pope's sandals . . . As to the others . . . One can always assign them diplomatic posts in European courts."

Some nymphs were painting their lips using the Palatine Guards' gleaming plates of armor as mirrors.

"In any case," added the Venetian nobleman, "I was referring to tradition. You will agree that, among them, the most important is our Catholic faith. Protecting it is the primordial objective of this entire undertaking. The Catholic House of Austria, a 'hammer for heretics' as it was called by Laurens Gracián, no doubt shares this philosophy."

Lady Night, covered with a star-studded blue velvet blanket, a mask in the shape of a full, smiling moon on her face, danced with a headless man who, judging by the head that a lackey bore on a silver salver, must have been Charles I of England.

43

The Venetian nobleman stopped, let go of the Roman senator's arm and jabbed him in the chest.

"I'm going to ask you once again to try to influence Vienna. It is imperative that His Highness, Archduke Ferdinand Maximilian, decide once and for all. That is to say, that he declare his decision publicly and officially, since we know that he's already been convinced."

"May I ask how *il Signor Procurante* knows this?"

"He has very good sources. Their Highnesses, the Archduke and Archduchess, are taking Spanish lessons several hours a week. Princess Charlotte devours books on Mexican legends and the Prince is absorbed in Humboldt, Mathieu de Fossey, and other travelers who have described the wonders and wealth of Mexico. And just wait until our illustrious Michel Chevalier finishes his report. I'll show you statistics that speak for themselves. For example, did you know that France exports five times as much to Mexico as they import from us? We can't risk losing that market, nor the enormous mining potential that Mexico provides. Yes, I know that some members of Parliament have said that Sonora's mineral wealth could be a myth, as was California's. But that will not prove to be the case, Walker and Raousset knew very well what they wanted. Sonora has vast amounts of silver. And, tell me, is Europe, are we, going to let anyone snatch away that wealth from us? The North Americans began Sonora's economic conquest long ago. They've invested millions of dollars there. And one of these days, perhaps, Juárez will sign another treaty and will give them the entire Sonora territory."

"Europe already has investments in Mexico. The English own all the silver mines in the central region."

The Venetian nobleman took the Roman senator's arm once again and walked with measured steps.

"Not only that. Exports from England to Mexico outnumber ours threefold. If we let them build any more railroads, they'll strip the place bare. But I'm surprised that you count the English as Europeans. In many ways, England is not a part of Europe. Let's say that we can consider the English to be Europeans when it's convenient to us, and see them instead as barbarians or Vikings or whatever you like when it suits our needs. When all is said and done, they, and only they, are to blame for the fact that America now contains twenty million Yankees, history's new vandals. These people want to steal the entire continent, beginning with its name, which they've already appropriated for themselves."

"Speaking of England, I confess that it seemed somewhat . . . somewhat strange that support was sought from a Protestant nation for an enterprise designed to uphold the Catholic doctrine . . ."

"Senator, one of the most valuable virtues in a ruler is pragmatism. Allow me to remind you that our illustrious Cardinal Mazarin assisted Cromwell, who was not only a staunch Protestant but guilty of regicide. And that Francis I sought and received the support of Suliman the Magnificent . . . And, if it's true that the English aristocracy is hoping for a Confederate victory, the Mexican Empire will be able to consolidate its interests. Yes, we needed the support of Her Royal British Majesty, and, thank God—or perhaps thank Albert—we secured it . . . An extraordinary woman, Queen Victoria, don't you agree?"

"They tell me that she's inconsolable since Albert's death."

"Oh, you can't imagine how much they both enjoyed their visits to France. Saint-Cloud always seemed a fairytale palace to Victoria. And in Versailles, where, by the way, they met Bismarck, they almost wept for joy at the magnificent fireworks that climaxed with a reproduction of Windsor Castle. We had also planned for fireworks tonight, but—well, you see how it's snowing. Another time, perhaps. To get back to Mexico, did you know about the arrival of French ships in Campeche? The people poured out into the streets in support of the monarchy. According to my calculations, Lorencez must have already landed in Veracruz with another four thousand men. So we won't only have 'blue trousers' in Mexico, but 'red trousers' as well. They tell me, moreover, that Carrera is ready to join the Mexican Empire . . . as soon as there's a Mexican emperor of course."

"Carrera?"

"Rafael Carrera, you will remember, is Guatemala's 'President for Life,' as he calls himself. A petty dictator like so many others that crop up in those lands . . . Soulouque, Rosas, Santa Anna . . . Ah, would you allow me to remove my mask a few moments so that I can breathe? It makes me very warm, and it's melting the wax on my moustache."

The Venetian nobleman removed his bird mask, revealing the face of Napoleon III.

"Who would've thought . . . ? What a great honor, Your Majesty, to have chatted . . ."

". . . with a senator from the Republic of Venice. But now I will allow you to address the French Emperor, if, of course, my dear Senator, you will reveal your own identity as well."

45

The Roman senator removed his white silk mask, behind which appeared the face of Prince Richard Metternich.

"Oh, oh, what a surprise. Prince Metternich, our dear Excellency, the Austrian Ambassador, son of the great Chancellor Clemens Metternich. I see it, but I don't believe it . . . Welcome to the Tuileries."

Flaubert's Salammbô was absent that night, since no one had dared wear that costume after the Countess of Castiglione appeared at a earlier Tuileries Ball intent on seducing Louis Napoleon, her upswept hair pinned by a diamond-studded tiara, her nude shoulders, arms, legs, and back exposed beneath transparent tulle, followed by Count Choiseul carrying the black velvet train of her cape in one hand. The Count had been dressed as an African slave, his skin painted black, and he'd carried an enormous sunshade—which on this occasion would have been a snow shade. But everyone else was there, including a Venus rising from the sea.

"Yes," continued Napoleon. "Set aside a few minutes next week to chat with me, my dear Prince. Let us decide on a time. As I said before, I want to show you several things. The Empress has ordered a set of dishes with the imperial monogram of Maximilian I of Mexico. That will be one of our presents to him. I've also asked one of our best tailors to design a parade uniform for the Mexican marshals—there will be such a thing as a Mexican marshal some day, don't you think? I myself have sketched some designs for uniforms suitable for the tropics. We have to think of everything. I've also ordered several tons of mosquito netting to relieve, as much as possible, the suffering of our troops in those unhealthy lands. You're aware that yellow fever is endemic to Veracruz . . . Of course if, Monsieur Pasteur's theories on germs hold true, we will soon eliminate yellow fever, malaria, and other diseases. I will suggest to the Empress that we invite Pasteur to Compiègne next autumn. We will stun rabbits so that he can hunt them easily. These scientists have no idea what a shotgun is . . . Are you acquainted with Monsieur Pasteur?"

"There are other germs that you would have to eliminate too, Your Majesty."

"Oh, yes, I can imagine to whom you are referring. That German journalist . . . What's his name, Karl Marx? A man who spends his life attacking England, among other things, but had the impudence to live in London for ten years. Did you know that he wrote in *Die Presse* that the Mexican intervention is one more ruse of mine to distract the French people from other problems? But no, I wouldn't have to eliminate these diseases. At least not in France. As long as we keep them under control, all these communists and republicans will be proof that freedom of expression is alive in France, that we are a constitutional monarchy. And that's exactly what the world needs, my dear Prince—liberal dictatorships. You see, here in Paris we allow Legitimists and Orleanists to say whatever they wish, and to criticize the Empire to their heart's content. The same with the followers of Blanqui and Proudhon—all of those types. Victor Hugo should really come home, so that he can see how much freedom one enjoys in the Empire. They tell me that he's taken to designing gloomy castles. But of course, it rains every day in Brussels and the Channel Islands. I too became melancholy in England with that eternal rain and those gray, gloomy days . . . Here Victor Hugo would recover his *joie de vivre* and that Marx fellow would learn to calm down. Here he would find good cuisine, he could speak his mind, he could drink excellent wines, he could enjoy the sun-drenched Paris boulevards, or the banks of the Seine, all of that. He could watch Cora Pearl dancing nude on a carpet of orchids. That's what I call the good life. And what I call democracy. Of course, we do have to be careful not to attack democracy. How could I, as the first European head of state chosen by a general election? How could I, when two years later the French people elected me their emperor by a landslide? In some ways—don't you agree, my dear ambassador—I had more right to govern France than Juárez had to lead Mexico when he came to power . . . Would you care for some champagne? Empress Eugénie loves pink champagne. Have you paid your respects to her? I'll tell you a poorly guarded secret that's already common knowledge: if you spot a Marie Antoinette carrying a basket filled with poppies and strawberries, followed by two lackeys dressed as cows with silver bells on their collars, you'll have found her. Although you never know with my beloved Eugénie. Sometimes she disappears in the middle of the ball to change costumes. I wouldn't be at all surprised if she had become, for example, a bullfighter . . ."

(In a suit inspired by Goya, her hair in a pigtail, carrying a two-color fighting cape, and followed by a lackey dressed as a picador's assistant, pushing a bull's head with nacre-inlaid horns on a cart.)

That night, every window in every room of the Tuileries was alight until dawn: in the Council Chamber, in the Salon of the Marshals, the private apartments of the Emperor and the Empress, the Green Room, the Pink Room, the Room of the Service Officers, the Room of the First Consul. At dawn a cart left the Tuileries with all the leftovers from the great banquet—pâtés, marrons gla-

47

cés, rabbit terrines, chicken fillets à la toulousaine, vol-au-vents à la financière, asparagus in hollandaise sauce—to be sold at the main Paris market, under a sign reading "From Last Night's Ball at the Tuileries," advertising to those willing and able to afford such a luxury that they could finish up the delicacies that a duchess, a prince, or perhaps even the Emperor himself might have touched with their fork, or left on a plate. When the lights finally began to fade, it was time for the other carts to head out to the Bois de Bondy, east of the city, and drop off the excrement gathered the night before in the Parisian latrines. The excrement dripped through the cracks in the carts and left dark stains in the snow. Sometimes the snow kept falling and blanketed the stains. That morning, this was not the case. It had stopped snowing in Paris, the temperature fell, and the dark excrement stains remained visible and frozen.

But if it had stopped snowing in Paris proper, it kept on snowing nonetheless above the city. A strong wind that kept the snow from falling blew it horizontally, up to the height of what, thirty-nine years later, would be the third level of the Eiffel Tower.

3. The King of Rome

Austrian Chancellor Clemens Lothar Metternich, nicknamed The Grand Inquisitor of Europe, and to whose persistence and good taste we owe the invention of the Viennese chocolate torte, or *Sachertorte*, once said that coffee should be hot as love, sweet as sin, and black as hell. Vienna had adopted the habit of drinking coffee thanks to the invasion of the Turks, who were defeated once and for all in 1683, that Year of Wonders, *annus mirabilis*, following the unsuccessful siege mounted by the Grand Vizier Kara Mustafa. This didn't keep the city from teaching the world forty different ways of preparing coffee, not always hot, sweet, or black. But Vienna, whose city walls had disappeared at the beginning of the century to give way to the beautiful avenue known as the Ringstrasse, is also the city originally founded by the Romans as Vindobona or Vindominia. It's the city where the stoic philosopher Marcus Aurelius died, and that was devastated by the plague in 1679. The plague was a scourge from God, and was often a crueler and better-aimed weapon than the infidel's scimitars and catapults: Saint Louis, King of France, died of plague in the final Crusade. Vienna showed the world the pomp and splendor of a triumphant and resplendent Baroque era that combined Gothic and Renaissance art, frivolity and exuberance, in temples like Karlskirche, in palaces like Schönbrunn, and in monuments like the Column of the Holy Trinity. The city always manifested its joy in living, its love for pageantry, and its gluttonous tendencies as well. It showed its love of nature in 1552 in the great enthusiasm that an elephant, a gift to the emperor from the Grand Turk, awakened in the Viennese; by the amazement caused by a giraffe bestowed upon Vienna by the Egyptian Viceroy (which resulted in a giraffe craze, consisting of dances, hairstyles, skirts, and makeup *à la girafe*); and by the admiration provoked when Captain Hadlock brought a pair of Eskimos from the North Pole—promptly put on display in Belvedere Park, to the endless amazement of the Viennese. Not for nothing did Franz Schubert die from typhoid fever and extreme poverty: Vienna turned to and then taught the world the delights of pop music—the dizzying waltz, the diabolical violin of Johann Strauss, as well as the mechanical tunes that seemed to come out of nowhere every time a clock struck the half hour (with minuets), or the quarter hour (with gavottes); every time, in short, that a window or a snuff box was opened, or an ivory ball was placed on the blue felt of a billiards table. In keeping with the times, the Viennese upper-middle class, who weekly ordered a vat of hot bathwater for their houses, also hung Aeolian harps from trees in their gardens to be played by the Alpine winds. But Vienna, this Vienna, which from 1556 had been the capital of the most illustrious emperors of the house of Habsburg—those founders of the principle of universal monarchy, whose control through the course of the centuries extended from Portugal to Transylvania, from Holland to Sicily, and to four-fifths of the American continent—had also taken it upon itself to teach Piedmont patriots how to dance to the sound of whip-cracks, and to the rhythm of falling truncheons. And this same Vienna had hanged Hungarian rebels so that they too could learn to dance, to the beat of a vulture's wings.

In that city, in Schönbrunn Palace, on July 6, 1832, Ferdinand Maximilian Joseph was born. He was the brother of the future Emperor of Austria-Hungary and himself the future emperor of one of those American countries where a dazzling sun still hung, then, from its zenith, illuminating a great vastness of tropics and deserts, albeit when this pale sun, shining on the Alcazar of Toledo and the cathedral of Vienna, had already begun to hide beyond the horizon. Better known by his second name, that of his notable ancestor Maximilian

I—patron of the arts, deer hunter, founder of the Spanish Habsburg branch via the arranged marriage of his son Philip the Fair to Juana the Mad, claimant of a lineage leading back to Priam, and aspirant to the papacy—Ferdinand Maximilian Joseph came into the world two weeks before the death (perhaps of consumption or from a poisoned melon), in that same Schönbrunn Palace, of a boy with a spirit of iron and a body of glass, called the "King of Rome" in some quarters. This boy didn't really have a chance to say very much on his deathbed, since his mouth was constantly filling up with a bloody mucus that Moll, his faithful servant, had to wipe away with a handkerchief. Some say his last words were "Poultices! Ampules!" Others say that they were "Harness the horses! I must see my father. I must embrace him one more time!" It's also possible, of course, that the King of Rome—who was never a king, and was never in Rome—had died of love for Maximilian's mother, the Archduchess Sophie.

On one occasion, the King of Rome's father had said that he would prefer to see his son pale and dead at the bottom of the Seine than captured and in the hands of his enemies. The conqueror of Wagram and Austerlitz lived just long enough to know that his son had indeed been captured by these self-same enemies and had been taken to the Viennese court, where they'd forbidden him to speak French, where those around him had been ordered never to speak of his father, where he had been stripped of all his keepsakes and titles, and where the things that Napoleon sent him from Saint Helena—his spurs and horse's bridle, his hunting pistol, his field glasses—never arrived. But the Great Corsican did not live long enough to find out, some years later, that his son had died, still a child, his skin rough, brittle, and white as paper, his thymus swollen and gristly, his fingers wrinkled, his chest reddened from emetic pomades, and his neck covered by the puncture marks left by leeches, still a captive in the room next to the bedchamber with the gold-trimmed Chinese lacquer from Schönbrunn Palace where he, Napoleon the Great, had slept with the Countess Walewska, after his troops had crossed the Danube on a bridge rigged together from boats in order to inflict his first great humiliation on the Habsburgs. The second great humiliation that he inflicted on the family was to marry Marie Louise, the daughter of Emperor Francis, because Bonaparte was far more interested in an heir with royal blood who could perpetuate his incipient dynasty than he was in Josephine's admittedly delicious and generous rump. History reports that when Napoleon studied the Habsburg family tree—a family that took its name from the falcon, and had adopted nothing less than the cross that redeemed the world as its scepter—he pointed to Marie Louise's name and said: "This is the womb I want to marry." Although Napoleon didn't go to Vienna for the prenuptial ceremonies, he sent the Prince of Neuchâtel as his proxy, also tasked with escorting Marie to Paris. The city of Vienna still had the opportunity to see what the imperial couple would look like, however, thanks to Mälzel, the genius who had invented the automatic chess player, and who, with infinite patience and miraculous cleverness, had created both miniature orchestras and tiny military bands, as he presented two huge dolls of the bride and groom on the balcony of a house on Kohlmarkt, their hearts and internal organs made with gears and springs. The crowd gave them an ovation and wept for joy. In Paris, Napoleon and Marie Louise greeted the townspeople—the men and women, young and old, seen from the balcony where they stood, seemed themselves like diminutive mechanical reproductions—and when the couple retired they were followed by great acclamation in the streets of the city. Less than twenty-five years before, another Habsburg—also an Austrian and also a French sovereign, also with a son who would never reign—had been jeered by the Parisian mob. Her head, which had turned white overnight, rolled from the guillotine onto the Place de la Concorde. This same mob, easily moved to emotional extremes, turned out in strength to extol the name of Marie Louise when Napoleon's heir was born. The child was born with a blue face, almost dead, and gave his first cry only when they wet his lips with cognac. One hundred and one cannon salvos and a rain of bulletins dropped from a balloon by the aviatrix Madam Blanchard all announced the good news with which the heavens had blessed France and her sovereigns. Ten thousand poets composed verses in honor of the King of Rome, who was also called Napoleon II from the time he was a child. But few knew all the names—Napoleon François Charles Joseph—that he was given, first in a private baptism in the Chapel of the Tuileries, and then later in the official state baptism held at Notre Dame in Paris. The latter occasion was the day when his father first showed the infant to the multitudes. The King of Rome was wrapped in gold and ermine as Napoleon raised him above his head, just as Edward I had shown the first Prince of Wales to the English people. Paris, all of France, lit up then, and the merchants poured into the streets to hawk tapestries, crockery, fans, folding screens, music boxes, medallions, parasols, colored pictures, and engravings, all commemorating the baptism. The Cross of the Legion of Honor was pinned to the cradle of the King of Rome and the Order of the Iron Crown hung above his head. Before he was three years old, he had been dressed in a French grenadier officer's uniform, and that of a colonel in the Polish Lancers. But these things wouldn't last, including the one name, François, that his father chose from all his other names and titles to use when he held him on his lap and kissed him, or made faces at him in front of the mirror and fastened his enormous sword around his son's waist and played war games with him on the carpets of the Tuileries, telling him, "François, you will be history's second Alexander—the day you stretch out your arms to the world, it will be yours." All this ended when the King of Rome left Paris with his mother, heading toward Vienna, never again to return to France, and his father headed alone for the island of Elba, carrying the miniature close to his chest that had accompanied him through the frozen fields of Beresina and the flame-devoured streets of Moscow, showing his son riding a lamb. The little King of Rome was no longer called François, and began to be called Franz—Archduke Franz. Later, for a time, he was Prince of Parma. Later still, until the day he died, he was the Duke of Reichstadt. He was also known as the Eaglet. There were poets who called him Astyanax—comparing him to the son of Hector, who was seized by the Greeks and whom Ulysses threw from one of the highest towers of Troy—when they found out that, snubbed by the House of Austria because the plebeian blood of the Corsican adventurer coursed through his veins, but envied by that same House of Austria because he also carried the royal blood of the Habsburgs, he had been given a palace for a prison. But in none of the bedrooms, nor the other enormous halls of Schönbrunn—not in the Carousel Room, nor the round China Room, nor the Million Room—did the Eaglet find the velvet chairs with the Tiber and the Seven Hills of Rome painted on their broad backs. Nor did he ever find the Sèvres porcelain that Napoleon had painted with famous battles, Paris monuments, extracts from the Napoleonic Code, and the Niagara Falls, on which the King of Rome was supposed to receive his meals. His beloved Governess, Madam Quiou, wasn't there to gather him in her arms and to bury her face in his golden curls, as she had been sent back to France on instructions from Metternich. His mother had gone to live in Parma on the orders of Emperor Francis I, where she was made a grand duchess and delivered body and soul to a one-eyed marshal with whom she conceived more than one bastard. She forgot about Napoleon, about the love the Corsican had had for their son, and the devotion he had always shown to her. The first proof of that devotion had been given to her the day she arrived in Paris after crying a river of tears to discover that the Emperor of France had ordered all the furnishings and objects she had had in her bedroom at the Hofburg moved to or reproduced at the Tuileries down to the tiniest detail. Her bed was there, as well her chests of drawers, chairs, rugs, paintings of her Papa Francis and her stepmother, and her shrine and vanity case; she also found her birds in their cages, her mirrors, and her curtains; even her favorite dog was there: alive, fat, and slobbering.

When Archduke Franz, alias the Eaglet, stretched out his arm, it wasn't to take possession of the world, but rather so that his mentor, Count Dietrichstein, could hit the palm of his hand with a stick, as punishment for speaking French. But these blows were far more painful to those French bards who still thought, as one of them wrote, that the little "Jesus of the Tuileries" would grow up to be the Christ of Schönbrunn. Besides learning German and those other languages that an archduke needed to know, as well as a smattering of the other languages a prince of the Empire that ruled, among others, Czechs and Magyars, Poles and Romanians, Italians and Serbo-Croatians; besides learning the history of the Holy Roman Empire—the crown of which the Habsburgs had possessed for almost three hundred and sixty years—and the art and intricacies of ceremony and protocol within the Austrian Court, and how he should behave not only as the grandson of the Emperor or as a future member of the imperial army, but also as King of Belgium or Poland, either of which he might be, someday: not with the haughtiness or the pageantry of what was once the Spanish branch of the Habsburgs, but with the dignity, the grandeur, and the generosity that had distinguished the Austrian branch since the reign of Maria Theresa . . . besides all of this, the Eaglet learned how to earn the love of his grandfather, of his tutors, of his step-grandmother, of the Austrian soldiers, and of the Viennese.

Blond, pale, his eyes big and blue, resembling his father more than Marie Louise, but more beautiful than either; quiet, serious, affectionate, obedient and judicious, the Eaglet was transformed into a splendid horseman, a careful student of artillery and the art of military architecture and logistics. He swore to crush not only the rebels of Parma who had risen against the Grand Duchess, but also all the enemies of the Habsburg Empire—among whom we might count Chancellor Metternich, one of the few people who never loved the boy, and who knew very well that the Eaglet would never dare to fight against France or the French. Metternich's spies had reported that the Eaglet, who had needed to relearn French, his forgotten native tongue, as though it were a foreign language, had translated "*Die Schlachten von Ligny, Quatre Bras und Waterloo*" ("The battles of Ligny, Quartre Bras, and Waterloo," wherein Count Anton von Prokesch-Osten had paid homage to the Great Corsican) into French in secret, so that he could learn it all by heart.

Unfortunate King of Rome, whose chest narrowed and whose face grew thinner as his legs grew longer! This poor François who, named infantry captain at age fifteen, lost his voice while giving orders to a battalion! Unlucky Duke of Reichstadt, who lost all color in his fingertips one day, and the next began to spit blood. He had dyspepsia, a chronic cough, and hemorrhoids. His neck and scalp were covered with scabs. After fainting in the middle of the street, he was no longer allowed to fence, nor dance lively waltzes, nor ride his horse on the banks of the Danube. That wretched Eaglet! When his legs could no longer hold him, his grandfather had made him a colonel. Dr. Malfatti's prescriptions and potions proved useless, as did the care and affections of his aunt, Archduchess Sophie of Bavaria: scarcely four years older than he, already nicknamed the "Amorous Archduchess" and "Madame Potiphar." Neither the mustard plasters, nor the jenny's milk in seltzer water, nor the Marienbad waters had any effect. On July 22, 1832, a traveler passing through Vienna stopped at the Schönbrunn, saw the two stone eagles that Napoleon had ordered placed at the main entrance of the palace to commemorate the fall of the old city, and that the Austrians had forgotten to remove, and said: "One of these two eagles has surely died on the Isle of St. Helena from sadness, desolation, nostalgia, or impotence, or perhaps from arsenic poisoning; but the other will soon take flight to reconquer France." At about the same time, the Duke of Reichstadt, bathed in perspiration, burning with fever, his legs ever more swollen and his mouth filled with fresh blood, suffering from an enlarged spleen, his mesenteric glands inflamed and hardened, and his eyes dancing in their sockets looking for the ghost of his father or else his life-sized portrait and sword—the only two mementos of the Great Man that Metternich had allowed the Eaglet to keep—died in a bedroom in that very same palace. Some said it was from tuberculosis; others that Metternich—who had never believed it was in Austria's best interests to have the throne of France occupied by someone who might one day turn out to be more a Bonaparte than a Habsburg—recognizing the fragility of the Eaglet, had secured for him the favors of the celebrated and beautiful Fanny Elsler, and other dancers and courtesans besides, like Mademoiselle Pèche and the Polish countess, in whose arms, thighs, breasts, and sheets the unhappy, unfortunate Franz had expended his life. Others still said that the same Chancellor had sent him a gift of poisoned melon and that the Eaglet had died a virgin. Yet others refuted this, insisting that he had been a virgin only until the moment that the Archduchess had realized he was becoming a man, and that if anything had poisoned his soul and consumed his body, it was this first amorous adventure with the Archduchess. And then . . . others said even more. Gossipmongers, for instance, spread the rumor that the Eaglet was the father of the child named Ferdinand Maximilian, who would, many years later, be Emperor of Mexico, and who was born a scant two weeks before the Eaglet's death.

The bells of St. Stephen's Cathedral rang in mourning. The boatmen who sailed the Danube toward the Black Sea; the conductors of the *Zieselswagen* in their short blue pants and top hats who strolled along the Landstrasse; the archdukes and princesses of the court; the Vienna Boys' Choir; the lackeys in three-cornered hats and jackets embroidered in gold; the café violinists; the cavalrymen in their long, sky-blue tunics, purple trousers, and plumed helmets; the burghers having picnics in the Prater; the musical clocks, the waltzes, the forests, the traveler who had stopped in front of the Schönbrunn; everyone and everything in Vienna cried for the Eaglet. Even the Emperor Francis himself sobbed like a baby when his adored grandson died. But nobody cried for him more than the Archduchess Sophie, whose grief was so enormous that it left her completely drained both of tears and milk. No one will ever know if Sophie and the Eaglet did more than touch fingertips when they walked in Schönbrunn's gardens and drank from its fountains. We ourselves will never know if, reading from Byron aloud together in the dark corridors of the palace, they went any farther than kissing each other's hands. And if it is indeed true that Ferdinand Maximilian was the Eaglet's son, we will never know if he was conceived after innumerable nights during which the two young people discovered, over and over, the heat and beauty, the youth and splendor and smoothness of their bodies, or if he was the product of one sudden, hasty, and shameful copulation that might have occurred behind a brocade curtain in a malodorous water closet, or atop the carpet of roses in the rococo theater where Marie Antoinette had tripped Mozart up, or in the log cabin in the garden that the Eaglet had built with his own hands as a child after having read Robinson Crusoe, imagining his father as another recluse, abandoned by mankind and left in the hands of God on another deserted and unreachable island. What we do know with certainty is that one day the Archduchess and the Eaglet knelt together in front of the altar in the royal chapel at Schönbrunn. She had asked him to go with her to pray together for God to heal him. He didn't know that this would be the last time in his life he would receive the Holy Sacrament, or that they and the priest were not the only people in the sanctuary. The archdukes and chamberlains and all the court dignitaries who were dictated by protocol to be present each and every time a prince of Austria received the final sacrament all stood silently behind a door. Almost oblivious, certainly incredulous, they were mute witnesses, almost accomplices, to this mock marriage—somewhat secret and adulterous, yet also somehow innocent.

Finally, other people entirely said that his death shouldn't be blamed on consumption, love, *or* poisoned fruit, because the King of Rome—the Eaglet who would never become a full-grown eagle—died, in reality, of nothing more than the shame of having been an orphan, a king without a kingdom, a prince without a principality, a colonel without soldiers, an emperor without an empire.

One can still view the Eaglet's cradle—a masterwork of precious metals, a marvel of sterling silver and mother-of-pearl, encrusted with Napoleonic bees—in a museum in Vienna, the city where he died. At one end it has a representation of heaven, at the other an eaglet poised to take flight. The King of Rome was buried in this city, alongside the emperors and princes of the Austrian House of Habsburg, in a tomb at the Capuchin Chapel. All the titles that Austria and destiny had seized from him were inscribed on the stone tablet of his tomb. Then, more than one hundred years after his death, an Austrian paranoiac who dreamed of being King of the World ordered that the remains of the King of Rome be taken to Paris, the city were he was born, and be laid to rest near the tomb of his father, Napoleon the Great.

III

BOUCHOUT CASTLE

1927

Is that why they expect me to sit still, staring blankly at the spiders as they build their webs? So that I won't find out that Alfonso XIII of Spain drives his automobile all over the world, running over cows and donkeys? So that I won't find out that your nephew, Archduke Otto, shamed your whole family riding his horse nude around the Prater in broad daylight?

I don't give them any satisfaction. Some afternoons I stay in place, perfectly still, letting spit dribble out of my mouth. Then they tell me that I have to wear a bib. They threaten to tie my jaw shut, as with the dead. They say that if I don't stop, they'll collect my spit in a jar and take it around to all my family—my nephew King Albert, my sister-in-law Henriette, my grand-nephew Prince Leopold—and embarrass me to death. You see, Your Majesty, they say, even Little Leopold, who's just a baby, has stopped drooling by now. Mind what you say, Doña Carlota, and keep your mouth shut.

Is that why they want me to count every single filament of every single cobweb, while I sit here and hold my breath? Just to keep the news from me that my nephew, Wilhelm II of Prussia, has become a puppet of Hindenburg and Ludendorff? Or that the Orléans and the Bonapartes were banished from France forever after the fall of the Paris Commune? Perhaps they'll let me breathe after all, but make me count every breath and sigh, while I sit on my balcony and stare at the sky. Do they expect me to keep track of every wisp and shred of cloud that goes by, morning and afternoon?

All night long, I sit, my legs spread apart and my nightgown hiked up to my waist, while I masturbate, nonstop, hour after hour. My slobber drops into the ooze from between my legs and falls to my feet in a white, viscous thread that reminds me of your sperm, Max. When they find me like that all hell breaks loose. "How shameful, how disgraceful!" they say. "An Empress must never do that!" An Empress, Maximilian. Tell me, whose Empress am I? Does my empire consist of a couple of Indians and an ape, just as Charles Wyke would have wanted? Am I still the Empress of a land that, for me, stopped existing long ago? Am I the Empress of my memories? Of your remains? Tell me, where are the palace guards whose breastplates—gleaming like mirrors—reflected the mounted figure of the Empress Carlota who reviewed the troops on her Arabian sorrel in the palace courtyard? Tell me, where did they hide my crown? Did they pitch it into the murky bottom of Xaltocan Lake so that toads could use it for a nest? Or could they have hidden it in the Lacandon Jungle for the iguanas to lay their eggs in it?

Perhaps what they want is for me to count the raindrops when the clouds turn to rain. When it stops raining, when a rainbow follows the sun, is it that they want me to remember every rainbow that I've ever seen? I never saw as many rainbows as in the Valley of Mexico. Remember, Maximilian? Tell me, then, whose Empress am I, since I will never be the Empress of the Rainbows? The Empress of your tarnished, green countenance? Of your decayed purple lips? Of your running crimson blood? Don't they understand, Maximilian? I'll never be anyone's Empress, since they took away my mountains and my rivers, my Papaloapan River and its butterflies. There will be no more river waters to soothe my tired feet after those long hikes through the forests of Oaxaca. They took away my Mount Iztaccíhuatl and its melting snow that quenched my thirst after I'd lived in a desert for so many years.

Shut your mouth, Doña Carlota. Put your knees together, Madame Empress. What more do they want, then? Do they want me to be quiet and still, not to laugh or to cry? Or if I do cry, do they want rivers of tears? Must I count every tear before I swallow it? Or would they prefer me not to drink my tears but to let them slide down my chin? Must I collect all my tears in a tower of thimbles taller than the tallest castle turret? Do they want me to topple the tower and empty out each thimble, one by one, into the moat, as I count each wave?

For whom, or for what, must I cry? Perhaps for Eugénie's cousin, Ferdinand de Lesseps, who died an idiot, a broken man after he failed in Panama? Or for Achille Bazaine who died a traitor despite his distinguished career as commander in Sebastopol, as an officer in Queen Cristina's Spanish court, and as Field Marshal in Mexico? No, they would rather I didn't cry at all, because then I might cry for everything that they've tried to hide from me all these years. Yes, I would weep for Concha Méndez whom the crowd pelted with orange peels when she refused to sing at the "Mamá Carlota Theater." I would cry, yes, I would, for the death of our little Prince Iturbide. I would cry because your internal organs ended up in a Querétaro sewer. I would weep rivers of tears for your entrails. I would take them in my hands, I would salt them with my tears. I would devour them with my kisses.

But I refuse to cry for the end of France's Second Empire. I will not shed a tear for Juárez's death, for Don Porfirio's exile, or for the fall of the Habsburgs. I will laugh at them all. I will cackle hysterically as I stroll down the Paris boulevards, arm in arm with the Grand Duchess of Gérolstein. I will keep laughing at my own madness until my teeth fall out.

They keep me locked up in here so that I can count my teeth one by one as they fall out, and string them up in a necklace; so that I can choke myself with that necklace until my tongue sticks out. Look in the mirror, Your Majesty. Stick out your tongue and count your taste buds. Close your mouth, scowl, and count every wrinkle on your forehead. Count your crow's feet, Doña Carlota. Strip down and count every mole and freckle, every freckle you got from the Yucatán sun. Count the warts that you got for being old and stubborn. Count the hairs that stick out from your moles, your nose, and your ears. Count all the things you got for being stupid and crazy. You should have known better and kept yourself young like your sister-in-law Sisi. Even at fifty, she had ebony hair, long and graceful like a comet's tail. And when she swam in Corfu waters, the sun stopped dead in its tracks and the fish fell in love with her beauty.

Or maybe they want me to walk around the castle, counting every corner and every step on every stairway, every crack in every step without ever letting me remember that I used to hide and pray and fall asleep in that corner of Laeken when I was a child. Or that my brother Philippe would find me and wake me with his touch. Or that the steps from Miramare to the docks reached almost to infinity, because it took me sixty years to find the bottom, to realize that I had strayed into my soul's own inner workings there, and that you were down there too, drowned and forgotten?

Is that the kind of Empress they want me to be? The Empress of Oblivion? The Empress of Froth and Nothingness? Is that what they'd like? Do they hope that my First Communion veil, that all the carpets made of seashells by my Mexican Indian women, that the spikenard wreath that adorned the Imperial Barge when we sailed the Viga Canal, that the red poncho, a present from

Garibaldi, will all turn into the same foam that comes out of my rabid mouth when I tell them, when I shout at them, that they are all stupid women, that I'm stupid for not having been satisfied being the Vicereine of Lombardy and Veneto, the Empress of Mexico, or even the Princess of Laeken, the beloved daughter of Leopold I of Belgium? Do they wish that they could stop me from drinking deep at the source of my memories? Or that the waters from the Trevi and Tlaxpana Fountains would stop trickling through my fingers, like the years and like my life?

Or do they want me to stick a thousand needles in a pincushion and to thread each one with one of my gray hairs, now that they've fallen out? Because I'm going bald, and blind. Remember, Maximilian, when you used to collect spiders and lizards with Dr. Bilimek in Cuernavaca? The other day the messenger from the Empire came disguised as Bilimek, his smock pockets full of jars and carrying his big yellow parasol. He brought me five black-widow spiders that nested in my wig and built their webs around my body. They covered me with a dense shower of thread and trapped me in a viscous web that clouds my eyes and keeps me paralyzed.

But why do they want me blind? So that I can't look out my window at the flowering nettles? So that I can't see those Prussian soldiers who invaded my beloved Belgium, killing and torturing so many innocent people? So that I can't see them take off their hats as they heed the warning at my castle's moat that herein dwells Emperor Franz Joseph's sister-in-law? Or see them keep their distance and respect my solitude so that I can't even tell when they're smiling? I know they're very respectful—not of my relationship to Prussia's mightiest ally, but of my being crazier than a loon. Tell me, is that why they all want me blind? So that I can't find the armoire where I keep you all to myself, so that you can lead me to your bed over and over, like the first time? Do you remember our honeymoon when we sailed up the Rhine and we passed Lorelei's rock and the echo repeated my moans of love and pleasure five times? Do they want me blind so that I can't read in the English newspapers (imagine the scandal!) how my brother, Leopold, King of Belgium, sneaks away to London to visit Miss Jeffries's brothels? Or so that I can't find out in the Gotha Almanac that your name has finally been listed among the dead? Or so that I can't visit the San Andrés Hospital chapel in Mexico to view your nude corpse with its blackened, brittle skin, yes, exactly as Juárez saw you? On that table of the Holy Inquisition where the Zapotec tyrant first saw you? The tyrant who never dared face you alive, and never visited you in your cell at the Teresitas Convent because he was certain that your very presence would humiliate him, not only because you were so tall and he was just a pygmy but also because you were a Habsburg Prince and he was an Indian, a lowlife, a plebeian. He would have had to look up to meet your blue, imperial eyes, so instead he chose to see you lying nude and dead, your skin the color of his Indian skin, and your eyes replaced with black paste, by his orders. Is that why they want me blind, Maximilian? So that I'll never find your real eyes? Tell me, Maximilian, tell me, what did the Indian do with your eyes? Did he put them in his waistcoat pockets? Did he store them in a strongbox with the national archives? Did he make a present of them to Colonel López so that he could wear them over his own treacherous eyes? Or did he throw them from Fort San Juan de Ulúa in a jar, so that the waters should carry them back to Miramare?

Or perhaps they want me blind so that I can't see how all of them, my physicians and ladies-in-waiting, my most beloved kinfolk, wait for the most minute distraction, a mere blink of the eye on my part, in order to poison me? Like Mathilde Doblinger, that idiot who tried to kill me recently by running a comb dipped in salamander spit through my hair. Or my half-witted brother Philippe who tried to knock me unconscious with a potion made with henbane so that I could be transferred clandestinely from Miramare to Terveuren and no one would know that I was with child. So that I should give birth in that unconscious, dreamless state. So that my eyes should never see and my arms never hold my child. So that I couldn't count his smiles, his tears, his words, his footsteps, his years, and his days. But it was all a wasted effort, because my brother Philippe never knew that my pregnancy would last a lifetime. That I would give birth to my child many years after Philippe had become deaf as a stone, after little Prince Baudoin died, and even after Philippe himself was dead—my poor foolish, kind brother, the Count of Flanders.

What those women don't know is that I'm already blind, because they took your eyes away from me. When they took them away, Maximilian, everything went with them: the blue of the Adriatic, the aquarium filled with red and gold fish that had been set above the grand staircase at Miramare. They took away everything that I saw through your eyes because it was through them that I learned to see and love the fields of Waterloo across which we rode our horses that day, remember? The day a peasant gave us a rusty, mud-covered rifle bullet with the initials of Napoleon the Great engraved in it. It was you, your eyes, that opened mine. Your eyes taught my eyes to love Laeken Palace, the green canals of Bruges, the forests of chimneys in Brussels. They taught me that those things had been made for me. You colored my childhood, Maximilian. Later, when you came to take me to Miramare, you colored my adolescence. You taught me that my fairytale childhood dreams would give way to that larger world in which you and I, the Archduke and Archduchess of Austria, the Viceroy and Vicereine of Lombardy and Veneto, would live together from then on to make our surroundings, the people and landscapes both, conform to our wishes. With your eyes you colored all of the years that I waited for you, unaware of my own desire, while my father, King Leopold, amused himself by making gold dust out of his generals' epaulets, and my mother, Queen Marie Louise, prayed with every Hail Mary to go to heaven once and for all. Remember the ceremonial garlands that people threw toward our barge as we cruised the Rhine? I remember those garlands, and your arms. The barges, laden with fragrant wood from Cologne; the Moselle wines that captains poured into the Rhine, mixed with sunbeams, to sweeten the waters; the barges and the wine, the ships' golden wake; the raucous storks swooping down along the river; the river itself. The river and your arms that circled my waist; the perfume from resinous woods, your breath, the sunset, and the castles' black silhouettes outlined against a sky crimson from the blood of the dragon Siegfried slew to become invulnerable; the columns of Charlemagne's Ingleheim Palace on which Heidelberg Castle was built, and where old Goethe fell in love with Marianne von Willemer; the Seven Mountains from which came the rock to build the cathedral of Cologne with all its myths: the relics from the eleven thousand virgins of Saint Ursula, massacred by Attila; the sepulcher of the Magi, who crept into my childhood bedroom at Laeken Castle on Epiphany Night to leave the world that had been made for me at my feet. The whole world with all its mountains and all its rivers, and among them the very river where I would see my reflection, gleaming in the sun, while I thought of you. To awaken, to open my eyes every morning, in Laeken or in Hofburg, in Schönbrunn or in Miramare, and see the light that filtered through the drapes, was to remember that the sun was made for me—as were the sky and the clouds and, farther away, the stars—invented solely for my pleasure. To see the stars before falling asleep—bidding farewell to Orion's lights, by which the Magi had traveled—to draw the curtains once again to get in bed and close my eyes was all to be born every night to a dream world that had also been created solely for me. Tomorrow would be another day, another dawn that the gods would forge for me during the night, and offer me in all its splendor: the newest day of all, at the foot of my bed, and with it, the greatest and most brilliant of all empires.

It was from you that I learned, when I was a child, and my mother was still alive, and my brother Leopold was teaching me Belgian history, and I was learning about the world from my father and my teachers, and they told me that Flemish knights would say farewell to their sweethearts beneath castle turrets before setting off to join Baldwin, King of Jerusalem, in his battle against the infidels (the infidels whose blood, spilling from their slashed throats, thickened the waters of the Red Sea), and that the knights themselves would go on to die in the blazing sands of the Sinai Desert, and that Calvinist mobs had looted the Monastery of Armentières and the Cathedral of Antwerp, burning effigies of Saint Gudula and Saint Amand in the plaza; that French Jacobins had rampaged through Brussels markets wearing red hoods, and skewered cauliflowers with the pikes they'd used to prod people when planting Liberty Trees—it was you, only you, who taught me the real history of Belgium: that it was a country that had been razed by Huns and Normans, destroyed by Philip II, devastated by Louis XIV, and invaded by Napoleon, but that had been created just for me, for my pleasure or pain, my anguish or my awe, and that from Belgium's history the history of the entire world emerged: the pirate Francis Drake, for instance, whose body was rotting at the bottom of Portobello Bay; or Alexander the Great, who crossed the Hellespont to conquer the Persian satraps; or Lady Godiva, who'd ridden nude through the streets of Coventry; or the War of the Roses, with the red rose of Lancaster versus the white rose of York; and then from these, all the flowers of the world: the purple corymbs of rhododendrons, the white crowns of water lilies, the fragrant lavender petals of lilacs—all created just for me; as in June, when the rhododendrons at Bouchout flowered just for me, so that my brother Philippe could gather them, and, kneeling down, put them at my feet; and it was for me that the water lilies in all the ponds at Enghien rose to the surface: only for me, and for the Countess d'Hulst to fill the vases in my bedchamber at Terveuren as I lay feverish with the croup, feeling that I would cough and vomit my life right out of my body, and with my life, the world, which would die with me, me, for whom the lilacs in Laeken had bloomed in triumphant bouquets.

That, Maximilian, was what you taught me. You were the one who created Mexico for me; the one who designed its jungles and its seas; the one who shaped, with your words, the aroma of its valleys and the fire of its volcanoes.

I've often asked myself what that Indian did with your tongue. What the Indian Juárez did with it, since he never accepted your invitation to speak with him because he knew that the moment you opened your mouth you would overwhelm him with your knowledge and your nobility, with your generosity. Tell me, what did the Indian do with your tongue, which Doctor Licea cut off in Querétaro? Did he put it in a cage that he suspended from a palace cornice to show the world what should be done with the tongues of usurpers? Did he send it to the Tuileries as a gift to remind Napoleon and Eugénie of their broken promises? Or did the Indian graft your tongue onto his own to embellish it, to speak to his countrymen with your voice about nations, freedom, equality, and justice?

When they took away your tongue from me, Maximilian, they left me nothing, since it was you who taught me to create the world with words. But, why did they want me mute? So that I couldn't tell them that José Manuel Hidalgo and Esnaurrízar had died forgotten, or that Prince Salm-Salm had succumbed to a French bullet, or that your nephew, Emperor Karl, had died, dethroned and heartbroken, in Madeira; or that my niece, Victoria of Germany, had died forsaken by her subjects, or that Van der Smissen, my son's father, had killed himself, or that you, you had been executed at Las Campanas Hill?

Or do they want me mute so that I can't remind them that, just as I've seen all these men and women buried, I will also live to bury the rest? You must know, Maximilian, that I buried all my ladies-in-waiting, Julie Doyen, Marie Bartels, Sophia Musser. The latter was the one who pulled me from Terveuren the night I set fire to the castle—if you could have seen, Maximilian, what tall and beautiful flames! You must know that I buried the other spies and guards whom Dr. Hart and Dr. Basch and Madame Escandón and Radonetz and Detroyat and you yourself set on me, Maximilian, and that I buried my brother Philippe, and my sister-in-law Henriette, who kept me walled in at the Miramare Gartenhaus; and that I will bury all of those who like me locked up inside my chamber and the castle, who want to keep me from visiting my mother's grave in Laeken and keep me from telling her that I've always honored her memory, that I still love her as though she were alive, and that I haven't missed a single day of reading Saint Francis of Sales's *Treatise on the Love of God* nor Saint Alphonsus Liguori's *Glories of Mary*. To keep me from telling her that I pray for her soul every night and likewise for the souls of Papa

Leopich, Grandpapa Louis Philippe, and Grandmama Marie Amélie, and that I have never forgotten the teachings of Father Deschamps, and that I am not as lazy as when I was a child and tired easily, because, believe it or not, Maximilian, they won't allow me to go to the Ducal Palace in Milan to check on my silkworms, nor to see if I can use that silk to make a rebozo that I can wear to pray to Our Lady of Guadalupe the next time I go visit her, nor will they allow me to go to Schönbrunn to visit the garden of the King of Rome, where your father, the so-called "Gentleman Gardener," cultivated violets as a child from the seeds Monsieur Célestin Chantepie sent and also grew those white violets that Napoleon liked so much in the Tuileries and *Les Invalides*. Nor do they let me play with the wooden rocking horse that belonged to my cousin, Princess Minette in Claremont, and not even in my wildest dreams will they let me go to Mexico—you're much too old, Doña Carlota, they tell me, for such a long trip, for so much excitement, they tell me, you would get seasick on the *Novara* on the way to the Sotavento Islands, and if one of your carriage wheels came off on the way to Córdoba, your bones would crack because they're dry and brittle, and you're much too old to swim, Doña Carlota, so you would drown in Lake Chapala, and your heart is much too old, so it would burst in Anáhuac Valley, and you have far too few teeth left, so they would crack if you were to eat taffy, and they would splinter if you ate nut brittle made from the honey that Captain Blanchot ordered to greet the Emperor; they tell me all that, but, Maximilian, on every anniversary of our departure from Miramare and our arrival in Mexico, I put on my crown and my purple mantle and my grand medallion of the Order of Saint Charles and I go down to the moat in Bouchout and I climb on the barge and I tell them, today we are going to Mexico and when they, my watchdogs, see me dressed like that, sitting on the edge of the barge, my eyes fixed upon the water as though I were counting the fish and the waterbugs, the lilies and the frogs, the spots on the frogs' skins, the scales on the fish, the tunics on the lilies, the tiny round leaves of the duckweed, the pebbles at the bottom, and the insects' wings, they don't believe, they can't imagine, Maximilian, that I know more than all of them; that I know everything because every night the messenger comes and tells me everything. Last night he was dressed as the Archangel Saint Michael and he brought the rain gods with him and he told me, and the rain god, the *chaakob* told me too, that I was going to have a child, and the Archangel covered me with his wings, all the gods covered me with a veil of water, and when they, my ladies-in-waiting, knocked on my door that morning, and they came into my chamber and said good morning, Madame Empress, why are you up already, Doña Carlota?, the archangel flew out the window disguised as the blue wind and they found me gathering the plumes that had fallen from his wings, and I told them, to mock them, that I had been counting all the down from my pillows and that was why all my pillows, my quilts and my cushions were all torn apart and shredded as I danced amid the feathers, counting each one as it floated down, taking each feather to my lips and blowing it away, out of the window, in a downy snowfall that blanketed the castle grounds and the moat; and I told them that I wanted them to bring me all the chickens from the castle so that I could pluck and count every one of their feathers, and all the hens that laid their eggs for me in the suite of the Albergo di Roma, the quetzal birds given to me by my Mayan priests in Tenabo and Hecelchakán, the cranes that escorted your train when you traveled to Bohemia, Maximilian, and the storks that disturbed your sleep in the plains of Blidah, so that I could count their feathers one by one, and for them to bring me the swallows that nested in the patios of the Teja Hacienda, and the vultures that circled above the wastelands of Las Campanas Hill, and the dove, Maximilian, from the song "La Paloma" by Concha Méndez, and the orange canaries that Grandfather Louis Philippe gave me when he was still the King of France; I told them to bring me a white hummingbird from the jungles of Petén, so that I could count its feathers one by one and pick the tiniest and softest one as the Archangel ordered me to do, to hide it in my breast and impregnate myself with it so that my round and luminous womb would grow, for nine months and sixty years, with the son that I will bear one of these days, Maximilian, and who will be grander and more beautiful than the sun.

Or do you think, Maximilian, that if they want me mute it's because they don't want me reminding them that they're all already dead? Do you think, Maximilian, that you and they, my jailers, my executioners, want me never again to take leave of either the castle or my senses—that they want me to remain locked up forever, counting the tendrils, the filigrees, and the roots of the moss that covers Bouchout's walls? Or the drops of dew that carpet its grounds? Or each angle, each filament, each protuberance, each crag on a rock, each juncture or crevice where scarabs hide? Or do they want me to count each scarab's wing-sheath, each of their wings and each of their legs? Do you suppose, Maximilian, that they want me to stop reminding them that I only speak to ghosts? You should know, Maximilian, I say it over and over again, a million times, that I've buried them all. I buried Prosper Mérimée, that idiot who told everyone—when I came to ask for help from Louis Napoleon and Eugénie—that of course they would feed me, but that they wouldn't grant me a single penny or a soldier. I buried Colonel Aureliano Blanquet, one of your firing squad in Querétaro, in Chavaxtla Ravine, and with him, the rest of the firing squad. I buried General Porfirio Díaz with the soil of Montparnasse Cemetery, and I buried Karl Marx in Highgate. I buried your brother Franz Joseph, and with him the whole of the Austro-Hungarian Empire. I buried the Romanov Royal Family in Ekaterinburg. With the soil of Heiligenkreutz Cemetery, I buried the bloody and rose-covered corpse of Baroness Maria Vetsera. I buried my brother Leopold, and Margarita Juárez and their children. I buried the century, Maximilian, and, if you behave, I promise to have the messenger come disguised as a gravedigger and bring you a sack of wet earth from Orizaba and the Valley of Mexico where the yellow *acahualillo's* flowers spilled forth like flaming lava as you rode to Cuernavaca. With those flowers and my very own hands, I will bury you, Maximilian, to see if you, who never learned to live in those lands that you claimed to love so much, to see, I was saying, if you will learn to stay dead once and for all in those lands where no one loved or wanted you.

I am Charlotte Amélie of Mexico, Empress of Mexico and America, Marquise of the Marías Islands, Queen of Patagonia, Princess of Teotihuacán. I am eighty-six years old and I have lived for sixty years in isolation and silence. Presidents Garfield and McKinley were assassinated and no one told me. Rosa Luxemburg, Emiliano Zapata, and Pancho Villa were born and died and I never found out. You can't imagine, Maximilian, all the great events that have occurred since your horse Orispelo tripped on the way to Querétaro and you and your generals were forced to drink champagne instead of water when republican corpses polluted the Blanco River. Gabriele D'Annunzio took over Fiume and Benito Mussolini and his Blackshirts swept triumphantly into Rome. Kemal Atatürk and Mahatma Gandhi were born; vitamins and ultraviolet rays were discovered. I am going to get a sunlamp to tan my body, to be more beautiful than your Indian brown-skinned mistress, my darling, my beloved Max. I am Charlotte Amélie of Belgium, Baroness of Oblivion and of the Foam, Queen of Nothingness, Empress of the Wind. Miguel Primo de Rivera overcame Abd el-Krim in Alhucemas and nobody told me. North American troops invaded Nicaragua, Niels Bohr discovered the atom, and Alfred Nobel

67

invented smokeless gunpowder, and no one ever told me anything because they think I'm mad, because they want me to be deaf, blind, mute, crippled, as though I were really some old woman with eroded, sagging breasts like the breasts of Raymond Lull's lover, and with hemorrhoids as big as partridge eggs, and with yellow, brittle nails, and silver pubic hair, stiff as a scouring pad, sitting in my chambers, my head bent over and my eyes half-closed. That's how they want to see me. And that's how they do see me, Maximilian—my hands in my lap, palms upturned. They think that I do nothing but count the lifelines and the lovelines, the lines of lies and forgetting, of dreams and laughter, and they see me dead, yes, old and cackling, mad with loneliness, laughing at nothing, my tears falling into my cupped palms, mixed with the dribble that falls from my lips like a stream of pulque, crying for no one's death—yours—across another ocean—the Atlantic—my eyes closed, looking inward, watching the darkness, imagining the convolutions of my brain, lost in them as in a maze, asking no one—everyone—to repeat a name to me that can never be uttered, Ferdinand Maximilian, quietly, my lips clamped shut, these lips that one evening at the Chiquihuite Hill I smothered with fireflies so that you would put them out with your own; lips that don't tell how these quiet hands of mine crowned your brow with daydreams on the Isle of Lacroma, how these hands were alive and warm and knew the contours of your chest, all the most fertile months of the year; how these nipples ripened like purple-blue grapes in the clear waters of Mount Xinantécatl; how these eyes reflected your face in iridescent greens—how these, and I, am all yours. I am all yours: my two legs that I bathed in lemon water and nacre dust, my legs that I scoured with pumice so that you'd find them glowing and smooth when you came back to Mexico City from your travels through the countryside. And these buttocks too are yours, which I dusted with roses and rice powder to make them fragrant and snowy for you, as you came down from your horse at the edge of the frozen lake to mount, see, feel, and kiss them. Likewise these breasts, which I wish had been firm and round, bursting with milk, milk to save your life, so that those Querétaro ladies wouldn't trick you with their oranges laced with arsenic, or the nuns with their poisoned almond cookies, or Princess Salm-Salm with her poppy-filled cakes. They would have rescued you, Maximilian, from your chef Tüdös's laudanum-laced dogmeat stew, or from Father Soria's poisoned altar wine. Every morning I would have visited your cell in the Teresitas Convent so that you could suckle my breasts, and they would always be bursting, and never lose their milk, as happened to Concha Miramón after Juárez told her that nothing could be done to save Miguel from the firing squad. I would have asked the messenger to come disguised as a lamb and I would have rubbed my breasts with wet salt so that he would be forced to keep on suckling.

If they only knew, Maximilian, if they could only imagine it, they would know that it is they who are insane, not I. Yesterday the messenger came from the Empire. He brought me your tongue encased in velvet. He brought your two blue eyes in a crystal box. With your tongue and with your eyes we're both going to recreate history. Meanwhile, they all dread to see you and me alive again, to see us relive our youth, while they've all been six feet under for so many years. Rise up, Maximilian and tell me what you want, what you prefer. To have been born, not in Schönbrunn, but in Mexico? Or just not to have come into the world a few steps away from the Duke of Reichstadt's death-bed, and the room where Napoleon Bonaparte had made love to Countess Walewska? Would you prefer, tell me, to have been born in the gardens of our Borda Villa, beneath the shadow of the *flamboyán* trees, drinking nectar from hummingbirds, lulled by the sweet breezes of the tropical climate? Would you prefer, Maximilian, not to have been executed in Mexico, so that you could have been the just, liberal ruler of a great, prosperous land, where peace would reign forever? To have grown old as a white-bearded patriarch and to die beloved by your Indians, by all those Mexican Indians whom we ourselves invented, whom we ourselves turned into ingrates, such ingrates, Max, that not a single, solitary one visited you, listen to me, Max, after you were taken prisoner, forsaken by God, condemned to death by Juárez? When not a single one deigned to come to your cell bearing even a chicken, or journeyed on his knees to the shrine of Our Lady of Guadalupe, wearing a cactus collar, to pray for your life and that of the Empire? Come on, Maximilian, arise. We're going to reinvent our lives. We'll go to Africa on safari with David Livingston so that you can cover the walls of Iturbide Hall in the Mexican Imperial Palace with stuffed elephants' heads. We'll go to Symphony Hall in Boston to hear Johann Strauss and a hundred orchestras and twenty thousand musicians and we'll bring them all to Mexico to play the "Emperor Waltz" at the Plaza de Ar-mas in the capital. If you want, Maximilian, we can leave a wreath made from houseleeks at Juárez's tomb in the Rotunda of Illustrious Men. We'll show the Indian that we monarchs can forgive, that resentment doesn't course through our veins. The other day the messenger came and he was Santos-Dumont. Did you know, Maximilian, that the airship and the airplane were invented and that London and Paris were bombed and that Santos-Dumont invited me to fly over the Eiffel Tower in a blimp and that from those heights I could see all of Paris, I could see myself playing with a red ball in the Tuileries, and I could see Grandpa Louis Philippe warding off golden bees with his black parasol? That I could see you in Satory on horseback beside Prince Oskar of Sweden? That I saw Versailles and the Grand Trianon where Marshal Achille Bazaine was tried? Or Saint-Cloud Palace, where I arrived on a stifling hot afternoon, my heart shattered, since I knew that—no matter what we did—it would all be useless, since everyone had forsaken us? Get up, Maximilian. Let's join General Pesqueira in his airplane and bomb Sinaloa. Let's fly around the Valley of Anáhuac in a dirigible with Santos-Dumont. Let's watch, from the air, all the people being massacred by General Sóstenes Rocha on Juárez's orders. Let's watch the triumphant entrance of the Golden Men of the North, or the blood of Madero and Pino Suárez covering the City. Come with me, Maximilian. The washing machine was invented, as were tricolor traffic lights, tanks, and—they kept it a secret—the machine gun. How can those idiot women think that I won't find anything out as long as they keep me locked up and alone when I'm the one inventing the whole world? Do you know what they fear the most, Maximilian? That I will reinvent you. That your ghost, that ghost which haunts the deserted halls of the Hofburg—abandoned by the rats and the falcons—the Chapultepec Castle terraces, and the Las Campanas Hill slopes, will be reborn as a prince grander than you were in life: grander than your tragedy, grander than your blood. Get up, Maximilian. But you have to promise me that you won't let anyone humiliate you ever again, that you will beware—pay attention!—that you will beware of Louis Napoleon and Eugénie, of Bazaine and Bombelles, and of Count Hadik and all your friends, all the ones who want to poison you. If you catch cold, listen to me, Maximilian, don't drink *tolú* balm. Beware, Maximilian. When you go to Puebla, turn down offers of eggnog in Alfeñique House or of port from General Codrington in Gibraltar. When you return to Smyrna, avoid smoking a hookah. Watch your back, Maximilian, beware of the sticks of gum that the cripple Santa Anna may offer you. And of liqueurs from Michoacán and Chiapas. When you make love to Amelia of Braganza, refuse to take an aphrodisiac. Don't drink the waters from Geyser Springs and don't eat the smoldering ashes of Mt. Popocatépetl. Should you return to Vienna, beware of cappuccino from the Blauen Flasche, and if you visit the Hofburg, stay away from its wine cellar, and from your great-grand-mother Maria Theresa's medicinal wines. Don't eat prickly pears in Capri, or candy eggs in Mixqui. During Holy Week, keep away from the rose-colored water they sell in the stands of the Parian Arcade. And when you go to baptize Miguel López's son, don't drink the holy water or toast him with champagne. Be careful, Maximilian, don't eat raccoon tails in Colima, and if you attend the Paris Exposition, don't drink essence of roses from Adrianapolis or acacia juice from Martinique. And when you go to Cuernavaca, don't drink from the lips of Concepción Sedano. Beware, Maximilian: those lips are poisonous.

IV

A MATTER FOR WOMEN

1862–63

1. *Partant pour le Méxique*

"Your Majesty: I've just received very important news from Mexico. Events are moving in our favor, and I think that the intervention and the Empire are now feasible. I would like to inform the Emperor."

"Your Majesty," in this instance, was Empress Eugénie. And the man who is said to have whispered these words in her ear was Don José Manuel Hidalgo y Esnaurrízar, a Mexican immigrant who lived—and very well at that, bon vivant that he was—in, among other cities of the Old World, Madrid and Paris.

It is also said that the former Eugenia de Montijo put her sewing aside, stood up, and walked towards her husband's office.

Her husband, Louis Napoleon, could have been doing anything, really, in that office. Perhaps he was reading—as Count Corti tells it—a letter from the King of Siam. Or perhaps he was thinking about a thousand different things, such as the life of Caesar, whose biography he was writing during his leisure time; or that he would play the exotic animal lotto that evening with Loulou, the little imperial prince; or about the medal collection that the Duke de Luynes had promised to donate to the Tuileries Library. Perhaps he was thinking about more important things, like the project proposed by the prefect of the Seine to build a new sewer system, or about European politics. It had been a long time since the subject of Italy had stopped bothering him, but maybe he was thinking about Spain; or perhaps, by coincidence, about Mexico; or about both: Mexico and Spain. In February of that same year, '61, he had spoken in Compiègne with his friend, the British prime minister, Lord Palmerston—who ten years earlier had provoked the ire of Queen Victoria when he had approved, without consulting her, Louis Napoleon's coup d'état—about the advantages of bringing down the Bourbons. Palmerston, who thought no Bourbon was worth a damn, wanted to put the King of Portugal on the throne of Madrid. Louis Napoleon, for his part, would annex the province of Navarre to France, and maybe the Basque provinces as well. But the idea of creating a continental Empire in Spanish America was, without a doubt, much more tantalizing than sending Isabella II into exile and thus emulating his famous uncle. Given that Spain had been appeased by the reconquest of Tetuan—Napoleon was, perhaps, thinking—he might be able to convince it to participate in the regeneration of Mexico, and at the same time compensate the country for the insignificant role it had been allotted in the expedition to Cochin China. Without a doubt, Napoleon already had some idea as to Isabella II's favorable disposition to join France in the Mexico enterprise, since, that summer, at the Vichy Resort, he had had the opportunity of meeting alone (secretly and not so secretly), with a Spanish grandee: General Prim, Count of Reus, hero of Morocco and Marquis of Castillejos.

Eugénie, always smelling of patchouli, could hardly fit through the office door because of the enormous crinolines that made her famous. When she became pregnant, she had tried to conceal the roundness of her stomach, which got bigger everyday—*la heureuse grossesse*—by having her crinolines grow proportionately, not only in width, but also in terms of new laces, silks, and velvets; and soon all of Paris, and all of Europe, was imitating the Crinoline Queen (as she became known). Her wide skirts created a vogue that lasted many years after the birth of the little imperial prince.

"José Manuel Hidalgo is here," said the Empress, "and he brings news about Mexico."

But perhaps—or less perhaps than certainly—whether or not Louis Napoleon's thoughts were far away from Mexico that September day, during which, by being at his leisure in Biarritz, he could have afforded to think about whatever trivial things caught his fancy, such as the next play Viollet-Le-Duc would present to the guests at Compiègne—in the last one, Loulou himself, with a long red frockcoat that touched the floor and nankeen pants, had played the part of a wise old man who thought he'd found Gallo-Roman ruins everywhere—the truth is that this news forced the Emperor, from that moment on and during the rest of his vacation, to think about Mexico like never before.

"Benito Juárez," Hidalgo had said, "has just stopped payment on Mexico's foreign debt."

Eugénie's crinolines were so wide that a man—or even two—could have hidden beneath them; thus, Hidalgo y Esnaurrízar could well have stuck his head out between the feet and bloomers of the Empress to give this news to Louis Napoleon.

If it didn't happen this way, because this is obviously a fantasy, or even if it wasn't actually Hidalgo himself who was the first to give the news to the Emperor—and if it wasn't, he must have dreamt it in his *Memoirs*—we'll still say that whoever it was, and however he said it, went on to add that the French representative in Mexico, Dubois de Saligny, as well as his English counterpart, Sir Charles Wyke, had respectively lowered their flags and broken diplomatic relations with Mexico after handing an ultimatum to Juárez to annul the decree. It might well, for instance, have been the Quai d'Orsay, in the person of its Minister, Monsieur Thouvenel, who was in charge of officially communicating the above information to the Emperor. But the point is, regardless, that it was during his stay at "Villa Eugénie," in Biarritz, that Louis Napoleon first found out that Juárez had offered him the excuse for his intervention on a silver platter.

Besides which, he could now count on England's support. And if Wyke thought that Mexico was hardly the victim of a tyrant, and that Juárez was far from being a satrap, and if the British Minister of Foreign Relations, Lord Russell himself, might predict, as indeed he did, that the intervention in Mexico would have tragic consequences, none of that was important—because, as Hidalgo said, or might have said, to the Emperor: "Sire, we now have what we had been hoping for: English involvement. At the sight of our three flags united, Mexico will tremble under the power of our alliance, and all its countrymen will proclaim the monarchy en masse."

Furthermore, Louis Napoleon could hardly have forgotten that on April 12th of that same 1861, the Civil War had begun in the United States between the abolitionist Union and the pro-slavery Confederacy. Therefore, the country had found itself incapable of enforcing the doctrine set forth by President Monroe in the twenties, according to which the nation declared itself the guardian of the entire American continent. "America for the Americans," was the essence of the doctrine, which warned that any attempt by European powers to intervene in Latin America, or to extend their political regimes there, would be considered a threat against the peace and security of the United States. Another doctrine, that of Manifest Destiny—which established the

God-given right of the United States to expand its territory at will—had been added to the first. Divine Providence intended that the latter doctrine be put to work for the first time just two years after having been coined, when, in 1847, at the beginning of the war in which Mexico lost half its territory (equal to one-sixth of the surface area of Europe) to the United States, the American General Winfield Scott disembarked in Veracruz as head of a three-thousand-man force and told the Mexicans: "Remember that you are Americans and that your happiness is not to come from Europe."

Eugénie went in search of Hidalgo after announcing him to her husband, and invited him to accompany her to Louis Napoleon's office. He followed her and the froufrou of her enormous crinolines. The French empress's hoop-skirts were so very wide that in one of the rooms of her private quarters at the Tuileries she had had an elevator built so that the clothes she wished to wear could be sent down to her from the top floor without damaging them as they went through the narrow doors of the service rooms. On this elevator there was a mannequin that would go up naked several times a day to another floor, and then would descend fully dressed, from head to toe, wearing a hat with ostrich feathers, a whalebone girdle, starched crinolines, the skirt from Lyon embroidered with brocade tulips and roses from Damascus, silk stockings, garters with gold filigree designed by Froment-Meurice, slippers with rows of diamonds, and the Swedish leather gloves that the Empress had ordered.

"Tell the Emperor what you have told me," she said to the Mexican.

President Lincoln was not one of the *manifesdestinistes*, as they were known in France. As a congressman from Illinois at that time, he had opposed the war against Mexico. However, as president, he declared that his country would not tolerate any deviation from the Monroe Doctrine, and by word of mouth from Seward, his secretary of state, he had warned Europe that the Union would consider the creation of a monarchy in Mexico as offensive and hostile. The legal, moral, historical, political, or imperialistic validity or invalidity of the doctrine that allowed the United States to assume such a role without consulting the nations involved never bothered Louis Napoleon. What he now knew was that as long as there was a Confederate soldier in Chesapeake, Richmond, or the Appalachians, who would defend himself against a Yankee soldier, even if he had an outdated maplewood rifle like those used by the Texas Rangers, and even if his uniform was a little ragged, he, Napoleon III, could continue with his Mexican adventure, and for "Manifest Destiny" substitute "Napoleon's Great Plan." Not for nothing was the United States, we have to admit, a feared power in Europe: besides de Tocqueville and Raousset-Boulbon, the Marquis de Radepont, ex-French minister in Washington, now resident in Mexico—and who, by the way, had his own candidate for the throne of Mexico, the Duke of Montpensier—was prophesying that the policy of the United States in the Americas was very much like the policy of Russia in Europe, that Europe would soon realize that the North Americans were already masters of Havana, and that they were getting ready to occupy Santo Domingo with their marines.

José Manuel Hidalgo y Esnaurrízar said what he had to say. Louis Napoleon lit a cigarette made of tea-washed tobacco and looked at his wife.

But let's not forget, and this is something else that had to be considered, Eugénie's crinolines were really quite enormous; if it was true that a man could fit underneath them, the Empress never had to turn to this type of subterfuge to hide her lovers, simply because she didn't have any; or, if she did have them, no one ever found out. She certainly would have been more than justified in taking a lover, given the many times Louis Napoleon cheated on her, though never with *les grandes horizontales*, as the high-class prostitutes in Paris were called, because he had several of the wives of courtiers and high officers at his disposal. He would meet them in his room dressed in a silk magenta robe with an embroidered gold Napoleonic bee. He never lacked for a princess, a duchess, or a countess, like that Labéyodère woman, or, of course, the most famous of them all, that Castiglione woman—who along with the Duchess of Hamilton and the Duchess of Pourtalés was one of the most beautiful of her time—and who besides having shared a bed with Victor Emmanuel, King of Piedmont and of Sardinia, and having sold her body to an old lord for one million francs, was sent to Louis Napoleon's court by Count Cavour to seduce the French Emperor and convince him to help Italy in its struggle for unity.

And the fact is that Eugénie was born to be faithful in several regards. Faithful to herself: "Never will I play the part of a La Vallière," she wrote to the Baroness Beyens in reference to the famous lover of the Sun King, when she told her that Louis Napoleon wanted to sleep with her before their marriage. Then, yes, she was faithful to her husband. And finally, faithful to the Bonaparte dynasty: she admired the first Napoleon deliriously and she thanked God for having been born on the exact day of the fifth anniversary of the Great Corsican's death on the Island of St. Helena. And being faithful all hours of the day and night must have been very tiresome to Eugénie. The Empress needed a lover to replace her librarian Saint-Alban who, to amuse her, would take all kinds of trinkets, candies, stamps, little tobacco boxes, and marbles out of his pockets. A lover with whom she could talk using the sign language that she herself had invented to communicate with the Mesdemoiselles Marion and De Larminat. In short, a lover who would accompany her on her tedious daily afternoon promenades through the Bois de Boulogne or to visit the big stores like La Compagnie des Indes in the Rue Richelieu or the Worth House in the Rue de la Paix where her favorite dressmaker had a series of flesh and blood mannequins whom he paid to remain perfectly still, not even to blink, and so they named the store's interior staircase "Jacob's Ladder," because it was said there was an angel on every step. But since she never had a lover, what Eugénie needed was something to occupy her other than worrying about the width of her crinolines: an idea. A great idea to fight for, now that the Suez Canal didn't make her heart beat faster any more, because—how awful!—it seemed that her cousin, Ferdinand de Lesseps, wasn't going to be able to finish it, not even in a thousand years. And it was the Mexican who gave her this idea.

"I have not yet received Monsieur Thouvenel's communiqués," said the Emperor to Hidalgo, "but if England and Spain are willing to go to Mexico and French interests demand it, we shall naturally take part. Although I shall only send a fleet, and not land any troops."

But neither this idea, nor the Mexican man, could have surprised Napoleon, who had already known them for many years, and who now saw them as merely confirming his belief that all Mexican politicians and intellectuals, conservative or liberal, went through life offering their country, or part of it, to foreign powers. Because, after all, only a few years before this, the Mexican conservative President Zuloaga had asked France for an army and a French general to pacify the country and protect its interests there. Not only Santa Anna, but, later, Murphy, a former Mexican Ambassador in St. James's Court, and now Hidalgo and with him Gutiérrez Estrada, another ultra-conservative Mexican who lived in the Marescotti Palace of Rome, wanted to make Mexico a monarchy and place a European prince on the throne—like the Priest of Dolores, the instigator of the Mexican Independence movement, whose troops had carried the emblem of Fernando VII on their uniforms. Even President Juárez himself had compromised the honor and territory of his unfortunate country on more than one occasion.

After Juárez's government had been installed in Veracruz in 1859, General Miramón surrounded it first by land, then to close the siege, mobilized two ships anchored in Cuba, the *Miramón* and the *Marqués de la Habana*. Juárez decided that since they weren't flying any flag, they could be considered pirate ships and any nation had the right to attack them. He then asked for the help of some American ships that were in the port's berths, and Commander Turner, officer in charge of the corvette *Saratoga*, and who also commanded the steamships *Indianola* and *Wave*, opened fire on Miramón's ships when, at their arrival in the bay, they refused to hoist a flag upon being requested to.

After Miramón was defeated in this incident, known as the "Antón Lizardo Affair," Juárez was securely in power. But if the cannon blasts from the *Saratoga* shocked Mexico, because for many it was humiliating and inconceivable for two foreign warships to engage in action in Mexican waters—not only with Juárez's blessing, but what was worse, at his behest—the noise and commotion caused by the McLane-Ocampo Treaty were even worse.

Hidalgo y Esnaurrízar tells us in his *Memoirs* that he dared to ask Louis Napoleon if he had a candidate for the throne of Mexico, and that the Emperor, after lighting another cigarette, answered: "No, I don't."

And yes, though it's not unlikely that he wasn't already thinking about his favorite candidate at that moment, at the same time it's more than likely that the Emperor had long since been convinced by this point of the necessity to intervene, and soon, in Mexico, lest Europe—and France in particular—lose a vital market for its products and a magnificent source of raw materials, since Mexico wasn't only important as a producer of silver, but it could also be made into an important cotton-growing country. It was fine that Louis Napoleon had ordered an increase in the production of cotton in the French property of Senegal, but that wouldn't be enough to feed the hungry textile factories in Flanders and the Vosges that were running out of raw material because the world's biggest producer, the United States, had stopped exporting due to its Civil War . . . And apropos of that war: as soon as it ended the Americans would again be a threat to Mexico, whatever the result might be, whether they remained united or disunited, because, as Prince Richard Metternich, Vienna's ambassador to Paris, had said, the possibility that in the end the North would annex Canada and the South would annex Mexico could not be ruled out. And apropos of Metternich: he did not support the candidacy of the Duke of Modena to the throne of Mexico, though the gossipmongers said that the one who was really opposed to the Duke was his wife, Paulina Metternich, famous for being homely, intelligent, and mundane—Prosper Mérimée had said she was two-thirds *grande dame* and one-third whore—and for smoking enormous cigars made out of the best tobacco, as rolled by the Chinese in Havana.

"A Spanish Prince would be ideal," Eugénie said as she opened up the fan she was carrying, "But I'm afraid there isn't anyone suited for the job."

Le Journal des Debate would soon blame Juárez and his government "for not having the least bit of shame in selling chunks of Mexican territory in order to maintain power." And Charles de Barrés would say, in *L'Estafette de Deux Mondes*, "Mr. Juárez has forgotten that the bones of his fellow countrymen are even now bleaching in the deserts of America and California." This wasn't just a French opinion—many Mexicans held it too, and among them several historians who would label Juárez a traitor from the minute it became known that his prime minister, Melchor Ocampo—his partner while in exile in New Orleans—and the American envoy, McLane, had signed a treaty in which Mexico had yielded its citizens, its troops, its assets, and its weapons in the Isthmus of Tehuantepec—as well as right of passage, from one ocean to the other—in perpetuity, to the United States. Because this treaty was signed a little before the Antón Lizardo incident, Juárez was accused of having orchestrated it in order to gain—at any cost, even if it compromised the sovereignty of a considerable portion of Mexican territory—the recognition and support of the Americans. Alarmed, the Minister of the King of Prussia wrote to Juárez that this was the "consecration of the Monroe Doctrine." And another diplomat, the Viscount de Gabriac—Saligny's predecessor—declared that in the long or short term the McLane-Ocampo Treaty would come to mean the exclusion of European trade on the American continent. The U.S. Senate didn't ratify the treaty—signed when James Buchanan was President of the United States—on Lincoln's coming into power. According to some, this was simply because they found the treaty to be ignominious. "It was the good Romantic era," a Mexican biographer of Juárez, Héctor Pérez Martínez, has said. But others, including their compatriot Justo Sierra, who otherwise echoed these sentiments, held that the treaty was rejected due to the hatred the Republicans had for the Democrats and for President Buchanan's politics.

Be that as it may, the truth is that Eugénie decided that the project to send a European prince to Mexico was a more important, more absorbing and, why not, even a more entertaining idea to think about than the width of her skirts or the color of her hat, even better than organizing the Empress's Mondays, when more than five hundred guests would arrive at the Tuileries and dance in the great Hall of Apollo; they would dine at the Gallery of Peace and the party would conclude with a cotillion; better than planning and spending her vacation at Saint-Cloud or at Chantilly or at Fontainebleau where the Empress would plough the waters of the lake in her gondola, guided by a real gondolier imported from Venice, and at her side the Imperial Prince would pedal a toy boat that looked like one of the steamboats that cruised the Mississippi; or in Compiègne where Mérimée would recite passages from Illyrian poems, Mallarmé would do the same with poems at random, and Le Verrier, the astronomer, would tell about how he had discovered the planet Neptune, without ever seeing it.

Autumns in Biarritz were something else entirely, because Eugénie liked to escape to Bayonne, only a short distance away, where she would attend a bullfight, and there, far away from the court and close to the land where she was born, the more she remembered she was a good-looking girl and a Spaniard, the more she forgot that she was an empress. And thus one day after she bathed in the ocean and began a trip to Bayonne, the city that invented the bayonet and the one in which King Carlos IV had surrendered the rights to the Spanish throne and its American possessions to Napoleon the Great, she met a gentleman who greeted her as her carriage passed by. She recognized him and had her carriage stop in order to chat with him and then had him sit at her side. It was a dear old Mexican friend, said to have been, in spite of his youth, the lover of her mother, the Countess of Montijo. During the parties at their Madrid residence, which the Montijos kept in Plaza del Angel, and likewise during those held at their farm at Carabanchel, this man had gone down on all fours—along with his other friends—so that the ladies (Eugénie, Paca, the Countess, and her friends), could climb on their backs and pretend to be knights engaged in a medieval joust. This elegant and attractive man with his black beard, a descendant of Andalusian noblemen, who'd traveled from Spain to France because, as the secretary of the Mexican legation in Madrid, he held the same position in Paris—and who in both of these courts and many others besides had wept before the royalty of Europe at the loss of his lands at the hands of Juárez's people—was the same man who now, four years later, how time flies! was once again in Biarritz to beseech France to send a European Prince to Mexico.

But who? A prince of the Orléans Dynasty? Or Don Juan?

"Did your Majesty know that Don Juan de Borbón was mentioned?" Hidalgo had asked the Emperor in 1857.

Or a woman? Lord Clarendon had said that if Isabella II of Spain were sent to govern Mexico, it would be good for that country, and her absence would hardly do Spain any harm into the bargain.

Meanwhile, with the passage of time and the accumulation of intrigues, the pleas of still other Mexicans had been added to the chorus—among them those of the man who was President Miramón's plenipotentiary in Paris, General Juan Nepomuceno Almonte, the biological son of José María Morelos, also a leader of the Mexican independence movement and who, being a priest, refused to recognize the child as his own, or give him his name, though he made him into a colonel when he was still a child; but time and the hardships of war finally did make it possible for the boy to get a name, since every time the priest had feared for the security of his offspring, he would say, "Take the child to the hills" (al monte). And by that time the whole world was learning about another Mexican, José María Gutiérrez Estrada, a wealthy hemp grower, who for more than twenty years, and without setting foot back in his own country during this time, had been living in a grand palace in the city of Rome, obsessed since 1821—back then it had been the Austrian Archduke, Charles, victor over the Napoleonic troops in Aspern, who was the candidate—with the idea of creating a monarchy in Mexico. He was inspired by the former Mexican dictator, Santa Anna, who, since he was serving one of his many presidential terms at the time, had given full authority to Estrada to discuss the project in Paris, Madrid, London, and Vienna. Eventually writing a pamphlet titled *Le Mexique et l'Europe*, which he handed out to Louis Philippe, Palmerston, and Clemens Metternich, among others, he went on to propose everyone from the other Bourbon, the child Don Enrique, and Carlota's two uncles, Prince Joinville and his brother the Duke d'Aumale, to Charles Auguste de Morny, the half brother of Louis Napoleon, as candidates for the position. He even nominated the Duke of Modena—rejected by Paula Metternich—who had become available due to the annexation of his country to Piedmont, and Leopold of Belgium, when he was still a Coburg prince living in England; and he continued to nominate candidates tirelessly by means of very, very long and ostentatious letters—some of them over eighty pages—wherein he quoted all the saints of Heaven and predicted in rather apocalyptic terms the debacle that would soon take place in Mexico if Europe did not intervene in order to exterminate that bunch of bandits and barbarians who violated altars and temples, gargled with holy water, lassoed priests, and played ball with the heads of angels, having first torn off whatever precious stones could be salvaged from these religious statues in order to mount them on the bandanas of their wide-brimmed hats, and naturally having melted down the gold tabernacles and other objets d'art in order to make coins stamped on one side with an eagle perched on a cactus and devouring a serpent, and on the other side with the face of another poisonous snake: that of the Indian Juárez.

In his book, *Die Tragödie eines Kaisers: Maximilian von Mexiko*, Corti tells how Hidalgo spoke of offering the throne to one of the Austrian Archdukes, so numerous that you were always running into one of them—though, of course, the Mexican didn't say so—gossiping at some banquet or other.

"The Archduke Rainer had been mentioned," he added.

"Yes, because it seems that Archduke Maximilian isn't willing to accept," murmured Eugénie.

Further, in order to speed up the intervention in Mexico, one had to give serious consideration to the rumor that a few days earlier had caused such a big commotion at the Quai d'Orsay when it was learned that the Juárez government was about to sign another agreement with the North American Union, and one almost as unbelievable as the McLane-Ocampo Treaty: Lincoln's new Representative in Mexico, Thomas Corwin, who in the forties had opposed the American intervention in Mexico so emphatically that he had been accused of being a traitor and was burned in effigy in the streets—having said at that time that he expected the Mexicans to greet the invading army with "bloody hands and hospitable graves"—informed the Juárez government shortly after it had suspended payments on its foreign debt that the U.S. government would be willing to make the payments on the interest of the debt for five years, if Mexico would agree to pay back the total loan amount plus interest in six years' time, with the single condition that the deal would include a specific tax on vacant lands and mining rights in the states of Baja California, Chihuahua, and Sonora—territories that would become the "absolute possession of the United States" in the event that, at the end of the specified time limit, "the entire debt had not been paid."

And, if all these arguments weren't themselves sufficient, neither Napoleon nor Eugénie had any real need to justify their grand enterprise in the eyes of history. Already there were some who were saying that the intervention in Mexico was urgent because Benito Juárez—that "uncharismatic Indian," who when visiting warmer climates would dress like any other peasant: white shirt and pants and a hat from Puebla—what that Zapotec Indian wanted was to provoke a caste war in his country in order to annihilate all the white citizens . . . because, moreover, if Maximilian were to accept—oh, if he were to accept the throne of Mexico!—it would be, for the Second Heir to the crown of Austria, for his country, a sort of compensation that France was giving it for the defeats of Magenta and Solferino.

And finally, it was all well and good after those two battles that the Papal States would never wield the same power again in Europe, but it was very bad indeed if Pope Pius IX should be holding a grudge towards Louis Napoleon after all the humiliations suffered during the war on the part of a unified Italy, among which the triumph of the Piedmontese over the Papal Army in Castelfidardo and the loss of Romagna and the occupation of Rome by French troops had been particularly painful, and therefore Louis Napoleon as well as Eugénie were happy to have the opportunity to console the Pope by undertaking a crusade for the Catholic faith in the New World.

Eugénie closed her fan. And if the story of the blow that the Dey Hussein gave the French Consul with his flyswatter is true, and not apocryphal, there's no reason that the gentle lash Eugénie gave herself in the chest with her fan at this moment doesn't also deserve to be officially recorded by history. And if the first stroke decided the future of Algiers, the second decided the future of Mexico—at least for some years—and of course that of one man: Maximilian.

This is because, after rapping herself in her chest with her fan, Eugénie said: "Something tells me that Archduke Maximilian will accept . . ."

Eugénie was the standard-bearer of the Mexican crusade by her own decision and because it was her great opportunity to let Louis Napoleon and France know what she, as a woman—and a Spaniard to boot—was capable of accomplishing. She was capable of much more than her little audacities, known by the entire court, such as dressing up as a man and drinking out of a wineskin during the bullfights at Bayonne, or inviting the twenty most beautiful women in Paris to have dinner with Louis Napoleon, so that she could show him—though it wasn't true—that his infidelities didn't worry her and that he could take all twenty of them to bed together, or else one by one, as he pleased. Neither was she worried for the time being about her servants, and not only her reader and her reader's assistant who would sometimes entertain her with history books, but also her instructor, her first chamberlain, her twelve palace ladies-in-waiting, maids of honor, and head maids, her hairdresser who wore short knee-breeches and a sword, her private secretary, or the librarian who would take rabbit feet out of his pocket; nor was she worried for the moment about her male and female dressmakers: Laferrière, who made her afternoon frocks, or Félicie who made her capes, or Madame Virot and Madame Libel, her milliners. For now, there, in the corner of her work studio, with its mahogany windows and walls with aqua-green tapestries and a marble chimney with bronze and lapis lazuli ornaments, on top of which there were two Chinese vases and the portrait of her lamented sister Paca, the Duchess of Alba, whose sudden death had affected her so much, next to the glass cabinet where she kept her husband's hat that had been ripped by Orsini's bomb, and the pacifiers, rattles, ringlets, and first shoes of the little Imperial Prince, on the other side of a gilded bamboo screen, and near the portrait of Louis Napoleon dressed in black and painted by Cabanel, in that corner, the desk where Eugénie, on her knees, wrote all her personal letters, because that's the way she liked to do it, yes, now, there, Eugénie could, with her goose quills, write much more important things than telling her mother the Countess how the construction of the new opera house was progressing, a building that would cap the "hodgepodge" of styles of the Second Empire, or how it happened that Loulou had gotten sick to his stomach after eating an Easter egg together with its silver red-flowered wrapping paper. By this time there was enough room not only for Mexico but also for the whole American continent under the protective skirts of Eugenia de Montijo, Eugénie, Empress of the French.

From that moment on everything would be resolved in a matter of a few weeks. Count Walewski, natural son of the Great Napoleon, who as Foreign Minister of Louis Napoleon had opposed a French intervention in Mexico some years before, now expressed his support after listening to Hidalgo. The Austrian Emperor, Franz Joseph, sent his Foreign Minister, the Count of Rechberg, to Miramare in order to confer with Archduke Maximilian. And Louis Napoleon wrote two letters: one to his Ambassador in London, the Count Flahault—father of his maternal half-brother, the Duke of Morny—instructing him to inform Great Britain of the intervention project, and advise it of the advantage of its participation for the purposes of recuperating the money lent to Mexico, putting a stop to the expansionist politics of the United States on the American Continent, and securing its future markets for Europe. The second letter was addressed to King Leopold of Belgium with the purpose of asking him to exert a double influence: on his niece, Queen Victoria of England, and on his son-in-law, the Archduke Max. Finally, Louis Napoleon informed the Spanish Minister in Paris of the contents of the letter to Flahault, and the Minister in turn communicated the intentions of the French Emperor to the Spanish Prime Minister, Calderón Collantes, who in turn wrote to his ambassador in London in order for him to inform the Court of St. James's that in Spain it was seen as inevitable that the navies of the three countries would occupy the principal points of the Mexican coast, not only to obtain satisfaction as to their demands, but also to organize a new government in Mexico that would deliver "security in the interior" and "guarantees in the exterior."

This is how it came to pass that on October 30, 1861, the three most powerful navies in the world—as the Mexican historian Fuentes Mares puts it, England "who could but did not want to," Spain "who wanted to, but could not," and France "who could and wanted to"—signed a tripartite agreement in London in which they each committed themselves to the immediate dispatch of troops to occupy the Mexican coast with the "ostensible" objective of pressuring Mexican authorities to offer more efficient protection to the persons and properties of the citizens of the three signatory nations, and further to demand that Mexico fulfill its financial obligations to said nations. As far as the second objective, the signatories agreed that they would not seek by means of the coercive actions stipulated in the pact any territorial acquisitions or any special advantages, and they committed themselves to refrain from exerting any influence on the internal affairs of Mexico, that is, "any influence capable of impairing the right of the Mexican nation to elect and freely establish its own form of government."

Overnight, the Spaniards turned into the hosts of the expedition. Francisco Serrano, Duke of la Torre and Captain General of the still-Spanish possession of Cuba, received orders from the capital to send a squadron consisting of eleven warships with 5,000 men on board—plus 100 lancers, 150 engineers, and a total of 303 cannons—to Veracruz. The Spanish warships anchored in Veracruz on December 10, 1861.

Suddenly, it appeared as though the fondest wish not only of the Spanish Prime Minister, Calderón Collantes, but also of one of the only two foreign representatives of Juárez abroad, his minister plenipotentiary in Europe, Juan Antonio de la Fuente (who thought—at least this is how Ralph Roeder tells it—that in order to save itself from France, the best thing that could happen to

Mexico was a Spanish invasion) were coming true. As for the Spanish representative in Washington, Matías Romero, he thought that if the intervention was inevitable, it was preferable that the United States should also participate, because they would tilt the balance toward constitutional legality.

But President Juárez had ordered the governor of Veracruz to surrender the port without resistance and withdraw. And a few weeks later the British commodore, Hugh Dunlop, arrived at the Mexican coast at the head of two propeller warships and four frigates with a total of 228 cannons. The French fleet was arriving at almost at the same time: fourteen steamships with a total of three thousand men onboard, among them a regiment of marines, a battalion of Zouaves, and a detachment of *Chasseurs d'Afrique* under the command of Admiral Jurien de la Gravière, astronomer and historian of the French navy.

General Prim also arrived, not only to lead his Spanish troops, but also with the (failed) intention of being elected Commander of the Tripartite Expedition. Finally, the two foreign ministers—French and the English—who had severed relations with the Juárez government, Sir Charles Wyke and Count Dubois de Saligny, also arrived in the torrid lands of Veracruz.

The 196 cannons of San Juan de Ulúa Fort and of the bastions of Concepción de Santiago, among which there were fifty iron cannons and sixty of English and Belgian manufacture, remained silent.

At the beginning of the second week of January 1862, the Tripartite Expedition began to crumble as the first disagreements among the representatives began to surface. The English and the Spaniards refused to back up the French demand over the now infamous Jecker bonds, and they declared that the French demands lacked any "real legal basis." General Prim insisted on the fulfillment of the Treaty of Mont-Almonte, which required that Mexico pay an indemnification for the murder of Spanish citizens at Chiconcuaque, and Commodore Dunlop demanded payment of the debt recognized by the British government in the custom houses of the main Mexican ports of the Gulf: that is, Veracruz and Tampico.

However, a short time later, in a bilateral declaration, the English and Spanish communicated to the Juárez government that their intention was not to seek redress for offenses, but to extend a friendly hand to Mexico to help the country come out of its chaos, and that at the same time they were hoping to witness its regeneration.

Benito Juárez suggested to his newfound allies that they pull back to Havana so they might watch Mexico's regeneration from there, and when this suggestion was ignored, he sent his ex-minister, Manuel Zamacona, to invite the invading commanders to the town of La Soledad to confer with his delegates: the Mexican foreign minister, Manuel Doblado, and Generals Ignacio Zaragoza and López Uraga. At the same time, the Mexican government authorized the invading armies to abandon the unhealthy port of Veracruz—by this time General Prim had had to send eight hundred of his men to hospitals in Havana—and provisionally move to Córdoba, Orizaba, and Tehuacán, cities with a milder climate: this with the proviso that if no understanding was reached during the talks at La Soledad, the foreign armies would return once again to Veracruz.

Meanwhile, Juárez had taken advantage of the indecision and the disagreements of the commanders of Tripartite Expedition to issue the "Decree of the 25th of January," according to which any Mexican citizen who collaborated with the intervention would be put to death.

Other characters also appeared on the scene: ex-President Miramón, who was not allowed by the English to disembark; Juan Nepomuceno Almonte; and, on March 6th, General Ferdinand Latrille, Count of Lorencez, who was coming to Mexico on the order of Louis Napoleon to take command of the French troops from the hands of Admiral Jurien de La Gravière.

President Juárez's conciliatory attitude, and his willingness to renegotiate the terms of Mexico's foreign debt and various indemnifications disarmed the Spanish and English representatives, who, signing the Treaty of La Soledad, accepted a peaceful resolution and withdrew from Mexico.

The Count of Lorencez, however, disavowed the Treaty of La Soledad, and searched for—and found—a reason to declare war on the Juárez government.

Nous voilà, grâce à Dieu, sans alliés!—"Thanks be to God, we've lost our allies!" Empress Eugénie would write to Archduchess Carlota when the news reached Europe.

And toward the end of April, Lorencez—in a letter addressed to the French Secretary of Defense—declared that the superiority in race, organization, discipline, and morality of the French army over the Mexican troops was such that, from that moment on, at the head of his six thousand men, he considered himself to be master of Mexico.

Having written this, he and his men headed straight for the city of Puebla de los Angeles.

2. The Archduke at Miramare

That tranquil and sunny afternoon, Archduke Maximilian was in the Salon of the Seagulls in Miramare Castle, in the vicinity of Trieste, the old city in whose cathedral, San Giusto—the burial site of so many Carlist pretenders who never realized their dream of becoming rulers of Spain—were entombed. The Archduke stood next to an easel with a cardboard-mounted map of the Republic of Mexico. On a table beside it was a small silver-inlaid lacquer box with marking pins.

Miramare was named this, obviously enough, because it faced the sea: the Adriatic, which is perhaps the bluest of all seas, though it seems a frozen and icy blue. One day when Maximilian was traveling onboard the warship *Madonna della Salute*, fearing an approaching storm, he was forced to seek shelter in the Bay of Grignano, where he spent the night in the humble house of a fisherman named Daneu. There, on a promontory, Maximilian decided to build the palace of his dreams, and he assigned the planning and the work to the architect Carlo Junker, who began construction in March 1856. This was the same castle that the poet Carducci described, with its white towers enshrouded in clouds brought by sinister angels. Romantic in origin, Miramare is considered to be one of the most rare and complete examples *di residenza principesca del pieno Ottocento*, of a mid-nineteenth-century princely residence . . .

The Archduke picked up a silver-headed pin and drove it into the place on the map corresponding to the state of Sonora.

"Sonora. If Herr Professor allows me to tell a joke, I can . . . I could . . . hmm?"

"Yes, Your Highness: I could, you could, he could . . ."

"I could say," the Archduke continued, "that the name Sonora is sonorous because of the great amounts of silver its land contains, silver that Napoleon wants. But we won't give it to him. It's for us Mexicans."

And the room where the Archduke stood was known as *La Sala dei Gabbiani* (The Salon of the Seagulls) because of the dozens of seagulls in flight painted on its ceiling. Each seagull bore a ribbon in its beak, and on each ribbon there was an inscription in Latin. There were also two paintings by Geiger that depicted Maximilian's first trip to Smyrna. In the same room, seated on a sofa, engrossed in a cross-stitch embroidery of the yacht *Fantaisie*, anchored in the Isle of Madeira, was Archduchess Marie-Charlotte, or Maria Carlotta as she wanted to be known since becoming vicereine of Lombardy and Venice. Of all the Latin proverbs conceivably adorning the ceiling—from *Gaudet tentamine virtus* to *Tempus omnia revelat*—one that would almost certainly have needed to be included was the one that Chancellor Metternich always applied in his policies, to honor the House of Austria: *Divide et impera* (Divide and Thou Shall Rule).

And standing nearby, dressed in a dark gray-colored frockcoat, light-blue trousers, white cravat, and a straw-colored velvet waistcoat, was a man with Indian features, spectacles, of medium height and curly black hair: *Herr Professor*, as the Archduke called him, or *Monsieur le Professeur*, to the Archduchess. They were practicing their Spanish.

"But at any rate, Madame"—Madame was one the many forms of address that Monsieur le Professeur used with the Archduchess—"at any rate, I believe that perhaps you should remove one of the *T*s in your name, and from now on write 'Carlota' using the Castilian spelling, with only one *T*."

The Archduchess raised her eyes from her embroidery and smiled at Monsieur le Professeur.

"A beautiful idea. Thank you."

Monsieur le Professeur bowed, and his eyeglasses slid to the tip of his nose.

"It would be a gesture that we Mexicans would appreciate very much. Now, shall we continue, hmm? with the conjugation: *Nosotros podríamos, vosotros podríais, ellos podrían* . . . hmm?"

Herr Professor crossed the salon taking long strides, his thumbs in his waistcoat pockets, and approached an enormous picture window that faced the Adriatic. Maximilian and his friend Junker had agreed that there wouldn't be a single room in Miramare castle without a view of the sea. One window had three panes, each of a differently colored glass: thus the Adriatic was a deep purplish blue seen through one pane, a pink-lilac through a second, and pale green through a third. Herr Professor approached the Archduke and looked at the map. Maximilian had another silver-headed pin in his hand. Herr Professor pointed to a place near the capital.

"And not only is silver found in Sonora, Don Maximiliano," he said, "but there, hmm? One can find other mines, among the richest in the world, in Real del Monte."

Maximilian pinned the spot. The Professor resumed his pacing.

"But to be honest," he continued, "the change will go unnoticed by most of my compatriots. I'm referring to your spelling of Carlota with only one *T*.

Unfortunately, we Mexicans who can read and write are very few, hmm?"

"*Davvero?*" exclaimed the Archduke as he lifted his eyes from the map.

"*Davvero*, Don Maximiliano, means 'really?,' and, unfortunately, yes? it is true. Now let's continue: *Yo podría, tú podrías . . .*"

The Archduchess put her embroidery aside and unfurled her fan.

"*Io* believe that those are . . . *¿Comment dis-tu*, Max? . . . *Des inventions? Des mensonges?*"

Monsieur le Professeur pulled a red bandana from his coat pocket and wiped the sweat from his brow.

"Falsehoods, Madame, hmm? Calumnies, lies."

"Yes, *Io* believe they are lies, Monsieur le Professeur, falsehoods, *Io* believe that there are many Mexicans who can read. But we did not mean to say zat Monsieur le Professeur would tell lies . . ."

"*That* the Professor would tell lies, Madame. On the other hand . . . would Your Highnesses allow me to sit for a minute? Thank you, hmm? On the other hand I would say, if you forgive me for the redundancy, hmm? I would tell lies, *Yo diría mentiras, tú dirías mentiras, él diría mentiras, nosotros diríamos mentiras, vosotros* . . . in short, that I would prefer . . ."

The Archduke smiled.

"Perhaps Herr Professor would prefer some wine. Nothing better than some cool wine on a warm day . . . *pétillant* . . . The Professor can serve himself a *piacere*," added Max pointing to a corner of the salon. "There are also Irish cookies that the Governatore of Gibraltar sent me. Dipped in wine *à l'anglaise* they are a *squisitezza*."

"How delightful, Don Maximiliano."

"Oh, have you tried them, Herr Professor?"

"No, no, I mean . . . that is to say yes, I have tried them. They are indeed a *squisitezza*."

Herr Professor walked over to the small round table inlaid with mother-of-pearl that held the wine and biscuits.

"Bravo, serve me some, *per favore*, and come here. *Übrigens . . . à propos*: tell me, where are the good wines bottled in Mexico . . . *Et toi, Charlotte, un peu du vin?*"

"*Non, merci.*"

Carlota had a glass of orangeade by her side. Herr Professor poured two glasses of wine. He walked to the table and gave one to the Archduke. He then picked a cookie with red frosting.

"Wines are produced," he said, and drove in the pin, "here in Parral, Don Maximiliano, hmm? but I am afraid that in Mexico we do not have what one could call—*yo llamaría, tú llamarías, él llamaría*—really good wines, hmm? We must import them from Europe along with many other items like coal, musical instruments, soap, weapons, paper, glass, and all sorts of foodstuffs. The warm season is usually long and, as a result, there is an excess of sugar in the grape . . ."

"*Est ist Schade*, Professor. It's a pity . . ."

"And they turn out too heady . . . So it is impossible to compare them to French or Italian wines . . ."

"Or to the German wines of the Rhine," said the Archduke lifting his glass, "*Am Rhein, am Rhein, da wachsen unsre Reben . . . Salute!*"

"*Le comparazioni sono tutte odiose*," chimed in the Archduchess.

"Or with German wines, hmm?" agreed Herr Professor, "*A votre santé* Don Maximiliano. With your permission, Doña Carlota, hmm? You see, the owners of the Real del Monte mines, Don Maximiliano, are English. The holder of all the cotton that Mexico exports is a Spaniard, José Pío Bermejillo, or something like that. Mmmmm . . . what an excellent wine, hmm? What did you say it's called? What I mean to say is that Mexico's wealth is in the hands of . . . Your Highnesses will not be offended as you will not be foreigners in my country? You no longer can be considered foreigners . . . The wealth, as I was saying, is in the hands of foreigners . . . hmm?"

"Iron, Herr Professor. Mexico has iron."

"Would Don Maximiliano allow me to take a pin?"

The Archduke handed him the box. Herr Professor picked up a black pin and pushed it into the map.

"Here in Durango, Don Maximiliano, Doña Carlota, there is a hill one hundred and eighty meters high, one and a half kilometers long, and three-quarters of a kilometer wide, which is estimated to be sixty-five percent pure iron . . . hmm?"

"We could make our own weapons," said the Archduke, "our own railway . . ."

"We will make, Don Maximiliano. *Yo haré, tú harás, él hará*. Now, if we set aside the cotton, the silver, and the iron, there will be little left to export, aside from the cow hides and goatskins that we export by the thousands to the United States every year . . . *nosotros haremos, vosotros haréis* . . . And this is because, during the three hundred years of colonial rule, Spain didn't allow any industry to be developed in Mexico that could compete with those of the homeland, Your Highness, hmm? Not even the cultivation of vineyards, the raising of silk worms, leather dyeing, nothing. This is why the Spaniards were so infuriated when Father Hidalgo y Costilla began planting white mulberry trees . . . Oh, I forgot, Mexico also produces a lot of cochineal . . ."

"To what is Monsieur le Professeur referring?" asked the Archduchess and closed her fan.

"Cochineal. In Italian it is *cocciniglia*, from the Latin *coccinus*, which means scarlet. The cochineal is a very prolific insect, hmm? which produces Chinese lacquer and wax such as in this box, that is to say, one of the species," said Monsieur le Professeur and picked up the pin box. "Others produce coloring substances, like the Mexican cochineal, hmm? Crushing the female produces a dust of an intense crimson or scarlet that is used to dye wool, silk, and velvet fabrics."

"And is it like . . . *la cocciniglia* from Madeira, Herr Professor?"

"The very same, Don Maximiliano, but it is native to Mexico. Sahagún used to call it the 'blood of the tuna.' Does Your Highness know what a tuna is— hmm? It's the fruit of the nopal, a cactus, hmm? and the cactus, hmm? is . . ."

"And, Monsieur le Professeur, can one dye an imperial cloak not with purple, but with cochineal?" asked Carlota.

"I had not thought about that, Your Highness, but I do not see why not . . . of course, yes, by all means. At any rate, the purple also comes from an animal . . . a mollusk, in fact. Yes, why not? Hmm? The only problem, I believe, with Your Highness's pardon, is that it would sound strange to speak of imperial cochineal rather than imperial purple . . . no? hmm?"

The Archduke smiled. Herr Professor sat down again, this time without asking Their Highnesses' permission.

"We could, yes, why not? hmm? But now we are going to practice this tense with a little exercise: To go to Mexico. Go ahead and conjugate, Doña Carlota: *Yo podría ir a México, tú podrías ir a México, él podría ir a México*, hmm?"

"*Yo podría* . . . but it is not a question, Monsieur le Professeur . . ."

"A matter, Madame?"

"It's not a matter of whether I am going to Mexico or not, because *Io am* going to Mexico, Max and I are going to Mexico—right, Max?"

"For God's sake, *mia cara* Charlotte, Carlota: Herr Professor only wanted to give an . . . *essempio*? *Ein Beispiel*?"

"An example, Don Maximiliano. But I could give another example, of course . . . hmm?"

The Archduchess slapped her lap with the fan.

"Hmm? Hmm? Hmm? The Professor could give another example, *tú podrías dar otro ejemplo, yo podría dar otro ejemplo. . .*"

The Archduke laughed, took a sip of his wine, and said to Herr Professor:

"As you can see, my Princess Carla has a sense of *umore*. I am German, *tedesco*, a gloomy *uomo . . .*"

"*Un hombre.*"

"*Un honbre.*"

"No, Don Maximiliano . . ."

"It's not . . . *ben pronunziato?*"

"It's not an *N*, but an . . . *M, hommmmbre.*"

"*Hommbre. Hommmbre.*"

"Perfect. And, you know, *hombre* in Spanish—perhaps mostly in Mexico—can express many different things, suitable to the occasion: surprise, happiness, incredulity, hmm? Hombre, there was a horrible earthquake! Hombre, what do you mean Mr. So-and-so died! Hombre, how sad!"

"For God's sake, Professor," said the Archduke taking another sip of his wine, "your *essemps* . . . examples are all gloomier than I."

Herr Professor dared to point his index finger at the Archduke.

"Your Highness has the gift of languages and is making astonishing progress."

"Yes, hombre."

"And like Doña Carlota, you also have a very good sense of humor. Let us now return to our verb. I could give other examples. I could imagine Doña Carlota going to the market to buy cherimoyas, mangoes, and sapotes, some of the most succulent and delicious fruit you will find in Mexico, hmm? and others that surely Don Maximiliano had the opportunity to taste during his trip to Brazil, but I could also imagine Your Highnesses being harassed by the Mexican Church and by the *Ultramontanes*, or suffering during your trips on the bad—very bad—Mexican roads . . . What I mean to say is that, hmm? I could, we all could limit ourselves to speaking only of the marvelous things that our country has to offer—I can't deny that there are many of these—without ever mentioning its enormous shortcomings, like those dangers and accidents that so large an enterprise as Their Highnesses' entails. But, from my point of view, that would be immoral, hmm?"

Carlota was growing impatient. She flipped her fan open and closed it again several times.

"Monsieur le Professeur is here only to teach us Spanish and nothing more . . . *C'est à dire . . .*"

"*Laissez-le parler*, Charlotte. We have much to learn besides Spanish. Though I could say . . . *Yo podría decir* . . . is this correct?"

"Yes, Don Maximiliano."

"I could say that Herr Professor, *quelquefois* . . . at times appears to be an envoy from Juárez to convince us not to go to Mexico."

"Nothing further from my mind, your Highness."

"We have been visited by a Mexican, Señor Terán, who was sent by the President to dissuade us from going."

"Juárez is afraid, your Highness."

"And that American consul in Trieste. What's his name, Carla?"

"Hildreth."

"Oh yes, Mister Hildreth. Charlotte has had to say that she is not in, that she is *malade* in order to avoid seeing him. He does not want us to go to Mexico—he has that *idée fixe*."

Monsieur le Professeur mopped his brow again with his handkerchief.

"He is not expressing his personal opinion, but that of his government, Don Maximiliano."

"We shall introduce him—right Carla?—to Don Francisco Arrangóiz and to Monsieur Kint de Roodenbeck in order to convince him . . . And tell me, Herr Professor, are you not a republican at heart?"

"Your Highness, I am a monarchist, hmm? I believe that only a monarchy can save my country from chaos. But the kind of monarchy I wish for Mexico is very different from what many other émigrés like Don José Gutiérrez Estrada and Don José Manuel Hidalgo want and expect, hmm? Though, to tell the truth, I am not an exile but only a man of science who has lived in Europe a few years in order to complete his education. Begging your pardon, Your Highnesses should, *yo debería, tú deberías, él debería, nosotros deberíamos, vosotros deberíais, ellos deberían*, hmm? realize that the liberal monarchy desired by the enlightened class in my country and by the Emperor of the French is not the kind of monarchy that those gentlemen, hmm? with all due respect to them, want for our nation. Neither does the Mexican Church, hmm? nor the Mexican Monarchist Party, if indeed it exists, because I allow myself to question its existence . . ."

"*Come dici* . . . ?"

"To call into question the existence of something, Don Maximiliano, is to doubt that it exists. And I believe you could call into question some of Señor Gutiérrez Estrada's ranting and raving . . ."

94

"Monsieur le Professeur, *je vous interdis* . . . I forbid you . . ."

"*Laissez-le parler*, Max . . ."

"Could we . . . *rinfrescare*?"

"Refresh, Your Highness . . ."

"Refresh the conversation with another glass of wine? Or perhaps Herr Professor would prefer to enjoy the ocean breeze? Want to come along Charlotte?"

Carlota preferred to continue her embroidering.

"*Come mi cara Carla, meine Liebe: Frisch auf!* Cheer up!"

It was a quarter past two on the beautiful Louis XIV clock carved with wooden garlands that sat in a corner of the Salon of the Seagulls. Max set his watch to it and stepped out.

•

Standing on a tiny pier at Miramare, facing the blue Adriatic, Maximilian caressed the carved head of the stone sphinx that he had brought from Egypt.

"Herr Professor, tell me: *Il y a* . . . Are there things like those we have in Vienna in the Imperial Mexican Treasure of Iturbide, or of the Spanish viceroys, things like . . . the crown of . . . *des Heiligen römischen Reiches*? . . . the Holy Roman Empire? . . . the one that lost the stone of wisdom? Or like the imperial crown of Rudolf II? The orb of Emperor Mathias? Yes, Herr Professor, so many beautiful historical things like the sword of Carlomagno? Charlemagne? the one given him by Caliph Harun al-Raschid . . . Are there such things in Mexico?"

"No, no, no, I'm afraid in Mexico we have no sword of Charlemagne, hmm? And as far as jewels left over from the Iturbide Empire or from the time of the viceroys, I know nothing . . . Wait, I am wrong, hmm? I now remember that Emperor Iturbide's sword is in the Hall of the Congress, yes, yes. The crown perhaps is there too . . . but, it occurs to me Don Maximiliano, that the real jewels of Mexico are the gifts it has given the world: tomatoes, hmm? the chocolate that your predecessor, Empress Doña Maria Theresa, made fashionable in Austria, and Empress Eugénie in Paris, tobacco, hmm? vanilla . . ."

"Noble idea . . . noble idea, Herr Professor . . ."

"Those beautiful trees native to Mexico, Your Highness: the giant ahuehuetes, the tule trees . . . hmm?"

"Oh, Herr Professor, *Io sono* . . . I am an *inamorato* of nature . . ."

"And the fruits of which I was speaking, Don Maximiliano: mangoes, pineapples, bananas, so extolled by Baron von Humboldt for their profusion, hmm? and for their nutritious value . . ."

"Ah, yes, yes, an *inamorato* . . ."

"The thousands of orchids, hmm? Though, I will tell you, hmm? we *have* had religious jewels like the Host of La Borda: a masterwork of solid gold, a meter and a half in height with a disk, imagine, Don Maximiliano, of around 4,500 diamonds, close to 2,800 emeralds, 500 rubies, over 1,800 pink diamonds . . . Its base alone holds some 2,900 mounted gems, hmm? though I am very much afraid that now with the sacking of churches by Juárez supporters . . ."

"Bravo, bravissimo, Herr Professor: you have a *prodigieuse* memory!"

"Memory, hmm? No, the thing is that I know the Tabernacle very well, Don Maximiliano. I have studied it. I am proud of my friendship with Don Manuel de la Borda, son of Don José, a miner from Taxco who was the richest man in America during the last century and who had the Host made, hmm? in honor of Saint Prisca . . . By the way, Don Manuel, the son has built some beautiful gardens in Cuernavaca . . ."

"Where?"

"Cuernavaca, Don Maximiliano: Cuer-na-va-ca, some fifteen leagues from the capital, hmm? very beautiful with lush vegetation, thousands of flowers, and teeming with butterflies, parrots, humming birds . . ."

"And . . . and could *Io* visit the Borda Gardens?"

"Yes, yes, Don Maximiliano, of course you could, *podría, podrías, podría . . . Su Majestad podría*, His Highness could even buy them . . ."

The Archduke turned his back on the waters of the Adriatic to behold the gardens of Miramare.

"Look, look Herr Professor: cypresses from California, cedars from Lebanon, fir trees from the Himalayas . . . I sent for all of them to adorn the Miramare gardens. But if I cannot bring tropical trees here like ceibas, baobabs, and paletuvios . . . *Io* have to go to the tropics . . . Do you know these lines from our poet Schiller: *Io* was also born in Arcadia? Well that's the way it is, Herr Professor: *Auch ich war in Arkadien geboren . . .*"

3. From the Correspondence—Incomplete—between Two Brothers

Acultzingo, April 29, 1862

My Dear Alphonse:

Forgive me for taking so long to write. You know that I have never been lax when it comes to writing letters but I become discouraged when I think how

96

long it takes them to cross the ocean. This is my first transatlantic letter! You can just imagine how long the trip seemed to me. I felt seasick for the first time in my life, and threw up overboard all day long, no doubt to the delight of the flying fish and dolphins that followed us along the way and who must have had a feast. At any rate, the smell of the ocean was preferable to the stench in the cabins that always nauseated me, especially after some giant cockroaches that let off an unbearable odor when crushed, invaded the ship in Martinique. So, I am guessing that when you read this letter I shall be in Puebla de los Angeles, that is, if a bullet from a Juárez supporter hasn't killed me first (an unlikely occurrence, since Mexican soldiers are all terrible shots).

In fact we are almost at the city gates. In the last few days we completed the ascent to the summit of Acultzingo, although some of the field artillery was taken across the Maltrata Pass, which is not as steep. As I write this letter, therefore, I behold a gorgeous panorama. It is almost nightfall and the evening sky is clear. From here to the east I can see the snow-covered tip of Orizaba Peak, bathed in rosy hues. It reminds me of those times when the Zermatt Valley is plunged into darkness and you can see, against the sky, the blood-red summit of the Matterhorn. To the west, with my telescope's help, I can make out the gleaming church domes of Puebla and its cathedral towers, as well as some of the many forts around the city of Puebla. But no matter how many fortified positions they have, we have no doubt that we will be able to occupy the city in one day. Of course, to do that we will have to find, very soon, some better means of transportation, because, when our troops arrived in Veracruz, all our mules had disappeared as if by magic. Or by a trick of the Juarists. The Spaniards planned to bring a shipment of mules from Cuba, but, as they ultimately decided to abandon the project, the four-legged beasts never made it. In any case it's for the best that the Spaniards are gone, along with the English who must now be marching around in Bermuda. Because of this the conquest and regeneration of Mexico will exclusively be the work of the French. Of course, with the welcome help of the Foreign Legion and the Nubians that we borrowed from the Viceroy of Egypt: their skin, black as coal, is the only kind, I think, that will fare well here in this torrid climate.

To tell the truth Prim had no business here other than to look foolish. First, he wanted to please both God and the Devil. As you know, in Parliament he objected to sending Spanish troops, to give him credit in case Spain considered it unwise to take part in the project. However, he also made it clear that he was unconditionally at the service of His Catholic Majesty, to take the glory of commanding the expedition forces, if Spain did decide to participate. And that is what happened. That is to say, Prim did lead the troops but reaped no glory as he soon not only realized that his dream of being Mexico's Emperor was impossible, but also that he would have to be willing to make too many concessions to Juárez's government in order to advance his Mont-Almonte Treaty. I don't have the slightest doubt that this was influenced by Prim's political relationship with Juárez. Or rather, not with Juárez but with one of the members of his cabinet. I understand that Juárez's finance minister is the uncle of Prim's wife, whom he brought to Mexico as a first class "*soldadera*." (Let me explain, "soldadera" is a term used here for the poor women who follow their men in military campaigns wherever they go, with everything—kitchen utensils and sometimes even a baby—on their backs. These women are unafraid of danger and at times they take part in the battles.)

To sum up, be that as it may, Prim's concessions gave rise to a series of absurd, if not ridiculous, decisions. The republican flag waving at La Soledad along with the three allied flags is something that Jurien de la Gravière should have never allowed. Nor did we come here to exchange gifts with the Juárez supporters, as happened when we sent Uraga (or maybe Doblado; I can't remember which one of Juárez's delegates) a shipment of French preserves and wines and they reciprocated (they sure got the better end of the deal) with boxes of some insipid candy that they make with *camote*, the local name for sweet potatoes, and some barrels of a whitish, slimy drink with a disgusting smell, like overripe cheese, which they call *pulque*. There are no good wines in this country. There is nothing I miss as much as the hake in béchamel sauce that we used to eat at the Durrieus', served with a bottle of chilled Chablis.

I apologize for the digression. If I also criticize our leaders, it's because they gave in to the dire influence of Prim and some of his generals, like Milans del Bosch, all of whom adopted a paternalistic attitude while in Mexico. They were to blame when the allied forces agreed to begin negotiations with Juárez, giving him the chance to proclaim the draconian law of establishing the death penalty for any Mexican who collaborated with us. What's worse, he had the time to organize his troops; although, truth be told, this did him little good. Here, in these same Acultzingo Mountains where I'm writing you now, and just a few days ago, we defeated and forced Zaragoza to retreat—the Republican general who's now cornered in Puebla, waiting for us. But I think I erred in calling them "troops." I have never seen such a ragtag, undisciplined army in my life. But this, I suppose, is probably due to the draft, or forced induction, since they have no other way to form an army here. None of those poor peasants who pass for soldiers has any idea of why or for whom he fights. There's a phrase from a famous letter that's often quoted here, from one Mexican officer to another: "Here's a group of shackled volunteers for you." There are also plenty of murderers in the Mexican ranks. And leading them as well—including the ones on our side, as in the case of Leonardo Márquez. This fearsome general was nicknamed "The Tiger of Tacubaya" because he slaughtered a bunch of unarmed doctors and orderlies in the town of that name near Mexico City. Besides this, there are groups of guerrillas here, and I can tell you that my having burned the midnight oil at Saint-Cyr studying trigonometry and logic isn't much help against them—since, as you know, I'm not one of the lucky ones who've been given the opportunity to really put their knowledge to use in the thickets of Saigon. Just to give you an example: there's a weapon they use here that we've never heard of before: the *reata*, a long rope tied with one end to a saddlebow, which the Mexicans, used to *jaripeos* or rodeos, handle with such skill that they can lasso anything from an animal to a rifle or a man, and at enormous distances. When it's a man, they drag him at a gallop without least hint of pity. I saw an African rifleman die like that, in pieces. The atrocities committed by the so-called Mexican "soldiers" have no parallel in history.

In any case, I can't fathom, as I was saying, why our allies came here. We've even heard rumors here of a protest that a member of parliament made in Madrid, asking why, having no business here, the Spaniards had bothered to come—and, then, if they'd really been needed here, why they're packing up and leaving. The fact is, that just like the English, their only real reason for coming was this: it's well known, and has been for a good while, that France's intentions are to establish a monarchy here. Well, I wish them bon voyage. Adieu, Count de Reus. Adieu, Marquis de Castillejos. They tell me that the name Prim has so much prestige (some will doubtless compare him with Murat) that even his enemies respect him, from the Rif to the Mountains of the Moon, where mothers quiet their children with the mere mention of his name, as if he were the boogeyman. But I can assure you, dear brother, that in a few years there won't be anyone here in Mexico who will remember that arrogant Catalonian.

All things considered, events have gone in our favor, although I confess that there are some minor setbacks. At some point it became known, I don't know how, that de la Gravière had received a secret letter from our Emperor, wherein he stated that the Mexican Monarchist Party would take up arms as soon as the allied troops arrived, and join up with us. I am beginning to doubt, however, that there are as many followers of the monarchy here as they say there are—besides that bunch of ragamuffins that I mentioned before, many of whom were chased away by Lorencez. I think now that the Englishman Wyke might have been right when, even before word of the secret letter got out, he stated that the majority of Mexican citizens (or at least the best-known ones, I suppose) are republicans. Even so, I'm convinced that only a monarchy will be able to save this nation from barbarism, and am glad to hear that Archduke Maximilian has accepted the throne of Mexico in principle, since other candidates, such as the Infante Don Sebastián, did not inspire the least bit of confidence in me. What I can't imagine is how this country of illiterates will be able to arrive at the "national consensus" that the Archduke demands for his final acceptance.

On the other hand, I can tell you that, while we're lacking supporters for a monarchy, there's an abundance of men who, like Prim, dream of being made emperor, or at least aspire to receiving a noble title; a prime example of which is General Santa Anna, who, they say, is willing to support the Intervention and the Empire provided that he be dubbed the Duke of Veracruz. This is the general who has been Dictator of Mexico several times—the one who lost his leg when Prince Joinville stormed San Juan de Ulúa, and who later buried that leg with great pomp. I'm sure you remember the painting at the Tuileries that depicts the "Pastry War," don't you? I have to tell you however, that not all Mexicans wear feathers as they are portrayed in that painting. In fact, I haven't seen a single one, though I hope to finally see some real costumed men if I get sent to Durango or Sinaloa, where there are apparently some Apache tribes who have the bad habit of collecting human scalps.

Things got even more complicated with General Almonte's arrival in Veracruz along with our own minister in Mexico, Count Saligny. The English saved us from Miramón, whom I suppose they haven't forgiven for robbing the English legation. As soon as he tried to set foot in Veracruz, Commodore Dunlop arrested him and sent him to New Orleans or Havana, or who knows where. Poor General Miramón. He was furious about the snubs that he suffered in Paris from the Emperor, machinated by General Almonte's maneuvers and intrigues. No doubt the bastard son of the priest Morelos is a cultured, refined man, but he shares many of his countrymen's faults—especially those who've spent twenty years away from their country. Not too long ago, for example, Almonte was furiously opposed to the establishment of a monarchy in Mexico, and especially to bringing in a foreign ruler. But now he's a happy standard-bearer for the Mexican Empire, full of airs and graces and even occupying the Regency till the Archduke arrives—and still wearing a halo of scandal since, they say, Almonte is among those who support a French protectorate in Sonora, and although this is an idea that I consider beneficial for both nations, many of the other Mexican conservatives have rejected it.

To top it all off, a group of Mexicans have refused to recognize Juárez's government, naming Almonte the Head of the Nation. He accepted, reputedly, "with the efficacious collaboration of the French army." Hence the request from Prim and Wyke—for whom it was the last straw—for his expulsion, which we refused. But apparently Almonte plots these little intrigues against anyone he can, as he did from the start with de la Gravière. Saying that the Admiral had asked Prim and Wyke for advice, instead of Saligny. If this is true, I'm glad, however improper it might have been, since Saligny—who's always drunk, or anyway putting on a good show of looking drunk, and with his hellish temper—is not only a sinister character, but an incompetent. Our real mission here, which by now has been clearly established, is not to settle accounts or recover old debts, but to regenerate this country once and for all. That stupid Saligny, however, refused to accept this, and so he kept on about that unfortunate business of the Jecker bonds and the punishment of those who supposedly tried to murder him in Mexico. The other problem that resulted from Saligny's ineptitude and stubbornness was the contradiction brought about by the Treaty of La Soledad, since by recognizing Juárez's government as legitimate, we were transformed overnight from an expeditionary force destined to bring law and order to an anarchic nation to an army of invaders dealing with a government that we ourselves had recognized. Therefore, there was no other alternative than to declare war, and that threw Lorencez's authority to do such a thing into question, since, according to international law (in Henry Wheaton's words), this right only "belongs to the supreme power of the State in every civilized nation." In any case, Gravière and Saligny finally focused on provoking an episode that would give them a *casus belli*. They managed to find it and they declared war on Juárez's government. During their retreat from Córdoba to Orizaba, the French rear guard ran into a small detachment of Mexican soldiers who were blocking the road near a place called Fortín. The Mexicans fled; our troops went off in pursuit. Well, I found this beginning to our campaign somewhat pathetic—not only because of the triviality of such an unnecessary encounter, but also because blood was spilled for no reason whatsoever at the "Battle of Fortín": the swords of our African riflemen took five Mexicans. It was a Sudanese battalion, not French, who started to create disturbances in Veracruz when the bulk of our troops moved to Orizaba and La Soledad, for instance. Nevertheless, all these divisions march under the same glorious flag that triumphed in Sebastopol and Solferino. We need to pay closer attention to such things.

And now, to keep from boring you with so many political matters, I'll sum up some of the things that have interested me the most. To begin with, I'll say that the end of our sea voyage didn't really provide me with any relief from my nausea, although the view of the red and black walls of the bastion at Ulúa is rather interesting, as is the intensely verdant and appropriately named Isla Verde, where you can buy some splendid coral for a few pennies. Likewise on the Isle of Sacrifices. But arriving in Veracruz, dear brother, is like arriving at Dante's Inferno. If this is where the future emperor will disembark, he will be greatly disappointed. From the ocean the port resembles the ruins of Jerusalem, except that it's far from being a holy city. It's not rich either, despite its original name of *Villa Rica de la Vera Cruz* (Rich City of the True Cross). The streets are unpaved and I hate to tell you how they get when it rains heavily, or even when they have what they refer to as a "light shower." A fellow soldier told me that he's only ever seen more mud and filth during the worst days at Pehtang, almost two years ago, when our troops first landed in the north of China. The entire city of Veracruz is an enormous sewer. The *alameda* or central park is in ruins, surrounded by fetid marshes. When it's not unbearably hot, there's a terrible wind they call the "norther" that covers the city with sand. Even in the Paseo de Malibrán, one of the better streets, you have to walk in sand up to your knees, and, of course, wear special goggles to keep from going blind. Not to mention the *pinolillo*, an insect with a truly terrible bite. And, by the way, before I forget, I wanted to pass on a curious fact: an English journalist who accompanied us on the ship and was "pretty groggy" during the whole trip, not because of seasickness but because of the large volume of gin that he drank, told me that the Isle of Sacrifices—which forms the port's triangular flood tide with Fort Ulúa and the Isla Verde—is named not because any sacrifices have taken place there, but because it was a place of "sacred fish." God only knows if that's true. To return to the streets of Veracruz (although I wish I never had to go back to that foul city), what struck me the most was the great numbers of birds of prey, the omnipresent *zopilotes*, those buzzards that no one shoos away, since they're protected by law: the Mexicans count on them to dispose of the garbage that the people throw out in the streets. You also see half-rotted horse and donkey carcasses all the time. Although, really, you smell them rather than see them, since they're generally covered over by swarms of black wings. In addition to this, there's the terrible heat, and the scourge of this region—one of the most unsanitary in the world—namely, the persistent yellow fever that's already begun to decimate our troops. They call Veracruz the "Garden of Adaptation." If you survive that city, you can survive anywhere else in Mexico. The hospitals are full and I feel sorry for the poor patients and doctors who also have to bear the stench of the burnt sulfur they use there to ward off the flies. And then there's still malaria and all the other diseases common to the tropics. Doctor León Coindet, chief medical officer of the Veracruz hospitals, once showed me a long list of patients, representative of the most diverse ranks and races—a Zouave drummer, an infantry corporal, a colonel of the African Battalion—who were all suffering from dysentery, tertian, or coma-causing typhoid fevers. They say here in Mexico that smokers are immune to typhus. I don't know if that's true, but since I heard it, I don't let go of my pipe. I've found very good tobacco in Mexico, and sometimes I add liquid amber to it, as Moctezuma did (by the way, they spell the Aztec Emperor's name as "Moctezuma" and not "Montezuma" here, and they say "Cuauhtémoc" instead of "Guatimozín"). At other times I mix tobacco and vanilla. It's the same vanilla we use to flavor our chocolate in France. But, of course, since it's so delicate and fine, I never imagined that it came from an orchid that grows in tropics so wild that they seem like they could have been invented by Bernardin de Saint-Pierre. Speaking of tobacco, I don't know how they managed to preserve it during the trip (I suppose that they'd come from Cuba), but the fact is that a French ship that docked in Veracruz had a cargo of Royal Poinciana flowers. As each officer disembarked he pinned one of those beautiful flame-hued blossoms to his waistcoat. I couldn't help but think of Jean Nicot—as you well know, he was one of the first to import tobacco from America to Europe, wandering around the European courts with a red flower, the flower of the tobacco plant, pinned to his breast. But let me go back to the yellow fever, or "the black vomit," as it's also called. Thanks to our being able to reach more temperate climates, we avoided repeating the tragedy of Leclerc's expedition to Haiti, where more French died from yellow fever than at the hands of Toussaint L'Ouverture's blacks. Although, I tell you, my dear

Alphonse, what affects and kills our troops are not only tropical diseases but also other and more malicious maladies as ancient as humankind's oldest profession, and whose existence in Mexico dates to when these were first brought from Europe by the conquistadors. At least, that's what the Americans say. An assistant to Dr. Coindet, whose word I cannot question, tells me that many of the patients who are crowding our hospitals, and who are far more numerous than you can imagine, are actually admitted with venereal diseases. The most common being syphilis. And treatment with either calomel or mercury vapors is frequently ineffectual. This has stopped me from having relations with the aborigines, among whom, as one gets used to the features of the race, there are indeed some whom you could call pretty. To be sure, there's a brothel with Irish prostitutes in Veracruz, but I've always preferred (inasmuch as is possible) to remain faithful to my beloved Claude. So when on leave, I usually play monte after supper at the Diligencias—the only hotel in all of Veracruz that can be called a hotel, and where one can get a more or less passable meal for about five francs. As to the rest of the local cuisine, it's repulsive, especially in those public houses that they call *figones*. Everything is literally swimming in grease and is too spicy. They say the Aztecs were forced to undergo a type of pagan confession and sometimes priests imposed the piercing of their tongues with long thorns (from a plant called *biznaga*) as penance. I had that same sensation, dear brother—of having not only my tongue but my palate pierced with thorns the first time I tasted chile, or goat pepper: *Capsicum*.

Now, if civilization has not yet arrived in Veracruz, there's no doubt that the lack of it goes well beyond the harbor. The highways are also in a deplorable state, and since the blessing of the iron road is limited to only one train for every two or three hundred passengers, and covers a distance of no more than fifty kilometers—from Veracruz to Camarón, from what I understand— most travelers are forced to take the "Stagecoaches of the Republic," which are painted up like circus wagons, and appear to imitate the style of the berlins of Louis XV's days. We should be calling them the "Stagecoaches of the Empire" by now . . . (Alphonse, do you recall the famous cookbook by Viard, who changed his name so many times and stopped calling himself "The Imperial Chef" when Bonaparte fell and Louis XVIII ascended the throne to become "The Royal Chef" instead, and, when Louis Philippe fell and the Second Republic was established, "The National Chef"? Tell me, is he still alive? Is he called "The Imperial Chef" again, now?) But to return to the stagecoaches, as I was saying, travelers suffer all types of discomforts in them and especially from the bouncing and the wobbling caused by an endless number of potholes, to which you can add the stubbornness of the mules, making the trip even slower since they only respond to being pelted with rocks. It's not unusual to see a conductor climb down from his stagecoach to reload his supply of projectiles. Even many pedestrians, especially young boys, join in stoning the poor beasts when the stagecoach goes by. And to make matters worse, the country is infested with bandits and highwaymen—and that's only mentioning the ones who actually admit to this profession, as opposed to the ones who disguise themselves as "soldiers." When you first travel through these regions, you notice wooden crosses placed here and there, at the edge of the road. I have been told that each cross represents a traveler murdered in that place. Of course, there are some picturesque elements along the roads, although these are also lugubrious in the extreme. You won't believe it, but in some places distances aren't marked by posts or milestones but by cow skulls impaled through their eye sockets on tree branches.

Although I love to experience new things, the remoteness of this place and my being exposed to such alien customs gives me a strong yearning for home, at times. I think of you a lot when I have my absinthe—which, unfortunately, has been very scarce lately. What can we expect? I can't avoid imagining you, yes you, happy mortal, Jockey Club dandy with your Austrian sideburns and with your square monocle and gloves like the Duke of Morny's, reading my letter, at the Tortoni, an absinthe at your side as well, then smiling and putting your letter down to plan your itinerary . . . Where will you go this evening, Alphonse? To the Brasserie des Martyrs, with Honoré Daumier? Or to the Brébant with a lady of high standing?

There are consolations. Ice is plentiful in this country. Not only from Popocatépetl (unpronounceable name), which used to supply Mexico City since Moctezuma's day, but also the ice that comes on ships from New Orleans. And, well, what more can I say? There are other compensations, of course. My lodgings are one of them. I live in the home of a wealthy Mexican family whose members treat me coldly, but no less hospitably for that, and who have a servant who's a genius at pressing uniforms. Many of our troops have lodgings in convents confiscated by Juárez's government. This is ironic, because it's understood—at least by Gutiérrez Estrada, Almonte, and their henchmen—that, among other things, we came here to restore the properties and the power of the Church. But one becomes accustomed very quickly to seeing churches turned into warehouses and the sight of confessionals bursting with cases of brandy, or of crucifixes lying among bales of cotton. Nevertheless, it's one thing to be a Catholic and quite another to be a fanatic. The conservative leaders who joined our army with the motto of "Long Live Religion!" (a sentiment that we of course do not agree with) haven't understood that the beauty of the French Intervention in Mexico is that it brings together two great traditions: the Napoleonic one of military glory, and the politically liberal one that grew out of the French Revolution.

The magnificence of the tropical vegetation, moreover, is impressive. The fruit here inspires nothing less than absolute lust. You would envy me if you could see me resting under a verdant dome of lianas and ferns, leafing through the *Italian Campaigns* of von Clausewitz, and feasting on a *guanábana*. I well know that Clausewitz does not interest you. But since you are a gourmet, Alphonse, you would love the *guanábana*, that fragrant fruit with its sweet white pulp, a unique flavor that I first tasted in the Antilles, and that here they make into a sorbet or ice that you eat—imagine how delicious—using an orange leaf instead of a spoon.

Dear brother, I have done my duty to bring you up to date. As I said at the beginning, I hope that my next letter will be posted from Puebla, a city that, according to my sources, is full of reactionaries, and for that reason we hope to be greeted with flowers and triumphal arches after a token resistance put up to save the city's honor. I trust that you are being cured of your socialist ideas, which will get you nowhere (don't get angry, this is an impartial piece of advice) and that could hurt the family. By the way, don't forget to put flowers on Mother's tomb. Magnolias were her favorites. If you do not want to go to Père Lachaise alone, ask Claude to go with you. She always accompanied me. Oh, and tell my beloved Claude that I've bought her a fan made from the wings of a beautiful bird called "Spatula." It will look much better in her hands than in those of the gold-toothed Veracruz negresses who spend the day smoking cigars and drinking chocolate and glasses of iced water. And belching to be polite. I thought only the Chinese and the Bedouins did that.

Wishing, then, for your good health, I send you warmest greetings.

Your affectionate brother,

JEAN-PIERRE

V

BOUCHOUT CASTLE

1927

Or, do you want the whole world to think that Maximilian and Carlota never made love in Mexico, that they slept apart after their first night at the Imperial Palace? That besieged by bedbugs, the Emperor slept on a billiards table and the Empress sat on an armchair, all alone, scratching her fetid welts until they bled? Yes, she was all alone, the Princess who crossed the ocean to rule a kingdom in the New World wearing a purple mantle and who found nothing, yes, absolutely nothing but the apathy and indifference of the Mexicans. She was left all alone that night, and a thousand others, alone with her own bedbugs, her eyes fixed on the silver wig case that those Indian women had given me, those women who had the nerve to embrace me and to smoke in my presence, who thought that their starched hoopskirts, silk petticoats, and diamond earrings had made them ladies worthy of my new court, just as you, my foolish Max, thought that by merely importing Gobelin tapestries, gold-encrusted ebony pianos, and Limoges china into Mexico you would create an imperial residence from that horrible edifice, those barracks that the Mexicans called a palace. There I was, alone, night after night, alone in those barracks, alone in the Castle of Chapultepec, and in the Albergo di Roma, alone, suffocating with disdain and hate, because you left me, Max, my arms and legs covered with scabs, my lips dried with the spit that drooled from my open mouth when I thought of the skin of my beloved Max, the skin that I so yearned to kiss, to cover with my kisses and my tongue, the white skin that covered your face, your shoulders, your thighs . . . to kiss it and fill my mouth with it, Maximilian, may God forgive me, as I wanted to do in Italy on the night that those Italian aristocrats refused our invitation to La Scala. To humiliate us, they sent servants dressed in black to our box seats. When I returned to the Ducal Palace I tried to give myself to you so that we could make love until the sun, gleaming from Saint Mark's golden domes, would surprise us, just to show those insolent people—the Dandolos, the Borromeos, the Addas, the Maffeis, and the Littas—and to show you as well—that you and I did not need, would never need, anyone else, as I lay there nude, on my back, with you inside me forever, until we died.

Tell me, do you want the whole world to know that I was an even bigger fool than you were for believing in you, in your love, in the fidelity that you swore to me so often, as if I didn't know that on that trip to Vienna on what you called viceroyal business you took showgirls into your bed? My only consolation now is that you will never be unfaithful, nor will you ever again be able to make love to that little Countess von Linden who visited your grave in the Capuchin monks' vault after she became the Countess von Bülow to put a bouquet of roses next to your mother's dry *sempervivi* flowers and the scroll with the Nahuatl-language greeting from your Xocotitlán Indians. It's no longer necessary for your family to send you away so that Vesuvius, or Smyrna, or Botticelli's *Birth of Venus*, or Michelangelo's *David*, or Sicily, or Naples, or the rock from which Emperor Tiberius cast his enemies, or the white tower from which he watched the stars, might make you forget her. Even if you returned, Max, if it were possible for you to come back to life, you would find that Paula von Bülow has also died, and that all you could do now would be to return her visit, to cry at her grave the same way you cried when we traveled to Funchal, Madeira. There you stopped at the house where Princess Marie Amelia of Braganza had died of consumption, the princess whom you had vowed to love eternally and secretly at the Gardens of Lumiar. If you returned, Max, if you came back to life and to Vienna, how surprised you would be, my poor Max; you can't imagine how ugly and dirty your poor city is, how changed because of that despicable Clemenceau and the Treaty of Saint-Germain that Austria was forced to sign after the Great War. If you could only see, Max, how humiliating it was for Emperor Karl to flee to Switzerland dressed as a gardener. Beggars and consumptives prey on Vienna's streets. Entire families live in ditches at the Prater. Apple tarts have disappeared from café menus, and instead of coffee you get chicory. People tear off the velvet upholstery from train seats to make clothing because they have nothing to wear. Milk and butter are a thing of the past. We have only potatoes and cornmeal. Come on, Maximilian, come to Vienna if you wish, to the Atlantis Café on the Ringstrasse to buy the love of a lesbian, or go to the heart of the old city, the Spittelberggasse where you will be able to chose a prostitute of any age or eye color that you desire, or one dressed as a nun or a schoolgirl, to take her and give her your death, since you have nothing else to give. Even the ulcers on your penis, Maximilian, the warts or canker sores, or whatever it was you brought from Brazil, even they have dried up; Maximilian, they are as dry as your skin and your tears, your tongue and your lymph. Do you want the whole world to know that Archduke Ferdinand Maximilian, second in line to the Crown of Austria and consort of Princess Charlotte of Belgium, brought back not only a jar full of scarabs with emerald- and tourmaline-encrusted shells from Brazil, and a live agouti, a cork and cane salacot, and poinsettia leaves pressed like red knives between the pages of a book, but also, in your trousers and in your blood, the ignominy of that incurable venereal disease you caught from a Brazilian negress, a musky slave with whom you coupled under a palm tree, beneath the screeching of macaws and the cackling of macaques? Do you want them to know that I will never forgive you for that, Maximilian? Everyone knew—how humiliating—all of Mexico knew why the Emperor and the Empress never slept in the same bedroom again. And that evil Abbot Alleau, conniving with that hypocrite Gutiérrez Estrada, published and spread the rumors that those bedbugs we found on our first night in the Imperial Palace, and the surprised eyes of the Indians who spied on us outside balcony windows, had only been the excuses that Providence gave you to leave me to sleep on a billiards table. You have never returned to my bedchamber at night, Maximilian, ever since that first cursed night you left me alone, deathly afraid on that armchair, with the terrible, interminable clamor of the fireworks outside and my heart's own beating. I was left alone until dawn, scratching my bedbug bites, licking my wounds like a cat. And how was your night in your felt and wood bed, Max? If at least you had become accustomed to sleeping on a field cot like your brother Franz Joseph, or as Papa Leopold on horsehair mattresses, you would have had an easier night. I dreamt the other night that you were lying on a bluegrass bed and that your penis was a long and varnished pool cue, and your testicles were two ivory pool balls, one white and the other red, can you imagine, Max, how hilarious? And that you hurt me when we made love, almost piercing my womb, almost tearing my uterus and skewering my intestines, popping out my eyes. But it was only a dream: the truth is that you left me alone, sitting in an armchair at the Mexican Imperial Palace, just like you'd left me on the eve of our departure for Mexico, when you locked yourself in the Miramare

Gartenhaus to write farewell poems to your gold cradle, just like you left me alone in a hammock on the Island of Madeira, overcome by the heady aromas of exotic fruit and flowers—American pineapple, Arabian coffee, Italian oranges, Persian lilacs, all brought together to an island that only needed the acid fragrance of your breath, your breath that smelled of tobacco, mint, and dense wine, your manly breath, to become a paradise.

Were you trying to make me feel pity when I left to visit my father in Belgium, when I left you alone at the Ducal Palace in Milan? You wrote your mother to complain that your good nature, your dangerous good nature, would turn you into a prophet of ridicule. Do you remember, Max, when we visited the slums of Valtelina to take clothing and food to their poor? Do you remember your projects to restore the Murano Dome, the Chapel of the Padua Arena, and the Ambrosian Library? Remember your get-well wishes to Manzoni during his illness? What good did any of that do you? Who thanked you, pray tell, for cleaning up the canals of Venice, or for your grief over the Lodi and Pavia floods? Who, pray tell, who appreciated your love for your Lombardo-Veneto subjects? I am a ridiculed prophet, you wrote your mother from Milan, scorned by Austrians and Italians alike—by Franz Joseph as well as Count Cavour, who feared that your good will would spoil the unification of Italy. At night you paced up and down the dark palace corridors, while outside there was merrymaking from the carnival and you waited for the first bell to chime at midnight so that the start of Lent, with its accompanying and properly soul-rotting anguish would silence that joy. Do you, did you, ever expect anyone to feel pity for you when you were left all alone in Querétaro at your cell in the Teresitas Convent, in your coffin, all alone at the San Andrés Hospital chapel in Mexico City, on the Holy Inquisition table? Or when you traveled alone to Europe in the *Novara*'s funeral chapel, and when, later, you were left alone on a barge, and on a high bier, under the wings of an angel, after you arrived in Trieste, all alone on the train that took you from Trieste to Vienna as it snowed, and later when your mother Sophie threw herself weeping on your coffin. She wasn't crying because of your death, Maximilian, but only for her own loneliness, her rigidity, her coldness, because then, as in forty-eight when Windisch-Graetz's troops recaptured Vienna, and the Odeon Theater burned to the ground—remember?—she had said she would rather lose one of her children than to surrender to the student masses. She was as responsible for your execution in Querétaro as anyone else, that whore who gave herself to Napoleon II and made him your father. When you wrote her from Orizaba telling her that you wanted to abdicate and leave Mexico, she replied, of course, that everyone missed you so much at Schönbrunn and the Hofburg and that all of Vienna, in Austria and Hungary, they all missed you. She sighed at the music of your Olmütz clock, and when she gazed upon the long, blond locks that they cut from your hair when you turned four, and when she caressed and smelled the little girl's skirts that you wore then; but you must remain in Mexico, she wrote you, because, my dear son, a Habsburg never quits, never. I remember, very clearly, I don't know why, that one morning you paraded by the Swiss gate at the Hofburg, in the uniform of Maria Theresa's Hussars, tall and slender under the arch that bore the coats of arms of Austria and Castile, of Aragon and Burgundy, the Tyrol eagle, you, your blond mane blowing in the wind, the lion of Flanders and of Styria, another eagle from Steiermark, the panther from Carniola, you and your blue eyes, my dear Max, here we all miss you tremendously, we got together with our four grandchildren on Christmas Eve, and the Emperor rocked our chubby little Otto. Franzi sat on a chaise next to Sisi, but, although we miss you terribly, you must remain in Mexico. Your situation here would be too embarrassing. On another unforgettable afternoon you got lost in the gardens at Schönbrunn. That day I cried out in despair, asking everyone, where is that little urchin—but stay in Mexico, my son, your situation would be untenable here—where could he be, dear Lord—stay, do not return. Better to be buried in Mexico than humiliated by French politics. Don't come back to Vienna, son. That morning you were not lost; no one had abducted you. You were sailing your toy boats in the Neptune Fountain and had fallen asleep next to the statue of the nymph Egeria, after drinking from the Schöner Brunnen brook discovered by Emperor Mathias, the palace's namesake. And when your brothers Viktor Ludwig and Karl Ludwig led your mother Sophie away after she had thrown herself upon your coffin, her face was covered with a mask of snow as fine as talcum powder where the tears had carved tiny furrows. Later, when you were left alone in the Capuchin vault she did not weep again; nobody wept, they all forgot you and the carnival went on, the party went on; not only the carnival in Milan and Venice but the carnival of the world, the delirious festival of history. As you know, that hypocrite Eugénie pretended to mourn your death so that on awards' day at the Paris World Fair, she refused to go to Vienna to give your mother and your brothers her condolences. She swore that she was trying not to appear too dramatic or histrionic, or the opposite, too indifferent. When she did go to Salzburg with Louis Napoleon a few weeks later, and rendezvoused with Franz Joseph and Elisabeth, they all wanted to forget you as soon as possible; they wanted to avoid a war between Austria and France. They preferred discussing Crete and the Middle East—or Garibaldi who was preparing his march into Rome and who would be defeated that same year by the French and the Papal troops in Mentana—to your death in Querétaro. They had to bury you quickly, once and for all, and when Eugénie tried not to let Sisi's beauty outshine her, Sisi, whom I shall never forgive for not going to Miramare to bid us farewell when we went to Mexico (she claimed to have rheumatic pains in her legs), or for calling me an arrogant, power-hungry Belgian goose, was more interested in outshining Eugénie and taking off for England to have another riding outfit tailored at Henry Poole's in Savile Row—and to hunt foxes, and another lover, at Northamptonshire—than she was in mourning your death, Maximilian, you who were her favorite brother-in-law, you who were always so kind to her. Yes, I regret to tell you, Maximilian, it's true, they all forgot you: your mother, who has not asked about you for the last sixty years. She knows you didn't fall asleep on the lap of the nymph Egeria. She knows that you aren't sitting in a corner of the Porcelain Hall in Schönbrunn, making up a secret language to imitate Albert II, the Lame, the first prince of peace among the Habsburgs; that you aren't walking through the eleven rooms of the Hofburg Treasure House, and stopping in awe before the Turkish crown of Stephen Bocskay, Prince of Transylvania, who was poisoned by the Austrians. She knows, Maximilian, because they told her where you went. You didn't go to the cabin where you saw yourself not only as Robinson Crusoe but also as a second king of Rome, who played the same game of conquering the world from that lonely place. And you hadn't gone to the bedchamber where the Duke of Reichstadt died to ask yourself once more, for the hundredth time perhaps, in front of Ender's watercolor showing him on his deathbed, if that prince with his eagle's heart and beak, that terribly pale prince who seems to be dreaming that he is alive, had truly been the one who sired you, or if all of that was a lie. No, your mother, the Archduchess of Love, knew very well, she always knew, where you had gone: to a scorpions' nest, a wasps' nest, Maximilian—Sir Charles Wyke had warned you—a mousetrap from which you wouldn't come out alive, as my grandmother Amélie told you, and I told you, Maximilian. Don't deny that now. I told you again and again that everything was for naught.

I do want to talk about you. I made up my mind never to forget you and that no one will ever forget you again. That is why I decided to stay in a dream; my eyes wide open. In a thick twilight peopled with ghosts who talk to me incessantly, who whisper in my ear or shout at me as I try to pretend that I'm blind and deaf and that these eyes that see them aren't mine, nor are these ears that hear them, nor is it my voice that calls them or begs them to leave me in peace, to leave me alone, that tells them I am tired of dreaming, of being someone other than myself. Only, it's too late. If I tell you that it's too late, Maximilian, I don't mean that sixty years is too long a time, because the day I chose to flee from Mexico, from Miramare and from Bouchout, from your death and my life—that day never happened. It wasn't sixty years, or even a moment, ago. No, it's from eternity that I summon all these voices, your voice and the voice of your conscience, the voice of resentment and tenderness, the voice that one day, more out of self pity than for your love, was able to proclaim you King of the Universe and place you on the throne carved by Indians in New Spain out of lava stone from Tlalpan for Viceroy Antonio de Mendoza. It is the voice that before or after, now and tomorrow, more out of self-hatred than resentment toward you, is able to leave you alone, riddled with bullets, in the dust of Las Campanas Hill. Or, if I wish, I can make liquid poppies or rivers of butterflies spring out from your bullet wounds. Or I can lace the golden rope through those holes that the Tamaulipas troops always carried to hang you from a tree just in case they captured you alive. I can string you up like a puppet and make you do the can-can in Mexico City's Plaza de Armas. I may be damned, but I am also privileged by dreams and madness to build, if I so desire, an enormous castle of words, words as light as air, which float like sugar paper, like cards, like wings, and then topple it with my breath so that my sweetest words will float with the wings of Concha Méndez's dove, so that they will fly to Querétaro, to bring you luck, Maximilian, and a portrait of the Empress Carlota dressed as the Queen of Hearts.

Because it's also the privilege of dreams to turn a mirror into a rose, and then a cloud, and then the cloud into a mountain, or the mountain into a mirror; if I want I can glue Sedano y Leguizano's dark beard on your face, or amputate your leg and replace it with Santa Anna's, or chop off the other leg and put Uraga's in its place, or dress you in Juárez's dark skin, or trade your blue eyes for Zapata's, so that no one will ever dare say that you, Ferdinand Maximilian Juárez, are not, or that you, Fernando Emiliano Uraga y Leguizamo,

113

were not, or that you, Maximilian López de Santa Anna, will never be a tried-and-true Mexican. You were as genuinely Mexican as those sugar skulls and bones that you can buy on the Day of the Dead at Dolores Market, where I saw the three tiled coffins that a gringo by the name of Chester Cuppia stole, along with our silver imperial tableware, to exhibit in New York, and where you had been made into a wax dummy, three wax dummies, still and pale and all dressed up, not in your blue cassock with gold buttons, black trousers, field boots, and the kid gloves that were completely ruined when your rotten flesh seeped into them in Querétaro; no, one of the dummies was in a royal purple uniform, appropriate only for an operetta colonel, the other in tails and a top hat; the third was almost nude, in a loincloth, just like Christ. I made those coffins and those dummies because there is no one in the world like me, Maximilian, no one else who can make you and take you apart. No else one like me who can craft you with my own hands, who can sculpt you in wax and melt you passionately with my body heat, to make your bones out of marzipan and eat them in little bites, or to carve you out of soap and bathe with you and rub your body against mine, to lick you until we melt into one tongue, one bitter perfumed skin. No one like me, either, who can shrink you down, if I so desire, to make you into a baby, still nursing, and then bury you in a display case, to make you a two-week fetus and then bury you in a matchbox. Who can make you unborn, and, one of these days, bury you alive, in my womb.

What I mean is that I am going to give birth to you any moment, so that they'll all know that your death is a lie. And it's for the same reason that the other day I took off with Countess Mélanie Zichy and my sister-in-law Henriette to the Paris World's Fair. Imagine, Maximilian, how much fun I had, all that I saw, how many things I bought! Sultan Mohammed Effendi was there, as was Eugénie, strolling arm in arm with her friend the Marquise of the Marshes. Behind them, also arm in arm, walked Louis Napoleon and the Imperial Prince, after visiting the Brighton Aquarium, but Loulou preferred the human aquarium at the Fair because there were divers eating, smoking, drinking, and playing dominoes under water. If you could see how fantastic, Max, that's what Loulou said to the Emperor of Solo and the Prince of Manko Negoro who rode through the Champ de Mars in carriages designed by Monsieur Hermans from The Hague. Eugénie told the Marquise of the Marshes all about her experiences at the Suez Canal inauguration, how impressive that marvel of construction was, built by her cousin Lesseps, who, of course, was also in Ismailia, and how proud she had felt aboard her yacht *L'Aigle*, followed by more than fifty ships, among them Franz Joseph's, one for each Royal Prince of Prussia, and then Prince Henri of the Low Countries. Maximilian, I pretended not to see nor hear them, since I was in a hurry and was shopping. I am tired of their gossip and their intrigues and their filth, so instead I asked Countess Zichy to come with me to the Amiens Pavilion and there I ordered fifty yards of blue velvet to make new curtains for your office in Miramare; I went to buy a cabinet made of pistachio wood for Prince Agustín's bedroom, but the truth is that I could still see and hear them all—I couldn't help it. And when your name was mentioned, and Sarah Bernhardt lent Louis Napoleon the tear-shaped diamond that was a gift from Victor Hugo, so that he could pretend to be crying for you, I couldn't bear it because you know very well what hypocrites they all are. Louis Napoleon would rather cry for forgetting to take the sapphire locket with a relic of the true cross that Caliph Harun al-Rashid gave to Charlemagne to Sedan and that would have guaranteed him a victory—as he said, before going on to complain of terrible bladder pains, of passing round, bloody stones like the pink pearls at the Fair in the Bermuda pavilion—than to cry for you, Maximilian. Henriette would rather cry over the fate of Stephanie than cry for you, Maximilian. This is the same Stephanie who, after Rudolf had died, married her second husband in our Miramare Castle and then sank into oblivion. She was never called Stephanie again, or the Rose of Brabant, homely as she was, with her big feet and her chapped hands—and so stupid!— no, the peasants in Transylvania never knelt down to her again as she went by to kiss the hem of her dress, nor did the people in Trieste shout, *Stephanie benedetta, Stephanie carissima*. Eugénie would cry in anger because Pope Leo XIII refused her an audience at the Vatican for having visited Victor Emmanuel I at the Quirinal twenty years earlier—yes, Eugénie would rather cry, Maximilian, listen to me, about losing her throne fifty years ago than to cry for you.

For that reason and to prevent the crocodile tears that they would have shed for you, I told them that you were there, that what they said wasn't true, and, I said it again, that you were in the Mexican pavilion and they would see you later, if they went with me. But first I asked Henriette to buy some Guesnu wrapping paper for the Christmas gifts I was giving the poor children of Trieste. I bought a load of Howitzer rifles for the arsenal of the Molino del Rey, and I said good morning to the Prince of Orange. And I went along with him, and the Prince of Wales, Princess Murat, Pauline Bonaparte, and my sister-in-law Henriette to drink cocktails in the United States pavilion because, you know, the mint julep was invented, Maximilian, along with sherry cobblers and brandy smashes. Then Louis Napoleon and Eugénie joined us and we all drank cocktails, Henriette drinking more than anyone else—one mint julep after another until she was quite drunk. I didn't want to tell her that her son, the little Duke of Brabant was there, soaked and trembling with chills, after falling into a pond, the little idiot. I didn't want to remind the poor woman that in a few days the little duke would die of pneumonia. I didn't want to tell Eugénie that if she looked carefully at Loulou's uniform, she would see that it was prickly with assegai spears. I wanted to keep the fact from her that, when the prince told her that his Woolrich cadet uniform would bring him closer to Alfonso XII, who wore the Sandhurst uniform, she would notice that his breath already reeked of rotting entrails. But I did warn both of them, you'd better not come around here with your lies, saying Maximilian this and Maximilian that. Maximilian is here, you hear? He is here, alive, at the Paris World Fair. And, I told Eugénie, if you ate pheasants stuffed with figs and wild-duck breasts in date sauce in Suez, on my way to Yucatán I found waiting for me, in Veracruz, a carriage lined in velvet and silk with gold fringes and clusters of mangoes, cherimoyas, pineapples, and mameyes. And just as they had once done with Max during one of his trips through the country, the people unhitched the Frisian horses and pulled the carriage themselves. And I told them that you, Max, had gone with me all the way to San Isidro, and that at El Palmar I had given medals to the Austrian soldiers for their bravery during the Battle of Tecomahuaca, and that when I arrived in Mérida, wearing a blue-trimmed white gown and a little black hat also edged in powder blue from which my golden ringlets peeked, the cannons from Fort San Benito roared and the bells began to peal. The locals were all there, all dressed in snowy-white linen, the children wearing paper wings, and they showered me with multicolored ribbons embossed with the words "Long Live Our Illustrious Empress," and poetry printed on scented leaflets calling me the "Protector Angel of Yucatán," and saying "God Bless you, Carlota." The Prince of Orange, I swear to you Maximilian, was quite impressed, but Eugénie pretended not to hear me, and she went on talking about the night that multicolored lanterns hung like shining coconuts from the palm trees in Cairo and she drank a pink champagne toast with the Egyptian Khedive to the future of France and the Canal, but I know she heard me, I knew that she was dying of anger and envy, as was Pauline Bonaparte, who began to tell us about a black slave with whom she'd bathed nude in a pool in Martinique. Henriette, who had drunk so many juleps that she had mint sprigs coming out of her nose, began to complain about my brother Leopold, to say that the older he gets the more libidinous he gets, although he's always been that way. He had barely returned from his honeymoon when he got involved with that showgirl—what was her name?—Aimée Desclée—and now he has a little sixteen-year-old whore for a mistress, Carolina, called the Queen of the Congo. And I said, look, Henriette, you have no right to criticize Leopold because he's my brother and I love him very much even though at times he was cruel to me but sometimes he was nice. When I was a girl he read me the story of the Isle of Flowers, freed by the King of Athunt who slew all the witches, and the story of the flesh-eating diamonds from the *Thousand and One Nights*. But then, Maximilian, I saw my brother Leopold there, yes, at the Paris World's Fair. I saw my brother, Leopold II of Belgium in a pavilion of mirrored walls. He was nude, very old, his beard completely white, tossing around on a bed with a little girl who was also nude. The mirrors multiplied their nude bodies to infinity, and the hands of black Africans, their knuckles bloody, moved up and down his legs and back like enormous black spiders, but he kept on fornicating.

This is why, Maximilian, I don't want you to see them. Ignore them. Pay them no mind. Pretend they don't exist. Go to the British pavilion so that you will see the tables covered in penguin hides from the Sandwich Islands. Buy me some sandalwood combs in the Ottoman pavilion. Go to the Belgian pavilion to see the equestrian statue of Ambiorix, King of the Eburneans, and buy me a bottle of Guerlain perfume in the French pavilion. Go to the Tunisian pavilion so that you can see Arabs at the bazaar swallowing live centipedes and buy me a face cream made of crocodile glands in the Brazilian pavilion. Oh, Maximilian, I want you to buy me so many things: a Cordovan purse, a Bayeux lace veil, a Christofle tea service like the one that was stolen in Mexico, a beaded dress like the one I saw in the Austrian pavilion; a jar of *mate* from Argentina; a dagger from Toledo. And if you go to the Dutch pavilion, buy me the crystal goblet with the hidden celluloid doll that pops up when you fill it with wine, used to toast the birth of a child so that, the day that Eugénie and Louis Napoleon take me for cocktails again at the United States pavilion, I can shock them. That doll has your eyes and your face, your hair, the first diapers that your mother Sophie put on you, the milk from your wetnurse on its lips. And when that bunch of two-bit royalty and carnival princes and princesses who are always bragging about their jewels and their castles—Maria Cristina of Savoy who came to buy Shantung silks for the drapes of the Chinese Palace in Caserta where my great-grandfather, the King of the Two Sicilies, prepared sorbets for his guests and relations; Maria Pia who came to the Fair for china from Sèvres and Limoges so that her horses can turn them into shards for the arches of the Palace of Fronteira; Catherine the Great of Russia who came with her diamond tiara with a ruby the size of a dove's egg; Marie Clotilde Bonaparte who wore the black pearl earrings from Fiji that she inherited from Eugénie; and Ena from Spain, who brought the necklace of huge aquamarines that she used in the recent foot-washing ceremony in Madrid—tell me that we don't have a cent, that the coffers are empty, that you will have to auction off the crown jewels, I can say, no need, you're wrong, you're way off, can't you see Maximilian swimming in champagne? Haven't you heard, I said to Marshal Randon and the Count of Chambord, about the infinite wealth of Mexico, of its ores and precious stones? Who said that we'd have to sell your horses Orispelo and Anteburro to the slaughterhouse? Maximilian is swimming in the golden pleasures of the Western Sierra Madre. Maximilian is taking a *pulque* bath in his obsidian tub. Don't you know, I asked Princess Troubetskoy and your uncle, Prince Montenuovo, and my uncle the Duke of Montpensier, that there's no country in the world like Mexico, on which Divine Providence has showered so many gifts? Don't you know that Mexico has every type of fruit, of landscape, of flower? Who said that I have to fire all my ladies-in-waiting and half of the palace kitchen staff? That we're planning to sell the Aztec calendar stone to the Kunsthistorisches Museum in Vienna? Maximilian is seated on a throne of roses that General Escobedo gave him. Don't you know, I asked Count D'Eu and the Duke of Persigny, didn't you know the story of the viceroy who invited the King of Spain to visit Mexico and swore that from Veracruz to the capital, for one hundred Spanish leagues, his feet would step on nothing but pure silver? Who said we were about to pawn our gilded carriage at the National Pawn Shop? Don't you know that in Yucatán I walked from the dock, all along the beach, and through the jungle, on a path of seashells and conches that took my little Mayans a month to lay, that the path was bordered by trees of precious woods festooned with green wreaths, and that I stepped between two rows of Indian women who were dressed in white, like dark-skinned vestal virgins, and who fanned me with enormous palm leaves? Who's that saying we're going to have to sublet the National Palace? Don't you know that with all the conches and the shells from Mexico we could cover the bottoms of all the European lakes? Of Lake Como, where my father Leopold went to cry over his Princess Charlotte of Britain; Lake Starnberg where Ludwig of Bavaria drowned his crystal swans and peacocks; Lake Constance where Louis Napoleon skated in the wintertime and dreamed about being the king of Nicaragua. Who says that we're poor and that we have to raffle off Chapultepec Castle? Oh no, hear me once and for all, I said to Madame Tascher de la Pagerie, to Countess Walewska, and to Count Cossé-Brissac: Maximilian is napping on a hammock woven from silver threads by the ladies of Querétaro. Don't you know that we could rebuild all the sleeper coaches on the Orient Express out of ebony, cedar, mahogany, and Campeche rosewood from Mexico? That we could gild the entire Statue of Liberty? That we could cover Notre Dame de Paris in tortoiseshell, or the Egyptian Pyramids with deerskin? Doesn't the world understand, Maximilian, that we could fill the European skies with the stars from Mexico, carpet the Champs Élysées with the petals from its orchids, or the Alps with the wings from its butterflies? Oh no, Maximilian is not poor. Maximilian is taking an imperial cochineal bath in his onyx tub.

Did you hear that the Orient Express was built, Maximilian? We will ride it on our honeymoon from Paris to Istanbul. The Statue of Liberty was erected too, and one day I will climb with you to the tip of its torch so that you will behold the arrival of Lafayette. The automatic washer was invented so that I can wash away the blood that stained your waistcoat on Las Campanas Hill. Someone invented celluloid so I could mold you in miniature, give birth to you, so that you will float up from the bottom of my glass, up from champagne as though from the depths of a sacred pool. So that you can breathe again, and I as well. Because if I ever bear a child, Maximilian, as I said before, his father will not be Van der Smissen nor Colonel Feliciano Rodríguez, nor Léonce Détroyat, nor anyone else. I will be its sole creator. My words and myself.

And so that they all could see that you were alive, or reborn, you rose from the dead. I told them all, come with me, come see Maximilian here, here at the Paris World's Fair, sitting on a throne covered with vicuña and alpaca furs, wearing the uniform of an Admiral of Texcoco Lake, skin dusted with gold from Peru, on your face the mask of a Quimbaya chief, in your left hand a cluster of onyx grapes, in your right the orb of Emperor Mathias, on your lap a model of the frigate that won you your glory in the Battle of Lissa, on your head the crown of the Holy Roman Empire, on your right shoulder a stuffed toucan, on your breast a medal with your likeness that lights up, opens and closes its eyes and mouth; on your brow the orange shade of an Achille-Gruyer parasol; on your lips an artificial d'Invernois violet; around you, blue butterflies from Brazil; at your feet a carpet of red moss surrounded by the rinds left from an apple peeler; shards of frozen water made by an ice machine; rabbit skins for making hats that fly out of pneumatic cylinders; rivers of beer that overflow from Bier Hall; mineral water from the falls at Schweppes, at its bottom a salt statue of Charles V; to your left a thirty-kilo block of amethyst and in the center a horsefly made of ambergris; to your right, the aerolite from Yanhuitlán that your Mexican astronomers gave you, and resting upon it a gold Fabergé egg containing a grain of white cacao. I would have liked to see you like that at the Paris World's Fair. To show you off, alive, to the Prince of Wales who visited the pavilions on a silver swan from Bond Street; or to Doctor Bilimek who rode the hallways on a Nachet microscope. So that no one would know that the heir of Constantine and the heroes who killed Otokar of Bohemia to found an empire—as I told Eugénie, who left with her American dentist in a silver Rolls Royce belonging to the Baron von Rothschild; as I told the Prince of Saxony who stuck his head out of the smokestack of a locomotive—so that no one would find out that the noble Austrian who wrote, among his other aphorisms, may your spirit be of steel, your heart of gold, your soul a diamond—the one who invoked his ancestor Isabella the Catholic of Spain on the stairway of the Port of Barcelona, where she received Christopher Columbus's greetings from the New World, and the one who at La Giralda Tower remembered the powerful Habsburg ruler who besieged the Pope in the Castle of Saint Angelo, and who counted the King of France among his prisoners—so that no one would dare imagine that the Prince who would be heir to the glories of Lepanto and Pavia, who sat on the throne of the Aztec rulers, so that no one would know that when you realized that all was lost you tried to flee, your possessions packed up—furniture, books, the paintings that you stole from Mexico—and shipped on the *Dandolo* to Trieste, so that no one would find out that you were humiliated, Maximilian, by a trial held in a theater named after a fake emperor, and that you were condemned to death by a murderous colonel and six filthy captains who could barely read and write; so that no one will know that your body was wrapped in sackcloth and was put in a box that cost twenty *reales* and that a Mexican officer said there goes the Emperor but what difference does one less dog make; I told Princess Metternich who hid in a Jamaican rum bottle, or Johann Strauss who conducted an orchestra of violin-playing crabs; or Napoleon III, who stuck his head in a Krupp cannon; or the Duke D'Aosta who bought me another mint julep; or your brother Franz Joseph who greeted me from his equestrian portrait; or the Czar of All the Russias who came out of a soap mill; or Doctor Bilimek, who swallowed a silkworm; yes, that's how I would have liked to have shown you off, Maximilian, alive to quiet the rumors, to quiet the shouting, so that no one would dare say, Maximilian has died; so that no one would dare imagine you nude on a table in an amphitheater, your eyes out of their sockets and your entrails sticking out; so that everyone, Maximilian, would see you exactly as I loved you, at the World's Fair, alive in the largest and tallest pavilion, at the top of the Pyramid of Xochicalco, at your feet the Nubian slaves, who slather their bodies with avocado grease and who sleep on wooden pillows that the King of Egypt sent you, and the Kickapoo Indians who've brought a gift of alligator boots from Louisiana; on your left La Malinche with a censer, and before you, on his knees, Colonel Rincón Gallardo who brings you the head of Colonel López in an iron cage; at your side your secretary, José Luis Blasio, with your quills and inkwells on a silver salver. So that you can sign your imperial edicts with a quetzal plume from Moctezuma's headdress, so that you can write to Sisi, your sister-in-law, with a chicken feather. So that you can write a poem about my lips with a quill from a robin redbreast, or you can write to Pope Pius IX with a plume from a bird of paradise. So that you can write to your mother Sophie with a feather from a cockatoo, and an ode to my neck with one from a swan. So that you can sign the invitations to our palace balls with an ostrich feather, and with one from a swallow write a song about my armpits; a hymn to my buttocks with a flamingo feather and with one from a canary to the hummingbird tongue between my thighs. So that you will sign the declaration of war between Mexico and Austria-Hungary with an eagle feather, and, with one from a seagull, write in your logbook as you sail on the *Novara* through the islands of the Aegean. So that you will use a crow's feather to sign Benito Juárez's death sentence, ordering his execution in the Plaza de San Pedro.

VI

"A PRETTY BOY THIS ARCHDUKE TURNED OUT TO BE"

1863

1. Brief Account of the Siege of Puebla

It's true that many ran away like a flock of chickens at the warning cry, "The French Are Coming!"—much to their shame, and to the shame of those who didn't. Like chickens yes, but tossing away not feathers but kepis, trousers, rifle slings, shirts and jackets, canteen holders, and boots. Shedding their clothes as they fled, ran, disappeared in the darkness so that the French wouldn't catch them with their uniforms on, they threw into the air and onto the road behind them the chocks and long packthreads with whose wicks they were supposed to spike their cannons, light their gunpowder, and set off their mortars. And they even threw away their own rifles, instead of breaking them up as they'd been ordered by the commander-in-chief of the Eastern Army. They cast their stockings and leggings, belts and pennants to the wind; they vanished, it's true, but many more did stay at their posts, by their cannons, long enough to destroy them, to keep them from falling into enemy hands, and though some of the guns weren't destroyed on the first try, others blew to pieces right away—gun-carriages, swabs, limbers, mortar trunnions, size twenty-four Spanish and English guns and size fifteen Dutch howitzers, Coehorn siege mortars, and Belgian shell-firing cannons on Gribeauval gun-carriages, blowing to pieces from the tops of the towers of the forts and bell-towers of the convents and raining into the streets, onto the glacis and embankments, onto the rocks and rubble, onto the hands, legs, remains of the corpses mutilated by previous explosions, and into the flooded trenches where the bodies of the soldiers' women were rotting, their heads split open by other size twenty-four shrapnel cans, and hand grenades. General Mendoza, whose cheeks puffed up and whose mustache bristled when he became angry, dressed as always in his outlandish uniform—an overcoat with a huge collar and wide cuffs, a hat with a large rosette and thick metal-embroidered chin strap, gigantic spurs, and other eccentricities—had gone the night before to talk with General Forey and returned a few hours later with his sword between his legs (his sword, of which the fine Toledo steel blade had been split in half by the bullet of a *Chasseur de Vincennes*, yes, the sword that was rumored to have belonged to the sinister Duke of Alba), returned shamed to death and in a rage because Forey had turned down the petition of the Mexican commander-in-chief to allow his troops to leave the garrison with their weapons and their battle pennants in order to go to Mexico City; Forey had said no, the surrender had to be unconditional and so the Mexican troops were to turn in their weapons and give themselves up as prisoners, and if they refused, General Forey added, "We're going to attack the garrison and kill all Mexicans." And it was then that, so as not to leave arms or ammunition behind that could be used later, General Paz gathered all the artillery officers in the Convent of Santa Clara and told them that on the orders of the commander-in-chief, at four-thirty A.M. sharp, that morning of May 17, 1863, they were to blow up all the powder depots, destroy all the rifles, spike the cannons, saw the gun-carriages in half, and burn or disable all munitions, and four-thirty A.M. was the precise time that a great explosion was heard in one of the city forts, followed by others, and then many more, and the sky was lit up by the glare, like flashes of lighting, and at the break of dawn, black fumaroles, white fumaroles, and tongues of fire, immense tongues of yellow, red, and blue flames could still be seen rising from the forts and convents, as though all the streets and markets in the city—Los Locos, El Rastro, La Estampa, and La Misericordia—and all their buildings—the Cockfighting Ring, the Parián, the Hospice of the Poor, the post office, the cathedral built by the angels—were all ablaze, and with their houses all the soldiers and the corpses of those who had died during the siege, and the civilian inhabitants too: the women, the elderly, and the children.

General Forey put on his hat with its long white feathers, satisfied that the dishonor and the painful surprise that France had suffered almost a year before on May 5, 1862, had now been avenged.

On May 5, 1862, the French *Grande Armée*, the triumphant army of the Crimean War and the war for the unification of Italy, undefeated since Waterloo, was routed in its attempt to take the city of Puebla by the Mexican defenders of the stronghold: the Army of the East under the command of General Ignacio Zaragoza.

General Lorencez looked at some of the cannonballs that had been fired against the French from the forts of Loreto and Guadalupe and, remembering that Saligny had promised that Louis Napoleon's troops would be welcomed by the residents of Puebla with a shower of roses, said: "Here are the Minister's flowers."

"No, my dear general," the Emperor of the French would say in a letter to the defeated General, "the Minister did not deceive you. He told you that the flowers of the beautiful Mexican women of Puebla would fall at your feet when you entered the streets of the city—but he could hardly have issued military orders himself to solve the minor technical problem of making sure you actually reached said streets," and besides deeming Lorencez's decision to place his cannons in line at two-and-a-half kilometers from the enemy fortifications a ridiculous mistake, Louis Napoleon called the General a fool, and told him to start packing his bags.

The tale of the Zouaves' flag, once so glorious at Solferino, which fell into the moat of a fort in Puebla when the flag-bearer was killed, and which was later rescued by his comrades at the cost of several more lives, wasn't enough for the French troops to feel even slightly glorious on that evening of May 5, 1862—if anything, they only felt muddy, since the floodgates of heaven opened wide and rain poured down, rain which, along with the mud, the hail, the wind, the fog, and the darkness, General Lorencez tried to blame, at least partially, for his defeat at Puebla, and the death of 480 of his men, among whom there were many of the selfsame Zouaves, descendants of a race of intrepid men who had hired out their strength and their fierceness to the Berber princes, and whose memorable performance in the Battle of Isly made the *Revue des Deux Mondes* recall the campaign of the pyramids and Marius's war against the Cimbri. These Zouaves were the very same who had once trekked for weeks and weeks through the mud and snow of the Jura, their feet bound in strips of cowhide held together with hemp string. The Zouaves—with their baggy oriental outfits, their red turbans, and their scarves to protect them from the sun and the sand—much as they'd frisked about like panthers in the thickets of Inkerman, much as they'd romped through the swamps of Veracruz surrounded by rubber trees with black foliage and mimosas with their overbearing scents—who, yes, like cats, had climbed the escarpments of Alma—now clambered on the summits of the Sierra de Acultzingo, on their way to Puebla de los Angeles, marching to the tune of, yes, to the tune of "Père Bugeaud":

As-tu vu
La casquette,
La casquette?
As-tu vu la casquette
Du Père Bugeaud?

And still they bit the dust—in the mud, on the plains of Puebla.

The battle of May 5th has come down as a glorious day in the history of Mexico. "The French eagles have crossed the ocean," said General Berriozábal, "to deposit at the foot of the Mexican flag the laurels of Sebastopol, Magenta, and Solferino . . . We have fought against the best soldiers of our time and have been the first to conquer them."

However, the true Battle of Puebla—the great, heroic, tragic and magnificent battle of Puebla—did not last one day, but many more. In his letter to Lorencez, Louis Napoleon acknowledged that Prim had been right, that at least thirty thousand men were needed in order to conquer Mexico. The French legislature approved their dispatch, Lorencez returned to France, and two divisions under General Elias F. Forey arrived in Mexico boosting the number of French troops on Mexican land to twenty-eight thousand men. One division was under the command of the hero of Malakoff, General Charles Abel Douay. The other under Achille François Bazaine, future Marshal of France. These were reinforced by almost seven thousand men of the Mexican auxiliary forces under the command of Generals Almonte and Leonardo Márquez, and then the Egyptian and Nubian contingents. The reinforcement troops had boarded ship in Toulon and in Mers-el-Kébir, and included a detachment of the Foreign Legion.

At the beginning of March 1863, ten months after the defeat of May 5th, and after almost ten months mainly taken up with inactivity and inattention, Douay's column made its way toward Puebla over the summits of Acultzingo; the 99th Assault Regiment over the peaks of Maltrata; Bazaine via Jalapa and Perote. The Cavalry Brigade was under the command of General Mirandol. Along with their siege, reserve, field, and mountain guns, the French had fifty-six pieces of artillery with a supply of three hundred shells each. The 2,400,000-cartridge reserve of ammunition would soon grow with the arrival of new convoys.

Puebla, a city of 80,000 people at that time, depended on a 21,000-man garrison, 170 artillery pieces and 18,000 small arms. It was Mexico's best-defended town, and since May of 1862 several new forts had been added to the existing ones. No effort was spared in boosting its defenses, nothing had been forgotten or overlooked: mountain cannons hoisted to the upper floors of the Penitenciaría; neighboring Indians given the task of making gabions for the trenches; two workshop installations constructed, a foundry and a gunpowder factory, and as much niter, sulfur, and lead as possible for them; the upper part of Fort San Javier and the Penitenciaría fitted with loopholes; covering the fronts of the buildings next to the forts with earth-filled sacks, and, with earth leftover from the excavations, building an extensive glacis at Fort Santa Anita; demolishing the church at Fort Guadalupe and constructing a vault and a cistern; raising over a hundred breastworks on streets and buildings; buying forty thousand meters of canvas, five thousand shakos, and eight thousand blankets; using the wood from the bullring to build barricades with loose dirt in the streets leading all the way to the outskirts of the city; and for logistic reasons, ordering that all the plum, apple, pear, hawthorn, orange, and lemon trees be cut down without hesitation in the beautiful grove of El Carmen. Besides this, the city garrison was under the command of some of the most prestigious of Juárez's generals, such as Berriozábal, Negrete, Porfirio Díaz, O'Horan, and the Garibaldian Ghilardi. But the hero of May 5th, Ignacio Zaragoza, the general who had been born in Texas while it was still a part of Mexico, would not be found in Puebla, since he had died of typhoid fever only a few months earlier, helpless in his delirium: on his deathbed, he had dreamt he was still commander-in-chief of the Eastern Army, inspecting the lines, and mounted on his horse from Kentucky, giving orders to his different divisions. In his honor and in his memory, the city would one day cease to call itself Puebla de los Angeles and call itself Puebla de Zaragoza.

The new commander of the Eastern Army was one of the most prestigious Mexican officers, as well as president of the Supreme Court of Justice, General Jesús González Ortega, who soon realized that, though it was true that the defenses of the city were excellent, the supply of ammunition for both the artillery and the small arms, however abundant it may have appeared to be—it was calculated that there were 3,195,000 cartridges for rifles of fifteen drams, Enfield rifles, Minié carbines, Mississippi rifles, and musketoons—would not be enough to withstand a siege that would last over two months. He requested new supplies from the Minister of War, but Mr. Juárez's government thought the siege could not possibly last more than forty or forty-five days without either the garrison surrendering or the French succumbing, and did not satisfy his request.

The siege of Puebla lasted sixty-two days, two days longer than the famous siege of Zaragoza in Spain.

On March 10th, General González Ortega announced that the siege of the city was imminent, and he asked all citizens who could not help in its defense, as well as all French nationals, to leave the city.

The Mexicans thought that the French would start their attack on March 16th, the birthday of Louis Napoleon's son, the Imperial Prince. Since this didn't happen, as a greeting and as a warning to the French troops, on the morning of that day a cannon was fired from the Fortress of Guadalupe.

The French troops continued advancing. In some places the terrain had so many holes and ravines that the gun carriages proved to be more stubborn than the mules and the soldiers had to break ranks and put their shoulders to the wheels.

On March 18th, half of the enemy troops surrounded the city in the north. The other half, under Bazaine, in the south. General Elias Forey set up his headquarters in the southwest, on San Juan Hill.

On the 19th and 20th there were only isolated exchanges of fire. On the 21st, the battle really flared up. That day the enemy fired over thirty cannon shots against General Negrete's division located at the foot of Loreto Hill.

On one of those days, Colonel Troncoso asked Lieutenant Colonel Jesús Lalanne: "Comonfort's troops, what good are they?" Some of those troops, a cavalry detachment, had been routed at Cholula, to the west of Puebla, and suffered serious losses after fierce knife, sword, and bayonet combat with the *Chasseurs d'Afrique* under the command of General Mirandol.

Meanwhile, the besiegers began applying tactics introduced by Vauban; they chose a place of attack and initiated a gradual advance by means of successive parallel trenches. On March 26th they began building parallels seven hundred meters from the forts of the Penitenciaría and San Javier. The Mexican commander Romero Vargas mounted his horse, rode out of the fort to inspect the parallels, was shot dead, and a three-man ambulance waving a white flag picked up the body. A day later the French were building another parallel at three hundred meters and the fort was subjected to a heavy attack of concentric fire. The Mexican captain Platón Sánchez was wounded on one ear. On March 29th, after the French completed a fourth parallel and added two T-shaped wings to it, the fort surrendered. In the neighboring small bullring and streets, a fire spread all the way to the Penitenciaría, where many resident prisoners, who could not be freed on time, burned to death. On a patio of the fort, a group of Zouaves barricaded themselves behind a circular fountain crowned by an angel with outstretched wings. The Mexicans opened fire on them and some shots perforated the fountain, creating several unexpected gushers. Another shot chipped off a piece of the angel's wing; yet another blew off its nose. A Zouave got up to cross the patio, but was killed by another shot, he fell into the fountain, and the waters turned red with his blood. Finally, someone on one of the rooftops threw a grenade that destroyed the angel and killed several of the Zouaves who lay there covered with pieces of the angel's wings, face, tunic, and hair.

Nobody picked up the corpses and they began to decompose. But if it was like this; if those Zouaves were left there, abandoned and rotting along with the bodies of other comrades and those of the men of the 3rd Regiment of the riflemen known as the *Chasseurs de Vincennes*, and those of the French hussars who had crossed the tropics wrapped in mosquito nets and who, without breaking their horses' stride, had plucked bunches of bananas in order to stuff them into their coat sleeves, and likewise the bodies of many Mexicans from the brigades of Oaxaca, Toluca, and the Zacapoaxtlas, of the Rifle Battalion, the Reforma Battalion and of the Corps of Sappers and the Corps of Engineers; if all these bodies were there in Judas Tadeo Street and in many other city streets such as El Hospicio, Los Locos, Los Cocheros de Toledo, and La Santísima, where there was a cannon nicknamed El Toro because every time it was fired it made such a loud noise that it broke all the windows on the block; and if they were there abandoned, rotting, and if later they began to become fodder for dogs and cats, and if they began to disintegrate when the rains came, to liquefy, to become shreds, scraps, a thick goo, a gray and foul-smelling sap, it was because the siege of the city of Puebla, which began with the taking of the Penitenciaría and San Javier, and ended with the fall of Totimehuacán and Fort Ingenieros, had become, from the very first weeks, a battle fought block by block, lot by lot, house by house, floor by floor, room by room, and because of this—because oftentimes the enemy was just on the other side of the street, and the soldiers would fire at each other from door to door, from window to window—the bodies of those who died in the middle of that street were simply left there, as were the wounded who couldn't walk or drag themselves away and who would soon be corpses themselves.

When General Forey learned this, when he found out that it was necessary, day after day, to fight and take one redoubt after another, to machine-gun individual houses, warehouses, and stores, and lob grenades through windows, balconies, transoms, and skylights, and to break up barricades that had been built with everything imaginable—armoires, buckets, irons, crockery, barrels, crates, tables, frying pans, and soap—when he learned that in eight days only seven square blocks had been taken, not even one per day, and that one of the few options still available was to build underground passages, but that the rocky subsoil of Puebla was so hard that it would only be possible to do this in a few places, such as Pitiminí Street, where one morning six houses crumbled as though by magic after the explosion of half a ton of gunpowder, General Forey gathered his officers into a War Council. He spoke of the possibility of bringing the naval artillery from Veracruz, complained bitterly about his lot, refused to accept responsibility for their failure, and proposed that they lift the siege and proceed to Mexico City.

This was not done, however, to the detriment of Juárez and his government, and the battle continued; the French attacked Fort Judas Tadeo; they threatened Fort Zaragoza; they attacked the forts of Loreto and Guadalupe and fired their guns at the churches of Señor de los Trabajos and Santa Anita and the towers of the Cathedral. The latter, however, managed to remain intact, perhaps because the angels took an interest in them; the French also fired their cannons at the Church of San Agustín, which was consumed by flames from its foundations all the way up to its dome, and with it all the holy objects of the congregation, all the chasubles and the furniture stored there: chairs and tables, desks, easy chairs, recamiers; and the boxes of ammunition being stored there exploded as well, sending the strings, keyboards, and pedals of some pianos sky high with a roar; and then, among innumerable other acts of war, there were skirmishes, bayonet duels, heavy exchanges of fire, tactical burning of gabions and tarred barricades; and while the interior fortifications of the blocks of houses were doubled and tripled, Mexican stone-clearing mines exploded around the invaders, raining down hundreds of pounds of rock of various sizes and shapes, colors and sharpness, on Zouaves, Egyptians, and the *Chasseurs de Vincennes*, denting their skulls, breaking their teeth and jaws, and crushing their ribs and their spirits

When Captain Manuel Galindo ran out of ammunition at Moscoso Street, he decided to surrender. A Zouave treacherously killed him.

On Mesón de Guadalupe Street, a group of French soldiers was walking with their Mexican prisoners when, hidden behind some rubble, some drunken

Zouaves opened fire on them, killing one prisoner and wounding another. A furious French captain drove his sword into a Zouave's belly, disarmed the others, and took them prisoner as well.

On Father Valdivia Street, some girls or soldiers' women from Puebla had taken to coming out on a balcony to make eyes and blow kisses at the Zouaves and *Chasseurs* quartered in the house across the street, and they would even hike their skirts up to their knees so the French would come out and flirt with them so the Mexicans could get a clear shot. One girl, desperate because the French knew all about their tricks by then, and no one would show his face to admire her legs, lifted her skirt up to her belly button, and ended up taking a bullet that splayed her sex like a flower in bloom.

There were a few short truces to bury the dead. The Mexicans gathered up the French corpses and took them in wheelbarrows to the Portal de Morelos. Then they picked up their own fallen. Some of the bodies from both sides, were still in one piece. Others were so torn up that they had to be recovered with shovels. When the burial details arrived at the Del Carmen Cemetery, they found that some bombs had destroyed the tombs and vaults and exposed the cadavers of the civilians buried there, whose state of decomposition varied according to the weeks or months that they had been in the ground. The stench was unbearable. The sweet taste of the ashes of the long-dead lingered on their tongues.

On May 5th, the Puebla garrison's artillery fired a general volley against the enemy in remembrance of the triumph of '62. The French batteries situated in front of Fort Ingenieros intensified their shelling. Lieutenant Colonel Francisco P. Troncoso received orders to visit the fort, and he was able to verify that as soon as the barricades were rebuilt, they were destroyed again, and every day one or more artillery pieces were rendered useless by cannon fire.

On May 9th, Captain Matus showed Lieutenant Colonel Troncoso one of several enemy projectiles that did not explode. It was one of those American so-called turbine shells fired from a rifle-barreled gun. The Lieutenant Colonel knew that these shells had very sensitive percussion fuses and that it was recommended that the fuses be removed during transportation and replaced with wooden plugs, with the fuses then to be reinstalled when the cannons were loaded. It was implausible that the United States had sold them to the French; the shells could only be from General Comonfort's artillery, and it was for that reason that the French didn't know it was necessary to replace the fuses. And if they were his, Comonfort's, it meant only one thing.

One evening—at least this is how Ch. Blanchot, a colonel who wrote his memoirs when he was a captain in Mexico and a member of Achille Bazaine's staff, describes it—one evening, in the town of San Lorenzo, the Mexican General Ignacio Comonfort, Commander of the Central Army, decided that it was time to raise the morale of his officers by throwing a party. Comonfort, along with Generals La Garza and Echegaray, had received orders from the Ministry of War to lead four divisions and march to break the siege of Puebla. That same evening, General Bazaine in turn received instructions from General Forey to march against Comonfort, and, at the stroke of midnight, after refusing to take some laxatives that General Leonardo Márquez had offered him and other officers such as Colonel Miguel López—Achille Bazaine set out with Zouaves, some Algerian sharpshooters, the 51st Regiment, the cavalry, and the 81st Battalion toward San Lorenzo, where he arrived at dawn, avoiding the sentries on the roads and the barking of the dogs, and, in what apparently was not the first such incident for a Mexican army fighting against foreign invaders—according to the historian Justo Sierra, it was in fact *de rigueur*, and had happened at San Jacinto, Padierna, and Borrego Hill as well—he caught Comonfort's troops completely unprepared. For the Juarista army, the Battle of San Lorenzo represented a loss of two thousand men—dead, wounded, or taken prisoner—eight pieces of artillery, three flags, eleven banners, twenty wagons loaded with supplies and ammunition, four hundred mules, and many heads of cattle. General Forey sent a group of prisoners to General González Ortega so that they could tell him personally about the triumph of the French, and after ordering a double ration of *eau de vie* for his troops, he had all the captured flags and pennants displayed on the terrace wall at Fort Penitenciaría so that the enemy could see them. There were plenty of things that weren't taken as trophies, however—a lace handkerchief, for instance, and some patent leather boots—because according to Colonel Blanchot, Bazaine's troops—necklaces and back combs and some civilian clothes like a tuxedo and a white vest with golden buttons—had arrived at San Lorenzo when a dance—an orchid corsage among some huaraches and the kepi of a wounded soldier—when a dance at Hacienda Pensacola was just about to end, and perhaps the Mexican officers—ripped blouses of fine batiste—perhaps they had still been dancing when they heard the shots of the sentries and the warning cries that sounded during the steps of the final cotillion; and when the orchestra stopped playing and they came out of the hacienda to rally their troops and fight off the French, many of the women there—white mantillas with silver fringes, several hairpieces, and the leather and blue-silk embroidered belt of a dead colonel—with whom they'd been dancing came out along with them, all stirred up by the dancing and the habaneras, the punch, and their patriotism—a pair of kid gloves—and many were also left there in San Lorenzo, dead or wounded, with their pink silk stockings and their embroidered garters all bloodied, their velvet and beaded handbags scattered among saddles and dead horses—the poncho and the dress boots of some dead captain and a low-cut corset adorned with a triple band of Spanish lace—dead like the woman who had worn the corset, or another, her belly ripped open by the shrapnel from a grenade, her crinoline and her padded sash sprinkled with golden camellias torn in pieces and likewise soaked in blood.

To Colonel Troncoso's question, Lieutenant Colonel Jesús Lalanne had replied: "Comonfort's troops are good for everything and for nothing." Sent in an attempt to break the siege and resupply the garrison, they arrived too late, and besides the loss at Cholula, they had suffered two additional setbacks: one at Atlixco and the other at La Cruz Hill. Furthermore, since they always received their orders from the Capital, González Ortega could never use them as he wished while there was still some opportunity for them to help.

The defeat at San Lorenzo brought with it, as a consequence, the defeat of Puebla. Munitions they had, but they were completely out of food. It had been estimated that their stores would last three months, and these had already begun to be depleted even before the end of the siege. The garrison was eating parboiled horse and mule meat. In the final days of the siege, people broke into stores and warehouses that, moreover, were empty. All the dogs, cats, and rats disappeared, and not just because they couldn't find any food themselves; there were no more lambs, and no more vegetables: the tomatoes, spinach, potatoes, carrots, and fresh fruit that the mountain Indians had brought were now being sold to the French in Amatlán or in the hills of Tepoxúchil; milk and cheese became scarce; cows disappeared; pigs' feet, backs, ears, and snouts had vanished, as had whole pigs; and when people heard that a woman street vendor was calling out that she had the best meat tamales in town, despite there being no meat left in the entire city, the town gossips said that the body of a Zouave, of a very fat Zouave with an enormous belly, had disappeared from Judas Tadeo Street, and that the meat was human (and this notwithstanding the fact that most people didn't consider the Zouaves to be human at all—that they considered them to be demons), though nobody ever found a Zouave's fingers, fingernails, horns, or tail in those tamales, no matter what you might have heard; and then grains became scarce: beans, lentils, corn for tortillas and wheat for bread—and when a bomb fell on one of the few bakeries still open, puff pastries, breadrolls, trifles, sacks of flour, and loaves of French bread flew through the air, and it rained, it snowed flour from the skies, and to the horrendous stench of the decomposing bodies abandoned in the streets was added the new, awful odor of burnt bread.

On the other hand, and as in any other battle, the luck that both the Mexicans and French had during and after the siege of Puebla in 1863 went from good to bad, from abominable to miraculous, and back. Certainly bad luck was in abundance—as in the case of General Laumière, who got shot in the forehead riding next to General Forey, and fell off his horse, already dead, seeing stars without really seeing them. And then, also unlucky, if not to the same degree, was Captain Hermenegildo Pérez, whom the French saved the trouble of destroying his cannon during the retreat when they rendered it useless with a grenade that, having hit the bridgeboard, made it explode into thousands of wooden splinters, some of which embedded themselves in the captain's stomach and others in one of his eyes: he didn't lose his life, but that eye had seen its last day. There were cases of extreme good luck as well, as with Lieutenant Francisco Hernández, who, during the siege, was promoted to second captain and later to first, just for having survived in one piece despite having been wounded four times: the first time in his arm, the second time in San Javier, the third time in his leg, and the fourth at Pitiminí. To return to bad luck, though, the cruelest of misfortunes befell a French corporal named Saint-Hilaire, who, having survived a bullet that splintered his occiput and slid between his bone and scalp, coming out of his forehead, during a trip to Veracruz as part of the detail escorting Mexican prisoners, was bitten fatally by one of those poisonous snakes (rattler, coral snake, *nauyaca,* or whipsnake) that emerge unexpectedly in warm climes from grass, puddles, stones, or roots. Then, Colonel and Marquis Gallifet also had very bad luck when a bayonet caused his intestines to spill out. He picked these up with his kepi, wrapped up his belly, and walked to an emergency medical station. When the Empress Eugénie found out that the Marquis had been gravely ill because there was no ice in Puebla to place over his wound to help it heal, she ordered that no ice was to be used in the preparation of dishes and drinks on the menu at the Tuileries. And then, even those who survived those months to tell about the siege didn't exactly feel fortunate since not only had ice disappeared from Puebla, but also all the necessary drugs and medications for treating their wounds, including chloroform. For example, a lady from Puebla had her leg amputated: they cut through her flesh, muscles, ligaments, and nerves and sawed through her bone, all without anesthesia. And then, bad luck, the worst kind, befell a soldier who, on being ordered to destroy his rifle, picked it up by the barrel instead of grabbing it by the butt, and as he struck the pavement, set the gun off, firing a shot that, as in the case of General Laumiere, struck his forehead, and so he fell, and lay there, gazing like the General at the heavens, among the rocks and the mud, the picks and axes left behind by the sappers, the torn sacks filled with earth, the muddy banners, the wet petards and his Minié rifle, now split in two. And then, there was miraculous luck: for instance that of Sergeant Andrade, the day that one of those fuseless shells bounced off one of the breastworks at Santa Inés and made its way through the window of the warehouse and fell on a box of armed grenades, and all of them exploded and killed everybody there except Andrade, who came out with a blackened face and his coat in shreds, but unscathed. Naturally, we would have to count all those who lost an arm, a leg, or their eyesight as unfortunate. Also those who lost their hearing, like a lieutenant of the Mixed Regiment from Veracruz who was surprised by some *Chasseurs* who attacked him one whole afternoon with heavy fire while he hid behind one of three large bells that had been brought down from a temple to be melted. Good luck, though, rather providential, came to Generals Bazaine and Forey, who, one day, as they inspected the trenches on foot, were forced to jump like jackrabbits to dodge a volley of bullets that ricocheted on the rocks around them, but which missed them just the same. But it was bad luck—though not at all the worst—that came to the spy who sent messages on little paper boats from the La Malinche Hill down the San Francisco River to the outskirts of the city of Puebla, because, well before reaching the brickworks of Loreto, the messages were completely washed out, the little boats arriving at the Puente del Toro, where a *compadre* was waiting for them. And then *apparently* good but *actually* bad luck struck the Mexican prisoners who (during an intramural armistice) were exchanged for French prisoners in the first days of May, because instead of being safe and well fed in captivity they'd been released to starvation and terror. And then bad in one way, but very good in another—since he wasn't actually present at the time—was the luck of the owner of the fireworks warehouse that was set on fire by a stray bomb, causing the besieging troops to think that the Mexicans had suddenly appropriated all the fireworks, matches, rockets, and other such artifacts of optical telegraphy to send General Comonfort a volley of luminous signals; but then seeing so much sparkling rocketry—with Bengal lights, blue and red shooting stars, so many crazy girandoles and silver comets—they then wondered if perhaps the Mexicans were celebrating a national holiday, a feast to the Virgin, or else an imminent impossible victory, a successful escape and exit from their doomed city—though those who were on the inside knew that there was little left to celebrate or to illuminate with this conflagration, this deluge of little stars, sparks, and tiny balls of fire falling on Puebla and its dead—just like the bread, the burned flour, the stones and grenades, bombs and bullets, rubble, dust, pieces of angel statue and human parts had fallen before them. Or, more precisely, there was nothing at all to celebrate: there was nothing to celebrate when there was so much hunger and desolation, nothing to illuminate where there was so much misery.

When the white flags of capitulation had been raised in the forts, a few hours after the destruction of their troops' weapons, all the Mexican officers gathered at the Archbishop's Palace in Puebla. General Forey allowed the high-ranking officers to keep their weapons, welcomed them in the general headquarters, offered them cigars and cognac, praised the courage with which they had defended the garrison, and was amazed at the large number of officers and even young generals in the Eastern Army. He also said that the heavy exchange of fire of March 29th reminded him of the best days of Sebastopol, and that he had communicated this to the French Minister of War.

Out of the eight or ten thousand Mexican soldiers that are estimated to have been taken prisoner, five thousand of them were transferred, by force or by choice, to the imperial troops under the command of General Márquez. Two thousand of these were assigned by the French to destroy the trenches and barricades and to cleanse the city of rubble and human remains in order to prepare their triumphal entry. The rest, along with the generals and officers who refused to sign a document pledging never to take up arms against the Empire again—though signing it would have meant their immediate release—were taken to Veracruz to be shipped out of the country. Dubois de Saligny wanted them sent to Cayenne like common criminals. General Almonte, dressed from head to toe in a uniform bright with gold trim, requested that they all be shot. General Forey, however, ordered some sent to France and others to Martinique. And thus, on their way to the ships *La Cérès* and *Darien*, which were waiting for them anchored in the port of Veracruz, the prisoners went from Puebla to Amalucan Hill, to Acatzingo, to San Agustín del Palmar, to La Cañada de Ixtapa, to Acultzingo, across the colored plains covered with red and yellow soil that stuck to their sweaty faces, making them look like Mohicans—as described by Lieutenant Mahomet of the Turkish Battalion—some of them on foot and others in carts, sometimes sleeping in tents and other times in excrement-carpeted corrals, or, less often, in folding beds with clean sheets that ladies from Orizaba collected for them; from Orizaba to Córdoba, from Córdoba to Paso del Macho and Palo Verde, sometimes escorted by battalions of infantrymen, sometimes by Turks, still other times by the Egyptians, or "Black Panthers," who were very tall and very black and only spoke their own language, and who were mourning the death of their leader whose embalmed body they carried alongside his white horse—harnessed Arabian style—in order to ship both to Alexandria; or at other times they were escorted by legionnaires of all nationalities and trades: Poles and Danes; students and weavers; Italians and Swiss; doctors and gilders; Prussians and Bavarians; sailors and bison hunters; Spaniards and Württembergers; as well as some incognito princes and seekers of gold who later left for California: all with their dark-blue jackets, their neckerchiefs, their pants dyed madder-red, their crude fabric gaiters, their square-visored kepis and thick leather cartridge belts that earned them the nickname "leather bellies": two thousand in all under the command of Colonel Jeanningros and other officers in Hungarian-style black tunics with stripes who had traveled to Mexico with General Forey, bringing with them the tales of their feats and battles in the Carlist, Algerian, and Crimean Wars, of the cholera that nearly finished them off in the Balearic Islands, of the razzias and the *cafard*. And with them came the echo of the wailing of Algerian women when legionnaires who were taken prisoner were tied to a post to be eaten alive by Algerian dogs. And the prisoners of the siege continued from Palo Verde to La Soledad, from La Soledad to Veracruz, but not all of them arrived.

Out of the twenty-two generals who surrendered, only thirteen arrived in the port of Veracruz, and out of the 228 high-ranking officers, only 110 went aboard. The rest had managed to escape here and there during the journey, among them some of the most important Juarista leaders, such as General González Ortega himself, Generals Negrete and Porfirio Díaz, and a Colonel by the name of Mariano Escobedo.

In any event, Monsieur Dubois de Saligny spread a rumor that González Ortega had escaped, and Forey was happy to hear this, because he admired the brilliant and heroic manner in which the man had defended Puebla, and though he had made a triumphant entrance into Puebla on May 19th, with flags waving, drumrolls, bugle calls, and undulating pennants, the General, who had traded his field uniform for his dress uniform to show off his white hat, so that no one would doubt he was the Commander-in-Chief of the Expeditionary Forces, was welcomed by a dead city, almost in ruins. No roses, kisses, dahlias, perfumed hankies, or carnations were dropped from the balconies, glass windows, ironwork windows, pillars, or broken iron bars. However, at the steps of the Cathedral, where the French had gathered all the cannons that had survived the hecatomb, there was an American rifle-barreled, size-four gun that would soon be shipped to France as Forey's present to the Imperial Prince. There too, at the doors of the Cathedral, he was greeted with open arms by the Town Council, with their smiles, crosses, holy water, organs, incense, and golden canopies all brought out for the occasion, and greeted too by all the clergy of the city, and with them all their resuscitated nuns: abbesses, vicars, vestry sisters, and novices who sang a *Te Deum Laudamus* Mass. A French flag waved from one of the towers of the Cathedral, and from the other the Mexican Imperial Banner had been unfurled. When the French entered the nearby town of Cholula, where the African Light Infantrymen with their sabers had sent Comonfort's cavalry fleeing—as Colonel Du Barail tells it— churches rang their bells for three days (and it's well known that there were as many churches and oratories in Cholula as there are days in the year): they tolled their bells and vomited up their holy relics and majolica effigies into the streets, forming processions, with confessors and martyrs escorted by swarms of cherubs wearing clothing from the ballet. The Indians knelt down in the dirt, the cattle drivers crossed themselves, the women cried, and clarinets, bugles, trombones, kettledrums, and cymbals thundered, roared, and bellowed waltzes, polkas, schottisches, and mazurkas until at the end of three days General Mirandol, who had remained in Cholula minding the garrison, dispersed all the third-rate fiddlers, brass bands, dominoes, midinettes, contrabass players, Aztec emperors, singers, orchestra directors, Aztec Tiger Knights, pirates, sopranos, harpists, and drummers with a cavalry charge.

•

The real glory of the fall of Puebla went to General Achille Bazaine. What Elias Forey got from Mexico was the baton and golden bees of a Marshal of France, and the memories of his many dispatches and his triumphal entry into Mexico City next to the two people he hated the most at that time: Almonte and Saligny. A so-called General Salas gave Forey the keys to the city at San Lázaro Gate, and a short time later the French troops entered the city where they were received with triumphal arches, and a shower of flowers so thick that some of the horses became rowdy and frightened. Shouts of "*Vive l'Empereur!*" were frequently heard, and the balconies were decorated not only with French flags but also with the beautiful Mexican women who had been so scarce in Puebla de los Angeles. This reminded the French writer and politician Émile Ollivier of the reception the French themselves had given the allied troops when they entered Paris in 1814 to free them from Bonaparte's dictatorship. Excitedly, the Parisian people had shouted "*Vivent les alliés! Vive Guillaume! Vive Alexander! Vivent les Bourbons!*" Unlike that occasion, however, this one cost the French troops over ninety thousand francs; the greatest amount, it seems, was spent in transportation for cheering peasants. The French Captain Loizillon told his godmother in a letter that Almonte had hired the peasants for the reception at the price of three cents apiece, plus a glass of pulque. This technique was neither new nor particularly Mexican: several years before, for instance, when Franz Joseph and Elisabeth visited Milan, the Austrian authorities of Lombardo-Veneto had hired peasants and townspeople at the rate of one lira per head.

Forey's entry into Mexico City on June 10, 1863, coincided with the departure of the ships *Cérès* and *Darien* that carried the Mexican war prisoners and brought news to Fontainebleau of the fall of Puebla. The orchestra played the hymn "*Reine Hortènse*," Louis Napoleon cried with emotion, and José Manuel Hidalgo was reinstated at court in the Tuileries. No one could say, seeing him at a party, as they'd been doing now for some time, "*Ecco la rovina della Francia!*"—here is the ruin of France—at least for a little while.

The French column entered Mexico City from the east. After lowering the republican flag, Juárez fled to the west. General Negrete was at the forefront of the presidential transport with five hundred soldiers, and in the carriages that followed rode the President himself and the members of his cabinet, the judges of his Supreme Court, the members of the Permanent Commission to Congress, and those of the National Archive as well. Large quantities of arms and ammunition were left behind. Don Benito had invited the Diplomatic Corps, consisting at the time of the representatives from only four nations—Ecuador, Venezuela, Peru, and the United States—to go with him. His invitation was turned down, but the Peruvian Ambassador to Mexico, Manuel Nicolás Corpancho, who was hoping that Mexico would join the "American Union" proposed by his country to defend the independence of Spanish America, and who already had the backing of Chile and Ecuador, kept four rooms in the Capital for a time protected by the Peruvian flag, where Mexican liberals could seek asylum. Benito Juárez went to San Luis Potosí, the first stop on his ambulatory presidency.

Benito Juárez was accused of violating the international conventions of war when he abandoned Mexico City without naming any authorities to turn the city over to the enemy. The French had already forgotten that they had violated these same conventions when it was Lorencez, and not the Head of the French State—that is, the Emperor—who declared war on the Juárez government. At any rate, General Forey considered that having taken Mexico City, the conquest of the nation was complete. But Benito Juárez pointed out that the fall of Madrid and Moscow hadn't given the first Napoleon control of Spain or Russia, respectively, and that the government of the United Mexican States would be, from that moment on, wherever he himself happened to be, in San Luis, Matehuala, Monterrey, Saltillo, Mapimí, Nazas, Parral, Chihuahua, or Paso del Norte—Juárez had been invested with extraordinary powers by Congress before it was dissolved—as the military operations of the intervention spread.

Forey, promoted to Marshal, retired from Mexico leaving Achille Bazaine in his place, a military man who had distinguished himself in Algiers, in the Spanish Carlist wars, and in Solferino; a man who spoke Spanish and who a short time later would actually become Dictator of Mexico when Napoleon ordered Almonte to turn civil powers over to him.

General Miramón was allowed to return to Mexico. He was first assigned to Guadalajara and later called to Mexico City, where he was put on standby. Meanwhile, some of the liberal leaders, among them General Uraga, went over to the French side along with their troops. Another one of the liberal generals, Porfirio Díaz, remained loyal to the Republic and withdrew to Oaxaca in the south of Mexico. The Juarist general Comonfort died in battle. Bazaine organized the Mexican Imperial Troops in two great divisions: one under the command of the "Tigre de Tacubaya," General Leonardo Márquez, also called "Leopard Márquez" by some; the other under the command of a general who a few years later would share, along with Miramón, the destiny of Maximilian at Las Campanas Hill: Tomás Mejía. He was a pure-blooded Indian who was known as "Papa Tomasito" and had numerous followers in the Sierra Gorda. After Tampico's fall in August of '63 to the Imperialist Troops, other cities followed. Mejía defeated Negrete at San Luis, and along with Douay, he took Querétaro. Morelia, Guadalajara, and other garrisons fell later. When French ships began arriving on the Pacific shores, the Imperialists considered themselves rulers of a piece of national territory that ran from one ocean to the other. Still, this only represented about a sixth of the territory of Mexico. And this despite the fact that, at the beginning of that year, the total number of men who had arrived from Cherbourg or Toulon, Oran or Brest, Lorient or Alexandria, onboard the *Amazone* or the *Finistèrre* or the *Navarin* or the *Charente* or the *Tillsit* or the *Palikari*, already numbered more than forty thousand. The cargo that had been transported from Europe to Mexico weighed more than twenty-six thousand tons. Juárez's prediction—that if the enemy was concentrated in one place it would be spread thin over the rest of the country, and if it was spread out everywhere, it would be weak everywhere—had come to pass. Bazaine's nightmare was beginning: the Imperial troops would kick the Juarists out of a garrison and fall back, leaving a detachment at the garrison and taking most of its troops to attack another; soon the Juarists would reappear and retake the garrison they'd just abandoned. There were cities that were taken, lost, retaken, and lost again upwards of fourteen times.

Meanwhile, the anti-guerrilla troops concentrated themselves in the warm latitudes in response to the many groups of guerrillas fighting in Veracruz, Tamaulipas, and other Gulf states. All of these were considered nothing more than bandits and assassins, and, indeed, some of them were. Among them, the "Plateados" were renowned for their clothes—were overlaid, inlaid, and adorned with silver, from head to toe. The organization and the command of the counter-guerrilla forces—French in name only, since they were made up of the dregs of numerous nationalities: English, Dutch, Egyptian, Martinican, Turkish, American, and Swiss—was the responsibility of Colonel Dupin, who had taken part in the sack of the Summer Palace in Peking—and later being discharged from the French army for holding a public sale in France of the objects he'd stolen in China. He was later restored to the rank of colonel in order to be sent to Mexico. He was tall, with a long graying beard, an enormous hat covered with gold embroidery, and a wide ribbon band from which hung two metal plates with the face of a lion in each. He wore a loose, red, coarse cotton blouse, huge yellow boots with golden spurs, a colonel's cape, a revolver and saber at his waist, and numerous crosses, medals, and decorations on his chest. Colonel Dupin soon became famous for his cruelty and his dogs, who could sniff out anything. It was well known that no Mexican guerrilla fighter who fell into his hands ever came back alive.

Besides the constant battles and the never-ending taking and retaking of the towns and cities, there was an event—soon before the fall of Puebla—that has gone down in history as considerably more glorious than the circumstances actually warranted (because that's how the French wanted it). A captain in the Foreign Legion named Danjou had a wooden hand that he always kept covered with a white glove. His real flesh-and-blood hand had been amputated after a rifle that he had been holding to point out some scenery backfired. One day Captain Danjou offered himself up to be one of the volunteers who were to clear and secure the terrain along the route of a convoy that was carrying four million francs in gold as well as several artillery pieces destined for General Forey. Along with a few dozen men from the 3rd Company, he was surprised on the road between Chiquihuite and Palo Verde by over one thousand Mexican lancers. The legionnaires took shelter in the corral of an abandoned hacienda, called Hacienda de Camarón. Without food and water, the legionnaires were annihilated and only three or four of them survived. Inspired perhaps by Mac-Mahon—who upon taking the city of Malakoff in the Crimean War planted a French flag and said, *"J'y suis, j'y reste"*—Here I am, here I shall stay—Captain Danjou decided that, since he was in Camarón, he would stay in Camarón. That's where he died, separated forever from his wooden hand. The Commander of the Foreign Legion, Jeanningross, took the hand under his care and sent it to the General Headquarters of the Legion in Sidi-bel-Abbès. Later on it would wind up in a museum at Aubagne, near Marseilles. Since then, the Day of the Foreign Legion is known as Camarón Day, and every year on the anniversary of the battle, Captain D'Anjou's hand, with its mahogany wrist and fingers and palm of oak—and which, for some reason, perhaps due to the humidity, ended up looking like a claw, and growing discolored—is taken out of its crystal box, placed over a red velvet cushion on a pedestal in the middle of a great patio, and paid homage by the bands and cannons of the Foreign Legion, whose men parade in front of it. Later, the legionnaires toast to the memory of Camarón with sweet rum from the French Antilles.

QVOS HIC NON PLVS LX
ADVERSI TOTIVS AGMINIS
MOLES CONSTRAVIT
VITA PRIVS QVAM VIRTVSS
MILITES DESERVIT GALLICOS
DIE XXX MENSI APR. ANNI MDCCCLXIII

HERE, THEY WERE FEWER THAN SIXTY
PITTED AGAINST AN ENTIRE ARMY
ITS SIZE CRUSHED THEM
ON APRIL 30, 1863, THESE FRENCH SOLDIERS
LOST THEIR LIVES, BUT NOT THEIR COURAGE

2. "That's Correct, Mr. President"

"Did you say over six feet?"

"Yes, Don Benito, one meter and eighty-five centimeters."

"Then he's really tall . . ."

"That's correct, Mr. President."

"I must come up to his shoulder, at the very most . . ."

"At the most, Don Benito. Tell me, did you want me to put all these details into my summary?"

Benito Juárez put on his glasses and opened the report, or "summary," as the Secretary called it, to the second page and read:

> When on December 1, 1848, Emperor Ferdinand learned that his brother Franz Charles had renounced his succession rights, he abdicated in favor of his nephew Franz Joseph, older brother of the archduke Maximilian. This made Maximilian an heir to the throne of the House of Austria . . .

He then returned to the first page and his eyes went over the first paragraph once again:

> Ferdinand Maximilian Joseph, direct descendant of the Catholic
> Monarchs, Ferdinand and Isabella and of Charles V of Spain and I of
> Germany, was born on July 6, 1832, at Schönbrunn Palace.

"Details, Mr. Secretary? Like his height and that sort of thing? No, that was mere curiosity. Superfluous information, irrelevant. What I would like you to do is tell me about Schönbrunn . . . You've visited Schönbrunn, right?"

"That's correct, Don Benito. But only the gardens, which I liked much better than those of Versailles . . ."

"Why?"

"Why did I like the Schönbrunn gardens better than the ones at Versailles? Well, because . . . I don't know. I hadn't thought about it before. Actually, they're very similar. Perhaps I liked the ones at Schönbrunn more because they aren't flat but on a slope, and they go up to Neptune's Fountain, and it's as though they were part of the horizon. Am I making myself clear, Don Benito?"

"And, are they very big?"

"Huge, Mr. President. And so is the palace. It is said to have fourteen hundred bedrooms and over one hundred kitchens . . ."

Benito Juárez continued reading the report:

> His principal titles include Archduke of Austria, Prince of Hungary
> and Bohemia, and Count of Habsburg.

Then he looked at Mr. Secretary over his glasses.

"You know, I've always asked myself how would someone feel living in so large a home. Think about it, Mr. Secretary . . . Fourteen hundred. If you slept in a different room each night, it would take . . . Let me see . . . three . . . four . . . yes, about four years to sleep in all of them . . ."

And then he read on:

> Ferdinand Maximilian is the second son—the firstborn son is the
> present Emperor Franz Joseph—of Archduke Francis Charles and
> Archduchess Sophie.

He looked at his Secretary again over his glasses.

"Maximilian, son of Archduke Franz Charles? Don't people say he's the son of Napoleon II?"

"Well, that's right, Don Benito. That's what they say, that he was conceived out of the affair that Archduchess Sophie had with the Duke of Reichstadt . . . in which case the Austrian has Jacobin blood. Is that what you're implying, Mr. President?"

"Jacobin blood? Come on, Mr. Secretary. Napoleon I was never a Jacobin. He pretended to be one when it was to his advantage . . . But tell me, do they look alike?"

"Does who look alike, Don Benito?"

"I mean, does Maximilian resemble the Duke of Reichstadt, Napoleon II . . . ?"

"I don't know, Don Benito. All I do know is that the Archduke has blue eyes like the Duke of Reichstadt, but plenty of other Habsburgs do as well—though, on the other hand, if you put a portrait of the Archduke next to one of the man who supposedly was his grandfather, Napoleon I, you'll see there isn't the slightest resemblance . . ."

"And does the Austrian resemble the Archduke Francis Charles?"

"To tell the truth, Don Benito, I haven't paid any attention. I've seen several portraits of Archduke Francis Charles, but I haven't given much thought to his resemblance to Maximilian. What I can tell you is that Francis Charles is an epileptic and many consider him to be touched, just a little bit short of an imbecile, like his brother the Emperor Ferdinand . . . and Maximilian doesn't resemble either one of them because he himself is no fool . . ."

"Neither one of them?"

"No, Don Benito. The Archduke is an intelligent and educated man who has traveled extensively, as I say in my report . . ."

Benito Juárez leafed through several more pages of the report until his eyes came to rest on the following paragraph:

> The Archduke's character is closer to the Wittelsbachs than to the Habsburgs. He loves good food and wine, dance, poetry, music, and literature. He collects rocks and minerals. He is fond of archeology, history, and geography. In Miramare he has a library estimated at 6,000 volumes. On the other hand, Franz Joseph is the more Habsburgian of the two brothers. He is moderate. He is not interested in music, works standing up, and is frugal in his meals.

"The Emperor Franz Joseph is frugal in his meals?"

"That's correct, Mr. President. It seems that he has beer and sausages for lunch almost daily, and that he sleeps on a camp bed . . ."

"On a camp bed . . . You'd think he was living on a battlefield, not in a palace . . ."

"You're probably right, Don Benito. I understand that he's particularly fond of everything that has to do with the army and militia . . ."

"And Maximilian too?"

"Well, no. It seems that he does like to wear a uniform and it's true that he fought along with his brother in several battles, but I understand his real passion is the sea. At twenty-two he was already Admiral and Commander-in-Chief of the Austrian Imperial Navy. Yes, his passion is the sea. His office in Miramare, I'm told, is a replica of his office onboard the frigate *Novara*. He's also very fond of horse riding, Don Benito. Though, of course, like any prince of the House of Austria, Maximilian received extensive military instruction. He knows how to handle weapons, and he studied fencing . . ."

Don Benito took off his glasses and looked out the window.

"Tell me, Mr. Secretary, would you have liked to study fencing?"

"Fencing, Don Benito? Me? To tell the truth, I've never considered it. What about you, Don Benito?"

"No, not fencing, but I wouldn't have minded learning how to ride, and ride well . . ."

"It's never too late, Don Benito . . ."

"Yes, it's too late for many things . . . to learn these well, one has to be taught in childhood, or else when one is very young . . ."

"You're probably right, Don Benito. Not for nothing do the princes of the House of Austria have the best riding school in the world, the Spanish Riding School of Vienna . . ."

The President put the report down and went to his window.

"The only thing I can ride well is a mule, Mr. Secretary. Still, mules know how to tread better than horses on very rough terrain without losing their footing—isn't that right?"

"That's correct, Don Benito."

Don Benito, looking at the sky said:

"Sometimes, when I think about all those liberators of our America— Bolívar, O'Higgins, San Martín, even our priest Morelos—I tell myself that they were all illustrious men on horseback. But, Benito Pablo, if you yourself are ever mentioned in the history books, you'll have to be an illustrious man on muleback . . ."

"But as you yourself said, Don Benito, mules go farther . . ."

"No, it's you who have said it, Mr. Secretary. We mules go farther."

"Pardon me, Don Benito, I didn't want . . ."

"Don't argue with me. That's quite correct: we mules go farther. And now tell me, why, on the subject of Franz Joseph, did you write that 'he is the more Habsburgian of the two brothers' when there are four altogether, as you yourself say further on."

"Yes, of course there are four: Franz Joseph, Maximilian, Charles Louis, and Louis Victor, in addition to one or two girls. Yes, there should be six children altogether . . ."

Don Benito turned around: "And which of them did you say is effeminate? Charles Louis?"

"No, Don Benito. Louis Victor. But he is more than effeminate, Mr. President; he is a homosexual, a sodomite. This is why he refused to marry one of the daughters of the Emperor of Brazil, like Archduke Maximilian wanted."

Don Benito looked again at the gray sky. "There are too many gray skies here in the north. They make me sad. You have no idea, Mr. Secretary, how I miss the blue skies . . ."

"As I was saying, Don Benito, what I did is try to highlight the contrast between the two older brothers, Franz Joseph and Maximilian, and the political implications of this contrast. By the way, as I state in my summary, this contrast echoes that between other brothers of the Austrian Dynasty such as Frederick III and Albert VI, Josef I and Charles IV, Francis I and Archduke Charles . . ."

"Blue, blue like the sky, that's what my Godfather used to say . . ."

"What was that, Don Benito?"

"That's what my Godfather, Salanueva, used to tell me, may he rest in peace. 'If you marry, Benito Pablo, marry the daughter of white men, to see if you can have a baby with blue eyes, blue like the sky' . . . And, tell me, Mr. Secretary, is the Archduke very white?"

"Yes, Mr. President, Maximilian is very white, just like Princess Carlota . . ."

Benito Juárez went back to his desk, sat down, put his glasses on, and leafed through the report.

"Carlota . . . Carlota of Belgium. You don't tell me much about her, Mr. Secretary . . ."

"Well, Don Benito. I limited myself to the essential facts, which at any rate I imagine you already know: that she's the daughter of Leopold of Belgium, himself the uncle of Queen Victoria of England, that her mother is Princess Marie Louise, daughter of King Louis Philippe of France . . ."

"I beg your pardon, Mr. Secretary: Louis Philippe was not King of France but only king of the French."

"How's that Don Benito?"

"What I mean is that he wasn't King of France by Divine design, but King of the French by the will of the people . . . but go ahead."

"Yes, well, I was saying that Carlota's mother, Queen Louise Marie, left her an orphan when she was ten years old, that she has two brothers, the Duke of Brabant and the Count of Flanders . . . and that . . ."

"When I said that you didn't say much about Princess Carlota, I meant, Mr. Secretary, her character, her physical appearance . . ."

"As I told you Don Benito, the reason is that I considered some of these details not relevant enough to appear in my summary."

"Yes, perhaps you're right. But that's no reason for you not to tell me about them. Tell me Mr. Secretary, did you have a chance to meet Princess Carlota?"

"Well, as I was telling you Mr. President, I also visited the gardens of Miramare Palace, which are open to the public on Sundays, and on one occasion I saw the Archduchess on the arm of the Archduke, walking on the pier . . . And to tell the truth she didn't seem as pretty to me as they say she is. However, she looks good from a distance. As far as her character, a priest with whom I talked in Brussels told me she's a good Catholic. As you know, despite the fact that he himself is a Protestant, Leopold allowed his children to be brought up in the religion of their mother. The priest told me that Queen Marie Louise used to pray several hours a day and that she was known as the 'Angel of the Belgians.' It seems Princess Carlota has gained a reputation for her temperament and perseverance, as well as a precocious nature . . . and I believe I did mention her favorite reading in my report, Don Benito."

Benito Juárez leafed through the report and his eyes found a paragraph that read: "Her austere theological upbringing is nourished by her readings of San Alphonse of Ligorio and Saint Francis of Sales. She is inspired by Montalembert and she reads Plutarch."

Don Benito looked at the secretary over his glasses and pointed to the desk.

"It's nourished *with*, not *by*, Mr. Secretary."

"How's that Don Benito?"

"I said that you should have written 'nourished *with* her readings,' not 'nourished *by* her readings . . .'"

"You're always correcting my Spanish, Don Benito."

"I had to learn it very well, Mr. Secretary, with all its rules, because it wasn't my native tongue. And I learned it with blood and tears. Have I ever told you that when my uncle was checking to see if I had learned my lessons, I myself would bring the paddle so that he could punish me whenever I hadn't learned it well? The only reason I left my village to go to Oaxaca was to learn Spanish . . . *Castilla*, as I used to call it."

"You did the right thing Don Benito."

"Yes, I did well. I admit it. But it was very difficult, Mr. Secretary, and all because I was an Indian . . . a barefoot Indian. As I was sometimes called."

"Really, Don Benito?"

"Of course *really*, and you know it very well, Mr. Secretary: I've suffered much because of the color of my skin, and right here in my own country. Not to mention New Orleans, though over there people saw me as being almost white, next to the blacks."

Don Benito got up and began walking in slow circles around the room. He took off his eyeglasses and began waving them as he said: "I want to make something clear once and for all Mr. Secretary: why do you think I'm interested in the physical characteristics of the Archduke? After all, I shouldn't have to be concerned with how he looks, right? If his hair is blond—and it is blond, isn't it?"

"Yes, Don Benito. His hair and beard are blond."

"To make matters worse . . ."

"A long beard, split in two. But you've seen pictures of the Archduke, haven't you, Don Benito? They say that he grew a beard in order to hide the family chin. Come to think of it, yes, as a matter of fact, since the Archduke has a sunken chin, he couldn't possibly be the son of Napoleon II—right, Don Benito? That's a characteristic of the Habsburgs."

"Mr. Secretary forgets that if Maximilian were the son of Napoleon II, he would then be the grandchild of Marie Louise, the Austrian, another Habsburg."

"That's true Don Benito. And, of course, not everyone inherits those features of theirs. They say that Emperor Franz Joseph shaves his chin precisely to show that he has neither the hanging lip nor the sunken chin, and to that end he tried out several beard styles until he settled on a Prince Albert . . . But you were saying, Mr. President."

Don Benito was still walking slowly, swinging his eyeglasses slowly.

"Yes, I was telling you that I shouldn't give a damn what the Archduke looks like. But things aren't so simple, Mr. Secretary. You have to remember that the writings of Gobineau on race have had a bigger impact in Germany than in France . . . Why? Because the theory of pan-Germanic superiority goes hand in hand with the idea of the white race's superiority, even with the theory that a handsome face corresponds to a beautiful soul, and vice versa. As I was telling you, here in Mexico, we can't escape that prejudice. Why do you think, Mr. Secretary, I served dinner barefoot in the house of the family who would eventually become my in-laws in Oaxaca? Because I was a dark-skinned Indian. Why do you think that, when I arrived in Veracruz onboard the *Tennessee*—I've already told you about this, haven't I? No? Well, when I arrived in Veracruz they put me up in the Governor's Residence. One day I came out onto the small terrace there and I asked a black lady for a glass of water. Of course, she didn't know I was the President. You know what she said? I'll never forget it: 'What a bossy Indian,' she told me, 'What an arrogant, ugly Indian. If you want water, go get it yourself.' This is what happens to me, Mr. Secretary—because I'm a dark-skinned Indian."

"But it happens less and less, Mr. President."

"Yes, less and less. But it still happens."

"And besides, Don Benito, you've made us all proud of our Indian ancestors. I, for instance, am sure I have Indian blood in me."

Juárez stopped, smiled, put on his eyeglasses, and looked at the Secretary over them.

"Indian blood in you, Mr. Secretary. You're pulling my leg. You're only saying that to please me. You're so white you're almost transparent. But I was telling you . . ." Don Benito said, and he sat in front of his desk, took off his glasses, and pulled a cigar and a box of matches out of a drawer.

"I was telling you . . ."

"Allow me, Don Benito."

"No, no, it's all right," Don Benito said, and lit his own cigar. "I was telling you that to top it all off, they want to impose a so-called emperor on us who has all the characteristics that many people here consider attractive—like white skin and blue eyes. And you shouldn't forget, Mr. Secretary, that we live in a country that believes its benefactor god, we could say its ultimate god, is white, tall, and blond—and who promised to return some day."

Mr. Secretary placed an ashtray next to Don Benito and said, "Quetzalcóatl, Don Benito."

"Quetzalcóatl, Mr. Secretary."

"But surely you aren't suggesting, Don Benito . . . it would be an exaggeration . . . you aren't suggesting that our people could mistake Maximilian for a reborn Quetzalcóatl . . ."

"Many wouldn't, of course. Anyone who knows how to read and write knows very well that the Archduke is nothing more than Napoleon's puppet. But there's still so much ignorance in our country, Mr. Secretary . . . six million illiterate Indians. I was a rare, lucky one."

"You were strong-willed, Don Benito."

"I said I was lucky. I was decisive, I think, only in that I chose to overcome my own lack of confidence."

"But, do you really think that our people are going to take Maximilian for a god?"

"You yourself have told me that many Indians kneel before the portraits of Maximilian and Carlota . . . but to tell the truth, no, I don't really think they will. If the Archduke sets foot in Mexico, people will soon realize he's no god, nor anything of the sort. That's what happened when the Spaniards came. The problem is that all this nonsense about skin and eye color upsets me regardless, because they convince me, increasingly, of the overwhelming European arrogance . . . of the hypocrisy of all those who call themselves Christians and then make decisions as to who deserves what on the basis of the color of their skin. Do you remember what *Le Monde Illustré* said about me? 'The current president of Mexico does not have even a trace of clean, Caucasian blood'— and this in a newspaper that calls itself enlightened. And then there was that English newspaper, what's it called?"

"The *Times*, Don Benito?"

"No, a different one."

"*The Morning Post*?"

"Yes, that one. Do you remember, Mr. Secretary, that it called me a usurper, and after mentioning that the people of Mexico would have to be consulted, it said the word 'people' in this case was meant to refer only to European or part-European races?"

"Yes, I remember well, Don Benito. Don't you think that's outrageous?"

"Of course I do. It's outrageous."

Don Benito leafed through the report again and read at random:

> The Archduke is known to have had two intimate liaisons. One with the Countess Paula von Linden, and the other with Princess Maria

Amelia de Braganza of Portugal. The former was the daughter of Württemberg's Minister in Vienna. These indiscretions upset Arch-duchess Sophie . . .

"Archduchess . . . *arch*-duchess. You know, I've asked myself many times why these Austrians aren't satisfied with the title of 'duke.' Why do they have to be archdukes? There aren't any archcounts, archmarquises, or archkings."

"Yes, Don Benito. I understand your confusion, though I'm not sure what the reasoning behind the title is. I think it was Rudolf IV who decided that the concept of dukedom was obsolete, given the size of the territories under a duke . . ."

"Mexico, Mr. Secretary, is still a very large country in spite of all the terri-tory the Yankees kept—bigger than Austria, bigger than England or France, and perhaps bigger than all three of them together. So what? Am I going to start calling myself Archpresident Benito Juárez?"

The Secretary smiled. Don Benito puffed on his cigar and continued his reading:

> . . . Archduchess Sophie, who asked the Emperor to send the Arch-duke away on a long trip so that he would forget the Countess von Linden. The Württemberg Minister was reassigned to Berlin, and the Archduke . . .

"You know what? The only person I know who would have been capable of giving himself that kind of title is Santa Anna: 'His Serene Highness Antonio López de Santa Anna, Archpresident of Mexico,'" Don Benito said without taking his eyes off the paper.

> . . . sailed toward the Middle East accompanied by Count Julius Andrássy. On this and other, subsequent trips—besides the Middle-Eastern countries—he visited Sicily, the Balearic Islands, Pompey, Naples, Sorrento, Greece, Albany, the Canary Islands, Madeira, Gi-braltar, North Africa, and several Spanish cities like Barcelona, Mal-aga, Seville, and Granada.

"Tell me, does the Archduke have a mistress at the moment?"

"He doesn't seem to have one, Don Benito. He's isolated himself in his castle at Miramare for two or three years now . . . though people gossip about some es-capades in Vienna. The one who has and had several affairs is King Leopold."

"Is that a fact?"

"Yes, Don Benito."

"Even when the 'Angel of the Belgians' was alive?"

"I wouldn't know about that Mr. President, but it's possible. Nowadays, among the better-known ones, is a Parisian prostitute named Hortènse, and another called Arcadie Claret. He even had the nerve of marrying the latter to one of his courtiers, von Eppingoefen or Eppinghoven or something like that, and later assigned him to a post far away from Brussels. Leopold had two children with this woman, but the people don't like her. On more than one occasion they've pelted her carriage with rotten vegetables."

"Really? And what about Franz Joseph?"

"I don't know Don Benito, but he must have a mistress since he doesn't get along with Empress Elisabeth, or 'Sisi' as she's called. Believe me Mr. President: she is a truly beautiful woman."

"Yes, I think I've seen a portrait of her. Why don't they get along?"

"Because they have completely different personalities, Don Benito. She's cheerful, vivacious, likes open spaces, and loves to ride horses in the forest. When she was a child, people say, her father used to dress as a gypsy and take her dancing in the taverns of Hungary while he played the violin."

"I wonder if that's true?"

"Well, it could be, Mr. President."

The President continued reading, this time out loud:

> Archduke Maximilian traveled to France in 1856. His visit coincided with that of Prince Oscar of Sweden. The Archduke was the object of many welcoming events and a warm reception by Napoleon III and Eugénie. It was revealed later that the Archduke criticized the French court ferociously.

"How was this known?"

"How was what known, Don Benito? His criticism?"

"Yes."

"Oh, well, it seems Maximilian used ordinary mail to send letters from Paris to Vienna praising Napoleon because he knew they would be intercepted and read by French agents before reaching their destination. However, he sent other letters via secret courier with his real opinions about Napoleon and Eugénie. That's the story, anyway. How was this found out? I don't know, but as you can see, there are countless rumors in Vienna, and many have outlived their intended purpose or audience."

"That was hypocrisy on the part of the Archduke, don't you think? And now he's after their help—Louis Napoleon and Eugénie are his sponsors."

"That's correct, Don Benito. The Archduke's memory is very selective, especially if we take into account that it was Louis Napoleon who helped Count Cavour in his struggle for the unification of Italy, an action which resulted in Austria's loss of Lombardy."

"And now, Mr. Secretary, it is Carlota, Louis Philippe of Orléans's granddaughter, who seeks Louis Napoleon's help, when it was he who confiscated all properties that the Orléans family held in France. That's what I call losing one's self-respect."

"You're right, Don Benito. On the other hand, it's quite natural. They forgive everything between themselves, since they're all actually one big family. That's the reason for their degeneration and insanity . . . there have been quite a few insane kings, through the years."

"But Archduke Maximilian isn't crazy, is he?"

"Well, many people believe only an insane person would accept the throne of Mexico, but he's not loco-crazy. As I told you, the Archduke is known for his intelligence and sensibility, is even known to be a bit of a liberal. He's written memoirs of his travels and poems and even a book of aphorisms that people say are quite brilliant. And it's also known that since his youth he always carries a notebook with him containing moral precepts and codes of conduct that he's committed himself to following no matter what."

Don Benito looked at the secretary over his glasses and said: "And among these precepts, does the Archduke include respect for other people's rights, and the right of other nations to decide on their own form of government?"

"I suppose not, Don Benito."

"There can only be peace between nations when that right is respected, don't you think, Mr. Secretary?"

"That's correct, Don Benito."

"Don, Don, Don Benito . . . Don Benito this, Don Benito that. You can't imagine, Mr. Secretary, what it cost me to acquire the title of 'Don.' When I was born, I was a nobody, that's for sure. By contrast, as we were saying, these archdukes come into the world already addressed by all their past, present, and future titles. They're born with all their needs provided for. I didn't earn my 'Don' until I became a teacher of physics at the Institute of Oaxaca. But it wasn't a title I could keep for very long. In San Juan de Ulúa and New Orleans I lost my Don and became plain Benito again. But what can you tell me about Eugénie? Is she really such a beautiful woman?"

"It does seem that painters such as Winterhalter might flatter her a little in their work—but yes, it's true, people say she is very pretty. I suppose, Don

Benito, she takes after her mother, the Countess of Montijo, who posed naked for Goya, the painter."

"You are mistaken on that point, Mr. Secretary; it was the Duchess of Alba. The confusion arises because Eugénie's sister, Francisca, married the Duke of Alba, but it was the mother of that Duke of Alba, or his grandmother, who was the one who inspired Goya's *Naked Maja*."

"Oh, very well, Don Benito, if you say so . . . So much adultery and perversion."

"Yes, there is much of that."

"And then there are some other things that I found out but did not write down because I thought they were superfluous."

"Things like what, Mr. Secretary?"

"Well, I was told that when Carlota's father, Leopold, entered Paris with the Russian troops he'd joined in 1814, he was seduced by Queen Hortense, Louis Napoleon's mother."

Don Benito put down his cigar in the ashtray and leaned back in his chair: "What a surprise. Then Louis Napoleon could be the son of Leopold of Belgium?"

"No, Don Benito, Louis Napoleon was born . . . I think in 1808. He would have been six at that time."

"1808, two years younger than I . . . How old did you say Carlota and Maximilian are?"

"Maximilian is thirty years old and Carlota twenty-two."

"Twenty-two? So young?"

"Yes, Don Benito."

Don Benito puffed on his cigar again and put it back in the ashtray, setting his eyeglasses on the table. He got up, walked around the room again, and asked: "Did the relationship between Hortense and Louis Napoleon last very long? Sorry, between Hortense and Leopold, Mr. Secretary?"

"I don't know, Don Benito. It occurs to me—it's a joke of course—that all this adultery, all these children . . . and bastard children from the European monarchs, that it's all served the purpose of cleaning up their blood once and for all. People say, for instance, that Louis Napoleon doesn't have a single drop of Bonaparte blood in him."

"Which would give him a lot of incentive to send a man who could indeed have Bonaparte blood away from Europe."

"That's correct, but as I say in the report, Franz Joseph already has plenty of reasons to want to see his brother sent away. Jealously, among them. You can't imagine how upset he was to learn that Maximilian was a candidate for several European thrones, like Poland's, and very recently that of Greece. I was told that during the last uprisings in Poland the Viceroy of Galicia began shouting 'Long live Maximilian, King of Poland,' from the balcony of his palace in Krakow."

"Yes, I want you to give me more details about their rivalry, Mr. Secretary, and tell me, is the Archduke a Mason?"

"It seems he is."

"Of the Scottish rite, I suppose."

"Do you think it's the same in Europe as it is here, Don Benito? That the conservatives belong to the Scottish rite and the liberals to the York?"

"I would rather we say that it's the same here as it is in Europe, and not the other way around, Mr. Secretary. Everything else aside, vinegar will always be vinegar and oil will always be oil."

"Well, in that case I suppose he is: the Archduke must belong to the Scottish rite."

"You're contradicting yourself, Mr. Secretary. You were telling me a few minutes ago that Maximilian is a liberal, and now you're saying that he's a conservative."

"Don Benito, you're always catching me in my contradictions. I meant 'liberal' within his conservatism, if I make myself clear."

Don Benito stopped in front of a portrait on the wall depicting a bullfight. He said, "Three months ago Puebla fell . . . How time flies . . . First it was Poland, then it was Greece, and now it's Mexico . . . After a while those Habsburgs will propose creating another Holy Roman Empire."

"And as Voltaire said," the secretary declared, as Don Benito started pacing around the room again, "it wasn't holy, Roman, or an empire."

"Well, it was an empire. And it still is. As a matter of fact they've ruled over many nations: Italian, Spanish, Dutch, Scandinavian, French, Magyar, Slavic, and of course, Spanish American."

"Charles V said on one occasion, and very appropriately, as you know, that the sun never set in his empire—or was it Philip II, Don Benito?"

"Yes, I think it was Philip II. If they've been able to govern so many different peoples, it's precisely because the Habsburg Empire was founded on the negation of the idea of nationality. That is, all nationalities except one: German. And the confirmation of this policy, as you know, was at the Congress of Vienna, where the very sovereignty of nations was negated in the most cynical manner possible."

"You said, 'except German,' Don Benito? But Archduke Maximilian is Austrian, not German."

"Let's not pretend he's an Austrian, Mr. Secretary. All of them may have been born in Austria, the Palatinate, or wherever, but they're German at heart. What's more, they can't help being German. And as I was telling you, the Germans are a people who thrive on dangerous theories of superiority and world dominion. Have you read Fichte, Mr. Secretary? It's true he's a great philosopher, but he infected the minds of the German autocrats with the idea that since Bonaparte had betrayed the ideals of the French Revolution, the Germans were better qualified than the French to guide humanity toward the fulfillment of those ideals. What's absurd is that a short time after Fichte, Hegel rounded off the deification of the State, and thus deified tyranny. I ask myself, how can a person like the Archduke—who according to you is a liberal—reconcile the idea of the state as a social contract emanating from the consensus of the people with this mystic conception of the state as divine authority? How, Mr. Secretary? It would seem impossible, no? But nevertheless, it's apparently been done. And do you know why? Because they're capable of betraying everything, even themselves, for their ambition. As I was telling you, the Archduke is now bowing to the wishes of the same man who humiliated the Austrians in Magenta and Solferino, although Austria and her emperors are hardly known for keeping their promises—remember Andrew Hofer, the Tyrolese patriot. Austria swore to Hofer never to return the Tyrol to Eugénie, and it betrayed him. It ceded it to Bonaparte, who with the same ease as Caesar divided Gaul, shared the Tyrol among Italy, Illyria, and Bavaria . . . and poor Andrew Hofer ended up being shot by French soldiers. The same thing happened with Poland: Austria and Prussia had sworn to defend it against any attacks by other nations. What happened? As soon as Catherine invades Poland, the Austrians and the Prussians ally themselves with the Russians and split it up among the three of them. What about Louis Napoleon? Isn't he also a traitor? Where, Mr. Secretary, did his Carbonaro ideals go? The Carbonaros declared war on all tyrannies. And didn't Cavour say Louis Napoleon had betrayed him? Sure, Napoleon used the fact that the Prussians had begun mobilizing in the Rhine as a pretext—but then, hadn't Cavour sent the Countess of Castiglione to seduce Napoleon and convince him to aid the Italian cause? Nothing but shameless tricks, Mr. Secretary. Oh, and speaking of Germans, I forgot to mention Herder, who saw the world as a symphony of nations, but led by the Germans, taking it upon himself to teach his fellow countrymen to venerate their peculiar national characteristics. And what about Metternich? Rhenish! He was the creator of the German Confederacy, the *Bundestag*, a system designed to defend the sovereigns of the German states, always including Austria, not only from the French but also from internal liberal movements. Yes? And the irony of all this is that if it hadn't been for the first Napoleon, the Germans would have remained divided into some three hundred principalities, free cities, and ecclesiastical states. Bonaparte and his Code, Mr. Secretary, did the world the dubious favor of reducing that multitude of helpless entities to only about thirty. The Germans are shameless and have no dignity. And apropos Metternich . . . I have been accused of running away from Mexico. When have I ever run away from Mexico? I have only withdrawn from the capital . . . and I had to do it. Have they already forgotten how the Great Chancellor Clemens Metternich fled Vienna in 1848? Do you know how he managed it, Mr. Secretary? Hidden in the laundry cart."

"You know a great deal about history, Don Benito."

"Don't believe it. Ask me the names of the six wives of Henry VIII and you'll see that I can only remember two or three of them at the most. I have the occasional lapse in memory, but your report has helped me clarify some doubts I had about Maximilian's actions in Italy, in which I'm particularly interested."

"I'm happy to hear that, Don Benito."

Don Benito walked over to the table and put his glasses back on and leafed through the report and said, "Here where you say . . . oh no, this is about Leopold and Carlota." Then he read:

> It was during his trip to France that Louis Napoleon made the yacht *Hortense* available to Maximilian to go to Belgium. It was there that he met King Leopold and his daughter Charlotte, soon to be Carlota. Leopold's first wife had been Charlotte Augusta, daughter of the future king of England, George IV, who held the position of regent during the life of his father, George III.

Don Benito murmured, "Another insane king, George III," and continued reading:

> Through that marriage, Leopold hoped to become Prince Consort of England some day, when Princess Charlotte became queen. How-

ever, Charlotte died a short time later without bearing any children, and Leopold at forty-two married Princess Marie Louise, daughter of King Louis Philippe of France. When Princess Carlota was born, the Queen decided that she was to be named after Leopold's first wife. The Archduke and Princess Charlotte fell in love and a short time later the House of Austria asked for her hand in marriage. The wedding took place on July 27, 1857 in Brussels with the approval of not only Leopold and Sophie and Franz Joseph, but also Queen Victoria. On a previous trip to England before the wedding, the Archduke had charmed the English Queen and her husband, Prince Albert. Before this, Carlota had incurred the wrath of Queen Victoria when she rejected Don Pedro de Portugal as a probable husband. Another candidate for her betrothal had been Prince George of Saxony.

"But then," Don Benito said, "Leopold was wrong twice concerning his potential to marry into a ruling family. First his English lady dies, and then it's the Bonapartes and not the Orléans nor the Bourbons who are the ones who come to power in France."

"That's correct, Mr. President, his marriage to Marie Louise was a political miscalculation."

"Tell me," said Don Benito, and looked at his Secretary's eyes, "have you been in love many times?"

"Me, Don Benito?"

"I'm asking you because I don't know how one can love so many different women; or else, how many different women can love one man."

"Well, in the case of Leopold, it seems when he was a young man he was very handsome and quite charming. Today, of course, he's an old man. I was told that he not only dyes his eyebrows but also uses rouge and wears a black wig styled in the old-fashioned manner."

"That's as ridiculous as my powdering my nose, don't you think?" Don Benito asked, and kept on reading: " 'Shortly after his marriage, Franz Joseph named Maximilian Viceroy of the provinces of Lombardo-Veneto.' Ah, here's the Italy business. Yes, I'm very much interested in the job that the Archduke did in Lombardo-Veneto. What can you tell me about that, Mr. Secretary?"

"Not too much more than what I put in the report, Mr. President. There might be a couple of things, I suppose."

"What sort of things?"

"Well, for instance, the Archduke initiated the construction of the great plaza in front of the Duomo of Milan, and he restored the Ambrosian Library. When the poet Manzoni became ill, he visited him personally, and then, as I say in the report, the Archduke tried in vain to get Austria to liberalize its attitude toward Lombardo-Veneto, because Franz Joseph was always adamantly opposed to such principles, and never approved of the way his brother governed the provinces. People say, Don Benito, that Franz Joseph even sent people to spy on Maximilian, and that his mail was censored by the so-called Cabinet Noir of Vienna. The truth is that the Archduke went too far with his liberalism, if you'll allow me to call it liberalism. Count Cavour said Maximilian was the most formidable enemy the Italians had in Lombardy, and precisely because he took pains to become a just ruler, to implement the reforms to which Vienna was so opposed. Manin, on the other hand, said that the Italians didn't want Austria to become more humane—they just wanted Austria to leave."

"*Was* Austria becoming more humane, Mr. Secretary?"

"Well, not exactly. I was told that on one occasion—imagine, Don Benito!—the Military Administration of Milan sent City Hall the bill for the sticks that the police had broken on the backs of some demonstrators. What else can I add to what I wrote in the report? Well, yes, Maximilian and Carlota earned the affection of their Italian subjects, but only on a personal level. They stopped making public appearances, despite the fact that Carlota enjoyed going to La Scala, because they were tired of the jeering and the catcalls. Young Italian women even refused to dance with Austrian officers. It's said too that on more than one occasion the Archduke showed weakness—for instance during the rebellion of the students in Padua, and also, I was told, when he criticized the cruelty with which Radetzky suppressed the riots of the Milanese in 1848, when he executed and hanged several hundred Italian patriots for the simple crime of owning guns."

Don Benito continued reading, this time out loud:

> On more than one occasion the Archduke made it known to Vienna that the duality between military authority and civil authority was incompatible in a government, and he asked for direct command of the Austrian army in Lombardo-Veneto, but Franz Joseph refused. And when Count Cavour ordered his troops to march to Lombardy along with Louis Napoleon's army, the Emperor relieved the Arch-

duke of his position and named Count Gyulai military and political commander of Venice and Lombardy.

"The disasters of Magenta and Solferino follow on June 4 and 24, 1859, respectively, Don Benito."

Don Benito continued: "'The meeting at Villafranca between Louis Napoleon and Franz Joseph resulted in the liberation of Lombardy' . . . But not that of Venice.'"

"That's correct, Mr. President, and it's then that Louis Napoleon betrayed Cavour."

Archduke Maximilan and Princess Charlotte then retired to their castle at Miramare on the shores of the Adriatic, near Trieste. It is here that the Mexican royalists offer them the throne of Mexico.

"You were telling me about an island they visit sometimes?"

"Yes, Don Benito, the Isle of Lacroma facing the coast of Dalmatia . . . where Richard the Lionheart once got shipwrecked. Or, that's the story. They also say that Richard the Lionheart was a sodomite."

"You don't say. I didn't know that part, but of course they don't teach you those things at school. What a bunch of degenerates, like you said."

Don Benito put the report on the table.

"You won't believe it, but indulging in a conversation about these banalities, however germane, can make one forget that there are more important things to worry about. Did you know that people are blaming me for the defeat of Puebla now, because they say I didn't foresee that the siege would last so long? At any rate, I'm very thankful to you for your fascinating conversation, Mr. Secretary. When are you returning to Europe?"

"In about three weeks, Don Benito."

"Give my greetings and thanks to Émile Ollivier. The same to Victor Hugo, should you see him. Oh, if you run into Jules Favre, tell him not to compare Maximilian to Don Quixote. Don Quixote was an idealist. The Archduke is a man of boundless ambition."

"If the President will allow me to retire . . ."

"Yes, of course—but wait. I wanted to ask you something else. What was it? Oh yes, in your report you say that the Archduke had two love affairs, but you only go into detail about one, the one with Countess von Linden. You don't say anything about Amelia de Braganza."

"Oh, yes, I'm sorry, Don Benito, I didn't include her. The House of Austria would have undoubtedly approved that union, but she died of consumption very young, before her engagement to the Archduke could be announced. By the way, she died on the Isle of Madeira, the same place where Carlota would later spend a winter while the Archduke, her husband, was traveling in Brazil. They say—but it's also gossip, I suppose—that in Brazil a negress gave Maximilian a venereal disease. They say he's sterile because of it, and that this is why he and Carlota are childless."

Don Benito walked toward his window and said, "Sterile? Well, now you can see why I'm not offended when some people call me 'mule,' so long as it's only on account of my being stubborn, obstinate. That quality is all I have in common with mules. Mules may be sterile, but I'm not. I've had several children."

"That's correct, Don Benito."

"And some of them are quite handsome, as people say—not as dark as I. Imagine," said Don Benito, and looked out at the cloudy sky. "Imagine—prejudice as to skin color is so deeply ingrained in us that I've heard my own wife, Margarita, speaking about a nephew of ours, or of any child, really, 'He's very handsome, very white, and with blue eyes!' One of these days I'm going to write her a letter saying, 'Guess what, Margarita? Did you hear what a pretty boy our Archduke turned out to be?'"

3. The City and Its Vendors

Birdseed!

Ink for sale!

"In this here city there's lots of flooding but we ain't got no floods in my village. We ain't got no statue of a lion neither, like that one here on San Antonio Street. It has the water level from that 1629 flood marked on its head . . . In this here city there's tons of rats, that's the truth. In my village there ain't no carnival but here they got one. They throw eggshells filled with confetti and lavender water and streamers that tickle my nose. You ain't suppose' to eat the food they leave for you at the door 'cause it can have rat poison in it, that stuff they call muriatic powder, yessir. But here they got lots

161

of piñatas at Christmas time and they didn't have none in
my village. Even though they won't let me whack 'em, 'cause
I always break 'em, I always get to stuff myself with jícamas
and peanuts . . . And where else can you hear all them boleros
and habaneras all night long, even if you can't hardly hear
'em? Not in my village. And what about that French music
at the Plaza de Armas after vespers? Not in my village. Here
they look down on me and sometimes they knock my hat
off when a priest or a monk goes by, yessir. But where else
can you find a Tivoli del Eliseo with its Sunday picnics that
smells like sardine and sausage sandwiches? In my village, for
instance, we never had none of them scribes that writes letters for people like me who can't write none . . . Some day I'll
take you to see them at the Plaza Santo Domingo, so you can
see the ink made from huisache and you can hear the quill
scratch the paper . . . If you're good, I'll take you to the corner
where the House of Tiles is. It's got the coolest and smoothest
walls in all of Mexico. On Sunday I'll take you to the Alameda
so you can see the bench where Don Foré used to sit . . ."
Come and get your cakes and turnovers! Get 'em while
they're hot!

With time on his hands, a bit cockeyed all his life, and grown old over the last
few years, General Elias Forey came to sit on that bench every Sunday at the
Alameda Park and brought a bag of candy for the children. Getting ready to
return to France, he comprehended nothing of what was happening in those
days, since, in his sincere view, he had followed his Emperor's instructions to
the letter. He would ask General Douay: "Didn't I dissolve the government
created by Almonte? Don't I control Mexico, as Emperor Louis Napoleon recommended, unbeknownst to anyone? Have I not avoided taking sides, as the
Emperor demanded in a letter from Fontainebleau—with either the Liberals
or the Conservatives?"

Instead of hup, two three
We crabs go three two hup!
Instead of marching down
We like to go way up!

"Hear the song? Hear it? In my village nobody sings. Here they all sing. We made up a little song for Don Foré that goes like this:

> With Don Foré's whiskers
> I'll make a saddlebag
> For our brave Don Porfirio
> To put it on his good ole nag . . .

I wonder though who this Don Porfirio can be . . ."

General Douay nodded: "Yes, General. In one of your proclamations you said yourself, 'My fellow Mexicans, get rid of those liberal or reactionary labels. They bring nothing but hate and the spirit of vengefulness.'" To which General Forey replied, "Yes, that's just what I said."

> Soap from Puebla!
> Oven-baked gorditas!

"In my village there weren't no proclamations or edicts. At least not a long time ago, when I first came here. Here they have lots of them. There's always a new one. That's what reminds me of Don Foré, all his announcements and proclamations that Don Atanasio, the wine merchant, kindly used to read aloud to me. But you'll see on some corners that people read the proclamations posted on walls aloud, for us who can't read . . . The good thing about the French coming here is that now we have twice as many holidays—the Mexican ones and now the Paris ones too. The bad thing is that all the priests and monks are back out in the streets. When Don Benito was here the convents and churches were empty, and everybody who lived in them was gone, so I lost the habit of taking off my hat. That's why it's good to remember exactly where every convent or monastery is, like Recolletas, the Antonines, the Exclaustration, Santa Isabel, Regina. I know them like the back of my hand. If you can, it's also good to tell apart the noises that the sisters and the brothers make, even if there's so many of 'em that it's hard. The Bethlehemites, the Johannines, the Franciscans, the Hospitalers . . . But anyhow, in time you can learn to tell the difference between the rustling sound of the Saint Brigitte sisters' habits, or the clacking of the Sisters of Charity's rosaries, or the paddling of the Discalced Carmelites' bare feet . . . Me, poor as I am, I ain't never gone without my huaraches. Without them I would step on all the dog- and people-shit you find on the streets of this city. My village don't have so much shit . . . no sir. But there ain't no Café Inglés in my village or a Fulquieri restaurant where they give me scraps . . ."

Louis Napoleon had said to Lorencez, "It is against my interests, my nature, and my principles to impose a government on the Mexican people." Had not Elias Forey, who signed his proclamations, announcements and decrees as "Commanding General, Senator, and Commander-in-Chief of the Expeditionary Corps," not named a governing body of thirty-five citizens, presided over by the so-called Three Caciques—Juan Nepomuceno Almonte,

> *Amo quinequi*, Juan Pamuceno
> don't wear them kingly duds,
> 'cause a robe and crown sure don't fit ya
> like yer sandals and yer crate

General Salas, who had given Forey the keys to Mexico City, and Archbishop Labastida's proxy, a Mr. Ormachea—as well as a group of notables—215, ranging from doctors to diplomats, from sharpshooters to cobblers. This assembly, in turn, had proclaimed barely forty some days after the taking of the capital that . . .

Cottage cheese and molasses! Very tasty!

"I don't know why the song says 'yer' 'instead of 'your.' That's just the way it is. I learned all of Don Foré's edicts by heart from hearing them over and over again. The same with General Duay who came to tell us about twenty ways we would die if we didn't go over to the Frenchies' side. One day we'll ask the evangelists why it's 'yer' and not 'your' and what Don Foré really meant when he said 'I didn't come to wage war against the Mexican people. Only against a small bunch of *uncrapulous* men who govern by inspiring terror.' The fact is, I did contradict Don Atanasio when he said that Don Foré just ranted and raved against us Mexicans, but to me he was right sometimes. 'What do we see in your streets,' Don Foré's edicts would say, 'but polluted waters that contaminate the air!' He's saying that to me, who can smell things better than most people. 'What are your roads but potholes and mires?' You don't need to tell me about it. Ain't a day that goes by without me almost breaking my bones falling into open pits like the one at La Amargura Alley where they dig every day. 'What is your administration but organized theft?' Tell me about it! I've lost track of the times I've been robbed of my alms money . . . And you can also see the evangelists there. The ink made from the pink amapa flower smells nice . . ."

Butter, fifteen cents!

The Assembly had proclaimed that:
Number One: The Mexican Nation would adopt a hereditary and moderate monarchy. *Number Two*: The throne would be offered to Archduke Maximilian of Austria and his spouse, Archduchess Charlotte. *Number Three*: Were the Archduke to decline, the Mexican Nation would appeal to the kindness and wisdom of the French Emperor to appoint another Catholic prince to the Mexican throne . . .

"Do you believe that terror business? I don't see the difference but I can smell it. They used to tell me that when Don Hernán Cortés and his soldiers came, Emperor Moctezuma threw incense at 'em not 'cause he thought they was gods but 'cause they stank. They never changed those tin clothes even when they went up Popo to bring down sulfur for their cannons. Have you smelled sulfur? In my village there ain't no gunpowder factories. To me them Frogs is just like that. They stink more than the Injuns. They're also real tightwads . . . Or maybe you think they just don't understand me when I say, 'Alms for the poor'? Do I have to say it in French, like Pardiú? Them Frenchies is just like the Sisters of Charity; even with that name, they don't even give you the time of day. They just keep trying to take me to their convent to fix their chairs. But I don't like to give up my freedom . . . In my village you walks three blocks and yer in the boonies. Here you can walk and walk and you never get out. I'm gonna take you to Puente de Peredo, to Siete Príncipes, to the Calle Nueva, to the Carrera de Corpus Christi, to Calle Verdeja and Medinas, to the La Puerta Falsa of La Merced and Puente Quebrado and Calle La Joya so that you can see the fabric shops that smell like a wet goat right after it rains, and of benzene, like at the cleaners. You can tell the marble shops and the fencing schools by the noises, and you get a lot of different smells from the pharmacies, like rosewater for gonorrhea, paregoric elixir or aromatic vinegar for pustules . . ."

Excellent marzipan sweets . . . !

And even though Forey thought that those were Napoleon's and Douay's wishes, this was not the case. Or at least, not exactly—*pas exactement*. Among other reasons, this was because there was talk about some letters that a Captain Loizillon had written from Mexico to Louis Napoleon's godmother, Hortense Cornu. In these letters he said that Forey was turning the nation over to ultra-reactionary and ultra-clerical "elements"—indeed, most of the Assembly of Notables were both; many of them, moreover, were former members of Santa Anna's government. Cornu showed one of these letters to her godson, who decided to send Bazaine a copy, keeping the author's name from him. The general, in turn, had already conspired against Forey, complaining in his correspondence to the French Minister of War about the fact that the excessively generous commander of the expeditionary forces had begun distributing Legion of Honor crosses to Mexican officers with whom he was barely acquainted. It didn't matter whether it was true or not that Forey had a list of names in his pocket, compiled at the Tuileries and verified by Hidalgo, from which many of his Mexican "Notables" were selected. What mattered now was that Louis Napoleon insisted on a liberal government and Forey's way of doing things wasn't likely to bring one about, especially after he'd alienated the Mexican Liberal Party. After all, its members were educated and enlightened by those same French institutions, customs, codes, edicts, and decrees toward which the general was so partial—an example of which was the "Abduction

Law," ordering the confiscation of the property of any republican who took up arms against the French. Also, this wasn't the way to serve Mexico, but to cater to French interests; and, besides, in view of the Sonora Protectorate, to ban—as Forey did with a different proclamation—the exportation not only of coins but of silver and gold bars, was simply not acceptable . . .

Get your fresh coconuts!

"In this here city you can't walk on the streets from seven to nine in the morning 'cause they shake all the rugs over the balconies and they dump the piss from the chamber pots out the windows, yessir. But there ain't no rugs back in my village, much less balconies. I'm gonna take you to the lower floors of Porta Cheli so that you can hear the racket at the Munguía Press. There ain't no printing presses back in my village. And I'll take you to the Iturbide Hotel so you can hear the noise from the Recamié Restaurant and from the stagecoaches that come through every day. You hear them? Hear them bells? Them's the bells that tell when the Sacred Host is going out to some poor dyin' soul. Since Don Foré came we got back the contraption that holds the Sacred Host. You hear it coming every day 'cause here more people die than in the villages . . . That's why I like the city better than my village. For the smells and the noise and the vendors 'cause I like to hear 'em:

Water barrels, ten cents.

Frogs for sale!

and 'cause I like to hear the water in the barrels and the squeaky noises of the water-carriers' leather aprons. I don't like them frogs, though, not even the croaking they do when they're alive. I don't like how they smell when they's dead neither. Can you hear 'em? And the Cathedral bells? Ringin' matins. What a fluke! The Sacred Host just went by and the bells start up ringin' . . . In my village there weren't no bells that rang so nice . . ."

Quietly, every Sunday, he sat on his usual bench. Children rolling hoops shouted, "There's Don Foré! There is Don Foré!" since they knew that he always gave them sweets and candied almonds. The murmur of the fountains, the vendors who peddled pinwheels, feather dusters and tiny white fish:

Get your roasted juiles!

The organ grinders, the lottery-ticket vendors, the candle makers, the blind man who begged "*Alms, Mosié Don Foré, pardiú,*" and to whom Forey always gave a few coins—sometimes a whole *real*—and that sun, that marvelous yellow Mexican sun . . . Perhaps General Forey would have preferred to stay there, like that—peacefully—in that city filled with colors and noises so different from those of Paris—the vendors' cries as described by the Marchioness Calderón de la Barca; full of sensual and strange fruit like the very delicate mamey, or the mango whose aroma Captain Blanchot compared to that of the aphrodisiac terebinth—and would have preferred to live out his life giving orders to his generals from his office at Buenavista Palace, candy to the children on Sundays, sitting on this same bench in Alameda Park. But Monsieur de Radepont joined the campaign against Forey and his followers, claiming that he was a nobody, worthless, and soon after came the Baron de Saligny. The Baron tattled to Hidalgo that shortly before the fall of Puebla, General Douay had claimed the city to be impregnable and that the entire venture was folly created entirely by a woman's whim—*née du caprice d'une femme*—the woman in question, of course, being the Empress Eugénie. As a result, the Emperor finally decided to pull Forey out of Mexico and leave the expedition command in General Bazaine's hands. To accomplish this, he rewarded and punished Forey simultaneously. After giving him the title of Marshal of France, Napoleon said that there weren't enough troops in Mexico to merit their being commanded by a marshal, so Forey was ordered back to France. Forey left, never to return. He departed Mexico with a marshal's baton, and left behind the vendors' cries and likewise his own proclamations, in which he had extolled his nation's power over and again, and claimed that its expeditions to China and Cochin China had proven that there was no land so remote that an offense against France's honor would go unpunished, as well as chastising the Mexicans for their cruel fondness for bullfights (this despite the fact that there had been a cartoon printed in a newspaper in the capital saying that the French had had the luxury of fighting bulls as important as Louis XVI and Marie Antoinette: the executioner, Robespierre, dressed as a matador, was shown parading around the ring wielding the two monarchs' wigless heads, instead of the tail and ears of a bull bred on the Atenco ranch). Along with Forey, and likewise never to return, left the Baron de Saligny; the latter repeatedly ignored his summons from the Quai d'Orsay, since he didn't want to abandon his business interests in Mexico, nor jilt the woman he was planning to marry . . .

> "A little cup, a little cup
> gimme a drop for Saligny
> A little cup, a little cup
> gimme a drop for Saligny

. . . that was the song we wrote for him. You know, of all the Frenchies, Saligny stank the worst. It's not that I don't like the smell of wine. I just don't like the smell of drunks . . . I'm gonna take you down to Don Atanasio's wine shop some day. He's the one who reads me the proclamations and lets me stay there for hours to panhandle. At first you can't tell the difference in the smells 'cause they all mix together into one big one. Later though you can tell if it's raspberry, orange or, my favorite, guava likker. Then if you want you can put 'em all together again . . . Hear that? Hear that shout . . . ?

Colossir? Colossir?

it's them Indians bringing coal from the mountains and they're yelling: Coal for you, sir? Coal for you, sir? But it sounds like '*Colossir . . . Colossir*' . . . Yeah, our peddlers also add their perfume to the city . . ."

In the name of the enlightened principles that had taken so many to the scaffold, France's opposition to the Mexican imbroglio was represented by five French members of parliament, called *Les Cinq*: Ernest Picard, Émile Ollivier, Adolphe Thiers, Antoine Berryer, and Jules Favre. The latter was a noted politician who, regarding the war against Mexico, had declared: "There is only one road, to negotiate and retreat. Why make war? We should only do that against our enemies. But where are our enemies there?" As to the expected victory, he stated, "Afterwards will come responsibility. The government that you have created will have to be maintained." In turn, from his exile in Brussels, the novelist and poet Victor Hugo, who had played every political role possible—as a Bonapartist, a "Legitimist," a republican, and an "Orléanist"—sent a proclamation of his own to Mexico that read: "Both of us battle the Empire, you all from your Motherland and I in my exile. I send you my support as a brother." Benito Juárez ordered both proclamations—Favre's and Hugo's—translated into Spanish and posted on the walls of Mexico City, Puebla, and other cities. Further, Forey just couldn't understand why, considering that the war had been waged to collect Mexico's debt to France, Louis Napoleon had told him to start off by forgetting the matter of the debt entirely. He understood even less why, if the war was meant to export a Catholic prince, as requested by the Mexican reactionaries and clerics, in order to restore the faith, the orders from the Tuileries were to proclaim religious freedom and to ignore the matter of the confiscated Church properties that had been sold to private citizens. Naturally, with the arrival of the French and the coming Empire, the Church thought things were going to go back to the way they'd been before Juárez came to power. When the Church saw its error, however, facing Forey's proclamations, and then, after Marshal Bazaine's departure, it began to compose, print, paste, and hang proclamations and exhortations of its own against the French, against Louis Napoleon, the authorities, and the Intervention, on the very same walls where, first, Juárez, then Forey and Bazaine, had posted their decrees and edicts in turn—on Vergara Street, famous for its steamed corn dumplings,

Come and get your steamed dumplings!

and then on the Portal de Agustinos, always fragrant with almond candy; and on the walls of the Girls' School; and on the walls of the San Lorenzo or Santa Teresa la Antigua convents: complaints against the French, against Napoleon, against the authorities, and against the Intervention; nor should one forget Bilbao Alley, always smelling of Chapala whitefish and pinto beans, and on the façades and doors of all the bars and cafés where French soldiers ate, drank, and sometimes gambled—where one could always hear cards, pool balls, and the rattling of chips out in the street. And there was also Monsignor Antonio Pelagio de Labastida y Dávalos to be reckoned with, who, having been expelled as a bishop by Juárez, had returned as an archbishop after becoming a Prince of the Church in Rome and Paris. Afraid of contracting yellow fever in the tropics, he had chosen to return during the "norther" season in Veracruz.

Despite the fact that Bazaine himself returned his Episcopal Palace to him in perfect condition, refurbished his seminary, and rebuilt his country house in Tacubaya, the Monsignor still wasn't satisfied—even though the only thing the General had failed to do was replace the olive trees in the orchard that, brimming with fruit, had disappeared during the war.

Delicious jerky!

"I scratch a little bit and find another one under it. Then I scratch that one and there's one more. I like to pull them off, to grab a little edge and pull it off, in strips. You can only do that late at night, when you're pretty sure they ain't watchin' you. Like I said, I know all the corners and all the churches where they paste them up by heart, like here at Escalerillas and Tacuba, or at La Profesa. But now I have to be careful 'cause the priests, who don't really like the French, wait for night to come to put up their own announcements. This one is still wet. I'm sure the priests put it up there on top of Basén's latest one. And Basén's is on top of the one put up by the Green Bird and that one's on top of a decree posted by Don Foré. And Don Foré's is right on top of Nepomuceno Almonte's, Almonte's on Don Victor's and Don Hugo's. And Don Victor's and Don Hugo's is on top of Don Benito's proclamation. Don Benito's is covering Echegaray and Miramón's Christmas Plan. The Christmas Plan is on top of one of Santa Anna's pronouncements, and so on . . . It's never-ending. And, you know, I left my village ages ago and when I came to the capital the walls were covered with the Iguala Plan proclamations that soon ended up under Emperor Iturbide's announcements. They covered these up with the Casa Mata Plan proclamations. So, I was telling you, all you gotta do is scratch a little bit . . ."

Soil for your house plants!

In any case, the Mexican Church, determined to recover its properties and privileges, banned all work on Sundays. Every one of the priests, monks, and clerics who had vanished during Benito Juárez's administration returned to the streets of Mexico. Processions and church bells added their fanfare to the cries of the merchants: junk dealers who traded urns for used clothing; vendors offering quail, sweet potatoes, chestnuts, fried bananas, or soap from Marseilles; door-to-door barbers; butchers selling roasted lamb heads crowned with bay leaves or else selling chickens; and with all this the bustle of vehicles: broughams, barouches, cabs from the Seminario and Mariscala taxi stands; calèches led by plump, silver Frisian horses; stagecoaches departing from the Callejón de Dolores to all the cardinal points; mule-drawn streetcars and sedans; the multitude of colors from storefront flowers and fruits complementing all the activity: the pistachio-green waistcoats worn by dandies and fops; the black fur overcoats sported by gentlemen and other bluebloods; gray military capes; the ochres, maroons, and dark-blues worn by notaries, tax and bill collectors, drivers, shopkeepers, lamplighters, petty civil servants, domestics, and representatives of every trade or skill; the pink and pale yellow tulles and crinolines worn by ladies and young women, their backsides enlarged with horsehair-stuffed bustles; the magenta and iridescent olive capes and skirts of Geneva velvet worn by future Mexican marchionesses and court ladies—and all of these were enhanced in turn by the colors worn by brides of Christ who had renounced the world and all this nineteenth-century ostentation: the sky-blue mantles of the Sisters of the Conception; the Teresians' brown tunics; the Recollet nuns in gray habits and white-ribboned wimples with five scarlet disks sewn on the ribbons to represent the Savior's Five Wounds. The monstrance was carried through the streets again. The Virgin Mary—virgin among virgins, in her sky-blue mantle, sprinkled with stars and the inscription in gold letters, *Tota Pulchra est Maria*, amid clouds of organdy and lamé, and multicolored zephyr rainbows through which angels and cherubs peeked—returned to the city center in her beautiful ceremonial carriage drawn by bishops and other high clergy, through Empedradillo and Plateros and San Francisco, led by graceful life-guards on proud sorrel steeds, followed by musicians, schoolchildren, fraternities bearing standards and insignia, religious orders, and secular clergy.

Get your pralines!
"You hear, you hear that 'rizz, razz'? Let's get movin'. They're comin'! Hear 'em? Those're the convicts sweepin' the streets. The noise you hear is the brooms when they sweep back and forth, rizz, razz. The other noise, clink clank, is the shackles they got on their feet, and the chains that go from one to the

other on their feet. They always leave the prison at dawn, and they line up single file and they all sweep together, first thisaway, rizz, then thataway, razz. Get movin'. One day one of them fellers paid to shovel mud and trash out the manholes onto the street to dry threw a bucketful at me and gave me a shit bath. The foreman and the guards just laughed at me. They're assholes . . .

Come on. Get movin'."

To be on the safe side, Bazaine decided to remove the Archbishop from the Regency Council and left for Guadalajara. Monsignor Labastida took advantage of his absence, called a meeting with the Archbishop and five other bishops who had returned to Mexico. Joined as a synod, they composed a document that addressed Generals Almonte and Salas, rejecting the authority of the State to confiscate Church property, and they excommunicated (irrevocably—including *in articulo mortis*, in case of death) not only the authors and implementers of the sacking of the churches, but also those who refused restitution of those properties to their legitimate owners. Since the blame for this wasn't limited to the State, but was also attributable to French officers and, in the final analysis, to the entire French army, the Church determined that it was no longer necessary to celebrate military High Masses every Sunday. Labastida announced that from that point on, the Cathedral's doors would be closed. General Neigre, whom Bazaine had appointed commander of the capital, replied that if the doors remained closed his cannons would blast them open. At seven the following Sunday morning, Neigre ordered a cannon placed before San Hipólito Cathedral. A few minutes later the doors were opened and Mass was sung. When Bazaine found out, he thereupon ordered an artillery barrage to coincide with the elevation of the Host during the Mass that he and his officers were to attend in the Cathedral of Guadalajara.

Sweet tamales, chile and lard tamales!
"Yessir, in this here city there's a lot of racket. In my village it's not the same. There the padres don't do like they do here getting all of us street people and beggars together so we can make lots of noise with our rosaries and our cans and our medals and our tin cups to protest Don Foré's and Don Basén's proclamations and announcements. There's lots of earth-

quakes here too. In my village it shakes sometimes but since all the houses are made of adobe, one crack is the same as another. Here it's different. The cracks on the Inquisition Palace's lava-rock are not at all like the ones that the last earthquake left on the stone of the Belén archery. That's been leaking for about a year. You know somethin' else? There's no trees in my village. Here in this city was the first time I could touch a whole tree, from the branches down to the roots. That was when the Santa Cecilia earthquake knocked down a great big eucalyptus. I filled my pockets with the little seed pods. They smell real nice. In this city there's lots of things to get hold of. Not in my village. I know the Archbishop won't let me touch his big hat or that amethyst cross that they say he wears on his chest, but one day he let me kiss the buckles on his shoes. Pure silver, they are—or so they say. I've felt the softness of the kid gloves the ladies wear when they give me money, and the coldness of the patent leather of their boots that's as smooth as water and makes a real nice squeaky sound. I like to touch the rough skin on the mamey fruit and the prickly skin on the pineapples. You can't find them fruits in my village. Like I said before, one day I'll take you to Alameda Park. I like to hear the water in the fountains there and I like to touch the lions' heads when they spit. I'll show you Don Foré's bench. Today we'll go to the Main Plaza. Next to the Metropolitan Chapel there's the Paseo de las Cadenas. The chains ring when the wind blows, and nearby there's that Aztec stone they call the calendar. I like to touch it because it's real bumpy . . . I remember the Santa Julia earthquake, in '58, the worst one of all 'cause the cisterns flooded and lots of churches was damaged, like the Chapel and the Church of San Fernando. That earthquake knocked down a statue of the Mother Country. They let me touch it too, and they laughed when I touched its tits . . .

—In my village there's no Mother Country statues with their tits exposed . . ."

Get your matches!

174

Having settled in Buenavista Palace in Mexico City, after placating the Church, General Bazaine ordered the departure of a Turkish detachment to surround the Port of Acapulco by land, while by sea it was attacked by an Algerian detachment under Maître Salar, a freebooter who, nine years before, had led a ship packed with mercenaries to Sonora in a belated effort to save Raousset-Boulbon's life. Captain Blanchot, Bazaine's aide-de-camp, resented not being sent to Acapulco, since he had heard that in colonial times, shipments from Asia had arrived there, and, after being taken crosscountry, were repackaged in Veracruz and delivered to the capital; when an interminable series of rebellions, demonstrations and coups had interrupted traffic in Mexico, some valuable shipments had been left behind in that Pacific port. Rumor had it that, besides those coolies who never arrived in Havana to work in the cigar factories—whose Spanish masters, unable to pronounce their names, gave them such Greek names as Socrates, Protagoras, or Alcibiades, and who ended up staying in Acapulco—there were packed warehouses where one could buy treasures that would make Colonel Dupin green with envy very cheaply and that would probably not be seen again for a long time, since no ships were coming in from China and the Philippines: sandalwood and lacquer boxes, ivory figurines, maybe even Golkonda diamonds, Lahore shawls, Manila shawls, and scarves from Kashmir. However, General Bazaine consoled Captain Blanchot by charging him with two projects. One was to redesign the Spanish garden in Buenavista Palace, as the general was partial to English-style landscaping. Among other things, therefore, Captain Blanchot diverted a nearby stream to form several babbling brooks. But since the stream was crawling with water snakes that now were wriggling into the garden, Blanchot had to ask for help from a local chieftain. This man, whom he called "the 'nabob' from Chapala" in his memoirs, sent thirty cranes by return mail. In a few days, the cranes had devoured the snakes. The other consolation Blanchot received was to organize the gala that the French army would be giving to celebrate the arrival of Maximilian and Carlota in Mexico City. The captain calculated that, in order to pitch a sky-blue tent over the whole of the great courtyard of Buenavista Palace, he would need several kilometers of cretonne, an army of seamstresses, a dozen or more tubs to mix white lead paint with aniline dyes, an equal number of brooms to use as paintbrushes, and a small detachment of French sailors from Veracruz—mast carvers, sail makers, and carpenters equipped with saws, rigging, cables, and everything else needed to raise the blue cloth ceiling—the bluest possible—and to suspend a great golden eagle, with widespread wings, from its center.

"I'm gonna tell you two things for you to remember: one is that I ain't gonna take you to Mixcalco Plaza because at dawn every day they shoot one or two Juárez men there. We could have bad luck and catch a stray bullet. Have you heard La Llorona? It's the ghost of a woman. She died of sorrow because they killed her children in Mixcalco, so she goes around at night screaming: 'Oooh, my poor babies . . . Oooh, my poor babies . . .' When I hear her I feel my heart shrink. They say that she's got a long mane and a white nightdress that she drags along the ground . . . The other thing is, listen to me: I don't know if you're from a village or from a city. But if you wanna go aroun' with me and you want me to give you your bones and tortillas, and to let you sleep next to me, and to pet you and scratch you, you have to behave and not bark at nobody but them Injuns and them bums. Watch out you don't bark at no priests: you just wag your tail at 'em. They're mean fuckers. Watch out you don't snap at nuns and wag your tail at 'em. They're mean too. Just like with them monks and ladies, and with Basén's police. Only you better not wag your tail at the Sacred Host . . ."

Shoes need mending . . . ?

Buy custard and hot chocolate here . . . !

I buy used clothing!

Roasted chestnuts, ladies and gentlemen!

Get your chestnuts here!

VII

BOUCHOUT CASTLE

1927

Go on, Maximilian, have the guts to bring back all the Maximilians that you were at one time or another. The little poet from Schönbrunn Palace, who spoke to the statues in the garden avenues, called them by their names and recited their legends aloud: Artemisia, who mourns the death of her husband and brother Mausolus; Mercury, the inventor of the flute and the lyre; Olympias, with her son Alexander the Great, who so resembled both Emperor Joseph II, and his wife Isabella of Parma; Diana, the hunter goddess who became the Countess von Linden the day that she shot an arrow through your heart— go on, Maximilian, take out that cotton stuffing from your nose that keeps you from breathing the scent of the chestnuts that flower in May at the Prater, or the aroma of the melons from Jojutla that Sara York gave us; Maximilian, remove the lacquer from your face that keeps you from smiling as you used to in Albania when you received the envoys of the Aga from Ismid, under a tent, in a burnoose. The varnish stretches your flesh and keeps you from smiling as you once did after you fought beside your brother Franz Joseph at the Battle of Raab, when Budapest fell, its one hundred most notable citizens hanging from its street lamps, and its women lashed in the streets by Baron Hayman's orders. You cried with fury and impotence, remember? Go on, Maximilian, take the cotton stuffing out of your ears so that you can hear the roar of the cannon that Prince Salm-Salm won for you in Querétaro; or the sound of my breath, or my words that are sweeter than the echo of the blue cave of Linderhof where mad King Ludwig of Bavaria dreamt that he was Lohengrin, its water clearer and purer than the foaming Usumacinta River waters. Rise, Maximilian, and put on your cork hat with the moths that you caught as they slept under the tall and dense trees of Mangueira Lagoon. Put on your miner's suit and the tarred helmet with a candle on it as you did when you went down the black hole of the silver mines in the Hacienda de la Regla. Put on the admiral uniform that you wore the afternoon when you spoke with the ghosts of the Duke of Alba and Philip II of Spain under the heady orange trees of the Lonja in Seville. Go on, Maximilian: cut your veins open so that the embalming fluid will run like the port that you drank in Gibraltar. Cut open your entrails so that the sawdust and lavender will pour out, along with the undigested chicken breast. Put on the waistcoat and the cassock that you wore when you left the Convent of the Teresitas on the most beautiful day of the year. I cleaned them myself with benzene and I sent them to the invisible tailors so that they would mend the bullet holes. Take out those eyes made of paste and put in your own two blue eyes, those that stopped looking at me when you were thirty-five and I was twenty-six. If you don't put them in, Maximilian, if you don't put your own blue eyes back in their sockets, the eyes that marveled so at the huge goldfish at the Caserta Hatcheries, oh, and if you don't put those eyes back in that so delighted in the snow-covered volcanoes of Anáhuac, which they saw through the moist and violet mists of Cuernavaca dawns, I swear to you, Maximilian, that you will never see me again as I looked when I was twenty-six. When I was twenty-six my face was smooth and soft and fresh, my tresses were still black and reached my waist. I wove them with multicolored yarn so that they would resemble the braids of a Mexican woman, fresh from the hills of Oaxaca. Go on, Maximilian, get up and put in your eyes, and comb your hair, and brush away the plaster from your brow and cheeks that was left on your face from the death mask that Dr. Licea made for you. Brush your whiskers to clean them of lint and cobwebs. Brush your teeth. Gargle with champagne to get rid of your zinc chloride breath, Maximilian. Bathe in your granite and lapis lazuli tub and rid yourself of that death smell you picked up from the Medici mausoleum where you found the Michelangelo sculptures so vulgar and repulsive. That death smell you picked up in Granada when you visited the tombs of Ferdinand and Isabella, of Philip the Fair and Joan the Mad, and from the table in the Holy Inquisition courtroom in the chapel of San Andrés Hospital in Mexico City.

Go on, Maximilian, take off the sponge soaked in Egyptian wines and dragon blood that they stuffed in your mouth and tell Drs. Alvarado and Montaño to put your tongue and your uvula back in so that you can talk to me again, to tell me your secrets and that you still love me. Get up, Maximilian and tell me—and if you tell me what you, your open heart, imagined on top of Xochicalco Pyramid, I'll tell you what my sleeping heart dreamed in the shadow of Tajín Pyramid. Come on Maximilian, don't play dumb or deaf. Tell me, what kind of cactus needle did they use to sew your lips shut? From what beehives did they get the wax to stuff in your ears so that you couldn't hear, not my screams, but the hummingbirds that built their nests under your balcony, flapping their wings, or the poisoned words of Concepción Sedano? Go on, tell me how your life has been beneath lead sheets, and I'll tell you about mine, how I've lived through it all, how I've borne up; how I've almost forgotten that day, a long time ago, in my childhood, when I stopped being a girl and became a princess; in exchange for which, my mother said, pointing her finger at me, you will have to learn to love God—and she would point at the sky—and to love your country, not only the country of your birth—and she would point to the window—but also, she said, the Angel of Belgium—and again she pointed at the sky—whom God, someday, will place at your feet—and she pointed at the floor; and so that you will succeed, she said, you will first learn to know the color of your blood—and she pointed at her blue veins on her wrist with her white, long and thin finger. I learned from that day that I carried the blood of Saint Louis and of your great-grandmother, the Empress Maria Theresa of Austria, and of Louis XIII of France. The same blood, Louis Philippe told me, which covered the scaffold in the Place de la Révolution the day that my father, your great-grandfather, who was called Philippe Égalité, was beheaded. And if he was the family traitor, you must realize, my little Charlotte, in return, he not only died like a man and as a prince, dressed in his best bottle-green frockcoat, his recently starched, piqué waistcoat, his freshly polished patent leather boots, but also as the great glutton that he was his whole life, because he refused to go to the guillotine before stuffing down a dozen oysters washed down with a good claret, my grandfather said, eyes shining with both tears and laughter. And he told me about his exile in Switzerland where he taught mathematics and in London where he bought the cheapest clothes he could find, my poor grandfather who left behind seven hundred thousand francs in a dresser drawer and ran out of the Tuileries via the tunnel that Napoleon the Great had built so that the King of Rome could escape if the Revolution came. My grandfather who, sitting on the throne that the mob had defiled, put me on his lap and told me that no one had been so many things before being king: a soldier, an immigrant, a republican, a teacher, a traveler to America, and a Sicilian nobleman, Prince of Orléans, and a British knight. He didn't know then

179

that, having ignored my grandmother when she begged him not to abdicate, to die like a king, he would be a nobody, a nothing, *after* being a king. Poor Louis Philippe. He would have been better off beheaded like his father Philippe Égalité, or Charles I of England. He would have been better off shot to death like you, Maximilian.

Tell me, where did those springs go? Those springs, tall and clean, like the Adriatic sky? Those springs who knelt down to kiss the tip of the whitest table linens and who, furious and happy, poured their thick sap into my mouth when I was a child, Maximilian, when I was just a child who embroidered pillows with her dreams of greatness, with fables and happy surprises, with tears and fairy tales? That child who promised God, on my mother Louise Marie of Orléans's life, that I would sew my eyes to the clouds, keep them always looking up at the clouds? I was a princess and hadn't met you yet. My saliva was chaste. I baptized my purest thoughts with it. You hadn't arrived yet, Maximilian, on the yacht *La Reine Hortense*, to take me riding in the fields of Waterloo or to escort me to the Opera to see *I Vespri Siciliani*. I had never looked lovingly at any man other than my father and my brothers. In those days I was a serious and dour princess, silent, without tears; words barely grazed my lips with the tips of their wings. I was a chaste princess with her clothes-pressers who ironed in the palace edicts, her laundresses who washed out her desires in the green canals of Bruges. When I woke up in the morning, all the bells in Brussels woke as well— those same carillons, Maximilian, that now hang from my neck and choke me with anxiety and deafen me because they ring in unison at all hours of the day, at all the hours of my life. Oh, Maximilian, the crown that you gave me melted on my forehead and its golden rivulets burned and singed my breasts and my womb. Oh, Max, Max, my dear, my lovely Max. Where are those dragon-breath summers, those days pretending to be as wide as the world, burning my cheeks with their flames when I was a child who played with the wind, whose hair waved in the wind and who ran after the wind, when I was a princess and prayed every day to Saint Hubert, patron of the hunters of Ardennes, so that he would never let me fall into temptation or get caught in the burning webs of desire. Maximilian, when I was just a child and insolence still hadn't settled in my heart, and the shadow of desire hadn't burned my thighs, when all I needed to do was to raise a finger and my lackeys would tear live birds off the trees at Laeken, and my ladies-in-waiting would bathe me in oatmeal water and helio-trope paste, and dry me with white lily leaves and the wings of larks.

I was slow to learn pride and shame. I could forgive Philippe Égalité for voting to execute Louis XVI, since he paid with his own head; and my other great-grandfather, Ferdinand I of the Two Sicilies too, who liked to hawk fish at the markets and who threw fistfuls of spaghetti to the beggars every Holy Thursday from his box at the Theater of St. Charles with his own hands—at least he had the wit or the good luck to marry my great-grandmother Marie Caroline, who turned Naples into one of the most culture-rich cities in Europe. But how could I forgive that pig for cheating on her so many years with that whore whom he gave the title of Duchess of Floridia? How can I forget, tell me, Maximilian, all of my father's transgressions? How can I forgive the man whom I adored my whole life, that Nestor of rulers, my beloved Leopich, Queen Victoria's mentor, the only monarch in all of Continental Europe who kept his people united during the '48 revolutions—that beautiful, intelligent, and handsome Leopold I of Belgium, a Lutheran, a moralist; tell me, how can I forgive him for deceiving my sainted mother, the most beloved queen of the Belgians when she was alive and most mourned when she died, as demonstrated by her peasants and her weavers, her soldiers, all of the people who bowed before the funeral train that bore her remains during the entire journey from Ostend to Brussels, who blessed the memory and prayed for the soul of the guardian angel of Flanders and Brabant, Limburg and Hainaut, Namur and Ampères, Liège and Luxembourg? How could I forgive my father for tainting the Saxe-Coburg blood of which he was always so proud with the peasant blood of the harlot Arcadie von Eppinghoven, and for giving me so many bastard siblings? How can I, Maximilian?

I know every corner of Bouchout. I knew every corner of Miramare and of Terveuren, of Laeken, and at times I think that my life has been nothing but an eternal roaming through houses and castles, rooms and hallways; and that it was there, in their solitude, in those stairways and dark corners—and from the mouth of ghosts, not the lips of my nurses, teachers and governesses—that I learned not only what mathematics and geography couldn't teach me (nor history, Maximilian, that history which my parents, my aunts and uncles, my cousin Victoria and Prince Albert, full of immortal names and battles that had drenched all of the European dynasties in glory; those dynasties whose blood fed that noble and burning spring that my father didn't respect and that I swore to keep pure, clean, and pristine, same as my conscience and my doll house), but that my father was a liar, that his blood had been dirty from the beginning of time. And I didn't believe this because I put no stock in the foolish lies of those who said that a so-called Maria Stella was the true daughter of Philippe Égalité; that my grandfather, Louis Philippe, was really the son of a Tuscan police chief. Those were nothing but stupid stories. If they'd been true, I wouldn't have had Orléans blood running through my veins. No, I believed that my father was tainted because one day, at Castle Chaumont, I saw the ghost of Henri II of France make love to his mistress, Diane de Poitiers, under the drawbridge, although I kept quiet about it; and because another time I saw the ghost of Jacob I of England in Edinburgh Castle, lying nude on the tile floor, shouting to the Duke of Buckingham to fornicate with him but I did not tell my cousin Victoria because she would have called me a madwoman. And because one night, in the temporary vault at the Escorial, I saw Don Carlos of Austria sucking at the breasts of Isabel de Valois, his stepmother. I didn't say a word because I understood that those were my ghosts, that they only appeared to me and that no one but me could exorcise them, and only if I could make myself forget the liquid that had begun to seep out from between my thighs, that liquid which could only be a corrupt and foul-smelling blood, foul as the blood of Louis XIV's brother, Philippe of Orléans, who left his wife in the amethyst baths at Schwetzingen Palace to make love to the Chevalier de Lorraine, who poisoned his first wife, Henriette Stuart. Yes, the same liquid ran out from between my thighs for the first time the afternoon that I rode my cousin Minette's hobbyhorse at Claremont because I felt like a child and I liked to play at it and I thought suddenly that I was urinating but I was not. When my grandmother saw the dark red, almost black crust on the hobbyhorse's back, she cleaned it herself with a wet cloth. She asked me to wrap my arms around her neck and she muttered, "My poor Charlotte, my poor Bijou, you are no longer a child nor will you be one again." And if I bathed daily with cold water and slept with my hands under my cheeks and I did not put my hands under the sheets and said the Nicene Creed—I believe in God Almighty, who is in Heaven and Earth—over and over again until I fell asleep with exhaustion, I would frighten off those specters of disgusting kings and adulterous queens and I would never again dream—awake or asleep—about any of the palaces and castles and houses that I knew or would know in my dreams, about those beasts with two backs, those monsters, naked and panting, sweating and foaming at the mouth, that rolled around their purple and ermine beds, penetrating each other with their tumescent and slimy organs. Only thus would I be able to dream of angels again.

But you came, Maximilian, you came one day in the yacht *La Reine Hortense* that Louis Napoleon had lent you. You recited Victor Hugo's ode to the Great Corsican and your eyes filled with tears when you thought of the defeat of that man who might be your grandfather, and you knew it, although no one mentioned it to you. I told you that I also had been moved to tears when I saw the flag that Wellington had taken from the French troops displayed at Windsor Castle, the flag he had taken from my dear soldiers, in their red trousers, from the army that in Austerlitz defeated two empires and that in Jena, in six hours, humiliated a whole kingdom. You came and brought youth and joy, and I knew that Laeken and my life had a new light in it that you sparked with your good humor and your smiles. You spoke of Paris—remember?—and you swore that if Paris was a city of emperors, only Vienna, absolutely only Vienna, was the imperial city par excellence. And you stated that the protocol of the Tuileries was one of interlopers and you told my father Leopold that, despite the parade in the Champ de Mars, which had been splendid, the women's dresses at Louis Napoleon's court were outrageously indecent, and that Prince Plon-Plon, the Emperor's cousin, had the look of a secondhand Italian opera bass. You can't imagine, Maximilian, how I thank you for making fun of the court and the pretentiousness of the man who robbed my grandfather, Louis Philippe, of his throne. I thanked you with my laughter, remember? I almost burst out laughing when Papa Leopich asked you what the Countess of Castiglione was like and you replied that, although she was very beautiful, she looked like a Regency ballerina raised from the grave. How grateful I was to you, Maximilian, how grateful that when you arrived in Brussels in your white Austrian fleet admiral's uniform, you brought with you all the splendor and magic of Vienna to the gloomy Laeken Palace. You brought in your wake a flock of lackeys who chewed lily petals to freshen their breath; with you came the horsemen of the Spanish Riding School of Vienna, in their tricorn hats, their maroon riding coats, and high black boots, the tails and manes of their stallions braided in gold, stepping to the rhythm of the *Radetzky* and *Turkish* marches. In your eyes fluttered the blue violets that grow at the base of the Tyrolean Alps; in your voice sang the hallelujahs of the bells of St. Stephan's Cathedral, and in your arms, oh Maximilian . . . do you remember the *Langaus*, that whirlwind waltz popular in Viennese ballrooms, that went faster and faster, until the couples fell exhausted to the floor and old men died of apoplexy? . . . In your arms, Maximilian, I fell into an even more intoxicating and dizzying whirlwind, a dark, dense, warm whirlwind that took away my childhood and my innocence because those arms and those eyes, that swollen Habsburg lip that I wanted to bite, and those long, strong hands that I wanted to feel around my waist, feel lifting me to the sky—these weren't the eyes, nor the mouth, nor the hands of an angel but of a man. No, Max, the whirlwind waltz didn't kill me, I didn't collapse onto the floor at Laeken, blinded by that vortex of light, by the splinters and crystal bolts that whirled around us faster and faster, as though I were motionless in your arms and the whole world and the sun and the universe were whirling around us. I almost, almost died of love and desire, of tenderness and lust for you that night when I was alone, in my room, and my hands crawled under the sheets. I wanted to ask you to disappear with me into the Laeken gardens, to run with you and hide in a Tivoli circle, to undress and make love under the willows, to crown you with myrtles and kisses, to pull out the grass with my teeth and spread it on your body, to blend it with the hair on your chest and your belly. I wanted to swim with you nude on the beaches of Blankenberghe and to lie afterwards on the shore on a moonless night. There, under the stars, I wanted to lick you all over, like a lamb thirsty for love and salt, to lick your stomach and your thighs and fill my mouth with your penis and to feel how you grew inside me, how you throbbed, how you emptied out quickly into my throat, and how your sour, warm milk ran down to my belly. That night, alone in my room, I asked God and my mother for forgiveness, I begged them to wrench these base desires from my flesh and my mind, and I even tried to do it by flagellating myself, I spent the night on my knees, I clawed my flaming breasts and my moist cunt until they bled. Then, then, poor pitiful me, Maximilian, I thought of you again and I knew that I was making love to you and that the more I scratched at my thighs, my breasts, and my vagina, the more you loved me, the more I loved you: I saw you on my bed, naked, still, immensely pale, your black eyes wide open; I smeared my blood onto you, on your skin, to lick it back off again. Oh, Maximilian, what I would have given to be in Querétaro, beside you, at Las Campanas Hill, and to cleanse your wounds with my tongue, with my saliva, to wash your body and your bowels. I would have rinsed your intestines in orange water. Now I'll macerate your body in wine, I'll bathe your eyes in collyrium; I'll order Baron Lago and Princess Salm-Salm to give me your arms so that I can wave them in the wind. I'll tell our friend López to give me your hands so that I can put them on my breasts. I'll ask Benito Juárez to give me your skin so I can live inside it, to put your eyelids on me so that I can dip into your dreams. Oh, Maximilian, how I would have loved you!

If I'd only known then what a hypocrite and liar you were. If I'd found out that in your letters to Vienna you said that my brother, the Duke of Brabant, was Machiavellian. And as for my father, whom you called the matchmaker of Europe, you said that you abhorred his paternalistic air of superiority, and that his endless pontifications and advice bored you senseless. If I'd know that at Tournai, Ghent, and Brussels you looked sadly at the remains of the former Austrian subject state, and it hurt you to think that such a fertile nation, with its grand, noble, and industrious cities, was no longer under the power of the Habsburg Empire. If they had said that you, you who had described the guests at the Tuileries Ball as burlesque characters and libertines, later faulted the Epiphany Day Ball that we offered at Laeken because, as you wrote, cynically, to Franz Joseph, the Belgian nobility had deigned to socialize with tailors, cobblers, and retired English shopkeepers. If only some gossipers had told me—although I would have never believed it at the time—that the man who claimed to love me so much never once mentioned his beloved Charlotte in his letters to Vienna—Charlotte, the greatest love of his life.

Because you lied, Maximilian, because you were such a hypocrite, because you boasted of things you did not actually possess—a noble, generous, and universal spirit, for instance, and a heart capable of loving all the people on Earth—God punished you and sent you to Mexico so that you would choke on your lies. Tell me, Maximilian, yes, you, Maximilian Ferdinand of Habsburg, stooge of Hidalgo and Eugenia de Montijo, marionette of Gutiérrez Estrada and Father Fischer, puppet of Napoleon III, tell me, how, when, why, and whence did your love of Mexican Indians originate? You who were offered the throne of Greece, who replied that you would never be the ruler of those cretinous, depraved people; you who said that the Italians were degenerate descendants of Rome, because what attracted you most about Italy was not her people but the Neapolitan palm trees with their luxurious crowns; just as what attracted you to beggars and lepers was their picturesque appearance—like the sweet Madonnas of Raphael Sanzio and the bronze lamp of Galileo Galilei—not their sores or their poverty; you who in Lisbon marveled at the homeliness of the women but were spellbound by the verdigris plumage of the parrots and the breast marks of the toucans at the Palácio das Necessidades aviary; you, who in Madeira were repelled by the islanders' faces but were seduced by the geraniums with their dense umbels and the wines made from Malvasian grapes, and the palanquin rides through the sunny streets of Funchal, scented by the perfume of Amelia de Braganza. Tell me, Maximilian, who said that Algiers and Albania deserved not only different rulers but different populations—because while you were visiting those countries you were only interested in eating roasted gazelle surrounded by dwarves and buffoons, and hunting ostriches, dressed as a Bedouin, on camel-back; who, in the Canaries Islands, was more interested in the mummies of the Guanche kings shrouded in goatskins, the volcanic rock, and the four-thousand-year-old dragon tree in Tenerife than in its living people; who was more fascinated by the seashells and snails that you collected on the beaches and the lilac-tinged white flowers of the bitter pumpkins in Saint Vincent than its women, whom you described as black scarabs, and their children, whom you called little chocolate-colored beasts; who wrote in your memoirs that in Bahia one didn't see Ceres and Pomona walking the streets but only mulattoes and blacks with horrendous faces not demonstrating a single drop of intelligence; because you preferred to pay attention to the tarantulas in Bahia, the giant fireflies, the macaque whiskers that hung from tree branches, the lianas that were like garlands of woven roses, and the casuarina that resembled a huge witch's broomstick. Maximilian, what happened to you in Mexico? What made the love of an exotic land flow inside you, a land so foreign to your customs, so alien to the color of your skin? A land so strange to the immaculate Germanity that Rudolf of Habsburg exalted after he defeated the King of Bohemia? That Germanity of which you boasted in your diary and that so concerned Maria Theresa when she told my great-grandmother Marie Caroline never to stop being a German at heart, even if she had to pretend to be a Neapolitan. Tell me, what potion did they give you in Miramare, Maximilian, to make you abandon your most sacred ties to the land where your ancestors were buried and where you spent the loveliest years of your childhood and adolescence to go to the other side of the world to rule a nation of thieving priests and mangy peasants, a nation of corrupt military men and politicians, of inquisitors and reactionaries, or Indians in feathers and illiterate peasants who wear necklaces made of coyote teeth, who eat cactus leaves and bull testicles? Did they make you drink a *toloache* tea? Or did they give you a wine made from *ololiuque*, that herb that makes your eyes pop out? Tell me, Max, what potion, what cordial did you take in the town of Dolores that made you so willing to expose yourself to ridicule, dressed as a Mexican *charro*, celebrating with a nation that wasn't your own on the anniversary of its emancipation from the greatest empire the House of Austria ever had, your House, Maximilian, the House that God spread over the Earth and exalted it in order to exalt His Church? And in Querétaro, when you walked on the Plaza de la Cruz dictating the new tenets of courtly behavior to Blasio, and when you put your dog Baby on your lap and played whist with Prince Salm-Salm, tell me, what spell, what charm had been cast on you to make you think you could ever return to Mexico City alive? What made you imagine that, just like Count Radbot, who built Habichtsburg Castle without walls—the castle that gave its name to the Habsburgs—because he knew that overnight, with only one command, his subjects would form the best walls possible, walls of human flesh, alive and vibrant—what made you think, tell me, that those Indians and peasants would flock, by the hundreds and the thousands, to Querétaro, to offer their love and loyalty to you, a foreign prince, to protect your white body with their brown ones, to spill their Mexican blood so that not a drop of Aryan blood would be shed, that same Germanic blood that coursed through the veins of the king who founded your dynasty under a red cloud shaped like a cross that spread its wings over the Cathedral of Aquisgrán on the day of his coronation? What elixir, what poison did you drink in the eyes of Concepción Sedano that kept you from seeing that she also was an Indian, alien to your race? What curse were you the victim of, which made you refuse to see that there were no gods in the streets of Mexico but fifty thousand beggars; that the Apollo of Belvedere never set foot on those streets—only Indians with dark skin and black, bright eyes like those of a deer, those eyes that watched us from the balconies of the National Palace, that still spy on me through the keyholes and the windows of Bouchout, that appear at the bottom of the washbasins and flutter through my room at night like tiny obsidian suns? What drug did you take, Maximilian, that made you blind to the fact that, just as in Brazil, where the barefoot negresses who dressed in European clothes looked—I'm quoting you—like circus monkeys, the Mexican court ladies, in their gigantic balloon-like crinolines, were like Eskimos protruding from their igloos, dripping with curtain scraps and tinsel fringe? What kept you from realizing that the people who refused to respond to your call after you responded to theirs could only be called perverse and dishonest? Was it nothing more than hypocrisy and lies?

To die, of course, is easier than to keep on living. To be dead and glorious is better than being alive and entombed in oblivion. For that reason, for that reason alone, and to throw your own lies in your face, I travel back in time every night. Alone in my dark bedroom I see you, time and time again, a thousand times, succumb silently to the bullets of a silent barrage; I've seen you kiss the dust of the hill and to open your mouth without saying a word; I've seen the officer who points to your heart with the tip of his sword, and the soldier who gives you the silent coup de grâce, and the flames that rise from your frock-coat. Silently and alone, every night—not a leaf moving in the garden poplars, not a log crackling in the castle hearths, not a ripple disturbing the water in the moat—alone in my darkened room, time and time again, a thousand times, I've reversed time and seen you open your eyes and come back to life and get up; I've seen the bullets leave your body and return to their rifle barrels; I've seen the blood evaporate from your chest, and the hole from the last shot in your scapular close up. I've seen the wings of your beard come back together, and the firing squad return the twenty gold pesos that you gave each man so that they wouldn't shoot you in the face. Oh Max, if only you could see how amusing it is to undo time, to undo the foothills of Las Campanas Hill, to see you jump back into the black carriage, to see General Mejía's wife run back-ward, her baby in her arms; and if you could see your chef Tüdös, how shocked he looks, since he can't understand, could never understand, no matter how many times I explained it to him, he could never understand that time is going backwards now, could never understand how it could be possible that you've returned from the dead to reenter your cell in the Teresitas Convent, and how the four lamplighters have come back, carrying lit candles, your field cot, the ebony table on which you read the *History of the Italians* by César Cantú and wrote to Father Fischer so that he would send you some cases of Burgundy wine from your Mexico City cellar. The glass of sugar water, covered with a cloth to keep the flies off, that Dr. Basch prescribed for your diarrhea, reap-pears, as does the crown of thorns that you found under a lemon tree in the con-vent garden, and the silver crucifix and basin that those thieves stole from you.

The cinema was invented, Maximilian. The messenger came and brought me a light-and-shadow camera, and a long, silver, celluloid ribbon. He was Char-lie Chaplin and I went with him to California to dig up gold nuggets the size of Hesperides apples, to eat grilled filet of shoe leather. Another time he was Ru-dolf Valentino and I made love to him to the sound of fifes and tambourines on a white gazelle skin laid on the sands of the same desert where your friend Yusuf—remember that he offered you roasted lamb cutlets as though offering you a delicate flower?—put up his tent. Are you listening, Maximilian? But if I could really reverse time, as though time were a celluloid reel being wound backwards, don't think for a moment that I would want to see you walking on the streets of Algiers again, flirting with the Loretas and the Grisettes in their rose-colored kid gloves, scented with patchouli; or sitting in the Marabout that belonged to my uncle Aumale, the Viceroy of Algeria, under the stained-glass ceiling, smoking a hookah, under the ostrich eggs painted with verses from the Koran that hung from the ceiling to keep out the evil eye. Don't think that I would, Maximilian.

The cinema was invented and it is as though all of our photographs and daguerreotypes and paintings have come to life. As though all the Austrian, French, and Mexican flags in Cesare dell'Acqua's painting, in which he immortalized our departure from Miramare toward Mexico, started to wave in the wind, and the oarsman began to paddle, and my heart began to beat again, overexcited. It's as though the waters of the Adriatic, so like a mirror on that day, and which barely moved under the *Novara*'s sails, were swollen now by a recent wind, gusting softly and coldly, voluptuously, brimming with omens and azure promises. Or as though our little Prince Agustín de Iturbide were winking, or smiling, or flashing his teeth at us from that photograph that was stolen from me and taken to Hardegg Castle. Poor Agustín. After becoming the heir to an empire greater than France, England, and Spain together, he died old and alone—first becoming a Spanish professor at Georgetown University, and then a monk. Did you know that, Max?

But I never want to see you in Cuernavaca again. I don't want to see you at the bullring in Seville, throwing purses full of silver coins at the matador's feet. I don't want to see you at Sydenham Crystal Palace arm in arm with Queen Victoria. I only want to see you and to have you forever in your cell at Las Teresitas Convent, in your cell with your cot and your chamber pot. If it's necessary for you to jump out of your pine box, that coffin for a smaller man, which your feet stuck out of—if that's what has to happen in order to make time go backwards and for me to get you back in your cell, locked up, then jump Maximilian! Run back to the carriage, to the convent! And if, to undo the years, the milk must return to the breasts of Miramón's wife, and life must return to General Mejía, then by all means let them return, Maximilian. But Tüdös's teeth, which were knocked out by a bullet at Calpulalpan's, will not return to his mouth; the soldiers of the Empire who were knifed by Galeana's hunters at the foot of San Gregorio Hill will never rise again; nor will the clear and cold water that you used for washing your face every morning run back through the aqueduct arches on the Chinese Hill—because all of this occurred before they locked you up in your cell at Las Teresitas. It's there, there in that cell and nowhere else, neither before or after, that I want to keep you frozen, so that you'll never escape from me again. In your cell, with your crucifix and your spyglass and your mirror and your brushes and your scissors.

Or perhaps you think that, if it were up to me to undo these last sixty years of humiliation and being forgotten, those who are to blame for my isolation and madness would be allowed to relive the most beautiful times of their lives? No, Maximilian. If Colonel López imagines that I would like to see him beside me again, on his horse, on the way from Veracruz to Córdoba, an orchid bouquet in his hands, tall like one of those Aryan gods whose absence so disappointed you in Brazil: handsome and blond among the crowd of Africans from Sudan, Nubia, and Abyssinia that the Egyptian Khedive sent us to Mexico . . . tell him, when you see him, that he is very wrong. I only want to picture him—and forever—in his last days, when he was dying slowly from a rabies bite, of suffocation and thirst, choking in his own fear and spit. I don't want to see Benito Juárez entering Mexico City in triumph, president and dictator again. I prefer to see him on his deathbed, his chest bare, an endless stream of boiling water pouring onto it. And, as you can imagine, I hardly want to see Eugénie or Louis Napoleon during their own moments of glory. I don't want to picture her swathed in a cloud of verbena perfume, shopping in the Lumière Salon of the House of Worth, crowned with the wreath of violets that Louis Napoleon gave her in Compiègne. I want her forever in Zululand, destroyed by the memory of the imperial prince who, at three, in a grenadier's hat and coat (but also in a white skirt, because they still dressed him like a girl) reviewed the French troops victorious in Magenta and Solferino; I want to see her furious because that stupid Victoria denied her the pleasure of touching, eating, and kissing the dirt where her Woolwich cadet, who never became Napoleon IV, finally succumbed. And I refuse to see Louis Napoleon before the French National Assembly, the last will and testament of Napoleon I in one hand and in the other the sword of Austerlitz. I refuse to see him in his triumphant visit to the Sahara, as twenty thousand Arabs cheered him and cleaned his boots with their mustaches. No, I shall always imagine him in Chislehurst; on the wooden horse that he was forced to mount every day so that he would not became unaccustomed to riding. I want to keep him pale, trembling, his cheeks rouged as they were in Sedan, overcome by the pains of his hypertrophied prostate and gallstones, while on the other side of the Canal, in his beloved France, the marble crosses, angels and garlands of Père Lachaise Cemetery were spattered with the blood of the one hundred and forty commoners that the troops of Thiers and Mac-Mahon executed at the Communards' Wall, while Leon Gambetta, the man who had proclaimed the Third Republic at the Hôtel de Ville fled, that coward, in a hot air balloon over the skies of Paris.

No, I shall never tire of repeating, a thousand times, over and over: I want you in your cell, as I told you before, prostrate on your iron cot, eaten up by the bedbugs that—in their blood, and in your blood as well, bore the name that you borrowed from the city of Querétaro. Or else, I want you pacing endlessly and measuring the infinite and devastating distance between the four walls of your prison, the smallest room you ever had to sleep in, the smallest room you'd ever bared your nightmares to, the smallest room you'd ever filled with the pestilent vapors of your green and liquid shit that dysentery made you leak out five, seven, ten times a day into your chamber pot. That's where I want you, sitting on your chamber pot. You'll see Tüdös's fear, his expression of surprise when he realizes that I've made time go backwards, back until the last days in Querétaro when, with no paprika, salt, or oregano, and no wine, he prepared a pie made with cat meat for his Emperor and for General Miramón; and he made donkey-liver sausages for General Mejía and Prince Salm-Salm. Just like during the Siege of Puebla (this time it was your turn to be besieged, my poor Max), the mattresses had all disappeared because their stuffing was being used to feed the horses; and then the horses were gone because they'd been slaughtered to feed the officers; and then the corpses were gone because the dogs ate them; and the dogs were gone because the soldiers had eaten *them*; and the bronze medals for your Mexican hunters were gone as was the bronze intended for cannons; there were no heroes nor cannons to protect you from Escobedo's troops; the sulfide for your gunpowder was gone and there were no fireworks or rockets to celebrate the triumph of the Battle of the Cimatario; and then the doors and windows disappeared because you put a tax on them just as Santa Anna had. So, when you rode through the streets in your black carriage, on the most beautiful day of the year, preceded by the Battalion of the Supreme Powers, there was no one to cheer you, Maximilian, or say God Bless You, from the doors and windows in Querétaro—and since the lead had disappeared from all the printing presses when you needed it melted down to make more ammunition, there was no one able to print your story, or post flyers on the walls of the City of Querétaro calling Juárez a murderer. The bells too had disappeared when you melted them down to forge more cannons so, on the most beautiful morning of the most beautiful day of the year, when you went by in your pine box, your feet sticking out, along those same silent streets, with their blind doors and windows, Maximilian, on the day you died, there weren't even any bells to toll for you in the City of Querétaro.

VIII
"MUST I LEAVE MY GOLDEN CRIB FOREVER?"
1863–64

1. Cittadella Accepts the Throne of Tours

Louis Napoleon sent Bazaine a letter asking him to confirm the rumor that Juárez had bribed Jules Favre. Richard Metternich wrote the Austrian Minister of Foreign Affairs, Count Rechberg, to tell him Empress Eugénie hated Miramón and that the intervention was doomed to fail. From Madrid, Don Francisco de Paula y Arrangóiz wrote to his namesake Don Francisco Javier Miranda telling him that Queen Isabella of Spain preferred a Republic headed by Juárez to an Empire under the Archduke. The Archduke wrote Louis Napoleon congratulating him on the fall of Puebla and the taking of Mexico City. From the Isle of Saint Thomas, General Santa Anna wrote Gutiérrez Estrada to offer his services to the Empire. In a letter from Mexico, Lieutenant Colonel Loizillon told Hortense Cornu that he had broken the mouthpiece of his amber pipe and that a Mexican had shown him how to dissolve the pieces in a mixture of oil and terebinth essence in order to rebuild it. Gutiérrez Estrada received a letter from Miramare in which Ferdinand Maximilian assured him that he had always had a deep interest in the fate of Mr. Gutiérrez Estrada's beautiful country, but that he couldn't help with the salvation of Mexico unless a national public referendum showed, beyond any doubt, the people's desire to place him in the throne. From Chantilly, the Mexican General Adrian Woll d'Ohm wrote his friend, Colonel Pepe González in Havana, in reference to Leonardo Márquez, that the truth was, "In our wretched Mexico, terror gives prestige," and not to forget to send him a lottery ticket every month. From the Palacio de Buenavista, General Bazaine wrote to the French Minister of Defense, Marshal Randon, to inform him that General Castagny's division had successfully occupied the cities of León and Lagos. In Brussels, King Leopold received a letter from his daughter Carlota in which she complained that the Mexican Clerical Party was very reactionary. At Miramare, Carlota received a letter from her adored Papa Leopich in which he reminded her that once a person had gained the trust of such a party, it always remains faithful to that person, unlike the Voltaireans. "The Spanish and Criollo Voltairenism was a sad thing." From Carlsbad, Prince Carl von Solms received a letter in which the former *chargé d'affaires* of England in Mexico, Sir Charles Wyke, told him he hoped the Archduke would not put his head into that wasp's nest. Louis Napoleon wrote his new Ambassador in Mexico, Montholon, recommending to him that he negotiate the project with the Regency of turning the State of Sonora into a French Protectorate. Maximilian sent Richard Metternich a letter to be delivered to Louis Napoleon in which he praised the genius of the French Emperor and stated that his acceptance of the throne of Mexico was subject to the support of England. In Miramare, the Archduke received a letter from the American Commodore Maury in which he offered his services as Grand Admiral of the Mexican Imperial Fleet. From London, Sir Charles Wyke wrote to Stephan Herzfeld about the audience the French Emperor had granted him in Paris and how he had told the Emperor that, given the circumstances, Maximilian would not be welcome in Mexico. In a letter in which he called Maximilian "Sire" and "Your Majesty," General Almonte assured him that by the time he read the letter, six million Mexicans would have voted for a monarchy. From Compiègne, Eugénie wrote Carlota to tell her that, unfortunately, in that beautiful country—Mexico—there were nothing but republicans who burned to satisfy their hatred and resentment. Maximilian wrote a letter to Pio Nono that His Holiness considered inappropriate because in it the Archduke dared refer to the Mexican Church as corrupt. From London, the former correspondent of the *Times* in Mexico, Charles Bourdillon, wrote to Maximilian telling him the English banks were not too eager to participate in the financing of the venture. Also from London, Karl Marx wrote a letter to Frederick Engels, written half in English and half in German, in which he told him that Louis Napoleon was not only very hesitant but also "in a very ugly dilemma with his own army," and that between Mexico and his genuflections before the Czar, which Boustrapa (instigated by Pam) was performing in *Le Moniteur*, he could easily bust his head. "Pam" was Palmerston, and "Boustrapa" was Marx's nickname for Louis Napoleon, formed with the French names of the three cities in which he had tried to gain power: Boulogne, Strasbourg, and Paris. And if at their castle in Nantes, a certain Cittadella and Blanche received a letter from a certain Julien that said, for instance, "Cittadella has already had the opportunity to verify that, guided by Divine Providence, and without Bourdeaux and Rouen's help, Metz's army has conquered Tours, to the grief of the conservatives and jubilation of the liberals; what's needed now, however, is—besides confirming the support of Orléans—for Jean to pressure his Legislative Branch to obtain new testimonies devoted to the enterprise, to convince Adolph to deliver the cotton," this meant that, at their castle at Miramare, a certain Maximilian and Carlota were actually receiving a letter from a certain Gutiérrez Estrada, written according to one of the secret codes invented by the Mexican to communicate with the Archduke, who in order to decipher it had to substitute some names for others in accordance with a cipher by which Nantes was Miramare, Cittadella was his Imperial Highness Maximilian, Blanche was her Imperial Highness Carlota, and Julien was the very same Gutiérrez Estrada—and Bordeaux was England; Rouen, Spain; Metz, France; Tours, Mexico; the conservatives, liberals; the liberals, conservatives; Orléans, Vienna; Jean, the French Emperor; testimonies, money; Adolphe, the House of Rothschild; cotton, the loan—and, finally, Louis, Paul, Charles, Julie, Daniel, Richard, Le Havre, which were, respectively, Eugénie, the Pope, Almonte, Franz Joseph, Miramón, Santa Anna, and Veracruz—though Divine Providence was always just Divine Providence, which like God and all His saints always appeared in Julien's letters under their own names and attributes.

Dozens, hundreds of letters like this traveled from one place to the other in Europe and across the Atlantic from Europe to America. During 1862 and 1863 and in early 1864, letters came and went: some by ordinary mail, by donkey, by stagecoach, via the ships of the "Royal Mail Steam Packet Company," and others by special delivery—some innocent, others lies, secret, written in code, interminable, optimistic—in the hands of private or royal messengers. And because even this wasn't sufficient, everyone was always traveling from one place to another to give his opinion, his advice, and his warnings. Maximilian sent his former *valet-de-chambre* and now his private secretary, Sebastian Schertzenlechner, to Rome to ask the Pope for his advice, and at the same time give him a model of the funeral chapel of Jerusalem carved from the wood of an olive tree taken—of course—from the Mount of Olives itself. King Leopold sent the former Belgian Minister in Mexico, Monsieur Kint de Roodenbeck, a specialist in writing reports that pleased his superiors, to talk with his son-in-law about the viability of a monarchy in Mexico. Louis Adolphe Thiers, the historian, said it was all madness. Carlota had the uniforms for her future imperial mansion made in Brussels. Maximilian complained that while the relatives of his wife, the Coburgs, were taking throne after throne, the Habsburg family had recently lost two: Modena and Tuscany. The Mexican Archbishop Pelagio Antonio de Labastida y Dávalos asked Louis Napoleon's permission to have Marshall Forey travel to Miramare to talk to the Archduke, and Napoleon denied it. At Miramare, the Archduke read a communiqué from the American Consul in Trieste, Richard Hildreth, in which he assured him that Mexicans had a terrible and congenital aversion to kings and aristocrats. Monsieur Kint de Roodenbeck went to Paris with the mission of making it clear to Napoleon that the Archduke was willing to accept the throne as soon as the cities of Morelia, Querétaro, Guanajuato, and Guadalajara declared themselves in favor of the Empire. Louis Napoleon told Metternich that in Mexico it wouldn't be advisable to resort to a universal suffrage. Santa Anna wrote the Archduke Maximilian assuring him that not only one party, but also the great majority of the Mexican people yearned for the restoration of Moctezuma's Empire. Sir Charles Wyke said the Archduke Maximilian would be elected by a majority in places inhabited by two Indians and a monkey. King Leopold warned his son-in-law, *Cher* Max, that those who knew the inhabitants of Mexico well unfortunately held them in very low esteem. Señor Arrangóiz traveled to Miramare to tell the Archduke that though it was true the best form of government for Mexico was a monarchy, it shouldn't be a permanent one. Louis Napoleon sided against the idea of returning the confiscated properties to the Church; Maximilian wrote the Regency Council instructing them not to make a decision regarding the Church properties until his arrival. Spain's Queen Isabella bemoaned the fact that her daughter had not been considered as a possible Empress of Mexico. And just like the Duke of Brabant had previously written his sister, Carlota, in Miramare, that if he had a son old enough, he would try to make him King of Mexico, Eugénie told the American Ambassador to France—who assured her that in his country, the North would be the victor and everything would turn out badly for the Archduke—that if Mexico weren't so far away, and Loulou, the Imperial Prince, were not a child, she would lead the French army personally, and write one of the most beautiful pages of the history of their century with her sword. The Ambassador told her to thank God—both for Mexico being so far away, and because

Loulou was still a child. Señor Arrangóiz traveled to London, as Maximilian's representative, charged with convincing the English Court of St. James's that the Archduke was far from being a fanatic in religious matters. Maximilian invited Sir Charles Wyke to Miramare for talks, but on Lord Russell's orders, Sir Charles declined this invitation. General James Williams of the Confederate Army wrote the Archduke—who in his reply asked the General to convey his greetings in turn to the President of the Confederacy, Jefferson Davis, and to tell him that he was fond of the South. In a letter to Maximilian, Louis Napoleon told him that what Mexico needed was a liberal dictatorship, because a country beset with anarchy couldn't be rebuilt with anything more than a bunch of parliamentary freedoms. Cittadella, that is Maximilian, and Julien, that is Gutiérrez Estrada, met secretly in Merano; there, Cittadella, who was traveling incognito, told Julien that he wasn't demanding voter approval of all citizens of Tours, that is of Mexico, but that the vote of only a fraction of the population of the capital would be insufficient. Julien was still very excited, as evidenced by a comparison he made known to Count Mülinen between Mexico and Austria; for him, both were "like a maiden waiting honorably to be married." Though, on the other hand, Julien was disillusioned because Richard, that is Santa Anna, whom he had proposed as the Regent of Mexico, that is Tours, had betrayed them, and along with his son declared himself against the invading army of Metz, that is France. Finally, Julien was quite alarmed, because in France, which is to say Metz, there was already talk of there being another candidate to the throne, Prince Joinville, Carlota's uncle; this move would surely calm the feared Orléanist opposition in the parliament of Metz. (In this context, "Orléanist" did in fact mean the supporters of the House of Orléans, or the Orléanist Orléanists, to put it another way). Julien went on to say that he was very upset because the Orléans press (and here Orléans meant Vienna) was critical of Maximilian's—that is to say Cittadella's—eagerness to accept the throne of Tours (Mexico). What was worse, an assemblyman had said that if Maximilian left Europe, he would first have to renounce all his rights to the Austrian succession, and this had worried Cittadella and Blanche quite a bit, who in their castle at Nantes on the shores of the Adriatic were weighing all the pros and cons on a daily basis, now.

•

The Archduke loved his six-thousand-volume library very much. It included texts on art, history, and literature: the novels of Walter Scott; the *Storia uni-*

versale of his dear friend, professor, and protector, César Cantú; Leonardo's studies on the flight of birds; Byron's poems, which he had promised himself to read aloud on the shores of the Black Sea. He also loved, they both loved, the Castle of Miramare very much, with its superb park which covered twenty-two hectares, its *Saletta Novara*—an exact replica of the *quadrato di poppa* of the *Novara* frigate—with its Swan Lake, its *Sala della Rosa dei Venti*, thus named because there was a gigantic gyrating nautical rose in its ceiling that pointed in the direction of the wind without having to be out of doors; with its library and the busts of Dante, Homer, Goethe, and Shakespeare; with its *piazzola* containing the cannons that Papa Leopold had given them; with its magnificent *Sala di Regnanti*; and so many other things as well. Maximilian wondered, "Should I leave all this in exchange for pure ambition and uncertainty?" and wrote a poem:

> You fascinate me with the bait of a crown
> And confuse me with nothing but chimeras
> Should I listen to the sweet song of the Sirens?

He also wondered about leaving Vienna, his beloved Vienna, the Hofburg, Schönbrunn, yes, most of all the splendid Palace of Schönbrunn that Maria Theresa's husband had turned into one of the marvels of art and rococo architecture inside and out, which only the uninitiated could ever stoop to comparing with Versailles or Caserta. Perhaps he would never see them again, if he were to leave for Mexico. "Must I leave my beloved country forever?" . . . leave the make-believe Roman ruins at the Castle of Schönbrunn where he used to play hide-and-seek, the Hall of Mirrors where Maria Theresa accepted the oath of allegiance from her ministers and where Mozart had given a concert when he was only six years old . . . the beautiful playground of my early years . . . the white and gold room with its red damask curtains and the clock with its cherubs, the walls with sky-blue tapestries and the stuffed lark, the land where he was born . . . What you want me do then is leave my golden birthplace forever, the land where I spent the *brightest*, most wonderful days of my childhood? And he remembered with a bit of a shiver the Baroness Sturmfeder, who had always loved Franz, his brother, more—he would never be able to make the Baroness, whom he called "*aja*," in Portuguese, love him. He also remembered the beautiful Countess von Linden, and the day he'd bought her a rose bouquet in a flower shop at the Ringstrasse, which she wore that night at the opera. When the Archduke looked at her with his binoculars, she buried her face in the roses. He also remembered that his brother had presumed to separate him from the Countess, to end that adolescent affair. It was here that he experienced those exquisite feelings of early love. Later on, however, he forgot her, he forgot the Countess because he had become a tireless world traveler. And then: if he accepted the throne of Mexico, he couldn't travel the globe anymore. It's true that other great monarchs had abandoned their countries for long periods of time in order to learn things: Peter the Great, for instance, spent almost a year outside Russia. And Eric XVI, the lunatic King of Sweden, had managed to visit, incognito, the most sordid taverns in London. It was also said that the new Sultan of Turkey, Abdul Aziz, was planning a trip to Vienna and Paris. Even so, it wouldn't be the same to travel as a Sovereign as opposed to a mere archduke. Only a few weeks ago he had said to his sister-in-law, Elisabeth, more beautiful than ever, that he would like to travel to India, Tibet, and China in a balloon. It would be impossible for the Emperor of Mexico to embark on such a trip. He remembered the nakedness of the women of Nubia and Barbary, which had so disturbed him at the slave market of Smyrna that he'd had Geiger, the official painter of the *Vulcain*, the ship that was taking them from Trieste to Greece and to Asia Minor, paint them, this Geiger had done masterfully. Precisely because he was only an archduke, a nobody, he was able to bribe the customs officers at Seville so they wouldn't search his luggage; and precisely because he was only an archduke that he'd been able to undress in order to bathe *in conspectu barbarorum*—as he wrote in his memoirs—on an Albanian beach, shaded by the rugged cliffs of Escutari, in plain sight of those barbaric Albanese in their red Turkish hats, their caftans with embroidered petticoats, and pistols and daggers at their waists.

On the other hand, however, there were many possible advantages to taking the throne. Carlota could hardly go on painting oils and watercolors for the rest of her life, and Maximilian himself couldn't just sit around playing the organ until he was an old man. And, anyway, wasn't Mexico a very large country, containing all the climates of the world, and landscapes: deserts, jungles, snow-capped mountain ranges, and coniferous forests? He would travel the length of his Empire, he would go to all its provinces, bathe in all its oceans. Besides, if the Great Project, the greatest of all—that of creating an Empire that would stretch from the Río Grande to Tierra del Fuego—came to fruition, he could travel to Honduras and explore the Darien; he could visit Venezuela, the land of Simón Bolívar; he could go down the Amazon River just like Orellana did first; he could climb to the summit of the Aconcagua; in Valparaíso he could drink dark red wines from the Maipú region . . .

Another one of the problems he foresaw, financing the enterprise, would take care of itself, once he was installed: Mexico was a country with infinite resources. Mexico, or The Imperial Mexican Treasury, would be able to pay for everything: the transportation of the French troops, their board, their salaries, and of course all the expenses of the campaign for however many years it would last. It would pay for every bullet, every mortar or grenade used or in reserve; new uniforms as needed, the fodder and dry hay for the horses and draft animals, the victory celebrations, everything. In a letter to the Archduke, Louis Napoleon confirmed that the French army in Mexico would gradually be reduced, so that by the end of 1865 there would be 28,000 men on hand, 25,000 by the end of 1866, and only 20,000 by the end of 1867—and that 6,000 Foreign Legionnaires would remain in Mexico for eight years. "Whatever happens in Europe," Louis Napoleon said, "France's aid will always be present for the new Empire." This aid, according to calculations, would cost the Mexican Treasury 270 million francs until July 1864. In addition, the Empire had to satisfy the claims of the Jecker House, along with all the other claims filed by Monsieur de Saligny and the allies of the Tripartite Convention in Veracruz. However, Maximilian would never acquiesce to Louis Napoleon's wish to create a French Protectorate in Sonora: a "Protectorate," which, to be sure, would have grown to encompass quite a bit more than that state, since according to Montholon's orders, it would take up a significant slice of Mexican territory, from the Gulf of Mexico to the Pacific, including large portions of Sinaloa, Chihuahua, Durango, Coahuila, Zacatecas, Nuevo León, San Luis Potosí, and Tamaulipas: in other words, half the country. But this wouldn't happen, Maximilian decided. Mexico's silver belonged to Mexicans, and there would be more than enough to finance the expedition and the Empire. Yes sir, he would show them. When Philip II was building El Escorial, hadn't people in Europe said that he would never finish it, because all the gold in Spain wouldn't be enough to pay for it? Philip II *did* finish El Escorial, however, and to show his critics that he had more than enough money, he'd set a large piece of gold on one of the towers. Carlota and Maximilian would do something similar in Mexico . . . after all, the gold for El Escorial had come from Mexican silver.

What bothered them most, however, was another problem. Between 1848, the year Franz Joseph was crowned Emperor, until the birth of Prince Rudolf in 1858, Maximilian had been first in line to the Austrian throne. In 1853, Max was prevented from becoming Emperor of Austria by nothing more than the gold embroidery along the neck of Franz Joseph's uniform—or had it been the buttons?—which deflected Libényi's knife. The Archduke hated to think about his brother's death, his brother whom he loved so much, or that of his nephew Rudolf, but he couldn't help it. It was necessary to have one's feet on solid ground, after all, and the death of both, or either, was a possibility—or two possibilities. If this was to happen, he would have to abdicate the throne of Mexico and return to Europe: it would be impossible for him to renounce his rights in Austria. He remembered the ugly rumor that had spread in the court when the attempt on Franz Joseph's life had been made: the Emperor hadn't interpreted Maximilian's haste in traveling from Trieste to Vienna to visit him in his sick bed as an act of love. According to Franz Joseph, Maximilian had merely been anxious to see with his own eyes how badly his brother had been injured, to gauge his own chances to succeed to the throne there and then. Neither did Franz thank Maximilian for his efforts to initiate a collection to erect a votive church on the site of the murder attempt, a *Votivkirche*, as an expression of thanks to God for his brother's having survived. Really, the most incredible thing had been Franz's dismissal of Maximilian from his post as governor of Lombardo-Veneto. He, Maximilian, would never forgive him for that. He who had been born in that castle—twice the general headquarters of Napoleon the Great; site of the sumptuous festivals of Joseph II and the endless dances of the so-called Vienna Dancing Congress of 1815, when the Eagle had been a prisoner at St. Helena and the Greats of Europe were redrawing the map of the continent and conspiring to suppress any possible revolutionary movement. He, Ferdinand Maximilian of Habsburg, who had learned to value the greatness of the House of Austria and the Empire in the long corridors and huge salons of Schönbrunn, shining with lacquers and brocades, in its immense gardens, in its squares, from the tower of which one could admire the north side of the palace and the Vienna Woods, and then, to the south, the foothills of the Alps; he, Ferdinand Maximilian, who had dreamed of becoming one more of those renowned emperors: another Rudolf II, collector of dwarfs, painters, and an astronomer with a silver nose; another Maximilian I, model of nobility, patron of the arts, a Renaissance man; another Frederick III who had incorporated, into innumerable objects and buildings, the magnificent bilingual motto of the five vowels, AEIOU—*Austria est imperare orbi universo—Alles erdreich ist Oesterreich unterthan*; another Charles V of Germany or Charles I of Spain, who after having ruled half of the planet, retired to his monastery to assemble clocks, eat ostrich eggs, and contemplate his own coffin . . . and why not?

Only yesterday—how time flies—he had met with his brother in Venice and things seemed to be progressing wonderfully. They had agreed on almost everything: that he would take the name Ferdinand, Ferdinand I of Mexico, and not Maximilian; that he would travel to Mexico aboard an Austrian warship, perhaps the frigate *Novara*; that Santa Anna would receive the title of Duke of Veracruz or Tampico, as he wished, and a salary of 35,000 a year. Franz Joseph approved the idea that Maximilian and Carlota visit Rome and Paris, and that they ask the Pope to bestow the rank of Cardinal or perhaps Patriarch upon the Mexican Archbishop, as well as to provide a loan of twenty-five million dollars for the purpose of recruiting volunteers among the ranks of the active officers of the Austrian army, with the condition that they all be Catholic and not-Italian. Discussion of the very delicate issue of the succession had been postponed for a year, and Max thought Franz Joseph would end up giving in. They were so happy together, talking in Vienna; they touched on the theme of the Vienna Congress of 1815, which had been so expensive for the Austrians, though it must have been magnificent, and lots of fun besides. Beethoven had directed a gala concert in the Rittersaal of the Hofburg, there had been tournaments and parades in the Prater, hunting expeditions, the parties thrown by the Esterházys, the Auerspergs, and the Liechtensteins, and then all the general ostentation and luxury . . . and yet, what good did it all do? They asked themselves, what was the point? Not only had Vienna become inundated by journalists and charlatans, beggars, street vendors, and prostitutes, but also, as someone had said, "The Czar of Russia had made all the love that was to be made; the King of Prussia had thought everything that was to be thought; the King of Denmark had spoken all that there was to be spoken; the King of Bavaria had drunk all that there was to be drunk; and the King of Württemberg eaten all that there was to be eaten. Oh, and the Czar danced forty nights without stopping!" Who had paid for everything and everyone? The Emperor Franz of Austria, 50,000 guldens every day. What was it all for, if Congress couldn't even avoid the catastrophe of 1848? (Though Franz Joseph should have been thankful for it, since that catastrophe had put him on the throne . . .) Nor did it do anything to stop the crumbling of the Holy Alliance, and it couldn't even keep France from reemerging as a European power. This conversation, their conversation, was taking place because times were hard, because money couldn't be squandered like that anymore—and for nothing. Maximilian agreed. "Though the House of Austria will never abandon you," Franz told his brother, and assured him that he would continue to receive his endowment of 150,000 florins a year; 100,000 to be paid in Vienna and the remaining 50,000 set aside to pay off several debts like those incurred by the construction of Miramare, and of course the Mexican enterprise. The brothers also agreed to restore the Order of Guadalupe when Maximilian was established in Mexico—the order founded by Emperor Iturbide, which had disappeared and then been resuscitated later on by Santa Anna, only to disappear again—and also establish two further orders: that of San Fernando, and then, for the ladies, and in honor of the Patron Saint of Carlota, the Order of San Carlos. And, yes, definitely, Maximilian must make his journey to Mexico in that beautiful 1,500 ton frigate, adorned with fifty canons, whose name, *Novara*, commemorated the defeat of Sardinia by the Austrians, and with its defeat, the final demise of the possibility that the Republic of Venice might rise again.

That said, they moved on to the subject of the visit Carlota and Max had made in May 1862 to consult with Leopold in Brussels regarding the unsavory circumstances that had come about when Otto I was expelled from Greece and England thought that the ideal solution would be for Maximilian to occupy the vacant throne, and Queen Victoria wrote Leopold to convince the Archduke, and the Belgian monarch found it a splendid idea, though possibly only because he himself had aspired to that throne in his youth and dreamed he walked in the shade of the Parthenon and rested under the canopy of a blue silk puptent on the plains of Eleusis. But Maximilian was upset, even though the English Ambassador in Vienna, Lord Bloomfield, had promised that if the Archduke accepted the throne, the seven Ionian Islands would be incorporated into Greece. The Archduke wrote a letter to the Count of Rechberg in which he stated that he would never accept a crown already offered unsuccessfully to a half a dozen other princes, while Carlota, for her part, wrote her mother-in-law, the Archduchess Sophie, that accepting the throne of Greece would almost certainly mean the adoption of some prudish kind of religion for her dynasty.

What was happening? Was it a conspiracy to get rid of him at any cost? Would he also have had to relinquish his rights in Austria if he'd accepted the Greek throne? *You tell me about the scepter of power*, he wrote, *Oh, let me follow my dark destiny among the myrtles in peace! Work, Sciences, and the Arts are sweeter than the glint of a crown . . .*

However, it was said that the Archduke had sent cloth samples and various buttons to London and Paris that could be used for the uniforms of his future Mexican servants, and according to what the American Ambassador to Vienna learned, he also had a crown made out of papier-mâché to see—standing in front of a mirror—how he would look when he was Emperor of Mexico. And Carlota, already committed to making any sacrifice on behalf of her future adoptive country, wrote: *But, is it that we are here in this world only to live the days of silk and gold?* She went to Brussels to talk to King Leopold, hoping for his help and advice. At the meeting the King had said, the Empire must be constitutional; the French are in your hands not you in theirs; likewise you must convince the Mexicans that they need you, and that you don't need them; citizens must be equal before the law, and the freedom of worship must be respected; a Mexican Monarchy does not contradict the Monroe Doctrine; and in regard to the succession, Leopold advised them to be ready to compromise, but get guarantees that—in case it was all a fiasco—Max would be given back all his rights in Austria. But Franz Joseph insisted: *Mein lieber Herr Bruder, Erherzog Ferdinand Max*, he said in one of his letters. "My Dear Sir Brother, Archduke Ferdinand Max, if I were to die during Rudolf's childhood, how could you be a regent from Mexico? Would you abdicate the Mexican Throne? And if you were willing to do so, don't you think you would be a total stranger to Austrian politics at that point?"

Empress Eugénie had stationery made with the Habsburg crown over a Mexican eagle. Maximilian sent Baron de Pont, another one of his secretaries, to Paris. Carlota read Monsieur Chevalier's book, *Le Mexique Ancien et Moderne*, which Louis Napoleon had sent her, and she was surprised to find out that Lake Chapala was over three hundred thousand hectares, and she thanked God that Mexico City's summer was as mild as the three months of fall in Paris, since temperature rarely exceeded thirty-two degrees centigrade. The Archduke was told that the Mexican expedition was becoming more and more unpopular in Paris. The Austrian delegate Ignaz Kuranda said that the Reichsrat, the Imperial Assembly, would demand Max's renunciation to his succession rights as a *condicio sine qua non* to his acceptance of the throne of Mexico. The case of the Duke d'Anjou, grandson of Louis XIV, who gave up all his rights in France to rule in Spain as Philip V was cited. Max countered with the example of Henry III, King of Poland, who abdicated to become Emperor of France. General Santa Anna arrived in Veracruz aboard the English packet boat *Conway*, and a few days later Admiral Bosse had him on his way to Havana aboard the corvette *Colbert*. Lord Palmerston said Mexico was a witch's cauldron. Almonte wrote Maximilian telling him that Juárez and his followers had been completely defeated, and that the Mexican Indians took their hat off in front of the pictures of the Archduke and Archduchess. Louis Napoleon wrote Almonte warning him he would not allow Mexico to be swept by a blind reaction that, in the eyes of Europe, would be a dishonor to the French flag. Max thought of sending Schertzenlechner to Mexico on a secret mission. Sir Charles Wyke told Stefan Herzfeld that the Mexican people rejected the intervention. As an example of the corruption of the Juárez government, Monsieur Kint de Roodenbeck cited the fact that the Convent of Santa Clara in Mexico City, worth one hundred thousand piasters, had been sold to the Chief of Police for only seventeen thousand. Carlota read that Humboldt had said one banana tree was sufficient to feed one hundred people, in Mexico, and that the great astronomer Laplace was astounded when he discovered that the Aztecs knew how to measure the year better than the Europeans. In London, Don Francisco de Paula y Arrangóiz told Palmerston that if Maximilian didn't accept, he would offer the throne to a Bourbon prince, and Palmerston replied that there wasn't a single Bourbon worth a damn. Maximilian reread the Memorandum or Protocol he had signed when General Almonte visited Miramare in February 1863, and he was satisfied with its provisions which stipulated: the French troops would remain in Mexico until a ten-thousand-man national army was formed; that a loan for one hundred million dollars at five percent interest would be solicited and that the Church's assets as yet unsold would be offered as guarantee of repayment; that it would be prudent to establish a Senate and a House of Representatives; that in order to assure the services of the Conservative Party leaders and perhaps those of other political parties, a sum of two hundred thousand dollars would be made available; that titles of nobility among Mexican families be recognized and new titles be issued with the proviso that the number of barons be kept below twenty, and marquises and counts below ten. Maximilian received Don Jesús Terán, a special Juárez envoy, who told him that the Assembly of Notable Citizens was a farce, that the proceedings of support were an imposture, and that the Juárez government was legitimate. Carlota was afraid when she read that in the arid plains of northern Mexico, which resembled the Tartar Steppes, there were Apache tribes that inspired a terror similar to that once caused by the barbarians around the Roman provinces of the Rhine. Max wrote his agent, Bourdillon, in England, asking him to show that great commercial nation the financial advantages of the establishment of a Monarchy in Mexico. Monsieur Bourdillon warned the Archduke and the Archduchess not to trust in the promises of Mexicans because there wasn't a single one who wouldn't betray his dearest principles for five hundred dollars. Colonel Loizillon wrote to Paris complaining about the dust at Quecholac, which went right through people's clothing, and said his Arabian horse could be sold in Mexico for fifteen thousand francs when it cost only five hundred and fifty in Africa. Maximilian said his experience in Lombardy, where his subjects had loved and respected him so much, would be very useful to him in Mexico. Mr. Richard Hildreth told him, at Miramare, that anyone who aspired to the throne of Mexico should consider himself lucky to escape with his life. And if Eugénie, faced with an upcoming visit from Max and Carlota, could hardly have written to her sister Paca—as Bertha Harding tells us she did, in her book *The Phantom Crown*—to ask Paca to buy two scarlet fans, one for her and the other for the Empress of Mexico, and that if necessary she should send all the way to Cádiz for them—if she couldn't have done this for the simple reason that Paca had died several years before—at any rate, Eugénie was still captivated with the idea, especially since the fall of Puebla; and besides the stationery, she had already ordered silverware for Max and Carla stamped with the Imperial monogram. It was already too much for Maximilian, too many conflicts, too many worries. Though perhaps Sir Charles Wyke had exaggerated in what he said about the Indians and the monkeys, there was no proof that a majority of Mexicans really wanted an Empire; England was undecided in giving her official support; and the Rothschilds still weren't ready to open their purse—that is, for a loan. At the same time, the Mexican delegation charged with offering him the throne had already departed for Europe; Louis Napoleon asked Max to receive it as soon as possible; and though he and Carlota were both still trying to learn Spanish—and it was time for the irregular verbs, some as difficult as "*ir*," which would always begin in a different way: "*Voy a Esmirna*," "*Iba a París*," "*Iré a México*"—it was closer to Carlota's native French than to German, "*je vais*," "*j'allai*," "*j'irai*," so she had the leisure time to read books about Mexico by Chevalier or the Marchioness Calderón de la Barca, and learn that in Mexico the roads had innumerable potholes but that they were picturesque nonetheless because on them one would find herds of the pinkest and fattest pigs in the world, and mules bearing aromatic loads of vanilla that perfumed the air, and Indian farm girls with flowers woven into their hair and embroidered blouses like the Arab *gandouras* who sold exotic birds in iridescent colors in bamboo cages; while he, Maximilian, had no time for such trivialities.

And then, my God, there was so much more he had to learn, so many lists: the one detailing the equivalence of measures and coins, which he frequently had to consult in order to find out what the Mexicans were talking about—how many meters in a *toesa*; how many miles in a Castilian league; how many piasters make a florin; how much a piaster is in dollars; how much a dollar in francs; how much a franc in kreuzers; how much a kreuzer in *tlacos*. And "*tlaco*" was a word that appeared on the vocabulary list from the Nahuatl and Mexican Spanish, which their Spanish professor had given them—a list that omitted the native word for obsidian, the glass with which the Incas made their mirrors and the Aztecs the knives they used to tear out the hearts of their victims, which was similar to Icelandic agate, and on top of that a word of Latin origin; but it did include words such as "adobe," which is a clay brick similar to Kashmir bricks—the French were already calling the expedition, "the War of the Adobes" thanks to the parapets that were being made with such bricks to defend military installations—and others that were just unpronounceable, like "xoconoxtle," the fruit of a cactus used in Mexican cuisine, or "tezontle," which was a volcanic and porous gray or dark-red rock that was used in construction, as for instance in the Palace of the Inquisition (this is enough to drive you crazy, Carla!). And to top it all off, Max had to read Julien's, that is Gutiérrez Estrada's, interminable letters. He would get up to three a week, sometimes, and some of them as unbelievable as the one in which, a few months later, Julien, via Eugénie—that is, the Baron de Pont—suggested that he travel to Tours—that is, Mexico—and that from there he should tell Rouen, Bordeaux, and Orléans—that is, France, England, and Vienna—that he had not been accepted by a majority of Mexicans, and that because of this, he was returning to live in peace at his Castle in Nantes—that is, Miramare. And Maximilian, who had memorized the entire code invented by Julien, still had to decipher the message: Arteago was Hidalgo; Joseph, Archbishop Labastida; Ernest, Prince Metternich . . . and Cittadella . . . well, of course, he knew that one, Cittadella was he, Maximilian, at least until the Mexican decided to change the entire code, as had already happened once: Maximilian had been Nuñez, and Miramare, Bolivia.

But what the Archduke of Austria, Prince of Lorena, and Count of Habsburg also knew, was that the moment that he renounced his titles, he would stop being all of these thing—Archduke, Prince, Count—and he would have become just another citizen of the Empire, a nobody. Or would they also ask him to give up his Austrian citizenship? Would his own brother go to that extreme? Would he become stateless? Would he be condemned to a civil death?

•

Hall XIX of Miramare Castle, situated between the Chinese and Japanese Salons and the old Throne Hall, is called "*La Sala di Cesare dell'Acqua*," because several paintings by the Istrian painter can be found there. One of them depicts the construction of Miramare by Maximilian, and in it, among other things, there's a woman with a feathered headdress not very different to an Aztec's, who offers the Archduke—dressed in a purple robe—a pineapple: the tropical fruit par excellence, which was represented in Maximilian's coat of arms crowned by the motto "Equity in Justice." In another painting, Cesare dell'Acqua depicted *L'offerta della corona a Massimiliano*. This offer made by the Mexican Delegation, presided over, as expected, by Mr. Gutiérrez Estrada, took place in Miramare on October 3, 1863. Carlota wasn't present during the ceremony, and Maximilian appears in civilian clothes, without any decorations. José Manuel Hidalgo, Tomás Murphy, General Adrián Woll d'Ohm, Joaquín Velázquez de León, Francisco Javier Miranda, and Antonio Escandón were also part of the Delegation. A short time before, Maximilian had traveled to Vienna so he could discuss the matter of the succession rights with his brother, and Carlota had gone to Brussels. Back in Miramare, Carlota wrote a memoir, over fifty pages long, titled, *Conversations avec Cher Papa*. Leopold was very happy that he'd regained his favorite role—that of the tutor to future emperors—and he insisted that she should neither resign the throne of Mexico nor her rights in Austria. On the other hand, Franz Joseph's instructions were very clear: the Mexican Delegation should be accorded official but private recognition, and in his replies to them, Maximilian was in no way to mention the name of the Austrian Emperor. As expected, Gutiérrez Estrada's speech was overflowing with bombastic hyperbole: He, Mr. Gutiérrez Estrada, born in a country faced with a disastrous future, synonymous with ruin and desolation, prey to republican institutions that were nothing more than a font of the cruelest misfortunes, was presenting the crown of the Mexican Empire, that the people, in the full and legitimate exercise of their will and sovereignty, by means of a solemn decree of the Assembly of Notables, ratified by such-and-such provinces, and that according to all predictions, would be ratified by the entire nation, with the hope that Mexico would finally awaken to happier times—Mr. Gutiérrez Estrada was offering the crown to the most worthy offspring of the illustrious and renowned dynasty, which, among its many achievements, had first brought Christian Civilization to the very country that was now longing to welcome him, Maximilian of Habsburg, who had been blessed with so many gifts from Heaven, a man of rare abnegation, the privilege of men who are called to govern, and with him his August Wife, distinguished by her lofty talents and exemplary virtues; together they could establish, in this nineteenth century—given their many titles—the government, the true freedom, the happy products of that same civilization, in Mexico.

In his answer, Maximilian asked them to take the necessary steps to ask the Mexican people what kind of government they wanted for themselves, because he was not willing to accept the throne without having the entire nation ratify the vote taken in the capital. Maximilian's speech was sober and direct, very different from that of the Mexican, though one word in particular that he used, the verb "demand," with regard to the guarantees that would assure the integrity and independence of the Empire, would cause the Archduke a headache, and his first humiliation in the Mexican affair: the French Minister of Foreign Affairs censored the translation of the speech, whose publication in *Le Moniteur* of Paris was only authorized after Monsieur Drouyn de Lhuys changed "*j'exige*" to "*je demande*." The Archduke, then, was no longer demanding guarantees; he was limited to asking for them.

With or without sufficient guarantees, with or without England's support, with or without the vote of the entire nation, Maximilian and Carlota had already decided, as of Christmas 1863, to accept the throne of Mexico. The only remaining detail to clear up was a final decision as to the succession rights. At the beginning of March, and a few days before their trip to Paris, where they had been invited by Louis Napoleon, they received the so-called Arneth's Memoirs in Miramare, which was a document produced by the Austrian historian Alfred von Arneth under the instructions of Franz Joseph, and in which, after citing several historical examples, it was stated that in all previous occasions in which the dominions of the Habsburgs were divided, it had always been possible to bring them all under one crown, and that this would not be feasible in the case of an emperor living in Mexico and trying to govern Austria from there. Arneth concluded that for the benefit of both the Austrian and Mexican interests, the Archduke should renounce all his privileges.

In Paris, Maximilian and Carlota were greeted with imperial honors. Louis Napoleon and Eugénie were in a splendid mood. At a grand banquet in their honor, the chef of the Tuileries made an immense sugar Mexican eagle devouring a serpent. Carlota posed three times for Winterhalter, the Court's painter. Eugénie gave Carlota a Spanish mantilla and Maximilian a solid-gold medallion of the Virgin. They arrived at the Tuileries Chapel accompanied by the grand marshal, the grand maestre, the commander-in-chief of the palace guard, and the officers and ladies-in-waiting of the imperial houses of Louis Napoleon and Eugénie. There, they heard a Mass sung by the students of the Conservatory, and Carlota noticed that the French Emperor didn't stop twisting his moustache for a single moment. They dined several times in the Louis XIV Salon decorated with suns and horns of plenty and the slogan *Nec pluribus impar*, served by *maîtres d'hôtel* dressed in sky-blue silk uniforms, frockcoats whose collars were embroidered with imperial flowers, and three-cornered hats with black plumes tucked under their arms. In the center of the table was a large, beautiful Sèvres, and behind Eugénie a motionless Nubian servant in Venetian attire. Louis Napoleon showed off his favorite cane covered in rhinoceros skin with a golden eagle in its hilt. They spoke a bit about everything: about Puebla, about Juárez fleeing the capital, about the brilliant campaigns of General Brincourt; that you had to go through Veracruz very quickly to avoid being infected with yellow fever or black vomit; Eugénie told them that at Paulina Metternich's last ball, she, the Empress, had dressed as Juno, and Count de Fleurier as a Haitian coconut seller, and then Maximilian said France should ask England to return the Rosetta Stone; but then the Egyptians would ask you for it, he went on, and the Greeks would seize the opportunity to ask the English for the Elgin Marbles. The what marbles? The Parthenon friezes, Eugénie, who knew a lot about history, clarified. Splendid, but then, said Louis Napoleon, but then, you, the Austrians would have to return the Scanderbeg Crown to the Albanese; we better leave things as they are. There was also a grand parade in Maximilian and Carlota's honor through the new avenues of the modern Paris, designed by Baron Haussmann, and Maximilian reviewed the French troops. The Squadron of the Hundred Guards slammed the butts of their rifles against the ground, an honor accorded only to the Emperor and Empress of France and foreign monarchs, and Eugénie said that one time she had smacked a guard to see if he would move, but he hadn't even blinked, and the same thing happened when Loulou spilled a whole package of sweets onto another guard's boots, and Louis Napoleon said that since 1858 he had eliminated the practice of having one of the members of the Squadron sleep at his bedroom door. Eugénie and Carlota, their faces covered by thick black veils so no one could recognize them, visited several temples, and with a bit of laughter and disgust Eugénie told her that once she went to a church incognito, accompanied by Hidalgo, and that she had had to put her lips on a crucifix after a black had kissed it, but she kissed it anyway because in so doing she was fulfilling a religious vow she had made, praying for the fall of Puebla, and she did not regret it. Eugénie told Carlota she loved to go out disguised and that she wished she could go like that to see Offenbach's *Les Géorgiennes*, because people said it was a delicious operetta, but that this would be almost impossible. At any rate, it was almost spring and the City of Lights lived up to its name, there were fire-swallowers and musicians in the streets, acrobats dressed as harlequins, children with Scottish skirts and glengarries in the boulevards and in the parks, and everywhere Carlota went people applauded and shouted, *Bon chance, Madame L'Archiduchesse!*, Good luck, Madame Archduchess! and Carlota didn't know whether to be happy or sad because she couldn't stop remembering that as a child she had played there in the Tuileries, in those same corridors and salons like the *Salle de Travées*, the *Galerie de la Paix*, the *Salon des Maréchaux* with the portraits of France's twelve marshals and the busts of French warriors and sailors, and the Diana Gallery which ran next to Eugénie's quarters, and in the Hall of the King her grandfather Louis Philippe would sit her in his lap and tell her that the magnificent gentleman in front of her, drawn with color threads, was none other than Louis XIV, and that the scene embroidered in the tapestry commemorated the occasion in which the Sun King presented his son to the Spanish Grandees. But on those same streets of Paris the same gossipmongers who had already taken it upon themselves to call the French Expedition, "Duke Jecker's War," said that Maximilian was not an Archduke but an *Archdupe*.

A few hours before Carlota and Maximilian left for England, where they would visit the Court of St. James's and Carlota's grandmother in Claremont, Louis Napoleon and the Archduke signed the so-called Miramare Convention. In it, the French Emperor ratified the terms expressed in his previous correspondence with the Archduke. His future Mexican subjects were to pay France the two hundred and seventy million francs covering the expenses of the expedition through July 1864, and a thousand francs annually for each French soldier remaining in Mexico after that date. Maximilian also agreed to satisfy the Jecker's demands. In exchange for this he rejected, outright, Louis Napoleon's project to make Sonora a French protectorate for fifteen years.

In England, Queen Victoria decided not to accord them imperial honors, but she gave them a friendly reception and commented that Maximilian seemed anxious to get rid of the *dolce far niente*, and that Carlota would undoubtedly follow him to the end of the world. In Claremont, Marie Amélie, Carlota's grandmother and Louis Philippe's widow for seventeen years, lost her composure and begged them, sobbing, not to go to Mexico. Her daughter Clémentine with her long Bourbon nose, counting the beads of her rosary over and over again, and the Countess of Clinchamp, and Carlota herself, and the little princess Blanche d'Orléans, all tried in vain to calm her down. The raving grandmother shouted: *Ils seront assassinés! Ils seront assassinés!* They will be killed! They will be killed! Blanche, the little princess who was six years old at that time was surprised to see that it was a man, Maximilian, who cried at this spectacle, not Carlota, who remained impassive.

From England, Maximilian and Carlota went to Brussels to say good-bye to Papa Leopold and the Duke of Brabant and the Count of Flanders, and there, together with generals Chazal and Chapelié, they spoke about the formation of a one-thousand-man body of Belgian volunteers that would be known as the Empress Guards. The next stop was Vienna.

•

Another one of Cesare dell'Acqua's paintings in the XIX Hall of Miramare Castle is titled *La partenza per il Messico*. Maximilian and Carlota are standing in the eight-oar boat that took them from the pier to the *Novara*. At the distance, in the bay, the frigate was adorned with gala banners. A Mexican Imperial flag waved on its mainmast. There was another one in the smaller boat, and one more up in the castle's tower. The French ship *Thémis* that would accompany them to Mexico and the imperial yacht *Fantaisie*, as well as the Austrian gunboat *Bellona* and the six Lloyd's steamships that would escort them part of the first day's journey, were all close to the *Novara*. According to the Belgian historian André Castelot, Carlota pointed to the French flag aboard the *Thémis* and said to Maximilian, "It's the flag of civilization accompanying us," and Maximilian didn't reply. All of Trieste had come to bid them farewell, and from the pier covered with flowers, the townspeople, men, women, and children blew kisses, shouted hoorays, and wished them the best of luck. The municipal band played the Imperial Mexican hymn first and then the *Gott erhalte, Gott Beschütze. Unsern Kaiser, unser Reich!* Maximilian and Carlota were accompanied by, among others, Count Franz Zichy and his wife Mélanie; Countess Paula von Kollonitz; the Marquis de Corio; Count Bombelles, son of Maximilian's former tutor; the Belgian engineer Félix Eloin, sent by Leopold; Sebastian Schertzenlechner; Angel Iglesias and Joaquín Velázquez de León; General Adrián Woll; and Herr Jacob von Kuhacsevich. From the deck of the *Novara* Maximilian saw the Castle of Miramare for the last time. *Comme il pleure, mon pauvre Max!* How my poor Max cries, Carlota told Countess Zichy.

Between the morning of April 14, 1864 and the date Max and Carlota left Claremont, the dream of the Mexican Empire almost remained just that: a dream. On March 19th, Maximilian and Carlota arrived in Vienna where they were accorded imperial honors. The following day, the Count of Rechberg visited Maximilian in his private quarters and gave him, on behalf of the Emperor, a document titled "Family Pact," that contained the resignation of Maximilian and all his descendants to the succession rights in Austria, including the right to tutor any Austrian prince. Max refused to sign it and Rechberg told him that in that case the Emperor could not authorize the Archduke's acceptance of the Crown of Mexico. The following day, the Supreme Chief of the August House of Austria sent his brother a written note confirming everything his foreign minister had said. Max was upset and in his answer he said he would be very sad to have to tell a country of nine million people—a country that had put its trust in him to build a better future, putting an end to the devastating civil wars that had already lasted for generations—the reasons for his resignation. A heated discussion followed this epistolary exchange: Max told his brother he would sail on a French ship at Anvers and Franz Joseph answered that if he dared to do that, he would erase him from the list of princes of the

House of Austria. *Sophie* became indignant and sought refuge at Laxemburg Castle where Max and Carla caught up with her on March 24th. There, Carlota insisted again that Austria should simply recognize a historical right: Mexico, after all, had belonged to the Habsburg dynasty, and this enterprise was nothing more than a matter of recuperating it. Two days later they went back to Miramare, and five days after that, Maximilian's cousin, Archduke Leopold, arrived at the castle to inform him Franz Joseph was urging him again to sign the declaration of his resignation. On March 27th, Maximilian told the Mexican Delegation that was staying in Trieste that in view of the insurmountable obstacles that he was facing, he had decided to retire his candidacy to the Mexican Throne. Carlota proposed they secretly board the French ship *Thémis*, and as soon as they arrived in Algeria or Civitavecchia make public their acceptance and thus safeguard Max's rights in Austria, but the Archduchess's idea was not taken seriously. Max, on the other hand, said he would travel to Rome to explain the situation to the Holy Father. Hidalgo sent a telegram to Paris that turned the Tuileries and the Quai d'Orsay upside down. That same night Louis Napoleon had Richard Metternich awakened at two in the morning through a messenger who gave him two letters: one from the Emperor and another one from Eugénie, both full of reproach, warning him of the scandal that was about to explode. Early the next day Metternich showed up at the Tuileries and stated that his government was the first to lament the situation. Louis Napoleon sent a telegram to Miramare to inform Maximilian of his dismay and said that a refusal, at that stage of the game, was impossible. That same morning of March 28, 1864, Louis Napoleon sent his aide, the Inspector General of Artillery, General Charles Auguste de Frossard, to Vienna and then to Miramare with the mission to speak first with Franz Joseph and then deliver a handwritten letter from the French Emperor to Maximilian. The letter included a paragraph that Louis Napoleon would come to regret, a few years later: "What would you think of me," it asked, "if once Your Royal Highness were in Mexico, I should suddenly tell you I couldn't fulfill the obligations to which we have agreed?" And then, too, the phrase that would, he hoped, force Maximilian to reconsider his position: "It's a matter," said Louis Napoleon, "of the honor of the House of Habsburg." In Vienna, Frossard's attempts were of no avail: Franz Joseph made it clear that Austria couldn't be governed by a Prince who had been thrown off a throne—because this possibility would always be present, in Mexico—and that, should the adventure succeed, he didn't want to accept the possibility that, with time, a Mexican descendant of the

Archduke might think that he had any rights to the Austrian Crown. When at Miramare Frossard insisted that the honor of the Habsburgs was at stake, Carlota intervened and told the General that they were doing Louis Napoleon a favor by going to Mexico. Frossard replied that the favor was at the very least reciprocal. On April 2nd, Maximilian received three letters from Franz Joseph. The Archduke had previously told his brother that he would accept the Family Pact, if his inheritance was not included in his renunciation, and if a secret clause was added in which the Emperor promised to reestablish the Archduke in his former rights if he renounced or lost the Mexican Throne, and along with this the restitution to him of all the rights pertaining to Austrian archdukes, or, if necessary, the rights due, in any case, to his wife and children. In the first two letters, Franz Joseph confirmed what the two brothers had agreed to in Venice with regard to the annual one hundred and fifty thousand florins and the recruitment of a contingent of Austrian volunteers. In the third, Franz Joseph promised to do everything within his power, as long as it was compatible with the interests of his Empire, to ensure that Maximilian or his widow and heirs would keep their position in the Empire, in case Maximilian abandoned the Mexican Throne of his own free will, or was obliged to do so by circumstances.

Since this alone wasn't sufficient, Carlota traveled to Vienna to speak with Franz Joseph. The Archduchess also failed. The inflexible Emperor limited himself to making what in his opinion was a very important concession: he would go to Miramare in person to deliver the Family Pact.

Franz Joseph's Imperial train arrived in Trieste the morning of April 9th. The two brothers locked themselves up in the library of Miramare Castle. There was a moment when Maximilian left the room to walk alone in his garden. A short time later, Count Bombelles went looking for him, and the discussion continued. Several hours later the brothers came out of the library. It was evident that both were very upset, and that they had cried.

In the Grand Salon, and in the presence of their two brothers, the Archdukes Charles Louis and Louis Victor, Ministers Schmerling, Esterházy, and Rechberg, Archdukes Charles Salvador, William Joseph, Leopold, and Rainer, the three Chancellors of Hungary, Croatia, and Transylvania, and other high dignitaries of the Empire, Franz Joseph and Maximilian signed the Family Pact.

Franz Joseph left Miramare immediately. Before boarding the train he turned toward his brother, opened his arms and shouted, Max, the two brothers embrace for the last time!

The following day, April 10th, Count Hadik went to look for the members of the Mexican Delegation, who were staying at the Consistorial House of Trieste.

It was Sunday, the day the gardens of Miramare were opened to the public. Maximilian was wearing his dress uniform of an admiral in the Austrian Navy, as well as the emblem of the Order of the Golden Fleece. Carlota was wearing a pink silk dress, the black ribbon of the Order of Malta, and her diamond archducal crown. Gutiérrez Estrada took it upon himself to make a cumbersome speech in French in which he made reference to the Habsburg slogan that appeared on the triumphal arch in front of the palace in Vienna, *Justitia regnorum fundamentum* (Empires are founded on Justice), and he affirmed that God's hand was visible in the enterprise. Maximilian read his answer in Spanish in a shaky voice, and in his speech he declared that, thanks to the votes of the Notables, he would now consider himself elected, that he accepted the crown, and that further, thanks to the generosity of the French Emperor, the Empire could count on the necessary guarantees. He insisted, once again, that his intentions were to establish a constitutional monarchy in Mexico.

When Maximilian finished, Gutiérrez Estrada jubilantly knelt before him and said, "Long live His Majesty Fernando Maximiliano, Emperor of Mexico." He did the same in front of Carlota, "Long live Her Majesty Carlota Amelia, Empress of Mexico." The imperial Mexican flag was hoisted at Miramare and saluted by the cannons of the ships anchored in the port. Lacroma's Abbot approached in order to take Maximilian's oath. The Emperor knelt down, put his right hand over the Gospels, and swore to preserve the integrity and independence of his new fatherland. The Miramare Convention was signed afterwards, and Maximilian I began issuing a series of orders, among them the designation of new Mexican Ambassadors to several European capitals. He also sent a letter to the First Magistrate of Trieste in which he informed him that he had awarded him the Cross of Knight-Commander of the Order of His Empire, and had ordered to have twenty thousand florins lent to him, and that the interest earned on the loan was to be distributed among the neediest families of Trieste during Christmas.

A congratulatory telegram from Louis Napoleon arrived before the ceremony was over, according to some historians. Others, like Gaulot, state that the telegram arrived the following day, that Carlota received it and took it to Maximilian who was having breakfast with Doctor Jilek and that the Archduke threw his fork down and said: "I've already told you I don't want to hear about Mexico at this time." Maximilian locked himself up in the *Gartenhaus* and refused to see anyone. Dr. Jilek said the Emperor was exhausted and needed to rest. Carlota had to receive the delegations from Trieste, Venice, Fiume, Gorizia, and Parenzo, and she had to preside over the official banquet at the Hall of the Seagulls. At the *Gartenhaus* Maximilian finished his poem and decided to postpone his departure to the following day, the 14th; thirteen was bad luck. And thus, the morning of the 14th, after having walked once more through the halls and gardens of Miramare, Maximilian and Carlota bid farewell to their servants. Once again, Maximilian was moved to tears. Richard O'Connor in his book, *The Cactus Throne*, says that Miramare's majordomo preferred suicide to accompanying his Emperors to Mexico. At the last minute, Maximilian received a telegram from his mother Sophie: "Good-bye, receive our prayers and our tears. May God protect and guide you. Good-bye forever from the land of your birth, where we will never see you again. With a distraught heart, we bless you once again."

The *Novara* weighed anchor and headed toward Pirano bordering the Istrian Coastline.

2. "Camarón, Camarón . . ."

Camarón, Camarón . . . I can't say I was happy, but I wasn't sad either; I can't say I was awake, but I wasn't asleep either. I was carried away, watching a horned hummingbird hanging in the air so it could suck the nectar from the flowers in the Virgin's gown, where I was hiding. I was really hiding good when I saw them come in, with their square-visored kepis, neck-covers, blue jackets, madder-dyed pants, and their leggings, all but the officers, a captain, or someone who seemed to be a captain with his black cape and gold bars, and believe it or not, a wooden left hand, and then I said to myself, these have to be the legionnaires, but it doesn't matter what I say to myself, I said to myself—it's the Colonel I need to say it to, that's why he paid me: to tell him who they are and how many. I began counting them with my fingers: one, two, three, and when I got to forty the hummingbird got scared and I lost count, but I started up again and got to around sixty. I could hardly even see the dust behind them when I started running, but they sure as hell didn't see the dust behind me, 'cause nobody runs faster than I do. I found the Colonel in the shade of a carob tree but he hardly even thanked me for the information 'cause his wife was digging out some chiggers that had gotten under his toenails and he looked like he was about to explode from all the itching . But as soon as he put his boots on, his mood changed: he thanked me properly, patted me on the back and said, very well, you estimate about sixty legionnaires, very well, we're going to finish them off. Come with us so you can watch us beat the shit out of those Frenchmen. But a well-read captain of his said, I beg your pardon, Colonel, if they're legionnaires, if they're the same ones who, I understand, came to Veracruz on two ships from Algeria under the command of Colonel Jeannin-gross, if those are the same ones, he said, it's more than likely that there are more Germans, Prussians, and even Italians in the troop than Frenchies. It doesn't make any difference in this case, the Colonel said. And he was right. It didn't make any difference in this case because everyone on their side was a foreigner and we were all Mexicans on our side, with the advantage that they were only sixty men, more or less, and, without exaggerating, we were about a thousand. If we'd only known about the convoy then, if we'd known that those legionnaires were only there to scout out the road for a convoy packed with gold and cannons for General Forey, or whatever his name is, then instead of going after them we could have waited for the carts to go through. After all, there were lots of us and half of all the gold we got would've gone to the Government of the Republic and we could have kept the other half ourselves. We deserved to get it, or at least that's what I would've ordered if I was a colonel but I'm not even a sergeant 'cause I'm not even a soldier. I get paid for spying, for keeping quiet for days at a time just like what I was doing under the blue mantle of flowers, almost not breathing, and I get paid for running, like I told you, and I get paid for being a taster. I taste the cactus leaves to make sure they're not bitter, and I try the *capulín* cherries to make sure they're not sour, and I taste the mushrooms to make sure they're not toadstools even though I already know that they're not, but they don't know that I know, and that's why, I was saying, I get paid, 'cause I know all the nooks and crannies for five leagues around Chiquihuite, and all the springs and rivers like the Arroyo de la Joya where I saw the legionnaires that day, and like the Arroyo Camarón that runs next to the hacienda of the same name where those sons of bitches dug-in that night. Camarón, Camarón . . . A shrimp that falls asleep, my father used to say, is swept away by the current. It's not that the legionnaires fell asleep since we didn't give them time for that, but they rested on their laurels, that's how I'd put it, they were too confident, like our Mr. Well-Informed Captain had said, because of their victory at Sebastopol, or Whatchamacallit, and they thought they were back among the Turks, that we'd be easy pickings. So, instead of re-treating, which personally is what I would have done, if I was a soldier, which I'm not, the captain with the wooden hand whose name was Captain D'Anjou or something took them to the corral of the Hacienda Camarón and there, in the corral, we corralled them. What I mean is, they, our soldiers, corralled them, 'cause I was hiding behind some geraniums at the time, because I wanted to see what was happening, and to write it all down for somebody, for whoever would pay me more. I can't actually read and write, mind you, but I write it all down in my head. You couldn't imagine all the things I've written there. Some-times I can't even imagine it myself. And I know how to read the rocks and the trails, the mountains and the ferns. That day I read the clouds. I mean, I read the sky 'cause there wasn't actually a single cloud up there and I told myself it wasn't going to rain, not a drop, for a long time, and now those legionnaires were going to find out what heat really is. Not desert heat, no sir, but the heat of the tropics, of "the warm latitudes," like the name says, the yellow-fever heat that had already been giving them hell 'cause the hospital tents were filled with filthy legionnaires throwing up that black, smelly mess that comes with the fever—I saw them. I also saw Captain D'Anjou and others smoking cigarettes like those Mexican officers do who aren't natives of the tropics but only pass-ing through, smoking to keep mosquitoes off them, but believe me, those cigarettes don't do a thing to scare bullets away. The first shot we fired knocked the cigarette out of an officer's mouth; the second killed a horse right between a legionnaire's legs. I won't say anything about the third shot and the others that followed 'cause I didn't have time to count them all. We went after the le-gionnaires till they got in the corral and, like I said, I was hiding behind a ge-ranium. I don't have to smoke to scare the mosquitoes away: they already know me and know I have bad blood. I can stay still for hours at a time, with-out even blinking, and if I get hungry, I eat whatever's handy. I can go for days without water, but they can't, as we found out later. Those idiots forgot to fill their canteens and when we trapped them in Camarón, they didn't have a drop of water; all they had was a bottle of wine for about sixty men, imagine, not even enough to sweeten the taste of their deaths. I saw the bottle going from mouth to mouth. The Captain with the wooden hand took a swig. Two other officers and a few more drank. "Hey, give us a drink, you sons of bitches!" one of our Mexican lancers shouted, and I saw one of the legionnaires piss into the bottle, put the cork back in, and throw it at us, saying something in a language I didn't understand. He would've been better off saving his piss for later, but he didn't realize that yet. That bottle was the signal to start shooting. We may look shabby to you Europeans (or maybe I should say "they" look shabby, since I'm not a soldier) in our tattered shirts and dirt-covered pants; at first sight we don't scare anybody, but in a real battle anyone seeing us at full gallop, howling louder than the Egyptian battalion and the African zephyrs put together, anyone who saw us coming, charging closer and closer, well, they wouldn't piss politely into a bottle, like that French legionnaire—they would shit their pants. The only problem was that our lances and our horses weren't much good, at that point, and no matter how brave and experienced the cavalry was, we weren't very good fighting on foot, if I'm honest. One of our mounted soldiers was taken down by the first French shot. But when Fate's on your side, everything turns out all right. The legionnaires had two mules loaded with supplies and ammunition; they were the kind of mules that don't need a bridle or a halter, and are trained to follow a male. When they saw the stray horse that by chance happened to come up to graze right outside the hacienda, the mules went running after him. Camarón, Camarón . . . Those legionnaires were pretty damn careless. They started shouting like madmen at the mules to get them to come back, and I told myself, these guys have to be really stupid. How can Mexican mules understand French? It's not that mules really understand what you tell 'em, but they do respond, if I'm making myself clear. And well, I'm not even a soldier, let alone a French legionnaire, but if I'd been one, I would've shot the mules right away, so that no one else could've used the supplies and ammunition. As it happened, the legionnaires now had no food as well as no water. But our smart captain told us then that those legionnaires are like devils who can put up with everything, that they get their strength and virility from absinthe, and from a wine as red and thick as blood. He told us that they know how to ride camels and that they kill Bedouins as quick as mosquitoes. But when the Bedouins catch those legionnaires in turn, and, they say, tie them to posts so that dogs can eat them alive, the legionnaires don't say a word. And, our captain said, all of them are sick with the "sylphis" or whatever you call it: every one of them is a living sore from head to toe, but this condition is also what makes those demons so damn strong. But not here,

Captain—we've already seen that they can't take it, I told him, or, I mean, I wish I could've told him, 'cause who am I to contradict a captain, who am I to talk back to an officer? Anyway: not here. Here in Camarón we're going to kill 'em all, if you can put any stock in pure numbers, 'cause over there on that side there are only sixty men, and here, on this side there are a thousand of us. I should've had the nerve to tell the Colonel: even if Napoleon sent twenty thousand soldiers, there's a million of us here; and the Emperor, that Frenchie, and that damn Austrian they want to send us, well, they would've been better off, would've been better served if they'd just sat down and done some counting, 'cause numbers don't lie. Nobody taught me how to add or subtract: I can't read numbers or write them on paper, but I know how to count flowers and buzzards. I know how to count down the days and the dead. And I never miss. Buzzards never miss either. That's why this time—it didn't matter that our losses were worse than theirs, since there were so many of us—the buzzards began circling, not above us, but above the Hacienda Camarón. Maybe the buzzards are starting to like that white French and German meat better: they're getting spoiled. I said our losses were worse, there were many more dead on our side, the Mexican side, 'cause out of every twelve bullets the legionnaires fired they put one in a Mexican, they were such good shots. One of the other eleven bullets disappeared into thin air; another one took a dip in the *arroyo*, skipping upstream like a silvery salmon; another bit the dust and twisted like a fire cracker; another buried itself in the trunk of a mahogany tree, sending out blue sparks, and another one, you won't believe me, but I saw it, it killed the hummingbird I was looking at earlier on, and let me tell you, it's not easy to shoot down a hummingbird, they're smaller than a bullet and just as fast. But that was a lucky shot and all that was left of the poor thing was a small spray of feathers; what else could have been left? I started counting our dead soldiers but there were too many and they were scattered all over, I started counting the legionnaires and like that song about the beer bottles, I said: sixty legionnaires in the troop, sixty legionnaires—one was shot dead, and then there were fifty-nine, fifty-eight, etc. When I only had a few left, I lost count, It was noon. The legionnaires stopped shooting and we did the same. There was silence, a huge silence that seemed as big as the world. But when I say silence I don't exactly mean that, 'cause the rainforest is never quiet. If those legionnaires could've lasted longer, if they had spent the night at the Hacienda de Camarón, they would've seen, or better, they would've heard, that at night the forest is more alive than in the daytime. The Colonel tied a white hankie to a spear, and raised it above some brush; next he showed himself and asked for the legionnaires' unconditional surrender. A howling monkey was the first to answer us. Then a legionnaire that I had already seen before, crouching on a rooftop—I just don't know why the bullets hadn't even touched 'im—this was a blond guy that our smart captain had guessed was a Pole 'cause of the way he talked—stood up and asked those below him how to say "Shit!" in Spanish to answer us. The Colonel pretended not to understand and waited to see what the Captain with the wooden hand would say. But those idiots refused to give in. They said legionnaires never surrender. Camarón, Camarón . . . One of those birds you can always hear laughing but can never actually catch sight of answered them back. And then there was another belly laugh like the first one, but it wasn't a bird, it was our Colonel. Then a captain laughed, and the rest of us joined in, and in a few minutes there were about a thousand "birds" laughing at the trapped legionnaires, those starving and thirsty legionnaires, with the square-visored kepis, those legionnaires and their captain in his black and gold cape, and his wooden hand. We uncorked our bottles and shouted at them, Cheers Frenchies! We tossed crackers from our rations up in the air so they could see we had more than enough. We drank out of our canteens, gargled, and spit out the water so they could see we didn't need any. We tied white rags, tulips, underwear, birthwort plants, and *colorín* tree branches to our spears and bayonets. Then we shouted at them, here's the peace that you turned down, you sons of bitches—we're going to stick it to you, and you know where! Next we grabbed the bullets from their two runaway mules, and since we couldn't use them 'cause they were too long and sharp for our Spencer rifles— though later, after we got their rifles, we did end up using them—we tossed them up in the air by the handful to show them that we didn't give a damn about bullets either. But like I already told you, when I say we did this and that, I really mean that it was them, the soldiers, 'cause I'm not a soldier, just a spy. Not only can I freeze for hours at a time but I can also crawl along the ground and not make a sound, not disturb so much as a leaf, like a feathered snake. I took advantage of the truce and the noise from the laughing birds to crawl out in search of dead soldiers. You just can't make a living out of telling stories. People pay me almost nothing, when they do pay me. I make more money from the dead than from the living. I can get more for a gold ring than from telling someone everything I had to do to get it out of a dead man's tight fist. I can get more money from a silver chain than from telling how I choked the dying man who was wearing it and helped him get to heaven a little quicker. I get a few pesos from almost every battle, and two or three gold teeth, silk handkerchiefs, and Cuban cigars. But what I wanted most out of the Camarón siege was a legionnaire's kepi, some French boots, a blue jacket, and some madder-dyed pants. Well, what I really wanted to get out of the Camarón siege was not the kepi, nor the boots, the blue jacket, or the madder-dyed pants—what I really wanted was Captain D'Anjou's wooden hand. I'll give it to the highest bidder. I have it here in this bag. I didn't even have to rip it off the man—it jumped right out when a bullet hit the Captain in the chest: he went one way, and his hand went the other—I saw it leap as high as a bird, and like a wounded bird I saw it fall in the dust, and like a dying bird I saw it shake on the ground, until still another stray bullet grazed it and made it jump again, after the Captain was already dead. And then the heat began to die down, but by that time the legionnaires were dying of thirst; they were licking each other's sweat and they were crawling so they could drink the blood of the wounded, and even though they didn't really have the urge, they were trying to piss into their canteens so they could drink it. Then we heard a bugle or what we thought was a bugle—the legionnaires thought the same thing—and the Colonel got anxious 'cause he thought that other legionnaires were coming to break the siege. But nothing happened. Nobody came to help them, and I thought maybe since there's a laughing bird there's also a bugle bird. And we began imitating the French bugles and the French trumpets getting ready for the final charge, pointing our bayonets: out of the fifty-eight legionnaires that I'd had left, one was killed by a bullet that went into one of his cheeks and came out the other end pulling a row of teeth and a chunk of his tongue behind it, so that left me fifty-seven; and then out of those fifty-seven, one was killed by a bullet that went in through his armpit without even tickling him, so that left me fifty-six; and then out of those fifty-six, fifty were accounted for by another fifty bullets. When there were only six legionnaires corralled in the Hacienda Camarón (six or maybe fifteen, if I counted wrong, but anyway no more than what I could count with the fingers of three hands) the Colonel said, that's enough, let's finish them off, and we charged the corral. I mean, they did, they began the assault 'cause I was hiding quietly behind the geraniums, just watching so I could tell you what happened, not because I'm afraid to die but because, among other things, I make a living out of telling stories, and if I die, ladies and gentlemen, I can't tell you how I died. If I died, I'd be the only dead guy that I couldn't make a living from. One time I got some field glasses that belonged to a dead captain on the battlefield, and I sold them to another officer 'cause I don't need field glasses to see a long way off—I'm used to it. I jumped out of the geranium bed and climbed to the top of a *capulín* cherry tree so I could see what was happening close to the corral wall facing the river. I jumped down from the cherry tree to hide in some hawthorns so from there I could see what was happening in the rooms facing the corral. I climbed a *colorín* tree 'cause from there I could see what was happening at the entrance to the corral that faces the main road. On the *capulín* tree I filled my pockets with cherries and I kept very still so I wouldn't scare off a *Jalapa* cardinal that was pecking its feathers for fleas. I was the one that got scared at the hawthorns 'cause when I took a shit there I got my ass full of thorns. On the cherry tree I took advantage of the situation and began eating the cherries and spitting the pits out, trying to hit the open mouth of one of our dead below to see how many I could get in. From the *capulín* tree I saw how some legionnaires were trying to escape by climbing over a pile of bodies almost as high as the wall facing the river, and I saw them jump over that wall, but on the other side some of our soldiers ran them through with their bayonets, like chickens. From the hawthorn I saw how one of our men drove his bayonet into a legionnaire's neck, and I saw the spurt of blood that came rushing out, and how, in revenge, a legionnaire drove his bayonet into the bladder of one of our other men, and how a stream of urine came spurting out. From the *colorín* tree I saw a Mexican and a Frenchie fighting with daggers and I saw how they embraced in order to stab each other in the back. I saw how they fell dead, still embracing, like they were making love. Then I remembered that our well-informed captain had said that since they go such a long time without seeing women, many legionnaires end up making love to each other, but that the officers look the other way 'cause they don't care if they're not manly when they make love, so long as they're manly when they fight us. And they are. They're devils, monsters. From the fifteen or so legionnaires that were left, one died from a bayonet wound, and then all I had left were about fourteen. From those fourteen-odd soldiers I had left, one died from a knife wound and all I had left were thirteen, more or less. And since thirteen is an unlucky number, when you have luck, only three or four were left alive at the end of the day, and our men took them prisoner. All the rest are still there in Camarón or, I mean, they were. I waited till everything was over and night fell. I closed my eyes but I didn't fall asleep. I never fall asleep even when I close my eyes. And now, gentlemen, let me show you what I have in this bag. These are the pits from the actual cherries from the Battle of Camarón, gentlemen, the pits from the very same cherries I picked with my own hands when I was on top of the *capulín* tree watching how the legionnaires died. These are the actual feathers from the hummingbird at the Battle of Camarón, gentlemen, the very same feathers I took with my own hands after the poor creature was killed by a French bullet. These are the actual flowers from the *colorín* tree of the Battle of Camarón, gentlemen, the very same flowers I picked with my own hands when I was on top of the *colorín* watching how the French were being killed. Like I say, I didn't bring back kepis, leggings, blue jackets, or madder-dyed trousers, not just 'cause I wasn't interested in kepis, leggings, jackets, or pants, but 'cause when our men had left and I tiptoed to the hacienda's corral I found that the bodies were all naked 'cause our men had already taken all their clothing, and worse than that, gentlemen, all their money, all their rings, all their silver medals, and their gold teeth. Those poor devils were so naked they didn't even look like legionnaires anymore but like ordinary Christians—but at least they couldn't feel the cold or the heat anymore. I kicked the rats and the dogs away from the corpses. This rat pelt you see here, ladies and gentlemen, is the skin of an authentic rat from the Battle of Camarón. But what I really wanted to find and finally found, Captain D'Anjou's wooden hand, was still there after all, half-hidden among the corpses. It was still warm, so to speak. And I have it with me gentlemen. And if someone tells you that I've sold Captain D'Anjou's hand more than once, it's true, but it's also a lie. Since you can't make a living just from telling stories, like I told you, I got into the business of making wooden hands like Captain D'Anjou's. I sold one to a priest who wanted to use it as a bell ringer. I sold another one to a Frenchman who knew almost as many stories as I do—not from having witnessed them in real life, but from having read about them in books. I sold another one through the mail to the widow of Captain D'Anjou herself. I don't know who else I sold the others to, but I got good money for them. But look, this, right here, is the real hand from the Battle of Camarón, the authentic wooden hand of Captain D'Anjou. Look at it, it has the same road dust on it that you'll find on the road to Hacienda de Camarón. Yes, this hand here, among the *capulín* pits and hummingbird feathers and the petals of the *colorín* flowers, is the wooden hand Captain D'Anjou used to smash the

Berbers' faces at Mers-El-Kébir. This is the hand that a carpenter from Constantine made to replace the hand of the hero of Kabylia and Magenta, of the illustrious soldier of Saint-Cyr who lost a hand without glory or danger in Algeria. Look at it. Look at the blood of that same Captain D'Anjou. Look at the splinters made by the bullet that made it jump that the second time, like I told you. This is the hand that slapped the face of the despairing legionnaires, rousing them from their stupor; the hand that struck the map of Veracruz when the Captain said: Here is Camarón, here we've arrived, and here we stay. Look at it, ladies and gentlemen. This is the authentic hand that was left without a Captain who was left without a hand. It has been certified by the Mayor of Chiquihuite. My witnesses are God and the moles, all the Saints and the mahogany trees. It's been certified by a Polish deserter who took off for California searching for gold nuggets the size of pumpkins; it's even been certified by the very same Captain D'Anjou, who found time to autograph it just before dying. And I'll exchange it, gentlemen, I'll exchange this authentic hand for ten silver pesos, if you're rich, or for a bottle of rum, if you're poor; I'll even trade it, if you want, for another story that I can take away and sell, gentlemen—with only one condition: that it's a better story than the one about Camarón, Camarón, Camarón . . .

3. From the Correspondence—Incomplete—between Two Brothers

Paris, April 25, 1864

My dear Jean-Pierre:

Thank you for your prompt letters; I appreciate them. It's always a pleasure to hear from you. However, I get somewhat overwhelmed when I receive a second, sometimes a third, letter from you before I can reply. I don't know how I can call myself a historian and think that I can write a three or four volume history on the Thirty Years' War when apathy keeps me from sending a few lines to my only brother on the other side of the ocean. I beg your forgiveness and I promise to write more often.

The news that you've married in Mexico came as a surprise, as you can probably imagine, but it was also of great comfort for reasons I'll explain here. You will remember that a long time ago you suggested that I take Claude with me to Père Lachaise, to put flowers on Mother's grave. I did ask her and, afterwards, I ventured to invite her to lunch. We returned to the cemetery several more times, at her insistence. A great friendship grew between us based mainly on our mutual love for you—she as your fiancée and I as your brother. But Claude was very bored, and your stay in Mexico became so long, that I thought the least I could do was ask her to go out with me, to distract her a bit. From then on we started to see each other—more and more often we went to the theater and the opera (always chaperoned by one of her sisters), as well as the botanical gardens and museums. I will not say, "You can figure out the rest yourself." No, don't even think about it, my dear Jean-Pierre, there was no betrayal. We always talked about you, of your letters, of how happy you and Claude would be after your marriage. I even tried to persuade her to travel to Mexico. Finally—what can I say?—we fell in love like a pair of adolescents. Neither of us had the nerve to confess it to the other. And this is the reason I can say that I was relieved to hear about your marriage in Mexico, as no doubt you too will be relieved to hear that Claude did not suffer when I told her the news. She asked me to send you and María del Carmen her best wishes for your happiness. The same goes for me.

And now, my dear brother, I'll take the liberty of continuing the epistolary discussion that we started almost two years ago about the Mexican imbroglio. Despite the fact that our sublime Lamartine insists that it's a likewise sublime idea to establish a kingdom "as vast as the ocean"—what else can one expect from a man who said that abandoning Algiers was equivalent to renouncing our mission and our glory?—enthusiasm has already begun to wane not only among the general public but also those politicians who favored intervention, who consider the enterprise audaciously conceived, but find its execution too timid and indecisive.

Poland is another factor that distracted us from the Mexican venture. Although the press hasn't abandoned Mexico as a topic for discussion, including those in the opposition—*L'Opinion Nationale* frequently prints segments of Favre's speeches, and *Le Courrier de la Gironde* has made a point of publishing Juárez's most important declarations—last year, when Wielopolski's politics brought about an uprising in Poland, we French stopped thinking about Mexico and Latin America almost entirely, and shifted our attention to the Poles. The same old story: Mickiewics, Chopin, and other Messianic émigrés in Paris, almost all of them Polish, made France believe itself to be the self-appointed apostle of all nations, and the guardian of freedom. The police of the world. Of course this distraction gave an even freer hand to Louis Napoleon with regard to Mexico.

But perhaps what most displeases me about all this is realizing that this régime—Napoleon's—is so totally lacking in moral authority. You tell me that you miss the marvelous Parisian life. I understand you perfectly. It seems marvelous to you and to those of us who have privileges, for all who can spend the afternoon at the Café Bignon, or go to the Clay Pigeon Shooting Club at the Bois de Boulogne on Sundays, or to those who can afford the luxury of losing two thousand louies in one evening of baccarat. It's marvelous for the Duke of Gramont Caderousse who recently gave his paramour a giant Easter egg, so large that it held a life-size horse and buggy inside. Yes, Parisian life, at least that life that Octave Feuillet describes in his novels and Offenbach in his operettas, can be lovely if you are a courtier, a nouveau riche (or a *vieu riche*, an aristocrat who still hasn't lost his wealth, as we have), if you are Prosper Mérimée and you prepare gazpacho at Compiègne tea parties (how far will people go, for Heaven's sake?), or you are one of the five thousand "lucky ones" who are invited to the lavish masked balls at the Tuileries, or, finally a well-off petit bourgeois who can have the luxury of eating well, drinking fine wines, and following the latest fashion trends (I ask myself if it was people like this who helped make the colors named for the sites of our past victories—magenta, solferino, Crimean green, and Sebastopol blue—so fashionable. I imagine that now we will have fabrics in Puebla yellow or Tampico green soon). What else can I say about a city that you know as well as I? But someday I would like to invite you to visit the Paris of the Goncourt Brothers—the City of Lights known as the Brothel of Europe— so that you can see firsthand its poverty and prostitution. So that you can go to Belleville and Ménilmontant or to the filthy Rue Harvey with me. The Goncourts, who have attended rat-hunts (Paris is infested with these disgusting rodents), speak of other horrors in their novels as well. It's believed that there are more than thirty thousand prostitutes in Paris. There are some quarters the police dare not patrol. Baron Haussmann estimates that four-fifths of this marvelous city's population live in poverty, not to mention the drunks that you find lying in the streets, out of their minds from drinking absinthe, and the children whose parents hire out to beggars so that they'll be able to seem all the more pitiable.

You probably wonder how relevant all this is to the Mexican affair. Very much so, I say. I am unable to see how we can justify invading a nation in the name of social justice when there is so much corruption and inequality right here in France. Every colonial enterprise that boasts a civilizing mission is only a miserable fraud, as the most praiseworthy Jean-Jacques Rousseau has said. Nor do I understand how Louis Napoleon dared address the Mexican people in almost the same words as the Allies used in 1814, when they invaded our own country to "free us from a tyrant," who was of course none other than our Louis's own uncle.

We find fault with Mexico in every way. In Europe we laugh at Santa Anna for having imposed a tax on windows, when the window tax was an English concept from the 1830s. We also deride Santa Anna for having created a miniature court on his little Danish island. However, Napoleon did the exact same thing when he created his little kingdom at Elba, with its very own ministers, national anthem, and flag designed by the "Great Corsican" Himself. But of course no one dared laugh at him, because, even there, he still terrified them.

It is also said that a proof of Mexico's political instability is the large number of governments it's had. But Achille Jubinal has reminded us that during the last seventy years we ourselves have had more than twelve régimes in France (I think he's miscalculated, actually, since, just counting Louis Philippe's reign, we've had seventeen different cabinets in eighteen years). And what about the number of different régimes in Spain under the rule of María Cristina and Doña Isabella II? I think that we can safely say there were dozens of them, as well as a long succession of military dictatorships.

They call Juárez a tyrant because he has implemented a mandatory draft. I oppose such a measure, as you can imagine. But Juárez did not invent the draft. Instead, as you well know, it was our Committee on Public Safety in 1793, under the auspices of Lazare Carnot, who did this. Moreover, Napoleon I implemented that selfsame law in all the nations that he conquered. Of the seven hundred thousand soldiers who made it to Moscow, only a third were French. Later, the Austrians dragged peasants out of the Lombardo-Veneto provinces to induct into the armed forces that invaded their own lands. And think of all the deserters from the Egyptian battalion in Mexico. Those poor devils are deserting because we the French stranded them there by force, as we did not long ago in Dahomey when we formed Hausa marksmen battalions in Madagascar, without the right—as indeed Juárez has, and legitimately—of citing the need to defend the integrity of our own national territory as a motivating factor.

Another frequent topic here is that of the Mexican atrocities. In one of your letters you yourself said that there are many more atrocities occurring there than in any other country at war. For God's sake, Jean-Pierre, how can you make such a statement when you, as well as I, know the infinite number of cruelties found throughout history, among which *il sacco di Roma*—when lansquenets committed such outrageous abuses and inconceivable crimes as raping nuns and beheading priests and friars for a whole week—and the St. Bartholomew Day's Massacre are only two examples. I could also list the Afghan massacre of the British in 1841; of Christians by the Druze in 1860; of Turks by the Greeks at Khios in 1821, and the Greeks by the Turks in '22; the Poles by the Russians in Warsaw only two years ago; not to mention the massacres during the mutiny in India. (By the way, this was an uprising the British stifled aided by conscripts from the Punjab). In any case, I'm not going to write out a whole catalogue of atrocities here (a Universal Encyclopedia of Infamy would contain too many volumes!), but I'm certainly interested in clarifying some things . . .

I'll never forget (I was six or seven at the time) that Christmas afternoon we spent with Grandfather François at Perpignan (remember?) when he suddenly decided to tell about the horrors of the Revolution, which he witnessed when he was barely a child. Two scenes persist in my mind, as though I had witnessed them myself. First are those children and women on the night of the fall of the Bastille, bearing torches and dancing around three beheaded corpses. The other is the sight of the mob that undressed and quartered Princess Lamballe and stuck her head on one pole and skewered her heart on another, raising them below Marie Antoinette's prison window. It was very painful for me to learn that we, the French, were capable of such monstrosities. You could argue that in the case of Princess Lamballe, as in many others, it was irrational behavior perpetrated by a hysterical mob. We cannot forget, however, that our Revolution had leaders like Robespierre and other intellectuals, who were responsible for many terrible iniquities. In the name of fraternity, equality and liberty ("Liberty, how many crimes have been committed in thy name!" said Manon Roland at the foot of the guillotine) more than forty thousand were summarily executed en masse in Paris, Vendée, Lyon, and who knows where else. And for what purpose? To betray all the ideals of the Revolution and to submit us to that "Robespierre on horseback," as Mme. de Staël referred to Napoleon I? In the name of civilization and the glory of France—a nation that, being Catholic, should be ruled by the principle of the universal equality of men, but which nonetheless undertook the extermination of the black rebels of Haiti, as though they were animals? The letter in which Leclerc told his brother-in-law Napoleon that the best course of action in Haiti was to slaughter all the black mountain people, including women, sparing only the children under twelve, is widely known. I need not tell you anything about the other infamous acts committed in Europe. You are well aware of the ferocious repression by Cavaignac of the June Days Uprising here in France in '48 and, to cite another example of a country involved in the Mexican venture, the atrocities committed in Bréscia and Hungary in the name of Austria by General Haynau, whom Palmerston justly nicknamed "General Hyena."

And now, my dear Jean-Pierre, didn't you mention that at the end of the Reform War in Mexico, a victorious Juárez declared a general amnesty and did not order a single execution or reprisal of any kind? That after the May 5th victory he released all the wounded French soldiers and had them transported to Orizaba? That Lorencez received the medals of all of those who died in battle so that they could be sent to their relatives in France? Is it to combat this man's government ("a man worthy of Plutarch, that any country would be proud to claim," as described by Émile Ollivier) that we have sent officers such as Billault, who, as you know, has spent his life setting fire to villages and destroying whole cities; such as Berthelin, known as an assassin, or Potier, denounced for his numberless excesses? Among these rogues, Colonel Dupin no doubt wins first prize, as you well know. It's irrefutable that Juárez's men commit atrocities at times, but we must also keep in mind that many bandits hide under the republican flag to carry out their crimes without retribution. I was told that a group of Liberals once buried some enemy soldiers alive—standing up, up to their necks. Later, those Liberals attracted Dupin's men by firing shots so that their horses would trample those same poor devils' heads. This was unarguably a savage act, but it is not so unlike the methods applied by Dupin, the looter of Peking Palace, and his followers: Mexican guerrillas buried alive in the dunes at Alvarado; men thrown into the Tamesí River with stones tied around their necks; others mangled by bloodhounds in Veracruz tidepools. (I have been told that there's a bounty not only on Dupin's head but also on his mastiff's—two thousand pesos). There are also the men he had hanged from lampposts in Tampico squares. All of those victims of barbarity incite a desire for brutal vengeance and reprisal. And please don't tell me that those officers are exceptions. You can't forget that a man whose hands are covered in blood leads the expedition. Yes, I am referring to Marshal Bazaine, so admired these days, who was sent to Mexico not only because he speaks Spanish but also because of his actions in Algiers. That is to say, because he distinguished himself in subduing a nation fighting for its freedom. It's not a secret that Bazaine, expert participant in sallies against so many annihilated villages in Kabylia, was one of those responsible for burning and asphyxiating five hundred Algerians of the Ouled-Riah tribe, including many women and children, inside a rocky Dahra cavern. By the way, since the number of soldiers who aren't French in the counter-guerrilla forces and in the Foreign Legion is so large, so huge, does Louis Napoleon honestly propose to defend the "Latin Spirit" in the American Continent with such a motley rabble of Prussians, Dutch, Württembergers, and Martinique Africans? And what about Catholicism? Will he defend it using these same Protestants and Moslem Egyptians, the latter of whom still kneel in prayer toward Mecca right after cutting off their Mexican prisoners' ears?

Speaking of a "Latin Spirit," I shall digress briefly here. You know that the Tuileries is filled with dreams of greatness—Eugénie pictures herself as another Isabella the Catholic—and Louis Napoleon speaks openly of the other American republics that can be transformed into monarchies, besides those that, he says, are already leaning in this direction, like Guatemala, Ecuador, and Paraguay. But notice that these republics aren't called "Spanish" or, much less, "Ibero" or "Indo" American. No, there's a new term—apparently originated by Michel Chevalier—which is much more convenient for the purposes of France. Mexico, Colombia, Argentina, etc., fall now under the term "Latin" America. Obviously Louis Napoleon could hardly pass himself off as defender of the "Spanish American Spirit." The problem is easily solved when one substitutes "Latin" for "Spanish," and now one can also incorporate all the French-speaking present and future Caribbean colonies into the same America . . .

Of course, it's not my intention to suggest that we, the Europeans, are responsible for history's greatest atrocities. I don't think that there is a single nation or race that has the doubtful privilege of a monopoly on barbarity. I am far from agreeing with Fourier's claims that our ships travel the world only to introduce savages and barbarians to our vices and passions. I don't believe in the "noble savage" myth to which Columbus contributed so much when he wrote the Catholic Monarchs that he had found the best land and the best people in the world. But neither do I share the philosophy of Bacon, Voltaire,

Hume, and others, who did not recognize the equality of the "degraded people" of the New World, those who apparently upheld Aristotle's idea that war
is naturally just when it is waged against those born to obey and who refuse
to do so. No, we white people are in no way the only ones who have made this
world a more sinister place than it is by its own nature. Montesquieu tells us
that Egyptian priests sacrificed every white man who fell into their power. All
you need is to take one look at the history of slavery to be horrified by the fact
that Western African tribes fought among themselves constantly to capture
prisoners of war to sell as slaves to the Portuguese or the British. Haiti's King
Christophe is notorious for his cruelty. And yes, of course the Aztecs were also
cruel, were they not? They performed human sacrifices. That, of course, was
wrong. But what we Europeans cannot allow is to keep being shocked by those
sacrifices when, at the same time they were being committed, the Inquisition
was at its horrible peak in Europe. There was one difference—the Aztecs had
a religion based on cruel gods, so their sacrifices, albeit morbid, had a certain
logic. We Europeans tortured the innocent and burned witches at the stake in
the name of a God who was all mercy and love. Slavery was also at its peak—in
1517 Spain gave the Flemish the monopoly over the trade of Africans—and it
remained big business for many centuries thereafter.

But, of course, if we started enumerating the horrors of slavery, my dear
Jean-Pierre, we would never stop. Europe's insatiable need for sugar, cotton,
tobacco, indigo and other raw materials was the cause of what no doubt was
the most inhumane commerce in history. Most at fault were not only the soul-
less traffickers who took chained slaves to the Caribbean, Brazil, and North
America, but those who, in power—kings, pontiffs, the entire system—allowed and encouraged this monstrous trade. Did you know that our illustrious
Colbert recommended the slave trade as indispensable to the progress of the
French merchant marines? Do the English know that their just as illustrious
Admiral Nelson—who always took ten- and eleven-year-old boys to service
his cannons—opposed the abolition of slavery since he thought it would cause
the ruin of the British Navy? What about the ruin—physical and moral—of
the torture, the humiliation, the suffering, and the death of millions of human
beings? No one cared. The system required it, and still does, because abolition
did not end slavery. I'm not referring here to the fact that trafficking continued
after abolition was implemented. Indeed, it brought about worse atrocities,
because, as you know, the captains of illegal slaving ships prefer to dump their

human cargo before being caught in the act. The case revealed by Benjamin Constant—of the ship *Jeanne Estelle*, whose slaves were thrown into the ocean in sealed coffins—is only one among many. No, I speak of the type of serfdom denounced by Lamennais in *Modern Slavery*, and by Charles Dickens, and, recently, the Goncourt Brothers, in their novels. The fact that there is no longer a Duke of York to brand his initials on the buttocks of the three thousand slaves that he sent to sugar plantations every year doesn't mean that the inhuman conditions that turn a majority of men—women and children too—into beasts of burden to serve a small privileged minority, do not still prevail. It's difficult to believe that in the 19th century, in civilized England, during the rise of the so-called Luddite movement, during which the British government was forced to send more troops to Nottinghamshire than Wellington sent to Spain, the death penalty was imposed after the destruction of a textile mill. Capital punishment was already in existence in any case, as a reward for poaching pheasant and sometimes for cattle theft. The English were even crueler toward their colonized subjects, often starving them to death. You and I had already been born when the notorious "Corn Laws," designed to protect English farmers, were the cause of a famine in Ireland that wiped out hundreds of thousands of people and forced millions to immigrate to America, crowded in the bilges on Cunard steamships.

But there is quite a bit more to say about this. We need only think of the horrors that followed the conquest of America to be ashamed of Europe's history. Here I want to clarify that I have learned many things about America from a Mexican scholar who lives in Paris. Consequently, one of these days I'm considering abandoning my studies on the Thirty Years' War—on Gustavus Adolphus, Wallenstein, and the Defenestration of Prague—to turn toward Artigas, the bloody epics of the "Bandeirantes," and Leona Vicario; that is, if one can cover that wide a field. But as I was saying, it is sufficient to know about the colonization of the Americas in all its cruelty: the slaughter perpetrated by Cortés in Cholula, and Pedro de Alvarado in the Main Temple of Tenochtitlan. Or Atahualpa's torture in Cajamarca at the hands of the illiterate brute, Francisco Pizarro. Or in Cuzco, that of Tupac Amarú, whose head and limbs were distributed to the four cardinal points in Peru. Of course we can add the torture of Cuauhtémoc, the persecution of Indians by Balboa and his hounds, the desecration of tombs in Colombia to extract emeralds from the bellies of corpses; the hundreds of thousands of lives sacrificed to the extraction of gold in the hills of Potosí . . . In any case, I don't intend to get into an endless list of atrocities. Las Casas's statement that Indians preferred to go to hell so that they would not run into Christians in heaven, as well as their committing suicide to escape the inhuman slavery in the mines, is more than explicit enough, and more moving than any story I could tell you. And we must add to Spain's crimes those of Great Britain—for example the systematic annihilation of the Redskins in North America. This didn't stop with the slaughters in Wyoming and Arapahoe, but it goes on to this day. Did you know that Minnesota's governor has just published an edict offering twenty-five dollars for each Indian scalp brought to him? By the way, this was a practice wrongly attributed to Indians—it was actually invented by their Anglo-Saxon conquerors. Yes, I know, the Indians were no lambs. The Iroquois tortured and burned many Jesuits. Some people even say that they fed on their flesh. But what can we expect? Valdivia's torture in Chile at the hands of Araucanos is no small thing either. When I find out the details of this I will let you know, since I need to corroborate what I've heard. Some say that Valdivia was forced to drink melted gold. Others claim that the Araucanos cut off his limbs and pieces of his flesh little by little, as they ate him before his very eyes.

By the way, speaking of the English, there's something else that we never seem to learn. No nation wants a foreign army to help it—without an explicit invitation to do so—to free itself either from local tyrants—in the case of Mexico, I suppose this would be Juárez and his Liberal party—or foreign oppressors. Among the few exceptions that I recall there is, no doubt, the case of Lafayette, Rochambeau, and the Franco-American alliance. But as for the rest, foreign intervention has never had good results. It's different when it concerns one individual, as happened with Garibaldi in Argentina and Uruguay, Lord Byron in Greece, or Francisco Javier Mina in Mexico. But you'll remember how Popham and Beresford's venture in Argentina turned out in 1806. (This was the mission that made the British Parliament resound with the shout of "Rejoice!" and the *Times* to publish the news that "from this day on, Buenos Aires belongs to the United Kingdom." Popham and Beresford thought that all they needed was to land in Buenos Aires, claiming that they had come to liberate its citizens from their Spanish oppressors, to be received with open arms. But you saw what happened—they were thrown out, both that time and when they came back the following year. Even women and children fought against their English "liberators." They were met with sticks and stones, buckets of boiling water, and the contents of many chamber pots, thrown out of the windows of Buenos Aires.) I would not add the Frenchman Liniers, the hero of that little war between England and Argentina, to the list of Byron, Garibaldi, and the rest, because he continued to support the Spanish Crown.

Oh, by the way, I just found out about Ghilardi's death. Ghilardi, as you probably know, was an Italian-born Mexican who fought with Juárez during the Reform War. Later he joined Garibaldi's forces in Italy and returned to Mexico to combat the French. I heard that he was shot in Aguascalientes.

In any case, the die is cast. That sparkling "Mexican" emperor is on his way to America, amid—I'm not exaggerating—an aura of scandal. On one hand, the unproven rumor that Juárez has bribed Jules Favre to have his support has created great indignation in political circles. At the same time, the Interventionists want to justify Maximilian's payment of two hundred thousand dollars to buy off Mexican Liberals. And this is not a rumor. It's written in the so-called Convention of Miramare. On the other hand, people who've given the matter some thought—who, unfortunately, are not too numerous—are amazed that Mexico, the invaded nation, is going to have to pay for its own invasion, down to the last penny. To add insult to injury, the French protectorate project in Sonora would guarantee that Mexico is robbed of all its silver (though we'd leave them ten percent as charity!). But of course, money is the real reason behind the invasion, not stopping the advancement of Saxon infidels, as Charles Martel did with the Saracens. This is all because enormous sums of money are needed to continue sustaining the insolent luxury of the French Court—so that the Observatory's winged dragons will continue to spew *eau de cologne* and colored water when a foreign "dignitary" visits us. So that Madame Rothschild may continue to dress as a bird of paradise; so that our Emperor can reward, with proper gifts, the favors he gets from his functionaries' and courtiers' wives. Things have become so good-naturedly cynical here that each lady who visits the Tuileries knows to put a ring, an earring, or a jewel into a designated basket; if the jewel belonging to that lady is drawn, she is chosen to spend the night with Louis Napoleon, who awaits the lucky winner at a predetermined time every night in his chambers. That's how things are. It's all prostitution. Even Leopold, the future Empress Charlotte's father, comes to Paris to bed the best courtesans. Sometimes Hortense Schneider makes him wait up to an hour outside her hotel. Everybody knows it. How can we possibly tell the Mexicans that we're invading their land in order to civilize them and end corruption in their nation? Tell me, has Juárez ever been accused of squandering his country's treasury on lovers and prostitutes? Or even on his wife? To placate Eugénie's jealousy, Louis Napoleon has to be very generous with her. On a recent afternoon, at the Gardens of Saint-Cloud, the Empress found a four-leaf clover covered in dew. She radiated happiness. A few days later Louis Napoleon gave her a brooch that he had ordered from one of the best jewelers in Paris. It was a four-leaf clover carved from emeralds with diamonds as the dew. In the meantime, a mediocre novelist such as Octave Feuillet turns into the darling of society and the *demi-monde*. Gustave Flaubert, on the other hand, is criticized. A painter such as Renoir starves while a Winterhalter (whose latest painting depicts Eugénie accompanied by her court ladies—a "bouquet of the most exquisite flowers," said a critic) rolls in money.

Last but not least, as the English say, even though the Archduke was fortunate to be rid of Santa Anna, many Mexicans who surround him and support him are far from enjoying an impeccable reputation. Those who live in Europe, such as that caricature of Cato, Gutiérrez Estrada—made wealthy from the sweat and tears of his hemp-picking slaves—or Hidalgo y Esnaurrízar, who had the audacity to increase his own salary by many thousand piasters the moment Maximilian named him ambassador to Paris, are as bad as those who live in Mexico, such as Leonardo Márquez, the Killer of Tacubaya. To make matters worse, the ones crossing the Atlantic with the Archduke aren't much better. For example, there's General Adrián Woll D'Ohm, a former card-dealer in a casino, who left his wife working as a cook in the French Legation; and Francisco de Paula y Arrangóiz, accused of theft ever since he gave himself an exorbitant "commission" (almost seventy thousand dollars) when he represented Santa Anna at the Treaty of La Mesilla. Again, I have received all this information from my friend, the Mexican scholar.

This letter appears to be an endless diatribe. But please understand, Jean-Pierre. None of this is directed toward you. I understand very well that you are a patriot and, as a French military officer, you are only doing your duty. Perhaps it's distasteful at times, but it is, after all, your duty. I only ask you to reflect a bit on what Victor Hugo said: "The war against Mexico is not waged by France but by the Empire." I should also dedicate more space to personal matters, to talk about what everyone always discusses in letters—the weather, our health. Well, Claude and I are both fine although she has just recuperated from a cold that kept her in bed for almost a week. We are enjoying a beautiful spring (although by the time you get this letter, I'm afraid, we will be burning up). I chose a luminous afternoon to show Claude your letter. We were at the Luxembourg Gardens, walking on a path that was virtually covered in flower petals. In a few days she will have her wedding gown. I am very happy that Carmen is an excellent cook, as you say, and that you have learned to enjoy Mexican food. My scholar friend claims that it's quite varied and (in all seriousness) on par with French or Chinese cuisine. I will reserve judgment until I find out personally. I agree with you that everything has its limits. If eating armadillo or iguana sounds bold, a dish of mosquito eggs and agave worms is foolishness.

As always, a loving hug from your dear brother,

ALPHONSE

P.S. Two appropriate items to clarify: Yes, I'm attracted to the work of von Clausewitz, but not because I am interested in strategy but in its political content. After all, he was the one who said that war is nothing but a continuation of politics, didn't he? Now, whether Fort Perote was or was not fortified in the Cormontaigne style as the squares of the Moselle, as you state in one of your letters, tells me absolutely nothing. Please, Jean-Pierre. I have never used a square monocle. The one who uses (or formerly used) one, as I understand, in order to imitate Morny, his protector, was Dubois de Saligny, who, by the way, has fallen from Louis Napoleon's grace. Again, love.

A.

IX

BOUCHOUT CASTLE

1927

When I tell them that one of these days Benito Juárez is going to show up at the Vatican dressed as a Mexican peasant, claiming to be that Indian Juan Diego . . . that he will ask the Pope for a breakfast audience and, when he unfolds his cactus-cloth cloak in front of Pius IX, I shall appear as Our Lady of Guadalupe, I shall stand on a half moon made of ivory, borne by cherubs whose wings will have the Mexican tricolor, and the Pope will be so startled that he will choke on his cocoa, he'll spit out a pink foam and get onto his knees to kiss my feet and the hem of my sky-blue cloak, embroidered with silver stars; just as, many years ago, at the Vienna Mondscheinsaal balls, roses suddenly fell from the ceiling at midnight, the dome at Saint Peter's Basilica will split open and it will rain roses; they will take over the Vatican: roses, thorns and all, will drown the Pope's hot chocolate, they will engulf the Sistine Chapel, they will bury Michelangelo's *Pietà* in their petals, they will flood Rome and will stream down Trinità dei Monti; those roses and their perfume will overcome the Villa Borghese; they will cover Pauline Bonaparte's statue, recently bathed in donkey's milk; they will rush through the Appian Way and they will jump and take a dip in the Roman fountains and the Tiber . . .

Or when I tell them that I shall take the ice-making machine I saw at the Paris World's Fair to Mexico, to freeze Lake Chapultepec on a sweltering summer day like those when Aztec emperors had to bathe three times, while the band plays "Over the Waves"—the waltz composed by Juventino Rosas whom you did not know because he was born two years after I went mad and died more than thirty years ago—you and I will join hands and skate on the lake's frozen, blue waters, me dressed as a *china poblana* and you as a *charro*; though on your head will be the Aztec Emperor's feather headdress that you wanted so badly to take back to Mexico, but which your brother refused you—the headdress that you found as a child between Schubert's square piano and the Egyptian figurines, Joseph Haydn's clavichord and the Polynesian masks; its long, green quetzal feathers, bright and iridescent, dusted with gold, awing you—the most beautiful plumes you had ever seen—and you had never seen anything like it so you mistook the headdress for the largest and most sumptuous fan in the world, the fan that belonged to the Queen of Sheba; but the headdress is still in Vienna, you'll be surprised to know, at the Hofburg Ethnological Museum, with the Far East bric-a-brac that our dear yacht, the *Novara*, brought to Europe; there you can also find the Brazilian collection of Don Pedro I, and a few of the things of yours that weren't stolen or destroyed in Mexico, along with Captain James Cook's memoirs from the South Seas (as you know, Maximilian, he was beaten and stabbed to death by the Hawaiians for the same reason that you were executed in Querétaro, having believed in the nonexistent guiltlessness of savages).

(Though, at the Hofburg Museum, I haven't seen those buttons that the ladies from Querétaro made of Sierra Gorda opals for your nightshirt, I haven't seen the bleeding heart that your brother Franz Joseph gave us as a wedding present—that's what they called it, because it was a very large heart-shaped diamond bordered with rubies, remember?—I haven't seen it for a long time. They stole everything, Maximilian, our honor, my jewelry, your portraits, my happiness, your smiles, my life savings, despite the fact that Prince Ligne swears that my wealth grows daily. He claims that my money is invested in the rubber plantations my brother Leopold set up in the Congo. But I know that's a lie. Everything has been stolen. They have left us nothing. How do you want me to finance my voyage? I ask them. Those Burmese rubies that I left in Chapultepec while hurrying to come to Europe were lost as well. They told me that some Mexican nouveaux riches who left Mexico during the Revolution on a ship that sank in Chesapeake Bay took them.)

Or when I tell them that I shall write to Madame Tussauds wax museum to send me Grandmother Marie Antoinette's head, and Robespierre's and Father Hidalgo's . . . that I will put them in my bedroom at Bouchout and converse with them every morning; that I will put blush on Marie Antoinette's cheeks so that she won't look so pale, and will dust Father Hidalgo's head with rice powder to cover the black spots that came from hanging in a cage outdoors—every night I'll put the heads in a glass case; and I'll also ask for the head of Charles I of England, and of Frederick the Great's friend and lover, Von Katte, beheaded by his father, the King Sergeant, before Frederick's eyes; and the head of Mons, Catherine the Great's lover that her husband Pedro I gave her to keep in a glass case so that she would never forget her betrayal . . . poor Catherine of Russia, she never overcame being a servant, a Lithuanian peasant . . . when I ran into her at the Fair she was falling-down drunk . . .

When I tell them all of this, Maximilian, then they can truly think and claim that I am mad.

Or when I suddenly get up in the middle of the night and I order them to light up the entire castle and to unveil the birdcages so that the birds think it is daylight and sing . . . When I make my ladies-in-waiting dress as every one of the Carlotas I have been in my life—one in the bridal gown that I donned to marry you in Saint Gudula's Cathedral; another wearing the Order of Malta and the pink crinoline that I first wore when you accepted the crown of Mexico; and a third in the cherry-colored silk dress that I wore when we entered Milan—then they can truly say that I am mad. Let them say it, Maximilian, although I know that I do not say such things, and that every time that I make the servants wear those clothes they follow me around and torture me and shout at me and remind me how happy I was when I was nine and Uncle Aumale told me how he defeated the Emir Abd al-Qadir in Algiers; they put their cheeks next to my face so that I can smell my mother's perfume and lily breath; when I wake up in the morning they're all there, in my bedchamber, the same as always: Mademoiselle de la Fontaine at the head of my bed, wearing the black dress and broad-brimmed white hat that I wore when I went to drink from the Fountain of Bees; at the foot of my bed, Charlotte de Brander wearing my First Holy Communion gown, a rosary in her hands; standing at the open window, bathed in sunlight, is Anna Goeder, dressed in the garments that I wore when Winterhalter painted my portrait in Paris when I was twenty-two. Now quietly, now mutely, they thus remind me of how innocent, proud, beautiful, and slim I once was; how my eyes sparkled and how they changed colors from dark chestnut to light green when I looked out my bedroom window at Laeken and the sun hit my face. My brothers thought that I was contemplating the horizon but my eyes went beyond that, beyond the Soignies and d'Afflinghem Forests, and the bell tower at St. Gertrude's in Louvain, and the Hôtel de Gérard le Diable in Ghent, and beyond all the domes, the turrets, the pillars, and the bell towers of all the churches in Brussels, Courtrai, Charleroi, and beyond my dreams.

The other day when I stood next to my window, Maximilian, I saw a sub-marine come out of the moat at Bouchout. I said that Commodore Maury, the Mexican Navy commander had sent it, so that we could rescue the rubies that sank in Chesapeake Bay. That you and I, hand in hand as when we skated on the lake, would dive together on giant seahorses, in golden diving suits embossed with the Imperial monogram, followed by our palace guards in their white-plumed silver diving suits, to the bottom of the sea. There we would find the rubies that came from the drops of blood spilled by Asura during his battle against the King of Lanka, the enemy of the gods. Afterwards, we will return to Mexico in that submarine which will emerge from the waters of Veracruz by Fort San Juan de Ulúa, in a dark, shining whirlpool, dripping with algae and lilacs, with yellow honeysuckle and dewy bougainvillea. It looks like a whale, I told them, but it is even better than the mechanical whale that so amazed the guests at the wedding of Marguerite of England to Charles the Bold One in Bruges.

Yes, when I tell them all of this, I shall allow them to say that I am crazy as a loon, mad as a hatter.

Or if I tell them that I am going to have a child—that child, Maximilian, which will not be yours, nor Colonel Rodríguez's, nor Colonel Van der Smissen's. This is because, if I have ever had anything living inside me, it's not a human being but an *axolotl*. I know it because, when I sit in my rocking chair with my head lowered, I see it growing in my womb, shining and round like a fishbowl. But no one—you hear me Max?—no one made me pregnant. That *axolotl* was the one Baron von Humboldt fished out of Texcoco Lake. I swallowed it by accident the other day at the Paris Zoo when I went with my uncle, the Duke of Montpensier. I was so thirsty from running through the Luxembourg Gardens after the golden hoop that my grandma Marie Amélie gave me that I drank from the aquarium with both hands.

Let them go ahead and say that I'm crazy, but not when I tell them, when I swear to them, that I live my life at the hour of your death. I have ordered every clock in the castle set at seven o'clock in the morning, the time that those bandits ended your life at Las Campanas Hill. There is no bedchamber at Bouchout, not a room in this castle where I'm kept locked up, not a hallway, not a window where it isn't seven A.M., July 19th, many years ago: the day, Maximilian, that your blood ran down the hill, through the streets of Querétaro, through all the roads in Mexico, to cross the ocean. The moon can shine

on the turrets and parapets of Bouchout; the moat waters can reflect the sway-
ing rays of the sun, Maximilian, but in my castle and my bedchamber, in the
clock with the blue angels on my nightstand, in your beloved Olmütz clock,
and the one from the Island of Lacroma, and in my eyes and in my heart,
Maximilian, it's always seven A.M. Sometimes I wake up and I'm sure that it's
high noon, by the sweat that wets my breasts, by the sun that blinds my eyes,
and I ask my ladies-in-waiting who are always watching, always by my side,
standing guard, what time it is. Tell me, it must be noon, why didn't you wake
me? And my ladies, their eyes always wide open, always alert and attentive,
say, no, Doña Carlota, how can you imagine, Your Imperial Majesty, Empress
of Mexico, that it is time for you to rise, it is only seven in the morning, time
for you to wash and dress and eat breakfast, my ladies say, and they dance
around my bed, one wearing my spectacles and the other one my dressing
gown and another in my astrakhan slippers. I say, but there is too much light,
don't you see the sun high in the sky, don't you see its rays filtering through the
castle barbicans and playing on the windowpanes? My ladies-in-waiting say,
certainly, Doña Carlota, Regent of Anáhuac, it's just that it's always summer,
and they put on my spectacles, and you couldn't see the sunrise because everyone in the castle was asleep, they say and they put on my slippers and I tell
them, it's just that it's always summer, and they reply, yes Your Majesty, it is,
and they put on my dressing gown, the world has been burning, Your Majesty,
for sixty years; I ask them why sixty years and they say, it's just that it started
burning when Don Maximiliano's vest caught fire when he received his coup
de grâce at Las Campanas Hill, and everything has been on fire ever since;
Your Majesty, the Empress of America, must know that the charity bazaar at
the Rue Jean-Goujon where your niece the Duchess d'Alençon was burned to
death has been in flames for ages now; and the City of Chicago burned down
because of a cow that kicked a paraffin lamp; the *Ciudadela* in Mexico City
burned down during the Ten Tragic Days; all of Europe burned because Archduke Franz Ferdinand was gunned down by Gavrilo Princip in Sarajevo; the
Lusitania burned when the Germans sank it, and Terveuren burned, Doña
Carlota, because you yourself set it on fire. The villa in Biarritz where Empress
Eugénie and Don José Manuel Hidalgo invented the Mexican Empire also
burned, as did Paris, for five days, from the fire set by the Second Commune;
the Tuileries burned, destroying the figures that the little imperial prince had
dressed in the military uniforms from throughout French history. The world

will keep on burning, engulfed in flames, until Your Imperial Highness, Doña Carlota Amélie Clémentine, God forbid, dies. God will allow it one day, though, my ladies say, and I order them to take down every mirror in the castle, to put them all against the windows to reflect the sunlight toward every corner of all the palaces and castles where we have lived so that your portrait as an admiral can burn, as the Hall of the Compass Rose, the sphinx at the Miramare wharf, the portrait of Catherine of Medici, and everything that we had or could have been, Maximilian, all our memories and our aspirations, my dear, beloved Max, will burn too. Then I close my eyes and I dream of the world in flames, I dream that my heart is a glowing ember and when I awake I think that it is midnight from the darkness that weighs on my eyelids, from the cold in my bones and the pit of my stomach, and I sit on the bed, I search for a candle, I light it, I wake my ladies-in-waiting who sleep by my side on the rug and I say to them, wake up you bitches, tell me what time it is and they rise, shaking, their eyes stuck shut, and they tell me yawning and stuttering, those lazy useless women, oh, Your Majesty, oh Your Empress of America, it is time to get up, it is seven A.M., rise and shine, Your Majesty, say my ladies, and they bring my corset and my artificial fingernails, they bring my woolen stockings and my false teeth, they bring my wig. I tell them, but look how dark it is, can't you see the stars trembling in the sky and spreading their light in the fountain waters? Don't you see the darkness creeping along the castle drawbridge and licking the stones in the wall? My ladies reply, yes Your Majesty, Empress of Mexico and America, yes Doña Carlota Amélie, but it is wintertime and you cannot see the sunrise, that's why it is so dark that it seems to be the middle of the night, but it is seven A.M., we swear to Your Majesty, we swear by all the saints and angels in the heavens and I tell them that it is always winter, is it not, always winter? and those loafers, who fall asleep standing up, leaning against each other, their eyes shut, say, yes Your Majesty, yes Doña Carlota Léopoldine, it is always winter, Your Majesty, and it has snowed for sixty years—it began to snow on Don Maximiliano's coffin when he was taken from Veracruz to Trieste aboard the *Novara*; it snowed on the foam of the waves and the backs of the dolphins that accompanied him; it snowed on the gold trim of Admiral Tegetthoff's uniform (he was the same who stood guard by the body throughout the trip); it snowed on the Austrian war flag that covered the cedar coffin Don Benito Juárez had made for him; it snowed when they took him by train from Trieste to Vienna. Snow blanketed the tracks, the train, and the trees along the way, blanketed the funeral car where Don Maximiliano journeyed, very still. Since then it has never stopped snowing. It snowed when they sent Dreyfus to Devil's Island, Your Majesty; it snowed on the soldiers' corpses from the Battle of Celaya; it snowed on the corpses of the Armenians slaughtered in Constantinople; it snowed on the Brooklyn Bridge; and it snowed, Doña Carlota, it has snowed all this time on the Ardennes peaks that your nephew, Albert I, the King of Belgium, scaled dressed as a Tyrolean; it snows in the paths and the ravines of the Pyrenees where Empress Eugénie went, accompanied by her ladies, to gaze at her beloved Spain from France; it snowed on the smokestacks of the ship *Ipiranga* on which Don Porfirio Díaz wept at his exile. Rest in Peace, Doña Eugenia and Don Porfirio Díaz, all of them Rest in Peace. It will keep on snowing, God forbid, but he will not forbid it, and it will keep on snowing until Your Sacred Majesty, Your Highness, the Imperial Doña Carlota dies, my servants tell me and they fall asleep standing up, those useless women. Then I think of you, Maximilian, I imagine you standing by the frozen Chapultepec Lake, the castle behind it, its terraces and stairways covered in snow. I see your tears like sleet sliding down your frosty skin, your icy crystal eyes gazing on pyramids covered in ermine, the snow-covered banana groves; the rivers of cold blue lava that run down the volcanoes. While my ladies keep sleeping on their feet, leaning on each other, I open the castle window to let in the snow. Then it snows inside the castle, in my room, I say. It snows in my eyes, I shout. It is snowing in my burning heart, I moan. They open their eyes and say, yes, Your Majesty Carlota, yes Your Highness Amélie, yes Your Grace Léopoldine, yes Your Most Serene Clémentine, yes Your Empress the Mad, yes Your Archduchess, the Archcrone, yes, those cursed, treacherous cunts. As if I didn't know that they're always waiting to catch me unaware, to pounce on me and undress me, to force me to bathe and smother me in creams and perfumes and clean clothes; to take me to bed again and say, now, Your Majesty is very pretty and clean and nice-smelling. Your belly and your buttocks are powdered; put on your wig since we brushed it with salt all night to leave it shining. You will please Don Maximiliano very much. Put on your nails. We left them in nacre powder all night in a silver goblet. Don Maximiliano will climb down from his coach and will dust off the flamboyant petals and the duckweed leaves from his boots. Put on your bloomers that we washed in soap root, Doña Carlota. He will brush the dust of the Apam Plains from his golden epaulettes—put on your eyelashes that we curled with hot irons—and he will bring, in his big white felt sombrero, masses of red roses that he cut during his last trip to El Olvido. Put on your teeth that we left soaking all night in a cup of milk, my ladies say to me. Go on, don't be squeamish, eat a little. You need it. See how thin you are. Your Majesty looks like a skeleton. And I ask Dr. Jilek what time it is, tell me doctor, for the love of God, what time is it? It is seven in the morning, Your Majesty, breakfast time. Please, eat something, he says and I throw my spoon at him. Egg hits his spectacles and you can't imagine, Maximilian, how I laughed, to see that long, yellow, quivering snot running down his nose. You can't imagine how much I was reminded of Maria Vetsera, her eye hanging out of its socket, in a viscous liquid. I imagined her dead, coming down the Mayerling staircase. And from thinking about Maria Vetsera, whose scalp had to be pinned to her head after the bullet pulled it off, to think of her and of your nephew Rudolf, nude on the bed beside her, his brains spilling out—what a pity that you never saw him again, Max, you would have been so proud of him—I almost vomited in front of the doctor. But I had nothing left in my stomach, only the fire of frozen resentment. I refused to eat and I ate nothing all day, Max, but it wasn't the nausea. Nor did I regret having thrown the egg on that fool Jilek's face. No, it wasn't that.

When Jilek, Basch, and all the other doctors who locked me up here, and my companions, and Marie Henriette and the Baron de Goffinet all see me here, sitting down quietly in my bedroom, when they see that I spend every hour and every day sitting here, they think that it's because they ordered me to do so, because they taught me to sit still, because they threatened me, because they scold me if I move. But what they don't know and will never know is that it was all my idea. Since I was a child nobody could ever sit still better than I, could sit unmoving like a rock, not moving, never blinking, barely breathing, Max, my chest still, not swallowing, not even a glimmer in my eyes. I lie still, as though I were asleep with my eyes open or, even, as if I were dead, or even more, as if I had never existed, as though that Maundy Thursday afternoon I had not gone with my brothers, the Duke of Brabant and the Count of Flanders, to Saint Jacques Church; as if I had not said aloud, my lips barely moving, the Holy Week prayers; as if I were not there, in the gardens of Laeken, with my two brothers, Leopold and Philippe, playing freeze. Like me, they stood still, very still, turned into statues by a magic spell, until a bee lit on Leopold's forehead and he became very frightened and swatted it with his hand, cursed, and was out. Philippe laughed, called him a coward, and also was out. They both looked at me but I had not moved a muscle. The bee lit on my head but I didn't swat it. I didn't move my head, didn't even close my eyes, so I won. I've always won at playing freeze, Maximilian. Ask my father Leopich, ask him if when he scolded me for something I'd done wrong and said that I must behave like a princess, and someday like a queen, ask him if I moved even a finger. Ask him if later, when he was sorry and kissed my head and said over and over that I was his little sylph, the winged joy of the palace, the Angel of the Co-burgs, ask him if I said a word, if I smiled, if I threw my arms around him and kissed him. Ask him if I opened my mouth to tell Denis d'Hulst that I didn't want my mother to die, when the Countess put me beside her every afternoon to write letters to my aunt, the Duchess of Nemours. In the letters I told her how sick my mother was, how she was paler and weaker every day, and how her face had become sharp, her long Bourbon nose growing more and more pronounced. Ask Mademoiselle Genslin, my English teacher, Madame Claës, my arithmetic tutor—ask them, Maximilian, if either of them ever saw me blush when I didn't know the answer to one of their questions; ask my father, Maximilian, if I cried when they laid my mother, Queen Louise Marie, to rest in Laeken Chapel. There I was, the bee on my head. My brother Philippe, Lip-chen, always so good to me—you can't imagine how I miss him—died from overeating and smoking. I danced six times with him at a court ball. How my counts and duchesses applauded us! My uncle, Prince Joinville, lifted me up to the ceiling so that I almost touched the palace chandeliers. That night my mother read *Sleeping Beauty* to me and I was very still then too. Philippe was there but that time I refused to dance with him again. He danced around me making faces to make me laugh. Since he did magic, he took a rose from behind my ear and said, "Here, m'lady, thou hast the proof of my burning love," and made the rose vanish as he threw it up in the air. He pulled out three knotted colored scarves from his sleeve and got up and said, "M'lady, this is the rope that thou will use to escape the castle and fool the dragon," and then he tickled himself and rolled on the ground laughing. But I did not join him. I did not even move a finger. And I didn't open my eyes in fear when my brother Leopold, who knows so much, told me how Gottfried the Hunchback, the Duke of Lotharingia, was assassinated in Zealand. Nor when he came up to me so violently, as though to scratch my face. Nor was I surprised when he reminded me that when they found Charlemagne in a cellar of Cologne

Cathedral, eight centuries after his death, he was sitting on a throne, his body intact but for a piece of his nose that they replaced with gold. He reminded me of this so that I would open my mouth, but I didn't move, as if I hadn't heard him. I didn't smile either, nor did I show my teeth, as he wanted me to, when he began to tell me the story of Isengrain the Wolf and Renard the Fox. I didn't get angry and I didn't frown because he knows very well how much I loved the French—since our grandfather was French—when he told me that Marshal Villeroi had bombed Brussels for two whole days, or when, a hundred years later, during the Revolution, the French had destroyed Saint-Lambert, the cathedral at Liege, and demolished Orval Abbey, the most beautiful in the world, and I didn't so much as quiver when he reminded me of the Dürer etching of the Four Horsemen of the Apocalypse that hangs in Laeken and that's always frightened me so. No, it was as though he wasn't even there and didn't raise my petticoats, pretending to lash at my legs with a thorny branch he had in his hands. My legs didn't shake, nor did I blush, which is what he wanted. It was, Maximilian, as though I hadn't heard him whisper in my ear, so that Philippe wouldn't know, and so that I would get sad and cry, that he hated our father. He would say what a pity that Grandpapa Louis Philippe hadn't died when Fieschi tried to blow him up with a bomb nor when Lecomte tried to assassinate him that day I said that I was sure that the man didn't know Grandpapa was in his carriage. I didn't cry, I didn't shed a single tear. My brow was uncreased, serene, both then and when Leopold finally bit me on the neck so hard that he left tooth-marks. I didn't react when my good Philippe shouted indignantly that he was a brute. Why did you bite Bijou, as he always called me, and threw himself on Leopold and began hitting him. Leopold, always a coward, ran off whimpering so Philippe went after him, promising—oh beautiful lady!—that he would return to save me from the spell that had frozen me, but only after slaying the dragon who was disguised as Leopold. On the way he would kill the Duke of Alba to avenge Count Egmont and, of course, after that, he, Philippe the Brave, from Brabant, would expel the invading Huns or Normans from Flanders or would hang them from the trees of the Carbonary Jungle. But Philippe forgot me and I remained still, frozen, in the garden, not crying. I remembered the folk tale then Leopold had told me about a fountain where the Virgin, surrounded by white lambs with scapular-shaped black stains on their backs, appeared to Ermesinda, Countess of Luxembourg, and asked her to build a monastery on that site, later called Clairenfontaine. Just thinking of the fountain, I got terribly thirsty, as thirsty as I have been for the last sixty years. But I didn't move; not even my dry lips trembled. I remained still, deep within Laeken Garden, in the somber Enghien Garden, lost deep in Soignies Forest, and standing in Miramare Garden. Only when it began to rain was I able to cry because my tears blended with the raindrops. Only then could I drink from that rain and those tears than ran down my face.

Lipchen returned many years later and I was still there, not moving, almost not breathing. He took me by the hand and we walked in the garden. Under the shade of a fir tree he said that I was the person he most loved in the world and then he declaimed a poem by Heine. I remember: I was sixteen, almost a child. It was very hot and the palace guests rode down the Boulevard Botanique and the Rue Royale to the Place de Palais. In the vestibule by the window that looked out on Trieste, the Istrian Coast, and Punta Salvore, Philippe told me that I was still the most beautiful of all the women he'd met. I saw you, Maximilian, in the Conversation Chamber in Miramare. You were gazing at the statue of Daedalus fixing Icarus's right wing. I saw you in the Novara Room, writing a letter. In front of your desk was another sculpture: Dürer's wooden effigy of Maximilian I. Philippe pointed to the Adriatic and told me that there was news from the other side of the Ocean. We went up the Rhine, in the Stadt Elberfeld, through Mayenne, toward Nuremberg, and you told me that in Bulgaria one of your brother Franz Joseph's children had just died from the measles. Philippe told me that he would never make me cry like that scoundrel Leopold. Forgive me for calling him that, he said. With his back to Miramare's ivy-covered façade, he swore that I was still the most beloved Empress in the world. In his right hand he had a dove that took flight toward Havana. I remember that I walked with you in Laeken Gardens on that afternoon when you described Miramare. I turned my head and saw you in the depths of the forest, wearing your blue frockcoat full of wax, a strange crown on your head, something like a bloody turban. I realized that you had been crowned with your own entrails. Philippe told me that there was news from the other side of the ocean. I swore that I would always follow the motto of the House of Coburg, that I would be faithful and true in my love. You told me that your mother Sophie used to call you Monsieur Maigrelet because you were so scrawny. Philippe said to me, Maximilian's been imprisoned in Querétaro. After the wedding we visited—remember how funny it was, Max?—The Manneken Pis. Maximilian was betrayed, my brother Philippe said to make me cry, despite what he had promised me. The people did not betray him; it was a single man, Miguel López. And there was a concert at the Théâtre de la Monnaie and a Venetian nautical party. Maximilian, Philippe said as if trying to make me laugh, was never in prison. When he was supposed to walk in his Teresitas cell, he was really walking in the Plaza de la Cruz and asked pedestrians for a light for his cigar and greeted the dark-eyed Querétaro ladies and the servants who brought him a box supper of vermicelli soup, beans, and rice pudding cooked at Señor Rubio's hacienda. He said hello to the sisters who took him bed sheets and to the colonels who took him blue ribbons for the six white mules of his carriage. When he sat on his stool in his cell, he was really sitting in his Imperial Palace office and planning his upcoming trip to Guanajuato. He gave instructions on rules of courtly behavior to be included in his *Court Ceremonial*. He said to Blasio, write this down: the cardinals' skullcaps will be like so, and the admirals' chevrons. When he lay down on the cot in his cell, he was really lying in the hammock on the terrace of his villa in Borda. He threw breadcrumbs to the swallows. He asked one of his Gallo Club servants to bring him a glass of Hungarian wine. Listen, Carlota, listen to me Charlotte, Lipchen said to me. Maximilian was condemned to death in Querétaro, but not by his people. It was by a single man whose name was Platón Sánchez, Philippe told me, as though trying to make me cry. He said more: Listen, Bijou, pay no mind to the Gotha Almanac. If Maximilian doesn't appear among the dead, it's because the almanac that Maria Henriette gave you is a fake. Maximilian was executed in Querétaro, but his people didn't execute him. It was a single man who did. Then Philippe took out a bullet from his waistcoat and said: It wasn't the firing squad who delivered the coup de grâce, it was Juárez. It was Benito Juárez who killed him. I didn't move a finger, Max; I didn't lower my eyes. I remained motionless, almost without breathing, as though I were sleeping with my eyes open. All I wanted then, all I could have wished for, would have been that the cold, rainy wind that took us to the Istrian Cape, that tore the red tapestry in the Chamber of the Ambassadors, that stirred the irises in the lake and that clouded the window panes in the Throne Room, Maximilian, that that wind would fill my face again with rainwater, although Philippe told me and swore to me, as though to make me smile: Don't mind me, Princess, because Maximilian is alive in your heart and mine; he's alive in the weeping willows and the paths of Miramare Garden; he's alive on his knees before Rubens's *Assumption* in the castle chapel; he's alive in the Room of the Princes and in his golden crib in the Danube where his father, the King of Rome, rode on horseback. Dr. Jilek said to me, Doña Carlota, we'll never get anywhere if you behave in this manner, and he wiped off the yellow snot that was running out of his nose. Your Imperial Majesty can't travel to Mexico in this state. Look at your protruding cheekbones and ribs, your sagging double chin. Look at your spiny elbows. What will the mayors say? Or the Hussars? What will the palace guards say, Your Majesty? Will they say that we starve you at Bouchout? I'm going to write a letter to Don Ferdinand Maximilian, said Blasio. He took an indelible ink pencil from his briefcase, wet it on his tongue, and asked, his teeth stained purple, What shall I say, Your Majesty? Why doesn't Your Majesty tell me what I can say to Don Ferdinand Maximilian, the Emperor, Your August Spouse?

My dear Maximilian. My beloved King of the World and Lord of the Universe. Don't believe anyone who tells you that I am mad because I refuse to eat. They are lying. The other day I told my servants that you were coming to lunch at the castle. I had them bring out the English marmalades that you liked so much since you first tasted them in Gibraltar, the afternoon that the Moors and the Christians fought in Ceuta and you watched the battle through a telescope from overseas. I remembered that once, in Valencia, they showed you a giant magnolia that had grown in a Capuchin cemetery and you said that the clergy probably made good fertilizer so I had several bunches of wild asparagus brought from Père Lachaise Cemetery. I remember that during the war with the Turks, Emperor Joseph II had water from Schönbrunn brought to him at Belgrade, so I ordered several bottles brought from Tehuacán. The messenger brought a basket of mangoes and guavas and a pitcher of milk, white as jasmine buds, bubbly as champagne, like the goat's milk that a German goatherd gave you in the Canary Islands, as he kissed your feet. Your mother, Archduchess Sophie sent me some poppy-seed and honey cakes and a jar of milchrahm. From the Miramare cellars came a shipment of those mild Rhine wines and those strong Rioja wines that you savored so much. Princess Paula Metternich sent you a box of your favorite havanas from Paris. I ordered Tüdös to make a Brunoise soup, salmon tartare, and grilled filet with Richelieu sauce. I asked the musicians and the singers to rehearse the *Fantasie Brillante* that Jehin-Prume composed in honor of my father Leopold, as well as *Lucrecia's Toast*, *La Paloma* and the Mexican Imperial Anthem. I waited for you, Max, seated at the table, all afternoon, but you never came. I waited fifteen years.

I have waited, seated, but you never come. In the meantime, here I am, Max, refusing to take a bite. It's not because I am crazy that I won't eat, Max—that's not true. Don't believe them if they say so. How can I not want to eat when I'm starving? If anyone had to put her hand in a pot of boiling soup at San Vicente Orphanage to take out a meager piece of meat, it was I, Maximilian. If anyone had to put her fingers in the Pope's cocoa mug, Maximilian, it was I, and not you, because I was starving, because they are all trying to poison me. If anyone had to drink from the fountains of Rome, if anyone had to take hens to her hotel so that I could eat only the eggs that they laid before my very eyes and that I could crack and cook with my own hands, it was I. If anyone had to leave Bouchout Castle at midnight to drink water from the moat and to eat clover and roses from the garden, it was I, Maximilian, I, Carlota Amelia. It is I who crawl down the castle hallways to eat spiders and cockroaches because I am starving, because they all want to poison me. They say that I'm mad because I eat flies, Maximilian. They say that I'm crazy because I would like to eat what's left over of your body, because I want to go to Vienna, to the Capuchin Crypt, and devour your coffin and your glass eyes, even if I cut my lips and tear my throat. I want to eat your bones, your liver, and your intestines. I want them cooked in my presence. I want the cat to taste them to ensure that they aren't poisoned. I want to devour your tongue and your testicles. I want to fill my mouth with your veins. Oh, Maximilian, Maximilian. Don't believe anyone who tells you that I'm like a small child because I eat the dirt from flowerpots. Dr. Bohuslavek got angry with me because I told him not to worry, that I always wash my hands before I eat dirt. He told me I was an idiot because I gnaw on the carpets. He said, We're going to remove all the castle rugs, because I eat blankets and coverlets. He said, Please Your Majesty, we can't leave you uncovered, because I'd eaten my own clothing, Blessed Virgin, said my ladies, we can't have you bald, because I'd pulled my hair out and ate it. No, that we can do, Dr. Riedel told me—we can shave your head and your underarms and your pubic area if you don't stop eating your hair. That we can do.

Isn't it true, Maximilian, that no one told you that aspirin and the typewriter had been invented? With aspirin I can get rid of those terrible migraines that I suffer every time I think of Mexico. And I will use the typewriter to write a very long letter to General Escobedo so that he will let you leave Querétaro. I will also write a poem about your trip to Seville, the day that you lunched by the Guadalquivir River in a little lemon orchard bursting with golden fruit.

I bet no one told you that a new magic contraption was invented to see and photograph live people's bones and entrails. They can see if you've swallowed a foreign object that can hurt you. You must know that your mother Sophie swallowed the ring that you sent her with Dr. Basch. The ring melted in the poor woman's stomach and burned her intestines. Also, Louis Napoleon swallowed the letter in which he promised you to be true to his word. Your brother Franz Joseph swallowed the Family Pact, so both almost died of anguish. Our friend Colonel López swallowed the twenty thousand gold coins that he received in exchange for his betrayal. They turned to air in his mouth. Eugénie swallowed a lead toy soldier dressed as an English officer who'd pierced his heart with his sword. And I, oh, I, Maximilian . . . the other day Jilek, Bohuslavek, and Riedel came to see me. They scolded me and said, Oh, Your Majesty, we can leave you bald and without drapes but not without soap since then we wouldn't be able to wash you. Please don't eat the soap. Please, it will taste bitter. And don't eat your face powder—it will give you nausea, Doña Carlota. And if you eat the fireplace embers, you will get hoarse. Your mouth and your throat will be covered with sores. Maximilian, I told them then that I had swallowed the bullet that took your life at Las Campanas Hill. It was the same bullet, I said, that my brother Philippe had given me at Miramare to make me laugh, to make me cry, to make me live, mad and lucid, asleep and awake, dead and alive, for sixty more years. If you could see, Maximilian, all the excitement at the castle. They thought that the bullet would pierce my intestines. Dr. Bohuslavek felt my stomach. Dr. Riedel gave me an emetic. Dr. Jilek—Pardon me, Your Majesty— gave me an enema. Clots of blood and phlegm mixed with half-digested rose petals came out of my mouth. Silk threads in many colors, and soap bubbles, came out of my nose. A white fur ball and the two diamonds from my wedding tiara that I ate the other day came out of my anus. But the bullet never came out. Since then, every morning after my bowel movement, Dr. Jilek and Dr. Riedel and Dr. Bohuslavek take my high, gold and porcelain chamber pot to the Hall of Audiences, place it on a lacquered table, sit down, and split my shit into three little soup bowls. With the little ivory hands that my maids use to scratch my back, the three doctors pick through it to look for the bullet. My ladies dance around with incense and atomizers that spew out clouds of cologne. This morning I surprised them. When they came to get the chamber pot they found it empty because I was so hungry, Max, that I ate my own shit. Dr. Jilek's cheeks trembled with fury. Dr. Bohuslavek told me that he would tell Queen Victoria. Dr. Riedel said that from now on I have to defecate in the presence of my ladies. I was so humiliated to have to do it in front of them, Max, despite the fact that they are so good to me that they start singing to keep from hearing the noises that I make. They put their fans in front of their faces to pretend they aren't looking, but I know that their fans have holes for them to spy. I was so ashamed and—especially—so furious that I decided to get even, so I defecated on my bed, I defecated in a castle hallway, I defecated in a fountain in the garden, I defecated in the tureen of our Imperial china.

X

"MASSIMILIANO: NON TE FIDARE"

1864–65

1. From Miramare to Mexico

"Blue? Blue as in France? Or green? Dark green as in the Mexican flag? Green is also the color of the Prophet," said Don Joaquín. "What Prophet?" asked the Countess of Kollonitz. "Mohammed, my lady." A hard and cold northwestern wind, albeit favorable to their voyage, was blowing. Maximilian spent his time thinking, imagining, asking questions, and writing. The mayors, he said, patting Mr. Iglesias on the back, will wear a flag-green coat with silver embroidery and a hat with black feathers. "Are you satisfied, Carla, Carlota?" However, in spite of the wind, the usually turbulent Adriatic was like a mirror on that day. "The key," Max said and raised his hand as if he were holding it, "the key to the Imperial Archive will always be in the possession of the Crown Treasurer. Write this down, Sebastian." The yacht *Fantaisie* was at the head of the fleet. Next came the *Novara*, and in its wake, about 250 fathoms behind, the *Thémis* under the command of Captain Morier.

The waters of the Adriatic were never bluer. The squadron paraded past the city of Trieste behind the ships anchored in the bay decorated by their flags. All the coastal batteries saluted the squadron. The cannon salutes seemed endless as the *Novara* crossed them in turn. The Lloyd steamships took their leave and the squadron continued toward Pirano, where the *Novara* encountered a multitude of fishing boats that surrounded it as a farewell gesture to the departing Prince and Princess. "And if you agree," said Maximilian dipping a cookie in his sherry glass, "the royal chamberlain will wear court tails at the public hearings that will be held every Sunday, and where I will see anyone who wants to see me. He will wear a white tie and display his medals." The Countesses Zichy and von Kollonitz threw coins to the fishermen and Maximilian took Carlota's hand and whispered so low that she could hardly hear him: "The day the son of a crowned prince is born, one of our children, Carla, the Emperor will not be dressed in mourning, but will have his palace chamber, antechamber, sofas, and armchairs draped in purple, as well as their covers, pillow cases, and tapestries. I shall also place a purple bow on my sword's hilt and the silk sash around my arm will also be purple." "What are you saying, Max?" The Count de Bombelles sighed deeply and they went on sailing down the Adriatic, still serene, plying over the tenuous foam. Carlota retired to her quarters well into the night. She had waited for the sunset, after which she quietly contemplated the tiny lights of the Istrian and Dalmatian coasts. Arm in arm with General Woll, Maximilian was deciding on the uniforms for the ranks of his troops during a battle, a parade, and an inspection, respectively. Maximilian was thinking: kepi, frockcoat, and dragon-green wool pants for his Staff Special Corps. Maximilian was writing: seven dull-gold leaf epaulettes on the tip of the brim of his brigadier-generals' hats. Or perhaps, for the dress uniform of his Palace Guard, the Empress's Guard, his beloved Charlotte—the princess was sad—would prefer the men to wear polished silver helmets with a gold, spread-winged Imperial Eagle? Sad yes, but not only for leaving Miramare. And white patent leather chinstraps? She was also sad for not having bid farewell to Lacroma Island. And red waistcoats, white chamois pants and gloves, black patent leather boots creased at the calf? Yes, Carla? Is that how you would like it? But Carla, *cara* Carla, don't you realize that in order to get to Ragusa we would have had to veer off course and waste precious hours? "And the Grand Marshal will be charged with the conservation of the court furniture, including the dining room set, the china, the tablecloths, and the gardens. I said it before and I say it again, Carla, we're very fortunate! We have a kingdom at our feet!" As they were sailing toward Otranto, that yellowish, uncivilized Cape that made Maximilian think of his first early-morning marine guard, when he first felt the hot Italian sun of Sicilian blood on his skin—poisonous, he called it. The Countess von Kollonitz commented that the coast of Calabria was very ugly, and Félix Eloin, the engineer, agreed. Maximilian was sketching. Maximilian asked for color pencils and charcoal pencil, to sketch the hat of a functionary of the Appellate Court: black felt with a moiré ribbon, black plumes, and a green, white, and red-striped cockade. "Just like the Italian Flag!" Carlota exclaimed. "Did you only now realize, *carissima mia*, that the flags of Mexico and Italy have the same colors? This has to be a good omen." Once they were far from the snow-capped peaks of the coast of Albania and had bid farewell to Corfu, Maximilian remembered that during a feast of Saint Sylvester at Schönbrunn he had once received a miniature basket with mangoes, bananas, and pineapples as a surprise gift, and the fact that, under its delicate zinc cover, under its molten wax, the collection of fruit appearing on a snowy evening in Vienna had also seemed a magnificent omen. A tropical omen, said Mr. Iglesias. And when in the morning Commander Morier had sidled the *Thémis* up to the *Novara*, at arm's length, the passengers on both ships shouted greetings from gunwale to gunwale, and Max and Carlota appeared on the stern. Once again they heard the good-byes and saw the handkerchiefs. Later, as the *Thémis* pulled away, Max watched her through his binoculars, and signaled Captain Morier to criticize some of the maneuvers of the French ship, which would surely cause the *tripes à la mode* he'd had earlier to give him indigestion, Max said. He went down to his office, looked at the sextants, at the compasses, lit a cigarette, and through the smoke he saw, he imagined, his Cabinet Members in light-blue frockcoats, of course, like the French? Nonono, Carlota would say; in green. All right, green, but light-green with thick gold buttons on the breast. Splendid; and the eagle engraved on them. *Das ist recht.* And black trousers and waistcoats? He took the pen, dipped it in the inkwell, and wrote:

"Awarding of skullcaps to Cardinals." The *Novara* was entering Mediterranean waters. "The skullcap placed on a gold platter." And they sailed around the Italian boot. "The platter placed on a table covered with red velvet." And they rounded the Cape of Santa Maria di Leuca and entered the Gulf of Tarento. "And the table placed next to one of the lateral walls of the presbytery." Maximilian's thoughts interrupted him: during his first trip, within sight of Leuca, to the left of the ship's battery, they had rigged up a chapel made from Austrian flags, but the Chaplain was sick and Mass was suspended. Can it be an involuntary sacrilege to vomit the Body of the Lord, to feed the sharks with His transubstantiated flesh? And it was the morning of Sunday the seventeenth already, a very limpid morning, Count Zichy confirmed, and Etna could be seen to the right with its snow-capped peak, though the black-ore vein was hidden by the morning mist, and Maximilian told his companions about that other trip along the coast of Calabria. He heard a shout, "*Un uomo è caduto in acqua!*" and it was true, a man had fallen off the maintop. "Did the poor fellow drown?" asked the Marquis de Corio. "The *salva uomini*, the lifesaver, was not properly thrown," said Maximilian, "but we rescued the man with a lifeboat, thank God." While they were steaming toward the Strait of Messina,

Maximilian, who had written in his memoirs, about Mount Etna, that it had been "witness to so many past ages and to the degeneration of powerful nations," now wrote, on an immaculate sheet of paper, "When a Vice-Admiral visits a warship for the first time, he will be given a nine-gun salute." "Remind me of this, General Woll, as soon as we get to Mexico. Remind me also, *bitte*," he asked his brand-new secretary, Sebastian Schertzenlechner, "to get in touch with Commodore Maury." And since Eloin, the engineer, was green with envy due to Schertzenlechner's new assignment, Max told the Belgian that he would head the secret police. "So, what color, what embroidery would you like for the secret police frockcoats?" Carlota asked in jest. Max answered, "Oh, that's a secret we will write with invisible ink." "All the ships of the navy will be battleships, of course, and since there will also be a senate, how should they dress?" "In blue frockcoats," said Maximilian, "not green because it would be too much." Carlota resigned herself: "Blue then, with palm tree leaves intertwined with oak branches embroidered in gold." "And the swords?" "Gold with mother-of-pearl handles." Maximilian instructed Schertzenlechner to take note, while Carlota remained rapt and leaned over the rail trying to locate the whirlpool that had swallowed the ancient mariners lost in the Strait of Messina—her brother, the Duke of Brabant, had told her about it when she was a child. Max showed his secretary the map of the Mexican National Imperial Palace, along with design number eight for the Great Court Balls. As they passed near Reggio, far from Messina, and through the currents of the Calabrias, they could see the lush greenery. And Maximilian said, "At midnight the monarchs shall retire to their quarters from the Emperor's Salon preceded by a small Honor Service." Sicily's mountainous coast was on the left; the Benedictine Monastery of St. Placid towered above the strait. He ran his index finger across the map, "and they will cross the Dining Hall, the Gallery of the Lions, the Iturbide Gallery, the Gallery of Paintings, the Yucatán Hall—write this down." Scylla, a lighthouse. Carybdis, an enormous and old castle. And not a single whirlpool in sight, nothing to remind the traveler of Schiller's "The Diver." On the contrary. "The ocean was so beautiful," Carlota noted in her diary, "first an emerald color, then lapis lazuli, then emerald, and so on." At twelve they arrived at Stromboli, its crater spewing off thick smoke clouds. "Then," Maximilian thought, "the entourage of the first two groups will leave the palace via the Empress's Staircase," and he ran his fingers across the stairs on the map. "Everyone else will exit by way of the Emperor's Stairs." And as a concession to Carlota he said: "Would you like *cara*, dear Charlotte, for the regular frockcoats of the Palace Guard, the Empress's Guard, to be of dragon-green cloth with blood-red endsleeves so that, with the white buckskin gloves, they will have all three colors of the imperial Mexican flag on them?" "Of course. *Es bleibt dabei.*" And because when they left the Lipari Archipelago they were sailing too close to shore, they did not see Ischia or the coast of Naples or the peaks of Abruzzo. Besides, Eloin would also be the Head of the Imperial Advisory Council, and the Count would be the Head of the Civil Advisory Council. The Neapolitan Coast disappeared along with the memories of another afternoon when the golden waters of the Gulf of Naples had bathed the shores of Castellamare, and Sorrento appeared surrounded by orange groves in bloom. A violet cloud had surrounded Vesuvius, and Archduke Maximilian, guided by a Capuchin monk, had visited the ruins. He commented that it was a city of miniature houses or temples: Greek, Egyptian, Gothic, Roman. He had heard the whisper of the cypresses; he had inhaled the aroma of the myrtles, he'd drunk Chianti and Lachryma Christi; he'd traveled to Capri; he'd visited the ruins of Tiberius's Palace; and with his mouth full of icy cold prickly-pear juice, he'd admired a woman with the smile of a bacchante, who allowed herself to be carried away by the fiery, vertiginous wave of the tarantella. However, this had been several years before. Now, Monday, April 18th, at one o'clock in the afternoon, the fleet entered the port of Civitavecchia, where it was received with bands, salutes from the cannons on the ships anchored in the port and from the French occupation troops, and the special train that was to take the party to Rome.

There, in the Eternal City, as Count Egon de Corti said, Maximilian lost the chance to clarify the situation of the Church in Mexico. Maximilian asked Count Giovanni Maria Mastai Ferretti, also known as Pius IX, to send a papal nuncio of "reasonable principles" and, shortly before giving Holy Communion to Maximilian and Carlota, the Pontiff pointed out that the rights of the State were unquestionably great, but the rights of the Church were even greater and more sacred. "The Emperor Maximilian"—as Mr. Velásquez de León told Tomás Murphy, the Mexican Ambassador in Vienna, from the *Novara*—"answered the Holy Father as follows: that though he would always do his duties as a Christian, as a sovereign he would always defend the interests of his State." It is possible that at that time Maximilian was thinking about *Christ of the Tribute Money*, the Titian painting that had so impressed him at the Dresden Museum. But Rome was throwing a gala in honor of the Mexican Imperial Couple; the crowds loved them. Gregorovius, the German historian, wrote that the Pope had never before blessed a prince with so much emotion, and his coterie was so numerous—an eyewitness said that the French looked after him with such zeal because they knew they wouldn't soon find another simpleton who would accept the crown of Mexico—that it was best to forget about the Church, the nuncios, Juárez, and the properties taken away from the Church until they arrived in Mexico. Gutiérrez Estrada felt like a peacock because not only had the monarchs stayed at his Palazzo Marescotti, but also because Pius IX had deigned to visit him. And then, of course, there were the pine trees and Rome's white camellias, the speeches and feasts, the masses in the catacombs, the small lake, the terraces, the flower beds of the Villa Borghese; from there, the panorama of the whole of Rome and its marvels made everyone happy. Maximilian and Carlota, accompanied by their entourage, walked all over the city; they went up and down the steps of Trinità dei Monti several times; they walked along the Avenue of the Magnolias; they visited the ruins at night, and Carlota wrote her grandmother Marie Amélie in Claremont that she was in love with the Coliseum under the moonlight. They dipped their hands in all the fountains: the Trevi Fountain, the Fountain of the Moor, the Fountain of Neptune, and in the Fountain of the Rivers—so named, Maximilian told his darling Carla, because in it one can find the four rivers of the world, which are . . . "The Nile?" "Yes, the Nile." "The Ganges?" "Could be, Carla, could be." "The . . . The Amazon?" "Nonono: the Danube." "And what's the other?" "Take a guess." But Carlota didn't guess. "The River Plate, woman." "But why not the Amazon? Why not the Mississippi? Why not? Why not the Yang-Tse-Kiang? Why the Danube? Why?" "Because they were the rivers, *cara*, of the four continents, *mia cara*, Carla, that were under Papal authority at that time, when the brilliant Bernini built the fountain, Carla, *carissima mia, meine Liebe.*"

Once they were back at Civitavecchia and at the *Novara*, a poem began circulating, a lampoon, first hand-to-hand and then by word of mouth:

> *Massimiliano, non te fidare*
> *torna al Castello de Miramare.*
> *Il trono fradicio di Montezuma*
> *è nappo gallico, colmo di spuma.*
> *Il timeo danaos, chi non ricorda?*
> *Sotto la clamide trovò la corda.*

But of course at this stage Maximilian and Carlota were committed to moving forward, to having faith, to never again seeing Miramare Castle. Who during such a festive time could possibly have anticipated that there was a gallows hiding under the royal purple mantle? What gallows? And besides, as Mr. Iglesias said: evil-minded and envious people are never in short supply. Never, Count Bombelles agreed. It's all rubbish. And everyone admired the dolphins that escorted them for a long stretch of the way to the Isle of Caprera, so loved by Garibaldi, and like General Woll said, without any need for French bayonets. Carlota locked herself up in her cabin, which she hardly left, absorbed in her readings of Father Domenech, of Baron de Humboldt, of Chevalier. And Maximilian would write, dictate, talk, and daydream. He would write: Gold braid in black velvet strap for the headdress of the auditors. He would dictate: The order of the small and large entourages for the Easter Saturday ceremonies will be as follows . . . He would say: "The master of the Emperor's Horse will have the care and handling of stables, harnesses, and riding saddles. Oh, I forgot to mention, take note, *bitte*, the length of the division generals' swords will be eight hundred and thirty-five centimeters and their hilts made of wood," as they sailed between Corsica and Sardinia, "wood bound with toad skin." "Toad skin?" asked Carlota with a grimace of revulsion. "Yes," Max answered her as they sailed past the strait: the Sardinian Kingdom and malaria to their left, to their right the birthplace of Napoleon the Great, "out of toad skin and covered, take note, Sebastian, with eight turns of strong gold filigree twine. Women, Carla, know nothing about swords." "Perhaps not about swords, not about rifles or epaulettes, but we do understand about colors and designs," Carlota complained. "And I am not convinced about the vine leaves and the wheat stalks embroidered in gold over gray cloth for the financial inspectors. Why don't we make up a design with Mexican, instead of European, plants?" she said as they left the Balearic Islands behind and headed toward Gibraltar. He took her by the shoulders. "For God's sake Carla, you aren't thinking, I suppose, about golden cactus leaves for the headdresses of the generals, right? You wouldn't want *me* to wear a feathered headdress like Moctezuma's, I hope." "Oh, Your Majesty can't imagine how overcome with emotion I was," Don Joaquín said, "the first time I saw the headdress in Vienna." "Well, I read in a book," Carlota said, with that gigantic, bare, sunburned, and bald Rock of Gibraltar as a backdrop, "that Mexican priests have included the designs of Aztec and Mayan frets in their chasubles." "In the final analysis, we must be thankful to Queen Victoria for something," Maximilian said to General Woll, who had already been named the Emperor's first aide-de-camp, when they were received by the British fleet with Imperial honors. "Do you see, Carlota, do you see? That perfidious Albion is paying us tribute." To the left, the dead white Ceuta, and one of the columns of Hercules, Mount Hacho. Max handed Carlota his binoculars. "Look, the famous monkeys of Gibraltar are there. I told you already, on our way to Madeira that time—didn't I?—how, when the last monkey disappears, the English will abandon Gibraltar?" "They will never leave," said Don Joaquín. "They would start importing monkeys from Timbuktu." Everyone was delighted with the banquet, a magnificent tea party that the Governor, General Codrington, gave the Mexican monarchs and their entourage. In turn, everyone was pleased with the banquet that they, the monarchs, offered the General on board the *Novara*, as well as with the horse races on shore. Maximilian was surprised by how green the track looked, like a piece lifted from St. James's or Richmond Park and brought through the air like a grass magic carpet to land at Gibraltar. Maximilian told Schertzenlechner: "You see, Sebastian, wherever the English go they take their grass, their delicious marmalades, their curries, and their teas with them." "And their English women, clumsy as always," the Countess von Kollonitz (she preferred the Von to the Of) said. The Countess, who almost fell off the boat that brought her back to the *Novara*, but who nevertheless had enjoyed her visit to the Caves of Gibraltar, agreed with the Emperor that of course the ones at Adelsberg were better. They got a good laugh at the grotesque statue of Elliot, the defender of Gibraltar, who withstood a nearly three-year-long siege by the Spaniards and French: it wore an enormous three-cornered hat; it had spindly legs and a pigtail wig and the golden keys to the city in its hand. But a cloud darkened Maximilian's thoughts then, even though the green marine phosphorescence of the strait fascinated Carlota. This was due to a letter that had somehow slipped by Schertzenlechner, self-appointed intercepter of all disagreeable correspondence. It had come in a mailbag shipped from Gibraltar and, judging from the language, it came from an Austrian anarchist who had remained anonymous and called Maximilian a usurper; he claimed that no tyrant had ever escaped him, that he had a rifle and was a good shot and, as soon as Maximilian set foot on the American continent, he would show him. "But your Majesty is not a usurper," Count Bombelles said. "And I will never be a tyrant," added Max. "No one will ever dare attempt against His Majesty's life," Señor Iglesias said. A few hours later the anonymous letter was forgotten, or so it seemed, and, lying in his cot, *Guten Nacht*, and with his eyes wide open, Maximilian daydreamed. "The entourage from the Palace to the Cathedral: a carriage, two horses, four spaces for the second secretary of ceremonies, the service chamberlain, and two ladies-in-waiting. A second carriage, two horses, two seats for two palace ladies-in-waiting." The next morning, *Guten Morgen*, after having done his ablutions and combing his long blond beard, as ever parted in two, and with the *Novara* already in the Atlantic, he went on to "the third, fourth, and fifth carriages." "To our right," the Count Zichy said to his Countess, "is Trafalgar, where Admiral Nelson acquitted himself so gloriously." When they left the deserted islands behind, inhabited only by goats, on their way to Madeira, and after all enjoying a good cup, a nice cup, of Earl Gray tea, provided by Governor Codrington, Max reached "a sixth carriage: four horses, four seats for the palace's first lady-in-waiting, a service lady-in-waiting, the Grand Master of Ceremonies, and the Civil Service's Quartermaster General of the Civil Register." And Max commented, "How intelligent the English are. Along with their armies and their warships, they bring others loaded with oxen and milk cows." "Six palace guards will follow on horseback, six orderlies, two aide-de-camp generals, the Court's Grand Marshal, the division generals." "Impossible, Your Majesty," Don Joaquín said. "Why impossible?" asked Carlota, taken by surprise, and just at the moment that Maximilian was about to get to her carriage, the Empress's, which was going to be number seven: six horses, Her Majesty, the Empress, and her grand chamberlain . . . ! "I'll show you, Sire," Don Joaquín said, and he drew a map of Mexico's Main Plaza. "The National Palace is here. I beg your pardon, the Imperial Palace. And the Cathedral is here. As you can see, the distance between one and the other is very short, much shorter than the length of the entourage." "So that when the first carriage arrives at the doors of the cathedral," Maximilian said, "the carriage of Her Majesty, the Empress . . ." "would still be at the palace," finished Mr. Iglesias. "Exactly." And Maximilian did some figuring: and besides all the ceremony chamberlains, the horsemen, the doctors, the other chamberlains, and ladies-in-waiting. "Impossible." But when Madeira came into sight, with its scented, multicolored flora—mimosas, purple-flowered aloes, pelargoniums—Maximilian remembered the painting that shows Isabel of Parma, Joseph II's fiancée, as she entered Vienna. All of the hundreds of carriages were able to fit in the Hofburg courtyard because they followed a zigzag pattern, like a waving snake. "What we could do," Maximilian said, "is to have the entourage turn left as it leaves the palace, circle the entire plaza and arrive on the other side of the cathedral." "*Magnifique*," Carlota exclaimed, and everyone applauded. Maximilian proposed a toast, in English, imitating General Codrington: "*Gentlemen, will you charge your glasses, please!*" and he promised that the next day they would draw up a list of the wines and menus for the banquets that would be offered to heads of state, plenipotentiary ambassadors, and so on. However, Madeira saddened Max and Carla a bit. Carla for two different reasons. First because she had spent several months alone on that island while Maximilian was traveling in Brazil. Secondly, because she knew that Princess Amelia de Braganza—and this was the reason for Maximilian's own sadness—was buried there. Maximilian remembered having written in his memoirs that, on that unforgettable island, "a life I had thought would some day assure the tranquil happiness of mine" had died. And something else—what was it? Oh, yes: "A pure and perfect angel who had departed to her true native land," which was none other than heaven, of course. To make Carlota happy he said: "I have thought of every detail," kissing her hand, "except one." "What?" Carlota asked. "The *baciamano*. Didn't I tell you? In Gaeta all the important people of the Kingdom of Naples knelt before me. A ridiculous ceremony that has no hand kissing because they limit themselves to extending their right arms." Meanwhile, the ecstatic Countess von Kollonitz contemplated Madeira's flora and mumbled one of Heine's poems, the one about the snow-covered spruce that dreams of being a palm tree, or something like that. After Mass onboard the *Novara*, Maximilian said, "When I say everything, I mean everything: if in the Café Europa at Naples the butter cubes are embossed with the Bourbon Fleur de Lis, in Mexico it will bear the imperial eagle and the snake." As he was helping Carlota put her shawl on, he said: "Remind me to have the molds made." Madeira's coastline was disappearing in the horizon. Max, who on his first visit to the isle felt like a modern Ahasuerus, a restless wanderer, had confirmed that the most exotic fruits and flowers of all the five continents came together in that one piece of paradise. "It's a pity, yes, it's a pity that its inhabitants are so unsightly." "And the ice, Max? What about the ice. Will the ice swans that adorn the tables at our banquets become ice eagles devouring ice snakes?" "And why not?" answered Max. Yes, why not. If there had been sugar eagles at the Tuileries, why not have ours made out of ice or butter or nougat, of *alajú* paste, or cactus fruit jelly? And though in reality it was only the custom to celebrate when crossing the Equator, the crew of the *Novara* decided to honor the Tropic of Cancer in the same way. This meant that sailors, captains, officers, the Emperor, Carlota, and all her ladies-in-waiting, had to dress as Neptune, amphytrites, nereids, tritons, and other sea creatures, gods, and goddesses. And no one, except the ladies, was allowed to escape the baptism of seawater. Everyone was wet and happy. (Well, the Emperor was also spared. Who would have dared pour a bucket of seawater over him? *"Dawider behüte uns Gott!"* May God Forbid!) "The Emperor's naval aides will replace the chamberlains, and take over their responsibilities," Maximilian wrote, and then he asked General Woll, "Do you think princes have the right to make their servants wear the national emblem without a plume?" A moonless night in a dead calm, Orion sparkling over the Mediterranean, as were Andromeda and Eridanus. But Carlota, it seemed, was no longer interested in the seascape, the sunsets, or the evenings. She spent her time in her cabin reading and writing letters. Its sails motionless, the *Novara* hardly made three knots per hour. "And take note, Sebastian, so we won't forget anything," Max said: "for the Lent sermons, for the washing of the feet on Holy Thursday—and let's not forget Palm Sunday—the palace ladies will wear the Empress's monogram and high-cut black silk dresses with mantillas, the Order of San Carlos, and, during services in the warm latitudes, the Emperor's Civil Corps attire will be white frockcoats and ties. What are we missing, Sebastian? Read this, Mr. Eloin, and tell me what you think, please." "At this rate, we'll never get to Veracruz," said Don Joaquín. "Forget Veracruz," Mr. Iglesias said, absorbed with the flying fish, "we won't even get to the Windward Islands," and, at Maximilian's request, they cast their nets and pulled out one of the jellyfish that was floating like a marine rose near the frigate. Having run out of coal the only thing they could do was to have the *Thémis* tow the *Novara* to Martinique. And so it was—and the Countesses Zichy and von Kollonitz, and Schertzenlechner (in sum, all the Austrians on board, including Max himself) felt humiliated. The French were towing the monarchs to America. "How shameful, isn't it, Don Joaquín?" "One shouldn't take it to heart," the Mexican said, "but laugh." And they did, and when they were in Fort-de-France, in front of the statue of Empress Josephine, who was born in Martinique, the Countess von Kollonitz was amazed at the gigantic earrings and the brightly-colored turbans the black women wore, and she admired the coconut trees and the cassavas, the bread trees, bamboos, and other flora she had never seen before. They had forgotten about the incident. Once again they were accorded Imperial honors; part of the retinue climbed the mast of the *Vauquelin*, and a crowd of natives went aboard the *Novara* and brought coal the color of their skin in big baskets. The Countess von Kollonitz said that black people were offensive to the European eye, nose, and ear. Soon they bid farewell to Fort-de-France and they headed toward Jamaica, described by Columbus as a crumpled sheet of paper. They disembarked at Port Royal and penetrated—to quote the Countess's memoirs—into the mysteries of black squalor. From there, Sir James Hope took them to Kingston aboard the steamship *Barracoutta*. There they had ginger preserves and enormous muscatel grapes for lunch the following day. They bid farewell to Jamaica in order to leave finally, finally! for Mexico. Good luck! *Glück auf*!

•

It was useless for her to close her eyes. She would still see the clouds of yellow sand and the whirlpool of black vultures that had greeted them at the Port of Veracruz. Staring fixedly at the silver wig holder that sparkled with the reflection of the fireworks, she cried and remembered. It was just as useless to cover her ears. She knew she was doomed to hear the dreadful noise of the rockets and fireworks the Mexicans were setting off to celebrate the advent of their sovereigns at the Plaza Mayor through the night. She cried and she remembered. She also scratched herself. She scratched until she bled, but the only thing she managed to accomplish was spreading the acid poison further under her skin. She had welts on her thighs, on the backs of her knees, on her arms, on her insteps. Something was wrong, very wrong. At the beginning, a few hours before the snow-covered summit of the Pico de Orizaba could be seen in the horizon, everything was happiness and optimism aboard the *Novara*, and both of them, she and Max together, had counted the number of designs they had created to date, and were meant to appear in the *Ceremonial*: twenty-two, twenty-three, twenty-four, yes, almost all of which would be necessary for functions, concerts, grand receptions, the Empress's social gatherings, her birthday, etc. And when Veracruz appeared, under the cloud-covered Pico de Orizaba, Carlota wrote her grandmother, Marie Amélie, who was fascinated with the tropics and dreamt only of butterflies and hummingbirds, "It seems to me that it's an error to call this the New World simply because it lacks the telegraph and a bit of civilization." She wrote that Veracruz resembled Cadiz, but was a bit more oriental, and that when she saw Fort San Juan de Ulúa she thought about her uncle, Prince Joinville; she thought about him very much. Their designs and plans had been possible, and Maximilian was thankful for that, because he had been given maps to the main floor and the first floor of the palace. Also another map of the Emperor's Hall, and still another one of the Imperial Chapel, then one of the Metropolitan Cathedral, and of course, one of the Collegiate Church of Guadalupe. At any rate, on that afternoon of May 28, 1864, the Emperor and Empress of Mexico were greeted by the sight of San Juan de Ulúa, the Isla de Sacrificios, the Isla Verde, the pier, and the remains of a French ship run aground in a coral reef; by a smell that began creeping aboard the *Novara*, a smell the Countess von Kollonitz described as pestilential and which must have been from the swamps that surrounded the city; and by the silence and desolation, and by the gusts of sand, and by the buzzards. Schertzenlechner and Eloin almost got down on their knees in order to sing the Mexican Imperial Anthem. Maximilian thought that if his dynasty didn't as yet have a historical museum in which to exhibit the great artifacts of his court, he said, such as Saint Stephen's bag, the famous giant ruby known as "The Jacinth," or the phaeton of the King of Rome—may he rest in peace—his Mexican kingdom would soon acquire enough pomp, dignity, and splendor to overshadow the courts of London, Vienna, Madrid, and Paris. "Take note, Sebastian, the Emperor's aides-de-camp will not be on horseback while carrying out their functions, except when the Emperor himself is to appear mounted. Take note, Sebastian, the sashes of the Appeals Court vice presidents will be crimson silk with silver acorns. Remember, Sebastian, to remind me to read the Messidor Decree of the Year Two of the Revolution, which regulated the precedence of the court's high dignitaries and functionaries in France—which of course we're not going to copy, but rather take into account. You remind me to do this too, my love, *mia carissima* Carla, if you remember."

As it happened, in Veracruz, no one knew the exact date of the arrival of Maximilian and Carlota. Fearing the spread of yellow fever, General Almonte had camped out in Orizaba. Maximilian refused to disembark and he ordered the *Novara* to anchor far away from the French ships, which, after all, were an invading force. A short while later a distraught Rear Admiral Bosse came to the *Novara* to protest this decision and Carlota said she was not willing to tolerate the Frenchman's bad manners. At night the stormy tail end of a norther knocked down all the triumphal arches, unfurled flags, wreaths, and floral carpets that had been set up in Veracruz. Almonte arrived and urged Maximilian to leave the port quickly to avoid an infection. Maximilian decided to disembark at six in the morning after hearing Mass onboard. The ladies and young ladies of society in Veracruz hardly had any time to comb their hair and put on their jewels, the men to wax their mustaches and get dressed, and the mayor to get into his formal attire so as to present the keys to the city. Neither did the garbage collectors have time to collect the torn and shredded sateen paper ornaments, like wilted flowers half-buried in the sand. Will we use sateen paper to print the invitations to the Empress's social gatherings? Muddied laurels and palms, multicolored streamers tangled in the buzzards' feet. However, the Emperor and the Empress did manage to find time to dress up. Maximilian decided to wear black tails, a white waistcoat and trousers, and black tie for the *Te Deum* Mass at the Veracruz parish church—where Countess de Zichy was amazed to see men use fans, but Max told her that he had seen men, real men, keep cool with those same devices at San Carlos Theater in Naples—and later, as he descended from his train in Tejería, he wore white from head to toe, and, still later at the *Te Deum* in Mexico City Cathedral, a Mexican general's uniform. On the other hand, Carlota thought it was a good idea for her new subjects to know from the beginning that she liked blue and that there was no other color—not even imperial purple—that suited her better, and most of all under those pure, transparent, and blue skies that, she had been told, covered the Valley of Mexico.

And it was true, that's the way the skies were in the Valley of Anáhuac, but they weren't so beautiful and transparent in all of Mexico. Maximilian had hardly disembarked, and the imperial declaration which began, "Mexicans, you have asked for me!" had hardly been made public when at La Soledad a messenger gave Maximilian a letter signed by one of the many Mexicans who, of course, had not asked for him, President Benito Juárez. The letter had been posted from the city of Monterrey, and one of its final paragraphs read: "Sir, man is given to attacking the rights of others, to seizing their property, to making attempts on the lives of those who defend their nationality, to making their virtues seem a crime, and to making a virtue out of his own vices. But there is one thing that is beyond the reach of such perversity, and that is the terrible verdict of History. *History will be our judge.*"

And history, in lowercase, tells it like this—that Maximilian, during the entire voyage from Miramare to Mexico, forgot the pain caused by leaving his white castle on the shores of the Adriatic, his golden Austrian birthplace, his parents and brothers, and he spent his time not only dreaming about a *Court Ceremonial*, but also dictating it or else writing it with his own hand. A Ceremonial which, when printed a few months later in Mexico, was over five hundred pages long. The fact that the ceremony of presentation for a cardinal's skullcap had one hundred and thirty-two clauses or paragraphs devoted to it is an example of how detailed it was. One of the few times in which the brilliant Emperor interrupted his task was when, with the help of his wife, he drafted a document that caused yet another scandal: a protest against the Family Pact, which had stripped Maximilian of all his rights. In the document the royal couple called the pact, "an attempt to usurp," and Maximilian and Carlota both swore they had never read it.

History also says that on their way to Córdoba, the carriage in which Mr. Joaquín Velásquez de León was traveling overturned somewhere between La Cañada and El Palmar, and that Don Joaquín and five other gentlemen had to climb out a window, and, as though this weren't enough, one of the wheels of the imperial carriage broke, leaving Maximilian and Carlota to continue their trip aboard a stagecoach of the Republic. Maximilian said that up to that time he believed no carriage could wobble as much as the light carriages of Valencia. History also says that the imperial retinue arrived exhausted in Córdoba in the middle of a downpour; Maximilian asked for an umbrella and walked with Carlota to the Municipal Palace; the Prefect Soane fainted, and Max himself helped him get up. History says that, in honor of the sovereigns, amnesty was granted a few prisoners of war, and that, the following day, in that same city, Maximilian, who on a trip to Brazil had tasted chili peppers and written in his memoirs, "Now I know that in Purgatory there will be American food with pimentos and cashews," had to pay homage to a Mexican national dish called *mole*. Don Joaquín said, pointing to a black sauce, "it is made out of peanuts, chocolate, and fourteen different types of chilies or peppers," and added, "it is served on fowl meat which is none other than the *guajolote* or turkey, a bird native to Mexico. Try it Your Majesty, it's delicious, and afterwards wash it down with a glass of pulque." "From Mexico?" asked Carlota. "Then why do the English call it turkey?" "I suppose they think those birds come from that country, Your Majesty." "Oh, it's the same thing with turquoises," the Emperor said, and Count de Bombelles raised an eyebrow and wiped off a drop of mole dripping down his beard. "There are many turquoises here in Mexico," Prefect Soane said.

"But let's leave behind those foul, torrid regions and move on to the temperate zones to be able to look at the Indians clearly and closely, those flesh-and-blood specimens of the bronze race, *la race cuivrée*, with eyes like a doe's," Mme. Kollonitz said, though Maximilian said they actually reminded him of the eyes of the gazelles of the plains in Blade. And all the flora is magnificent: sugarcane, coffee shrubs, banana trees, the agave that the English traveler described as "a brobdingnagian asparagus," and an infinite number of flowers of all imaginable colors: the violet of the jacarandas that stand out against the reddish purple of the bougainvilleas or against the canary yellow of the gold rain spilling over the walls and on the roadside the scarlet of the flowers of the *aretillo* that hung from the branches like lanterns below the blue of the sky in the *manto de la virgen* or *coleus blumei*, at her feet the pale orange of the small bell-like flowers of the grenadine, and let's turn finally to the profound emotion of the travelers as they left the magnificent snow-capped volcanoes, Popocatépetl and Iztaccíhuatl ("Though only the Popo is a volcano and not the Izta," said Mr. Iglesias—but let's call them both volcanoes so that we can admire the Valley of Mexico in all its glory in a single clause). The Countess von Kollonitz got a bit of a nosebleed from the altitude and Count Zichy was a bit short of breath, but still, everyone was close to tears from the sight of it all. These marvels and the welcoming receptions that kept getting more enthusiastic as they approached the capital caused Maximilian to regain his good spirits. Carlota was also happy, and a few days later, in her letters, one of them addressed to her beloved sister the Empress Eugénie, she wrote that Max and she had heard Mass in the chapel erected atop the Pyramid of Cholula where the Aztecs used to offer human sacrifices in the past; and, she wrote, the Cholula plains reminded her of Lombardy, just as the countryside in Córdoba was very much like that of Tyrol, and in Puebla de los Angeles she had donated seven thousand piasters from her own purse for the Orphanage for the Poor, and besides, she wrote Eugénie, the people are supremely intelligent and almost all the Indians know how to read and write.

In Mexico City not only were there no hurricanes to topple the innumerable triumphal arches, flags, pedestals with symbols of the Arts, Commerce, Music, and Agriculture, or the busts of the Emperors and Empresses of Mexico and France, or the rows of Venetian lanterns and of glasses that hung from balcony to balcony, but the imperial party was greeted by a multitude that cheered them and recited poems under the hot sun—in Spanish and Latin, in French, in the ancient Mexican language—written by Don Galicia Chimalpopoca. All the Church princes were waiting for them, the cannons thundered in their honor, bells rang at full peal, and, in the domes of the Metropolitan Cathedral, the notes and the lyrics of the *Domine salvum fac Imperatorem* were heard for the first time. In other words, and at long last, they were enjoying a proper parade or imperial procession: their solemn, impressively solemn, triumphant entrance into Mexico City. After spending the night at the Village of Guadalupe, Maximilian and Carlota's retinue was followed by over two hundred carriages carrying Mexico City's society elite, who had traveled to the Gate of San Lázaro to greet them. The entourage traveled to the palace by way of streets called La Santísima, El Amor de Dios, Santa Inés, Moneda, and Arzobispado, and was followed by private citizens on horseback, by students, by the lottery vendors' union, by porters and water carriers waving stalks and poles with multicolored streamers. Thus was the entrance of the sovereigns into Mexico City as described by the newspapers of the time, such as the *Cronista de México*, which on that day was printed on sky-blue paper. Perhaps Max would have liked to have Sebastian Schertzenlechner at hand in order to take some dictation: "Artillery Salutes. For the Mexican Princes twenty-one cannon volleys; for the Ministers of the Army and Navy, nineteen. Fifteen for the others." Or perhaps he had already had him write this down. Yes, perhaps he'd done it as they were leaving Martinique to the sounds of the *Chant du Départ*. The Empress's Lancers, under the command of Colonel López, were at the head of the procession. The African Hunters and the Hussars were next, followed by the rococo carriage of the Imperial couple, General Bazaine to one side and General Neigre on the other, both with drawn swords and on prancing mounts. But nothing was closer to a true court ceremonial than the mourning observed, a few days later, on the demise of Her Imperial and Royal Majesty, the Duchess of Bavaria. The instructions for the mourning and half-mourning protocol that the court was to observe appeared in the *Official Daily*. Thus, for the ladies, mourning meant black silk, velvet, and gloves, with only diamonds and pearls allowed for ornament. The half-mourning called for black and white with purple and gray, and jewels of all colors—emeralds from Colombia or rubies from Burma, sapphires from Ceylon or turquoises (not from Turkey but from Mexico): marvelous opportunities to turn dead letter on a page into live ritual. General Juan Nepomuceno, whom Maximilian stripped of all military and political power when he gave him the ornamental title of

Grand Marshal of the Court and Minister of the Imperial House, signed the instructions.

But after the celebrations and the cheers, after the first audience in the Hall of the Throne, Maximilian and Carlota did not, after all, get to sleep on a bed of flowers that first night. The National Palace, as described by the Countess von Kollonitz and other travelers of the time as a sort of barracks or a third-class European hotel, not only didn't have a hall large enough for the receptions Maximilian had dreamed about, but its bedrooms were like hallways, narrow with low ceilings, and most of them, having been uninhabited for a long time, were covered with dust and cobwebs. "I am sure Chapultepec Castle, built by the viceroys on a hill surrounded by centenary *ahuehuete* trees, will be more pleasing to Your Majesties," said Don Joaquín. "The whole valley can be seen from its terraces, there is a lake at the foot, and through its slopes runs the spring in which the Emperor Moctezuma bathed. *Chapultepec*, Sire, means 'hill of the *chapulín*,' which is to say, hill of the locust." In order not to alarm Maximilian, Don Joaquín abstained from telling him that it had been in one of this selfsame hill's caves that the last Toltec king had committed suicide. At any rate, that night there was no other alternative but to sleep there, in that barracks called a palace. And some of the things history says happened to Maximilian and Carlota that night can be verified, others not. It's difficult to know, for instance, if it's true that behind the red curtains and bedroom windows they were being watched by bright, black, cunning eyes—those same dark doe eyes, those amazed and sweet eyes filled with fear whose fixed and astounded gaze had greeted them when they alit from their bogged-down carriage on their way to Córdoba among the mangroves and marshes, the cactus groves, and the blue convolvulus. The eyes of their new subjects watched in amazement as the emperor and empress went through their imperial bedtime rituals, because, rumor had it, some palace servants had sold the curious the opportunity to spy on the country's brand new sovereigns from the balcony.

On the other hand, there is no doubt whatsoever about the rockets and fireworks that began exploding when Maximilian and Carlota entered Mexico City—almost under the legs of the horses pulling the imperial carriage. One day the Spanish Monarch Ferdinand VII asked a Mexican visitor, "What do you think your countrymen are doing this minute?" "Setting off firecrackers, Your Majesty." A few hours later the Spanish monarch repeated the same question and the Mexican gave the same answer. This happened several times. And Carlota found out that night that this was far from being hyperbole. Every fiesta or commemoration—any excuse whatever, really—was an opportunity to set off deafening firecrackers for hours, for days, for years, forever.

And that's the way it was until the early hours, though the noise wasn't the only reason the Empress couldn't sleep a wink that night. The story of the bedbugs is true. As soon as Maximilian and Carlota were ready to go to sleep they began to feel their stings. They called the servants, lifted their blankets. The imperial bed was invaded by bedbugs, dozens of them, legions, some pale and flat, others red and fat, shiny, already satiated with Bourbon and Habsburg blood. Carlota spent the night in an armchair. In search of another bed, Maximilian walked through those rooms, halls, and galleries he had traveled with his fingers on the map of the palace: the Paintings Gallery, the Hall of Charles V, the Yucatán Hall, the Dining Room. Finally he found a billiards room. He looked at the bare walls and remembered the one at Schönbrunn with its two murals commemorating the creation of the Order of Maria Theresa following the victory of Frederick II in the Battle of Kolin. Later he clambered onto the table, and there on that billiard table carpeted in blue felt, the Emperor Ferdinand Maximilian I spent his first night in Mexico City. "And the Minister of Public Instruction, should he wear a purple silk robe embroidered with gold palms, and an ermine cape, Don Joaquín? And the decorations for Civil and Military Merit brought on a silver platter, General Almonte? And the sash of the president of the Court of Appeals in white silk with golden acorns as in France? Because you're not suggesting that we change the acorns for green prickly pears or chayote squash with thorns, right, Carla, dear Carlota, *mia cara carissima*, Carla?"

2. With Your Heart Pierced by an Arrow

The big barge was in the middle of the river, held fast by ropes tied to both banks, and Colonel Dupin was in the center of the barge. He was sitting on a leather chair placed on top of a wooden crate. He wore a sombrero with a very wide brim and a high crown richly trimmed with looped cords and gold arabesques. Pinned to it, like the veil of an old-fashioned bride, was a mosquito net hanging to the floor and surrounding him completely.

The prisoner was kneeling down in front of him, bare chested, his arms stretched out crucifixion-style, and his wrists tied to a pole behind his head.

On the floor, next to him, there was a gray felt Texan hat studded with a multitude of metallic ornaments.

The Colonel said: "*Dis-lui que mon chapeau est plus grand que le sien.*"

The interpreter translated: "Colonel Dupin says: My hat is bigger than yours."

Besides the interpreter, who was next to the Colonel, there were five or six other men in the barge, rocking there together on the Tamesí River. They all wore Mexican straw hats with high crowns, but unadorned. Some were smoking while squatting. There was a full moon and the night resounded with frogs and crickets.

The Colonel added: "*Et que ma moustache est aussi plus grande que la sienne.*"

"The Colonel says: And my moustache is also bigger than yours."

Colonel Dupin, Commander of the French counter-guerrillas and military governor of Tamaulipas, had a long salt-and-pepper beard besides an enormous moustache. As always, he wore his big red Hussar's dolman with leather cuffs and gold loops, like those on his hat; likewise his white trousers, huge yellow boots, and large spurs. From his waist hung two guns and a saber that, since he was sitting, touched the floor.

His black mastiff slept next to him.

The Colonel pointed to the gray felt cowboy hat and spoke through his interpreter:

"Where did you get that hat?"

"General Santa Anna gave it to me . . . a Gringo prisoner had given it him at El Alamo," the prisoner answered.

"With the little stars and all," asked the Colonel.

"Yes with the little stars. I added the relics later."

There was an intense scent of oranges and the sound of someone grinding coffee on the riverbank.

"Where are you from?"

"From Ciudad Victoria," answered the man.

"Ciudad Victoria," the Colonel said, "would fit completely inside the Place de la Concorde."

Then he opened up the mosquito net, placing his hands in front of his face, as if he were peeking out from behind a curtain, and ordered the prisoner's hat brought closer to him. He looked at the tiny metal stars for a moment, the pins, the medals and small charms pinned to the brim and the crown, the brooches shaped like eagles, anchors, or roses, and the diminutive gold and silver hearts and legs, hands, and ears. Then he pointed to the end of the barge and gave another order.

Two of his men got up, went to a pile of sacks and boxes, and placed several objects at the Colonel's feet.

"This is only a fraction of yesterday's loot," the Colonel said. "Look how pretty: the command baton of the Mayor of Güemes, an American drum, a trombone, and an infantry pennant. I'm going to keep everything, except that gold and silver embroidered cavalry flag. I'm going to take that one to Paris so they can put it in Les Invalides. But how in hell should you know what La Concorde or Les Invalides are? Tell me, what's your name?"

"Juan Carbajal," answered the man.

"And do you know where the Mayor who held this baton in his hands yesterday is now?"

The prisoner didn't answer.

"He's hanging from a tree in the Plaza de Güemes."

The Colonel opened up the mosquito net again, took out a cigar from a pocket, and lit it.

"I hang some of Juárez's supporters and enemies of the Empire," he said. "I hang them from posts or trees; others, however, I throw to the dogs, to be torn to pieces. The other day I caught one. I had his feet tied and lowered into one of those wells that you've poisoned with arsenic and the bodies of dead mules. We lowered him in and brought him back up; we put him in and took him out. We didn't know if he died from swallowing so much water or from ingesting so much poison."

"How are you going to kill me?" asked the prisoner. The interpreter translated the question, but the Colonel didn't answer.

"From Peking, you know what Peking is? It's the capital of China. I brought back a lot of things from here: a jade scepter in the shape of a sacred mushroom that they call *ling-chi* and some small porcelain dolls. I also brought some jade hooks the Empress of China used to string mulberry-tree leaves to feed her silkworms . . ."

The Colonel let out a big puff of smoke and raised his eyes to the sky. At that moment a cloud covered the moon and a bird let out a cry.

"Let's see what else I can take with me from Mexico . . . for the time being I'll start with your hat so I can hang it on my living-room wall, alongside my other hunting trophies . . ."

The Colonel remained silent for some minutes. The moon shone again and the Colonel got up. Standing on the crate he looked like a giant. He took a folded piece of paper out of a pants pocket and ordered:

"Stand him up . . ."

Two men lifted Juan Carbajal off the ground. The Colonel unfolded the paper and showed it to the prisoner. Then he spoke loudly, almost shouting, and the interpreter translated:

"And now, you son of a bitch, tell me, what does the note that you hid in the meat say?"

The Colonel was referring to a piece of beef that was hanging from the saddletree of Juan Carbajal's horse. They'd found a coded message from Juárez's supporters inside. Colonel Dupin's mastiff had already taken care of the meat.

The prisoner answered:

"I don't know what it says. I don't know the code."

Colonel Dupin tossed out his cigar, and it made a luminous curve in the night before sinking with a slight hiss into the waters of the Tamesí.

"You're a liar, but I'm going to get the truth out of you, you son of a bitch."

The Colonel sat down again and opened his mosquito net.

"Besides, you're a damn fool. You don't even know how to hide a secret message. You probably don't know anything about the story of the Orlov diamond, right? Well let me tell you. It's on the Russian Imperial Scepter now, but it came from a temple in India. Do you know how they got it out of India?"

The prisoner didn't answer.

"It was a French soldier. With his knife, he made a cut in his own calf, put the diamond in there, and then sewed up the wound. Later he sold it to Prince Orlov . . . That's how these things are done. Hide what's precious in your own goddamn skin, not in a piece of beef where anyone can find it—right?"

The prisoner didn't move his lips. The Colonel said:

"You're very quiet. Me, I distrust a close-mouthed man. Let's see, where were you coming from? How many of you are there?"

The Colonel held his nose and shouted: "And get that dog out of here, he's farting! . . . Well, then, you're not going to answer me? I have many ways to make mutes talk . . . you know that, don't you?"

"Yes, I know that," answered Juan Carbajal.

"Let me think what I'm going to do with you so you'll talk . . . let's see, let's see . . . Oh, yes, I have an idea. Let me see his hat."

The Colonel opened the mosquito net, took the hat, and turned it around very slowly. "You know," he said. "I'm going to be good to you. I won't take all your little stars, or all the little silver and gold hands and feet from your hat. I'm going to let you keep some . . . so you can wear them yourself."

He then chose a star.

"This one, I like this American star. You, take it off."

One of them took the hat and pulled out the star.

"And now," said Colonel Dupin, "now we're going to reward you with the Order of the Idiot Who Doesn't Know What's Good for Him . . . you there, pin it on his chest."

The man came up next to Juan Carbajal. The prisoner closed his eyes and tightened his jaw.

"What's the matter?" the Colonel asked. "Don't tell me his skin is that hard."

"No, Colonel. The pin is half rusted."

"Push harder then."

The star shone on the bare chest of the prisoner. A trickle of blood oozed from it.

"And now, are you going to tell me how many of you there are?" asked the Colonel.

"I don't know. I was only told to take the message."

"To whom?"

Juan Carbajal didn't answer.

"To whom? Where?"

The Colonel rubbed his beard.

"Why are you so stubborn? Do you enjoy suffering? Life is so short. Look, if you don't talk—and you will talk, eventually—and then, later on, I'll probably—but if you talk, look, you can come over to our side, and you'll have lots of fun."

On one of the river banks, behind the black silhouette of the trees, some moving torches were shining.

"Look, look over there . . . The other day we were told that the Juaristas had hidden weapons in a theater in Tampico. We confiscated them all: a bunch of Colt revolvers, Sharp carbines, and lots of ammunition. But we also found a box filled with women's wigs, and sometimes my men get drunk and wear them, and they dance at night with lit torches and they have lots of fun. Tell me . . . would you like to wear a red wig and dance a habanera with one of my men? One of them is a gigantic Dutchman who could break your waist with only one arm."

The Colonel asked for the Texan hat once again.

"You're an atheist, right? People bring these little silver hands and legs and these gold hearts as thanks to the Virgin or to the Lord, who've cured them with a miracle . . . but then you go and steal them from the Virgin . . . Don't you fear God?"

"What God?"

"Oh, you're a blasphemer on top of everything else," Colonel Dupin said, and took off a small silver leg.

"Take it," he ordered one of his men, "and pin it to his lips so that he'll learn not to blaspheme."

The man came up next to Juan Carbajal, pulled out his lower lip and pierced it with the pin. The prisoner barely complained.

The Colonel again took the paper from his pocket and unfolded it.

The interpreter translated the Colonel's words: "If you don't tell me what it says here, I'm going to pin a little star on you for each letter in the message. I'm going to make you see stars. Let's see, pull the prisoner's pants down."

Another trickle of blood dripped down Juan Carbajal's chin and neck.

The Colonel stuck his head out of his mosquito net.

"Bring the hat to me. Let's see . . . yes, take off that Mexican buzzard."

"It's not a buzzard," said Juan Carbajal. "It's an eagle."

"*Ces't un* buzzard," the Colonel insisted.

The interpreter translated: "It's a buzzard."

". . . and stick it into his foreskin," the Colonel added.

"In his what?"

"In the skin that hangs out of the tip of his dick." Colonel Dupin said, and buried his face back into the mosquito net. "In a little while we'll find something else to stick in his testicles."

The man came close to the prisoner, pulled out his foreskin, and pierced it with the silver eagle's pin.

"You Mexicans," the Colonel said, "besides being very stubborn, are very stupid. You know who Napoleon Bonaparte was?"

"Yes," answered Juan Carbajal.

"Well, the emperor we have in France is also named Napoleon Bonaparte, because he's his nephew. And our Emperor is responsible for bringing France nothing but glory, in battles like Magenta and Solferino, like Sebastopol . . ."

"We defeated you at Puebla," said the prisoner. The Colonel kept on talking as if he hadn't heard him.

"And we've brought civilization to many places: Cochin China, Senegal, Martinique, Algeria, . . . and now that we want to bring it to Mexico, you don't want it."

"Do you know who Benito Juárez is?" asked Juan Carbajal.

"Oh yes, he's an Indian. A stubborn Indian, like you. Why are all of you so stubborn?"

"Napoleon wasn't French," the prisoner said, "and Benito Juárez is Mexican." Colonel Dupin got up and opened up the mosquito net.

"You miserable son of a bitch. And what is it to you? Come on; grab him tight because this one is going to hurt. That one, that pin with the little yellow stone, stick it in one of his testicles . . ."

Juan Carbajal curled over with pain. The man was pinching his testicle, which kept slipping out of his grasp, over and over again.

He was finally able to grasp it and he pierced it with the pin.

"Splash his face with water to wake him up," said Colonel Dupin who sat back in his straw chair and closed the mosquito net once again.

Juan Carbajal opened his eyes.

"I made you scream this time, right? Like a sissy. Pin a star in each of his buttocks so that he'll look like a pansy."

The men turned the prisoner around and carried out the Colonel's order. Everyone laughed, not counting the prisoner. Two streaks of blood dripped from Juan Carbajal's buttocks.

"OK, OK, that's enough. Be quiet. Turn him around . . . Tell me; are you going to tell me where and to whom you were carrying that message? Or do you want me to decorate your other testicle too?"

Juan Carbajal's knees were buckling. The men held him up. He was shaking, and his sweat mixed with the streaks of his blood.

"I already told you—I can make anyone talk. I was told that the *plateados*—you've heard of them, right?—those bandits who're covered with silver from head to toe, hence the name? I was told that they're very brave. Well, not only did I make one of those *plateados* talk, he ended up on his knees, begging me in my mother's name to spare his life. I was also told that those other bandits, who wear heavy leather jackets and trousers because they're always in areas covered with brambles and thorns, are also very tough. But, look, everyone who's ever fallen into the hands of Colonel Dupin's counter-guerrillas have even told me how they came into this world . . . and, in turn, I tell them how they're going to leave it."

Colonel Dupin filled his lungs with the hot night air and snorted.

"Look here, I'm being very patient with you," he told Juan Carbajal. And then he told his men, "Let him loose."

Juan Carbajal collapsed to the floor of the barge. The Colonel's mastiff opened his eyes and pricked up his ears. Soon he fell asleep again.

"Stubborn, yes, you're very stubborn. Besides, you don't know how to make decisions. One must always choose. One can't have everything. You for instance, you will have to choose between being a live traitor or a dead asshole. Which do you prefer?"

Juan Carbajal lifted his face, but didn't answer. The Colonel leaned out of his mosquito net and pointed to both banks of the river.

"Look, look," he said. "I like all of this: the jungle, the lianas, the orchids, the shrieks of the monkeys, the call of the parrots, the flight of the toucans. Only one thing bothers me: the mosquitoes. Otherwise I like everything about the jungle, the heat included . . . I even like the warm waters. Then, why don't I stay here forever? Why don't I have a red granite house built on the summit of Chiquihuite and cover it with orchids? Oh, because I also like Paris. You've never been to Paris, have you?"

Colonel Dupin stroked his mustache and then he licked his lips.

"Paris . . . Paris. Paris is the most beautiful city in the world, and more so since Baron Haussmann filled it with very wide boulevards, which, besides being pretty, facilitate cavalry charges against troublemakers . . . The charges of our *Chasseurs d'Afrique*, for instance, who had the Juaristas on the run at Cholula. Come on. Pick up the prisoner. Make him kneel. That's right, and give me the hat again."

The Colonel began turning the hat around slowly.

"Oh, I like this one. Look at this pretty thing: a silver heart pierced by an arrow? Did your girlfriend give it to you?"

The Colonel took out the pin and looked at it for a while.

"I'll give you one more chance. Where were you taking the message?"

Juan Carbajal didn't answer.

"Stubborn. I mean stubborn like those mules you people shout *macho! macho!* at. Come on, stick it in his left tit. You know, once we tied a chinaco's arms to the saddle of my horse. I had him running behind me all morning long. Every time he fell I would stop my horse and shout *macho! macho!* And we threw rocks at him like you do with the mules. But one time he didn't get up and so I had to drag him. I dragged him for many hours until I left him at the gates of hell. I was riding a horse from La Panocha that time, one of the ones that have hooves so hard they don't need horseshoes. Tell me, would you like to die like that chinaco?"

The jungle was beginning to fill up with sounds and whispers unlike those that usually sounded at night. In the horizon, toward the mouth of the river, a pale white glow appeared. A streak of blood dripped down from Juan Carbajal's left nipple.

"You know, I even let some of you, those who behave, choose their own deaths. I ask them if they want to die by firing squad, or if they prefer to be quartered by four horses. Or drowned. Sometimes I allow the ones I hang to choose the tree they like the most. And, here's something you may not know: Colonel Dupin never hangs more than one man with the same rope. Each person I execute gets a new rope. What do you think of that?"

"How are you going to kill me?" asked Juan Carbajal again.

The Colonel pretended not to hear.

"Though I must confess, I myself have a favorite tree, which I've used over and over again. A very tall and wide one, very leafy, very green. It's at the Plaza de Medellín. I've hanged more than twenty men from it. But, sadly, I can't take every condemned man back to Medellín, can I? Oh, what I wouldn't give to be able to have Paris next to a warm sea with white sand . . . are you listening?"

Juan Carbajal's head was bent and his eyes closed.

"You, give him some mezcal."

The Colonel had said anisette, but the interpreter translated it as mezcal. One of the men took Juan Carbajal by the hair to get his face up, and with the other hand he brought a bottle next to his lips. The mezcal ran down the prisoner's chin. He kept his eyes closed.

"Raise one of his eyelids and stick one of those tiny hand pins through his eyebrow so that this son of a bitch can see me with at least one eye."

Some monkeys began screaming. The Colonel's mastiff yawned, pricked up his ears, opened his eyes, stretched, got up, and walked to the end of the barge to drink from the river water. The black and silvery water had begun acquiring a pink and purple hue toward the east, toward the mouth of the river. A new streak of blood went around Juan Carbajal's eyelid and began dripping down his cheek, to his lips.

"Can you see me now? Can you hear me now?"

The prisoner nodded vaguely.

"Yes, what I wouldn't give to have banana groves on the Champs Élysées. Do you know what the Champs Élysées is? It's the most beautiful boulevard in the world."

The mastiff lay at the Colonel's feet.

"And yes, I'd love to see the Seine bordered with coconut palms. Look, day's breaking," said Colonel Dupin as he peeked out of his mosquito net, "and when it comes, I won't have any other choice but to kill you. You are forcing me to do it. Tell me, where were you taking that message?"

The prisoner didn't answer.

"And the Bois de Boulogne . . . how wonderful to fill it with lianas and ferns, bamboo, mangoes, and so on . . . Do you hear the bell-ringer bird? It's like he's ringing the hour. It must be around five. What time is it?"

One of the men checked his watch.

"*Il est cinq-heures, mon colonel.*"

"But I can't have both. I have to choose, and I choose Paris. I'm going to die there. As soon as we finish all of you off and have Emperor Maximilian firmly on his throne, and we civilize this territory, I'm going to ask to retire from the army, and I'll go back to France. Though I know, pacifying you won't be easy because you're very slippery people, aren't you, and Mexico is very big. Listen, have you heard of La Barragana?"

"People say she's a guerrilla fighter for Juárez."

"Guerrilla fighter? She's a bandit. All of you are bandits, not guerrillas—an important distinction. I understand she's very brave, and it's only because of that that I don't know quite yet what I'll do with her if we catch her alive. I don't know if I'll have her breasts cut off so that she'll look more like a man—since living and fighting like a man is what she wants, after all—or if I should just pardon her in memory of our Saint Jeanne d'Arc. What do you think?"

The Colonel's mastiff got up, ran to the edge of the barge, and jumped into the water. He swam ashore.

"He must have caught scent of a mole . . . he loves moles," the Colonel said, "at any rate, I'll take some local plants with me to Paris to see if they grow there, and some animals too, like one or two blue macaws. Tell me, would you like to die drowned in the Tamesí?"

Juan Carbajal raised his head to look at the Colonel, but didn't answer.

"There are many things about this country I don't understand," said Colonel Dupin. "For instance, why do you call this river by the same name as the

English river, the Thames, when they don't have anything in common? Or why—and I was thinking about this just the other day—why do some of you Indians bathe every day, while others never bathe at all? Their faces covered with crusts of dirt like tree bark. Also, I don't understand how you people can eat so much muck. I'm tired of so many tortillas and beans. Outside of Mexico City's Recamier Restaurant and Tampico's Café Reverdy, there's no place in this entire country where you can get a decent meal. I'm tired of stinking drinks like pulque and those poisonous so-called brandies of yours. In my house in Paris I'm going to have a cellar filled with wines from Bordeaux, from Sauterne, absinthe, Pernod, crème de cassis . . . but I'm sure you don't know what I'm talking about, right? And now, now I'm tired of you."

Colonel Dupin stuck his head out of the mosquito net and looked up, smiled and pointed to the sky.

"Look, look. Above your head—the fireflies!"

Above the barge a luminous cloud of fireflies went by like an elusive constellation of green stars.

"Fireflies, fireflies," said Colonel Dupin and got up from his straw chair. "I would love to have them above me when making love in Paris at night—I would like to see a cloud of fireflies come in through the window and stay there circling above the bed . . . but one can't have everything."

The Colonel got down from his box and lifted up Juan Carbajal's face with one hand.

"The same with you, you see. You had to choose, and you chose. You're an asshole, but I note that you're a man. I don't understand that either. Some Mexicans cry like women when I'm about to kill them, and others like you, don't even blink. An English Colonel told me that India's Sepoys are like that, indifferent to death."

"How are you going to kill me?" asked Juan Carbajal for the third time.

The Colonel asked for the hat again.

"What a beautiful gold rose . . . It's gold, right? Where did you steal it? I'm certainly going to keep this one. I'm going to give it to a girlfriend of mine in Paris, and I'm going to ask her to wear it in her navel. How am I going to kill, you ask? Let's see, let's see, we'll see."

The Colonel walked slowly around Juan Carbajal. Thin lines of blood dripped from the prisoner's face and neck, his buttocks and his legs, his chest and stomach. The first rays of sun gave the Colonel's mosquito netting an orange glow that surrounded his face. Like the fireflies earlier, a flock of raucous, noisy green-yellow parrots crossed the river above them. The Colonel stopped in front of the prisoner, stroked his beard and his mustache, and said:

"I have an idea."

He reached for the pin that they had stuck in Juan Carbajal's left nipple. He grabbed it and with a sudden jerk pulled it out. The prisoner screamed. His breast was left hanging, almost torn off, and a streak of blood, thicker than the others, oozed from the wound.

"I have an idea—but you know, before I kill you, I've decided you won't be wearing anything. You hear me? You don't deserve it. I'm going to put everything back in the hat, the hat I'm taking to Paris. You and you, take off everything you pinned on him: the stars, the buzzard, everything, one by one, and with a good tug, without opening the pins first. Let this be a lesson to him."

Then he looked into the prisoner's eyes.

"And if you want to know how I'm going to kill you, Juan Carbajal, you'll find out right now. I'm going to kill you like I've never killed anyone else before."

The Colonel looked at the brooch he was holding in his hands and whispered, "*Ces't beau!*" and added: "*Faites venir l'Indio Mayo et qu'il apporte son arc et ses flèches.*"

The interpreter translated:

"Have the Mayo Indian come with his bow and arrows."

3. Scenes of Daily Life: Mexican Nothingness

"The Papal Nuncio, flying out the window!"

Louis Napoleon, fixing his eyes on the map of Paris, contemplated the past, present, and future projects that would make it the most beautiful and modern city in the world. Thanks, of course, to the Baron Haussmann and to geniuses like Charles Garnier and Viollet-le-Duc. The Champs Élysées. The iron and crystal pavilions at Les Halles. The Holy Chapel. The Opera. The sewers . . .

"The Nuncio, flying out the window?" whispered Louis Napoleon, leaving his cigarette in one of the two ashtrays Maximilian had given him: they were the oval shells of a mollusk called an abalone, admired for its iridescent beauty: "For those cigarettes, which so aid in our meditations," as the Emperor of Mexico had written him.

For her part, Carlota had promised to send Eugénie a photo album of the Toltec and Maya ruins and monuments—the Pyramids of the Sun and the Moon, the temples at Uxmal and Chichén Itzá—in the province of Yucatán, which she wanted to tour immediately; and also of those monstrous giants of Tula that must have been palace guards of the bloody Huitzilopochtli, the god who devoured human hearts.

"Yes, Louis, flying. Imagine, how amusing!"

Eugénie was referring to what Carlota had said to Bazaine: that many times she'd a mind to throw Monsignor Meglia, Bishop of Damascus and the only Papal Nuncio Mexico had ever had, out the palace window. The conversations with the Nuncio had given Carlota an idea of what hell must be like: if Carlota and Maximilian said something was white, Monsignor Meglia said it was black, and vice versa. All reasonable arguments slipped past the prelate "as if on polished marble." For him, as for Franz Joseph, there was no such thing as a *mezzotermine*, a compromise: *le juste milieu*, as her grandfather, Louis Philippe, had spoken of so often.

"Besides," added Eugénie, "Carlota says that to tell the truth, His Holiness, Pius IX, is an *iettatore*: any business in which he intervenes turns sour. His Holiness, an *iettatore*!"

Eugénie burst out laughing.

•

In the Hall of Ambassadors at the Mexican Imperial Palace, Maximilian was supervising the stripping of the ceiling. The bedbug incident had been very unpleasant, so he was having every last corner of the place fumigated, including the roof. The ceiling had covered some splendid cedar rafters that no one had noticed before; Maximilian ordered them to be left exposed forever. That night he said to Carlota:

"They're breathtaking. It was a complete surprise, like the many others that this nation has given us, and will continue to give us in future."

Aside from the surprises, the Mexican Empire that Carlota had hoped would keep Max truly busy, and that the latter had thought would keep Carla amused, very soon became a nightmare. Despite that, it was a pleasure to ride through the streets of the capital in the golden imperial carriage, a gift from their former subjects in Milan, or in the Daumont driven by a coachman wearing an enormous white hat, a green velvet Spencer, and a tricolor poncho, and pulled by six Isabelle mules with zebra-striped flanks. It was a pleasure for both of them to ride on their own at seven-thirty in the morning after the Daily Accord, on the Calzada de la Verónica or the other avenue that would someday join the castle with the palace, and that would be more beautiful than those Champs Élysées of which Louis Napoleon was so proud . . . The avenue would be called, yes, it would be called Calzada del Emperador, or, even better, the Empress's Promenade. Or, then again, the Calzada del Emperador?

•

At the Tuileries, Eugénie said to herself: "I'll write Carlota to tell her that Monsignor Chigi assured me that Meglia is not as inflexible as he likes to appear, and if he seems to be, it's only so he can give in with honor later on."

And Eugénie kept thinking that, if Monsignor Meglia had only had the opportunity to participate, along with the Emperor and Empress of Mexico, in the Maundy Thursday ceremony of washing the elderly's feet, and had had the opportunity of seeing Maximilian and Carlota getting down from their carriage and bowing in the street when they came upon the Holy Viaticum being administered, just like any commoner would, the truth is that the Nuncio would have no reason to doubt the sovereigns' devotion and piety. Perhaps Carlota was right when she said that Meglia was only a puppet, the marionette of Archbishop Labastida.

"The problem, Your Majesty," Hidalgo y Esnaurrízar said to Eugénie, on an afternoon in which a sand-laden breeze blew gently over the beaches at Biarritz, "the problem is the Decree that Emperor Maximilian issued to restore the freedom of worship in Mexico. Moreover, he has confirmed, de facto, the nationalization of Church property. Some have begun calling his decrees Juárez's policies without Juárez."

Eugénie sighed . . .

•

At Claremont Castle in England, Marie Amélie sighed as well. She sighed every time she remembered her childhood and the eruption of Vesuvius that had so disturbed her. She sighed when she remembered Louis Philippe, his sad coronation in the Chamber of Deputies, the throne draped with the French tricolor. She sighed when she remembered her firstborn Chartres, dead at such a tender age, when he jumped from his coach. And she sighed whenever she remembered Charlotte, whom she had warned would be killed in Mexico, along with Maximilian. And now Charlotte, her sweet granddaughter Charlotte, barely twenty-three and having arrived at that faraway savage land only a few months before, had written her that she was aging. She was aging, yes, because everything in Mexico was corrupt or corruptible. Because governing Mexico was a task for Sisyphus. And, if indeed some Liberals had attached themselves to the Empire, it was, according to Charlotte, because they, as hungry bees, found more and better honey in Maximilian's hives than in Juárez's wild flowers . . .

Marie Amélie remembered then that it was time to take the honey and lemon the doctor had prescribed for her laryngitis.

"They will be killed, they will be killed," she muttered.

"What's that you were saying, *Maman*?" the Duchess of Montpensier asked.

•

The Duke of Brabant wrote his sister Charlotte that he was riding through the streets of Paris with Louis Napoleon, when suddenly he saw a great crowd. He asked the Emperor if it was a funeral procession.

"No, my dear sir," Louis Napoleon answered. "That's the Contract Office for the new government loans to Mexico. It's the opposite of a funeral—it's the birth of an Empire. The extremes of life touch each other, as ever. Parisians are eager to buy stock."

•

"Nevertheless," Carlota said to Maximilian after she read the letter. "They tell us the opposite, that the Jecker bonds have crumbled and that they are being sold in France for a few pennies. That is, when they do sell. And we're so short of funds here."

Carlota placed the letter between the pages of the *Guide to the City of Mexico* by Marcos Arróniz, to concentrate on her Spanish-language grammar, by Herranz y Quiroz, while Max gave her a lengthy account of his travels around their new nation. He told her how amazed he had been to find out that some of the villages he'd visited hadn't seen a priest for ten, fifteen, or twenty years. Couples lived in mortal sin and many children, even youths, went unbaptized. He added that he'd had the pleasure of chatting at length with that blond, blue-eyed colonel, Miguel López, the one who had escorted them from Veracruz to Mexico.

•

It was raining that afternoon, as it did almost every day, in Brussels. The King confessed to Eloin that he didn't understand the matter of the dressed fleas and the jumping beans.

"But, are these fleas alive?"

"No, Your Majesty. They are dead," Eloin added, as he tried to explain to the Belgian monarch that Mexicans had conceived ways to dress fleas as brides and grooms, as *charros* and *tehuanas*, whatever they wished. He added that they could be seen with powerful magnifying glasses. There were fleas in skirts and trousers; Lilliputian veils and shawls were cut to fit those dead, dried fleas. They carried canes and wore spectacles, boots or slippers . . . And the beans, well, it was very simple. Because each one had an insect larva hidden inside, it jumped and twirled in the palm of one's hand as well as on a flat surface.

"Oh, I see. Yes, yes, of course . . . A larva, you say?"

Eloin had not come to Laeken to talk about dressed fleas or jumping beans but to inform Charlotte's father of the objective of his European journey: Maximilian had assigned him to ensure the support of the European nations against the ambitions of the United States. Lincoln was dead and, along with him, the hope that Max and Carla harbored that the President (assassinated by John Wilkes Booth on the night of April 14, 1865) would have come to recognize the Mexican Empire, sooner or later. On the other hand his number-one man, Seward . . .

"That Yankee was very lucky wasn't he, Eloin?"

Yes, on the same night that Lincoln had been mortally wounded in his box at Ford's Theater, William Henry Seward had survived an attempt on his life. A man had burst into his house and his bedroom and knifed him while he slept. With Seward, however, the Monroe Doctrine survived. The new president Andrew Johnson, "The Plebeian," had named himself the defender of that policy. Eloin told Leopold with regret that Johnson had refused a letter of condolence from Maximilian.

"He even refused to receive the messenger, Your Majesty. I told Emperor Maximilian too that the fact that Emperor Napoleon has suddenly lost interest in the Sonora Protectorate is not a coincidence. He clearly intends to remove the French troops from the border to avoid a *casus belli*. As to Montholon, Your Majesty knows . . ."

Leopold of Belgium interrupted Eloin with a gesture; he took Baroness Eppinghoven by the hand and he asked her to go to his chamber with him. He said that he was suffering a new bile attack.

Eloin left. On the morrow, in any case, he would tell the king that Maximilian had become the enemy of the present French Ambassador in Washington.

•

Nevertheless there were pleasures. *Cajeta*, a confection of caramelized goat milk, dark and thick, sinful and very sweet, was one of the Empress's delights. The arrival of the handsome Colonel Van der Smissen—heart of gold, iron arms, and brainless—at the head of those Belgian volunteers who wore waving blue tunics embroidered in red, green, or blue "brandenburgs," and felt hats with rooster-feather crests, was another reason for joy. And since a special kind of pleasure was to learn some of the humble customs of the people, Carlota learned to drink from a gourd, to bathe using a sort of sisal sponge called *estropajo*, and, although she was amazed at how poor some people were, to the extent that they ate mosquitoes, ants, grasshoppers, and water bugs, she sampled tortillas—round, flat bread that resembled the Indian *chapati*, according to Sir Peter Campbell Scarlett. Made with a meal that resembled Italian *polenta*, the French *cruchade*, the Argentinean *mazamorra*, and the Paraguayan *abatí-atá*, the tortilla had a flavor that, although simple, was unique. Perhaps it would be good to adopt it for second-tier banquets, in which the dishes—in relation to the great, official, first-class dinners—not only varied in nature and quality, but also in language of origin. So that the *dinde au cresson*, the *vol-au-vent financière* and the *boudin à la Jusienne*, those dishes offered during the dinner in honor of Bazaine's promotion to marshal, became *costillas a la jardinera*, *croquetas de arroz*, or *budín de Sagú*. In any case, when her dear Max grew weary of the *lenguado a la holandesa*, the *cartuja de codornices a la Bagration*, and other delicacies prepared by Monsieurs Bouleret and Masseboue—in either language, French or Spanish—one could always have a goulash, simple and unassuming, but with all its ingredients intact, beginning with an adequate portion of paprika, made by the faithful Hungarian cook Tüdös, who had taken to dressing as a Mexican gentleman rancher of the time: short waistcoat with epaulettes and trim, breeches open at midcalf, lace-trimmed underpants, red sash, and low-crowned, wide-brimmed hat.

•

The terrible heat did not seem to affect Eugénie's mood that morning at Saint-Cloud. Perhaps because, as a native of Madrid, she was accustomed to those "six months of hell that follow the six months of winter" in the Spanish capital . . .

"Come on, Louis, play it on the piano and I'll sing . . ."

Louis Napoleon, who believed that he had inherited some musical talent from his mother, Queen Hortense, agreed happily. He began to play Concha Méndez's song on the piano while Eugénie sang:

> *Si a tu ventana llega,*
> *Ay, una paloma . . .*
> *Trátala con cariño,*
> *Que es mi persona.*
> *Cuéntale tus amores*
> *Bien de mi vida;*
> *Corónala de flores,*
> *Que es cosa mía . . .*

"They tell me Charlotte loves this song . . ."

Yes, at that time Carlota sang "La Paloma" because she was enchanted by it. She had fallen in love with it the first time she heard it at the Imperial Theater. Made popular in Mexico by the Mexican singer Concha Méndez, the song had been adopted by the Mexican Empress: she said it was her favorite song of all time.

> *Ay, chinita que sí,*
> *Ay que dame tu amor,*
> *Ay, que vente conmigo,*
> *Chinita,*
> *A donde vivo yo . . .*

"La Paloma" was one of those sweet habaneras that were in vogue in Spain, in Mexico and other countries. Coming from Havana, they were called habaneras, of course. They had a slow, sweet rhythm, so slow and sweet, with dance steps so lazy and loving, so pianissimo, that, as Captain Blanchot said, couples did not dance, but sighed to it, in unison.

•

Pope Pius IX and Monsignor Meglia walked, very slowly, through the Sistine Chapel. They walked under *Moses's Journey into Egypt* by Pinturicchio and Perugino.

"I could not agree more with Your Holiness," Meglia said. "The only solution is to sign a treaty with Mexico like those we finalized a year ago with El Salvador and Nicaragua . . ."

They walked under *Moses and the Daughters of Jethro,* by Botticelli.

"In those treaties, as Your Holiness must know, we designated the Catholic faith as the religion most appropriate to those nations . . ."

They walked under the *Crossing of the Red Sea*, by Cosmo Rosselli.

"But Emperor Maximilian's attitude renders this impossible. Does His Holiness know that one of his ministers, Pedro Escudero, I believe, referred to a letter that I published before I went to Guatemala, as a *'lettre insolente'*?"

They went under *Scenes of the Life of Moses*, likewise by Rosselli.

"The only thing in that letter was the truth—that the decree for the freedom of religion subjects the Mexican Church to public whim . . ."

And they walked by the *Punishment of Korah*, by Botticelli.

"I ask myself how His Majesty, Emperor Maximilian, could have dared to decree that any rescript, brief, or bull from Your Holiness might only be published under the Imperial exequatur?"

Pius IX stretched out his arms and shrugged his shoulders.

"I don't know. But we'll make that lost sheep return to the fold," the Pontiff said, and raised his eyes, which rested for a few seconds on one of Michelangelo's frescoes: *God Separating the Light from the Darkness.*

•

"Iturbide? I didn't know that Mexico had had an emperor before . . ."

It was the second or third time that the Viscount Palmerston had told Queen Victoria that Mexico had indeed had another emperor, Agustín de Iturbide. At the moment, at Balmoral Castle, he was telling her that an Agustín II might rule Mexico someday, in addition to the aforementioned Agustín I.

Like Marie Amélie, Victoria missed her late husband, Prince Albert, terribly. But she listened carefully to the questions that Palmerston was posing: Did Maximilian have a mistress, or several mistresses, or not? Was he sterile, as a leaflet written by a so-called Abbot Alleau claimed, or not? Was Carlota venting her frustrations from her childlessness by ruling in his stead? Whether or not Maximilian was impotent, as many suspected, the case was that the consorts did not have marital relations, and this was leading them to pursue adoption as a means of ensuring the succession to the throne. The chosen one, Palmerston told Victoria, was the grandchild of Emperor Iturbide. He was three years old at that time (1865), and he was an intelligent, handsome child with only one—correctable—flaw. Because his mother was a North American, the child, Agustín—God willing, someday to be Agustín II of Mexico—spoke half Spanish, half English. He would say, for example, "*Me gusta* a lot *el cake.*"

"My Darling Vicky . . ." Victoria had stopped listening to Palmerston in order to review, mentally, the letter that she intended to write her beloved daughter as soon as she was free. Vicky was married to Prince Frederick, heir to the Prussian throne: a tall, handsome, richly bearded man . . . Few European princesses like Vicky faced such a bright future.

"My Darling Vicky . . ."

•

Eugénie was the only one who understood, or seemed to understand, all of those exotic Mexican customs to which Carlota referred, perhaps because she was a Spaniard and because Don José Manuel Hidalgo y Esnaurrízar had undertaken the task of giving her all the necessary explanations. This is how, one morning, on her way back to the Tuileries from a brief stay at Compiègne, Eugénie learned that *piñatas* were made of clay, that they could be given any shape possible with three types of papers—papier mâché, crepe paper, or tissue. A *piñata* could be a silver boat, a red carrot, or a rainbow-tailed comet. Blinded with a scarf, people hit them with sticks until they broke. Its delightful bounty of fruits and nuts with strange names—*tejocotes*, *jícamas*—and flavors as strange as their names, *cacahuates*, *capulines*, fell like manna from heaven . . .

"They have a unique flavor, Your Majesty, that I could not describe . . ." Hidalgo said to Eugénie. "Although one could say that the capulín is the Mexican cherry, darker and stronger flavored."

Eugénie thought that anything could happen in such a land, a country as strange as Mexico where on All Souls' Day people ate marzipan skeletons, and sugar skulls with their names spelled out on the skull's brow; where birds sat on their eggs not to keep them warm but to cool them; where in one state alone (Michoacán) there were more than four hundred craters that could become volcanoes at any moment and cover the entire continent with a sea of burning lava. Because all of that happened in Mexico, besides earthquakes and the noise, the constant noise: firecrackers, pyrotechnics, rattles made of wood and even of iron and silver, and the Holy Week rite of exploding "Judases," those enormous cardboard figures stuffed with gunpowder that hung from sticks like a great vineyard of corpses . . .

Because of all that, it could happen, for example, that in the final analysis Mexico would not be the easy conquest that the French Empress had imagined. Because Eugénie—who at the beginning, with that enthusiasm she always displayed to learn the history, the conquests, and the heroes of what she called Columbus's Cuba, Ponce de León's Florida, Pizarro's Peru and Valdivia's Chile—had asked herself, how could it be possible that thirty thousand men wouldn't be enough to subjugate Cortés's Mexico? After all, the great Conquistador himself had done it with very few men—one hundred? Five hundred? With time the Empress had been persuaded that the opposite was true, and now she was thinking that they would need perhaps three hundred thousand men to conquer such a vast territory. Was this the moment that Louis Philippe had chosen to suggest the departure of the French troops? Yes, it was true: Eugénie knew that the Mexicans could no longer tolerate the French. Many of the latter committed crimes with impunity because no Mexican soldier or policeman was allowed to arrest a French soldier. The third Zouave regiment had become regrettably notorious for severe pillaging in Huauchinango. Potiers, Berthelin, and Dupin had earned their own notoriety very quickly, although Maximilian had succeeded in having France recall Dupin, after the latter had committed many atrocities in the name of civilization, including burning down the city of Ozuluama. But what would Maximilian do without the French?

"Organize a Mexican army. It's about time," replied Louis Napoleon. "He can accomplish that if he starts allocating more funds to his military instead of wasting his budget on so much foolishness . . ."

•

Well, enough about Montholon and Schertzenlechner. King Leopold only wanted to hear about matters that interested him. Or be filled in on what he did not already know. He knew very well that Maximilian had earned Montholon's animosity when he removed the Chancellor of the Empire, Mr. Arroyo, who had finalized the agreement that, with Almonte's help and thanks to the pressure exerted by Montholon's own, had given France the right to exploit the mines in Sonora. Louis Napoleon had lost interest in the Sonora silver mines at the conclusion of the American Civil War, so this adversarial act had been in vain . . . Montholon left for the United States and Monsieur Alphonse Danó was put in his place in Mexico.

As to Schertzenlechner . . . well, the Belgian monarch was indifferent to the fate of the former lackey who had lost the battle against Eloin. An Austrian and a Belgian respectively, they both had conspired against the French; when that bored them, they conspired against each other. Finally, Maximilian had to choose between them, and he picked Eloin. Schertzenlechner left Mexico without bidding farewell to Maximilian, despite the fact that the Emperor had pardoned him and spared him for starting alarming rumors. Seven thousand Indians, Schertzenlechner had claimed, were marching toward Mexico City to defend their cause. But the seven thousand Indians never arrived.

The matter that did interest Leopold greatly, on the other hand, was the Iturbide child's adoption. He could not be resigned to Maximilian and Charlotte's lack of an heir, to the prospect that the Mexican Empire would belong to a stranger and not to his grandchild, a Coburg.

•

Prince and Princess Iturbide were crossing the ocean toward Europe. The only one left in Mexico was Princess Josefa. The Iturbides' exile was one of the conditions of the secret agreement between the family and Maximilian. In exchange, besides little Agustín and his brother Salvador, each of them—including their aunts and uncles—had all been granted the title of prince and princess, and a settlement of one hundred and fifty thousand pesos, besides a lifetime pension. In accordance to other terms of the agreement, no one was allowed to return to the Empire without Maximilian's authorization. The problem was with Alicia, the mother, whom Maximilian considered a bit crazy because she did not want to leave her child; in his view, the child's grandiose future was based entirely on this separation. Moreover, her concessions to the pressures from her family were clearly temporary. In any case, it was quite a privilege to observe little Agustín swinging from the branches of those ancient ahuehuetes that dripped with Spanish moss in Chapultepec. Or to place him on one's lap when one—namely Maximilian—nestled in a hammock under the golden cages of the toucans, while the four dogs imported from Havana—like "La Paloma" and all the other habaneras—frolicked on the terrace or chased butterflies, and wise Dr. Bilimek, carrying an enormous yellow parasol, grasping tweezers, and wearing a sort of pocket-covered apron—jars in every pocket—went in search of lizards, worms and scarabs.

"Provided, of course," thought one of the Iturbide princes, as Fort San Juan de Ulúa faded in the horizon, "that Maximilian and Carlota don't have a child of their own."

As long as, to that effect, they persevere their celibacy. Well, celibacy as regards what went on between them, anyway, because it was said that Maximilian was not in the least impotent. Quite the contrary . . .

•

It was clear that the European museums and galleries (the Vatican included) that Maximilian had visited in his pre-imperial life all held more important and more numerous works than what the Emperor saw when he visited the Art Academy of San Carlos in Mexico City; on the other hand, however, it was such a delight to sail down the La Viga Canal in his imperial gondola, surrounded by poppy-crowned canoes, and to behold a *St. Francis of Assisi* by El Greco and *Susannah and the Elders* by Rubens. This compensated for the setbacks and displeasures. It was the same with his daily swim in the pool at Chapultepec—after paying the guard five pesos, to set a good example. And, likewise, his rides through the plains of Apam amply compensated him, as did Rembrandt's *Ahasuerus and Haman at the Feast of Esther*, Titian's *Bacchus and Ariadne*, and Tintoretto's *Judith and Holofernes*. All of this despite the fact that he'd once whispered to the Countess von Kollonitz, "*Nichts Lächerlicheres, als solch'einen Anzug selbst zu erfinden?*" (Isn't it laughable to find oneself wearing such attire?) The truth is that Maximilian seemed happy in those clothes— dressed as a modified Mexican *charro*—in an enormous gray felt sombrero, a silver hatband, serape, blue cloth pants trimmed with silver buttons, and spurs from Amozoc—a knight in a cowboy's saddle, on his spirited steed Orispelo, or the more docile Anteburro. *Our Lady of Mercy* by Luis de Morales, the Divine Morales, portraying a Virgin Mary whose tears appeared to be made of melting wax, and then the sinister *Saint Augustine* in his long black beard, next to a *Mary Magdalene* whose beautiful face reminded him of Empress Carlota (in both paintings by Zurbarán), all made him forget, for an instant, the splendor of Pitti Palace. In San Carlos he gazed, with great interest, at several paintings by a talented Mexican contemporary artist whom he decided to summon to the Court.

"Note this down, Blasio. We must summon Juan Cordero."

José Luis, Maximilian's Mexican secretary, wrote with an indelible pencil. When one wet the tip of this pencil with some water—or spit, in Blasio's case—what seemed to be lead or graphite became purple ink when it touched the paper. Blasio would do this also on the way to Cuernavaca, when he accompanied the Emperor in the carriage that had been built on the orders of Colonel Feliciano Rodríguez. This carriage contained a multi-drawered desk. Blasio always ended up with his tongue and lips tinted purple and this amused Max a great deal. But that was much better, no doubt, than to take an inkwell on the journey, since with so many potholes we would end up ink spattered, would we not, Blasio? Besides, how would we blot the letters and the edicts? You would have to air them from the windows—and then what if they flew away? What if the Emperor's edicts turned into birds?

·

It was as he sighed to a habanera with Pepita Peña that Bazaine—named Marshal of France after his Mexican campaign—fell in love with the little seventeen-year-old Mexican girl, and married her. Carlota, somewhat alarmed, somewhat amused, wrote Eugénie: "When men like him fall in love, they become demons."

"Carlota's observations are quite correct, as usual," said Eugénie.

Louis Napoleon, as usual, wore a sleepy parrot's expression, but he listened to Eugénie. In any case, what worried him more than Carlota's observations on Bazaine's love life were the other comments that the Mexican Empress made in her correspondence with Eugénie, or that the Emperor received from other sources. Carlota had said that the word "impossible" wasn't a part of the French vocabulary, and that, thank God, and thank Louis Bonaparte, they still had their dear red trousers, *les pantaloons rouges*, in Mexico. She had asked all the French officers for their portraits, to put into an album. With the help of the French army, one could, no doubt, bring peace to the Empire. In Mexico, Carlota said, the dissidents are a ghost army. The bands (they're nothing but groups of bandits) recruit any man who rides out of town carrying a rifle, seeking his fortune. One charge from the "red pants" or the African Hunters is sufficient to disperse them. Moreover, as her dear Max said, "The more I study the Mexican people, the more I am convinced that I have to make them happy in spite of themselves."

Louis Napoleon was gratified to hear Carlota describe the French troops in such terms. But it was necessary to reiterate that the French could not stay in Mexico indefinitely. Maximilian, therefore, was going to have to take action in that regard.

But in a country where anything could happen, as in Mexico, one could do nothing. A few months later, Carlota said so: In Mexico, besides chaos, people worship *nothingness*, a *nothingness* made of stone, "Immovable, as old as the pyramids."

Napoleon decided that the lovely afternoon merited a stroll through the Tuileries Gardens. But when he passed the Hall of Ushers, he felt a cold draft and determined, instead, to ride in his phaeton. When he appeared in the vestibule the Swiss Guard tapped his halberd on the floor as he shouted, "The Emperor!"

•

The Emperor, that is to say, the one in Chapultepec, became furious when he realized that Marshal Bazaine only obeyed orders from the Emperor—the one at the Tuileries—and not his own. That was intolerable. As a first measure, Emperor Maximilian decided to tell Emperor Louis Napoleon, perhaps by means of the letters between Carlota and Eugénie, that what they had in abundance in Mexico were not troops but one marshal too many. This was in reference to Bazaine, who would do well to return to France and take his Pepita Peña with him. On the other hand, Douay, who was in Paris at the time, should return to Mexico as soon as possible, to replace Bazaine. Douay was the same man who had derided Bazaine's suggestion to reduce the French troops by the repatriation of several units in June of 1864, the same month of Maximilian and Carlota's arrival. He was an apt, simple, energetic man, and not a dreamer like Bazaine. The latter stated, for example, that the guerrillas had been eliminated in entire regions, though d'Hérillier had assured him that the opposite was true, since he himself had had to face large groups of guerrillas at the very gates of the capital more than once. It was also true, as the Count of Corti tells us, that at times one could hear shots being fired in a battle taking place in the city sewers during one of Carlota's Monday *grand soirees* . . . Moreover, nothing that Maximilian did or decided was approved by Bazaine. The marshal acted as though he was Maximilian's tutor, and then acted surprised not to be received in Chapultepec, but only in the National Palace.

The Empress—the one in the Tuileries—received a letter from the Empress—the one in Chapultepec—singing the praises of General Douay's actions . . .

•

Carlota remained as regent of Mexico City when Maximilian went off to Cuernavaca to gather herbs and collect butterflies. But it was said that he also went there to do other things. Rumors arose that at night at the Borda Villa the Emperor received certain ladies who entered his private chamber through a secret ivy-covered garden door. At court the names of some possible visitors began to circulate. Other mistresses in Mexico City were mentioned, along with a certain Señora Armida from Acapatzingo with whom, historians claimed later, Max had several offspring. It was also rumored that in Cuernavaca he did at the very least have one mistress, if not a harem: a beautiful, dark-skinned woman, the daughter perhaps, or the wife, of the gardener-in-chief of the Borda Villa.

Now then, when Carlota stayed behind as regent, one couldn't say that there was really an emperor in Mexico City. But neither was there an "*empeorador*," someone who makes matters worse, as some had nicknamed Maximilian. To make matters worse, the nickname and pun also worked in French, "*un empireur*." This type of insult drove Maximilian mad. The satirical periodical *La Orquesta*, for example, ran cartoons that just infuriated him. In one, the Emperor smoked a giant cigar, a "*puro*," and the drawing suggested that Maximilian was another "*puro*," a name also given to diehard liberals. In another, Maximilian was depicted hatching from an egg, and the caption read: "We've got ourselves a '*güero*'!" It was explained to Maximilian that *güero* has several meanings in Mexico. A *huero* or *güero* egg is an unfertilized egg, but you could call a blond man like himself a *güero* as well. Further, the expression, "We have a *güero*," indicates that the speaker has a failed or impossible project on his hands.

In any case, when Carlota remained as regent in Mexico, things got done and Mexico really had a decisive ruler. Carlota, although something of a *pura* herself, had not, however, come out a "*güera*."

•

Aside from other positive things, such as Juárez's continued, seemingly endless flight farther and farther north, the excellent season of Italian opera in the capital city, and the good theater being set up with actors brought down from Martinique—as well as the detailed description of the court balls directed to the Mexican envoys in Europe—the garden at the Borda Villa was one of Maximilian's favorite topics in letters to his friends. And so, that was how Baroness Binzer found out that the Valley of Cuernavaca resembled a vast golden blanket, surrounded by enormous mountains tinted in all possible colors, from pale rose to purple and violet or the deepest sky-blue; some as rocky, dark, and steep as those off the coast of Sicily; others as dense with forests as the green mountains in Switzerland; and among them all, the most beautiful were Iztaccíhuatl—called the Slumbering Lady because it resembled a supine figure hooded by a shroud of snow—and Popocatépetl, her beloved (or murderer?) kneeling by her side. According to the legend, Izta and Popo were giants, and the male giant had slain his beloved out of jealousy. But that was immaterial. The important thing was that from those two mountains' melted snow came the iciest, most delicious water in the world. The Valley of Cuernavaca must be the most beautiful place in the whole world—or perhaps in all of creation—Maximilian swore to Baroness Binzer. There, in the heart of the valley, was the Borda Villa, with shady terraces, swinging white silk hammocks; whispering fountains under thick, green canopies formed by dark orange and banana trees; bowers thick with perennial flowering tea-roses; walls carpeted by fiery red vines; birds that sang through the day; and fireflies, multicolored butterflies, royal poincianas; and, in all the shades of red, reaching to royal purple, burgundy, and dark lilac, there were those marvelous creepers named bougainvilleas, in honor of a renowned French traveler.

•

It was a quiet evening at Saint-Cloud. Loulou, the little imperial prince, was calculating how many Algerian soldiers he would kill with his next cannonade, and he told his father that he figured on twenty.

Louis Napoleon adopted a comically resigned expression. On the gleaming parquet floor, the cardboard toy soldiers were acting out the Battle of Isly.

Louis Napoleon reread the note that Maximilian had sent to Paris, Brussels, London, and Rome. In the note, Maximilian had attributed the initiative of first offering him the throne of Mexico, and then convincing him to accept, to his own brother, Franz Joseph.

"I shall instruct the Quai d'Orsay," the Emperor said to Eugénie, "to pretend that this note never arrived. And you know what . . . ?"

"It's your turn, Papa," Loulou said. Louis Napoleon did not like to play at staging battles that he and his uncle had not won. Such was the case with the Battle of Isly, the glory of which belonged to Louis Philippe. But the Imperial Prince adored battling the red soldiers of Abd al-Qadir. When he played, he wore a hat that most resembled the one worn by Père Bugeaud.

"Do I know what *what*, Louis . . . ?"

Louis Napoleon said that he would kill ten French soldiers with his next cannon attack. Loulou complained, so they reached a good compromise—six dead and four wounded.

"Forgive me . . . what I wanted to tell you is that I shall write Franz Joseph begging him not to aggravate Maximilian's situation. It is a delicate matter. That Family Pact is giving us nothing but headaches. Franz Joseph never should have published it in Austria, and, in turn, Maximilian erred in having that article published in *L'Ère Nouvelle* in Mexico asserting that all the 'most distinguished jurists' are denouncing the validity of the pact from a constitutional and legal point of view . . ."

Loulou continued calculating . . . if he attacked the right flank . . .

"And now they tell me that a document called the 'Venetian Letter' appeared in the same periodical, maintaining a critical view of Vienna's behavior toward its subjects in the Lombardo-Veneto region . . . All we need now is the end of diplomatic relations between Vienna and Mexico."

This time he would kill thirty Algerians. Louis Napoleon gave up. In any case, it was a lost battle. Marshal Bugeaud was destined forever to be victorious at the Battle of Isly.

And Louis Napoleon surprised himself, humming "La Paloma" . . .

> *Si a tu ventana llega,*
> *Ay, una paloma . . .*

Eloin would have liked to tell King Leopold that his absence from Mexico was due as well to the fact that Maximilian wanted to distance him from the nation. According to the Military Chief of Staff Colonel Loysel, Eloin, his civilian counterpart, had tried to grant himself too much power.

Eloin would have liked to complain about Loysel to King Leopold, about that imbecile's going out of his way to make his, Eloin's, life impossible.

Eloin would also have liked to describe Maximilian's office to the Belgian monarch. Since Maximilian disliked blotting powders, Blasio placed all his manuscript pages on the floor, one by one, to sit until the ink dried. So the Emperor's study ended up carpeted in papers from wall to wall.

He would have liked to describe that office because, according to rumor, Loysel had taken advantage of Eloin's absence to suggest to Maximilian that he close the passageway that joined the Emperor's private quarters to Eloin's office. Maximilian had deemed it a good idea and, at the same time, also closed off the passageway that joined his quarters with Loysel's office. Starting then, he decided that he was only going to receive information in writing, and that he would give all of his instructions in writing as well, to prevent misunderstandings. The result was that the number of documents floating around multiplied prodigiously overnight. So the description of Maximilian's office—the floor and the hallways covered in letters, notes, edicts, messages, memoranda, flyers, party and banquet invitations, orders from Saccone and Speed, changes to the Court Etiquette, budgets, legal projects—was the main evidence Eloin wished he could give to Carlota's father as an example of Maximilian's absurdities, and of the chaos that was prevailing in the Empire.

But, on the one hand, he didn't dare criticize the monarch's son-in-law. On the other, as usual, Leopold was always more interested in other matters. Why had Don Francisco de Paula y Arrangóiz, Mexico's official representative to Brussels, The Hague, and London, resigned his post, for example?

"He didn't agree with the Emperor Maximilian's attitude toward the Church, Your Majesty. Your Majesty will remember that in an open letter, Don Francisco had written to the Emperor: 'Your Majesty, everything with His Holiness's consent. Nothing without it . . .' and His Majesty, Emperor Maximilian, deemed his attitude antipatriotic."

A Lutheran all his life, although not a religious fanatic, Leopold looked displeased. He also wanted to find out why Monsieur Corta, the Finance Minister whom Louis Napoleon had assigned Maximilian, had left Mexico against Maximilian's own wishes. From Paris, in parliamentary sessions, Corta had given himself the task of talking up the fabulous wealth of Mexico, a wealth that no one knew exactly where to find, since what money they had wasn't going far enough—the Emperor's food expenditures alone were over three thousand eight hundred pesos a month—or even how to administer, since Corta was soon followed by another minister, Bonnefond, and the latter, in turn, was quickly followed by Monsieur Langlais . . . and then, of course, Boudin.

"Why doesn't anyone take action?" asked Leopold.

The man that Eloin was looking at was not the monarch he was. The English novelist Charlotte Brontë described him as "a silent sufferer—a nervous, melancholy man . . ." And that, indeed, is how Leopold looked at this time. He had been deeply affected by the death of his nephew, Prince Albert, and he was pale and sickly. Eloin decided to speak about this plainly in a letter to Empress Carlota.

•

Once again Pius IX walked with Monsignor Meglia. As before, they walked on the same side of the Sistine Chapel. This time, however, they walked toward the altar.

They went under the *Punishment of Korah*, by Botticelli.

"Why does Emperor Maximilian send General Miramón to study artillery in Berlin, and General Márquez to Constantinople and the Middle East to study the Holy Sepulcher in Jerusalem? Why does he send away the very people who can be most useful to him?"

Monsignor Meglia had no answer to the Pontiff's questions.

They walked under the *Scenes of the Life of Moses,* by Cosmo Rosselli.

"Why does he want to take more than one hundred thousand Africans and Asians to Mexico? Does he want to fill up the country with Buddhists and Confucians? With voodoo worshippers?"

They went by the *Crossing of the Red Sea,* likewise by Rosselli.

"I imagine, Your Holiness, that they will convert them . . ."

"Yes? And what about all those American Confederates, those Protestants that Mexico wants to use for colonizing? Are they going to convert them also? By the way, who is this Father Fischer, the German pastor who's converted to Catholicism and whom Maximilian has named honorary court chaplain? Is it true that this priest promised the Emperor that, if sent to the Vatican, he would return with a treaty in his pocket?"

They walked under *Moses and the Daughters of Jethro,* by Botticelli.

"He is a false convert, a hypocrite Your Holiness, an immoral man who fornicates and has illegitimate children in Durango. He is a schemer, a former California prospecter. What more can I say, Your Holiness."

"Nothing. Tell that man Fischer that I do not wish to see him . . . But if he is Maximilian's official representative, what else can I do . . . ?"

And they went by *Moses's Journey into Egypt* by Pinturicchio and Perugino.

•

Under the shadow of the equestrian statue of Emperor Franz Stefan of Lorraine, in the gardens of the Imperial Palace, the Hofburg in Vienna, Archduke Karl Ludwig read a letter from his brother, Maximilian . . . In his letters to Karl Ludwig, to Doctor Jilek, Count Hadik, and the Baroness Binzer, the Emperor of Mexico did not say the same things that he said to Napoleon—that there were no capable men in Mexico—nor did he tell them the many unpleasant things that had happened to him and his empress. It's true that Carlota quickly overcame her shock when one of her future Mexican ladies-in-waiting took her in her arms. Carlota rejected her indignantly because she was unaware that such a gesture—an embrace—was a custom in that country. But she was more offended when an aristocratic lady of the city of Puebla, where the Empress was celebrating one of her birthdays, replied, after she was asked to become one of the court ladies, that she would rather be queen in her own home than a palace servant. In addition, it bothered the Empress to see women smoking, and especially that some of the guests at the second-class banquets—and even at the first class!—stole the silver service that Louis Napoleon himself had admired when it was displayed at Christofle in Paris before it was sent to Mexico. It bothered her that some guests scratched their heads with their forks, and that, after parties, there were always doorknobs and curtain tassels missing. At the balls, the chandeliers were so poorly made that the guests ended up covered in wax. Maximilian also neglected to mention in his letters the many ailments from which he suffered: tonsillitis contracted during his tour through Mexico; a subsequent laryngitis; hepatalgia, an illness of the liver, or so he had been told, for which the recommended cure was the *ajolote,* a very strange amphibian, a Mexican salamander, that an amazed Humboldt had taken to Europe and that fascinated Carlota when she saw it for the first time at the Bois de Boulogne greenhouse. But the little creature was repulsive. How did one take it? Fried? Dried and ground up? An *ajolote* infusion? Besides the fact that, for liver ailments and those terrible diarrhea attacks that he suffered, the best medicine, perhaps the only one, was to improve the condition of things in the Empire. Probably his premature baldness wasn't the result of a nervous condition but the fate of so many Habsburgs. In any case, he would try out the recommended quinine ointment mixed with rum. Thanks to that good man, Commodore Maury, quinine had arrived in Mexico in those three packets of *cinchona* seeds that the Clements Markham Company of the West Indies had sent. Maximilian wondered how long it would take for the plants to grow.

No, Maximilian said nothing about any of this to his brother Karl Ludwig. What he did describe was his marvelous tour around his new nation: León, Dolores, Morelia, Silao, Toluca . . . Dressed as a Mexican landowner, he had reenacted the *grito* ceremony in the town of Dolores, where Hidalgo had proclaimed Mexico a free nation. The industrious city of León was full of beautiful women; he hadn't seen so many beauties since he was in Andalusia. Querétaro was splendid. In Morelia too he had been greeted with much excitement. In one of the many towns that he'd visited (he couldn't remember which), the people had unhitched the horses from the Emperor's coach and towed it themselves. Carlota had met him in Toluca and both had gone up to the frozen lake in the Nevado crater. At any rate, everything was going as well as it possibly could. Carlota ruled in his place, prudently and wisely. (He also forgot to tell Karl Ludwig that he rode his magnificent English carriage during part of his journey, or on proud Mexican steeds . . .)

Archduke Karl Ludwig felt the August heat on his face and he moved a few inches to stand, once again, under the shade of the equestrian statue of Emperor Franz Stefan of Lorraine, in the gardens of the Hofburg, the Imperial Palace in Vienna.

•

On the way to Cuernavaca, Emperor Maximilian also asked himself many questions. Hadn't his father-in-law Leopold advised him to surround himself with natives in order to spare the Mexicans' feelings? Didn't he have a Mexican at his side—that intelligent, honest young man of twenty-two, his secretary José Luis Blasio? Hadn't he been able to persuade a Mexican Liberal, Don Fernando Ramírez, to accept a post in his cabinet? And wasn't the court almoner, the Bishop of Tamaulipas, not only Mexican, but also a full-blooded Indian? Hadn't Max hosted two senior and renowned Republican generals, Uraga and Vidaurri, at his table? Besides several friends of Benito Juárez himself, who had stated that, if not imperialists, they were at least "Maximilianists"? Hadn't he and Carlota demonstrated their love and compassion toward the Indians, to the point that, somewhat seriously, somewhat in jest, his people were now talking about their sovereigns' "Indian mania"? Hadn't Carlota named a descendant of Emperor Moctezuma a court lady? Hadn't he done the same when, in the course of one of his tours, he met an Indian woman who assured him that she was a descendant of the poet Nezahualcóyotl? As to the foreigners who surrounded him—among them Father Fischer and Commodore Maury, that world-renowned oceanographer who would bring exiled American Confederates to colonize unused Mexican wastelands—weren't they all honest and intelligent men? What could one say against the Count of Rességuier, who was plotting with him to annex Central America—perhaps including Belize—to the Mexican Empire? Or his head stableman, the Count of Bombelles? Or the bursar, Jakob von Kuhacsevich? Or his faithful valet, Antonio Grill?

On the other hand, while Eugénie was telling Carlota that one had to govern Mexico like the other Latin nations, with an iron fist in a velvet glove, Louis Napoleon was advising Maximilian to try to preserve his absolute power as long as possible. How, then, could he create a liberal, constitutional monarchy, if he allowed himself to be turned into a dictator? Leopold himself had stated: "Only dictatorship can dictate that there will be order and light." But what light? What order? Could that madman Santa Anna have been right when he called for the destruction of the Empire from his Caribbean refuge on the Danish island of Saint Thomas, and when he said that the only form of government that now existed in Mexico was an amusing kind of anarchy?

It was better to act without the French and to assemble a Mexican army. Write it down, Blasio, write it down so I won't forget. I must summon the Austrian ambassador, Count Thun, so that he can help us plan this out. And Blasio spit on the indelible pencil and wrote down: "We must take advantage on the growing discredit to Juárez's reputation." To his endless flight, Juárez had added the dishonor of an agreement between Matías Romero, his envoy to Washington, and a certain General Schofield. Romero said that, to stop Mexico from being flooded by Southern carpetbaggers, it was best to form an army at whose head they could place General Ulysses S. Grant, the hero of the War of Secession. This "auxiliary army" would then answer to Juárez. Its officers and soldiers would be rewarded with land, cash, and the opportunity to adopt Mexican citizenship. Apparently Romero had written the agreement without Juárez's knowledge. Whether Maximilian knew this or not was immaterial. An invasion of Mexico was in the works, as the historian Justo Sierra would write years later, which would be even more devastating than the French one. To lead it, Romero couldn't think of anyone more appropriate than a soldier who had himself taken part in the 1847 American invasion.

Toward the end of '65, a false rumor that Maximilian very much wanted to believe brought him—on a silver platter, yet—the motive he'd been needing to take draconian measures in order to bring peace to Mexico once and for all. Benito Juárez, it was rumored, had crossed the border to the United States, having abandoned Mexican territory. Maximilian thus published the "Decree of October 3rd," to which Bazaine added an unofficial clause so there would be no mercy for any prisoners taken. It is, said the Marshal, a war to the death. And it was. "The Black Decree"—as this decree was known—stated that anyone who rebelled against the Empire could be tried summarily, and summarily executed. Among the first victims were two Republican generals of spotless reputations, Carlos Salazar and José María Arteaga. Their execution, conducted in Uruapan, Michoacán, without Maximilian's knowledge, raised a tide of indignation. It was useless to argue that the guilty party was the Imperialist General Méndez, who—an enemy of both these generals and looking for revenge—had decided to carry out the execution without his superiors' knowledge. It was likewise useless to try to prove the impossible: that, had the Emperor known beforehand, he would have pardoned the victims.

"I would have done it, Blasio," Emperor Maximilian said to his private secretary on the way to Cuernavaca. "How can they think that I would've dared sanction the execution of two honest Republican generals, patriots in their own right? I would have pardoned them. I would have asked them, perhaps, to help me put together an army. I honestly don't know what the Marshal is up to. We've been here more than a year and still can't count on the Mexican army. I've proposed to Bazaine to name Brincourt or d'Hérillier in charge of organizing it, and he refuses. Then I call Count Thun and order him to form a brigade that will serve as a model for the other Mexican brigades, and Bazaine takes it as a personal offense. But tell me, Blasio, what can I do? The Marshal obeys Louis Napoleon and not me. He has the audacity to tell me Napoleon's opinions on my policies—oh, indirectly, of course. For example, he said that I should use fewer state funds to build palaces—what palaces?—and spend more on order and public safety. You know, the Empress wrote Madame de Grüne and assured her that she is perfectly capable of leading an army and that she has battle-experience in her blood. If people wouldn't disapprove so strongly, I would charge my beloved Carla with the organization of Mexican troops. But, regardless, for that we would need the cooperation of the Mexicans. What do they do, however? Nothing. *Rien. Rien du tout.* The secret reports from Commodore Maury are quite explicit on that point. And of course, this is why I've lost weight, why my moods are so erratic. Add to this all my other ailments, Blasio—like this dysentery, which comes back again and again . . . But here the officers have no honor. All the judges are corrupt and the clergy has neither morals nor Christian love in them. And as the Empress said, Blasio, during the first six months, everyone was perfectly enchanted with my government. Later, she wrote Empress Eugénie, 'Touch anything, change anything, try to start your work, and suddenly everyone damns you . . .' For my part, I assured my good father-in-law, King Leopold, that upright people must indeed learn to obey before they learn to talk. Here, however, all anyone does is talk and give me their opinions. There's a Swedish madman who proposes that we abduct Juárez. Others suggest that I bribe Romero. But no one actually helps me . . . To think how much I've done for these people—I've ridden through the jungles for eight hours, my horse sunk to its flanks in the turbulent and muddy river waters, I've climbed mountains, covered entire ranges just to meet and get to know my people . . . I've visited hospitals at dawn, as well as prisons and bakeries . . . And the Empress has done the same . . . But then they criticize me for commissioning Rebull to paint my portrait, to ask the architect Rodríguez to design a monument to the Independence in the Plaza de Armas . . . A nation, Blasio, is also its spirit . . . Yes, my beloved Carla is right. In a nation where everything can happen, nothing happens. Tell me, Blasio, have you read the works of that illustrious Mexican conservative, Lucas Alamán? Alamán said that as a nation Mexico was a freak, a monster . . . Sometimes I think that he was right . . . But please, don't take offense, Blasio, I beg of you, because if this little truth hurts you, it hurts me as well. Perhaps me even more than you, because this is the country that I have chosen, my adoptive country. Every drop of blood that runs through my veins is Mexican blood . . . Write that down, Blasio, write it down . . ."

And Blasio sucked on his ink pencil and wrote. By this time, as usual, his lips and teeth—without overstating it—were the color of the darkest of all bougainvilleas.

XI

BOUCHOUT CASTLE

1927

So that I wouldn't find out that Theodore Roosevelt, the inventor of "big stick" politics, was given the Nobel Peace Prize? So that I wouldn't go to Ypres to see the thousands of Belgian soldiers, poisoned by the Germans' mustard gas, crawling blindly through the streets, choking to death, their skin burning with sores? So that I wouldn't find out that the heir to the throne of Brazil died in exile? Tell me, Maximilian, is that why they want me to spend my days counting the grains of sand in an hourglass, the little turquoise drops of poison oozing from the hydra in the moat, every flake of snow, and the days I have left before I die? So that I will never find out that Alfonso XII died without seeing his son? So that I'll never know that the Count of Paris and the Count of Chambord died before they could reign in France, as my grandfather Louis Philippe did? Is that why they want me to count the falling autumn leaves and string them on a silk thread, or to spend my life counting piano keys? So that I won't get to know that during the Second Commune the Paris rabble who took off their hats every afternoon as the little imperial prince rode through the Tuileries Gardens in his Daumont carriage, escorted by Algerian sepoys whose wing-caped uniforms bore the French tricolor, that this same rabble forgot all about him after his death in Zululand? Don't they know that the messenger arrived a few days ago and he was Houdini the magician, and he told me that the helicopter was invented, and then he turned into a nautical compass, and he turned me into an aviatrix, and he turned the castle into a silver-bladed helicopter, and in that helicopter I took off for the North Pole with my nephew Louis Philippe of Orléans, and with my uncle, Prince Joinville, to South America? Don't they know that when I was a child, my uncle Joinville, who died when he was very old, deaf as my brother Philippe, showed me the Paris mob setting fire to a scale model of the *Créole* in the Tuileries Palace and then sailing it in a palace fountain while he told me that it had been on that very ship that he had had his own baptism by fire when my grandfather ordered him to fight against the Mexicans in Veracruz? Why are they doing all this to the person who saw the royal frigate cross the ocean, its sails swollen by the breeze I made with my fan? The one who saw French sailors bid farewell with their caps, and saw my uncle disembark on the Anton Lizardo beaches in a dinghy propelled by fur-covered oars—and it was I, I and no one else, Maximilian, who saw the *Créole*'s miniature cannons fire and saw how one of its shots blew off one of General Santa Anna's legs. Are they going to ask me to spend my life washing lentils, counting every lentil? Scaling fish, and counting every scale? Are they going to force me to spend the whole day embroidering hydrangea bouquets on pillowcases, and wallflowers on napkins? Or is it that they want me to blow bubbles all day long and with your butterfly net chase the bubbles through the corridors and the gardens of Bouchout? Me, the one whom no one told that Gaetano Bresci assassinated Humberto I of Savoy in the streets of Monza, because I knew about it before his birth, and the one whom no one told (you can imagine the scandal) that Prince Pierre Bonaparte fatally shot Victor Noir, because I'd known that for centuries, many years before the same Pierre Bonaparte murdered a Papal envoy and then went to fight alongside Simón Bolívar. Tell me, do they intend to put me inside a soap bubble, to have me locked up in a bell jar dressed as a virgin, when the fact, Maximilian, is that I learned from childhood, looking through my window on rainy days, I learned, let me tell you, to see the whole world in a drop of water? I, the one whom no one ever had to tell that her mother would die when she was barely ten, because I visualized her death even before she became ill. I heard her dying words, I felt her dying breath on my face, and I saw myself at the gates of death; I visualized my own death; I attended my own funeral: my arms were crossed and a rosary was put between my fingers; I wore a white lace bonnet and with its ribbons they tied my jaw shut. I don't remember who closed my eyes but I do remember that there was a sky-blue baldachin and that someone put flowers at my feet. Snowflakes were whitening the horses' black plumes on the funeral carriage, because it was snowing, Maximilian, just like on the day your dead body arrived in Vienna, and snow whitened the caps of the six Belgian legionnaires who were all as old as I, having outlived not only those poor boys who succumbed on the plains and mountains of Michoacán, murdered by General Arteaga's and Nicolás Guerrero's men, but had also survived the century, and just as they once accompanied us to Mexico, they were also with me on the day of my burial, bearing my coffin on their shoulders to Laeken Chapel where my mother lay, so that I might fulfill the promise that I had made to myself the day that I knew that with grandpa dethroned and dead, my mother, abandoned by my father Leopold, would not live much longer. I knew that if she died, I would die soon after, to be at her side forever. I did not see my son, General Weygand, at my funeral: I imagined that he was probably still fighting in Poland against the Bolsheviks. Your son Sedano y Leguizano was also absent—but then I remembered that Maxime Weygand hadn't been born yet when I was ten, and that Sedano y Leguizano was executed by a firing squad at Vincennes for spying for the Germans. I saw all that, Maximilian, inside a teardrop. In a single teardrop because I was a princess who had learned to be sad without showing it. To appear happy without being so. In just one tear that I wiped away with the back of my hand.

Since then I have not wept again and I shall not do it for anyone, not even you. So you'd better take care of yourself, Maximilian. Pay attention if I tell you not to eat the burro meat that Tüdös cooks for you at the De la Cruz Convent, nor to taste the marzipan sweets or the angel hair that nuns make in Querétaro. If I advise you, Maximilian, not to drink goat milk when you go to Chalco . . . and if I ask you, Maximilian, to watch out for the chicken and the bread that are brought to you for your breakfast on the morning of your execution . . . if I warn you, Maximilian, to beware of Bazaine, of Miramón, of Sophie, even of me, and of your own shadow, it's because I know perfectly well what awaits you. Listen and don't forget this: One night many years ago, after I had escaped Paris and the air that Napoleon III polluted with his perversity from Cape North to Cape Matapan, on the way to my Miramare Castle and then on the way to Rome where I would kiss Pius IX's sandals to beg for his help, my train stopped for a moment at the edge of Lake Bourget and an old lady gave me a ribbon for my hair and a young altar boy gave me a postcard of Haute Combe Abbey, the burial ground of the House of Savoy. As I came out of the Mount Cenis tunnel, a beggar threw a rose at me. In Milan, General Della Rocca came to see me in the name of the King of Italy and brought me a letter. In Villa d'Este, I went to Mass in the crypt of San Carlo and a priest honored me with a blessed candle. Later, in Desenzano, General Hany boarded the Imperial train to greet me in the name of Garibaldi who was suffering from the wounds he'd received in Aspromonte, as the General said, and he presented me with a red flag. In Padua, Victor Emmanuel himself stopped by and gave me a portrait of my great-grandmother, Carolina of Naples. I know that the old woman at the lake was Pepita Bazaine in disguise. The altar boy was José Luis Blasio and Della Rocca was really Hidalgo y Esnaurrízar. The Count of the Valley of Orizaba was General Hany and you, Maximilian, pretended to be the King of Italy. I knew that because no one has ever been able to fool me. But listen to me, listen carefully and look. Not even in Mexico when a Mayan maiden gave me cactus juice diluted in the limpid water of a sacred well to drink from a sea shell did I succumb, since I knew it had stramonium in it to drive me crazy. Nor when Concepción Sedano gave me poisoned cactus milk mixed with custard apple to kill me so that she could stay with you, so you would be only hers. Nor when even you tried to poison me with chocolate and antimony so I would have to stay in Mexico, so that Mexico would belong only to you. Listen carefully. When I was a child I learned to beware of everything and everyone. I never knew if my uncle Joinville was really he or an assassin in disguise. So that when he gave me a drawing from the album he made when he traveled to the island of St. Helena to bring Napoleon the Great's remains back to France, I washed it, just like when I arrived at Miramare I washed the rose the beggar gave me, every one of its petals, every one of its thorns, and would have washed the whole rose garden—and I also washed the ivy that had covered the whole bower in the garden, and I would have washed the entire valley, and with it your grandfather's first tomb; I would have washed each plank and rope and sail of *La Belle Poule* in which my uncle retrieved what was left of the first Emperor of the French; I would have washed the wings of the seagulls that perched on the ship's yards and defecated on the catafalque; I would have washed the catafalque; I would have washed the entire Invalides as I washed the ribbon that the old crone gave me and the postcard of the House of Savoy crypt and the blessed candle from Villa d'Este and Victor Emmanuel's letter and Garibaldi's flag and the picture of my grandmother, as I washed the telegram that you sent me from Mexico after the fall of Tampico and the assassination of the imperial governor, and as I washed the issues of *La Estafeta* that Almonte sent by post, and the wilted roses that he gave me at Saint-Nazaire, and when I arrived in Rome to see the Pope, I would have washed his sandals and Saint Peter's ring before kissing them, I would have washed the entire Vatican and its gardens, the Appian Way and the Trevi Fountain, its tiles, and the heads, eyes, manes, and necks of its marble horses, the beard of Neptune, before my lips touched its waters. Do you understand me, Maximilian? Do you understand that I'm telling you not to drink blackberry wine when you go to Tenancingo and when you go to Tabasco don't eat monkey meat? Beware, Maximilian, and if you get indigestion, don't drink cinnamon tea—and if you marry, don't drink orange blossom tea. When you go to Sinaloa, don't eat iguana breast. If they toast your good luck, don't drink clover wine. If someone takes you to Tampico, don't drink octopus ink. If you get lost in the mountains of Maltrata, don't drink condor blood. Beware, Maximilian and help me wash everything I have to wash. At Chapultepec Castle, we have to wash the benches and the stained-glass window of Diana, the inlaid-wood cabinets, the malachite pedestals, the blue drawing-rooms that Porfirio Díaz turned into guest rooms, Benito Juárez's presidential bed, the balcony where the Child Heroes died. At Miramare we have to wash the chapel, the altar, the windows, the pews, and the confessionals, and the prie-dieus of Lebanese redwood, and also the paintings of Cesare dell'Acqua. At the Hofburg we have to wash the rococo imperial carriage built for my great-grandfather Francis of Lorraine. We have to wash the hooves of his eight Kladrup horses, as well as the eleven thousand silver-headed nails of the mule-drawn litter on which the Austrian archdukes' hats traveled from Klosterneuburg to Vienna each time there was a new ruler. At Querétaro, we have to wash the tiled dome of the Church of Santa Rosa of Viterbo, and the three squat columns of the chapel at Las Campanas Hill erected in your memory and to Miramón's and Mejía's by the architect Maximilian Van Mitzell; and the cross that was carved out of the *Novara*'s wood. And above all, listen to me, we have to wash the keys to Mexico City, presented to us by its officials at the La Concepción stagecoach stop. Beware, Maximilian. Don't lick the gold or the enamel on the keys. Don't lick the diamonds on their handle; don't kiss its imperial eagles.

And do you know why? Because everything is poisoned. Because they want to poison you and me as they've done to so many others. Don't let them tell you that your grandfather, Napoleon the Great, died of homesickness in St. Helena. He was poisoned, Maximilian, on the orders of Louis XVIII, and I found out about it when I washed his bones and discovered arsenic on the one lock of hair he still had left on his skull. Don't let them tell you, Maximilian, that your father, the Duke of Reichstadt, died of tuberculosis. Metternich killed him with a poisoned melon. I knew it because the Eaglet's breath smelled of bitter almonds. Nor did Porfirio Díaz die of sadness. Venustiano

Carranza poisoned him. It was the same with all of them. Boris Godunov was poisoned, as were Andrew Hofer and William Tell. The same with Princess Sophia of Saxony, Ferdinand VII's third wife. And Philip II had William of Orange poisoned, as Princess Isabella did with my niece María de las Mercedes, and Ferdinand of Aragon with Philip the Handsome. Heed this, Maximilian, and never forget it: Prince Luitpold poisoned your cousin Ludwig of Bavaria with water from Lake Starnberg. Ravaillac murdered Henry of Navarre with a poisoned dagger. General Guajardo did likewise to Emiliano Zapata with a hundred poisoned bullets.

They say that I'm crazy because I began to clean all the objects in my bedchamber. But it's because I knew that they were poisoned, that with a mere touch of a doorknob, a painting canvas, a mirror frame, or a drawer pull, poison would enter my body. For a long time I also washed my clothes with my own hands: my crinolines, my sky-blue and navy-blue petticoats, my handkerchiefs, my capes, my Amiens lace bloomers, my tunics, my nightcaps, my *china poblana* costume, my gloves, my slippers, my silk shawls. I also washed all the whites: sheets, pillowcases, and napkins. I washed the walls and the chairs, the hallways, the granite balustrades. I washed the ceiling of the Rosa de los Vientos Salon, I washed the swans in the pond, the purple wisteria that covers the pergola, and I washed the cauliflowers. I told myself that no one should think that I was going to let myself be killed like a rat, so I washed the goblets, the dishes, the reliquaries, and the lamps. I rejected a box of chocolates sent from Perugia by my own brother, the Count of Flanders, who once took me from Rome to Miramare. From my sister-in-law, Marie Henriette, I refused a Kashmir shawl. I threw the boxes of milk candy in the trash that Blasio brought me from Mexico. I poured the ginger wine down the drain that Lord Kitchener sent me for my birthday. I made a bonfire in the Bouchout courtyard with the camisoles I bought in Alençon and the gloves that Sisi brought me. I also burned a book on the history of Mexico that a foreigner passing through Brussels had given me, because I knew that all of its pages were poisoned. I crumbled the biscuits sent by your mother Sophie into the castle's corners and passageways to poison the rats. Until I realized one day, Maximilian, that I couldn't escape. That the water I used to wash the stairways was also poisoned; that the soap I used to wash the walls, the columns, the trunks of the cypress trees, and the banister was poisoned too. I stopped playing the piano for many years because I knew that the keys were poisoned. I stopped playing the harp because I found out that they'd rubbed the strings with mercury sublimate. I stopped painting, Maximilian, because I knew that they wanted to poison me with verdigris and cobalt blue fumes. I never again dusted my cheeks with rice powder or my wigs with crushed fava beans. Moreover, I never wore a single one of my wigs again because I knew they were poisoned. Until I realized, as I told you, that the sponges I used to scrub the towers at Bouchout and our imperial carriage wheels and the cloth that I used for cleaning the armoires and the chests and the nests that swallows build every spring under the Miramare balconies, they were all contaminated with the same poison. But when I speak of poison, Maximilian, I don't mean of the poison of the Hydra that made the waters of the Thermopylae boil, nor of the hemlock that froze the heart of Socrates. King Mithridates took some drops of a potion daily, containing seventy-two different poisonous substances, in order to make his body immune to them. No, I refer to a different poison. Not the one in black widow spiders. Not the one in Amanita mushrooms. Not the one in the fangs of the rattlesnakes or the *vinagrillos* that the guerrillas in Veracruz used to hide in the packs of Colonel Dupin's men. It's not in the shade of the Java tree that the Dutch invaders lie in to take a nap with death. No, Maximilian. I know perfectly well that if the Widow Miramón brings me peach preserves, I must give them to the dogs to taste. You know perfectly well that if you go to Puebla and they give you a tea made from tochomitl flowers for diarrhea, you must make Colonel López taste it first. I know perfectly well that if Señora del Barrio brings me silver earrings from Taxco, I must put them on Mathilde Doblinger first; and if Eugénie gives me another fan from Valencia, I first must fan my cat with it—just as you know, or should know, that before washing your hair in Cuautla with palobobo flower tea to prevent baldness, you must invite the Duke de Morny to do it first, so that you will not be the one whose hair is poisoned, and that before smearing your hemorrhoids with the milky juice of yellow oleanders that they give you in Temixco, you must make Marshal Bazaine try it first, so that you will not be the one poisoned through your rectum, and that instead of rubbing your skin with ointment made from zephyr flower in Guanajuato to remove liver spots, you must give it to General Márquez first so that you will not be the one poisoned through your pores. But still, it's not that kind of poison I'm speaking of, and not even, Maximilian, of the scent of the poppies that poisoned you with love in Cuernavaca. Nor do I speak of Nero's poison, that Emperor Claudius threw into the Tiber, carpeting its waters with dead fish, nor of the poison into which Xenophon dipped his quill to tickle the same Claudius's palate in order to kill him, nor the poison that Agrippina poured into the cup of her son Britannicus. Listen to me: the Queen of Ganor killed her husband with a poisoned nightshirt on their wedding night, and the Chevalier of Lorraine killed Henriette, the daughter of Charles I of England, with a poison he mixed with chicory water. But I am not speaking of the arsenic used to poison Pope Alexander Borgia, nor of the poisons with which Madame de Montespan, paramour of Louis XIV, wanted to kill her rivals. No, I am not speaking of cyanide, nor of belladonna, nor of the curare used by Brazilian Indians to kill Portuguese slave traders, nor of aconite, with which the Ghurkas poisoned the wells in Nepal to kill the English soldiers, nor of the hellebore that Solon used to poison the wells from which the Spartans drank. I am speaking of something else. Of what I discovered one day—which was this: that everything, Max, the sky, the air, the wind, the light of the sun, the mountains, the rain and the sea water were all saturated with that venom that finished you off, that killed your dreams and my sanity, that ended your life and our devotion and our illusions and all the beauty and grandeur we wanted for Mexico. The worst poison of all—the lies.

•

I confess to you, Maximilian, that I lied too. Did I tell you that before being with you my body had never known desire or pleasure? Maximilian, listen to me carefully, even though you may be dead: that was also a big lie. You don't know, Max, you don't know, you never knew nor could imagine how much I would have loved you, how you would have loved me if I could only have dared tell you who I was, who I am, of who I'll always be. Listen to me, Maximilian, listen carefully, even though it's too late: My body was born for love. I'm going to tell you a story. When I was eleven or twelve, I was lying on a divan one afternoon. I fell asleep with a basket of fruit on my lap, my lips still moist with the sweet juice of a peach. Madame Genlis had left me alone for a few moments. It was almost the end of summer and the windows were open. A warm breeze came in to play with my hair, and my hair brushed and caressed my brow. I always loved to feel the caress of my own hair. On my face, on my neck. I woke up almost immediately, with a strange sensation on my lips—but didn't open my eyes. I realized that a fly had landed on my lips and was sucking the peach juice mixed with my spit. I let it alone. I let it walk all over my lips with its delicate legs and its mouth, parting my lips very slightly so as to give it more juice and more spit, to feed it, to feed my own pleasure. I had discovered that my skin was alive in a new and different way: that foul caress didn't resemble anything I had felt before. Or perhaps it did, yes. It resembled what I felt when I brushed the fringe of the drapes on my bare forearm so that the thread barely touched my skin, causing a very vague, tickling sensation, and chills that went up to my shoulder and spread all over my back. My skin and I were born for that, to be caressed by flies' legs, by curtain fringes, by flower petals. I live in a forest, nude, and when cherry blossoms fall, their pink petals bathe my body and embalm my flesh with their kisses. I remember that when we rode to Saint Gudula Church in an open carriage, I loved to feel the wind on my face and sometimes it made me feel like opening my corset, ripping it open so that the wind would touch my breasts. Since then I live in the nude, in a cage, exposed to the wind—and the wind, with its heavy cold breath, climbs up from my ankles and my thighs, follows the outline of my body, surprises it in its deepest hollows. On another night when it was very hot I asked Countess d'Hulst to leave me a plate of honey. When I was alone I opened the windows, I undressed and lay down on my back. I put a bit of honey on my lips and on my nipples. I put a bit more on my navel and on the hair that had sprouted between my thighs. I closed my eyes and summoned the flies.

I remember when Colonel Van der Smissen helped me get down from the imperial carriage. We had visited a textile factory in Cuajimalpa where they'd made a throne for me that seemed to be made of snow, since it was all tufted with cotton balls from its base to its high back. I tickled my nose with one of those puffs the whole way. Later I brushed it behind my ear. When we arrived at Chapultepec, the Colonel dismounted and opened the carriage door. I took his hand and, as I stepped down, I put it against my chest and held it there a few minutes, pressing against my breasts. I always liked Van der Smissen's smile, and the gleam in his eye. But that time more than anything I liked the warmth of his hands. My body, Maximilian, was made to feel the warmth of men's hands. My skin was born to be loved by clouds, by butterflies. I walk nude in a room full of blind butterflies that caress my belly, my thighs, my buttocks, and the rims of my eyelids with their wing tips. You know something? I was always forbidden to slide down banisters. I was told that it was dangerous, that I could fall and be paralyzed. I liked to do it just to feel the hard wood between my legs. That's why I would have liked to learn to ride horses as men do, to have something hard between my legs, something to rub against to soothe

the itching. Did I actually tell you that I'd never desired another man before I met you? I tell you again: it was a lie. I mean that it was a lie and also not a lie because at the time I didn't know the meaning of desire: a soft itch, almost a stinging, an uneasiness, between my legs. I didn't even know that to take my hand and touch that fleshy part there, to discover it, to feel it become hard and to rub it until I saw the face of one of Philippe's friends, I didn't know, as I was saying, that it was satisfying a craving. When I finished I no longer saw my brother's friend's face: it disappeared with the pleasure and the daydream. I never saw it again after I met you. I forgot it, as I forgot his name. From then on, every time I made an effort to remember it, only your face appeared to me. My flesh, Maximilian—you must hear this, even if it's too late—my flesh was made to be loved by water too. I walk naked in the world and rain bathes me with caresses and hail turns into streams of melted wax that slide down my body and lick it and set it on fire. And my flesh was born for seawater, yes for seawater, so that its warm, blue tongues and its bitter foam may drink from my belly and my thighs. Also for your hands, your white, long, fine hands—but they never knew it. I spend my life naked, Maximilian, and bathed in pollen, in a chamber full of dragonflies that sometimes covered all my skin and turned me into a seething mass of diaphanous wings and scented spittle. Do you remember, Maximilian, that when I returned from Yucatán I spoke to you of those living jewels that the Mayas use? They were called *maqueches*, those scarabs with heavy shells inlaid with precious stones. During the day the insects were leashed to blouses so that they could crawl on Indian women's breasts. Someone gave me one of those, capped with an emerald the color of my eyes. I asked General Uraga to keep it for me since it made me queasy. But that night I was so tired, and it was so hot, and I felt I'd been blinded by the dusty, sandy roads, I felt that I was choking with anguish at the Church of the Knights of the Mejorada, I was deafened by the cannonfire from Fort San Benito, I was serenaded at my balcony, and I had to go out. In the plaza people climbed the trees and palms, and the window bars of the Municipal Palace, all to see me; everything was full of noise and lights, an unbearable din; I swooned and dreamed that, over my bare skin, I was covered from head to toe with a dress made of live insects: bees with opal bodies, worms with backs inlaid with strings of amethysts, spiders with tourmalines, bedbugs covered with tough red shells polished like carbuncles. They moved, wriggled around, danced on my skin, caressing it with their velvety legs and their slimy bellies and they stung me and sucked my blood and lymph; they injected their nectar and their luminous poison with stingers fine as eyelashes; they covered me with tiny bubbles, with a thick, milky liquid. I awoke covered in sweat, rivers of sweat that slid down my body, that dripped from my brow down my neck, that poured from my underarms. My thighs were soaked with sweat and also with something else, a hot liquid. I sensed an acid smell. I was thirteen years old again and had just summoned the flies. And the flies, with their turquoise wings, heeded my call.

You can ask my brother Lipchen if he remembers that I also liked to play at being a witch to scare him. I chased him, riding a broom, through the halls and passageways at Laeken, in the bushes and flower beds in the garden. I went after him on my broom, and with me rode my restless yearning, moving the broomstick up and down until I started to moan and poor Philippe looked at me unnerved. I said it was nothing Philippe don't be frightened. It's only my heart. Look. Touch it, see it jump, and I placed his hand on my chest. My breasts had begun to grow by then.

Someone whom I always found repellent was Achille Bazaine. I remember those evenings in the Iturbide Salon when we had to dance the honor quadrille—I danced with the Marshal and you with his wife—with nothing but disgust. I thought the torture would never end. But afterwards, when I had Colonel Van der Smissen's arm around my waist, barely touching it but moving with a gentle insistence that invited—or commanded—my body to press against him to feel his warmth, oh Maximilian, I would forget that I was in Mexico and that I was Empress Carlota. I would forget you; I would be a child again, on the verge of becoming a woman, and I would again chase my brother Philippe and press him against the drapes, and touch his face, his chest, his legs and only after I was sure that it was Philippe I was touching and no one else, despite his objections and his swearing that it was he, and his begging me not to tickle him any more, only then would I take off my blindfold. It was his turn then. He was the blind man and he had to find me in the dark. When he found me, he had to touch my whole body, run his hands all over it, over my shoulders and my legs, over my face, until he was sure that it was I, Charlotte.

I am Carlota, the madwoman of the castle. They think I'm blind because cataracts cloud my eyes. When I walk I stumble on the furniture and I crash against the walls. When I look out the window I don't see the women who come from Louvain, Antwerp, and Courtrai every morning to wash my skirts and my camisoles in the moat at Bouchout. They think I'm blind because I can't see the bridge that the Ostend fishermen made for me to escape when everyone least expects it. Or because I didn't see how the moat became filled with the roses that the pilgrims that went by Bouchout tossed into its waters, those roses that you send me from Mexico, that Garibaldi sends from Caprera, and your cousin Ludwig of Bavaria sends from the Isle of Roses, and that have formed a carpet so thick that, barefoot, I could walk on it, across the water, to get away from here—when they least expect it. They think I'm blind because I prick my fingertips when I try to thread a needle and because I knock the goblets off the dinner table. Because I don't recognize anyone. The other day Blasio came to see me. I found out it was him because he told me so, because he swore that he was the very same José Luis, your former Mexican secretary. And he wanted very much to say hello because he hadn't seen me in quite a few years, although I know he's a liar because whenever I stroll through the gardens of Bouchout he spies on me from behind the trees to see if I'm really crazy. Blasio brought me an album of photos but I didn't know the people in them. "I can understand," Blasio told my doctors later, "that the Empress didn't recognize that bald general with the long whiskers, since she never knew Castelnau. I can also understand that she didn't recognize the white-bearded man without a mustache, because she never saw Father Augustine Fischer. Nor Felix Salm-Salm. But the fact that she didn't recognize Empress Elisabeth—as beautiful as she was on her trip down the Danube, waving good-bye to the musicians who played a waltz for her from a bridge overhead—or that she didn't know that the long-bearded man clutching a flag on a ship sailing—not on the Danube, but on a stormy sea—was her own, august husband, the Emperor Don Maximiliano, means that Empress Carlota has lost her memory or that Empress Carlota is blind." Blasio closed the album as he said this to Jilek, while he was sitting next to me, thinking, perhaps, that I was also deaf. Or a deaf-mute, since I didn't say a word. Or deaf and mute and paralyzed because I didn't even nod nor shake my head when they asked me, does Your Majesty know this gentleman with the little goatee? And do you know, Doña Carlota, this bespectacled general? And does your Imperial Highness recognize this blue-eyed colonel?

Did they, did our friend Colonel López know, as he looked at me with his blue eyes, that I was asking him with my eyes for something he never dared give me, because, apart from being a traitor, he was a coward? Did that ignoramus George of Saxony, whom my cousin Victoria wanted me to marry, realize that I was one of the most beautiful princesses in Europe? Did Léonce Détroyat know, when we were on the way from Veracruz to Saint-Nazaire, that I muttered his name at night, and that I'd summoned him with a whisper to my stateroom, so that he would take me in his arms? Did Captain Blanchot realize that on the way to Toluca to meet you he helped me off my horse and one of my thighs brushed his shoulders? Tell me, did it occur to him that under the velvet skirt and the starched crinolines of the Empress there were women's legs, two warm thighs that could squeeze his hips until he died of love, on his knees? Did José Luis Blasio realize the day he offered me candied strawberries that, under the Dutch linen blouse, under the silk and lace camisole of his Empress, there were two women's breasts, sweeter and warmer than any fruit? Did my palace guards ever realize, when I reviewed the troops at the National Palace, that the Empress reflected in their gleaming silver helmets, that the Sovereign who had designed each and every detail of their uniforms with her own hands, was a woman who could use those very hands to take off their black patent leather boots and undo the gold buttons of their red waistcoats, to kiss their feet and their chests, to lick their nipples and leave tooth marks on their necks? No, Maximilian, because they were the blind ones. You too—since, besides being blind, you were one-armed. And crippled, like your effigy.

Because they let me keep you. Since they think I'm crazy, they let me make a life-size dummy of you and lock it in my armoire. I would have liked to send a messenger to Versailles so that, from the closet where Louis XIV kept his wigs, from all the wigs the king kept there, the ones he wore morning or night, when he attended Mass or hunted, from all the wigs the Sun King took off at night when he slept with Louise de la Vallière or the Marquise de Montespan, he might choose me the finest and silkiest, the blondest of all, so that I could make a beard for you. I would have liked Dr. Licea to bring your death mask to Bouchout, the same one that he refused to turn over to Princess Salm-Salm because he had already been offered fifteen thousand pesos for it, to paint it with pink powder and to make it be your face. But I had to manage on my own. God only knows how I put you together, from old stockings filled with rags for your legs and your arms, and from pillows and cushions for your chest and your belly, and from thread and string and pins and the stays on my corsets to tie you up, to bind you so tightly that you wouldn't fall apart. I improvised a beard for you from gold drapery fringes. Not having your plaster mask, I would have liked Countess de Courcy to go with me to buy dentures from Dejardin and glass eyes from Pilon like those I saw at the Paris Exposition, to put them into that face of yours that I'd made from a white silk stocking stuffed with cotton. But I had to be content with the only thing they left me: my imagination. On the other hand, I had no problem dressing you because they let me use some old boots and your mint-condition Austrian Fleet Admiral's uniform to put on your new body. It's as though the years haven't touched your uniform at all, as though it were only yesterday that you traveled to Messina to try to recreate, in your head how Don Juan of Austria's fleet, sent to demolish Mehemet Siriko's, disappeared on the horizon when they headed toward the Levant. That was the uniform you wore when you visited Virgil's tomb and the love nest of the Nymph of Capri, and when you walked through the streets of Minorca among the hordes of drunken English sailors, and when you cut the agapanthus and *Strelitzia reginae* with tongues like sky-blue lances, and the Indian azaleas, white as Himalayan snow. I put those same flowers on your breast, and my jailers know it. They also know that every night I see you and I caress you and talk to you of many different things—I almost always feel pity for you and try to be nice. I would like to reproach you some days, as when I recall that Napoleon I took all of Marie Louise's furniture to Paris so that she wouldn't miss her room at Schönbrunn. I'd like to ask you then why you didn't take my bedroom from Laeken to Miramare and from Miramare to Mexico, and from Mexico back to Miramare—especially, Maximilian, after I brought your tomb to Europe, for which you've never thought to thank me. But no, I'd rather tell you pleasant things. I'd rather make you believe that time has stood still. That my grandmother Amélie did not die at Claremont, that the Prussian troops did not lay siege to Paris, that the Russians never crossed the Danube and the Americans will not invade Nicaragua to fight General Sandino. My jailers never hear me talk to you of such things, but of the Borda Gardens, the Pompeian villa in Cuernavaca where you went to cure your longing for the sea, and of the time you bought the Hacienda of Cuamala to add to your lands in Chapultepec. Of that, and of the love that I have had for you these sixty years.

What they don't know—because they think that when they undress me and then dress me in my nightgown and put me in bed and turn out the light that

I forget you're in the armoire and think that I won't be able to speak to you until the next morning—what they don't know is that as soon as they leave I get up to see you. I open the armoire and I take you to bed and I remove my nightgown and I make love to you. I make love to the stick that I place between your legs. One night I hemorrhaged—I almost pierced my vagina and ripped out my uterus—but I kept making love to you all night, until I fell asleep from exhaustion, next to you. When I woke I barely had time to put you away before those idiots arrived. When they saw that the sheets and my nightgown were covered in blood, they had a fit, they asked me what had happened and they started screaming, "Quick, call Dr. Jilek, tell Dr. Bohuslavek to come right away, the Empress is bleeding to death!" But I said no, nothing happened, I don't have to see any doctor, just call Don Maximiliano and tell him, "Hallelujah, hallelujah, Imperial Highness, your wife, Doña Carlota, the Empress, has begun to menstruate again. Her patron saints came to see her—Saint Ursula who arrived with the eleven thousand virgins, Saint Hubert of the deer head with a shining cross between his antlers—and the eleven thousand virgins kissed Doña Carlota's brow, and Doña Carlota touched Saint Hubert's antlers and the miracle occurred: Doña Carlota, hallelujah, is menstruating." That's what I told them to tell you, Max. I wish you could have seen the look of incredulity and envy, of hate and fear, of surprise and terror that those imbeciles gave me, may God pickle them alive.

They took away my stick. They took it away. They ripped you apart, Maximilian. God knows what happened to your penis . . . Maybe, like your intestines and your spleen and your pancreas, it was washed away in a sewer in Querétaro, or, like your heart, it was chopped to pieces and scattered all over the world in jars filled with formalin. But in my room I have the hunting knife that you used to split open coconuts in Algiers, the shotgun that you hunted rabbits with in the Hacienda Xonaca, and the telescope you looked at those boys through, from the train, those boys who came out of the sea in the Nocera Valley and rolled around wet on the black sand until their skin itself was black as coal. I also have the sword that you gave General Escobedo in Querétaro. I've used all those things to make myself bleed, but always thinking of you and no one else, I swear to you, Maximilian, not of Van der Smissen or of Colonel Rodríguez, or of my brother's friend, because I've forgotten them all. Sometimes I think that I've forgotten you too; but you, on the other hand, I can call to mind, and not them. Because I can't bring them back to life—only you. You live again every time I name you, every time I speak your name, Maximilian. In my bed, on the billiards table in the castle, on the terraces—everywhere I've called out your name, you've appeared and there, and with you inside of me, I have bled. "What a mess!" they said, "The sheets are stained, the blue felt is stained, the carpets and the stones are stained, how horrible, how shameful, the honor of Empress Carlotta has been stained! How embarrassing! What will Dr. Jilek say, Your Majesty!" screamed my ladies-in-waiting. "What will your Majesty's brother, the Count of Flanders, say? What would Emperor Maximilian say if he were alive? What would he say if he were here?" said my ladies, and they clapped their hands to their heads, they pulled their hair, they boiled water as though I was in labor, and I, you won't believe it, Max, I laughed my head off and I didn't bear a child but a piece of candle that had stuck inside me and that Dr. Jilek pried out with forceps. If you could only have seen how hard he had to work and how red his face was, like it was about to burst. Once I put a bottle inside me and it got stuck and they took me to the bathroom where they had to break it, and, how horrible, how frightening, the floor was covered with blood, but no, what nonsense, it wasn't blood but your favorite burgundy and my ladies stopped me from licking it up. How I would have relished filling my mouth with its color and with all those glass shards, but they didn't let me. They forbid everything and I am dying while I wait for you with open legs. They've taken away the candles, the knives, the bottles of wine, the spools of thread. Yes, one time I put one of those spools inside me. Dr. Jilek was able to reach only the very end of the thread with his forceps and, how ticklish, Max, while the spool turned around inside of me it seemed as though the doctor would never finish getting it out. They took away your telescope and your cigars and your sword. What do those bitches think, that I can't lie nude on the grass and make love to the garden hose? Next time I'll put a rat inside of me. I'll tell them, don't call Dr. Jilek, call a cat. Do they think that I can't go into the Neptune Fountain in Navona Square to make love to the water jets the Tritons puke out? Next time I'll put a carrot in me and say, don't call Dr. Jilek, call a rabbit. Do they think that they can keep me from lying nude in my bed and making love to a tulip stalk? Next time I'll insert a banana. I'll tell them, don't bring Dr. Jilek, bring a chimpanzee. What do those cunts think, that I'm insane?

XII
"WE'LL CALL HIM THE AUSTRIAN"
1865

1. "He's Like Jelly . . ."

"Then, Mr. Secretary, Marshal Bazaine is almost thirty-five years older than his *Pepita* Peña?" "That's right, Mr. President." "Well, he could be her grandfather . . . but tell me . . . wasn't Bazaine already married?" "Yes, Don Benito, but his wife, who stayed in France, committed suicide. It seems she had a lover, an actor in the French Theater, and this man's wife found some compromising love letters, and after warning Bazaine's wife, she sent them to the Marshal. But, I understand, Don Benito, that one of Bazaine's officers destroyed them before they got into Bazaine's hands. They say Pepita Peña is very intelligent and pretty: some men are just lucky, Mr. President." "I don't call that luck, Mr. Secretary. Luck is all I've had my whole life through, until very recently, but I'm lonelier every day." "I understand you were terribly saddened by your son's death and being separated from Doña Margarita, but in his fight against the Empire, the President is hardly alone, he has the whole nation on his side." "I was telling Pedro Santacilia: Santa, oh Santa, I don't know how I can endure the pain. Two children dead in a year . . . sometimes I feel I don't have any energy left to endure so many catastrophes . . . and Margarita's illness worries me . . . with the cold weather in New York." "I understand, Don Benito, I understand." "I asked Santacilia to send pictures of my children. I'm afraid I'll forget their faces. Are you saying, Mr. Secretary, that the whole nation is with me? Unfortunately that's not the case. As you can see, instead of coming to help me, González Ortega accused me of abandoning the country and proclaimed himself president from New Orleans . . . If the Yankees didn't apprehend him aboard the *Saint Mary* and lock him up in Brownsville, we would have one more enemy here . . . Imagine, having the nerve to declare himself president while in a foreign country . . . It's true, I went all the way to the border, to Paso del Norte, but I've never left Mexico since the invaders arrived—you know it, everybody knows it . . . Even the Archduke knew it, and nevertheless he spread the rumor I'd fled to Franklin City as an excuse to issue that damned decree and assassinate Generals Arteaga and Salazar. His pretext was that he was executing a few old enemies, but in reality it was an act of vengeance, pure and simple, because it was Carlota's countrymen who did it—from the Belgian Legion." "They say, Don Benito, that all those Belgians are very young boys, badly trained." "Not everyone is a Belgian in that corps of volunteers. Didn't you say so yourself? Didn't you tell me that because of all their crimes, the French say that the motto of the Belgian Legion is—what was it?—'Theft and rape?'" "Yes, Mr. President, '*le vol et le viol.*'" "And secondly, or perhaps firstly, what must have hurt Carlota the most, is that Captain Chazal, son of the Belgian Minister of War, was killed in Tacámbaro . . . that's what it was. At any rate we've lost two more generals loyal to the Republic who could have helped us fight this war. I mean, these two wars." "Two wars, Don Benito?" "Yes, Mr. Secretary: one is Mexico against France, the other one is the Republic against the Empire . . . And you see, Zaragoza died, and Comonfort is also dead, and his remains were desecrated by the priest of Chamacuero who had them exhumed because he said the poor man had no right to rest in consecrated ground." "That was a scandal, Don Benito; the clergy has lost all sense of proportion. Did you know that the former Belgian Minister, Baron de Graux, was denied spiritual assistance on his deathbed because he'd acquired nationalized Church property?" "Manuel Doblado is also dead, in New York . . . well, he was killed by his doctor, Quiroga, a traitor, and it was the same with Cortina. Uraga and Vidaurri are also on the Empire's side; though it's true that at any given moment I was never sure if Doblado and Vidaurri were my protectors or my jailers." "But, Don Benito, you have Don Sebastián Lerdo de Tejada on your side, and the support of governors Trías and Pesqueira. You have General Escobedo. Oh, and of course, General Porfirio Díaz." "Díaz? Oh, yes, he's a good boy. But he's very far away . . . besides, he lost Oaxaca. What I admire is his talent for escaping from jails." "Getting back to Generals Arteaga and Salazar, Don Benito, I understand their execution was carried out without Maximilian's knowledge, and people say that had he known, the Archduke would've granted them a pardon." "A pardon? What was their crime? Is it a crime to defend your fatherland against invading forces?" "No, no, of course not, Don Benito. But it was in his hands to grant mercy." "And has he granted mercy many times since then? According to what I hear he decided that he didn't want to hear about the sentences of military courts. If this is true, he's given up his right to grant mercy." "That's true, Mr. President. He washed his hands of it. He washes them as often as he can, Don Benito, always running away to Cuernavaca." "To catch butterflies, you were telling me." "That's right, Mr. President, to catch butterflies at the Borda Gardens while Carlota remains head of the government." "Strange fellow, this Archduke." "Absolutely, Mr. President . . . but do you know what? I don't think we can call him 'Archduke' anymore." "And why not—that's what he is, an Archduke, isn't he?" "No, Mr. President, Ferdinand Maximilian lost all his titles. The moment he renounced his rights to the House of Austria, he not only renounced all the dowries, family lands, properties in trust, actual and future lordships and serfdoms—such as Prince of Lorena, Archduke of Austria, Count of Habsburg, Colonel in Maria Theresa's First Regiment of Hussars, etcetera, etcetera—but also his rights to all royal and ducal crowns in Bohemia, Transylvania, Croatia, and I don't know how many more, Don Benito." "When I was studying history in Oaxaca, Mr. Secretary, the number of titles Charles V held astounded me. I tried learning them by heart: King of Castile and León and both Sicilies, of Jerusalem, of Granada, of Navarre, of Toledo . . . what came after Toledo? Sardinia, Gibraltar . . . Count of Barcelona, of Flanders, Duke of Athens and Neopatria . . . it was a never-ending litany. I ask myself if Charles V himself knew all of them . . . But then, Mr. Secretary, if we can't call him Archduke, what are we going to call him? Only 'the Austrian,' just like that?" "That seems fine to me, Don Benito, we'll call him 'the Austrian,' even though . . ." "Even though what?" "Even though he doesn't consider himself an Austrian anymore. He considers himself to be a Mexican." "Oh, yes, I've heard that story. The Austrian not only adopted Mexican citizenship, but he also feels Mexican, is convinced he's a Mexican." "His hypocrisy has no limits, Don Benito." "Yes and no, Mr. Secretary . . . the Austrian's soul will always belong to the Germanic race, as I've told you in another occasion, but the divine right that according to the Habsburgs allows them the privilege to govern other nations, allows them to place themselves—we spoke of this too, if I remember correctly—above nationalities and change one for the other, just like you'd change your suit." "Like someone who takes off his Austrian Fleet Admiral's uniform to dress as a *charro*." "That's correct, Mr. Secretary. But the worse thing is that there are nations that accept, or resign themselves to such absurdities. History is full of examples. Without going any farther, why is Napoleon III a Frenchman? And his uncle? Not only was Bonaparte a Corsican, but he was born in Corsica only a year after Choiseul bought it . . . if the French had taken a little longer to buy it from Geneva, Bonaparte wouldn't have been a French subject by birth . . . And when he himself, through his First Consul, in England, expressed his desire to see peace between their two countries, the English governor responded that the best guarantee for peace would be the restoration of the legitimate French monarch . . . Do you know what Talleyrand answered then?" "No, Don Benito." "Talleyrand burst out laughing, because the King of England, who had set this condition, was a German who didn't even know English, and who was occupying the Stuart throne . . . and—you see?—they even sow discontent among the nations already under their dominion: while German patriots fight against Czech autonomy, the Croatians and Slovakians are more interested in gaining independence from the Magyars than from the German governors who are their true masters." "That's the way it is, Don Benito." "When they told me that the Archduke, that's to say the Austrian, had put on a *charro* suit to reenact the Cry for Independence at Dolores—by the way, I was told people had stolen the clappers from all the town's bells before he arrived, is it true?" "I don't know, Don Benito, but I don't think they would have dared steal the clapper from Father Hidalgo's bell." "At any rate, as I was telling you, when I heard this, I looked at myself in the mirror. And there I was, the President of Mexico, in a black frockcoat, black hat, white shirt, black bow tie . . . Oh, you don't know how much I miss Margarita, she would always fix the knot in my tie—I always get it crooked . . . I should've brought some of the ones that come pre-tied. They fit me better anyway. Well yes, as I was telling you: I imagined myself dressed as a *charro* and I came to the conclusion I would look ridiculous for the simple reason that I'm not a *charro*, nor a hacienda owner, but a civil functionary. It's even more absurd for an Austrian to do it, a European Prince, isn't that so?" "That's right, Don Benito." "Since I became governor, I abolished the custom of wearing a special hat in a special way during public ceremonies, and I adopted, as you know, the common attire of a citizen, and I lived at home without guards or any kind of escort." "I know it, Don Benito, I know it." "And do you know why? Because I'm convinced that the responsibility of a ruler comes from the law, from his proper conduct, and not from suits or military gear more appropriate for the stage." "But they need those things, Mr. President." "Who does? You mean Maximilian and Carlota?" "Yes, Don Benito, they need the ostentation, the pomp, because that's what they are, rulers on a stage." "That's quite correct, Mr. Secretary." "The golden carriage they brought from Milan, the silver china with the imperial monogram, the orders and decorations . . . all those things are part of the show they need to put on, Mr. President. As you can see, Maximilian sent Louis Napoleon the great collar of the Aztec Eagle, and after the Oaxaca campaign, Carlota asked her father to send Bazaine King Leopold's great cross." "So, besides getting a Marshal's baton and a child bride, he also got a new decoration." "And Buenavista Palace as a wedding gift." "The Palace, yes. Tell me, Mr. Secretary, how can it be that a foreign usurper can decide to give to another foreigner property that belongs to the nation?" "I don't know, Don Benito, the boldness of these people knows no bounds . . . but I think Bazaine's marriage has helped the Republican cause." "How's that?" "Because they say the Marshal is so captivated with that Pepita Peña that he only wants to spend time with her, and so is neglecting his military campaign. Allow me, Don Benito, to repeat the old saying: 'A pair of tits will pull you farther than a hundred carriages.'" "The day, that is, the night the Austrian reenacted the Cry for Independence at Dolores, I was sitting on the grass under the moonlight at one of the banks of the Nazas River. This was a few hours after we ourselves reenacted the Cry for Independence at Noria de Pedriceña. I wanted to be by myself, surrounded by silence. I remembered how, once, when I was a shepherd in Guelatao, I fell asleep on the shore of the Laguna Encantada. You know the story—the patch of land I was sleeping on detached itself from the mainland, and at dawn I found myself floating in the middle of the lagoon. When I got home I got a spanking. Well, don't laugh at me Mr. Secretary, I felt that night as though something similar was happening to me. Since I left Mexico City, I've felt adrift, and as though I'm going to wake up to a very different reality, any moment now—all alone, in a vast void. Yes, this continuous coming and going has allowed me to get to know my country and its greatness, and all its beautiful places—like the Plains of Zacatecas, Mapimí Lagoon, the Concho and Florido Rivers flanked by cotton fields, and, on the way to Paso del Norte, the undulating Desert of Samalayuca. But sometimes I still see myself on my black carriage, on some dusty plain, trailed by the eleven oxen-pulled covered wagons that we'd packed the Public Records in, and which we've now left behind in a cave. Can you imagine, the National Public Records in a cave? But what I wanted to say is that at times I ask myself if I really know anything about all this . . . that is . . . I don't know if I'm making myself clear. Look, that night next to the Nazas, far away on those majestic mountains, bathed by the moonlight, if I may say so, I suddenly heard some birds singing. As a child, Mr. Secretary, I didn't speak Spanish, but I did know the language of the birds—or so I thought. That night, on the shore of the Nazas, while the Austrian, dressed as a *charro*, was reenacting the Cry for Independence, and the people applauded and cheered him, I found out I had forgotten their language . . . and this made me wonder if perhaps I'd also forgotten how to understand what this country, the land, and my compatriots are telling me. Does Mexico, do the people, really want *that*? The big show? Third-class monarchs?" "Don Benito, it's been over a year since Maximilian and Carlota were newsworthy . . . This last September 15th, I understand there were as many shouts of '¡*Viva México!*' as 'Death to Maximilian!' And I don't need to remind you about that journalist's article in a North American daily denouncing the French authorities for making all storekeepers in Mexico City close their shops the day Maximilian and Carlota arrived, and how the municipality threatened everyone who refused to decorate their homes and put lights in their windows." "Yes, yes, but the fact is that every day we fight, I'm lonelier— or perhaps I should say *we* are. It was Melchor, wasn't it? Melchor Ocampo? Who used to say 'I bend but I don't break.' Well, at times I think I'm going to break someday soon. And Melchor is dead too, of course. What good does it do me to have been named a 'Distinguished American' by the Colombian Congress and to have had my portrait put in the National Library in Bogotá if the fifteen thousand men General Mosquera promised to send from Colombia never arrived? Just like the five thousand men promised by the Continental Alliance proposed by Peru. The Alliance and the Treaty of Corpancho disappeared, just like the American dream came tumbling down under Bolívar's feet . . . and Corpancho is also dead." "But the War of Secession has ended, and the United States is on our side. Oh, and if Lincoln hadn't died, Don Benito . . ." "Lincoln didn't deserve such a sad ending as that. But Lincoln offered us his help against the Intervention and didn't keep his promise. As I've told Romero: we cannot depend on the Yankees to help us win. Up until now all their help has consisted of is toasts and speeches . . . sterile well wishes. Did you know that Romero even considers Seward an enemy of Mexico? Maybe he's exaggerating slightly, but as you can see, he's gotten sick and tired of protesting the passage of French troops through Panama to Seward—all they do is ignore us.

It's just as urgent that they enforce the Monroe Doctrine as any of the rest of us—and yes, it's true that President Johnson has started to come around to that opinion, but not because the United States is really with us—only because they're against the French being in Mexico. They don't want them here. They're against Frenchmen on American soil, not against France. Do you think France would've stood for what they did to us—allowing us to purchase arms in America and then not letting them through the Customs House in New York? We'd already ordered, as you may remember, close to thirty-five thousand rifles, eighteen million bullets, five hundred tons of gunpowder, God knows how many pistols and sabers, and after the Secretary of the Navy gave his approval, the War Secretary stopped the transaction dead . . . No, Mr. Secretary . . . they wouldn't have stopped that shipment if it had been ordered by France or another European country, like England. And, Mr. Secretary, you're familiar with the best example of this attitude, the *Rhine*. The *Rhine* sailed from San Francisco to Acapulco loaded with contraband weapons for the French troops, without so much as a protest . . . I'm thankful, of course, for the deferential treatment the American government has extended my wife and children, as well as to Romero—who now, to make things worse, has come up with this absurd deal with Schofield. For God's sake! What ever prompted him to think that causing one problem could solve another? Oh, Romero, Romero: if Seward doesn't interfere and send Schofield to Europe, I don't have to tell you that we might also end up being invaded by the Yankees . . . By the way, remind me to ask Romero to keep sending me newspapers from New York. And yes, as I was telling you, the attention the White House has shown my wife is one thing, but their refusal to deliver the weapons we've already paid for, or their claim that we actually have an American Ambassador—well, those are quite another. Of course, they're right—we do have an ambassador; he just doesn't dare leave his own country. What kind of Ambassador is that? And so, here I am, in Paso del Norte, without a diplomatic corps, without a Congress, without an army, and my presidential chair is made of *capulín* wood with a straw seat . . ." "The President said that the presidency, the executive power of the nation, would be wherever he was . . . that they would travel with him." "Yes, I said that, but at times I still feel ready to break . . . Please, Mr. Secretary, I beg you, not a word of this to any one. I have to overcome these moments of weakness. I don't want anyone to know. I must be strong, because the respectability and efficiency of a government also come from one's personal strength. And, yes, I will be strong, even if I'm left entirely alone in the end." "Don Benito, I would say that the one who's really alone, or anyway who's being abandoned, is the Austrian." "No, no, all the would-be aristocracy supports him . . . he has a thirty-thousand-man army . . ." "But, look, Don Benito, he himself is pushing away everyone who could be most useful to him. As you know, he sent Miramón to Berlin to study artillery, and he sent Leonardo Márquez to the Holy Land on the pretext that he needs to study the Church of the Holy Sepulcher in Jerusalem because the Austrian wants to build a replica in Mexico . . ." "He did the right thing there, Márquez is a dangerous man . . . and Miramón isn't far behind . . . but to send a man who murdered those defenseless doctors and nurses in Tacubaya in cold blood as an ambassador to the Holy Land . . ." "And, don't forget, who hanged several female Liberals by their breasts from the trees, Mr. President . . ." "And I also was told that Márquez took the Order of the Aztec Eagle along with him to present to the Sultan of Turkey. Why on earth is Mexico bestowing an order on the sultan of a country that's of no interest to it whatsoever? Tell me." "There's nothing to tell, Don Benito . . . but, as you know, the fact is that the Austrian also stripped Almonte of his power when he named him Grand Marshal of the Court." "Juan Pamuceno must be furious." "Of course, Don Benito. And that's exactly the way the Austrian has been thanking all the men who helped him the most, distancing them from the country or from positions of power. He also turned down Santa Anna's offer to help him . . . though people say Santa Anna wants to join the Republic now . . ." "Santa Anna? I would never accept his support. I would rather trust the Austrian's word than Santa Anna's . . . Besides, I'm sure he hates me. When I was working as a servant for my in-laws, the Maza family, Santa Anna came to dinner once, and I waited on him. He'll never be able to forget that the barefoot little Indian who served his food went on to become President of Mexico . . . *his* President . . . those were the days, Mr. Secretary. Did you know I almost became a priest? If it weren't for the fact that almost all the Bishops in the Republic had left by that time, and you had to go to Havana or New Orleans to be ordained, I probably would've been. But because of this, my godfather Salanueva allowed me to study law. And also, I almost became a businessman. My godfather sometimes allowed me to go to Montoya Lagoon, where I made a diving board out of barrels, boards, and grass. I charged four centavos a jump. I used to buy candy with my profits. But it didn't work until the second time I tried the scheme, with a friend's help. When I tried it the first time it fell apart and I almost killed myself . . . but then, like I told you, I've always been lucky. And since you mentioned Miramón . . . Terán just wrote to inform me that he would like to offer his services against the Empire. Incredible, no?" "Yes, Don Benito . . . and in reference to that would-be aristocracy, if you'll allow me to continue with this theme, well that's what they are, people who call themselves aristocrats and are happy with all the pomp and circumstance, with the *Court Ceremonial*—a hefty book as thick as your arm, Don Benito— and with the soirees that the Empress, pardon me, Carlota, offers every Monday imitating Eugénie de Montijo. But there is more and more criticism now for the excessive expenses of the Austrian's government, like those ten- or twelve-course banquets with over twenty wines to choose from. They say the Austrian had a very fine crimson tapestry brought in from Europe to cover the Ambassador's Salon of the National Palace, and that he's spent a fortune on chandeliers and silverware and the uniforms of the Palace Guard . . . He also had the patios in the National Palace repaved, and has made many modifications at Chapultepec Castle . . . and of course, because there are masked balls in Vienna and in the Tuileries, we now have them in Chapultepec. By the way, the 'Regulations for Masked Balls' have just been published in what's now known as the *Empire's Daily*. Curiously it's forbidden to dress up as a priest, a nun, a bishop or cardinal." "More than curious, I would say, it's redundant, because it's only forbidding masquerading behind a mask, since that's all a cassock and those other religious trimmings are: theatrical costumes. What a friend of mine used to say about the Jesuits—perhaps the most dangerous priests of all—comes to mind: 'Under the black cloak of Ignatius of Loyola,' he would say, 'hides the sword of Iñigo López.' You know, Mr. Secretary? One of the things that irritates me most is all this hypocrisy . . . Charles III expelled the Jesuits and many in Europe consider him to have been a great monarch, perhaps the best Bourbon king. I expel a few bishops and they call me the Antichrist. The separation of Church and State was enacted in France towards the end of 1700 . . . I do the same in Mexico, and they call me a demon, a heretic trying to found an atheist state . . . as if a state could be an atheist. That makes no sense. Only individuals can be atheists or deists. The state is secular, right?" "That's correct, Mr. President." "And tell me, the government of Carlota's grandfather, Louis Philippe, was Constitutionally Catholic—but wasn't it led for many years by Guizot, a Calvinist, and then by Thiers, a Voltairean?" "That's correct, Don Benito." "You knew, didn't you, that Garibaldi had a grand welcome in London, and that Lord Shaftesbury, or however you pronounce his name, compared him to the Messiah? In Belgium, Carlota's homeland, the works of Proudhomme circulate freely . . . Oh, the winds of liberty are blowing in Europe, Mr. Secretary, but here in Mexico that very same Europe wants to revive the obscurantism of the Middle Ages. I wouldn't go as far as to quote Zarco and Mata and those others who claim that there's somehow a fundamental unity between the Mexican Constitution and the Gospel. Those two things cannot and should not be compared. But the truth is that my government has never persecuted dogmas or beliefs, isn't that right? And it's not my fault that a guerrilla fighter like Rojas drafts priests into his army and shaves their heads . . . I have no control over that. If you pay close attention, the reactionaries have provoked all our civil wars, from the Plan de Jalisco to the Plan de Tacubaya. Did I say we were only fighting two wars before? No, it's not two, it's three—since in Mexico, like in so many other countries, including those in Europe, all these internecine wars have been nothing more than campaigns between the Guelphs and the Ghibellines, between civil and ecclesiastical jurisdiction, between the Emperor and the Pope." "That's right, Don Benito, between the Emperor and the Pope. Maximilian is in serious trouble with the Church because of what we already know: he didn't make any concessions to the Papal Nuncio, the matter of the confiscated Church property is still pending, and he decreed freedom of religion . . . which is why, in his vain attempt to create a liberal monarchy, the Austrian has fewer supporters than ever . . ." "Come, come, Mr. Secretary, I mean liberal in quotation marks, as we said. Besides, there have been some popular monarchs who favored democratic ideals. But at any rate, if you understand a liberal ruler to be one who tries to establish, let's say, a more organic, more complete relationship between the government and the community, then yes, the Austrian is somewhat 'liberal.' But he's not going to establish that relationship trying to be another Harun Al-Rashid or another Louis XVI and showing up—because you've heard that story, haven't you?" "Everyone has, Don Benito." "—unannounced at midnight or at dawn in the jails and police stations to find out how justice works in what he calls his country . . . Did you know about the bakery?" "Yes, that he started banging on the doors of a bakery saying, 'I'm the Emperor Maximilian, let me in,' and they didn't believe him and even threatened to call the police to take him away . . ." "That's known as making a fool of yourself, isn't it, Mr. Secretary?" "That's correct, Don Benito." "At any rate, I think the Austrian's actions have been instigated by Louis Napoleon. I don't consider Maximilian an enlightened prince or anything of the sort, least of all when he's under the harmful influence of Gutiérrez Estrada . . ." "But Gutiérrez Estrada fell out of favor with him . . ." "How's that?" "Because of the Abbot Alleau scandal . . ." "The man who everyone thought was a secret agent of the Vatican?" "The very same one, Don Benito. You probably remember that they found a pamphlet on him claiming that Carlota's obsession with governing is due to her profound frustration at not having any offspring, this having been caused by the Austrian contracting a venereal disease that made him sterile during his trip to Brazil . . ." "Yes, yes I know the story. But what does that have to do with Gutiérrez Estrada?" "Oh, because they say that they also found a letter from Gutiérrez Estrada on Abbot Alleau inciting the clergy against the Empire. The Austrian must have been hurt by that act of treason." "Yes, of course, naturally. But I insist, Mr. Secretary, the Austrian is acting the way he's been acting due to pressure from Louis Napoleon, who's always been interested in creating a liberal image for himself. Here, in Paso del Norte, I've been reading the first volume of his *Life of Caesar*. It seems he wrote it as a eulogy for his own life. But I doubt very much that he can excuse his own actions to himself, or even understand them. For instance, the coexistence, in one mind, of the Principle of Nationalities and the Holy Alliance, and at the same time, the plebiscite and the bayonets. And he boasts of being the first European chief of state whose mandate is based on the universal vote. Nothing but nitpicking, like that of his uncle Napoleon who created a sort of scientific despotism based on referendum. You know the story. Three times he gained power from his people: first as First Consul, then as Consul for Life, and finally as Emperor. But he did have much more going for him than his nephew, for instance his size . . . no, not that. He was almost a Caesar and he behaved like one. It wasn't a coincidence that, like Caesar, he divided the Gauls, he divided the Tyrol, and . . . at any rate, he ended up failing. He didn't even get to be—like they said—the new Charlemagne, who would unite the Teutonic and Latin races under the same crown. Insofar as his nephew is concerned, well, he's not only a little Napoleon, but also even less of a Caesar. He found his Rubicon in Mexico; he will not cross it . . ." "And he will find his Brutus, Don Benito." "Oh, that won't be me, Mr. Secretary . . . He's already found plenty of brutes, like Maximilian, and also those who keep him in power . . . though, they must not be so brutish because all of them have become rich . . ." "That's right, Don Benito." "Well, I was telling you, Louis Napoleon won't find his Brutus, but his Bismarck . . . pay close attention to what I'm telling you, Mr. Secretary; his Bismarck. And his life won't end with a knife, but his Empire will end with a Prussian needlegun, or a Krupp cannon." "That Bismarck is terrible, Don Benito; do you know he says a man shouldn't die until he has smoked one hundred thousand cigarettes and drunk five thousand bottles of champagne?" "He's said something even more serious, Mr. Secretary—you probably remember that as soon as he was named prime minister, he said, 'Today's great problems will not be solved by means of speeches or majority decisions, but with blood and the sword.' And he won't rest until he humiliates France with those same items. Five thousand bottles of champagne? That's incredible. I don't like champagne. I find it a bit salty. I do enjoy tobacco, as you know, but in moderation. And sometimes when I smoke, I remember my exile in New Orleans, when I used to work at the cigar factory and had to spend the day rolling the stuff up. For a while they allowed me to do the work at home, but not for long. They made me go to the factory and they seated me at a table where there were many Negroes idling away their time singing psalms in English. I must confess that Africans have an odor, especially in the summer—a bit acid, not very agreeable. Oh, New Orleans . . . How about I tell you an anecdote about my exile in New Orleans, Mr. Secretary." "Yes, Don Benito." "One day I was walking with Ocampo and I stood still next to the ocean—well, that's what I thought, that it was the sea—looking as far as I could. And Ocampo asked me, 'What's the matter, Benito? You're so deep in thought.' And I told him, I like to stand by the seashore and watch the horizon because I know that far away, though not too far, is Mexico, my country. And Ocampo told me, 'Come on Benito, you have to learn a bit more about geography. In the first place, this isn't the ocean, it's Lake Pontchartrain, and secondly, you're looking toward the north. One day we will go to the Mississippi Delta, to very end, and there, yes, if you face southwest, you can imagine your gaze traveling in a straight line, to the coasts of Mexico.' And I said, 'Come on, Melchor, you have to learn a bit more geography yourself,' and he asked me why, and I told him, it doesn't matter where I stand and gaze, since no matter how far we imagine my gaze traveling, it would never get to Mexico, since a gaze travels in a straight line and the world, you know is round. And Melchor laughed." "You certainly got the best of Don Melchor, Mr. President." "Yes, yes, yes, Bismarck is a man to be feared. And not only because he knows his own strength, after Denmark, but also because of what you and I were saying once of Hegel; do you remember? Hegel transformed the State into God, and as a result the logic of tyranny has now been embellished with the beautiful cloth of blood sacrifice. In a unified Germany, Bismarck could well embody the son of that God which is the State. But changing the subject, Mr. Secretary: I'm told that José Zorrilla, author of *Don Juan Tenorio*, is here in Mexico, and that he's a very good friend of the Austrian . . . is that true?" "That's right, Don Benito." "And what is Zorrilla doing here?" "Well, Don Benito, I suppose that he's here to compose eulogies and odes for Maximilian and Carlota . . . And plan a new National Theater, because the Austrian is very much interested in all those things. They say he's thinking of building an art gallery with the pictures of all the rulers and leaders Mexico has ever had, viceroys as well as presidents." "Including me?" "Oh, I wouldn't know about that, Don Benito . . . and that he's determined to beautify the city. The Plaza de Armas, you know, is now filled with trees, flowerbeds and small paths. And I'm told there are artificial floating plants in the fountains." "Artificial plants in the water? And how is it they don't fall apart?" "Oh, I don't know, Don Benito, they're probably made out of rubber." "Yes, it must be rubber or something like that . . . floating artificial plants . . . and the Austrian is wasting his time with all that?" "With those and many other trivialities, but what's irritated the Austrian's supporters the most is not all that—after all, in that sense, he has quite a bit of company—but his flirting with Republicans. First he called Ramírez into his cabinet, and now he's shocked the conservatives by wearing a red tie when he dresses as a *charro*—the Republican color—as he did I think in Michoacán." "If all of this weren't tragic, Mr. Secretary, it would be funny." "That's right, Mr. President. And if all that weren't enough, the Austrian is indiscreet in his remarks. For example, he's known to have said one day, 'I'm a Liberal myself, but that's nothing in comparison to the Empress, who is positively red . . .'" "Carlota red? How is she red?" "Well, Don Benito, a woman who said she felt like throwing the Papal Nuncio out the window—and that's another choice phrase that's become legendary, now; all of Mexico knows it—a woman like that could hardly be called ultramontane." "Throw the Nuncio out the window . . . what a good idea. But what did Maximilian and Carlota expect from Monsignor Meglia? What do they expect from a Pope who's condemned all the modern philosophical and political ideas in the *Syllabus*? Yes, there was a time when one could have expected more from Pius IX, who at the beginning seemed like a liberal Pope. But then he changed positions. The Italians were also fooled when everything seemed to indicate that Pius IX was blessing the unification of Italy; they never thought a Pope would ever support a war against Austria, the most important Catholic country in Europe." "Well, imagine, Don Benito, the Church's surprise when the Austrian decreed that, without his approval, no Papal Bull would be valid in Mexican territory . . . They say Monsignor Meglia left Mexico without saying good-bye to the Emperor . . . that is to say, the Austrian." "And have you any idea why he went to Guatemala from here?" "No, Mr. President, but I do know that he meant to complain to Carrabus, the French consul . . . to get all his anger and grief out of his system." "He must also be inconsolable, Mr. Secretary, because with President Carrera's death—who was always ready to become viceroy of Guatemala, with the backing of France—Louis Napoleon's dream to establish an empire from Mexico to Cape Horne has been destroyed . . ." "A dream also adopted by Maximilian. Bolívar couldn't achieve it, but an Austrian dares to dream it. But that attitude only reflects the eternal arrogance of Europeans. The idea that Jafet's race is destined to rule the world, to divide between them the 'islands of nations,' as it says, if I remember correctly in Genesis. They have always taken upon themselves the right to draw and redraw the political map of the continents . . . including their own. The right to share the world among themselves as they did in the Treaty of Tordesillas, the Treaty of Utrecht, and so many others. Have you ever stopped to think, Mr. Secretary, why the Near East and the Far East got their names?" "Well, Don Benito, because they are near and far . . ." "Near to what and far from where?" "Well, from Paris, Madrid, London, and Vienna." "But they are not far or close to each other. Do I make myself clear? History has been measured with only one standard: the iron standard with which European man has subjugated nations . . ." "It's true, Don Benito, but there have also been very distinguished European intellectuals who have spoken out against colonialism, Adam Smith, for instance . . ." "Oh, don't give Adam Smith as an example, Mr. Secretary. What worried Adam Smith was that the monopoly of the metropolis rendered his law of free competition ineffectual. And Bentham was worried that the colonies had become a useless and dangerous burden and that they provoked too many conflicts between the European countries . . . And Lamartine . . . Look, if Lamartine has asked for humanitarian reforms in the French colonies, it's because he knows very well that with those reforms the colonial system will be consolidated . . ." "I hadn't thought about that, Mr. President." "Well, do that, Mr. Secretary. Think about it. And besides, we have to distinguish between two concepts: colonization—that is, the founding of colonies like the pilgrims of the Mayflower did—and conquest—that is, to subjugate and steal. For instance, I'm not against fomenting immigration. I've always believed that having immigrants of different religious beliefs in the country can work in favor of freedom of religion. But it would have to be done in moderation, and not like the Austrian wants it now . . ." "You mean . . . the Confederates of Ciudad Carlota?" "Not only them, but also the one hundred thousand Africans and Indo-Asians that Maximilian and that Maury want to bring into Mexico. And besides, that's not colonization, but an attempt to restore slavery here. And I, having been to Havana and New Orleans, I, Mr. Secretary, know what slavery is . . . they can't fool me . . . And you tell me the namesake of the city that will symbolize the restoration of slavery is 'a red'?" "Please, Don Benito, I didn't call her a red. It was Maximilian himself who called her that. Besides, it's not my intention to defend anyone, least of all the Austrian and his wife. I only want to convince you that the person who's more and more alone each day is Maximilian, not yourself. You know, it was Engineer Bournof's report . . ." "Oh, yes, Bournof, the Finance Minister, the one who reported seeing peons shackled in chains, and families dying of hunger, and men lashed and bloodied . . . Yes, yes, perhaps it's true in some cases . . . But in any case it's the legal government of the Republic who should be the one to administer justice, not a usurper." "Of course, Don Benito, but they say it was that report that made Carlota convince the Austrian to institute the rural laws protecting the peons, and those reforms have completely alienated him from the landowners. So, add it all up, Don Benito: the Church is against Maximilian. So are the landowners. The ultramontane conservatives are abandoning him, and he hasn't been able to bring the Republicans to his side because, obviously enough, what we want is a republic and not a monarchy. He can probably count on the support of the French troops for only a short time longer, and really he's never actually had it, except in name. The emperor Bazaine serves under is none other than Louis Napoleon. And the people with whom the Austrian surrounded himself at first—that Belgian, Eloin, who King Leopold imposed on him, along with the Austrian Schertzenlechner—did nothing but foment discord between Maximilian and the French. The Austrian, Mr. President, is alone . . ." "Yes, perhaps you're right, Mr. Secretary . . . Tell me about the adoption of Iturbide's grandson—this would seem to confirm that the Austrian is impotent, right? Since they've lost all hope of having an heir . . ." "Not necessarily, Don Benito . . . Firstly because there are many rumors that the Austrian has had intimate relations with several women here in Mexico, among them the daughter or wife, I'm not sure, of the Chief Gardener of the Borda Villa in Cuernavaca. Secondly because, at any rate, the Austrian and his wife don't have marital relations . . ." "And how can you know that?" "Well, you know, Mr. President, kings, emperors, all of them, are surrounded by many people during the day, and at night they sleep in separate guarded bedrooms. And it's a fact, at least since they arrived in Mexico, that the Austrian has not paid Carlota a single conjugal visit . . . or vice versa." "Oh, I see, I understand . . . of course. But tell me one thing, Mr. Secretary: have you ever lost a son?" "No, Don Benito, I've been lucky . . ." "It's probably some of the worst pain you can have in life. But at least I've had several children, to whom I can leave, not a throne, but something more important and sacred: my principles and my love for my Fatherland. And also what I learned from Plutarch: respect and admiration for life. Some have died, yes, but others are alive and they will survive me . . ." "Of course, Don Benito . . ." "You don't know how much I want to see my granddaughter, María . . . I love little girls . . . When my own little girl died, I buried her myself. The law that forbade interment in the temples exempted political leaders and their family members, but I didn't want to take advantage of that privilege. I, myself, alone, carried her casket, a little white casket, this small, to the Cemetery of San Miguel . . ." "Yes, Don Benito . . ." "But at any rate, what do I know, I have to bear up, Mr. Secretary, and somehow act consistently and devotedly . . . as Vicente Guerrero would've done. Don't you think? After all, I have a sacred duty to fulfill toward my fellow citizens . . ." "That's right, Mr. President." "Everything is going fine . . . *tout va bien*; that phrase summarizes all of Voltaire's *Candide*, and for a long time now I've used it to cheer me up. The truth is that *not* everything is well, but perhaps you're right about many things. Yes, our army is trustworthy and we have better war resources. And how can I forget the great Italian patriot Mazzini's support for our cause . . . though the European legion that he was supposed to form to combat the invader never quite made it to Mexico . . ." "It's true, Don Benito. But you also had the congratulations of that association of Belgian democrats . . ." "That also must have hurt Carlota very much, don't you think? And, well, I've received so much enthusiasm from the people, and so much support in Allende, Hidalgo del Parral, Santa Rosalía, and Chihuahua . . ." "That's what I wanted to tell you, Mr. President. We lose some garrisons but win others. We have Saltillo and Monterrey on our side again." "Of course, of course, I myself wrote Santacilia telling him, I remember, that the imperialists are now like Saint Simplicius: as soon as they put out a candle, another one is lit . . . Yes, yes, I have to be more optimistic, isn't that right? After all, remember those who said that our enemy is like jelly: it moves but doesn't go forward. Tell me, Mr. Secretary, would you like to hear another anecdote about my exile in New Orleans?" "Of course, Don Benito . . ."

2. "A Man of Letters"

I'm a man of letters, gentlemen, and therefore almost peaceful. And I say almost because I've killed a man. I don't have a guilty conscience because I killed him in the war. But I paid for his death, and I paid dearly; I paid for it with those same letters I just mentioned; there are many more than you imagine, but very few at the same time. Or I should say there *were*, because, on one hand I once had more than three thousand different letters, but on the other I only had twenty-eight. I lost some after what happened. I had them in a trunk on a mule that traveled with me all over, from Sonora to Yucatán and from Yucatán to Sonora—putting my letters at the service of the Republic. I've never been entrusted with carrying a message hidden in a piece of jerky, and much less a message placed in the cartridge case of a bullet hidden you-know-where. But I wrote many such messages with my own hands. I've never given a speech or signed an edict or a decree, but I have written them. I can do this by myself, just me and myself, the two of us—and my love of letters has also led me to write posters of all sizes and colors. The first books I read in my life, which I still read, are *Don Quixote* and the *Arabian Nights*. But before I learned to read, when I was only six years old, my father, who worked in a print shop, took a case that held a shiny silver alphabet out of a cabinet, and with a pair of tweezers he plucked out each letter and lined them all up across the table, from A to Z. My father, who never drank except on special occasions, served himself a glass of extra fine Bacanora and told me that, even though he had never been a pauper—he reminded me that we had two cows, three pigs, and ten hens—he would not be able to leave me much in the way of real estate or land in the country, but that he would leave me the richest inheritance in the world: those letters, which were so valuable, not because they were made of silver—the best that could be found in the mines of the Arizona mountains—but, like my father said, for their intrinsic worth as letters. "With these twenty-eight letters empires and reputations are founded and destroyed," he said. "With them love letters are written, which are then scented with patchouli; and death sentences are drafted, inked in someone's blood. I don't know if Homer used them to write the *Odyssey* or Aesop his *Fables*, because both were blind, but, in any case, someone did. With these letters, newspapers and laws are made; with them the edicts of the French Revolution and our own Constitution were printed; and with them, I, your father, under the pseudonym 'The Eagle's Son,' wrote dithyrambs against Hyppolyte du Pasquier de Dommartin, one of the first of the many French thieves who sold their soul to the devil thanks to Sonora and its silver. Letters are used to give life to causes and men—and death as well. Sometimes having them face one way, and sometimes the opposite, in groups of two, five, or twenty, and lined up in rows—with them, my son, you will be able to help write the History of Our Land, just like that, in capital letters, and likewise you will write your own history, for better or for worse, to your honor or your shame." My father then gave me the first nine letters of the alphabet and told me: "In order to earn the other ones you will first have to learn the meaning of 'Spare the rod and spoil the child.' And so it was: when I lost my first baby tooth, a milk tooth, and I put it underneath my pillow, the next day I didn't find a coin there, but a silver *I*. When I lost the second one, I found the *J*, and so on, successively and subsequently, until I accidentally swallowed the last tooth, and as a result I had to look for the Z myself—not underneath the pillow, but next to some agaves, and, like my father said, in the dregs of the earth. My father, God rest his soul, passed away a long time ago: I myself wrote the famous epitaph that they carved according to my instructions, with Gothic lettering, in a serpentine marble stone. But the old man lived long enough to teach me to read and write and to instill in me an undying love for letters, to the extent that he arranged the typography of my first writings about the Fatherland and my diatribes against the Yankee William Walker and the French Raousset-Boulbon—because I also inherited a deep national distaste for filibusters from my father—with his own hands, and printed them himself, and went with me himself to hand them out in the city market, which was in Guaymas, because by then we had moved to the shores of the Pacific Ocean, to the world's most beautiful bay: how could Guaymas not be beautiful, since after only seeing it from afar, Walker elected himself President of Sonora, and Raousset thought he was a Sultan? I returned to Guaymas as to a lover after living in the capital for a long time, where I'd gone in order to get a better education, and to travel *in extenso* like I said, throughout the Republic, and to fight in the interim against Napoleon III's invaders, who brought us the Austrian—but I only intended to fight like my father had told me: not with the sword, but with the brilliance of my pen. How was I to know then that because of me, a man would be kissing—forever—the same golden and easily scattered sands that had been soaked by the pirate blood of Raousset-Boulbon? You can imagine my reaction, since just like President Juárez, I'd never held a gun or a rifle in my hands before, not even a blade for peeling oranges. First I was a poet who composed lyrics and eclogues to the forests of Guerrero, to the hills of Durango and the jungles of Quintana Roo. In the capital, I learned to be what people call an "evangelist," one of those guys who sit in the arcades in the plazas, at a blue desk, writing letters for those who can't write. And there, from ten in the morning to eight in the evening, I wrote thousands of letters—proposing and affirming someone's love, letters of resentment and spite, of eviction and of condolence, letters to lawyers and to senators, to parochial priests and town mayors. And I did very well, not only because I was good at it, but also because, along with his love for letters and the silver alphabet, my father had left me a list of writing conventions and forms of address, like *Dear Sirs, Esteemed Gentlemen*, and *Your Trustworthy and Faithful Friend*. He also left me a list of poetic words that I suggested to suitors, lovers, and prodigal sons so that their intended lovers, wives, or mothers would truly feel how cold their hearts had become, separated from them, or else be able to better visualize the local weather. My starting price didn't include the rosy tint of dawn, which cost several more *reales*, naturally. After learning to be a poet, and when I read the first installments of *El fistol del diablo* by Mr. Manuel Payno in the *Revista Científica*, what I wanted most in the world was to write a novel, and I have one in the trunk now where I carry my typography, my brushes, and my printed signs, but I don't know if I'm ever going to finish it, because I always stop liking some of the things I've written while I end up wanting to write about things I don't know when I'll be able to get around to, and as though that weren't bad enough, because of the events at the Bay of Guaymas, more than half of my novel disappeared. Anyway, writing novels—or, really, not writing them—took me not so much by chance as by causality, as my father might say, and helped me become a journalist—what I want to say in my pamphlets and articles, I say it fast, and I'm done. Even though being a journalist has its drawbacks: I'm tired of sending my articles to newspapers that don't publish them, I think out of pure envy, because my spelling has always been perfect and my grammar pristine, thank God. Or thank my father. Meanwhile, I've had to work at every kind of job to survive, and because, as you know, I have a knack for drawing, I combined it with my vocation for writing, and I started making signs and placards. If you go by Cocóspera, a small town in my home state of Sonora, I hope you'll see a *pulquería* named *La Consolidada*: I painted the sign, and I chose its lettering, which is fat and red with silver stripes, just as it should be, and as its name indicates: everything is consolidated. But besides Sonora, there's hardly a state among the nineteen that make up our nation, gentlemen, where there isn't a bar, a hardware store, or a grocery whose signs I haven't painted, using pica or sans serif fonts, red or yellow, Clarendon or Renaissance, blue and black, the typefaces that I've been collecting throughout my life and that I have in my trunk in order to serve the Republic. I want to make it clear that I don't like to promote myself, and that painting signs is not what I like doing best. It earns me a living, and sometimes, as my father would say, literally—which is not the same as "literary": when I lived in the capital the second time, on Tacuba Street, I painted a sign for the bakery called "Ile of Saint Louis," although I couldn't choose the lettering myself because the owner was a stubborn Frenchie who had already made his mind up, but for three weeks I got paid in sweet bread, with the additional advantage that in this case I could choose which-ever kind of bread I wanted: *semitas*, *alamares*, or *chilindrinas*, any kind. But of course, that was before the war. If a French baker had hired me to do that after his fellow countrymen had trod my native soil, as my father would say, I wouldn't have painted the sign; instead, I would've disappeared, and before going I would have spilled my paints on the bread, and there would have been another Pastry War. (I swear, in this second one we would've won.) Mean-while, during the three weeks that I was eating bread and water—if I can put it that way, in order to emphasize a good metaphor here—I wrote several letters to President Benito Juárez: Most Excellent Sir, I wrote, congratulating him on his Laws of Reform, and I sent an article to the *Monitor Republicano* that was never published, which made me think that maybe my work isn't published because it's too poetic—and I say that because my poems sound pretty when I read them aloud and because I think that they read better as poems than as

343

prose. Naturally, and because man doesn't live by bread alone, I like to be paid not so much in kind, but in hard cash; but once—and only once, as far as I can remember—I was actually paid in kind *and* in silver at the same time, when I painted a sign that said *Inglis Espoquen* for a silver shop in the city of Taxco, through which, years later, Emperor Maximilian would drive in his carriage with six white mules and coachmen in purple livery. Though, come to think of it, if it weren't for the moral principles that my father instilled in me, on another occasion they would have paid me in kind with the best possible thing—present company excluded—I mean, a woman. But when that woman in thick makeup and a red curly wig whom I met at a Tampico tavern asked if I could paint her a sign that said: "Fine Ladies," I didn't even deign to mutter an answer: I grabbed a pencil and wrote in very big letters, "No, sir," on the menu, even though she was a lady, if you could call her that. I'm also responsible for several menus. The prettiest one of all I made in that same city of Tampico, for the Café Reverdy, and I painted hanging pineapples and mangoes as decoration, which the owner liked very much. Another time I made a sign for a tobacconist who paid me in cigarettes. I've got in the habit of smoking them, since then; I wasn't going to waste my payment. Later I made a sign for a laundry and they told me that they could only pay me by washing my clothes for a month or so, but, since it was during lean times, and I had no other clothes than the ones on my back, I had to paint a sign for a store that sold pants and shirts and asked to be paid in kind by them as well so I could have something to wash. And I'll never forget the fun I had in a little town in the lowlands where they asked me to paint the sign for an ice warehouse; the ice was brought in on the back of a mule from Orizaba Peak, and when I finished they paid me with two blocks of ice, each the size of a barrel. People asked me, "What are you going to do now, throw a party to get some use out of them?" and for an answer I grabbed my mule, put the ice blocks on it, and left for a place called Hot Springs, where they have boiling sulfide water coming out of the ground, and I threw the blocks in to make the spring lukewarm, and thus became the first and only mortal, gentlemen, to ever have bathed in its hot, boiling waters. It was there, by the way, in the state of Veracruz, that I again placed my talents at the service of the Republic. And I say "again" because, as I mentioned before, I was very much against all invaders since I was a very young boy, be they the Comanches and Apaches of the Gila Valley, who every so often wanted to trample Sonora under their horses' hooves, or like all of the Yankee and French pirates who would come on boats to Guaymas, and who never learned from each others' mistakes: we kicked Walker out of Ensenada, woke Charles Pindray up with a bullet to his forehead, and executed Raousset-Boulbon in the Bay of Guaymas, but none of that did any good keeping Salar and de la Gravière and Castagny and Bazaine and all those other pirates from showing up. Well, after all my experiences, I knew who I was and whose side I was on. I saw it all with my own eyes: General Escobedo promised in a proclamation—this is true, and doubly true because I helped set up the type to print it—that his soldiers would get to keep all the loot from the towns that hadn't submitted to the government of the Republic by a certain date. It was also true, and I saw it, that wherever the French anti-guerilla forces went, there wasn't a crucifix or a silver cup left in the churches, and what's worse, there were hardly any virgins left either, and gentlemen, I don't mean the ones made of stone that you find in church. And it's also true that our men used what they called the rope torture on French prisoners before they executed them, though that's something I never saw myself. It's also true that the French would hang Juárez's emissaries from the trees; I saw them swinging like a bunch of bananas from the largest one in the main square of Medellín. And even if all that wasn't true, if I was making it up, well, that's why fantasy was invented, I say, to be used in the service of the cause—those same fantasies that I've had inside me since I first read *Don Quixote* and the *Arabian Nights*. Because of those books, you know, I've always been something like half Quixote and half Harun al-Rashid. Maximilian also was a little like that, I think, if I may be allowed to say so, and that's why I never really disliked the unfortunate Emperor; but I told myself, Juárez is the dark Indian born on Mexican soil, while the other is a blond Austrian interloper who came here uninvited; one is the President, the other is the Usurper, and without hesitating for a second, without batting an eyelash, I decided, as I've already told you, to put not only my pen, but also my brushes, my type, a portable printing press, and, above all, my talents, all at the service of the Republic—even though Don Benito never answered any of the three letters I sent him, and even though, thanks to those fantasies of mine, when I would see an Egyptian soldier in his white uniform and red fez, or a Hussar with his golden stripes, or a French soldier with his crimson pants, or the legionaries and the Abyssinians and the Janissaries and even the African hunters who are called blue butchers, I almost wanted to be on their side, if not in Mexico, at least in other wars, in far away places with strange names, surrounded by oases and camels, odalisques and Alhambras. But I was telling you that it was in the lowlands, in the Port of Veracruz, where I went to work for the Republic again. First I painted a sign that said "Killing Buzzards is Prohibited," but I didn't want them to pay for it because, as you might know, buzzards not only eat the decaying carcasses from the war, but also all the waste and trash the inhabitants scatter around, and which the northern wind stirs up. That was my contribution to the cleanliness of the city, and I would even say to the hygiene of the "circumfused," as my father might have said. I made my contribution to the war against the invaders the night I got up without anyone noticing and, in bad handwriting and with misspellings, as though it had been done by someone else, added "But Killing Frenchmen Is Allowed" to the same sign. Don't make light of these details—as my father used to say, the bed of the æquoreal sea is made up of tiny grains of sand. And it would have been fine by me if they decided to pay me in kind for the sign and the added statement, that is to say with live buzzards and dead Frenchmen, since the former would have eaten the latter: case closed. Some of my other contributions to the cause weren't so modest, but they all had to do with letters, one way or another. One of the times that President Juárez changed the capital of the government, I helped distribute the proclamation making it official, which said something like, "The capture of Madrid did not give Napoleon I victory over all of Spain, neither did the capture of Moscow give him all of Russia." Another time I spent three days painting signs that would give wrong directions to towns and places because, according to an idea I had, we wanted a Belgian detachment to get lost and if possible have it go around in circles—he hadn't foreseen, for some reason, that they would have brought their own fluvial and logistic maps. On another occasion I was given a big project, which was to put an enormous sign made with white-washed rocks that said "Viva Juárez" on the barren hill of a town, so that it could be read three leagues away, or at least from half the possible vantages three leagues away, since the sign only went halfway around the hill. Me and the assistants the mayor had assigned to me spent five days hauling rocks in a wheelbarrow because there were none there, and thenpainting them with whitewash. When we had finished with the "Viva" and were about to put the *J* in Juárez, someone told the mayor that some French troops were on their way, and so we got the order to put in an *M* for Maximilian, which I flatly refused to do, as you, sirs, might have gathered. Before I left town, I made sure to steal all the letter *A*s that they had in the official printing press; so until a new shipment of *As* arrived, they couldn't print anything about Maximilian, because if they'd wanted to print his name, it would have looked more like a year written in Roman numerals. My trunk got a lot heavier thanks to all those *As*, but I left happy with my contribution to the cause, and I promised myself that I would give my services to the cities or the municipalities that needed them the most, like Jalapa, Tlalpan, or Cosamaloapan. Finally, tired of all these adventures, I returned to Sonora at the time the French Pacific Fleet left Mazatlán under the command of General Castagny and headed for Guaymas—where I arrived almost at the same time as the French: I arrived by land, by way of Tepic, while they came by sea, of course, by way of the strait that opens between Punta Baja and Isla de Pájaros. The first thing I did was walk to the headquarters of General Patoni, who was defending the town square, leading a thousand men, to put my printing press and my talents at the service of the Republic; and, even though I was going to tell the General that I would print his long-winded speeches and remarks word for word, he couldn't see me, because he was so busy with war matters. I understood and, not taking it personally, *ipso facto*, I began working for the cause anyway. On the one hand, by that time—not so much because I needed money, but for the pure love of letters—I had begun printing posters, and I had a million of them, ranging from the ones that only get used once in a while, like "Furnished Room for Rent," to the ones that get used all the time, like "No Credit Today—Come Tomorrow"—and even some of the ones that are used, let's say, once in a lifetime, like "Closed Due to a Death in the Family"—and so I set my heart on printing others that might be useful in battles. On the other hand, because I knew the Bay of Guaymas by heart, with all of its islands—Isla de Pájaros, La Pitahaya, San Vicente, La Ardilla and the Islas Mellizas, as well as Almagre Grande and Almagre Chico, and the rocky and arid mountains that protect them from the winds—I set out to propose some ideas to the army that might be helpful to the cause as well as suitable to the topography of the area . . . but we couldn't put them all into practice. For example, I wanted to create a mail service via carrier pigeon that would fly from Almagre Grande to Almagre Chico, taking feet messages printed with my linotype inviting enemy soldiers to defect to the Republican ranks, and when one of the pigeons flew over the French ships anchored between the islands, we would kill it ourselves with one shot, so that it would fall like a stone with its rebel message onto the deck of the ship. But what I *could* do—thanks to the fact that I happened to know about night tide that flows from the tip of Playa de Dolores to Punta Lastre (a current which, as a child, would take me floating, face up through where the enemy ships were docked)—was to send messages in bottles that I bought at a liquor store in Guaymas that they were selling cheap because a barrel of Love Elixir had been riddled with bullets. There, inside those bottles, which were blue and long, and that I threw into the sea every night, I stuffed my messages, as well as a handful of fireflies, so that they would give off a practical light in the dark of the night, as well as the light of freedom. And one time the body of a messenger we'd sent to our detachment in the estuary of Cochore was returned to us by the ocean the next day, washing up on the beach at Punta Tortuga, with a sign in indelible ink tied to its neck that read: "Here's Your Fucking Mailman." Less than two days later, we executed a French spy, and by my own express order we took him to Playa de Dolores that night with signs around his neck that read: "And Here's Your Damn Spy." The water carried the enemy away, who didn't need to try and pretend to float like a corpse, because he was already dead. But actually, when we threw him in, he sank, and after we took him out and threw him back into the water and he just sank again, I had the brilliant idea to tie some bottles to his fingers and his toes and put not only one of my printed messages in each bottle, but also its corresponding and respective handful of fireflies, and that's how we did it. The dead man floated towards the French boats, his feet and legs open like those of an immense starfish with its tips filled with blue light. To make a long story short, I'll tell you what you already know: the Republic won the war against the Empire. Unfortunately, we lost the battle of Guaymas and General Patoni and his men had to retreat even though they tried to hold off the enemy down to the last houses; Castagny's naval artillery stopped them. That's how I once again found myself on top of that arid rocky mountain they call Tetas de Cabra, hiding in a cave with my trunk full of type. One morning I was thinking that if I were a publicist for the Empire I would've recommended that Maximilian call himself Meximilian instead, when suddenly I heard some noises. I tiptoed to the edge of the hillside and there at the bottom, ten meters away, just below me, I saw a French sailor crawling, though he was Mexican, if you know what I mean—and I thought he was going to aim at one of our captains who was nearby looking at the ocean through his binoculars. I would've liked to read an impromptu speech to this imperialist so he would come over to our side, I would've liked to read him a lyric poem about our Fatherland so that he would've stopped being a traitor, or I would've liked at the very least to shout a warning to the captain, who was somewhat nearby, but I realized the minute I opened my mouth that the son of a bitch, pardon the euphemism, would've fired at me instead; and I told myself, in a revolution a man of letters is worth at least as much, if not more, than a soldier—as my father would say—and because I thought of my father at that moment and what he'd told me about letters giving life to a cause and to men, whom you could also kill with letters, I got inspired, as you can imagine. I went back to the cave and brought out my trunk; I tiptoed back to the edge of the hillside and threw my trunk at the sailor; it fell on his head just in time, and he missed. And he is the man I told you I killed, and for which I paid so dearly, because the trunk opened and half the pages of my novel went flying through the air, as well as all my type, including the silver alphabet that my father had given me—and they either broke or scattered hopelessly on the mountain and the beach. Several weeks later, when my dear General Patoni and his men had vanished—I was, after all, only a civilian, and stayed at the port—I was still finding letters among the rocks, scrub, and hawthorns, and farther down in the sand, among the seashells; there were many, of course, that I never found, among them three of the letters that go in "Arizona": the *O*, the *I*, and the *Z*. This hurt me a great deal, and I'm still not resigned to having lost them. As far as the *M* is concerned I did find it, but I didn't get to keep it—I had seen it shine in the sand, very close to the rocks splashed with the blood of Raousset-Boulbon, the French count and pirate, novelist and author of Spanish romances who dreamt of being Sultan of Sonora; I had already seen the shining, I was saying, the shining legs of the *M* of Mexico and Maximilian, when, out of nowhere, I don't know how, an ill-omen appeared, a black bird. This was one of those magpies that take crabs out of their holes by pulling their claws with their beaks and it, that damned bird, took the silver *M*. I followed it with my eyes and I could have sworn that it let the *M* fall in the middle of the sea. But before that, before that long, and, as my father would say, fruitless search, and its resulting sorrow, I wanted to see the corpse's face, so I lifted my trunk off of him and I turned the body over. There, between all the blood and the letters of all sizes and shapes, from the *A*s that were in his ears, the *N*s and *X*s that were encrusted in his brains, the *O*s and *W*s, I saw that his eyes were wide open in an expression between incredulous and beatific, between impassive and stupefied, as though he had realized that one of the most unlikely and extravagant deaths of the war had snuck up on him. Because you, gentlemen, would have to agree with me that it's not every day that one can kill a person with the weight of his letters—and, as my father would say, not so much literarily as literally.

3. The Emperor at Miravalle

You could see the entire Valley of Mexico from the terraces of Chapultepec Castle, especially on such a clear, such a transparent afternoon. The Paseo de la Emperatriz ran west almost to the foot of the hill of the castle. To the north, Calzada de la Verónica. To the southeast you could see the snow-covered volcanoes. To the south, Ajusco Mountain. On such a clear day some of the towns nearby the capital were also visible. To the north, San Cristóbal Ecatepec; to the west Los Remedios and Tacubaya. To the south, Mixcoac with its colorful fruit trees, and then San Angel, and Tlalpan. A good eye could also pick out the rivers that appeared to be climbing through the mountains as well as the woods, thick with the Weymouth Pines that the Countess von Kollonitz liked so much, and on whose trunks—as she said in her memoirs—begonias would wrap themselves. For her, the American cedars that grew in Mexico were even more beautiful and ornamental than Lebanon's. At the foot of the castle, the trees from the Bosque de Chapultepec reached their dark greenness toward the west. The lakes of the valley were shining: Chalco, Xochimilco, Xaltocan, and Texcoco.

"And just as it's not possible, Commodore, to distinguish between one giraffe and another, or between one donkey and another, I could not, I swear, *parole d'honneur*, distinguish between one dark-skinned person and another; they all look alike to me. And now explain this to me . . . *Alle Länder gute Menschen tragen*: every country has its good men, yes, but where, where are the good Mexicans, Commodore? I must admit I told Louis Napoleon in a letter that in Mexico there are no competent men. The other day I also wrote him that there are only three types of men here: the old who are stubborn and rotten, the young who don't know anything, and then the foreigners, almost all of them mediocre adventurers. There are notable exceptions, of course . . . there is General Sterling Price, Governor of Missouri, who lives in a tent under the orange trees at the edge of the Veracruz railway, and who swears he's going to grow finer tobacco than the Cubans' on his lands. And we have Maine's

Brigadier-General Danville Leadbetter helping us so much with the building of the railway—educated men, Commodore, West Point graduates . . . Oh and he's also helping build Ciudad Carlota, which one day will be bigger than Richmond, you know."

"And New Orleans, Sire."

"And New Orleans, Commodore. Fighting Shelby also came with his iron brigade . . . Or what do they call it? His *Iron Cavalry Brigade* . . . I've asked Shelby to write his reports to me in verse, just like he did for the Confederate Headquarters. Did you know that he did that?"

"Yes, your Majesty . . ."

"And *of course*, we have you, such an illustrious, world-renowned oceanographer . . ."

The Emperor handed over his binoculars to this oceanographer and meteorologist, Matthew Fontaine Maury, and pointed toward the north.

"Take a look there. No, no, a little more to the left. Just a little. Do you see the sanctuary of Notre Dame de Guadalupe? It's always seemed a bit Muscovite to me. Don't you agree? And tell me what other country in the world can pride itself on having as director of colonization a man as distinguished as Commodore Maury."

"Your Majesty, I'm only . . ."

"The man who brought the quinine tree to Mexico and to whom one day we, those who suffer from tertiary fevers, will owe so much. Do you see that little rise next to the sanctuary, Commodore? I'd also like to acclimate to Mexico the alpaca and the llama . . . do you see it?"

"Yes, Sire."

"That's Tepeyac Hill, where the Virgin appeared to the Indian Juan Diego . . . They told me Commodore, the sort of things these Britons come up with! That the subjects of their African colonies are doling out the powders of the bark of the quinine diluted in water and gin. They're clever, aren't they Commodore? They're smart. Now look down there at those silver reflections—see them? They're from Lake Xaltocan."

"Yes, Your Majesty."

"As I was saying, I ask myself, what other nation can pride itself on having as its Director of Land Distribution a general like John Magruder? And there's Isham Harry, Governor of Tennessee, with his blacks that accompanied him to Mexico, and in short, we have all the foreigners who'd like to come here, to

351

populate our great land, and to help this grand territory prosper. The world is extending its hand to Mexico—my homeland, Commodore—and what do we Mexicans do? Nothing. Absolutely nothing. This is the Mexican nothingness to which the Empress refers. Oh, how I miss the Empress. I'd rather be with her in Uxmal, Commodore, than in Chapultepec. Poor Carla: the sun discolors her skin. It's so hot there, and so cold here! No, no keep the binoculars a moment, keep them please . . ."

"I understand the Empress had a magnificent reception in Yucatán."

"That's right, Commodore, *magnifique*! The Empress is the Guardian Angel of Yucatán. The fairy godmother. And she needs a distraction now that Countess Zichy and the Countess von Kollonitz have left . . . They're all leaving: nostalgia for Austria, the waltzes, the splendors of Vienna . . . But not me, Commodore, with the view of the ahuehuete trees, and the ash trees of the Avenida de la Emperatriz, more beautiful than *Les Champs Élysées* . . ."

The Emperor took Commodore Maury's arm.

"Come, come here. I'm going to show you the best view of the Valley of Anáhuac at this time of the afternoon. Not even the view of Sorrento is as beautiful . . . and as if that were not enough, Mr. Maury, there are those poor Belgian youths, badly trained, dropping like flies . . . *como moscas*. A little snuff, Commodore? The Emperor of Mexico is a heavy smoker . . . unrepentant . . . and when he's not blowing smoke, he's inhaling snuff!"

Commodore Matthew Fontaine Maury took a pinch of snuff from the little silver box, encrusted with blue gems.

"It's snuff from Seville, Commodore; strong, spiced. It came in the last shipment from Saccone and Speed . . . What would I do without Saccone and Speed, Commodore? What would all the monarchs do *in partibus infidelium*? A delicious blackcurrant liquor also arrived, blackcurrant marmalades and other delicacies, ah, and also the magnificent vermouth that I promised you: Noily Pratt."

"Yes, yes, it's been quite disgraceful, Sire."

"What's that? Pardon?"

"The death of the young Belgians, Your Majesty."

"It was brought up in the Netherlands, but this is *strictement entre nous*, between us, Commodore."

"I understand, Sire."

"They said that Bazaine prefers sacrificing Belgians to his own men. I'm not surprised, coming from someone who said that if his enemies were Mexicans, he was as much, or more, Arab than French—as if he wanted to justify his indolence! And it's well known that when the French withdraw from a town square, they leave Hungarian cavalry there and the *Jäggers* . . . *c'est a dire*, the Austrian hunters. Look there, down there you have Lake Xochimilco with its gondolas full of *adormideras* . . . the Empress loves to ride in the gondolas."

"Beautiful, Your Majesty."

"Yes, beautiful is the word . . . but for the Gog and the Magog of the valley, for the volcanoes with eternal snow: Popocatépetl and Iztaccíhuatl . . . Do you notice how well I pronounce them? I would use another adjective."

"Superb?"

"*Maestoso*, Commodore, majestic . . . Nothing in the world is as majestic as this view . . . And do you know what Marshal Bazaine has proposed? Forced conscription. Like I told him: Mr. Marshal, everything can be done with bayonets . . . except sit on them."

"Bravo, Sire."

"You think so? But what was I saying as I was leaving the terrace?"

"Your Majesty was telling me about his experiences in Brazil with the Negroes . . ."

"Ah, yes, yes, one looks just like the other. I think that American Negroes are another thing . . . different to the Brazilians."

"The American Negro has been in contact with civilization much longer, Sire."

"And there are examples of great fidelity and self-denial, Commodore, like the ones Baron de Sauvage cites in his report published in the *Empire Daily* about the slaves in the south that stayed to look after the properties abandoned by their masters."

The Emperor ran his hand through his blond hair, which the breeze had tousled.

"Do you know the story of Juan Diego and Our Lady of Guadalupe, Commodore? What more could I want than to cover this country with roses. But nothing can be done about it. We wanted to cover Mexico City with trees and what happens? The city floods every year, but there's still not enough water for irrigation. As I was saying—in Bahía, Mr. Maury, I didn't find any sign of real intellect in the eyes of the black people there. And, would you believe it? Their voices sound like those of animals; they have no modulation, no . . . nuance. That's what I wrote in my memoirs, which I will publish one day. There is no doubt, Commodore, like Michel Chevalier says. Do you know him?"

"Michel Chevalier? Chevalier, the one who fought with Lafayette at Yorktown?"

"Yes, as far as I know . . . but also the author . . . the author of *Ancient and Modern Mexico*. He says that the absence of Africans in Mexico is reflected by a higher average of intelligence among natives. Ah, the descendants of Shem in Brazil are so peculiar looking. You ask a Negro, what's your name? And he answers, 'Minas.' Where do you work? 'Minas.' Where were you born? And again he answers, 'Minas.' Everything is *Minas, Minas Gerais*, and the province. Many of those poor devils only survived because they knew how to swim: the Portuguese slavers would throw them overboard one or two kilometers off the coast. *Ainda que somos negros, gente somos, e alma temos*, says the Portuguese proverb, but there their masters ignore it, Commodore, because the only scepter that the Brazilian aristocracy knows is the whip . . ."

"The . . . ?"

"The whip, Commodore, what can you expect from people who talk with their noses and not their mouths? An ugly language, Portuguese, isn't it? . . . Because of them, we should balance out the number of Africans with Indo-Asians . . . not Chinese, Indo-Asians . . . The Chinese, Commodore, are superstitious and like to gamble and commit suicide. Look over there, Maury, that sparkle over there comes from the Cerro de la Estrella, a hill that had religious importance to the Aztecs."

"Did they sacrifice people there, Your Majesty?"

"Human sacrifice? Oh, I'm not quite sure, Commodore. I'll ask the Empress: she is very well informed . . . What I do know is that on that hill they celebrated the end of every Aztec century, which lasted fifty-two years, and the start of another. Speaking of which, *à propos* my adored Carla, there are rumors that my father-in-law, King Leopold, is very sick . . . Oh, there are so many burdens on my shoulders at once! This year, there were terrible floods in the Colima area—where a lot of game was lost, and the harvests were covered with sand. And there's no money, Commodore, the nation's coffers are empty. The banks issue more paper currency than we have funds to back it. And everything, everything has to be paid for by my government. I would like to have more funds for my Colonization Board, but look what we've had to pay for already: the expenses of the Mexicans that came to Miramare to offer us the throne—one hundred and five thousand pesos. And then one hundred fifteen thousand for our reception in the capital . . . Last year alone the mobilizations of Bazaine's troops cost us seven million francs . . . Oh, and the Mexicans, Commodore:

Hidalgo y Esnaurrízar is asking one hundred thousand pesos for indemnification, for God knows what. Add to that what the Iturbide family is costing us. Speaking of which, Alice or Alicia, the American, the little prince's mother, is crazy. She's not satisfied with anything; she only thinks about the boy . . . Oh, look, Commodore, the beautiful tints of pink and fuchsia that the snows of the volcanoes take on with the sunset."

"Oh, yes, yes, very beautiful."

"Really? Do you really think so, Commodore?"

"That's why, Sire, I don't understand the lack of cooperation from your Mexican officers. No offense, Your Majesty . . ."

"About the officials in my government, Commodore? Yes, yes, I admit, you have a point, unfortunately . . . And what do you think about the uncompromising attitude of the Church?"

"Ignorance, fanaticism, Sire. Look: It has been taught . . . or shown, that is, that with one hundred thousand tenant farmers in the lands that your people call *les terres chaudes* in the Gulf, five hundred million pounds of sugar could be produced, and the . . . the . . . income?"

"The revenue, Commodore . . ."

"The revenue would be thirty million pesos . . . Also, there are so many cotton planters attracted to the project . . ."

"With the one hundred thousand tenant farmers that we'll bring from Africa and the Asian southeast, Commodore, there will be money enough for everything . . . For the Imperial Fleet of battleships that you will command—it's a promise—for your new Virginia . . . for all of my big projects: the Academy of Arts and Sciences, the new drainage system for the capital . . . I've commissioned several artists to paint the history of the Empire, too. Are you familiar with *The Siege of Puebla* by Félix Philippoteaux? Oh, but there's really no one like Beaucé. Jean-Adolphe Beaucé? With his ample experience in Algeria and Syria, and who's painted the magnificent *Battle of Yerbabuena*, which was fought between the red squadron of the *contraguerrille française* and the First Mexican Regiment of Lancers . . . We have now commissioned him to do a large oil painting that shows the submission of the Indians of the Río Grande to the Mexican Empire, for the Iturbide Salon of the Imperial Palace . . . No, no, don't give up. I beg you, Commodore . . ."

"It's hard, Sire. We are humanitarians. We've set just compensation for the landowners. We passed a law in order to force the *masters* . . ."

"Don't say *masters*, Commodore, say landowners . . . Yes, a law that forces them to feed, clothe, and provide medical care for the workers and their children, Commodore, and to save one fourth of their salary, with five percent interest, on their behalf. We tell them this so often we're getting hoarse—and what happens, after we've fought for the rights of the peons? Mexico opens its doors to worldwide immigration, we offer freedom to any colored person who steps on Mexican territory, and they accuse me, Commodore, of reinstating slavery in Mexico! *Ludicrous*, as you would say, *completely ludicrous*."

"The Mexican Empire has many enemies, Your Majesty."

"Look, look here, Commodore, how beautiful! The Etna, the eternally smoking Stromboli, which is like a truncated cone, the Vesuvius where my peers and I used to cook eggs in the crater, we would slide down, rolling in the ashes, jumping like wild goats . . . Ah, memories of my youth. Like you, during your long trips, I know many volcanoes, but I have never seen, *never*, Mr. Maury, one as beautiful as Popocatépetl. Another one of my failures: I named Miramare Miramare because it faces the sea, and the name was inspired by a tusculum that had served as a refuge for Spanish kings in the Bay of Biscay. Well this Chapultepec Castle I wanted to call Miravalle because it faces the valley . . . But no one calls it that . . . I would have to issue a decree making it a law. Yes, yes, the Empire has enemies. But I think that if Lincoln were alive, he would have understood the humanitarian aspect of our project, Commodore, and we would have his support. But you see, President Johnson . . ."

The Emperor grew silent for a few moments.

"Yes, Your Majesty. President Johnson?"

"Yes, President Johnson . . . But what can I tell that you don't already know? There have been so many Americans who've backed down from coming here to help us because they knew they wouldn't be able to return to the United States without the personal permission of the President . . . So many, Commodore, who know that General Sherman's troops, by order of Ulysses Grant, patrol the border day and night so as not to let them come into Mexico. What are we to do, Mr. Maury?"

"And the Quai d'Orsay, Sire? What have they said?"

"Monsieur Drouyn de Lhuys recommends that we shouldn't insist on calling the tenant farmers confederates but *refugiés des hommes désolés*, and have them hand over their weapons at the border. And yes, we need weapons: this year my government bought six thousand rifles and fifteen hundred sables from Havana and ordered another fifteen thousand rifles from Vienna. But in any case it's better that Sherman takes their weapons so they won't be sold to the Juárez supporters instead, as has happened in the past. So, Commodore, the word 'confederate' is prohibited."

"I don't see . . . I don't see how President Johnson can fear the creation of a confederate force in Mexico."

"It was specified, Commodore, that we wouldn't allow any settlements, colonies made up of more than twelve confederate families. But they're not satisfied with anything up there. And here, the Mexicans themselves, my own countrymen, criticize me for ordering a few gold-trimmed, ebony pianos, some étagères from Boulle, and china from Sèvres. But the Empire has to have dignity, right? And if we didn't decorate the palace, if we hadn't ordered the ceilings removed, we would have never discovered those marvelous cedar beams! And now tell me, what do you think of Ajusco, also covered with snow? It's been a cold winter in the capital . . . and last week, I, Yours Truly, as the Mexicans say, really wanted a hot bath, Commodore, and what do you think happened? What do you imagine happened?"

"I don't know, Sire."

"Some pipes had been stolen from the castle, and we were left without any water at all for a couple of days. That's how the townspeople thank their Emperor for his work and efforts."

Maximilian again took the arm of Commodore Matthew Fontaine Maury.

"And I've done so much for them, Commodore, as you know. The decree as to the dress code and the emblems of the Mexican Army. The decree on Religious Tolerance. The decree on the Revision of Nationalized Assets. We signed an agreement about artistic and literary copyright with Bavaria. And what do the enemies of the Empire talk about the whole time? About the Decree of October 3rd, and, yes, unfortunately yes, it was a painful mistake to have executed Generals Arteaga and Salazar . . . but it seemed a necessary measure at the time. Now we have granted many pardons. We created the Orders of San Carlos and of the Mexican Eagle. This year we awarded the *Grandes Cruces con Collar* to four emperors and three kings. And *précisément*, on January 1, for starters we changed the *Official News*, which was published sporadically, into the *Empire Daily*. Mmmmm, such beautiful clouds. Do you remember Monsieur Poey's article—the one that contradicts you on the matter of the trade winds—about the azimuthal movement of clouds? I'm learning the names you've given clouds, Commodore, conventional, cirrus. Look at those, those over there, Commodore."

The Emperor pointed to some violet-tinted clouds in the direction of Lake Texcoco.

"Those are stratocumuli, right? *Et bien* . . . I'm not going to give you a catalog of our successes. Nor of my sorrows . . . Nor of the clouds. Like I wrote Baron de Pont, like Guatimozín, I'm sitting in a bed of roses, here: *j'ai mal à la gorge*: I have a sore throat . . . and I've had so many bouts of flu, so many pains in my liver. And it's no surprise, after the accusations of that cleric, what's his name, Alleau? And the return of Colonel Dupin—I've already told the Marshal I won't put up with that! Oh, if only the Empress were here to support me!"

"Your Majesty, the Empress is a wise ruler, Sire."

"*Bien dit, mon Commodore.* My beloved Carla knows how to govern. Without her, the Decree for the Needy would not have been approved. You saw the reaction of the landowners, Mr. Maury. And ours have only been modest attempts to do justice to the unskilled laborers of Mexico. The Empress was brought to tears when she read what Engineer Bournof wrote about the men beaten until they bled, the families that were starving to death, the day-laborers weighed down with chains. Mexico is the first country in the world, with legislation from my Empire, that passed a law protecting its peasants, and what happens Commodore? They accuse us of being pro-slavery . . . of stealing land. There wasn't even a Land Agency before I arrived in Mexico, Commodore . . . The lands were never surveyed! And they attack us for naming a firm, *particulière*, the Coutfield, to organize immigration. All we were doing was following the example of England and France, which granted Hythe Hodger of London and Regis Aine of Marseilles the privilege of introducing Indo-Asian and African immigrants into their colonies. Do you understand it, Commodore Maury? I don't understand at all . . . at all, I swear."

Coming down the Calzada de la Verónica, a cloud of dust rose up—it was a group of riders.

"Oh, let me see, let me borrow the binoculars, Commodore. Yes, of course . . . here, look, look."

"Are those . . . hussars?"

"Yes, yes, Hungarian hussars . . . what a beautiful spectacle! The French have imitated them since 1690, and later Spain created the Princess's Regiment of Hussars, but none of them are like the Hungarians, the first. You know, Commodore, I used to say only Austria truly has them because Austria has Hungary! But now we have them in Mexico as well."

The Commodore returned the binoculars to the Emperor and the latter put them away in the Russian leather case with the imperial monogram in gold hanging from his neck on a patent leather cord.

The shadows covered the Valley of Mexico. The top of Popocatépetl seemed to be on fire.

"*Nous dansons sur un volcan.* We danced on the summit of a volcano: that's what they told the Duke of Orléans in Naples, days before the rebellion of 1830 that forced Charles X, the last French king, a direct descendant of the Bourbons, into exile. Soon Commodore, perhaps, I will be dancing again on another Vesuvius, our Popocatépetl, ha-ha—but come in with me . . . It's starting to get cold and I can detect a delicious fragrance, can you smell it? The chocolate should be served soon . . . My doctor forbids it, but a little bit once in a while, nice and foamy, I say . . . And you Commodore, cheer up! Like I tell my beloved Empress, *cheer up. Let's be optimistic.* Your new Virginia will come to be, and the same with my Ciudad Carlota. You have my word! And our national navy too! I know about these things. With Tegetthoff, as you know, I modernized the Austrian fleet. We bought the steamship that we named *Radetzky* in honor of our hero at Piedmont from the English, and we built the *Kaiser*, and the *Don Juan de Austria*, and we fitted the *Novara* as a battleship. And I don't know anything about cotton, but we will make Mexico a large producer of cotton . . . of cattle too, of course. How is it possible that in England, not a cotton-growing nation, you can buy it cheaper than in this country, where it's actually produced? Five pence for a yard of cotton cloth in London and thirteen in Mexico. Tell me how? And once all the vanilla consumed in France came from Mexico; now the Isle of Reunion supplies a large part . . . But nothing can be done, Commodore, if like Charles Lemprière says in his book, every new cabinet repudiates the previous one's commitments, no matter how sacred. Mexico needs political continuity, and the Empire . . . will provide it. Yes sir!"

The Emperor extended his right arm and turned slowly on his heels as if he wanted to encompass the whole valley and what it held. The brooks, the immemorial ahuehuetes, the great shiny lakes; to the east the Sierra Nevada with Gog and Magog, Tecámac and Monte Tláloc; to the west, Las Cruces Heights and Monte Alto; to the northeast Lake Texcoco from whose surface foamy eddies would sometimes rise, while dust devils turned on its shores. The Emperor seemed as though he wanted to include the blue and transparent sky—in which, on dark and moonless nights, Sirius, Castor and Pollux, the Heart of Leo and Antares and a million other stars, would all shine as in no other part of the world.

"And in this valley, in the glorious valley of Anáhuac, we will grow a bluer grass than the bluest grass of Kentucky!"

Then he rested his hand on the Commodore's shoulder.

"Come, let's go drink some chocolate . . . I was telling you of my experiences in Brazil. It was there that I saw a Negro with elephantiasis: they get horrible skin diseases, you know. But there were compensations! The flora and fauna of Matto Virgem fascinated me. The iridescent humming birds, the darkness of the Amazon waters, the blackberry bushes with their prodigious foliage. Among other things, I took some very rare specimens to Schönbrunn. I also saw half-caste children there, Commodore, who brought to mind Corinthian metal: a mixture of copper, gold, and bronze. But it was in San Vicente, on the Windward Isles, where I had my first impression of Negro women being like beetles. It was truly *shocking* seeing those black slaves in the middle of the jungle wearing livery and frockcoats of red velvet embroidered in gold, and those black women in European dresses . . . They wore lace mantillas and crinolines and carried parasols; they combed their hair *à la Bordeaux* and went barefoot . . . *barefoot*! *À propos* of Negroes: Captain Blanchot was telling me that when Bazaine was coming to Mexico aboard the *Saint Louis* with the 95th Regiment they stopped at Saint-Pierre where he and his officers were offered a delicious banquet of Crèole and French cuisine and for desert they were served *une crème à la vanille*, a vanilla crème that, according to what their hosts told them, was made *avec du lait de négresse*: from a black woman's milk. And the captain would tell me laughing: *et pourtant elle était blanche!* And nonetheless, the cream was white!"

XIII
BOUCHOUT CASTLE
1927

Yes, Maximilian, it was a lie, it was the lies that brought us down. Max, here in my bedroom at Bouchout I have a chest full of lies that the messenger brought me. And some lies are so innocuous that they're like the dove in Concha Méndez's song, "La Paloma." Like doves, lies fly out when I raise the lid, and when I try to catch them by their wingtips they turn to ashes, just like Papa Leopold's letter. Some lies are salty and sparkling, Maximilian, like the seawaters that took the *Novara* toward the Mexican coast. Others are pious, like the Mexican Indians who dress as *hulanos* every feast of St. John, and, on Good Friday, as Herod, Pontius Pilate, Jesus Christ and Mary Magdalene. Some of your lies I'll never forgive. Do you expect me to forget the night that we spent in Puebla and you became indignant because they'd made up a double bed for us? You demanded a cot in a separate room and you spent the night there, under a painting of a prison, while I was left alone, under a painting of a hospital. Remember that, Maximilian? Such treatment from a man who claimed to love me so much. And some lies come embedded in other lies, like those pomegranates from Teziutlán, those clusters of crystallized blood; others hide between the pages of books and dry out, they lose their scent and the color that they seduced us with once, like the myrtle leaves and the garlands made from bryonies that I was given in Ragusa. I keep those in my hope chest, between the pages of the album with the eleven thousand signatures from the people of Trieste who wished us, the former Viceroy and Vicereine of the Lombardo-Veneto Provinces, good fortune in Mexico. Those were lies as well. After all, how could the Triestines wish anything but failure to the representatives of the same Austrian oppressors who made the Italian patriot Confalonieri rot in prison for fifteen years? Our downfall was that we believed in their love and their kindness.

Other lies are like the bright ribbons that I use to braid my hair or to tie the bows that I loop on the handles of the most unlikely door: the one that opens out onto the great cavern they call the Throne Room in the Cacahuamilpa Caves, for instance, or the one that opens into the ballroom at the Grand Trianon where Marshal Bazaine was sentenced for treason; the one that leads to the Corinthian pilasters at Saint-Cloud, with its statues of Strength and Prudence. But all of that was a lie too—strength and prudence turned to dust under General Moltke's steel cannons. Poor Bazaine—although he deserved to die that way, really, dishonored and exiled, for all the harm he caused us in Mexico—was made the scapegoat of the war, to hide the shame brought about by Mac-Mahon, the Duke of Magenta, whose stupidity was the reason that France, my grandfather's birthplace, lost Alsace. And that throne, ah, that throne of iridescent crystals that gleamed in the darkness of the cave, that glimmered in the light of the torches, was covered in stalagmites as sharp as those bayonets that, at your execution, cut your buttocks to ribbons.

Sometimes I take the ribbons and I sew them by their tips to my *china poblana* skirts and I fly them like the kites I flew as a child in Windsor Park with my cousins Aumale and Chartres, after making butter and cream at Frogmore with our cousin Victoria's recipe. Or like I fly them—please don't tell anyone, it's a secret—every time I sneak away to Mexico to fly kites with Señora Sánchez Navarro in the Valley of Tenancingo.

Go on, Maximilian, take a ribbon by its tip and dance with me and sing. Confess all of your lies. Pin the heart of a swallow on your chest and say that you lied when you swore to Benito Juárez—after he sentenced you to death—that you would happily lose your life if your sacrifice could contribute to bringing peace and prosperity to your new homeland. Go on, Maximilian, pin the tongue of a lark to your forehead and shout to the world that you lied when you gave your sword to Escobedo and you told him that if he allowed you to leave Mexico you would swear on Your Honor never to return. Go on, kowtow, kneel down, crawl, be an obedient little boy again, and I will call you "The Light of the Castle," the morning star of Cuernavaca, and I'll give you lemon drops and belladonna. I'll lower your trousers and whip you with brightly colored ribbons. I'll whip your lacerated ass so that you'll never lie again, nor believe the lies of others. Did you write in a letter to Dr. Jilek saying that in Mexico there was a healthy democracy, which didn't suffer from any of the same sick fantasies like the ones in Europe did? What a spanking you'll get for being such a liar! Brush your teeth with orpiment dust! Did you tell Baron de Pont that a Mexican had never worked so hard for his country as you did? Take *that* for being such a liar! Gargle with peyote and licorice! Didn't you write the Baron to assure him that if you were back at Miramare and they offered you the Mexican throne again you would accept it without a second thought? Take *that*, all of you, for being such liars! Give me your whip, Maximilian, give me your cock, and give me your sword. I'm going to whip all of the people of Chalco for being such liars and greeting us with carpets of flowers that spelled out: "Our Eternal Gratitude to Napoleon III." None of those words, those poppies, or those lilies was true. Lend me your saliva, Max, to spit in the yellow waters of the Río Grande. Give me a stick to beat the angels on the cathedral in Puebla because they lied and their stone wings weren't real. I'm going to beat your mother Sophie who swore that she would never marry Archduke Franz Karl, whom she called an imbecile because he was so slow, but went ahead and married him anyway, and with him conceived your brother and maybe you too, if you aren't, after all, the son of the King of Rome. Go on, Maximilian, lend me your teeth and wear Louis Napoleon's mask because, "Mustachoo," I'm going to skin you alive and bite off your stiff mustache with the King of the Universe's teeth. I'm going to make a rope from bacon slices to tie to your testicles and drag you by them under the Arc de Triomphe du Carrousel like a prize ox at a carnival. I'll drag you through the streets by your balls until you can't take anymore and you shout to the world that General Forey lied when he arrived in Veracruz and said that he wasn't waging war against the Mexican people but their government. And those poor little soldiers from Zacapoaxtla who died with their heads blown in by Forey's howitzers against the walls of Fort Misericordia de Puebla? Who were they if not Mexicans? Until you shout that you, "Mustachoo," you, Harlequin the Great, also lied when you said that France didn't wish to impose a government on Mexico that wasn't accepted by its people. And who were those soldiers who shot Maximilian in Querétaro but Mexicans? I'll drag you to the Council Chamber at the Tuileries so that you'll stand on the green velvet that drapes the oval table on which you signed the declaration of war against Kaiser Wilhelm I and his Prime Minister Otto Edward Leopold von Bismarck-Schönhausen, so that you will shout to all of France that you were lying when you said that you would only leave Fort Ham prison to go to the Tuileries or to your grave. You were lying because you ran off to England like Victor Hugo and my own grandfather, where Napoleon I himself wished he could have gone. Later you went to Chislehurst to die—not from bladder stones, but from the stones in your conscience.

Help me, Max, help me open the chest so that all the lies will escape like the misfortunes that darkened the world came out of Pandora's box, to see if I can find just one truth at the bottom. Only one. I want to know if it's true that I met my great-aunt, the Queen of Sardinia in the Turkish Hall at Palermo Palace, with its turquoise columns and opal chandeliers. If it's true that when we were married the servants at the Castle d'Eu gave us a Sèvres porcelain tea set that depicted the castles of the House of Orléans, a set that Louis Napoleon later stole. Beware, Maximilian, and don't drink the cinnamon tisane that Eugénie will give you in the cup with the Castle of Compiègne; be careful and don't wet your lips with the chamomile tisane that Madame Carette will offer you in the cup with the Castle of Neuilly. I'm warning you, Max, the thing about lies is that they don't seem like lies. There are lies as beautiful as my mother's face or Colonel López's eyes. There are sad lies and happy ones, like the story of Genevieve of Brabant that my brother Leopold told me so many times. And there are lies that resemble all the things I saw the other day: Limousin lacquers, rose-petal jam from Turkey, honey from Yucatán, Florentine cameos, leather cornucopias from Sudan, and many other things that I can hardly remember—tortoiseshell spoons from Romania, wax fruit from Mauritius, and the equestrian statue of Charles V, made of salt, at the Paris World's Fair.

Come, Maximilian, come and help me pry off the white violets you sent your mother from Corsica to place on your father's tomb and which have stuck to the bottom of my trunk. Help me shoo away the golden bees that are trying to drink the bitter honey that overflows the Eaglet's heart. There are lies like the spiny fish that the messenger brought me from the beaches of Mocambo. My doctors and my ladies-in-waiting would like to see me thread sequins and beads in its quills all day. Pull off one of the quills and skewer Colonel López's tongue, because he lied when he said that he had been to see Escobedo to win us some time to save your life. And plunge another into Eloin for having written you from Vienna that the Austrian people would have rather had you as their monarch than Franz Joseph. Stick pins into all of the people who told you at Miramare that you could form a Mexican government in exile such as the one my great-grandfather, the King of Two Sicilies, had created in Rome. Stick one into Hidalgo for telling Eugénie that the Mexican people belonged to the pure Latin race. Into Count Beust for having sent a telegram that said that your brother was ready to restore your place in the succession to rule the Austro-Hungarian Empire if you abdicated the Mexican throne. Into Baron Magnus because he promised you, in Querétaro, that he would put all the money you might need to bribe your guards at your disposal.

And that's not all. I have other things to show you: I kept this gold wire with diamond barbs that I commissioned from M. Fabergé for myself. I want you to tie my hands with it so that I can never write anyone letters from Mexico, ever again. Not my father Leopold, nor Countess d'Hulst, nor my brother the Duke of Flanders, nor my grandmother Marie Amélie, telling them that I'm happy, that our Mexican people worship us, that I don't know how to thank the good Lord for all that He has given us, and what a beautiful thing it would be to have a nation where all men are like Gutiérrez Estrada. And for you, Max, I have another present. Do you remember that afternoon in Miramare, in the Hall of Seagulls, when you had a map of Mexico laid out in front of you that you dotted with colored pushpins? A green one to mark the thick forests of Chiapas, with its *Lignum vitae* trees and mangroves? A blue pin in honor of the turquoise blue Gulf of California and its leaping dolphins? A silver pin to celebrate the silver mines in Guanajuato and the carvings that amazed the Spanish conquistadors in the Palace at Axayácatl? Today the messenger came dressed as Colonel Dupin and brought me the pins, Max, and he asked me to give them to you so that you can pierce your tongue, like your lies pierced it, every one of your lies, your white lies, your pink lies, your lies that were golden, like your dreams. Pierce your tongue for saying, as you did in Orizaba, that if the Mexican people decided to be a republic again, you would be the first to congratulate the president-elect. For having written that Austria was incurably ill from ennui and sadness, knowing that you were lying and that you would have preferred to be strolling in the Hofburg Volksgarten, listening to the joyous, crystalline peals of Johann Strauss's *Champagne Polka*, in Vienna's clean air, rather than in that horrible palace in Mexico City, tormented by the out-of-tune violins of those barefoot Indians, by their firecrackers and their rattles. Pierce your tongue, Max, because knowing that you were alone and forgotten, you whispered, behind a palace curtain, when you saw the French troops leaving Mexico, that you were free at last. And when you had been tried and sentenced, you said that you had never believed that you would be found guilty due to a situation that you had not created, when you knew that you were the only guilty party because there would have never been an Empire without you.

Pierce your tongue, Max, all the way down to your throat, with the black pin of one of your dirty lies for mocking Napoleon III, and marveling at the cynicism that he displayed when he told you at l'Orangerie, referring to the Crimean War, that perhaps it would have been better to slice Turkey up instead of coming to its aid, so that Austria could have annexed Albania and Herzegovina. You did this after you had written my father that Louis Napoleon's star had to fade, as with all of the lowly people of his class.

That's what you said about "Mustachoo," the greatest ruler of the century.

And for the Indian, Maximilian, for Benito Juárez, your assassin, who told a lie every time he opened his mouth—for saying to Princess Salm-Salm that he wouldn't let you live even if all of Europe's rulers begged him on their knees—we will save the hardest and sharpest stalagmite of all, the shiniest one from your throne made of salt and opal filigree and of aquamarine lace, yes, to drive into his chest. Because, if the Indian truly said that, it was because he had a circus Amazon, an arriviste, a fake princess on her knees in front of him, and not my cousin, the Queen of England. And because Princess Salm-Salm was an idiot. Why didn't she just offer herself to Juárez as she did to Colonel Palacios, who was so startled that he almost jumped out his window? Do you think that Juárez would have jumped off his presidential office balcony if Princess Salm-Salm had undressed in front of him? That swarthy Indian who, aside from his wife Margarita—whom he married in order to become a governor and minister, a president and hero—never succeeded in touching the sweet flesh of a white woman (save, perhaps, a prostitute's)? Do you think that he would have refused to touch the breasts of that Yankee princess? Do you think he would have been able to keep himself from pouncing on her as soon as she, Agnes Salm-Salm, showed him her garters and the lower ends of her thighs? And then, Magnus, along with Baron Lago and all the other European ministers who fled Querétaro, were not only cowards but imbeciles: they didn't know the Indian's price. My cousin Victoria should have offered him the Kohinoor diamond from the British crown, the one that she flaunted during one of her trips to Paris when she, the hypocrite, paid homage to Napoleon I, the greatest enemy that England ever had. But no, they could have dazzled the Indian with much less than that—perhaps with the emerald tiara that the city of Paris gave Eugénie when she married Louis Napoleon; or with the sapphires of the Duchess of Orléans, which they gave my great-great-aunt, Marie Antoinette; or with the tree, and its golden rose, that Pius VII sent Empress Caroline Augusta and that Sisi was going to take to Juárez. I would have taken it to him myself if they had told me, Maximilian, that they were going to kill you, but they kept it all from me and they locked me up in Miramare for months. I would have torn off the gold rose and would have undressed and lain on the divan in Juárez's office where Agnes Salm-Salm's lapdog snuggled. I would have put the rose between my legs and I would have told Juárez that if he kissed it with his dark lips, I would let him kiss the nest where the rose lay as well, along with its chestnut grass halo. Then it would have been he, the Indian, who would have begged on his knees. But they said nothing to me, Maximilian, and they all abandoned you. Sisi was only interested in wearing mud and mother-of-pearl powder masks to get rid of the wrinkles that she never lost or to wash her hair with cognac or egg yolks to bring back a shine that would never return. Your brother Franz Joseph, so busy with his mistress Katharina Schratt, didn't bother to cross the Atlantic to ask Juárez for mercy. Victor Emmanuel II of Italy couldn't forgive the fact that a ship named after you had sunk the *Re d'Italia* in the Battle of Lissa. Isabella II of Spain was busy amusing herself with Carlos Marfori. Alexander Nikolayevich was more preoccupied with collecting the prize he'd won at the Paris World's Fair for his thoroughbreds, and in recuperating from the shock when the Pole Berezowski shot him at Longchamp, than in your fate and that of your Empire. Because no one, Maximilian, not a single European monarch, not my brother Leopold, nor Luis I of Portugal, nor Kaiser Wilhelm I of Germany, not a single one of them, Maximilian, took it upon himself to go to Mexico to ask Juárez to spare your life, to flatter the Indian and inflate his pride, to addle him in his pettiness and ill will, in order to save your life. They all abandoned you. But if it gives you comfort, Maximilian; let me tell you that they are all dead. Your brother and mine and Victoria and Wilhelm all died of old age. Victor Emmanuel died at the Quirinal Palace as a gypsy had foretold, his face black from the ink that a barber used to tint his corpse's beard. Isabella of Spain not only died of old age but fat as a pig, a glutton and a harlot, and Luis of Portugal was assassinated in Cascaes. Alexander, who was found in the snow, mortally wounded by a bomb, died in the Winter Palace at St. Petersburg, his insides frozen. Only I remain alive.

And because I'm alive, and because I love you, I'll forgive all your lies if you promise me to be good and to respond truthfully to all my questions. Tell me, will your eyes ever see me again? Will your clear blue eyes see me, Maximilian, from the blue of the lake? Will my arms hold you, Maximilian, by the white balustrades of the Miramare balconies? Tell me, Max, do you remember when you caught the mumps and your grandmother gave you a cardboard fortress with lead soldiers and cap guns? Tell me, will your hands ever fire the toy cannons that will bring down the walls of Fort San Juan de Ulúa, so that they will crumble into the waters of Veracruz Bay to frighten the sharks and manta rays? Will you have the mumps again, Max, so that your brother Franz Joseph will send you secret letters written in his blood, with the tip of his sword? Oh, Maximilian, Maximilian of the ivory cradle under the stuffed lark. You planted violets, you raised crows. You planted ghosts, you raised a hail of bullets. Oh Maximilian, Maximilian of the lonely island of giraffes, and of the mumps, and of the cabin covered in wildcat skins and boa-constrictor drapes, Maximilian holding a pipe cured with apple peels and hyacinth tea. You planted dreams, you raised a coup de grâce. Oh, Maximilian, tell me, in the green silence of Venice, didn't sadness drink from the mossy mask of your lips? Under the bougainvilleas of Borda Gardens, didn't happiness drink from the blue butterflies of your eyes? On the beaches of Cartagena, didn't the wind speak to you from its ashes? Didn't the ashes have a son? Didn't the Alcázar in Toledo have a bird? When did the bird bleed to death on your sailor's breast? When did its beak pierce your neck? They kept it all from me, Maximilian. They've kept it from me for so long, the twenty-two thousand nights, Maximilian, that I have waited for you here in my dry lava bed I had sent from the Ajusco Lava Fields—in the dark, because I'm almost blind from the cataracts that won't let me see you as you were before, tall and blond, with the grand Order of the Golden Fleece hanging from your neck, and your winged beard that floated over the surface of the water when you swam in Chapultepec Lake. Do you remember, Max, those mornings so clear and newly washed with iris water, when I waved at you from the castle terrace, a letter from Papa Leopold in my hand? Do you remember when I came down to read it aloud to you from the banks of the lake? I went down the stairway that led to the chamber where my mother lay, and the ceiling was a dome embroidered with stars, and she, the Angel of Belgium, was very pale on her bed, three black swans from the Béguinage, with open wings, hanging from invisible, motionless threads. I came down, I fled, holding father's letter, and suddenly I realized that I was neither on the castle stairway nor at Laeken; that those stone steps on which a bluish-gray ivy crawled were the steps of the winding staircase to the round tower at Chichén Itzá. Later I found myself in the middle of a maze and I shouted for you but only the echo repeated your name, repeated it for an eternity, and I knew that I would only find the exit if I followed that red thread on the ground, but not the fresh blood that stained my cousin Minette's hobby horse, no, that other trail of warm blood that I left on the night we crossed the Tropic of Cancer on the yacht *Fantaisie* toward the Isle of Madeira. On a bed made out of planks, swept by sea foam, where the brooms and the bottles of port wine, your astrolabes and your compasses, the wind and the darkness of night, dancing around us, and you and I dancing too, nude, and that trail of blood, Maximilian, crosses the Isle of Lacroma, with its Mexican flags at half-mast and mourning garlands like black orchids. The imperial carriage that the people of Milan gave us and that was left behind in El Olvido drives by. It's overrun with mildew, honeysuckle has tangled in its wheels, and pheasants and quetzales with long, multicolored tails had made their nests in its interior. Ferns spill through its windows, and that thread, Maximilian, reaches your heart, as prickly as the porcupine quills the messenger brought me, or the star of coagulated blood that I have on my naked breast, wet with your kisses. Ah, Maximilian, Maximilian, child of the Florentine tiles of the Leopoldine wing at the Hofburg. Child of the soul scented by the Persian miniatures in the Million Room at Schönbrunn. Tell me, didn't the dust from the roads in Apam make you eat miracles? Little Maximilian, the child who slept on the Anáhuac Valley's silk thickets. Child of the loofah beard and the eyes of burnished oil— Emperor of Mexico, King of Xochimilco, Admiral of Lake Texcoco. Tell me, didn't you shed rainbow tears at dawn in Uruapan? The Blanco River, with its sweet and lovesick waters—didn't it kiss your thighs? Didn't Concepción Sedano's smile sprinkle down onto your face? Oh, Little Ferdinand, Master Maximilian, do you remember that one day you had the tails on your regiment horses trimmed English style? Do you remember when your brother chastised you for daring to defy the rules dating back to the time of Maria Theresa, who had commanded the tails to be long and braided? Tell me, will Franz Joseph never lock you up in your room again, under house arrest, so that in your loneliness the white studs of the Spanish Riding School—whose names you knew by heart—will buck and turn and twirl and trot at the speed of life in your imagination? Will you throw the memory of the time that he, the Emperor of Austria, cried in fear the first time he rode a pony, back in your brother's face, to his shame?

I kept going down the stairway, with Papa's letter still in my hand, and I realized that I had gone from our stairway to the winding steps that go up to the round tower at the castle at Chichén Itzá and that the stone sculpture of a reclining man with a bowl on his belly was the *Chac-Mool*, and that the animal with long fangs and a jade-encrusted body was the red jaguar, and I continued down the staircase and when I got to the bottom I knew that the gigantic circle of blue waters was a sacred well and not Lake Chapultepec. But I didn't see you, I only saw Blasio, who was carrying a large, white towel like a shroud, and who said something I couldn't hear, disappearing afterwards. I never saw him again because I was wrapped in a cloud of steam and the letter fell apart in my hands like ashes because it was the letter from a dead man, because my beloved father Leopold I of Belgium had written it a few days before his death, but I didn't get it until several weeks later, when I returned to Mexico City, my soul driven mad and poisoned with hemlock, from there, from Chichén Itzá, from the sacred pool. And I called to you, I told you screaming and sobbing that my poor father had suffered more than ten operations, that his feet had swollen monstrously, that on his last trip to England he could hardly speak with Victoria because he spent his time confined to bed at Buckingham Palace, writhing from the terrible pain of his gallstones, my poor father who sometimes had to sleep on his feet because of the pain, propped up by his armpits by mattresses nailed to two tables. I should have gone to Belgium to take care of him, to throw his mistress—that Eppinghoven woman, the only person he allowed to stay with him at his deathbed—out of his room; to shake him and wake him from his delirium and so be sure that, when he said Charlotte, Charlotte, my dear Charlotte, as he lay dying, he was referring to me, his little Charlotte, his Bijou, the Princess of Laeken, and not his first wife Charlotte of England, the daughter of the drunken, depraved George IV, whose name my mother gave me. I'll never forgive her for giving me the name of a dead woman whom my father loved his entire life.

It was then that I understood what Blasio had tried to tell me—that it was cold and that I should put on your towel. But I wasn't cold; the cloud of steam burned me, so I threw myself into the sacred well to cool off, and because I knew that you were at the bottom. First I lay on my back, floating on the water, very still, not even blinking. The sun above, at its zenith, and the blue sky, surrounded by the tall and dark walls of the well, reflected the trembling star of my orange skirt like a mirror, floating and twirling around me; the sea of liquid turquoise where I began to sink, almost inadvertently, as I used to sink into sleep when my mother read me some pages from *Fabiola*. I sank, very slowly, my eyes closed, like a sleeping bride wrapped in flames, down the long, deep well. When I opened my eyes I saw you lying next to me and I saw your face, so pale that it seemed made of plaster. But your hair and your beard were alive—they had turned to maggots. And your tongue was also alive—it was a purple fish tail. I devoured the worms, I swallowed the fish, because I wanted no one, Maximilian, not Dr. Licea nor Baron Lago nor Colonel Platón Sánchez nor Miguel López, to take locks from your hair home in lockets, nor pieces of your tongue in formaldehyde, as souvenirs of their evil deeds and their treason, of their cowardice and disloyalty. Because your heart was still alive too—in your rib cage a royal purple medusa was beating—and your penis was a luminous, slippery, burning eel between your legs, and your skin, Maximilian, the skin on your bones was like a blue, soft and trembling moss. So I undressed myself, to make love to you, although I knew they were watching us, that the Maya virgins who had been thrown down the well to conjure the rain gods were all watching us with their jet-black eye sockets.

But others were watching us too, Maximilian, and they are watching us with an awe too large for their empty eye sockets. If when they were alive and they fought for what they thought was their country, applauding your death, since you were a foreign usurper, once they were dead, they couldn't understand what it was that their own Mexican brothers had murdered them for. In the deep blue well, Maximilian, on an altar covered with marigolds and red *colorines*, were the skulls of those who were both the heroes and victims of a revolution that you never knew. Of a revolution that, like Saturn, devoured its own children. There, on that altar, I saw with my own eyes a skull covered with snakeskin, and another covered with puma hide, and yet another one covered with bullet cartridges; there I saw a skull covered with jade tiles, I saw the white, burnished skulls—radiating their own light as though they were lamps—of the Mexicans murdered in Mexico City, in Tlaxcalantongo, in Parral, in the Hacienda Chinameca. And they saw me.

But, I said, what does it matter if all of Mexico sees Mamá Carlota making love to Papá Maximiliano? Of course, I began to suffocate. I was choking, gasping for air, and even then I held my breath to keep making love to you and only when I began to feel what was at once pleasure and the greatest anguish of my life, and I could no longer bear it, I let the air out that was burning my lungs and my soul escaped through my mouth. Oh, Your Majesty Doña Carlota, we thought we had lost you. Was your windpipe blocked? Did vomit get into your lungs? Did you have a nightmare? asked my ladies-in-waiting, and I said yes, I had a nightmare. I was so tired of not being believed that I lied to them this once and didn't tell them that I'd just returned from a trip to Yucatán.

In any case, when those damned women least expect it, I like to hold my breath until I feel like I'll faint, until my face is purple, and then my ladies and my duchesses and my doctors are frightened, they think I'm suffering cardiac arrest, that I have emphysema, that I'm choking on my food, and they beg me to breathe, breathe Doña Carlota, for the love of God, they beg me, they command me, and they put a feather on my lips to see if it ruffles—bring a whistle, says Dr. Jilek, to see if she blows it—bring an oxygen tank because the Empress is suffocating, says the Count of the Valley of Orizaba—bring a soapy pipe to see if she blows bubbles, says Countess d'Hulst—quick, a tire pump, shouts Dr. Bilimek—and finally I couldn't hold it in anymore and I laughed. I burst out laughing because I imagined that they would blow me up like a balloon so I'd fly out the castle window and wave good-bye. And I flew through the clouds toward Mexico. But, no, no, if I ever return to Mexico with my belly about to burst it won't be because I'm pregnant from the wind or from you or Colonel Rodríguez but from tempests and hurricanes and whirlwinds so that the Mexicans will beat me with sticks as they do with their *piñatas*. And when I burst, Maximilian, all the misfortunes and tragedies that they deserve for being so ungrateful will shower down on them. And, as usual, tears follow laughter. With wet eyes I ask my caretakers why they want me to breathe so badly, why don't they just let me die? Why and for whom do I live like this, blind and crazy, old and alone, if the King of the Universe will never be back to see me, to touch and kiss me? They ask, but Doña Carlota, will Don Maximiliano be here for lunch? Will he drink from your hands, Doña Carlota, the clear waters of the wells of Yucatán, or the white poison of the rattlesnake? Will the Emperor be here to eat your *huevos rancheros* with Commodore Maury, on the terrace at Miravalle? Won't Don Maximiliano share a pitcher of hot chocolate with you? Will the Archduke be young again, to travel through the Habsburg Empire? Will the young women from Steiermark offer him a green felt hat? Will there be an edelweiss wreath and an eagle feather on the hat? Tell us, Doña Carlota, will Don Maximiliano be Emperor again? And General Oxholm, will he travel again from Denmark to Mexico to bring Maximilian the Cross of the Order of the Elephant? Will the Emperor display the golden elephant on a field of blue lacquer on his breast? And if the elephant is thirsty, will he raise his trunk to drink the sky? And when the elephant turns blue with happiness, will Princess Salm-Salm and the Papal Nuncio turn green with envy?

•

But more than your lies, my lies, and those of the others, more than the daily lies, Maximilian, what's killing me is the greatest lie of all, which is life, which is the world; the lie they never talk about, that no one mentions, because it deceives us all. When I told my doctors, for example, that yes, I had indeed had a nightmare, and had dreamed that I was drowning, they were very happy. That's the way it's been all these years. Every time I've answered one of their questions in a way they expect—when I say yes, I do dream, I hallucinate, I imagine things; or when I answer their questions as to my name, my age, the date of your death, Max—they look pleased, they smile, and later, they whisper in the hallways and in corners: The Empress is lucid today. May God keep her that way until the end of her life. What worries me, what I think could really drive me mad, is the temptation to try and understand all the delusions and the deceit from which they all suffer. And I become bored and tired of playing along and giving everything the names that they expect me to give them. "Who am I, Your Majesty?" Dr. Jilek asked one day. "Dr. Jilek," I replied. "And that over there, what is it?" he asked, pointing toward the mountains. "The mountains," I answered. "And this, Your Majesty?" he asked and he pointed at an embroidered image of the yacht *Fantaisie* that I cross-stitched about twenty years ago, and I answered, "It's a needlework replica of the yacht *Fantaisie* that I did a long time ago." That's when they say that I'm lucid—and they run, they fly to tell Leopold and Marie Henriette and my nephew Albert. Sometimes I almost feel pity on them, my poor doctors, and my pathetic ladies-in-waiting. And I say *almost* because the hate I feel for them prevents me from pitying their blindness. Perhaps it's not really hate, just scorn, because they understand nothing. Do you know where we are, Dr. Jilek? I asked him one day, like, one Sunday morning, I remember it very well, when Albert came to visit me, I asked him, Do you know who I am? We are in Bouchout Castle, Your Majesty, answered Jilek—You are my aunt Charlotte, Albert answered. No, I said, we are not in Bouchout, we are in Mexico, and I'm not your aunt Charlotte—I'm a miracle. And that's when—can you imagine?—they say that I'm mad. But didn't they—my brothers, my parents, my teachers—teach me again and again that I must believe in miracles? Didn't they speak to me throughout my childhood about the resurrection of Lazarus and of Our Lord Jesus Christ? Didn't Countess Mérode Westerloo tell me about how Saint Joseph's spikenard twig bloomed? Didn't Philippe promise to take me to the Cathedral at Köln one day to show me one of the goblets from the wedding at Cana that held the wine Jesus Christ had changed from water as his first miracle? Didn't my Vice Governor Louise de Montanclos talk about how Christ's own blood turned to wine? Didn't Cardinal Deschamps tell me to remember that the Holy Virgin's immaculate body had ascended from the earth to heaven intact? Didn't they take me, at St. Gudula, to see the miraculous communion hosts that have bled for centuries, after being cut by three Jews who then died, burned at the stake? Didn't Philippe promise to show me at St. Basil's in Bruges the grail with the drops of Christ's blood that evaporate every Good Friday? And now that they have a miracle before them, now that for the first time in their life they are able to stand in the presence of an actual miracle, Maximilian, they don't recognize it, they don't understand it, they don't see it. The only one for whom I felt some tenderness was Albert. When he was five I asked him the same question: Tell me who I am. And when I replied, no I'm not your aunt, I'm a miracle, he knew what I was saying. His eyes became bright, and he swore that he would keep the secret, but now that he thinks he's so important, now that he's a king, he's forgotten everything and become a cretin like the rest. Did you know, Maximilian, that after Albert flooded the Yser Valley to stop the German troops, it became an isolated territory of less than twenty square miles? And when they told him that it would be better to leave the country, do you know who Albert held up as an example? None other than a ruler who never left his own nation under similar circumstances—Benito Juárez! Albert, Albert my nephew said it to shame my family and me. Albert I of Belgium. But I was saying, now that they can all see a real miracle for the first time, they don't recognize it. It's not because they're playing dumb out of pure envy, because they'd like to gather all the days of their lives into one moment, as I'm doing now. Yesterday, for example, when we had the Spanish class at Miramare, tell me, how could we explain to our teacher his pupil wasn't just a young woman of twenty-three but also a middle-aged matron of forty, and an old woman of eighty-six? How could we make him understand that beneath that porcelain skin, under that beautiful face, rinsed in cologne and the millefleur perfume that made Colonel Van der Smissen fall in love, and that Gabrielle d'Estrées, Enrique of Navarre's paramour would have envied, there were ten or a hundred masks, each one less beautiful, much older, less fresh, more like parchment, until—well, he should see the one I wear today. How to explain to the Prince of Ligne, who's coming tomorrow to tell me the same story again—that I'm very rich, that we can continue to buy off the Congolese tribes with bottles of gin, and that England and Portugal have agreed to use the flag of the golden star on a blue field that Leopold invented, to fly it on both sides of the Congo River estuary—how to tell him not to be such a fool, that he's wasting his time, that he is speaking to a ghost, because sixty years will have to pass before I can be here with him; that underneath this octogenarian crone's face is lily-white skin of the Empress of Mexico, in Chapultepec. I'm there at one of my soirees and I'm talking to Lola Escandón, to Lola de Elguero and Pepita Bazaine. How can I tell him to wait a few minutes, that I'll be back, to be quiet, that I know everything he has to say about ivory and rubber, furs and diamonds, and that I want to hear nothing more about the Congolese, that I'm only interested in my Mexican Indians. How can I explain to our Spanish teacher—who, in any case, died so many years ago—how can I tell him that it does no good to talk about verb conjugations and tenses because I was never the Empress of Mexico, never Carlota Amelia, never the Queen of America, but only what I always am, have always been: an eternal present, without beginning or end—the living memory of a whole century frozen into one instant?

This is why, Maximilian, if they tell you that I'm lucid for hours, or even entire days—because they ask me the time and I tell them, because they ask me what day it is and I tell them the date, because I don't break mirrors and don't accuse anyone of wanting to poison me—don't pay any attention, don't believe them. It's only, as I was telling you, because I get tired. Only because I'm tired from coming down the stairs—but not the winding staircase that takes you to the round tower at Chichén Itzá, nor the wooden stairs at Laeken, nor the stairs at Chapultepec Castle, nor the stairs to the Sacred Well—no, the stairs that lead down to the castle where I live, the castle that is my head. I come down from a palace as big as the universe, with doors and windows that open out to all of history and all the world's landscapes. I come down and go out of my mouth and my ears, I look into my eyes, I pour myself out of the pores in my skin, only to realize that I'm locked up in a world that suffocates me, in a terrible, confining, incomprehensible reality that drives me mad.

And if they tell you that insanity has taken me over once again; that, gone mad with thirst, love, and light, I threw my breakfast at Dr. Jilek's face and told him that at night I was going to sneak out of the castle to drink from the fountains in the garden—don't believe that either. I'm not mad. Louisa, Frederick Wilhelm II's wife, who never slept at night because these glowing ghosts were always invading her bedroom—was mad. Caligula, who gave his horse Incitatus the title of consul—he was mad. Juana the Madwoman, who traveled with the corpse of her husband, Philip the Handsome, from the Carthusian monastery at Miraflores to the Cathedral of Granada, in hopes of finding a saint or a wizard to bring him back to life—she was insane. George III of England, who got confused and thought the Prussian ambassador was a tree—he was mad. Ludwig of Bavaria, who dined in Linderhof Castle with the ghosts of Marie Antoinette and Louis XVI seated at two empty chairs—he was mad. But I'm not mad. If I tell you that I've drunk from every fountain in the world, it's because I climbed onto the tritons of the Hofburg's Donaubrunnen Fountain to drink the waters of the Danube tributaries in a silver goblet crafted by Benvenuto Cellini—because I've filled the porcelain mug from which my great-grandmother, Marie Antoinette, drank her milk at Rambouillet with the icy water from the dragon cave that the Sun King had built at Versailles for his mistress, the Marquise of Montespan—because, whenever I want to, I go to Mexico and drink the water from the Tlaxpana, the Corpus Christi, or the Salto del Agua fountains in wooden gourds. The other day I went to Brussels to the fountain with the three nymphs whose breasts spurt out its water. I drank from each of their nipples. Then I went to the fountain with the child on it who's been urinating clear water for centuries, night and day. I put my lips on his tiny penis and I knew that the liquid that caressed my throat then wasn't the water from the Mosa, or the Sambre, or the Escalda, or any other Belgian river—it was the sweetest nectar of all, that comes from the rivers of milk and honey in Eden. And then I began to tremble, Maximilian, but not from the cold.

AN EMPEROR WITHOUT AN EMPIRE
1865–66

1. Court Chronicles

From the Protocol for the Honor Duties and Court Ceremonial, *Maximilian I of Mexico. Section Three.* Maundy Thursday.

23.
The prepared food shall be ready in the dining hall. As soon as the Emperor and Empress walk toward the table, the Ceremonial Stewards shall enter the dining hall, each followed by twelve men of the Palace Guard, who shall carry the first course on trays.
The First Ceremonial Steward shall tend the table of the elderly men and the Second Ceremonial Steward that of the elderly women.

After a very sad Maundy Thursday and Good Friday had come and gone, with the mourning, the Adoration of the Cross, and many Masses, matins, and vespers services, after Easter Saturday and Sunday, the members of the Court speculated as to whether Empress Carlota, whose profile more and more resembled that of her grandfather Louis Philippe, hadn't felt nauseated when she washed the twelve old ladies' feet. They wondered about what kind of an Easter egg Maximilian had given her (in France an Easter egg the size of a dove's could be stuffed with several rings and up to nineteen *louis d'or*, and one the size of a hen's could accommodate a two-thousand-peso necklace), and if the *Empire Daily* was right about the fact that potatoes from Galicia were more fertile and long-lasting, but that those from La Mancha were undoubtedly of higher quality—an opinion that Monsieur Bouleret, one of the palace chefs, was believed to share; and they wondered too how effective a product named Cupid's Secret, advertised in the same paper, was in removing unwanted hair, as Madame L. most surely wanted to know. Rumors spread that General Escobedo had captured a convoy of two hundred wagons carrying eleven million francs, and that a calendar decorated with ghosts and goblins had been published, and that a worried division general dressed in a dark-blue frockcoat with thick, braided epaulets had told Mr. Mangino y Larrea that, at a Mass in New York, thirty thousand Yankees had come out as Juárez supporters, and that an Easter egg the size of an ostrich's could hold as many as a million pesos' worth of diamonds.

24.
At this moment the Emperor shall hand his hat to the service aide-de-camp, and the Empress her scarf and her fan to the service lady-in-waiting.

25.
The service chamberlain shall take the dishes from the trays, and shall place them in the hands of the Grand Marshal of the Court, who shall pass them to the Emperor and to the Princes, who shall help him serve the table; the same procedure shall be followed when removing the dishes.

The somber black required for all these ceremonies definitely didn't suit the Empress well, since it made her look colder than usual, but after those days had passed, those days when the city was dead and the landaus, the berlines, and of course the Emperor's own phaeton were conspicuous by their absence, the palace parties and the Empress's Monday soirees—at which one could hear King Netzahualcoyotl's poems—were sure to return, and certainly Mariquita del Barrio's parties as well. At the latest of these, Concha Aguayo had looked radiant and Rosa Obregón seemed uglier and older than ever; Madame Sánchez Navarro resembled a virgin in a Murillo painting; there were colorful Venetian lamps, and others that gave off a dim light from sperm oil candles. "At the palace we shall again enjoy the delicious *quenelles* soup, and again hear the new habaneras: 'La Bella Elisa,' 'La Tardanza,' and, of course 'La Paloma,' the Empress's favorite." At Mariquita's party an interim *chargé d'affaires* from some obscure embassy announced that King Cotton had yielded to Goodfellow

Petroleum. Everyone had drunk the dry Madeira so favored by the Emperor, even though it was somewhat bitter, and the gossips said that the Empress would begin to fall asleep at the theater and that she would have to pinch herself to stay awake, but that, at any rate, she was very beautiful, and when the aforementioned *chargé d'affaires* chimed in that, sooner or later, Mexico would have to fall under the rule of the United States—"America must rule America," he added—Don Pedro Elguero and his namesake Don Pedro de Negrete called him an *agent provocateur*.

26.

The Empress's Grand Chamberlain and the service chamberlain shall take two dishes from the trays and shall present them to the First Lady-in-Waiting and the palace's service lady-in-waiting, who shall in turn place them in the hands of the Empress and the Princesses who shall assist her in serving the table; in the same way the plates shall be removed.

27.

The same order shall be followed with the other courses and the Ceremonial Stewards shall always fetch the dishes. There shall be three servings of four dishes each.

28.

After dinner, under the direction of the majordomo, the footmen shall enter to clear the tables.

"Well, she is not as beautiful as she is elegant," said Señora Arrigunaga, who was herself as beautiful as ever, referring to the Empress. She had heard Don Luis Robles Pezuela's compliments without blushing. "And not only does the dark clothing not flatter her but neither do all the diamonds; she does look good, however, wearing stones that highlight the color of her eyes, which are not blue as the poets have written, but brown, and very bright." "Would you like a glass of cherry cordial?" Señora R. whispered in the ear of her friend and confidante, the Marquise de K. "Lettuce soaps and arrow-root powder work miracles on delicate skin." "The Empress is aware of the problem with the color black, and that's why she did right in ordering the restoration of the other colors after the required—well, we now say *de rigueur*—mourning period following the death of her father Leopold, though some people say she did it to keep the little Prince Iturbide from being sad." "And the Emperor puts him on his lap when he rocks in his hammock at the Borda Gardens," said Lupe Cervantes. "Besides the news that Empress Eugénie is going to give Colombia a statue of Christopher Columbus for the city of Colón, the latest from Paris is that Gutiérrez Estrada denied the rumors that his son had criticized Maximilian, and that Napoleon III, besides being old and gouty, is very worried about the needle guns being developed by the Prussians, since they can fire three times faster than muzzle-loaded rifles." "Three times faster?" asked Concha Adalid, her mouth wide open.

29.
After the tables have been cleared, two ushers shall place a linen cloth over the feet of the twelve elderly men; another linen cloth shall be placed by two other ushers over the feet of the twelve elderly women, and under the linen their relatives shall take off each elderly person's right shoe.

30.
During this act, the First Almoner and the Chaplain Master of Ceremonies shall enter the room and position themselves near the Emperor.

31.
Two ushers shall have ready for the First Almoner and for the Empress's Grand Chamberlain the two washbowls and the water for the Maundy.

"And I'll never forget how funny, how ridiculous, I should say, Minister Lares looked the first time he danced a quadrille." "General Almonte's wife, *Die Frau Generalin*, as the Countess von Kollonitz dubbed her, had two left feet; she was so stupid and as usual so servile." "At any rate, feeding twelve old men and washing their feet, though they probably had them thoroughly cleansed beforehand and rinsed with eau de cologne and the most delicate of all tropical scents," noted Don Ignacio de la H., "is a chore that debases the royals and is only good for that smug Empress, so different from the Emperor." "He truly is handsome—*qu'il est beau, notre Max!*" "And what do we know about how to dance the quadrille here in Mexico? What do we know of the figures of the *Pastourelle*, the *Chassé-Croisé*, and the *Visites*?" "Oh, if only Mr. Johann Strauss could come to Mexico as *Ballmusik Direktor!*" "The really terrible thing, from what I've heard, is that the Empress now insists on putting these so-called typical Mexican dishes on the palace menus. I wonder if we shall live to see the day that turkey *mole* (God forbid!) will replace the giblets *à la Périgourdine*, and if we'll have *capirotada* instead of Berlin pudding or pulque instead of Johannesburg wines!" "I wouldn't say the Empress is arrogant—the other day she visited the orphanage and she kissed the little foundling girls. She put them on her lap and they showed her a chasuble they had embroidered in gold with their own hands." "In any case, truffle-stuffed turkeys are not as important as the latest news from Veracruz, because the packet-boat from Saint-Nazaire is bringing some sealed orders for Marshal Bazaine, and everyone's asking what these fabled orders might be about," said Doctor Carpena, interim First Almoner. It was a widely-known secret that Napoleon was ready to withdraw the French army from Mexico; there was even the rumor that Drouyn de Lhuys had written to Montholon requesting that he inform the American government that if it recognized, or at least respected, the Mexican Empire, the French would leave. Moreover, the Juaristas were ridiculing the French army, and rightly so, in a way. "It's not so easy," Commander Rudolph Günner claimed, "to conquer such a vast territory: the distance from Sonora to Yucatán is three and a half times that between Marseilles and Dunkirk . . ."

32.
At this time, the First Chaplain of the Court shall enter the Salon preceded by two other chaplains, all dressed in their vestments and accompanied by acolytes with candles and censers.

33.
The First Chaplain shall walk toward the altar erected for the occasion and shall chant the Gospel corresponding to this ceremony.

34.
The Emperor shall then take off his sword and hand it to the general aide-de-camp.

Lola Garmendia had planned a new post-Easter outing to Cacahuamilpa Caverns which, people say, are more beautiful than those at Antiparos and Fingal; Empress Carlota loved them, even more than the Mammoth Caves in Kentucky. "Foreigners are the ones who come here to show us the beauties of our own country," said Lola Elguero, whom everyone recognized for her musical talent. The Empress lost a shoe in the Chicle Passage, and baptized a rock formation Dante's Profile for its remarkable resemblance to the poet. The Court's artist, Herr Hoffman, did some beautiful sketches of the Salon of the Goat, the Fountain Gallery, and the Chinese Monolith. An assignment officer, also in a blue frockcoat with a plain, untrimmed collar, looked like he was going to say something, but changed his mind. The best-dressed women at Mariquita's party were, as always, the Countess del Valle, the Mier y Terán ladies, and the Lizardi woman, who looked gorgeous with a pearl tiara on her forehead that framed her face. "Though, if the French troops evacuated China, but left their navy there—"

35.

At the time the Chaplain pronounces the words "Cum accepisset linteum praesumpsit se," two chamber aides shall offer two aprons on silver salvers to the Grand Chamberlains who shall hand them to the Emperor and Empress who shall don them with the help of the Court's Grand Marshal and the First Lady-in-Waiting.

36.

Next, two other chamber aides shall offer two towels on silver salvers to the same persons who shall offer them to the Emperor and Empress.

37.

The chamber aides shall remain with their salvers near the Emperor and Empress in order to receive the towels and aprons as soon as the Maundy is over.

"—I don't see why they couldn't do the same in Mexico." "Yes, and I'm sure we'll all continue going to the theater, the opera, the zarzuelas—have you seen *La Isla de San Balandrán* yet?—and the bullfights in Atenco at the Plaza del Paseo Nuevo, but we're hardly going to fix anything in this country of idle and corrupt men just by amusing ourselves." "For my taste, the Emperor is not as handsome as people say, and even less so than I heard he was before all this began," said Señora M., a woman who'd recently married to a Belgian veterinarian. "Nothing will change as long as we continue to have only one street lamp in Alconedo Street, piles of trash everywhere, and open ditches filled with dirty water; even though it's true that they're constructing some paved avenues, they still haven't repaired the damage done to Belén Arcade from the earthquake two years ago, and this plan to build a trench around Mexico City to contain the floodwaters has been around since the viceroyalty." "Also, because he's bald, the Emperor has to part his hair at the nape and sweep it over his forehead." "Yes, but he's very tall," said Countess de Courcy, who sometimes accompanied the Empress to the sanctuary of Our Lady of Guadalupe, "as tall as the palace guards, who are so carefully chosen." "Why don't they just tell Carlota to drink the iron-rich water from the spring next to the sanctuary?" asked Señora Rodríguez de Esparza. "The Virgin has performed miracles for many barren women there, if I remember correctly." "In Vienna, public electricity was installed over twenty years ago in 1843." "Then you think the Empress really is barren?" "Nothing will change as long as thieves keep stealing everything out from under us—even our front doors, as was the case with a house on Relox Street—and as long as the palace guests help themselves to the silverware that Maximilian ordered from Christofle in Paris." "Is it true that the Emperor and the Empress haven't shared a bed since they arrived in Mexico?" "And most of all, nothing will ever change," said Señor Raygoza, "so long as all of us Mexicans don't unite under the flag of the Empire and make all the Juaristas and their followers disappear forever, along with men like General Vidaurri, who offered his military help to the Confederates in exchange for the presidency of what he wanted to call the Republic of Sierra Madre . . ."—"Could it be, as people say, that Maximilian is impotent?"—". . . and we start doing our own work, instead of bringing Chinese and Poles into the country, or Negroes from the Confederate States, as was suggested by Maury the oceanographer, whom, according to what I heard, the Emperor charged with reproducing the ambiance of Virginia in Mexico—or, I say, as long as we keep importing jacaranda wood pianos when we have so many jacarandas here." "Nothing will be accomplished," said a linguistics professor, a purist par excellence, "as long as we don't reaffirm our nationality with the correct use of the Spanish language and reject all these creeping Gallicisms, like *adieu*, *cachet*, *potpourri*, and *parvenu*, to name only a few." ". . . and when there's so much poverty here, it's nothing less than an outrage to spend so much money welcoming Angela Peralta back home so outlandishly, with over-decorated arches and gilt garlands of fruit, whether or not she's the only Mexican woman to ever sing at La Scala in Milan."

38.

When the First Chaplain utters the words "Coepit lavare pedes discipulorum," the Emperor shall kneel and wash and rinse the feet of the elderly men.

39.

The First Almoner shall pour the water, and the Chaplain Master of Ceremonies shall hold the washbasin.

40.

The Empress shall also kneel at the same time as the Emperor, her Grand Chamberlain shall pour the water, and a chamber aide shall hold the washbasin for her while she washes and rinses the feet of the elderly women.

". . . and another proof that the Empress is not arrogant is that, when she visited the *Colegio de la Enseñanza*, she showed true emotion as she accepted the canvas slippers for her and the Greek cap for the Emperor, both gifts embroidered by the students at the school." "Nothing will be accomplished in this country as long as Marshal Bazaine keeps spending so much time locked up in his Buenavista Palace, as he has been since he married that Pepita woman, that fraud of a marshal's wife, whose only ambition in life is to be introduced at the Tuileries; and if Bazaine leaves the palace, it's only on those rare early mornings when he can be seen on horseback, in a simple hussar's jacket and a white neck-guard under an insignia-free shako, undoubtedly remembering better days in Kabylia . . ."—"*Shako* is another Gallicism, though in reality it comes from the Hungarian *shakó*: why don't we say *morrión, adiós, distinción, olla podrida*?"—". . . and there's been no progress, either. I'm talking about a steadfast and visible progress, as long as—and I say this very, very privately, strictly between us . . ."—"Why don't we use *advenedizo* instead of *parvenu*?" ". . . as I was saying, as long as the Emperor pays more attention to subsidizing the farming of pearls, 'the most beautiful are for my dear Carla,' he has said—or silk worms, so that the Empress can wear her pearls on her silk dresses—than to running the country . . ." the wife of Don M. B. said. "And then when he does actually decide to do some governing, we're just as likely to get a harsh and much-needed edict like that of October 3rd, or else some nonsense about the creation of leech hatcheries, a waste of time." "And, did you hear? The other day a man swallowed several leeches and had horrible hemorrhages." "Still, let me tell you, the French have some Hispanicisms that would make your blood curdle—for instance, from the noun *novio*, fiancé, they've formed the verb *novioter* . . ." "And then the Emperor goes to Cuernavaca to hunt for butterflies—although, if I understand correctly, it's only one butterfly he seeks." "Then the Emperor isn't impotent?" "The one he *noviots*, that is, whom he courts, is a particular beautiful, black-eyed butterfly." "What? Are we going to have a Pompadour here in Mexico? A Diane de Poitiers?" interjected a beautiful young woman who, judging from the enormous décolleté that revealed the splendid turgescence of her white breasts almost in their entirety—and in spite of the yellow gap-teeth that not she but the Emperor always put on display, since his lips were always parted (another defect that betrayed his blue Habsburg blood)—would herself have liked, perhaps, to become another Du Barry.

41.

Having concluded Maundy, the Emperor and Empress shall take off their aprons in the same manner in which they put them on, and shall return the towels and the aprons to the persons who gave them to them, and who in turn shall return them to the chamber aides.

42.

The Emperor shall wash his hands at the foot of the platform, the service chamberlain shall pour the water for him, a chamber aide shall hold the washbasin, and the Court's Grand Marshal shall hand him the towel that another chamber aide shall hand the Marshal on a silver tray.

43.

The Empress shall also wash her hands at the foot of the platform; her service chamberlain shall pour the water for her, a chamber aide shall hold the washbasin, and the First Lady-in-Waiting shall hand her the towel that will be handed down from a silver tray by another chamber aide.

They spoke about the virtues of *anacahuite* pectoral syrup; about the scandal caused by Abbé Alleau, which shook up the entire Mexican upper class, when he mentioned that the Emperor had contracted a venereal disease in a Brazilian *bagnio*—this story being told by a brilliant English diplomat (who did not take it personally when someone pointed out that the professor seemed more offended by Anglicisms such as *meeting, lunch,* and *toast* than by Gallicisms like *homme du monde,* or *rastaquouerisme*); they talked about the designs and patterns of *La Mode Elégante* with which you could make fashions ranging from plush ties with black guipure lace to waistcoats with flexible whalebone and elastic ribbons for young ladies of twenty; about the Grand Ball at the Casino Español in honor of Saint Elizabeth and the *Te Deum* Mass in honor of Eugenia de Montijo's Saint's Day; about Chastreau's new French grammar; about the unbelievable insult "we suffered from Emperor Pedro I of Brazil when he made our Ambassador, Señor Escandón, wait almost a month to be received!"; of the equally unbelievable story that Monsieur Domenéch told about a Mexican anatomist and collector of skulls who had an Indian with an extraordinarily large head murdered in Yucatán so he could add the skull to his collection; about the steamship *Atalanta*, newly arrived in Veracruz from Le Havre with eleven cholera-infected people on board; about Don Joaquín de la Cantolla y Rico's Fencing Academy; about how terrible it was that the newsboys in the capital yelled out fake headlines in order to sell more papers, and likewise how awful it was that the female candy-vendors had taken to singing obscene songs in order to attract customers; about how the Emperor, conscious of the economic problems affecting the country, had disapproved of the excessive amounts being paid to the municipal police musicians, and had mandated cuts in the palace budget, with Carlota herself reducing the number of her ladies-in-waiting from twenty to fourteen, thus keeping a mere fraction of a proper entourage, if one took into account that the Queen of Spain had sixty. Also, the Emperor had forgotten all about his project to import fine horses to Mexico, since, after all, one could acquire a decent mount for oneself at the Hussar regiment's surplus horse sale that took place in the Main Square. With those horses, though, they say you have to check their mouths, since some have tumors on their lips, and they also say to watch out for overgrown hooves. As for today's prices, a Victoria wagon goes for eleven hundred pesos and it's eight hundred for a team of dapple-grays; a dark-chestnut pony costs fifty, and a ticket from Veracruz to New York up to one hundred and fifty gold pesos. Speaking of New York, fifteen thousand Mexican goat skins were auctioned off at ninety and ninety-five cents apiece. "Even more ridiculous," said the professor, "is what some people close to the Emperor and Empress do. For example, to keep from embarrassing them, these sycophants go out of their way to make the same errors in Spanish that our sovereigns do—so, after the first time Maximilian said *valso* instead of *vals* for waltz, everyone else started saying *valso* too, and since he said *dolce* for desert, it seems the whole palace says *dolce* now. They say: "Have you heard 'The Kiss,' a new *valso* for voice and piano? Have you tried the *dolce* made from milk that Empress Carlota likes so much?" "And, of course, they talk about how nowadays women use so much padding and so many artificial embellishments for their hair in Mexico, sporting single and double twists, braids and curls and wigs for hairdos *à l'Amazone . . .*" "No woman has any excuse for having a bad hairdo at the Empress's Monday soirees." "Carlota does speak better Spanish than Maximilian, since even as a little girl she had what they call *Sprachgefühl,* or linguistic intuition." "Besides, as another proof of her kindness, Carlota was seen quite affected by at the sight of those prisoners chained to one another, their feet in shackles, who early every morning were made to sweep and wash the streets of Mexico City: San Francisco, Capuchinas, La Perpetua, The Empress's Avenue." "And as though this weren't enough, some Frenchmen were so ignorant that they pronounced and spelled *pulque* as *pulgue, cangrejos* as *cancrejos,* and *chinches* as *tchinches,* to avoid saying *shinshes;* or they used double consonants that never occur in Spanish, as in *Coffre de Perote, Barranca Secca,* or *Passo del Norte* and—what's even worse—they spell the Empress's name as *Carlotta* even after she had it changed to the Spanish *Carlota,* with one *T,* which she did before ever leaving Miramare. But how nice it was that the Emperor has been so well compensated for these bad experiences with public festivals like the one held a few days ago to show him the project in the Plaza de Armas for the fountain with water jets that will crisscross in the shape of the imperial crown, or then the one with all the Mexican agaves, the finest of which has been dubbed *Agave Maximilanea* in his honor . . ."

44.
After drying their hands the Emperor and Empress shall return the towels to the persons from whom they had received them. These persons in turn shall return them to the respective chamber aides.

45.

The general aide-de-camp shall once again gird the Emperor with his sword.

46.

While the Emperor and the Empress wash their hands, the elderly men and women will have their shoes replaced by their relatives, and the ushers shall remove the linen cloth.

They spoke about all these things, they whispered, criticized, alluded, and ranted, and when the *chargé d'affaires* who had been called an *agent provocateur* had left, someone remarked that it made no difference whether Lincoln was alive or dead. Could something similar happen in Mexico? Would someone dare shoot Maximilian in the back at the National Theater in the middle of *La Traviata*? If the French were to leave and the imperial dynasty end, the Yankees would surely invade. They have their Butlers for Veracruz, their Sheridans for the Valley of Mexico, their Milroys for the inland cities, and meanwhile one hundred and one thousand pesos are being spent for the decoration of the Imperial Palace, and there are two thousand bottles of fine wines in the cellars, from Roederers to Fürst von Metternichs. "We should do as they do at the Court of Vienna: the girls go to dances wearing flowery percale and tarlatan dresses. They never part their hair in the middle," said Lola Garmendia. "Their mothers store their brocade dresses in camphor from one year to the next." "The United States will not rest until Mexican soil produces Connecticut walnuts." "General Leonardo Márquez, while a guest at the Palace of el-Woska in Alexandria, had his picture taken next to the tree that sheltered the Holy Family when they fled to Egypt." "My dear Marquise, I think I lived in Vienna long enough to be able to tell you that, even if we Mexicans are lazy, we don't come anywhere near the indolence of the Viennese, which is due, I believe, to the *Föhn*, the warm breeze that comes down from the Alps. This contradicts what Bazaine says when he complains about Mexican guerrillas being like wasps because 'they arrive, they sting, leave at the slightest reaction, and then return.'" They also talked about Albert Adler's lightning rod and about the new emulsified photography paper; they argued that rich Mexicans like Barrón, the president of Forbes Bank, as well as Béistegui and Escandón, should economize like the Emperor was, and that their women shouldn't be allowed to go to Europe to buy their jewels and gowns, especially now that fashions from the Champs Élysées were available in Mexico; and that there was no reason for Mexican seamstresses not to be able to reproduce petticoats in the Eugénie style along with the plunging necklines and bare arms that had so scandalized the Aztec capital at first; nor was there any reason—as a French industrialist told the Emperor's aide-de-camp, Bruno Aguilar, *sotto voce*—that one couldn't copy the *haute bicherie* of the Court of the Tuileries in Mexico as well. "The what?" asked Luisita Vértiz, but the industrialist wouldn't have dared to give a literal translation—"high-class whoredom"—in that company. All of this speculation was prompted by the installation of the new telegraph line between the capital and Cuernavaca; although it couldn't compare to the line between Siberia and Nicolajewski, it would at least allow the Emperor to send telegraphic love notes to Louise de Lavallière at Borda Gardens. "And what about the Empress?" "Oh, to criticize the Empress is a much more delicate matter—and to speak about her possible *affaires* with the handsome Colonel Feliciano Rodríguez, or with the commander of the Belgian volunteers, Colonel Van der Smissen," said Antonio Suárez Peredo, the grand chamberlain of the palace, who received a salary of 4,500 pesos, "it's not only a touchy subject, but possibly slanderous as well, since no one has any proof." "And what can you tell me about the Apache raids in Sonora, and about Delano's assertion that those lands are inaccessible, unusable, that there's no water there, and that the fabled silver there is nothing but a fairy tale, in spite of the Americans having invested millions of dollars in trying to conquer it . . ." And they went on to comment that not all Frenchmen, of course, were models of refinement: there was de Saligny, the drunkard, and then the Viscount de Gabriac, who was growing onions and turnips in the soil of the French Embassy in order to sell them at the market; and Bazaine, yes, the marshal, a man who himself had said, in alluding no doubt to his well-known indolence, that he was as much an Arab as he was French—well, he'd found his first wife out in an Algerian hovel, according to, I believe, Madame Magnam, and this was backed up by some of the other Frenchwomen like Madame de Rancy and Madame Blanchot, and then the American Sara York, all of whom took pride in their great refinement—and, to top it all off, some people were even saying that Marshal Bazaine, corrupt as he already was, had now received commissions from Los Precios de Francia, the most elegant and chic department store *de tout le Mexique.*

47.

Next the Emperor shall place around the necks of the elderly gentlemen purses with money that shall be handed to him by the Grand Marshal of the Court, who shall receive them from the Treasurer on a silver platter.

48.

At the same time, the Secretary of Administration shall present the First Lady-in-Waiting with a silver tray also holding purses with money with their cords arranged so that, as they are offered one by one to the Empress, she can place them around the necks of the elderly ladies.

49.

The aide-de-camp for serving shall hand the Emperor his hat, and the lady-in-waiting for serving shall hand the Empress her fan and scarf.

And finally someone asserted, and several people agreed, that even though you could equate justice *à la Française* with a smattering of injustice and repression, France was still the only hope for civilizing Mexico, with or without the help of the Church. "The Vatican should try to understand Mexican reality a little better." "The Emperor and Empress are very devout and the foot-washing ceremony on Maundy Thursday is only one of the many proofs of this," said the beautiful Lola Osio, somewhat overweight but still very pretty in her white grosgrain dress and Chambéry gauze petticoat of the same color and her tiny shoes, attending the party of Mariquita del Barrio. "I strongly believe that the only thing really needed in Mexico now is national unity, and that Maximilian really dedicate himself to his job, and take the bull by the horns," said Ciro Uraga, an orderly officer who liked to use bullfighting metaphors to silence the slanderers who were comparing Maximilian's reign to that of Joseph Bonaparte in Spain, claiming that—now as then—a free people would always strongly oppose any foreign oppression, presented with a monarch supported by nothing more than French bayonets. "That comparison is atrocious, since our Emperor has adopted Mexico as his new homeland and the Mexican people did in fact call upon him to take the throne, and will in the end support him; though it's true that Joseph Bonaparte made a mistake in not following Napoleon's advice to rule with an iron hand. Unfortunately, our Emperor is too soft, since the October 3 mandate—as draconian as it may have seemed—only served to have two rebel *chinaco* generals shot. Since then he's spared far too many Republican lives. But, thank heavens, the Emperor is not another Pepe Botella. Yes, he would do well to drink a bit less, since in my humble opinion he drinks a bit too much pulque, port, and Rhine wine, especially when he's in Cuernavaca. By the way, by no means will we ever have another Pompadour woman here, since I'm told the lady in question is the daughter—or is it the wife?—yes, the wife of a gardener." "A gardener?" an astonished young woman with round, white breasts and a diamond choker around her neck echoed, in her beautiful mezzo-contralto voice.

50.
At the conclusion of these ceremonies the Emperor and Empress shall come down from the platform and, accompanied by the Grand Entourage, shall return to their quarters, following the same protocol as when they entered.

"There were some French horses that began suffering from fatigue and other problems too, just as soon as they reached the high elevations, Your Majesty. We measured the rate of their breathing according to the number of palpitations on their flanks and their pulse by means of the glossofacial artery in the contour of the maxilla. Stick your tongue out, Your Majesty. A little more. Just like that. Undoubtedly for a doctor like myself who's only worked in Algeria and Indochina, it's a great opportunity to study the effects of the high elevation of Anáhuac on human and animal organisms. Say 'Aah!,' Your Majesty. Is your Majesty's uvula still numb? No? One more time, 'Aah!' Inhale, Your Majesty. Exhale, Your Majesty. That's good. Your Majesty can put your tongue back in now but please keep your mouth open. You still have several growths in the pharynx, and the roof of your mouth is somewhat irritated. That's why the horses born on the high plateaus are so hardy. Your Majesty can close His mouth. It's bad, the dust of Anáhuac, very bad, for the pharynx. Has Your Imperial Majesty seen those rotating columns of yellow dust, real whirlwinds, I would say, that rise up on the road between Chalco and Texcoco? A veterinarian colleague assures me that the only mules better than the French are the Arabian, and if there are better ones than those, they are the Mexican. Now we'll examine Your Majesty's chest. No, what Your Majesty calls white paste has nothing to do with the dust; it's a coating on the tongue. Please take your shirt off, Your Majesty. Among other things, your taste buds are not well lubricated. But I would definitely recommend that when Your Majesty rides a horse you avoid the dry flatlands with their sodium carbonate. How many bowel movements did your Majesty say he's had today? Six? Your Majesty isn't sure? Eight, perhaps? Let's say seven. Let's see, breathe in, Your Majesty. Breathe out, Your Majesty. That's right. Also, the reflection of the saline inflorescence of Lake Texcoco is hard on the eyes. Breathe in, Your Majesty—breathe out. But nature itself offers a cure. Did I ever prescribe mesquite-leaf juice for your conjunctivitis? Yes? Inhale. Exhale. Your bronchial tubes are a bit congested. People with bronchitis suffer more at high altitudes because they oxidize less than what they eat, which is likely to cause malnutrition. Let's look at Your Majesty's heart now. Take a deep breath. I'm going to prescribe ipecacuanha for your phlegm, but only in small doses, in order to facilitate expectoration. Inhale. Exhale. Once you've spit out the phlegm, I recommend that Your Majesty inhales and exhales several times to get rid of the nausea. Please, Your Majesty, cover your chest and bare your back. At any rate, any organopathic condition that hinders the regular exercising of the vital functions is more serious in Mexico City than at sea level. Inhale, Your Majesty. Exhale, Your Majesty. So, if Your Majesty has to vomit, don't let it worry you. Inhale. Exhale. The ipecacuanha stimulates the vomiting center of the brain, and has had good results in the case of chronic diarrhea when used as an emetic. Inhale, Your Majesty. Exhale, Your Majesty. Another example, Your Majesty, is that at high elevations such as Anáhuac's deaths due to pneumonia and pleurisy are frequent. That's it, very good. Your lungs, Your Majesty, seem to be in wonderful shape. Please, Your Majesty, cover your back and sit at the end of the table: I want to count Your Majesty's inhalations. Any fever? Has Your Imperial Majesty had any new fever attacks? No? In Africa I observed many varieties of larval fevers more difficult to diagnose than those found in the Valley of Mexico. Each region has its own peculiarities. Rest for a moment, Your Majesty, and tell me, any mucus? Has Your Majesty observed any mucus in your previous bouts of dysentery? In Cuernavaca? No. And in Orizaba? Not there either. For the time being I believe we can rule out lientery diarrhea: I didn't find any undigested foods in your last bowel movement, Your Majesty. Breathe easily, normally. Everything is different at high altitudes. Let's say, for instance, if we consider that the average surface of the body of an adult is seventeen thousand five hundred square centimeters, then on the Anáhuac Plateau, at an altitude of two thousand two hundred and forty meters, the atmospheric pressure is approximately thirteen thousand five hundred and eighty kilograms. Hold your breath for a few seconds, Your Majesty, and breathe again when I tell you. And in Paris, seventeen thousand nine hundred kilograms. Now, inhale, your Majesty. Exhale, Your Majesty. One. Some English doctors pretend that Mountain Diarrhea, inhale, Your Majesty, or Hill Diarrhea as they call it, exhale Your Majesty . . . Two . . . is a variety of malaria. Inhale, Your Majesty. Exhale. Three. The most curious thing is that Indians respond better to quinine . . . inhale, Your Majesty . . . than whites, or at any rate the bark of the *chicozapote* . . . exhale Your Majesty . . . Four . . . which, according to Jacquin, can be substituted for quinine entirely . . . exhale. At sea level, sixteen inhalations per minute are to be expected. Inhale, Your Majesty. Exhale, Your Majesty. Five. At the altitude of Anáhuac, twenty inhalations. Inhale, Your Majesty. Exhale, Your Majesty . . . Six. And this is because at high altitudes the air doesn't penetrate the air vesicles in the lungs in sufficient amounts . . . Seven . . . to fulfill the requirements for hematosis . . . Eight . . . in other words, the transformation of venous blood into arterial blood. Inhale, Your Majesty. Exhale. Nine. That's why blood at high altitudes is a bit thick and less consistent . . . Ten. Inhale, Your Majesty. That's also why emphysema is frequent in Anáhuac . . . exhale . . . due to the disruption of the equilibrium between inhalation—inhale, Your Majesty—and exhalation—exhale, Your Majesty. Twelve. As a result of this, lung hemorrhages . . . Thirteen . . . are rare, but it's not the same with lung clots. Fourteen. Those Mexican Indians have an incredible capacity, Your Majesty . . . Fifteen . . . several times a day . . . Sixteen . . . they climb Iztaccíhuatl and Popocatépetl and then walk down again carrying snow and sulfur. Seventeen. At those altitudes, as we're told by Sonneschmidt and the Glennie Brothers . . . Eighteen . . . people suffer acute pains in the knees . . . inhale Your Majesty . . . the eyelids swell . . . exhale Your Majesty . . . Nineteen . . . one more time: inhale . . . exhale. Twenty. Perfect: this is average for the Valley of Anáhuac, as I told you. Please lie down Your Majesty. Your lips turn blue and the face pales . . . we will now examine His Majesty's digestive system . . . there's foaming at the mouth . . . Please uncover your abdomen, Your Majesty . . . and the skin dries and becomes pulverulent. A captain of the 95th Infantry Regiment suffered a hemiplegia when he got to Fraile's Peak. About blood, Your Majesty. Has Your Majesty found any blood in His previous dysentery episodes? In Guanajuato? No? Your Majesty will forgive me if my hands are cold.

Fresh blood? Breathe naturally, Your Majesty. Digested blood? We can also discount the seasonal diarrhea that occurs during very hot seasons and is characterized by bilious fluids and is reddish and abundant. Inhale, Your Majesty. Exhale, Your Majesty. But Your Majesty must drink lots of water in order to avoid dehydration. Inhale, Your Majesty. Exhale. Not with meals, because the gastric juices are diluted. Inhale. Does it hurt here? No? Exhale. At any rate, better than the water from Santa Fe, which is oily . . . and here? I recommend the water from Chapultepec, which is light . . . it does hurt here? . . . A bit? . . . inhale . . . and has less calcium sulfate . . . exhale . . . and almost half the silica content. I also wanted to tell you not to go near the waters of Lake Texcoco when you ride a horse, because it's the repository of all the wastewater from the Viga Canal. That's right. Texcoco reminds me of the Pontine Region in the Roman countryside. Inhale Your Majesty. The Ancient Pontine Marshes. Exhale Your Majesty. It's true that there is no malaria in Anáhuac . . . can Your Majesty hear the percussion? . . . but sometimes mule drivers who come from the tropical zones bring it here. Does Your Majesty hear all right? It's what we call tympanitis: an inflammation of the inner ear. Your abdominal wall is distended and painful due to the accumulation of gases. No beans at all, Your Majesty. Inhale. Exhale. Do you expel gas through your mouth? Does Your Majesty belch often? Yes? We'll talk about pulque later, but you must drink it without champagne. Allow me to take the liberty of bending Your Majesty's right leg. Does it hurt there? No? Sometimes diarrhea becomes hemorrhagic at high altitudes and in that case lead acetate is recommended. Cough, Your Majesty. A bit more. Relax now. Any colic? Did Your Majesty say colic? Actually, I can hear the trajectory of the hypogastric colic Your Majesty is suffering from at this moment—it's climbing up the colon, accompanied by rumblings and flatulence. Gas problem, Your Majesty? Gas through the rectal tract? Very much? Yes? Forget about tamarind and watermelon drinks, Your Majesty, unless you want to suffer more diarrhea, and keep away from irritating foods like *mole*. Any urogenital disorders, Your Majesty? . . . according to Marquise Calderón de la Barca, a person needs to have a throat plated with tin in order to eat *mole*. If you're having trouble urinating, I recommend cold baths for the perineum. High altitudes must have other strange effects: I've never found . . . does it hurt here? . . . so many cases of leukorrhea, dysmenorrhea, and amenorrhea anywhere else . . . and here? . . . among women. Any discomfort in the groin area, Your Majesty? A woman's violent orgasm at high altitudes may cause congestion in the neck of the uterus . . . now Your Majesty must turn His back to me . . . and bring about a chronic condition . . . just like that, lying down . . . of fluxion. Forget about cocoa, Your Majesty. Now allow me to raise Your Majesty's gown up to the waist. For the same reason be so kind as to bend your knees until they touch your chest . . . spermatic waste is more debilitating in Anáhuac than at sea level. Your Majesty was telling me that in Taxco you were prescribed bismuth subnitrate for your diarrhea? It helps sometimes. Now Your Majesty will please allow me to examine your rectum. Inhale. Take a deep breath, Your Majesty, so that the examination is easier for you. The thing is that in Anáhuac the ladies are lazy. Inhale, Your Majesty. That's right. Exhale, Your Majesty. Slaves, I would say, to the *dolce far niente*. Inhale more air. More. Like the women in the Orient. The advantage of having diarrhea at high altitudes is that it has less of an impact on the liver . . . inhale, exhale, does it hurt here, Your Majesty? . . . than diarrhea in temperate or warm climates . . . and here? No? It hurts here. Inhale deeply, Your Majesty, and draw your knees closer to your chest. As for the pulque, as I was saying, if you drink it in moderate quantities . . . here? . . . it could be considered a tonic. There is no evidence of a tumor in Your Majesty's rectum. Inhale Your Majesty. Exhale. Neither did I find any trace of internal hemorrhoids. It only has seven liters of alcohol per hectoliter. Inhale. Exhale. Your Majesty's prostate appears to be good. Though some prepared pulques such as the strawberry one are particularly intoxicating. Inhale. Exhale. Does it hurt here? The usefulness of pulque is that it congests the intestines increasing their secretions. I am going to withdraw my finger from Your Majesty's rectum. Take a deep breath. Like that. Like thaaaat. Now we're going to apply an ointment to cleanse the area. Pulque also has an interesting amount of glucose: almost twenty-eight grams per liter, as well as gum and albumin. Your Majesty can now stretch your legs and pull down your gown. When I was in San Luis Potosí I had to organize daily walks with the city's chlorotic young women in order to overcome laziness. I'm going to wash my hands and meanwhile Your Majesty will please be kind enough to sit on the edge of the bed. I mentioned San Luis because they have good pulque there, but without a doubt the best is what comes from the so-called *maguey manso fino* from the plains of Apam. No, it's not necessary for Your Majesty to disrobe. Oh, and Your Majesty doesn't have to worry about rheumatoid arthritis: it's caused by heavy rains and almost always involves strictly temporary pain. Your Majesty will probably remember this piece of equipment, right? It's a pneumatometer. Ten months ago I took the liberty of measuring the capacity of your lungs with it. But as I was saying, there are some advantages to high plateaus. Your Majesty will please allow me to place one end of the pneumatometer in your mouth and you will hold your breath for a few moments. And one of those advantages is clear, clean skies, as brilliant as those in Anáhuac, whose blue frequently reaches the twenty-fourth degree in De Saussure's cianometer. Now Your Majesty will inhale through the nose. Inhale. And you will exhale through the mouth. Exhale. That's right. That's right. Through the nose. Through the mouth. And there's nothing to prove that at high altitudes there's any less oxygen being combined with the red corpuscles. Through your nose. Through your mouth. Who could ever say—for instance—that the inhabitants of the Himalayas, La Paz, or Tibet are nations of anemic people? Inhale through the nose, Your Majesty. Exhale through the mouth. But when a European isn't used to altitudes such as those in Tibet . . . through your nose, through your mouth . . . particular effects may arise. The autopsy of an infantryman of the first battalion in my division revealed crepitus of the lungs, serosity in the pericardium, inhale Your Majesty, exhale Your Majesty, a dark-red large intestine . . . through the nose, a lilac-colored spleen . . . through the mouth. Half a minute: almost three liters, very well. But those suffering from pulmonary tuberculosis, which here in Mexico is called Gallic Sickness and in France, the American Sickness, do much better and even find themselves cured at high altitudes. Inhale, Your Majesty . . . and another curious thing observed on the high plateaus . . . exhale . . . is that tears evaporate quicker, and the same with the aroma of flowers, which makes flowers seem less aromatic here. But besides the advantages I have already noted, Anáhuac and all of Mexico offer a marvelous variety of medicinal plants. The *pingüica* as a diuretic, Your Majesty, and the *tejocote* for the removal of obstructions in cases of dropsy are highly recommended. Inhale. Exhale. Even animals such as the *axolotl* or Mexican salamander, which we already have on display at the greenhouse in the Bois de Boulogne, are recommended for some liver inflammations. Through your nose. Through your mouth. The other day I was talking to Dr. Bilimek . . . through your nose . . . a man who knows so much about Mexican plants . . . through your mouth . . . he told me that the tea made from bougainvillea bracts is used as cough medicine . . . breathe like this, normally, don't move, Your Majesty, we already have four point nine liters . . . and that an infusion of Mexican sunflower leaves eases uterine contractions . . . through your nose . . . during childbirth . . . through your mouth.

Inhale. Exhale. Good, I shall now withdraw the pneumatometer from Your Majesty. If we compare today's reading of five point ninety-four to five point sixty-seven ten months ago, we find that for a person such as Your Majesty who has lived in Trieste, at sea level, for several years, your adaptation has been remarkable. As I've always said, horseback riding expands your chest and helps the blood circulate efficiently in the lungs, and no, I'm not going to ask Your Majesty to stop your daily dips in Chapultepec Lake; you should stop them only when suffering from laryngitis. Cold baths are only harmful to people with chest illnesses, those suffering from tuberculosis, laryngitis, or heart disease, and the elderly; and swimming is also very healthy. As I have well observed in Mexico and Africa, and Monsieur Dutrouleau has in Guadalupe, Guyana, and Senegal, mortality drops as practices of hygiene are developed and applied, and the best of them all is regular exercise. As far as dance is concerned, Your Majesty won't believe it, but I have come to the conclusion that habaneras, despite their slow rhythm, are quite enervating, at least for women.

Are you sure, your Imperial Majesty? If you feel you aren't done yet, Your Majesty, I will wait outside and you may recall me whenever you wish. Not necessary? Good. Then we shall examine Your Majesty's bowel movement. Yes, I think that we may also rule out a catarrhal diarrhea, which would be treated with doses of magnesium sulfate. Intestinal worms? Has your Majesty ever had intestinal worms? No? If we were to find lumbricoid ascarids, I wouldn't need to go to Japan, that is to say to the kuso flower, since in Mexico we have pulverized papaya seeds as a remedy. And now will Your Majesty please lie down with His back to me. If these enemas have proven effective after each bowel movement, there is no reason to stop using them. Yes, Your Majesty, as usual: some egg yolks dissolved in milk, kept lukewarm to keep them from cooking. Will Your Majesty please pull up your gown and bend your knees . . . a bit of starch, and some drops of laudanum. Of course one has to verify all these alleged therapeutic results . . . yes, that's it, Your Majesty . . . that are attributed to Mexican plants. You don't have to bend your knees so much now. I am going to insert the cannula. Inhale, Your Majesty. Deep. That's right, tha-at's right. To find out, for instance, whether it's true that the flower they call *yoloxóchitl* is a cure for sterility . . . now I'm going to start running the liquid through. Inhale, Your Majesty . . . or if an infusion of the "Virgin's mantle" (*Coleus blumei*) flowers . . . exhale . . . applied as a poultice, is useful against erysipelas. Has Your Majesty been drinking cinnamon wine as I recommended? Chocolate is out altogether. Hernán Cortés wrote an illustrious ancestor of Your Majesty's, Charles V, that one cup in the morning was enough to maintain the strength of a soldier for the whole day . . . inhale deeply, Your Majesty: it's only one liter and we already have a third . . . but that doesn't make it any less heavy a food for the stomach to digest. Relax, Your Majesty. Breathe deeply. More, still more. There is no doubt that each country has its peculiarities. In Mexico, for instance, there is no pellagra in spite of the fact that some writers have attributed it to corn. Perhaps it is because of the tortilla. Very well, very well. Control your intestines, Your Majesty: the powerful urge to have a bowel movement is natural. Inhale. Exhale. And I take this opportunity to recommend mouthwashes to Your Majesty with tincture of myrrh in order to strengthen His gums, and the use of fumigations to combat . . . inhale, exhale, we're almost done . . . the dryness of the throat caused by the dusty air of Anáhuac. And, I insist again, drink lots of water. Almost, almost done. Have water from the Río Prieto, which comes from the snows of Iztaccihuátl, brought to you . . . inhale, Your Majesty . . . and has a low salt level. And now Your Majesty, I'm going to take out the cannula. Inhale, Your Majesty, like this, like thiiis. And now I'm going to ask Your Majesty to contract your gluteal muscles and suppress the urge for a bowel movement, to allow the intestines to absorb the egg yolks and the laudanum to take effect. And if during Your Majesty's trips you are obliged to drink water with a high calcium carbonate content, and which can be recognized among other things by the fact that it doesn't cook vegetables well, nor dissolve soap, I recommend you add mineral salt. Does Your Majesty feel all right? And another effect of high altitude that we have had the opportunity to observe is that it affects the height of an individual. Did Your Majesty know that the Araucanians are taller than the Peruvians? Moreover, at the highest elevations in Peru the dryness of the air preserves and mummifies dead bodies . . ."

2. Seductions (I): "Not Even with a Thousand Hail Marys?"

"*Mea culpa*, it was my fault, Your Excellency, my very grave mistake. But I didn't leave the matter there. I asked her: Do you know the story of the Virgin of Zitácuaro? And she answered: The one that got bigger each time? And I said, exactly, when they were going to move her to a different church they lowered her from the altar and laid her on a table where the carpenter took her measurements to build the box she was going to be packed in, but when the box was built, negative: she didn't fit, the carpenter thought he must have made a mistake, and again, he took the measurements to make another box, and the same thing happened: the Virgin didn't fit, and they did the same thing over and over again until they realized that the Virgin kept growing as they transferred her from one box to the next, and they realized that she was trying to tell them she didn't want to be moved to a different temple, so they placed her on her altar again and that's where she is to this day, and, my child, that's what I think, and then she told me: But Father, I don't think the Virgin is all that tall, and I told her: Oh, it was when they put her back on her altar that she returned to her normal size, otherwise she wouldn't have fit into her original niche, but don't interrupt me my child, I was telling you, I said this to her, that we must accept the Lord and His mysterious designs as they are given to us and we should not try to understand them because, if you try to understand God, if you try to put Him into your mind, to close Him in there, well, He's always going to be bigger, do I make myself clear? And no matter how much you try to enlarge your brain to fit God in, He's always going to be a bit larger, do you understand? Our Lord and His intentions are to be placed on an altar, and contemplated from a distance—accept them as they are, let Him decide if Mexico should have a monarchy. I told her all these things and she answered that she wasn't too sure about that, and that she couldn't imagine how the glorious Morelia, that's what she said, or the heroic Zitácuaro could ever become monarchies, and I answered her, let's see, tell me why Morelia is so glorious. Because that's where Father Morelos was born Father, she replied. Morelos was a blasphemer, I told her. How can you say that Father, when Morelos was a priest? she asked me and I replied: Morelos was tried by the Court of the Holy Inquisition, in case you didn't know, and he died in disgrace. Now tell me, why is Zitácuaro heroic? Because Calleja burned it, she said. Because Santa Anna's men reduced it to ashes, she added, and I said, wrong, my child. Zitácuaro is a nest of heretics—and oh, I must have done something very wrong in my life—and oh, Your Excellency, now I've done something even worse, and I hope You will grant me absolution . . . But as I was telling you, I told her, surely I must have sinned many times, many many times, and that's why God has sent me to Michoacán to punish me. Yes, it's a punishment to be here listening to these blasphemies—that the Virgin is a Republican as you say, it goes in one ear, the ear that listens to your sins, but it doesn't come out the other. It comes out of my mouth, my child, my mouth, like a flame, oh my child, you will be damned. (Oh Your Excellency, I'm going to be damned.) And she argued: But Father, isn't it better to have a *chinaca* Virgin than one who betrays her homeland? And I said: My child, my child, stop your blaspheming. Heaven is the Virgin's home, and she's queen there, *Regina Coeli*. This land is a nest of heretics, and that is why—since I came here twenty years ago—my life has been a *Via Crucis* that began in Chucándiro and went through all of the towns in whose parishes I've served: Tzintzuntzán, Yurécuaro, Pátzcuaro, and thank God I'm a Basque, I told her. And she interrupted me again: but Father, she said, don't exaggerate. You can be a Republican and a Catholic at the same time, like me. That can never be, I said, it's a contradiction, and I was saying that if I weren't, if I weren't a Basque, I wouldn't have been able to pronounce my parishes' names. How's that, Father? she asked and I told her: I'm talking about all of those difficult names you have, like Tangacícuaro, Copándaro, Tarímbaro, Pajacuarán, Parangaracutiri . . . Parangaracutiri . . ."

"Mícuaro . . . Parangaracutirimícuaro."

"Mícuaro, yes Your Excellency, Mícuaro, yes my child, I told her, so I was telling You, thanks to being Basque, having being born in Guipúzcoa and named Belausteguigoitia. Belausteguiwhat? she asked. Goitia, I replied, but don't stray from your confession, my child, come, go on with what you were telling me because my ears can't believe what they're hearing. You were saying, I prompted her, that Colonel Dumaurier urinates on you? How is that? And, Your Excellency, she replied, Yes, he urinates between my legs. Between your legs, my child, and then? Then sometimes higher. Higher, where? Up to my breasts Father, he urinates on my breasts. And then? Nothing Father, because Colonel Dumaurier can't, he can't . . . And, Your Excellency, if I tell You all of this it's because I hope You will understand my situation so that You may grant me absolution, that's why I'm giving You all the details that she gave me, to be able to tell You everything without violating the secrecy of the confessional. I've ridden a mule through terrible rural royal highways, more than one hundred leagues from my diocese in Michoacán, hoping that You wouldn't recognize the sinner woman, even though I am the greatest sinner of all, yes, of all sinners, no one else. I am damned, Your Excellency. So please keep in mind that all the names I've mentioned to You are fake, beginning with Colonel Dumaurier's, yes, the man who couldn't get hard. Just like that, Your Excellency, she gave me all the details. The only thing he likes is for us to stand naked in a tub as he urinates on me—and when he does that he turns red, he starts to breathe heavily and moans, and when he's done, he orders me to get dressed and to leave. What was that, Your Excellency? Yes, yes, what You're telling me is exactly what I told her: Oh child, there is no salvation for you. But Father, she argued, if our own Jesus Christ forgave Mary Magdalene who had sinned so often. Yes, yes, Mary Magdalene sinned a lot, I answered her, but she sinned with the flesh. And I too, she argued—and I too, Your Excellency, I have also committed sins of the flesh. But you, my child, I said to her, you have committed sins of the flesh and of the soul. But not I, Excellency; I did not sin with my soul. Because if you had stopped at the sins of the flesh, I went on, I would absolve you—as I ask Your Excellency to absolve me. Give me whatever penance you wish, have me say ten *Credos*, twenty Our Fathers. It would do no good, I told her, absolutely no good. Fifty Hail Marys? she asked. Not even fifty Hail Marys, I replied. But why, Father? Why? Is it because of what I do with Colonel Dumaurier? she asked. Yes, because of what you do with Colonel Dumaurier, with Captain Desnois, and the other one, Lieutenant Galisomething, I replied. Gallifet, Father, she said. And then I asked her how it was that she could speak French so well, and she answered that she had been schooled at the Lyceum and is married to a Frenchie. Oh, a Frenchie, I said, you had not mentioned this to me, and if you hate the French so much, why did you marry one? Because my family ordered me to, Father, you know how those things are, she replied. Do you remember, Father? she asked—and do You remember, Your Excellency—those verses that say, *The fair one has arrived, how thrilled I am, oh my daughter, please give me a French son-in-law*? Well, my father sang that to me over and over again and didn't leave me alone until he got his way, until I gave him a French son-in-law. Your Excellency will understand my astonishment and indignation—then I said to her, moreover you're an adulteress, and she countered that Jesus Christ had said: "Let him who is without sin cast the first stone . . ." I said: Be quiet, no more blasphemy. Oh, Your Excellency, how was I supposed to know then, when I said to her, let's go back to what you do with Lieutenant Gallifet, which is also not his real name, Your Excellency. What I used to do, she said, because the lieutenant died six months ago in the hills at Copándaro. I remember saying, another victim of ungodly bullets, and she replied, no he died in an accident. His group found a cave where Melchor Ocampo or Father Morelos used to meditate, I don't know, and they went in carrying big pine torches and it turned out that the cave was full of crates of percussion caps, and the lieutenant brought his torch close to a crate that blew up in his face. Yes, yes Your Excellency, poor lieutenant, as You say, and as she said. The lieutenant was the only Frenchman she didn't hate, she assured me, because he was from Belgium and just a boy, she added. I believe this is why he liked sucking on my breast so much. I asked her, the *only* Frenchman? So you don't love your husband? She said: No, Father he stinks. Listen to this, Your Excellency. I'm so clean I bathe every day, she said. I told her, you worry about the cleanliness of your body, but what about your soul? Oh I feel so dirty, Your Excellency. One thing doesn't contradict the other, she argued, because what I do, I do with a clean conscience. You must be crazy, I said. No, I'm in my right mind, she replied, and bad odors offend me. Frenchmen smell almost as much as Spaniards. But, oh, forgive me Father, I forgot you are a Spaniard. Me? How is it that you speak Spanish like a Spaniard? she asked. So that I can communicate with all of you, I replied. My native language is *Euskara*, Basque, as I already told you. I'm Basque on all sides of my ancestry: Belausteguigoitia Amorrortu on my father's side, and on my mother's, Lamateguigoerría-Azpilicueta and Lazárragaguebara, I said. Guebara my child, Guebara. Lazárragaguebara, Your Excellency, and then she asked me: A Basque, Father? Like *Tata* Vasco? And I answered: Oh my child, just to think that Michoacán had one of the best bishops my country sent to the New World and that all the seeds of faith and devotion that were planted here in this soil, by the illustrious Vasco de Quiroga, turned to ashes in the dirt because not only Zitácuaro, but the entire state of Michoacán, is a breeding ground for heretics . . . I ask forgiveness for saying so from Archbishops Munguía and Labastida who are also from Michoacán and are the exception to the rule— right, Your Excellency? You know what? I asked her, Do you know why there are so many volcanoes in Michoacán, so many fumaroles? And she answered: No, Father. Do you know why, Your Excellency? Because Michoacán is closer to the eternal flames—or am I wrong, Your Excellency? Because all those sulfurous holes are roads that go straight to hell. It might not be true, but it is certainly possible, Excellency. Oh, how frightening, she said, and then I told her: Let's get back to that captain or lieutenant or whatever, who uncovered your breasts, as you were telling me. Only one breast, Father, she clarified, and he used to sit on my lap and suck on it, and at the same time he rubbed his thing all over his clothes until he was soaking wet and then he would leave, and You can imagine, Your Excellency, how uncomfortable all those things made me feel—I didn't do them for my own pleasure. How was that? I asked her—the lieutenant would leave? Yes, in his wet trousers. Oh child, there's no salvation for you—is there any hope of salvation for me, Your Excellency? Grant me absolution, Father, I beg you, for the love of God. It's no use my child, I answered her. It's no use. Give me a big penance Father, she begged. You too, Your Excellency, give me a big penance. Have me do whatever you want, to crawl on my knees from my house to the cathedral, or to say thirty Our Fathers and one hundred Hail Marys, she insisted—or two hundred, if you wish, Your Excellency. I told her she could not be saved with one hundred Hail Marys or even two hundred. And when she said that when she was with Lieutenant Gallifet she felt it was like playing with dolls, like breast-feeding a baby, I told her: You don't want to understand. I've told you many times that it's not the carnal sins—oh, the flesh is weak, Excellency—but the spiritual ones that will damn you. You are a heretic, an ally of the forces of evil, a spy for the Juárez camp, for the Reds. Father, don't say that, she replied. It scares me and gives me goose bumps. By then I too had goose bumps, Excellency. You should fear God and his wrath for selling your body, I reprimanded her, but you're lucky, my child, because God's wrath is slow, like His mercy. But I don't sell my body, Father, she argued, because I don't ask men for money or gifts. They give you even more in exchange for your favors, I said to her, something priceless: honor. Father, they're the enemy. My child, the true enemy is Benito Juárez. Does Your Excellency not agree? Juárez is the Antichrist. But some say, she argued, that President Benito Juárez is a Catholic. Oh my child, may the heavens spare us from Catholics such as he. Just like there are priests who are Republicans, she added. You haven't seen what's under their cassocks, I said. What do you mean Father, she asked. If you were to look under their cassocks, you would see a devil's tail—is that not true, Your Excellency? And then I asked her: Where did you do it with Lieutenant Gallifet, and where do you do all the other things? And she replied, sometimes at the barracks' canteen when no one can see us, sometimes in a hotel. Do you know the Gate to Matamoros? There too. Once at dawn in the bullring, Father. Do you know Las Jacarandas Avenue? At the Chicácuaro checkpoint, and once at the Cahuaro Ravine—and I told her, my child, *cahuaro* means 'ravine' in Tarascan. So it's as though you were saying the Ravine Ravine—as in the case of the ineptly-named Tepacua Plain, which means the Plain Plain, since Tepacua means plain in Tarascan. Is that all, where else? I asked. In a church as well? Never in a church, never, God forbid. So I said: At least you don't do it there—oh, Your Excellency, how was I to know at the time. And where else? I asked her. Well, I also do it at my house. I asked her astounded, how can that be. She replied: My husband travels quite a bit. And you desecrate your bed, your conjugal bed where you have relations with your husband? And she said: No, Father, I never have relations with my husband. He's not interested and he has his own lady friends. If I have defiled my bed, I have also defiled the sofa and the billiards table, but Captain Dubois liked to do it outdoors and during the day, so he would take me under a *ziranda* tree. So you have also fornicated in broad daylight, I said. Not always under the sun, she replied. A huge storm came over us one time as we were doing it in the cornfields and I got home all drenched. Tell me, I asked, what did you do with that Captain Dubois?—this is also an alias, Your Excellency. And she answered: Captain Desnois likes to do something that I don't like. What's that? I pressed on. Oh, Father, I'm so ashamed to tell you. I'm also ashamed to tell *You*, Your Excellency. I think it's called sodomy, isn't it? I replied: You don't even know the name of what you're doing. Yes, it's sodomy. It *was* sodomy, Your Excellency and I asked her why Captain Desnois had to do it like that when nature has provided the proper route, and she said: I don't know, Father, the Captain told me he spent a long time around Arabs and that he got used to doing it like that; not with women, but with men, even billy goats and ostriches. Oh, my child, there's no salvation for you, I said. What was that, Your Excellency? Oh, yes, later she told me what she did with Captain Dubois, but first I said: If you say you don't like it like that, it means, I suppose, that you like doing it other ways, at least that's my understanding, and she answered, Father, what do you expect me to do? When Lieutenant Gallifet sucked my nipples sometimes I felt a throbbing between my legs and my thighs would get wet. And when Colonel Dumaurier urinated on her?— Your Excellency, I also asked her—When he urinates on you, how does it feel? Well, it's not that I like it, Father, she said, but imagine how cold I feel, standing naked in that tub, so when I feel the hot stream it warms me up, and when he aims it between my legs up close, well, it's not that it makes me feel good but I don't feel bad either. My child, I said, not even after three hundred Hail Marys. You ask how cider enters into this, Your Excellency? Well, I asked her the same thing: How does cider figure into all this, child. And she said that another colonel who had gone north, a so-called Dugason—also an alias—liked to pour cider between her legs, and it made me really cold, she said. You ask why he poured cider between her legs, Your Excellency? Well, to suck it off later, she said. Oh, Your Excellency, Your Excellency, have me do any penance You wish. Order me to say one hundred *Credos* or five hundred Hail Marys, Your Excellency. To suck it, you say, to suck it? Those Frenchmen are evil, I said to her. See? Now even you are saying it, she chided me, but I assured her that in any event, they are our only hope. Don't you agree, Your Excellency? And what do you say about the Zouaves? she asked me, and so, Your Excellency, I—who have more than once soiled the hem of my cassock with the feces of those animals—could only reply that they were drunks and pigs. They accuse us of trying to poison them, Father, she said, but the truth is that they don't even know how to eat. They stuff themselves with *chirimoyas* and pork rinds and guavas, all together, and of course then end up shitting from north to south. But it's very difficult, my child, to get used to this food. I almost gave up the ghost twenty years ago when I arrived at the parish of Tzitzipan . . . Tzitzipan . . ."

"Dacuri, Tzitzipandacuri . . ."

"Dacuri, yes, Your Excellency. Dacuri, yes, my child, I said. Tzitzipandacuri. I almost died, I was telling you, from gorging on pork tacos and the truth is that it took a long time for me to get used to all these chilies and spices, my child, I craved baby eels *a la donostiarra* and codfish *a la pil-pil* so very much. And did you like it, I asked, when that colonel slurped the cider off your body? Oh, Father, you make me blush, she answered. I blushed myself, Your Excellency, as you can see. The truth is, Father, sometimes I did and sometimes I didn't like it. How can that be? I asked. Well, you see Father, she answered, when I had my eyes wide open and I saw him do it, it made me really mad and disgusted, but if I shut my eyes and imagined that it was my lover who was doing it, well then yes, Father, I did like it. Her lover? Yes, her lover, Your Excellency. I asked her the same thing: Your lover? You have a lover besides your husband? Which one? Are you talking about that rebel to whom you pass on all the secrets the French tell you—that scoundrel? Yes, Father, the same, she said, but he's not a scoundrel. Oh, if you could see him, Father, on his dark chestnut horse and wearing his German hat with its silver headband, his black trousers with mother-of-pearl buttons, his deerskin boots and . . . Stop! That's enough! Enough, I said, I'm not interested in how your lover dresses! and then I thought to ask her: I suppose you're one of those *Barraganas*, those rebel-camp followers! And she answered, me, a *Barragana*, Father? Please, I don't even know how to ride a horse, and I've never so much as held a gun. Besides, there's only been one true *Barragana*, Doña Ignacia Reichy. I replied that she was not a *doña*, but a demon, so evil that, as you can see, as Your Excellency can see, she lost her only chance for God to forgive her when she put a bullet through her heart. God does not open the gates of heaven for those who take their own lives. And she went on, I'm neither a *Barragana* in the mountains nor in bed, and I asked her, just what do you mean by that? She explained that, although a *Barragana* is a woman, she is so masculine that she sleeps with women too, and I don't do that. I only did it once, with a general's wife—yes, Your Excellency—just imagine, that woman wanted me, but she fooled me, she promised to tell me so many secrets and in the end she didn't tell me anything, and since then I've learned that you just can't trust women. And then, Your Excellency, I asked, who are you? I've already told you Father, she said, that I'm married to a Frenchman. A soldier? No, Father, an importer of wines and exporter of leather goods. I am a society lady. When Carlota came . . . You mean the Empress, I corrected her, the Empress Carlota . . . Pardon me, Father, but I can't call her the Empress. As I was saying, when she came to Morelia with Maximilian she asked me to be one of the court ladies at the palace and I said no. Only a fool would throw away a chance like that! I replied. But please don't remind me of the Imperial Couple's stay, I said. To think that we arranged for so many hurrahs and serenades, and we hung so many marquees, streamers and tricolor banners from our balconies, and we carpeted the streets with sunflowers, and the Emperor Maximilian wore a red tie, a *chinaco* string tie, do You remember, Your Excellency? And then she said: That's nothing, they say that Maximilian is more *chinaco* inside than his outfit, and I answered: Sometimes I don't doubt it, my child. Look how he turned down our *Te Deum* Mass—do you remember, Your Excellency?—and having the band in the plaza arcades play that song 'Los cangrejos' was mockery, my child. Yes, Father, a mockery of that sanctimonious bunch of fakes. And I said: My child, I forbid you to say that about true Catholics. But I'm one too, Father, she said, I'm a true Catholic and I repent for my sins. But I've already told you, I answered, that you are damned and would not be saved, going on like this, even if I give you a penance of six hundred Hail Marys. Oh, Your Excellency, give them to me, order me to say six hundred Hail Marys, six hundred or more, as many as You wish, seven hundred. And she argued: Archduke Maximilian is Catholic and you see, now you're complaining about him too, and I replied: My child, the problem is that you don't understand anything. This is the lesser of two evils. Wouldn't you say, Your Excellency? If I were to choose sides between Juárez and his mercenaries, and the Emperor and the French soldiers, I would choose the Emperor and the Frenchies, as you and your people call them, correct, Your Excellency? First, I said, because Maximilian's adopted child, Agustín de Iturbide, will succeed him one day, and then we shall have a Mexican-born emperor; second, because the French are going to leave here someday; and third, because Juárez will never change, and Maximilian will change as soon as the French leave. Don't You agree, Your Excellency? You'll see. His only choice then will be to seek the Church's protection, don't You agree, Your Excellency? And then she said: I don't know, Father, but tell me. If I said to you that my true sins are of the flesh, if I told you that in reality I do this not to hear their secrets but because I enjoy it, and that's my only reason, would you absolve me? Oh, no, you won't trick me like that, child, I said, not at all. Besides, I can't absolve you . . . What's that, Your Excellency? What did she do with the General's wife? Well, I forgot to ask her, and as I was telling You and I told her, I cannot absolve you because you have caused many deaths. How's that? she asked me. After all, thanks to Captain Clinchant having alerted me to the Imperialists' plans to attack Tacámbaro, we were able to defeat them. If he hadn't, imagine how many *chinacos* would have died. I countered: What about those poor Belgian boys, shot right there in Tacámbaro—weren't they human beings too? And then she came back with: Well yes, the poor boys, but they came to Mexico to fight. We didn't go to their country to provoke them. Don't argue with me, child, I answered, you still don't understand that they have a sacred mission: to restore religion in Mexico. Is that not so, Your Excellency? As well as ecclesiastic jurisdiction, yes? But if Captain Estelle hadn't told me about General Bertier's orders to attack the Quinceo, she insisted, they would've caught *La Barragana* alive; if Lieutenant Marechal hadn't told me that Captain de la Hayrie and his African Zephyrs were going to ambush Nicolás Romero in Zirándaro—no, not Zirándaro, Angangueo, I think—they would've killed him there, she said, and if Captain Dubois hadn't told me about the ambush that they'd planned for General Arteaga on the road to Tinguindín, when they were carrying the poor man on a stretcher after an epilepsy attack, they would've killed him, they would've killed the General for sure. So, Your Excellency, I said: Well, you see, because you've accomplished nothing, child, because after all these things happened, they all died anyway: *La Barragana* by her own hand, and Romero, Salazar, and Arteaga were all executed. Oh, poor General Arteaga, she lamented, he wrote such a nice letter to his mother before dying, and just imagine, Father, she said, the sorrow of his poor sainted *madre*. And I said, look, his mother may have been a saint, but that Arteaga was a son of a . . . Don't make me swear. No, Your Excellency, I did not utter that word I had on the tip of my tongue. Arteaga was a devil, my child, nothing more, and one less devil on earth is nothing but one more devil in hell. Captain Marechal? Lieutenant Estelle? What did she do with them, Your Excellency? I asked her that, but I was as confused as You are. Estelle was the Captain and Marechal the Lieutenant, she told me, Your Excellency—but in any case, those were not their real names. And Father, it was funny, she said, that those two always came to me together. And I asked: What do you mean together? Yes, both at the same time, Father, that's how they liked it. Just imagine, Your Excellency; and of course I said: I suppose that they didn't reveal military secrets to you because I imagine that each one would worry that the other would report them, right? And she answered: No, they didn't tell me anything. I was that one who gave them bad information. Good Lord, child! I said. You are very clever, but so was Lucifer. Intelligence is not a virtue. Doesn't Your Excellency agree? So, then, tell me, did all three of you go to bed together? Yes, Father. What was it that they did, Your Excellency? I asked the same question, and she answered: Oh, do you truly want me to give you the details? And I answered: Yes. Unless you tell me everything, how can I absolve you? And she said: Then you are going to pardon me after all? And I answered: No my child, goodness gracious, not even with all the penance in the world, not even after you say all the Hail Marys in the world. Not after eight hundred? she asked. Not even nine hundred, I answered. In that case, I'm leaving. If you're not going to forgive me I have no reason to be here telling you all this. I'll be on my way, she said. No, she didn't go after all, Your Excellency, but I wish she had. I wish I were not here with You, telling You all this, being contrite. No, she did not go; I told her that first we were going to talk about what she was doing with the lieutenant and the captain. I'm very ashamed to tell you, she said—and I am even more ashamed to tell You, Your Excellency—the Captain lies down on his back and I kiss his thing, and the Lieutenant gets behind me . . . Like Captain Desnois? I asked, and she replied: No, not all are like Captain Desnois. The Lieutenant puts it in, like you said, in the place that nature provided. When they both finish, they trade places and I'm still in the middle, like a pickle. Goodness gracious, child, tell me—it occurred to me to ask—was Nicolás Romero your lover? And she answered: No, Father, my lover is still alive, but I would have really liked to be Romero's sweetheart. He was so handsome. I used to see him go down the street with his hundred Zaragoza lancers while people shouted, Long live the Desert Lion! And he would do a somersault on his galloping horse, and the truth is, Father, that I melted. He's another patriot, she added, assassinated by foreigners. Not assassinated, child, I said. He was executed. No one is assassinated here; they are executed after having a trial. And then she said, Your Excellency, that it is well known that as soon as a *chinaco's* court martial begins in Morelia, Zamora, or Zitácuaro, they start digging his grave. And I said: That's enough, child. A man who takes up arms knows the risks beforehand, and for every Arteaga, Salazar, or Romero that the French have executed, Juárez's troops have murdered ten or twenty men. But she persisted, Your Excellency. She said: Oh, no, Father, just think about all the liberals who were shot at the Mesón de las Ánimas and buried in the stables. And when General Pueblita was defeated in Zitácuaro, a great number of *chinaco* officers and even privates were shot at El Calvario. And without going any further, there's the Plaza de Mixcalco in Mexico City, where they shot Nicolás Romero. Father, she went on, two or three Republicans die every day. And, by the way, did You know—that's exactly what she said; and did You know, Your Excellency?—that Nicolás Romero needed a coup de grâce to finish him off, and even *then* he didn't die, because, when they took what they thought was his dead body to the graveyard in a coffin, he suddenly knocked the lid open with a single blow, but then, yes, he finally died from the effort? You didn't know that, Your Excellency? No, I didn't know that, child, I said to her, but in the final analysis, he did die and was buried, did he not? And she said yes. Because, I continued, the devil, my child, does indeed fit in a coffin. I assured her of this, Your Excellency, unaware of the fact that the devil had taken over my own body by then. For the devil can enter any human body, is that not so, Your Excellency? A man's or a woman's. And then she said, Father, you know who I am. Do I? I asked. Yes, I'm the daughter of Don Aniceto Huitziméngari. Don Aniceto Huitziméngari's daughter, my child? Though this is also an alias, Your Excellency. Oh, I said, then you must be the blonde Huitziméngari girl, the one married to Don Antonio Dupont, the Frenchman. Of course, of course I know who you are. I remember you—and then, Your Excellency—she said, Father, is it true that I'm very pretty? Then the devil spoke through my mouth—not I, Your Excellency—it was the devil who said, You are pretty, yes, like an angel. And she said: Father, there's something I can do for you if you absolve me—And Your Excellency, I told her not to tempt me—But how can I tempt you, Father, she said, if I'm on the other side of the confessional? And I said, Tempt, as in temptation, do not tempt me Satan. Then she said, Father, I can grant you my favors. As you know, I am well-versed in many things. While I, I said, I don't know anything at all. Do not tempt me, do not tempt me. But now I know those things too, Your Excellency. Do not tempt me, I said. I absolve you, but who will absolve me? The Bishop, Father, she said. His Excellency will absolve you. And I said, Oh, no my child, he will never, ever absolve me. Not even after you say a thousand Hail Marys? she asked me. And I was quiet for a while and she asked me again, not even after a thousand Hail Marys, Father? And then—Do You remember, Your Excellency, the bell that Don Vasco de Quiroga blessed with his own hands, the one that's famous for calming storms with its ringing?—I wanted to hear that bell inside me because the storm was inside my body, but I couldn't hear the bell for all the devil's shouting, and the beating of my heart, almost bursting from my chest, didn't let me, and that is why, Your Excellency, I am here, humbly kneeling before You, and on my knees I beg You to absolve me, give me a very heavy penance, whatever You wish, whatever You tell me, all the Hail Marys You can assign me, as many as You think I need, Your Excellency, a thousand if that's what it takes . . .

3. From the Correspondence—Incomplete—between Two Brothers

Mexico City, April 25, 1866

My dear brother Alphonse:

Your last letter was very late in arriving. I had been given many assignments that required me to travel all over Mexico, and, as I found out later, the letter followed in my tracks but didn't reach me until I returned to the capital, where it might as well have waited all those months. They finally stopped sending me to the front. My ankle fracture didn't heal well, so I have been named "*messenger deluxe*." I will probably limp a little for the rest of my life, but that will allow me to ask for my discharge, and then I'll be able to turn my attention to managing my father-in-law's greenhouses.

I never told you about him and María del Carmen, have I? Well, short of sending you a portrait of my wife at this time let me say that she is nineteen years old and a typical Creole beauty, or rather, a mestiza with black hair and eyes and skin the color called "*apiñonado*" here: the color of the husk of a pineapple. You won't believe this, but she belongs to a traditionally liberal family. However, there has been no Capulet and Montague kind of tragedy. My father-in-law is an elderly, moderate, quite personable man—and a widower—a cultivator of orchids who, on the one hand, doesn't like Juárez, and, on the other, has a great admiration for France. This is a paradox being shared by countless liberals—having been invaded by the troops of a nation whose culture and ideals they consider their own. It must have been more or less the same for the citizens of Argentina during the turn-of-the-century occupations, if indeed the Argentineans were already the great Anglophiles then as they're reputed to be now.

I am awed, even overcome, by the substance and erudition of your letters, and sometimes you almost convince me that this Mexican intervention is unjust. But no, the more I think about it, the more strongly I feel—along with our Emperor Louis Napoleon—that this nation can only escape, not just chaos but a dire U.S. influence (now that the Union has triumphed and is pointing its claws in our direction), with a monarchy, and a monarchy with a European prince on the throne. The problem is that we lack good methods, patience and, especially, competent men. Starting, alas, with Maximilian the Emperor himself, and the people with whom he surrounds himself.

Among the latter, Eloin and the lackey Schertzenlechner are, perhaps, those who have done the most damage—since they not only hated each other, they hated us, the French, as well, and they influenced the Emperor's attitude a great deal. Can you believe that Eloin succeeded in keeping Maximilian from visiting our troops at a single army camp or hospital? Of course there has been a parade of very capable men such as Bonnefond, Corta, and several others, who have all tried in vain to put the Mexican Empire's finances in order, but it's all been useless. No one has paid them any mind, and that includes Maximilian himself. Besides, when all is said and done, there's no money available, neither for the conquest of this incredibly vast country, nor for the court's extravagances. And now that Schertzenlechner has been kicked out, unceremoniously, another sinister personage has taken center stage—a certain Agustín Fischer, a German Protestant pastor converted to Catholicism, and an adventurer, a California gold prospector, and the father of several bastard children into the bargain, who has a terribly pernicious influence on Maximilian. He's promised to reach an agreement with the Vatican and it's said that he was one of the advisors who convinced the Emperor to "adopt" (I would call it to "abduct") Agustín de Iturbide's grandson. If you add to this all the growing animosity between Maximilian and Marshal Bazaine (who for months has done nothing but give himself up to the delights of his endless honeymoon), you'll have some idea of the Emperor's precarious situation.

No, I don't believe that Maximilian will be able to reach a truce with the Church, nor with the conservatives. I even doubt that he'll be able to achieve any kind of inner peace with his lot, since by this time he must know that he's not here by the will of the Mexican people—a condition he set for his appointment. Not only are the innumerable hamlets of this country populated by illiterate Indians, but the large cities are also possessed of an Indian majority, not to mention the urban beggars, and the "*léperos*"—the local version of the Italian *lazzaroni*—who couldn't tell the difference between a Republic and an Empire if their lives depended on it, and wouldn't be much interested even then. Another part of the population is what we could call the well-to-do, who, as long as they are left alone, will greet French troops and Emperors with the same triumphal arches and kisses that they'll present to the Juárez forces the next day. Finally we have the really rich—almost all of whom are entirely self-absorbed and quite as ignorant as the peasants. The Countess von Kollonitz told me the other day that some of Carlota's ladies-in-waiting thought that Maximilian was French and so they couldn't understand why he spoke German—and they asked her where Vienna was, in Prussia or in Austria? And the fact is, for such ladies, there are only three European capitals: Madrid, because their ancestors are Spaniards, at least in theory; Paris, from where they order their clothing, which will be brought five thousand miles by sea and then two hundred and fifty by donkey; and, finally, Rome, because that's where the Pope lives. Of course there are exceptions, but not many. One such is Señor Escandón, for example, with whom I shared a long journey from Veracruz to his hacienda. But there is something very ironic here—the more distinguished and learned a Mexican is, the less Mexican he is, and the less he cares about his country's future. Such people prefer to live like Europeans and want their children to be educated accordingly. Witness the Escandón family, returning from a vacation in Europe, accompanied by a governess and a valet from England, a

Spanish accountant, and a French tutor. By the way, the Escandóns invited me to spend two days in their hacienda, which, like many Mexican estates, is practically a feudal property, an almost self-contained little city lacking nothing, including a church and chapel, and even an orchestra that plays on Sundays. I can give you some figures that no doubt will be of interest to you: a "*peón de raya*," or permanent farm laborer (hardly less than a slave) earns 285 liters of maize and 30 piasters a year. Adult day-laborers earn one *real* and a half per workday and children earn one *real*. Add it up—one real is an eighth of a piaster. The piaster, or silver peso, is thirty-five centimes more than five francs. Another interesting thing about the Escandón Hacienda is that all the food and drink I was served during my stay were home-grown, and that includes the coffee, rum, and sugar.

If we ask ourselves, therefore, who were, who *are*, the Mexicans who manifested themselves as the pro-Empire "great majority," as we were led to believe, we come to the conclusion that they are only a few wealthy and ultraconservative families who want nothing more than to be living in Europe (or else who are already there), aligned with what is perhaps the most corrupt body of clergymen in the world.

By the way, during one of my stays in the Port of Veracruz, I had the opportunity of meeting the Papal Nuncio, Monsignor Meglia. A most disagreeable and inflexible man who brought an equally inflexible message from Pius IX to Mexico, and who landed here making an enormous spectacle of himself, dressed in his splendid green and violet garments, and surrounded by Negroes—slender Nubians in long white robes, carrying long rifles, some of these lent by the Ottoman Empire as a tribute from the crescent to the cross. I must confess that I felt a bit sorry for the Nuncio, since, he told me, he'd suffered much seasickness during the journey, aggravated by the stink that—I think I mentioned this in my first letter—comes from those enormous cockroaches we have here when they get crushed; but also, on the same ship, there were some Cubans who spit everywhere even though there was a sign in four languages asking that this not be done. Apparently, however, the Nuncio found consolation easily enough in a light but excellent claret, of which he gave me several bottles.

As for Maximilian—as I was saying—it's a pity to admit that he's not the kind of man destined to govern a nation, especially one like Mexico, which is almost ungovernable. Let's agree on something, however—the Archduke is by nature a good man. He's also a cultured person, a lover of the arts, of letters and of science, but to such a degree that—ignoring the terrible economic problems of his administration—he spends much of his time on grandiose or useless projects. It was the same from the beginning: the inauguration of the Court Theater, costing 400,000 francs; an excessively sumptuous ceremony to unveil a monument costing 60,000 francs to honor Father Morelos, a Mexican Independence hero; and, finally, projects to create an Academy of Letters and Sciences as worthy as the one in Paris, for an art gallery that would include portraits of all the Mexican rulers (some of these are actually quite exceptional, such as the ones of viceroys, painted by Miguel Cabrera, and a Zapotec-like Juárez, whose style is reminiscent of Luca Giordano), for the foundation of university chairs in classical languages, natural sciences, and philosophy, and the editing of countless amendments to the *Court Ceremonial*. All of this is what occupies the time of the Emperor of Mexico, a man who has alternating fits of passion for botany, archeology, or literature. Also for entomology. When he becomes bored with the little he does to govern, he retires to a villa he has in Cuernavaca to catch butterflies and lizards. In the meantime, Empress Carlota stays at the head of the Empire, which is not at all a bad thing since she at least knows how to rule and to make decisions. She's been named regent twice already. Look, all you have to do is leaf through the *Empire Daily*. The pages of this publication usually reflect the same lack of proportion that characterizes Maximilian's rule. Frequently, the news items on the victories of the Imperial troops are so brief and slight that they almost go unnoticed. By contrast, you'll find pages and pages dedicated to the ceremonial activities that have to be observed on the Emperor's or the Empress's birthdays, or else to the description of balls held at the Great Hall of the Imperial Theater—"there were one hundred mirrors and the white carpet was dotted with sequins and white tinsel"—and other such vacuous accounts, like a list of what His Majesty receives from his goods providers, Saccone and Speed—but also Eduardo Guilló of Havana, Perrin et Cie. of Paris, and Francisco Toscano on Plateros Street in Mexico City (for cigars, weapons, fabrics, and fashions, respectively)— regulations for masked balls, an account of a journey taken from Marseilles to Corsica by the yacht *Geronimo* as it carried statues of four Bonapartes (Joseph, Lucien, Louis and Jérôme) to the family vault in Ajaccio, and endless treatises on such topics as cochineal bluing, or the speed and azimuthal rotation of the clouds. What tops it all is that the *Daily* has just published a naval code establishing Imperial regulations for all the ranks of Mexican seamen, from ship's captain to groom. Let me quote the sixth clause from the third section, entitled "On Sea Voyages": "In the event that the dimensions of the ship on which the Emperor is sailing are insufficient to hold his entourage, the latter will be spread out among other ships, according to the instructions of the general aide-de-camp." Of course the Archduke's entourage would not only be too large for one ship, my dear Alphonse, but also for the entire Mexican navy, since the latter doesn't exist. I'd be surprised if there are even three ships. And so that you don't think I'm prejudiced against the Emperor of Mexico, I'll describe him to you quoting Madame de Courcy and M. E. Masseras, verbatim. M. Masseras is above suspicion because he's the editor of *L'Ère Nouvelle*, a daily French publication in Mexico, and he's always been a fervent supporter of the Empire and the Intervention. I cite him from memory because, of course, he has *not* printed these words, but only spoken them, on several occasions, quite loudly in fact, in the palace corridors: Maximilian is "lightweight to the point of frivolity, erratic to the point of capriciousness, incapable of constancy, irresolute, obstinate . . ." And as for Madame de Courcy, I believe she's hit the nail on the head with the following: "It is tragic," said she, "that it is so easy to worship Maximilian, but impossible to fear him, since in Mexico one can only inspire respect through fear . . ."

And as though all this weren't enough, in addition to his excessive spending on ostentatious ceremonies, there are other Imperial disbursements that are even more difficult to justify—it's well known, for example, that Maximilian sent funds to Hidalgo to cover his personal debts, after the latter wrote Eloin saying that the loss of his country estates, devastated during the Wars of Reform, amounted to about 100,000 piasters. And then, in that vein, Loreto, Gutiérrez Estrada's daughter, wrote Empress Carlota asking for the restitution of funds for all sorts of losses caused by the Intervention. All of this has been interpreted as extortion—what else can it be? It's also common knowledge that the government promised Marshal Bazaine's wife 100,000 piasters should she ever be forced by circumstances to abandon Buenavista Palace—as though the concession, or gift, or usufruct, or whatever, of what was once a splendid national palace had not already caused enough of a scandal. Lastly, it's not common knowledge, but word is that the Emperor and Empress signed a secret pact with the Iturbides—on the adoption of little Agustín—that included a compensation of 150,000 piasters. Alphonse, do you realize what these amounts represent when we consider that a soldier's monthly pay is 30 piasters, and, as I was telling you, that a peon only earns that much in a year? The Emperor has spent what a soldier would earn in four hundred and fifty years and a peon in five thousand!

I'll repeat, however, that I still don't agree with you—although rereading the above I feel that I've almost been taking dictation from you. No, I do not share your belief in "socialist" utopias. I believe in God's will and I respect His desire that we have both wealthy and poor classes on earth. But sometimes I have to ask myself if it is also His will that the rich be quite *so* rich and the poor *so* poor. Still, I'm not certain what to think about this country, which has always been both immensely rich and utterly destitute at once. It was no doubt the knowledge of this very disparity and the inhumane treatment of some hacienda owners towards their peons—revealed by the engineer Bournof—that led Carlota to decree her reforms. Thanks to her, corporal punishment is banned, as well as excessively long workdays, and she's also made education mandatory for the peons and their children. But at the same time, these commendable measures—which the landowners are still resisting—have been obscured by some of the decrees related to the great immigration program planned by the Emperor and the Confederates . . . planned by that ineffable oceanographer, Commodore Maury—the inventor, no less, of the electric torpedo. Among other things, it's been mandated that peons be required to serve their landlord at least five years without permission to change jobs, and that escapees will be arrested and returned to their owners. And yet Carlota and Maximilian are surprised to be accused of bringing slavery back to Mexico! And then, besides the immigration of these veritable slaves—the one hundred thousand Negroes and East Indians already being planned for, and whose numbers they say might reach as high as six hundred thousand before the project ends— there's another issue too, which has already created profound unrest: namely, the planned and already partially initiated immigration of their masters, those Confederate landowners who, to the Mexicans, will always be the *Yankees* (despite the fact that they're Southerners) that took half their land. It will be completely impossible for the Mexicans not to resent the fact that these Yankee settlers will be exempt from military service for five years, and exempt as well from paying taxes on the importation of farm machinery, and, above all, that they'll be given slaves and land on a silver platter . . .

So, you can see how, in this blessed land where everything grows—from rubber to hemp, coconuts and tobacco, cotton and linen, ebony and vanilla, trees for dye—everything goes wrong for poor Max.

I must say that Mexico City has disappointed me deeply. I don't understand why Humboldt named it the City of Palaces—especially since the main one, the Imperial Palace, looks like a military barracks. Word is that Maximilian—who's ordered an architect to redecorate the Chapultepec Palace balconies in the Tuscan style—wants to redo the façade to resemble the Tuileries. But I doubt that he'll find the money to do that. Of course there are some beautiful churches here, built in colonial times, but others have suffered the terrible influence of the Churriguera Brothers, with rococo taken to extremes. And yes, there's still an impressive edifice to be found here and there, like the Palace of Mines, for example, the work of a brilliant Spanish architect named Tolsá, who also sculpted a magnificent equestrian statue of Charles IV of Spain. As for the rest, the buildings are dull, the city streets are squalid—and some are always flooded—gas lighting is unknown (they use only oil, petroleum, and very poor-quality candles that emit these noxious gases), stray dogs are as ubiquitous as in Constantinople—or cats in Rome—and mobs of criminals and dirty beggars congregate in the Paseo Nuevo, the Paseo de la Emperatriz, and the Portal de las Flores. They parade their sores and stumps everywhere, they panhandle, they moan in a sort of falsetto, while mothers delouse their offspring in public. Actually, they're not really *everywhere*, because they're banned from important functions in the churches, which leads one to assume that the Mexican Church doesn't consider all of God's children equal. It does no good for those "lepers" to show up loaded with rosaries and scapulars—something that's actually benefited the Church, when you think about it: Archbishop Labastida has organized more than one noisy demonstration using these beggars. Demonstrations, of course, to protest against Maximilian's policies on managing Church property, and for freedom of worship. So, it's not unusual for someone to witness such diverse spectacles—on the same day—as the Empress Carlota, elegantly arrayed "in a pearl and diamond tiara, and an iridescent fuchsia or lilac gown, with ruffles of English lace" (I quote the *Empire Daily*) reviewing her troops on horseback, escorted by Marshal Bazaine and his staff officers "in white burnouses and flowing toques," while the band plays a typical Mexican march, and then, a few hours later, to be surprised by a throng of "lepers," a veritable Court of Miracles, in an endless procession, with their scapulars, medals, and tin pots, making an infernal racket.

What's happening is that this Empire has become prey to an unending series of such spectacles. I was privileged to attend a banquet that the Emperor and Empress held at Chapultepec Park for a group of Kickapoo Indians who came from Louisiana to put themselves at the service of the Empire, and to request the right to live in Mexico. You should have seen Maximilian holding court, under those giant ahuehuetes, dripping with moss, next to those Indians in headdresses adorned with colored plumes and dressed in buffalo skins trimmed with pearls, and then Carlota chatting with their wives, small and homely—not at all reminiscent of Fenimore Cooper's Indian maids! The great Kickapoo chief, by the way, wore a large silver medallion with a portrait of Louis XIV, a gift from that king to the chief's ancestors during the time that Louisiana was our territory. The most amusing thing is that a few weeks later, at a costume ball in Buenavista Palace, some French officers dressed up as Kickapoos, and when the great chief arrived he knelt at Bazaine's feet and named him Viceroy of Sonora. The Marshal became enraged.

The rabble also make our lives more difficult generally. They curse our soldiers, they insult us in Spanish, and they spit on us as we go by. Their insolence has reached an intolerable level. But it's also quite understandable. We know that Dupin left Mexico at Maximilian's request—and now, at any rate, he's back—but his departure didn't help stop the atrocities and abuse being perpetrated by some of the French commanders. (You were right when you said in one of your letters that cruelty is not the domain of any one nation or race.) And some units are now boasting of how well they've adapted to Mexico—for instance, the much-admired Zouaves, who have energy to spare to perform heroic military feats, but also, I fear, for crime. This almost animalistic energy of theirs, which I think they get from eating that paste they make from powdered coffee mixed with cracker crumbs—or maybe from alcohol, since they always seem a bit drunk, despite the fact that our troops only get three wine rations per week and a daily ration of brandy with their breakfast coffee. I wouldn't be surprised if the Zouaves, who pass themselves off as Mexicans, aided by their skin color, have picked up tips from the locals, who are diabolically talented when it comes to smuggling and forgery. On one occasion we figured out that moonshine was being brought into camp by the candy-vendors, who were transporting it in long tubes, probably made from animal guts, woven into their braids. But what can you expect from a country where two or three mints for making counterfeit money are found and destroyed every month, and where this art has been practiced since the time of the Aztecs? I mean that forgery existed here even before there was money—they used cacao for commercial transactions (I just realized that it originally comes from Mexico), or rather the beans, which are pretty large; but there were Indians then who managed to open a hole in the beans, to take out the contents (which, of course, they then used to make chocolate), then plugged the hole with clay and covered up the slit. Further, I'm told that when Maximilian visited the pyramids, they took him on quite a ride. The Emperor had decided, on his way to Teotihuacán, to cross Lake Texcoco, a filthy lake, scarcely half a meter deep, its waters oily and teeming with mosquito larvae, in a type of gondola or imperial barge, with velvet seats and oarsmen dressed in red livery embroidered with silver—and then Maximilian himself was tricked, as was his companion and guide, Señor Chimalpopoca, into paying a fortune for some "pre-Hispanic" idols that of course, were fakes. By the way, it seems that Maximilian is very sad because Franz Joseph—although he's agreed to return some pre-Hispanic jewels to Mexico—refused to hand over Moctezuma's headdress, arguing that it wasn't in any condition to survive the long journey, and might fall apart, although the Aztec emperor's shield and a letter from Hernán Cortés to Charles V are soon to arrive. These things worry Maximilian more than a defeat for the Imperial troops at the hands of Juárez's army. You should have heard the fuss he made when the Ceremonial came out with two errors in its title (instead of "*Provisional Rules* para *the Service and Ceremonial* de la *Court*," it said "*por* the Service and Ceremonial *del* Court"). And I'm also told that Maximilian becomes extremely upset when he's reminded that there is no true aristocracy in Mexico, but that, since the government of this unfortunate country has been fought over between liberals and conservatives for half a century, any title that Maximilian could create—digging into the history of the independent Mexico—would be unacceptable for everyone involved. And even more so if he tried to glorify the leader of a successful military sally with a title of marquis or duke—it would be absurd for him to dub Miramón the Prince of the Ahualulco River, or General Márquez the Count of the neighborhood of Tacubaya. On the other hand, his joys are as childish as his sorrows: Maximilian was overjoyed at the recognition of the English throne, and the subsequent arrival in Mexico of its ambassador, Sir Peter Scarlett.

As I was saying about the capital . . . There are, indeed, some oases for foreigners here. We French enjoy plenty of these, of course. Germans can go to their club, *Das Deutsche Haus*, to drink Alsatian beer and to speak the language of the *Vaterland*, and the English spend their weekends at the Mexico Cricket Club, near Tacubaya, which the Blackmore firm supplies with that terrible, warm, bitter ale that the subjects of Albion enjoy so much. Tacubaya is a beautiful area, called Mexico's "Saint-Cloud." You must know that these comparisons have become very popular, and so now we call Xochimilco the "Venice of America," San Angel is the "Aztec Compiègne," Cuernavaca the "Mexican Fontainebleau," the city of León is the "Manchester of the New World"—Maximilian himself named it that—Chapultepec Castle is the "Schönbrunn of Anáhuac," etc., etc. All this besides the fact that this country has consistently been compared to Jauja (the Land of Cockaigne), the Hesperides, and Paradise, all in one. "If you look carefully," a distinguished geographer said to me recently, "Mexico is shaped like a horn of plenty." I only nodded, arching my eyebrows slightly, not wanting to tell the good man, first of all, that the Mexican territory got that shape when the North Americans stole half of it, and, secondly, that the horn's mouth faces upward, that is to say, toward the United States, perhaps as an indication of the destiny awaiting the riches of the country. As to the Mexican court, I could probably sum it up in few words: it's a kind of Malmaison combined with a *fête galante* of the Indies, the well-to-do tropics *à la Viennoise*. Moreover, since some French officers have brought their families, we now have enormous hoop skirts, bare arms, and great, tempting décolletages. At first this created a scandal, but it's caught on since, and now young Mexican ladies, especially those with beautiful breasts to show off, are delighted to use more and more fabric from the waist down and less and less from the waist up.

Finally, let me tell you briefly about the military situation, which is now more chaotic than ever, aggravated by the eternal rivalry between Bazaine and Douay, and to which inferno Maximilian and Carlota are always adding fuel, as does the laziness and disorganization that characterize the Marshal himself (please keep this comment to yourself). The truth is that Bazaine's triumphs are more impressive than long-lasting. They say, moreover, that last year's taking of Oaxaca would have cost far fewer lives and less money to boot if it had been initiated in advance of the campaign—which only wasn't done because of the Marshal's own apathy. As for Mexico City, although people vouch for its safety, the truth is that we are always on the alert here. We know, for example, that Nicolás Romero, a notorious Juarist bandit who was executed a short time ago, was able to carry out several raids just a few leagues away from the capital. Several of Colonel Potin's battles in Michoacán were represented as great victories, although this is hardly the case. Castagny, who sent very pessimistic reports on Durango, would have been imprisoned in Culiacán, were it not for the speed of the thoroughbred mare that brought him safe and sound to the walls of Mazatlán. And, well, it's probably already made the news in France that Bazaine has ordered a consolidation of the troops, and that so many outposts have been surrendered to the Republicans. No one is unaware of the fact that this is likely to be the first step before we withdraw our forces. Furthermore, no one could have expected anything different, after Lee evacuated Richmond and surrendered at Appomattox Court House. The pressure from the United States, which wants us to leave, is greater and greater, and I confess—not without some wounded pride—that I believe that Louis Napoleon will give in. The Monarchists were dreaming, when Lincoln took the presidency, thinking he might end up accepting Maximilian—it never would have happened: Lincoln was an ardent supporter of the Monroe Doctrine, and moreover his right-hand man, Seward, not only survived his stabbing by a would-be assassin, but also survived Lincoln's administration, so once again he's Secretary of State, this time for President Johnson. It's possible, in any case, that the withdrawal of French troops will be a relief to the Mexican people—and for Maximilian as well, but what will he do without us, since at the present moment there isn't a Mexican army to take our place? In any case, as I mentioned to you at the beginning of this letter, I hope to get my discharge and be left alone to live here in peace.

By all accounts, I fear that this whole enterprise is going under. A strange custom they have here, which I learned about a short time ago, made me think of Maximilian. There are, they say, some Indians who come down to the city carrying baskets loaded with fruit, and who at the end of the day, when they've sold all of it, fill the baskets with stones until they are as heavy as they were when they held the fruit, and—you won't believe this—go back up the mountains carrying the stones. "So as not to lose the habit," they say. The same thing, in a way, is happening to Maximilian. He has nothing left to offer and all he can carry now is a basketful of rocks. Yes, there can be no doubt: if Mexico was an Empire without an Emperor before Maximilian came, now Maximilian is an Emperor without an Empire.

That's the way things are. I don't even think Carlota can pull this ox from the ravine, firstly because she doesn't run the country regularly, only at times . . . and secondly, the death of her father, Leopold, and more recently, of her grandmother Marie Amélie, have affected her greatly. Poor Empress! She returned so happy from her apparently very successful trip to the Yucatán Peninsula only to hear the news of her beloved father's demise, and, in addition, that of the Baron d'Huart. D'Huart was the envoy of Leopold II, you will remember, who was bearing the official report of the Belgian king's passing and was himself waylaid and murdered by bandits in Río Frío.

And, well, I still have much more to tell, but I think that's enough for today. Please give my most tender greetings to Claude and tell her that María del Carmen is expecting a child, a little Mexican child, who, with luck, will inherit the family's blue eyes. For you, my dear Alphonse, a big hug and all my love.

Your brother,

JEAN-PIERRE

P.S. Tell Claude that María del Carmen wants us to name the child Claudia if she's a girl. Please don't forget to put flowers on Mother's grave at Père Lachaise. Oh, one more thing: the only small relief for the grim situation at the Treasury has been the death of Morny, since, as result, Jecker's claims seem to have become weaker. A nephew of Jecker's was here to demand a series of payments, but he was totally ignored. Of course, the first to oppose payment on the Jecker bonds was Langlais, but Maximilian's bad luck never ends. Langlais, one more on that long list of French financiers sent by our Emperor—Corta, Bonneford, and now Maintenant—was probably the only one who could have saved the Mexican imperial finances from chaos, and the only one aware of the damage done to Mexico by bankers from Paris and London. But you see, Langlais also died. There was a rumor here that he was poisoned, but the autopsy proved otherwise.

And once more, dear brother, till the next letter! Soon, I hope!

XV

BOUCHOUT CASTLE

1927

I, insane? The Baroness of Nothing, the Princess of Foam, the Queen of Oblivion? All lies. If I'm locked up, if they say I'm mad, it's only for this reason: to tell more lies. Because, Maximilian, I am the Empress of the Lie: of the great lie, the true lie, the lie that lights up at the mere touch of those viscous roses, the roses of Countess von Bülow. Of the lie that coils, like a barbed-wire snake, in the most sacred bread, baking in the ovens, and that sheds its skin when it touches the sea. This sea is the Adriatic and its blue skin is mine, the blue skin that reflects the frigate *Novara* with its banners in the wind. I am the Empress of the Lie, the lie that wafts from the grass to the sky and bursts like an air bubble. The grass is the Garden at Laeken and in the bubble are all my dreams about you and Mexico. Tell me, Maximilian, tell me, have you seen the lie, that damned lie, creep in from under a cloak of dreams, or else naked—horizontal and tame—as it draws its stripes on a tiger skin and unwinds its song? The lie is Concepción Sedano and your love for her. Look at it, Maximilian; it is a perfumed lie, suave, indivisible, like a book with blank pages. It's a lie that flies on dark wings, like a moth. Go to Cuernavaca, Maximilian, and try to catch the lie with your butterfly net, to pin it to your pillow. Clip its wings, those wings that unknowingly took away your best years, and forever. You will recognize it by its wind-burned cheeks and its ovaries decked out in their Sunday best, peering from behind a cluster of glass masks. I put on one of those masks, Maximilian, on the night that I danced with you at Laeken, crowned with mistletoe and yellow flowers and pink, transparent berries that dripped a sticky liquid. Remember, Maximilian? I wore one of those masks the day that I dropped to my knees twice at my mother's tomb before I left for Vienna with you. Go on, just you dare swallow that lie, the queen lie of the world, surrounded by its pygmy entourage who polish its ebony stumps with their tongues, the lie that sits on a toilet under an orange-peel tent where tarantulas and violets are cooked together. Violets grow in the Tuileries and Fontaine-bleau. Violets nest, also, in the decomposing heart of the King of Rome. Go on: make the lie yours, if you dare. It is a lie of coals and it wears a sheet, like a ghost's. Catch it if you can by its hide of snow and wash your face in that snow, wash your lies, wash your pride so that you, like me, can be a child again, and can find the lies in the cores of apples. Your mother Sophie brought you those apples in a basket when you were in bed with the measles. A lie, Maximilian, gets new eyes when it touches the stars. You saw those stars one night, from the top of the Pyramid of the Sun. The stars saw you at the Zempoala aqueduct and they bathed you in their lie-light. The stars wept for you when you left Miramare forever. But, Maximilian, you wouldn't be able to catch those stars with your butterfly net because all of them make up a giant lie inflated with black air, swinging like a half moon and hanging from the moon's ear, but forbidding you to bite the tips of its veins or to stroke the silver of its arches.

The messenger told me that I became an old woman overnight. With my eyes open at my birth I saw my mother's bloody thighs. With my eyes shut I saw my own death as it galloped to Damascus. And so, in the blink of an eye, my wig fell into a flour sack and turned white; my wrinkles arrived at night and clung to all my mirrors. But I have a secret mirror, a full-length mirror, that does not tell lies. The mirror is a door of air. I stepped through it and realized that I was in the hall at Neuschwanstein that led to the bedchamber of Bavaria's mad king, your cousin Ludwig. I realized it when I saw that the stalactites were lies, lies like the walls, which simulated those of a cave. At the end there was a door. I opened it. I found myself in the Tower of the Mouse, on the banks of the Rhine. I knew it because I saw the corpse of Bishop Hatto devoured by rats. I became small and went in through the hole where the rats came out. I found myself in the middle of the most beautiful ballroom in the world, the Henry II Gallery at the Palace of Compiègne. Then I became a bird and flew out the window over the sacred woods of Bomarzo and I went down a chimney at the Orsini Palace and was consumed by flames only to rise reborn from the ashes. Then I soared to the clouds, came down, and flew over the Castle of Chinon. I recognized it because on the ground I saw the bodies of one hundred and forty murdered Knights Templar and because there I recognized the imprisoned Eleanor of Aquitaine, and I flew over Helenental Park where Ludwig van Beethoven strolled, deaf to the birds' songs, and I flew over the Royal Pavilion at Brighton where the Prince Regent frolicked in the Chinese bed with his morganatic consort Maria Fitzherbert, and I flew to Brussels and saw myself at Bouchout and Terveuren, at Laeken, traveling down a dusty road, my eyes tattooed, my feet soaked in milk, and weeping round, metallic, fleeting tears of mercury. I followed my death's footsteps and I counted the cobblestones on the road. I counted each hailstone. I plucked the feathers off the birds with necks that the hailstones had broken. And I became so sad to see myself all alone, locked up in a room for sixty years, with nothing to do but thread sequins into the roses' thorns, or cover apples in red velvet, or bleach my pubic hair with peroxide, or draw your eyes on empty eggshells. I was so sad, Maximilian, when I remembered my father and my mother, my grandparents and my brothers, that I became a bird again and, with wings spread out, I swooped down upon the spire atop the Church of Saint Gertrude of Louvain.

I have a dagger piercing my breast. I have, piercing my breast, a dream. That dream is a lie. That lie, trying to look real, becomes a river, and it's so wide that it spills into the turbulent realm of the wind and into the idle promises of the moss. It's so great that it bursts out of its shrieking cage. This river is the Amazon, and I drank from its waters in the Fountain of Four Rivers when we went to Rome. The cage is made of glass, and inside it is your skull dressed in the feathers of the nightingales from Steiermark that you took with you to Mexico. The lie is so lazy that it sleeps in the yellow dregs of absinthe and only awakens on your lips when you speak of your Empire. The lie swims at the bottom of the most lavish dreams, but the lie is such a liar that it spins out of its own orbit and filters, like the saliva of heaven, like heavenly spittle, through the white scales of the clouds. It's then that armadillos roll with laughter on the peaks of Acultzingo and canoes glide engulfed in gloom through the waters of the Usumacinta River. The armadillos die laughing because you were executed on June 19th. The canoes, loaded with vanilla, are unable to perfume the mausoleum in the Capuchin monastery. Listen to me. If you want to know what a lie is, I will tell you again and again: you can recognize it by its propellers made of salamander skin, and by the unrelenting lightning coming off its copper palate, by the hideous surprise in its artificial eyes. A terrible taste stuck to your tongue when you realized that Juárez wouldn't grant your pardon, and those eyes aren't yours. They belong to Saint Ursula. Maximilian, if you want to know a lie, look at yourself in the mirror of my dreams, and you will see its image from head to toe. But you will not see yourself in that mirror—you will see me, coming from far away, moving through the wind and the years, through the waters of the mirror, to throw my arms around you. Don't be distressed if you see me wearing black, don't feel proud and assume that my mourning clothes are for you. I'm a widow, yes, but the widow of a dream, the widow of a century that died of old age, the widow of an empire that was left an orphan. Don't be frightened when you see me in white. I am the White Lady of the Habsburgs. The woman in white who sat at the bedside of Charles V at Yuste to foretell his death. The woman whom the Archduke Ladislas saw before he died during a hunt. The same one your father, the King of Rome, saw sitting at the foot of his deathbed, whose dress and even her skin he described as being whiter than the white waterfall in the Schönbrunn gardens. Maximilian, I will appear to you as well, but not to tell you when you'll die—to tell when you'll live: to tell the world that your death was a lie and that, if they haven't seen you lately at the Pyramid of Xochicalco or the Terrace of the Araucarias at Chapultepec Castle, if they didn't see you yesterday at the Giralda Tower, if last Sunday Baron von Rothschild didn't say hello to you in Naples from the gilded phaeton that he was driving himself, if they haven't seen you lately, then, like they told me in order to console me over your death, I'll tell the world that you shaved your beard in Querétaro, that you escaped the firing squad disguised as a Republican army captain, that you sailed on the *Susquehanna* to New Orleans where you now live incognito like a grand gentleman, that you sit in a white rattan rocking chair and in the shadow of a palm tree with an ivory trunk, that you listen to Negro bands playing jazz and dancing in the streets, and that it was not you who was shot in Querétaro but some poor devil wearing a fake beard . . . And if they tell me instead that they've kept you in Mexico, locked in a prison cell for sixty years, and that Juárez visits you every day in his black frockcoat and top hat and reads from the constitution of the United States of Mexico and blows his nose with scraps of the French flag . . . If they tell me that you really escaped and disappeared in the mountains of Chihuahua dodging bullets from Porfirio Díaz's men, or poisoned Apache arrows, and that many years later you appeared in Arizona and said you were Buffalo Bill . . . Or if they tell me that Juárez paid you a million pesos to keep you from coming back to Mexico and gave you permission to take Concepción Sedano and Princess Salm-Salm and your four Havanese dogs with you, and that he put you on a ship bound for Brazil, and that there you've grown old among the crab-covered mangroves and the aromatic coffee trees, wearing llama-skin slippers and a crown of ivy interlaced with diamonds, surrounded by your black slaves, and that Princess Salm-Salm dances nude for you on horseback while Concepción Sedano shoos away mosquitoes with a *ñandú*-feather fan . . . If they tell me all that, Maximilian, I shall believe it.

That's what they're afraid of and that's why they say I'm crazy—because they don't understand me. Nobody can stand the fact that their dark lives glow in the light of a lie that's as big as the sun. Nobody wants to hear, Maximilian, that when I speak about your life I am also speaking about my life and theirs. Nobody's ever wanted to understand these things, not through all the years I've been locked up in this room, knitting capes for the Hofburg falcons, or socks for the hounds that follow my nephew Albert when he climbs the Ardennes, or muzzles for the rats at Schönbrunn. They've always wanted to keep me sitting quietly, in total silence, still and bored, immensely bored as when I was a child and I was taught to bear boredom without showing it, as is every prince and princess destined one day to rule. I was bored to tears during those endless High Masses that my mother liked so much at Laeken Chapel. But I always kept a smile on my face, just as Countess d'Hulst taught me. And I was bored as an oyster with those recitals by Mademoiselle Sforlanconi that Marie Henriette organized every fortnight. But I kept my eyes bright, as my brother Philippe insisted I should. I had to bear Cousin Victoria's moralizing, year after year, with the same engaged expression, with the same hypocritical smile, the same sparkling eyes, as she repeated ad nauseam those endless sermons by my father Leopold, the Knight of the Blue Land, her revered Duke of Kendal, her mentor. She always said the same thing: that I must learn to be a princess, and that I would remember it all when I became queen. But Victoria was already Queen of England, and I was Queen of Nothing, of Nobody. So sad and bored, after playing and singing Schumann *Lieder* all afternoon, or painting oils of St. George's Church in Venice, or of the yacht *Fantaisie* sailing us to Madeira, to Istria and Málaga. I wrote to my father again from Miramare that the same clematis vines that covered the walls at Lacroma were creeping around Miramare Chapel, for, "As you know, Papa," I wrote, "we had the altar and pulpit, and the confessional, the pews and the beams all crafted from cedar, the red Lebanese cedar that my dear Max had brought to Miramare. I'm sure that you will love it because Miramare resembles Windsor Castle; its towers are like the turrets at Sintra Palace; its windows (when will you come to visit, Papa?)

are Moorish like those at the Alhambra." I was bored, I almost died of tedium when they made me put together jigsaw puzzles of famous battles: the Battle of Jemappes and the capture of Brussels, the defeat of the Duke of Orléans at Agincourt, William the Conqueror's victory at Hastings—and then puzzles with reproductions of the famous paintings of the history of the European dynasties: De Laurentiis's rendition of the twelve southern Italian provinces' feast in honor of Francis I; Gerard's painting of the coronation of Charles X of France at Reims; Winterhalter's portrait of my grandfather, Louis Philippe, with Victoria and Albert during their visit to France; the angels' gift of Maria de Medici's portrait, by Rubens, to Henry IV of France. Jigsaw puzzles of all the paintings by Titian and Velázquez that portrayed the Habsburgs' physical flaws. Yes, that's how they want me now, Maximilian, bored as an oyster, spending my days doing jigsaw puzzles or building a ship in a bottle, and because that's how they want me, they won't forgive me, they'll never forgive me for having escaped when they least expected it, right into the bottle and aboard the tiny ship, in the company of all the mad monarchs and princes—Maria I of Portugal; Saul, the melancholy king, at the helm; Erik of Denmark; Don Carlos of Austria locked up in the ship's bilge; George III of England; Charles VI of France sitting on the aftcastle in a throne covered in shit; Juana the Mad; and the open casket of Philip the Handsome—because, on that ship, inside that bottle, like one cast into the sea, escorted by dolphins and swordfish and flocks of seagulls and white stone curlews, I have taken my leave, determined to conquer the world.

I will reveal my secret to you, Maximilian, if you promise me not to tell a soul. One day at the Tuileries as a child, I found a paperweight collection. Inside each paperweight was a miniature reproduction of a castle: Ambras Castle, the Tower of London, the Alcázar of Segovia, Amboise Castle. I realized that if I sat and held one of those paperweights in my hands and put my hands on my lap and stared quietly, the castle came alive, with very small people much smaller than those in my dollhouse, and that these little people came and went through their doors, ate and danced in their ballrooms, went up their stairs, hunted for boar in their forests, and rode on horseback on the roads near the castle. It was like having a whole world in my hands. Each castle was enclosed in a crystal sphere; night fell in the sphere and the people slept or they made love, they turned the lights on and off. Or a day went by, like a gust of blue, and on my lap, right before my eyes, the sun, as small as a luminous lentil, traveled from one end of that celestial hemisphere to the other; then night fell again, sprinkling its constellations and stars like a silvery powder that shimmered on the surface of the glass. At times it snowed, or the dome got cloudy and I had to blow the clouds apart or make it rain. It rained at the Tower of London the afternoon I saw Queen Anne Boleyn cross the Traitor's Gate. On an autumn afternoon in Amboise I saw the bodies of a thousand decapitated Huguenots cast into the waters of the Loire on the orders of Catherine of Medici. It snowed at the Alcázar of Segovia the day Christopher Columbus knelt before Isabella of Castile. On a morning full of yellow flowers Ferdinand II invited me to visit his collection of giant armor and stuffed birds in his Castle of Ambras. I soon learned that all I had to do was sit alone, with empty hands, for a glass sphere to appear suddenly on my lap. Inside the sphere there would be an entire city, with all its churches and its houses, its smoking chimneys, its lampposts: Ghent and the hill where the god Wotan was worshipped; Bruges with its bridges and green canals; Brussels and its Martyrs' Square and National Palace, its fountains and cobblestone streets, on a morning cloudy with my breath. Wagons rode through those streets, people strolled, dogs scampered and history passed by as well. At the Municipal Palace in Brussels I saw the Brabant tricolor waving in the wind on Belgium's birthday. In the churches at Liège I saw Calvinists set fire to saints' effigies. In the year of the plague, I saw nude flagellants march through the streets of Louvain, tagged with red crosses, as they scourged their flesh.

Now that I'm old and alone, I spend whole days sitting in my chamber, my head bowed down and my palms turned up on my lap . . . all these years that my jailers have thought my head was as empty as my hands . . . if they could only see with my eyes, they wouldn't believe, Maximilian, how small and insignificant their lives look, and how infinitely great are my thoughts. With these I give shape and sense to a whole world that I illuminate with aurora borealis, with lightning, with white nights. Or with rainbows that I can hold in my hands, that I can lift and offer to you on my knees, to crown you. If only one of my jailers, or you Maximilian, if only you alone could hear, with my ears, the voices that I use to fill the universe, the singing of its stars, the murmurs of its ravines, the roar of its oceans. If only you knew that in the hollow of my hands I can hold the bluest and frothiest of all the seas, the Adriatic, and that if I raise my hands to my lips, with a simple puff of air I can make that deep blue sea bring you, wherever you are, cool water to rinse your eyes with, and make them bright and clear again, and that the foam that made white arabesque designs on your naval uniform will give your wounds salty kisses to stop their bleeding.

They will not forgive me because they don't understand that I can have a whole world in my hands and, by merely unclenching my fists, I can let it fall and turn to dust. Why can I penetrate these worlds at will and alter history? Did they ever tell you that a monk named Jacques Clément assassinated Henry III of France? That's a lie. I made love to the King last night and I plunged a dagger into his chest; mine was bathed in his blood. Did they ever tell you that Hannibal defeated Scipio in the Battle of the Ticinus? Lies. My spurs are still covered in snow from the Alps and the Pyrenees. Did they tell you that Louis XIII had Concini murdered? Lies. I had him killed and I'm going to make the Pope a gift of his head. What they will never forgive me for is that I can scatter all the jigsaw puzzle pieces I have assembled with just one blow. Or that I can put them back together however I wish and make villains into heroes, heroes into traitors, winners into losers, the humiliated and defeated into victors. A long time ago my life too broke into little pieces and everything flew up in the air. They say that I am mad because I crawl on all fours through the castle and they have to carry me to my bed and tie me down. But only I know what I'm looking for. They say that I'm mad because I broke my mirror with my fists— look, Maximilian, at the scars on my hands—and because at night I crawl up and down the castle corridors and I paw at the corners looking for the mirror shards. I saw you in one of them, dressed in your lancer's uniform. I tried to swallow it to fill myself with your memory. Look at the scars that were left on my lips. In another shard I saw you in the Tyrolean garden at Schönbrunn, and in another I saw myself in the Tuileries Gardens, on a spring day, and I was reading under a flowering lime tree, and then you and I were in the temple of the Pyramid of Cholula, and then we visited Les Invalides and we saw the Mexican standards taken during the siege at Puebla, and afterwards we strolled through the center of Mexico City and Plateros Street was carpeted in white flowers and with all those shards for Corpus Christi, Maximilian. I should have cut my veins, I should have taken my life, but I didn't do it. Look at the scars that I don't have on my wrists. In contrast, Maximilian, look at the ones I do have in my heart: the filthy alligators at Uxmal, lying in the sun; the stupid bird that perched on the *Novara*'s poop deck and followed us to Martinique; the wounded Belgian boys that I decorated at the Hospital San Gerónimo; the

Tabasco with its Italian and Moorish crew that took me to Sisal accompanied by General Uraga, who told me tales from the *Chilam Balam* and of the King of Itzá who would return from the dead to hurl foreigners into the sea. All those memories, Maximilian, are also stuck to my heart. On a path at Bouchout I found your hands and took them to my bosom. We sailed, as usual, down the Rhine and you caressed my breasts. I should have cut them off, Maximilian, I should have mutilated them so that you could drink from them as though they were goblets, and you could taste the milk destined for the son of another man. They say that I'm mad only because of that—because I want to pick up all the shards of my life and with them, as with a jigsaw puzzle, to put together a mirror where I can see my whole life in a single instant. Don't they realize that I'm running out of time, that I would have to live eighty-six years longer than the eighty-six years I've already lived in order to be able to remember every second? Don't they realize, Maximilian, that I can't remember the face of my governess, Madame de Beauvais? One morning, as I took some stockings out of a drawer that I once wore in Milan, I found a mirror shard from which my dearly beloved Maria Auersperg smiled at me. But I couldn't recover the face of Marie Auguste de Beauvais. Tell me, why don't they want me to hear my cousin Count d'Eu's voice any more, and jump rope and play snakes and ladders, and go see *The Imaginary Invalid* with him? Why, pray tell, don't they want him to whisper to me when I ride on horseback along the Veronica Causeway? Why don't they want me to have married you, as I did, in the temple of the Pyramid of Cholula, in its greenhouse where lemon trees flowered and the altar was alive, carved from the trunk of the widest tree in the world, in Santa María del Tule? In its hollow trunk, instead of saints, there were quetzal birds crowned with haloes, there were egrets dressed as the Virgin Mary and a crucified black swan, its beak and neck bent to its chest. Why not hang angel wings from its branches and the Mexican pennants that waved in the air stirred by the breath of alligators? Why don't they want a dodo bird to bear the train of my wedding gown? Why don't they let the fountain at the Hofburg, with its statues of the Danube and the Vindobona astride the shoulders of Tritons, be used as our marriage bed? Why don't they want me to marry that prince who, while witnessing a cockfight with a blind rooster in Spain, remembered the death of John of Bohemia at the Battle of Crécy? I can't find the portrait of the Burgermeister Charles de Brouckère and I'm forgetting his face. I want him to perform our civil marriage again. I want him to marry us in

Ayotla. I want to take the Grand Master of my court at Milan, Count Andrea Bartholomew, to Mexico, so that he can keep reading aloud from Tasso at Xochimilco Lake. I can't recollect his voice. Tell me, why don't they want to bring Maximilian the dreamer of Caserta back from the dead; why don't they want him to come back with the Prince who on the island of Madeira marveled at the Ethiopian arum with buds like ivory trombones and tasted the dark wine of the sweet Malvasian grape? Why is there no one with whom I can lay and make love under a tent made from the hide of a blind camel? Why, pray tell, don't they want my mouth to become a rooster's comb when I bite off your tongue? Why don't they want me to vomit it up as Malvasian wine, transubstantiated into the blood you shed at Las Campanas Hill? Pure envy, that's all. It's pure envy that makes damned women turn over in their graves, as their hearts turned over with envy in their breasts when they thought they were still alive. The other day the Archbishop of Malinas came to hear my confession. He said, My daughter, get down on your knees and confess your sins, and I laughed, I laughed out loud right in his face because he doesn't see that what I have to confess I already shout to the whole world every day: that besides masturbating every night thinking of men, I also do it thinking of Mexico, of its forests, of the cheap restaurants at La Merced market where white friars strolled and beggars danced to *malagueñas* and Jalisco *valonas*, and I masturbate thinking of the Empress's Dragoons, of Lake Chapala, and of your gold-banded *jarano* sombrero; for if I've ever stolen anything in my whole life it was the light of the Mexican sun, which I took to brighten my words, the scent of its pears from San Juan, which I took to embalm my life; for if I've ever been unfaithful to you, it wasn't with Colonel Van der Smissen, nor with the pommel of your sword, but with you yourself, with your dead body. Kneel down, Charlotte, my mother used to say, kneel before our Lord God; kneel down, Miss Empress—yes, that's what they all want, to see me on my knees, praying to Our Lady of Guadalupe to make me fertile with the waters of the Peñón, and on my knees in front of the Pope so that José Luis Blasio doesn't come to poison me disguised as an organ grinder—I recognized his acne-covered face—and on my knees in front of Benito Juárez to beg him not to execute you, on my knees forever, begging forgiveness for sins I have not committed, on my knees before Eugénie and the image of Saint Charles Borromeo, on bended knee before Huitzilopochtli and Napoleon III, kneeling before the Four Horsemen of the Apocalypse with stigmata on my hands and nail wounds on my feet. That's how they want me—a martyr among martyrs, buried alive in the sand like Saint Daria, murdered by her own father like Saint Barbara, decapitated like Saint Flora, or roasted alive like Saint Pelagia of Tarsus, but I am not, nor shall I ever be, a martyr to anyone. The Archbishop of Malinas also foamed at the mouth, because like my ladies-in-waiting, and my doctors, and even you, Maximilian, he was blind, all were blind and they never dared to see the miracle. Thus, no one saw me, from a Fontainebleau window, as I bid goodbye to Napoleon I, when he left for the Isle of Elba. Nor did anyone see me at Castle Laxenburg wiping Princess Isabella de Croy's tears as she left your nephew George of Bavaria forever, in the middle of their wedding night. Nor turned into an eagle as I proclaimed the victory of the Austrians over the French in the War of the Spanish Succession to Joseph I at the Hofburg. They missed me too as I mounted the lunar globe on the wreath atop the Amelia wing of the Hofburg, to peer through your telescope at the Battle of Celaya where General Obregón lost a hand. They never saw me open the door to my bedroom at Bouchout and sneak into Fenelon Castle: I knew I was there because I saw cauldrons of boiling marmalade pouring from a tower onto enemy soldiers. And I opened another door and I was in the Cacahuamilpa Caves: I knew it because I saw Dante's profile. And I descended a staircase made of iridescent glass and I opened another door and I found myself in the Chinese closet that Monsieur, Louis XIV's brother, had at Saint-Cloud. I knew it because he was kissing a palace guard. And I flew out a chimney and over Rocamadour Castle. I knew I was there because I saw, in a glass case, the parchment-dry, cobweb-ridden body of Saint Amadour, and I climbed through a window into the castle; I went down a staircase, always looking for pieces of my life and of my memories, your eyes in the Hofburg miniatures room, pieces of your heart in the Rose Room, your hands in the gilded mechanical clock that portrayed the wedding of Maria Theresa and Francis of Lorraine, ringlets of your hair in the chapel tabernacle with the miraculous ivory crucifix that saved Ferdinand II from a Protestant siege, and I opened another door and I realized I was at the Tuileries because some women were dousing the floors and the columns with petrol to set them on fire; everything was in flames: the letters and signatures of illustrious men in Eugénie's collection were burning, as were the lithographs of Les Halles, and Zola's "Cheese Symphony"; I ran madly through the Diana Gallery and the stucco chamber where the officers of the Emperor's House—burned to a crisp—were eating breakfast, and I descended the Empress's staircase and went to Miramare and I knew I was there because I saw my niece Stéphanie, because I saw you, Maximilian, and because I saw the crown of thorns that Dr. Jilek placed on your imperial crest.

But no one saw me. Nor did anyone see me go down the staircase at Miramare like a madwoman, and when I opened the door, and when I found myself in the Palace of Cortés in Cuernavaca, no one saw me cut a bunch of begonias and dahlias, carnations and daisies, to weave a chastity belt with them, because, Maximilian, I want to make it hard for you to love me, but not too hard, I want you to pluck me with those long, white fingers that played the harp during those endless afternoons we spent in Miramare. I want you to pluck me with those fingers, and not to pluck me with those hands that touched my breasts; don't deflower me; yes do deflower me and tell me with your lips that you do love me, with your teeth, that you love me madly—so I don't forget you, so I remember you all sixty seconds of all sixty minutes of all twenty-four hours in a day—I stand with my eyes wide open as you pull the petals off the daisies—or else that you only love me a little because I fall asleep after being up for three days and nights while you pluck the begonias and then I don't only dream about you but also about my grandfather Louis Philippe who made a tiny rocking chair in his woodshop for my uncle the Duke of Chartres—or else that you don't love me at all while you bite off the last petals of the last dahlias, you don't love me at all because sometimes I forget you for years at a time, and it's like you never existed, as if you'd never seen, at the Pitti Palace gallery, the unfortunate couple from England, as if two hundred carriages had never come to greet us on the plains of Aragon, as if, Maximilian, you had never been King of Mexico—to penetrate me thereafter with your tongue and impregnate me with it and your words, to make of me, Maximilian, the mother of the Divine Word, to be visited by the archangel. Then I would be on my knees but not in front of my executioners and my enemies, not in front of any god or virgin, but before all of Creation, before my creation, and not in the Chapel of Miramare, nor my mother's tomb at Laeken, and not in front of my father Leopold's crypt, which I never visited, may God forgive me, nor at the Collegiate Church of Guadalupe, nor in the Capuchin Chapel in Vienna in front of your sarcophagus; no, I am alone, alone, alone with my life, with my memories that have turned to flesh, to the water that I drink, to the air that I breathe, to the black velvet night, to the Imperial crown of warm-blooded birds that fly in circles over my head while I am transformed into one single memory, alive and beating, without beginning or end, on my knees, Maximilian, in the blue navel of Eden.

But now I am very, very tired. Even tired of being that—a miracle. I want to lie down and sleep. With Papa, with Mama, with Grandpa and Grandma. To forget that I've lived in the future. You know what else, Max? I liked nothing more, as a child, than sleeping with Mama. I also liked to imagine that I was in a great round parlor where we all slept, each on his own bed: Mama and Papa Leopich, my grandparents Louis Philippe and Marie Amélie, my uncles Nemours, Joinville, and Aumale. The beds' headboards were placed against the wall, in a circle, so that we could all see each other. We all pulled the sheets over us at the same time. It was a somewhat cold night, but we had a fire in the center and we were under thick comforters stuffed with wild duck feathers. After saying our evening prayers, Uncle Aumale told us how he had shot those ducks, on a gray humid morning, in the Enghien Woods. My aunt, the Duchess of Montpensier, told me how she had plucked the feathers and that she preferred doing that—plucking feathers from ducks—to embroidering flowers, every night after dinner, at the Tuileries or at Claremont, while they complained about Isabella of Spain's bad table manners and the stench she gave off. My grandmother Marie Amélie told us how she had stuffed the comforters with the feathers and how she had threatened her parents with becoming a Capuchin nun if they didn't allow her to marry my grandfather Louis Philippe. Grandmother had donned a nightcap trimmed with Alençon lace. My grandfather's cap had a gold fringe. My aunt the Duchess of Orléans explained how she had braided the gold thread to make the trim. Grandfather read the *Morning Chronicle* and talked about being exiled in Philadelphia when he strolled through the woods arm in arm with Prince Talleyrand, and he reminded us that Louis XVI and Marie Antoinette had taken him to the baptismal font, and after yawning he talked about the time that he was a captive, with his brothers, in Havana, and then, with a tear and the first gurgles of his snoring, he remembered his son, my uncle Prince Beaujolais, who died a drunk at the age of twenty-eight. Uncle Joinville, from his bed, told us that he had never written his Memoirs—he had sketched them. He showed us drawings of when he played with his classmates at the Lycée Henri IV, and of when, at the age of five, he visited Charles X in the Tuileries, and of the servants on a staircase taking dinner to the King in crates like children's coffins. My uncle had a pillow on his legs and on the pillow a notebook, and in it he began to

435

draw sketches of us, each in his bed: of Mama who complained of a back-ache and was almost hidden by her quilt, only her sharp nose showing; of Aunt Clementine who had not finished making the lace for her sheets and was mumbling that she wouldn't go to sleep until she finished, while promising Mama that she would apply suction cups to her the next day; of my brother Leopold who swore that he knew where the gold spurs scattered at the Battle of Courtrai were hidden, after the victory of Flemish troops over the French cavalry. At that time it didn't bother me that they only talked about war and death, that they told me the waters of the Meuse had turned red with the blood of innocents murdered by Charles the Bold and Louis XVI. For me the dead didn't exist because all my loved ones were still alive, and that's how they would be forever, every night, or perhaps for one, endless night. All in their plush, warm beds, in their nightcaps and their mittens, their nightgowns, their woolen socks, and with their hot water bottles. I was there to protect them, I who would stay awake to make sure they were all asleep and I would tiptoe over to kiss my mother's forehead and make sure she was nicely tucked in. To bless my father, to remove my grandfather's spectacles and Aunt Clementine's crochet needle from her hands after they had both gone to sleep. To pat my brother, Fat Philippe, on the head. To lull my little cousin, handsome Gaston, to sleep. To put the little Duchess of Chartres's rattle in her hands and to bless the little Duke de Guise, who was always so loving, and to put a pacifier in the petulant little Prince de Condé's mouth. To pick up the pencil that had rolled on the floor when Uncle Joinville closed his eyes and began to dream of sketching a dream. I would go back to my bed holding my breath to stifle the laughter caused by their symphony of gurgles, murmurs, and whistles. I would ask God then, I would ask Him to keep my loved ones always asleep and peaceful, and that if they dreamed that they should have quiet dreams about pretty things. The whole bedroom would then be filled with stars, the walls would turn into trees, and I would be there, in the white, circular clearing of an enchanted forest, thanking the Lord, with my face turned up to heaven and eyes wide open.

We're all here—you too. Other people I didn't invite have turned up as well. God knows when they got here, climbed into their beds, and fell asleep. The room is much bigger than I imagined and everyone is sleeping in total silence. Not a whistle or a moan to be heard, now. They sleep motionless, on their backs, their eyes closed and their arms crossed on their chests. Many years must have gone by, Maximilian, since they're all covered in a gray dust that's hardened and seems to have turned to stone. The flowers that Countess von Bülow brought to the Capuchin Chapel have also hardened, as has the jasmine bouquet that Sisi sent to Linderhof to be placed in the hands of Ludwig of Bavaria, as has the wreath of dried laurel that my niece Vicky placed on the breast of Frederick Wilhelm of Prussia—the same one she sent him after his victory over France. The two white roses that Katharina Schratt left on your brother Franz Joseph's chest have also turned to stone. We are all here, and I watch over them all, for I am the only one, Maximilian, who is not asleep.

Wide awake, on my back, naked with no sheets to cover me, my eyes wide open and staring at something like the dome of a temple—or is it the sky?—I am still free of dust. Naked and cold, with a chill in my bones that has not left me for over sixty years, I have grown tired of waiting for you to cover me with the tears of sadness you will shed when you see how old I have become, when you realize that you used to be ten years older than me but now I am half a century older than you. I am tired of waiting for you to cover me with kisses, lusting for my flesh, surprised to see me as a girl again, the little girl from Laeken Palace who opened her windows at night for the summer to come in and make love to her. I fell asleep one night not wanting to and I awoke (can you believe it?) feeling tingly all over my body. I had summoned the flies and they had come as ordered. I was a-swarm with blue, violet, iridescent flies, but so paralyzed with fear that I couldn't shoo them away. I couldn't close my eyes even though the flies landed on my lids and my nostrils, and the foul things crept about the flesh of my lips, and the sweet effusions of my cunt. Do you remember, Maximilian, those scorpions and centipedes, those earthworms and moths that covered the statue of a woman at the Villa Palagonia, on the way to Messina? That's how I am now, Maximilian, covered with maggots. Before they left, the flies laid their tiny eggs all over my skin and from those eggs they laid between my legs, in my mouth, in my belly, in my navel, on my brow and between my toes, in my armpits, the palms of my hands and in my eyes, the maggots hatched. One time I dreamed that—lying there, awake or asleep, it was all the same—on my back, naked, my legs apart, I was stretched out at night in the Borda Gardens and a cloud of fireflies got into me. I became pregnant with light, and in my womb, as in the celestial dome, fireflies traced the constellations. I dreamed that, if I floated down the river the poet called—remember, Maximilian?—as serpentine as the Seine, as limpid and green as the Somme, as mysterious as the Nile, as historic as the Tiber, as majestic as the Danube, that river in whose waters, shaded by seven mountains, I saw my face and that, after all, it was the face of a woman, a woman caressed and penetrated for the first time, kissed, with skin burned by a man's saliva, by his sweat, by your kisses, Maximilian, I dreamed, as I was saying, that it was all the same whether I was asleep or awake, or dead, like Ophelia, my wedding wreath of orange blossoms wrapped around my fingers, my hair braided in moonbeams, I dreamed that, if I floated down the river in that same way, on my back and naked, my legs apart, if in that way I were pierced by a flaming-red salmon that laid its roe in my womb, I would become pregnant with thousands of offspring that, when I reached the sea, would pour from between my legs to drown their thirst in eddies of salt. But dreams are only dreams. Today I'm not dressed in a cloak of stars, nor even in the dust of the plains in Tlaxcala, or the white sands of Antón Lizardo's dunes. I'm not dressed, Maximilian, in pollen from the roses of the Isle of Lacroma, nor in the snows of Iztaccíhuatl Peak. I haven't been covered by the dry, golden leaves of Soignies Wood nor by wings of swallows from La Teja Hacienda. Worms cover and clothe me with their silky webs, weaving my wedding veil—those worms that crawl into my mouth and my nose, my ears and my eyes. The worms that like warm, slimy caterpillars crawling towards my belly, devour the sweet flesh of my vulva, then fall asleep in their cocoons to dream, as I dreamed once, that they have sprouted wings. In a few months or maybe a few years—or, perhaps tomorrow—Maximilian, I shall give birth to a swarm of black butterflies.

XVI
"BYE-BYE, MAMÁ CARLOTA"
1866

1. On the Road to Paradise and Oblivion

"Yes, it's good for an emperor and an empress to humble themselves washing the feet of twelve elderly men and twelve elderly women, but it's something else entirely to humiliate the people as Prince Starhemberg and his courtiers used to do when they dressed up as beggars and brought dozens of peasants to their palace in order to ridicule them. They clothed them in courtly garments, put wigs whitened with lima bean powder on them, and had them wear swords, which made them stumble each time they tried to walk. And at a public ceremony one of the Estérhazy princes began pulling off the pearls from the embroidery on his frockcoat and throwing them to the crowd. But no matter, Blasio, we would have to forgive such excesses in view of the services these same individuals rendered the Austrian Crown. For instance, Starhemberg distinguished himself in his brilliant military feats against the Turks. Did you know that? At any rate, I say: self-respect above all. That's why at Huatusco, I wasn't offended by the Mayor's refusal to accept the thousand pesos I tried to give the town, saying they didn't have any poor people there. No, I wasn't offended, because I like a town with self-respect."

I was saying this to Blasio on our way to Cuernavaca as we rode in the coach drawn by six mules, white as snow, that Colonel Feliciano Rodríguez had built for me with a table and drawers for writing utensils, wearing a Scottish blanket over my legs that Blasio, being much less sensitive to the cold than I, almost never wanted any part of—and he, my good Blasio, always watching my lips, with his indelible pencil in hand.

"Take note, take note, Blasio," I was telling him. "We're going to ask Saccone and Speed to send us five or six grosses of English pencils, the best in the world (even though, as I once said to Lord Codrington, we mustn't forget that graphite was discovered in Bavaria!) so that you can write with them on our way to Cuernavaca without making your lip so purple."

That's what I was always telling him, but he insisted on using his indelible pencil, insisted on sucking away at it in order to write down everything I was dictating to him:

"Take note Blasio," I was telling him, "I must have them send us as many demijohns and siphons of Vichy or Plombières-les-Bains water as they can spare, because the water of Tehuacán disagrees with Empress Carlota. Take note, Blasio."

Blasio was taking down the order for Saccone on one sheet, while on another, the letter to Baroness Binzer, in which I was telling her that I had refused to let them take away the nests the hummingbirds had built under my window. "Oh, and on another sheet, Blasio, I want you to write down all the words you can think of that rhyme with Cuernavaca."

"Like *resaca, alharaca, matraca,* Your Majesty?" Blasio asked. I laughed heartily and told him: "No Blasio, don't be silly. Look, in Seville they have a saying, 'He who hasn't seen Seville has never seen a wonderville!'; and in Lisbon they say, 'He who hasn't seen Lisbon has never seen a thing this Bonnie,' and in Madeira I myself coined the following phrase: 'He who hasn't seen Madeira should go no place but there-a!' So, now, I want to invent one for Cuernavaca, like 'He who hasn't seen Cuernavaca . . .' But how can we can rhyme it with an ugly word like *matraca,* a pest?"

"*Hamaca,* Your Majesty?"

"A hammock? No, keep thinking," but I was happy knowing that that very night I would finally be stretched out on my own white hammock in Cuernavaca, forgetting all my worries for a few hours. Among them:

"We must write to Emperor Napoleon—take note, Blasio—to tell him that Baron Saillard is lying when he complains that we mistreated him in Mexico. Why did Saillard have to have the bad taste to interrupt my rest in Cuernavaca to give me the letter informing me about the retreat of the French troops, Blasio—why did he have such a lack of tact? Take note: regarding Domenech, who had the audacity to say that the time for a Joseph II hasn't arrived in Mexico, and that what we need here is a Cromwell, a Richelieu or a Committee for Security or Public Health, or whatever they called it, he should be firmly rebuked in the *Empire Daily*. Take note Blasio: let's start a letter to my friend,

Count Hadik, telling him this: I struggle with many difficulties, obstacles, but the struggle is my element—and tell him I keep losing my hair and I almost have a 'Hadikian' bald spot, eh? What do you think?" We could see the entire Valley of Mexico out the window beneath us, with snow-capped volcanoes in the background.

"And, Blasio, we must tell Degollado in a letter that I find it impossible to believe that the wisest monarch of the century and the most powerful nation in the world—because France still is, Blasio—would yield to the Yankees in such an undignified manner, yes, just like that, in such an undignified manner, and also take note Blasio: in a letter to Marshal Bazaine, written not in French, but as always in Spanish, say this to him: 'How is it possible, what will the people think of us when it becomes known that a whole state, Michoacán, located a mere fifty leagues from the capital, has not been subdued yet?' And take note Blasio, in another letter to Louis Napoleon (this is just the gist of the thing, later we'll give each word careful consideration), tell him not to think that France can keep control of all Mexican customs houses for an indefinite time, in order to take half their income, as he intends . . . and besides, yes, we also need to tell him—correct, Blasio?—that the customs houses of Tampico, Mazatlán, and Matamoros aren't producing any profits for us because our communication with those ports has been interrupted by the Juaristas. And meanwhile, what is Bazaine doing? Tell me, do you think that his inertia has to do with the fact that his wife, Pepita, has many relatives who are Juárez supporters?"

And Blasio licked the tip of his pencil and wrote with purple ink: "Ask the administrator of Miramare castle to send us the marble bust of Queen Louise d'Orléans, which is . . ."

And after fifteen or twenty words the ink of the pencil ran out and Blasio had to lick the tip once again to continue:

". . . which is at the Salotto dei Principi—Salotto with two t's Blasio—you're a lost cause," and he smiled, showing his purple teeth and finished the phrase: ". . . to give Empress Carlota a surprise."

That's what I told Blasio to write on our way to Cuernavaca, and we had already left the Churubusco Convent far behind us, and the enchanted city of Tlalpan and the beautiful Xochimilco, with its eternally blooming flowers of all shades and fragrances, and the undulating road climbed like a snake, surrounded by huge pines—up to that high plateau, so monotonous and sad and cold, called Las Raíces . . . and at that point Blasio did accept my offer to share the Scottish blanket.

What I didn't tell Blasio was that my *cara, carissima* Carla needed to be cheered up. It was sad for her after her trip to Yucatán, where she had done so well, to get the announcement of the death of her beloved father, King Leopold II, who had written me a letter only a few weeks earlier, saying, "What is needed in America is success. Everything else is just poetry."

"But what's life without poetry?" I asked out loud. "What is it, Blasio?" I asked, and then I said: "Take note Blasio, I must write a letter to Friedrich Ruckert thanking him for writing me a poem after I granted him an Order. It starts like this, if you haven't heard:

Der edle Max von Mexico

'The noble Max of Mexico!' And it ends with:

Und der gesetzt hat Deinen Thron
Lässt fest ihn stehn und nicht im Sturme Wanken.

'And may he who has founded your throne keep it steady so it won't totter in a storm.' Yes, Blasio, remind me to remind 'he who founded my throne,' Louis Napoleon, that he promised to leave the men from the Foreign Legion in Mexico for a few more years when the rest of the French troops are pulled out. Don't forget, Blasio."

Nor did I tell Blasio that it was a tragedy and a shame that Baron d'Huart, a close friend of Leopold II, had been assassinated by some bandits at Río Frío when he was coming to announce the coronation of Empress Carlota's brother—and apropos Leopold II, I told Blasio:

"Please note too that I have to question his refusal to receive Eloin when he was in Claremont; and apropos of Eloin, remind me, Blasio, to ask him to explain why people in Paris don't want to know anything about the Mexican bank, and ask him if he thinks his mission has failed; and apropos of missions, remind me, Blasio, to write Count Rességuier asking him to tell me what it is that Santa Anna is doing in New York, and why he bought a house there, and if it's really true that he's plotting an uprising, and above all to ask him to explain to me why he's been saying (I mean Rességuier) that opposition to my throne has waned in the United States when Father Fischer wrote to me from there saying that a war between Mexico and the Union could hardly be avoided, and apropos of *that*, Blasio, take note . . ."

I was telling Blasio and Blasio was licking the indelible ink pencil, his mouth filthy with purple but his handwriting clear and beautiful as ever:

"Remind me to thank Fischer not only for all his confidential dealings at the Vatican, trying to put together a concordat between my government and the Holy See, but above all for his long and entertaining letters in which he relates so much amusing gossip . . ."

I also didn't tell Blasio what some of that gossip had been about, for instance the story that Cardinal Alfieri—as Fischer told me in his letters—would sell his body and soul to whomever could guarantee him the papal tiara, and that Cardinal Antonelli—who would imagine it?—had a lover—but it wasn't necessary for anyone to imagine it because everyone already knew. And, anyway, what was this little peccadillo of the cardinal's when compared to the harem— over fifteen women!—that, according to Colonel du Barail, a priest of Cholula has at his service? What I *did* tell him when we were on our way to Cuernavaca and we had already passed the Valley of Anáhuac was:

"Of course I'm grateful to Fischer for his letters, because—if after his defeat at Pavia, Francis I of France said, 'All has been lost, except honor'—I say, and take this down Blasio, 'Everything has been lost, except humor.' But no, don't take it seriously, Blasio, it's only a joke; we shall never lose honor, never ever. Scratch that phrase out Blasio, scratch it: it's not worthy of a Habsburg; it's not worthy of he who said 'The silver of the earth cannot be extracted with bayonets.' Do you like that? Yes? And here's another one: 'Fear and ambition are the motors that make the world turn' . . . but don't write those down, Blasio, it's not necessary. I know them by heart; I wrote them down four or five years ago—imagine how ironic, some of them seem even more significant now, in Mexico, than when I first coined them. 'The old nations', I wrote then, 'suffer the affliction of remembrance', and, 'After a while, force and power become a right.' All of those phrases are mine, just like the twenty-seven rules of conduct that I always carry with me. I've read them to you, Blasio, haven't I? But I also know them by heart."

I was saying all this to Blasio on our way to Cuernavaca after we had left behind the cold and arid plain known as El Guarda with its few miserable huts that make the landscape even more desolate and we reached the Monte de Huichilaque fragrant with ocote pines that raise their green tips into the clouds which were so low that we couldn't see three meters in front of us and I was afraid, I told Blasio, that we would be held up by some bandits as happened to Baron d'Huart, may he rest in peace, and once again I recited my precepts of conduct:

"'Never lie; never complain, because it's a sign of weakness; always be measured in temperament; hear everyone out, but confide in few; do not blaspheme or use obscenities; exercise two hours daily; never joke with the subordinates . . .' Although you shouldn't take this last one very seriously." I told Blasio, "You, my good, my patient Blasio, are something more than a subordinate—you are my Mexican friend . . ."

And my Mexican friend smiled with his purple lips and teeth and what I didn't tell him then was that he looked like a smiling cadaver, I only said this to myself as we were crossing Huichilaque, a village of hunters and thieves, beyond all the gloomy plains covered with black rocks, and in the distance there were steep ashen crags, behind us the Cruz del Marqués and ahead, oh! just ahead and very soon the landscape would change into an earthly paradise as soon as my carriage with six white mules harnessed in blue and equipped with a desk and drawers for writing material—what a good idea of Colonel Rodríguez's, I said to myself, and I laughed silently at the dismal appearance of poor Blasio, as soon as—yes, as soon as my carriage would begin its descent into the Valley of Cuernavaca.

"What I mean, Blasio," I continued, "is that with you I can allow myself to poke a little fun at things, like—do you remember?—on that afternoon in Cuernavaca when I told you that whichever one of us lost the billiards game would have to crawl under the table, and it turned out that I lost! Luckily your brother, the Capuchin monk, was there, and so I was eventually able to pass the punishment onto him. And you will forgive me, Blasio, I hope, for the time I told Venisch to ask you to leave the table, because there were thirteen of us, and, as you know, that's bad luck. Though of course, deep inside I'm not superstitious, it's just that I avoid the number thirteen almost by habit—and remind me, remind me, take this down, Blasio, in my next letter to Gutiérrez Estrada I have to tell him that because of the clergy, poor people in Mexico are indeed highly superstitious—remind me, take a note, to tell Gutiérrez Estrada that priests here sell these stamps with which, supposedly, souls can escape Purgatory." I was telling Blasio this, and also telling him to jot down that I had to tell Estrada that just because Empress Carlota and I didn't enjoy praying novenas and the rosary or because we rejected nocturnal flagellations, this didn't make us any less Catholic because of that. And by the way, Mr. Gutiérrez Estrada, please be informed that the Emperor of Mexico has the intention of buying a small church in Rome, yes, yes, in Rome, to consecrate it to the Virgin of Guadalupe, no less.

And halfway through our descent into the valley, past the fog of the high plains and with all the colors of paradise ahead of us, I was reading in Blasio's notes: "*hamaca, petaca*," and I told him:

"Yes, of course, they all rhyme with Cuernavaca, but we can't use any of them, tell me, Blasio, why the Mexican cities I like the most don't have pretty rhymes? What are we going to rhyme with Morelia? Ofelia? Cordelia? What are we going to rhyme with Guanajuato? *Gato, garabato*? And what are we going to rhyme with Cuernavaca? *Vaca flaca*?" Yes, I said this to Blasio and we both laughed, we laughed heartily.

I also said: "Take note, Blasio, when I get back I have to inquire, query, demand—in writing or in person—an explanation from Bazaine as to how it's possible that he hasn't sent reinforcements to General Mejía, who is being harassed at Matamoros by General Escobedo. And further, I'd like to know how he can explain the fact that there are over sixteen thousand guerrilla fighters scattered throughout the country, as I've been told. Also, I must tell Bazaine that it's no longer possible to tolerate the fact that no Mexican policeman or soldier is allowed to arrest a French soldier. And, more, we must tell Louis Napoleon that I cannot forgive him for having authorized Colonel Dupin's return to Mexico. And we must tell my friend, Baroness Binzer, that the compliments Prince Grillprazer paid me when I granted him the Aztec Eagle are an incentive to future achievements. We must tell my teacher and friend, the historian César Cantú, that, as always, I continue reading him with great interest and delight. And then, we must tell my brother the Archduke Louis Victor that one of the things that make me happiest is to see myself surrounded by good people like you, Blasio—don't be modest—or like Schaffer, the Governor of Chapultepec who married a pretty little sixteen-year-old Mexican girl; yes, remind me to tell my brother everything about every one of you, about Günner, the lion of the capital, or old Kuhács, fat and round as a ball on his fiery steed—what a spectacle, Blasio—and of course about Ursula, yes, the great Ursula, the former *mandriera*! And we must tell Eloin that the command of the army will very soon be my own responsibility; and as to my brother, the Emperor Franz Joseph, we must demonstrate to him that a sailor like myself can also organize a land army. And, further, we must ask my brother how it can be possible that his ambassador in Washington, Wydenbruck, didn't leave the table when the vice-minister of the Yankee navy—his name is Bancroft, isn't it?—referred to me as 'the Austrian adventurer.' As to Barandiarán, our representative in Vienna, tell him we cannot expect anything from a government as short on loyalty as that of Austria. Also tell Barandiarán to inform Herzfeld that while it's good for him to take his secret mission with regard to the Family Pact very seriously, let him be very careful about what intrigues he stirs up. He must tell Herzfeld this himself—take note, Blasio."

And Blasio licked the tip of his indelible ink pencil and went on to write:

"Have Herzfeld begin a press campaign in Vienna to refute: *One*, that the Emperor of Mexico has become a Mason—I, a Mason, Blasio, how ridiculous!—and *Two*, to deny that I am willing to accept Mexico's going back to being a republic, so long as I am president—a president, Blasio, what a waste!"

What I meant, as we were descending into the Valley of Cuernavaca, inundated by white and yellow butterflies, was that an Emperor has to know, and be able to do, many more things than a president. That a prince from a European dynasty like the House of Austria has to learn, besides geography, history, mathematics, philosophy, botany, and so many other things, so many languages, and that's why, besides my maternal language, German, I speak French and English, Italian to address the Pope, and a little Hungarian and Polish, and now, of course, Spanish, Blasio. Imagine: all our paper money has its denomination written in ten different languages—those that are spoken throughout the Empire. And in preparation for the day in which our Empire will extend from the Río Grande to Tierra del Fuego, I still need to learn Nahuatl and Mayan, Quechua, Guaraní . . . oh, I remember the names of all my teachers well, Blasio: Esterházy taught me Hungarian, Count von Schneider mathematics, Baron de Binzer political science—I remember them all; and besides, a president doesn't need to know fencing, doesn't have to be acquainted with terms like hand parry, lunge, or foil touch; and a president doesn't need to know—and moreover no president knows anything—about the Viennese Spanish Riding School, and you have to promise me, Blasio, that when I send you to Europe on a special mission you will do two things when you arrive in the city where your emperor was born: one, listen to the

Vienna Boy's Choir, and two, visit the Riding School, and as homework you will learn the names of all the steps and movements of the horses and of the most appropriate music for parading each of them. Oh, for a Pluto Capriola, there's nothing better than Boccherini's "Minuet;" for a Siglavy Flora, a Strauss waltz—which information, I need hardly tell you, a president would find superfluous, but an emperor understands the necessity for these things. He has to know how to dance waltzes, gallops, mazurkas, everything—and how to hunt. I told Blasio, I've hunted deer and rabbits in Compiègne, beccaficos in Algeria, boars in Gödöllő, bears in Albania, ocelots in the Mato Grosso. And do you know why? Do you know why an emperor, a prince, has to learn all that, but a president doesn't? Because in addition to watching over the order, peace, justice, and democracy of his land, as a president does, a prince also has to keep watch over beauty and tradition, over elegance. Yes, elegance, Blasio! I was saying all this to Blasio on our way to Cuernavaca and because the zigzagging descent is quick, and the climate immediately began changing, I did away with my Scottish blanket and I took off my scarf, because I am cold-blooded, it's true, but not so very much—and to our left we saw the flat granite mass of the Cerro de la Herradura, and in the background the houses and the churches loomed up among the fruit trees, and we decided to stop for a snack. Meanwhile I told Blasio:

"Take this down, Blasio, take note. Getting back to Herzfeld: tell him to do a good job organizing the press campaign. Did you know, Blasio, that in 1858 or '59, I don't remember exactly, a German journalist, Julius Reuter, managed to have an entire speech of Louis Napoleon's made public in England only an hour after it was given? Oh, when the interoceanic cables finally come to Mexico and its Emperor's speeches can also be known an hour after they're given, that old and rotten Europe will have to respect us more. So, take note, on another page, Blasio—and please wash your mouth and your hands before we eat—jot this down: We must create a Mexican Press Cabinet for Europe. Yes, a cabinet. And do you know what, Blasio? We're going to work with two primary motivators: money and decorations." I told him all this and I asked him to hand me the briefcase that I always carry on my trips, and my good Blasio did as he was asked.

On our way to Cuernavaca.

On our way to the heat and the butterflies that were already fluttering around us.

On our way to the orange flamboyants and toward the shade of the bougainvilleas in the Borda Gardens.

Or our way to rest and oblivion.

"Yes, *oblivion* . . . that's why I decided to name the villa the Empress likes so much 'El Olvido,'" I told Blasio. "First I wanted to name it for the famous recreational villa of Frederick the Great in Potsdam, Sans Souci . . . but since Haiti's Black King, Christophe, built a palace that he named Sans Souci, well, the appellation lost its charm . . ." That's what I told him, and I opened the briefcase where I sometimes carried spare Orders of Guadalupe and Aztec Eagles, but above all a good number of gold watches with blue enamel covers and on them the monogram and the Imperial crown lined with chips of diamond in order to distribute them to officers, mayors, provincial judges, and other minor functionaries, and I also told Blasio:

"If we had a business manufacturing noble titles, Blasio, we would be rich . . . And if someone were to say that these were only fake titles for a fake nobility, I would respond: After all, the dukes, counts, and marquises created by Bonaparte are almost all as plebeian as the humblest commoner . . ."

And actually I shouldn't have told Blasio that, because a prince also needs to be discreet, and know to whom he can say something and with whom he ought to remain silent. So, I kept my mouth shut and reviewed my twenty-seven rules: "At each step, think of the consequences." "Everything has its time." "If reason is with you, steel your energy, etc., etc.," and then I decided to add a new one: "With your subordinates, discretion, discretion, before anything else." Yes, it would make a good addition to the list, but I didn't tell Blasio to write it down.

But to Blasio—who, while smart and a good fellow, is still only a secretary—I *could* say, as in fact I did:

"Besides which, Blasio, a sovereign must know the lives of the great monarchs and emperors of the past by heart, in order to follow their example. *À propos*, the life of Frederick the Great. That of Charles III of Spain. The lives of all those illustrious Braganzas, such as Pedro V, who was very much loved by his people, or John V, the magnanimous patron of the arts, and of course his antecessor, John IV, who was a great musician, a great composer, as was Prince Alberto, who decreed that monarchs should *not* wear their crown, but that it should rest on a cushion next to them . . . And among the Habsburgs, not only Maria Theresa, but also, of course, her son, Joseph II."

What I couldn't and didn't tell Blasio was that if I had to wear the crown in Cuernavaca, I would also put it aside, set it next to me, so as not to sweat and look as though I was nervous, and also to avoid getting any balder . . .

Because that is exactly the sort of joke that should *not* be made with a subordinate. Likewise the truth, the sad truth, that the Enlightenment or *Aufklärung* of which the French philosophers spoke didn't help my illustrious antecessor Joseph II at all, because he died without being loved by his people and failed in everything . . . and because he was intelligent, because he recognized his failure, he wrote his own epitaph as follows: "Here lies a prince who had honorable intentions, but who had the misfortune of seeing all his ideas come to naught."

Since, like the Mexican saying I admire so much advises, one shouldn't "wash your dirty linen in public."

Blasio's clothing was also dirty. Every time we went to Cuernavaca, on account of the indelible ink pencil—since he not only got his mouth painted purple but also his fingers, and he would stain his shirt, his coat, his trousers, his handkerchief . . . luckily, his table clothes were impeccable. Venisch made us wait a while because his mules were slower than my white ones, but when he arrived at last we began to set the marvels he had brought out on the tablecloths: fresh cheese, turkey stuffed with truffles, potato croquettes, smoked ham, mangoes and prickly pears, candied citron—and when they offered me bread, I said no, thank you, I prefer tortillas, and I remember telling Blasio that an Emperor must also learn to eat everything his subjects eat:

"Imagine, I was the one who, after eating chili at Bahía de Todos los Santos, had such pains in his mouth that I swore never to eat another hot dish again, and now, as you can see Blasio, I eat more chili than you and many Mexicans and I learned to eat *mole* just as in Algeria I learned to enjoy the national dish of the Bedouins, the couscous, which should be eaten with your hands, as you probably know, and even though I didn't get to attend any of the sumptuous parties that Aumale used to give when he was Viceroy of Algeria, I enjoyed my trip very much. In that torrid heat, Blasio, there's nothing better than to take refuge in those dark, cool tents made of camel hair and drink the sweet water that the Bedouins carry in goat skin canteens and that Yusuf served me in silver cups, although I always thought I saw some of the deceased goat's hairs swimming in the water . . ."

And we shared our lunch as well as our wine with our escort, and I told Blasio as I myself filled his glass:

"It's incredible, the number of things an Emperor has to take care of. Did you know Blasio that one day, at a banquet in Chapultepec, I found a wine named 'Montebello' on the wine list? We had to reprint the menus right away, and with precious little time, because, imagine, how could I offer my guests a wine with the name of two battles in which the French defeated the Austrians? How, Blasio?"

What I didn't tell him, because it served no purpose, was that in the first Battle of Montebello, fourteen thousand French sent eighteen thousand Austrians running all the way to Alessandria. That was shameful. But I *did* tell him this:

"I promise you, Blasio, that I'm going to let you eat in peace and that I won't do any more dictating until after dessert, but this, this is important, take note—in the Saccone order—but please don't put that pencil in your mouth while we're eating, dip it in water. Here, please, a glass of water for young Blasio."

And Blasio obediently dipped the tip of the pencil in a glass of water and wrote:

"Twelve bottles of tandoori curry, which I promised Commodore Maury. English salts for the Empress. Oh, and also for the Empress—heliotrope pills. And paprika, Blasio, paprika for the kitchen and the goulash of my faithful Tüdös!"

By this time the water in the glass had become a lilac color, and I remember raising the glass high and I said:

"*Crème d'Amour*, Blasio, this is the exact color of *crème d'amour*—have them send us several boxes. And also of the Malmsey wine from Madeira, the *Vinho das Senhoras!*"

And I almost said, the *Vinho das Senhoras par excellence*, but I didn't, because if it's all right for an emperor to use some expressions in other languages in his conversation, I had decided not to do it terribly often, though one of life's ironies, the more I try to speak Spanish, the more my court functionaries try to learn phrases in French; *tant pis*, I said to myself, making fun of myself, but like I'm always telling Carla: "Patience, my dear Carla, patience, *da tempo al tempo.*"

And because I'd promised Blasio not to make him take dictation while we were eating, I kept telling him about my trips to Algeria between each bite and each sip, but what I didn't tell him was that I discovered a secret affinity there with my illustrious predecessor Rudolf II, when I discovered that I was delighted to see myself surrounded by black dwarfs, hunchbacks, and other kinds of freaks—though when I decide to publish my memoirs, the whole world will find this out. But what I *did* tell him was:

"Don Julián Hourcade is already making plans for the first ice factory. Don Luis Mayer has proposed to build installations for extracting flammable gas. We've adopted the decimal-based metric system. In Sierra de Huauchinango, we're carrying out archeological explorations . . . oh, remind me Blasio, to go over the scale model of the Temple of Xochicalco that we'll be sending to the Paris Exposition with Monsieur Médehin . . . I've been told that the Viceroy of Egypt will send a scale model of the Great Temple of Edfu; our scale model of the Temple de Xochicalco has to be bigger, don't you think? And, as I was telling you, Don Génaro Vergara invented a motor run by wind. We founded the Ministry of Public Instruction and Worship and we've established mandatory and free primary education. Meanwhile, we consolidated the Empire even more with the addition of Baja California. We're going to build an oil refinery. And what does all this mean? That your Emperor, Blasio, has to take care of many serious things, and not only, as the malicious gossipers say, of poetry and butterflies . . ."

But what I didn't tell Blasio when we were already at the outskirts of the city and I was wearing my white Panama hat with its gold ribbon was that those same malicious gossipers were accusing me of having numerous lovers: Lola Hermosillo, Emilia Blanca, a so-called Miss Armida, another one nicknamed *La India Bonita* (Luz Bringas), and God knows who else—but no one, no one will ever know whether or not I've really had or have a lover. If I could talk freely, Blasio, I would tell you that I, your Emperor, am sometimes very weak. Since that time at the slave market of Smyrna, when I discovered the upsetting beauty of women's bodies . . . ah, Blasio, since then . . . Look, I adore the Empress, but I like to imagine that when I arrive in Cuernavaca, Blasio, in Cuanáhuac, the city where the Marquis of the Valley of Oaxaca, Hernán Cortés, built himself a palace, that there, just as La Malinche waited for the Conqueror, that I, the King of Tula, shall be greeted by Xochitl, the Queen of Flowers, with a bowl of fermented agave juice distilled from her lips . . . and between her thighs. I am frail in matters such as these, yes—but not in politics. My weakness is not the kind that Turgot referred to when he told Louis XVI that it was Charles I of England's political weakness that had led him to having his head cut off by his subjects . . . oh, no!

And because we would soon be entering the city, and my boys from the Rooster Club would surely be waiting for us—a club that, as I was saying in a letter to Count Hadik, is a group of volunteers who make up my Honor Guard in Cuernavaca, wearing a uniform that consists of black pants, a blue blouse, a gray felt hat with a white feather, and a golden rooster on the chest—wanting to escort me to my Borda Villa; and because, once there, I would have to offer them wine; and after they had left, I would lie in my white hammock and not feel like dictating anything to Blasio for hours, maybe even days, I hasten now to tell him:

"Take note Blasio, take note quickly: I must tell Emperor Napoleon that I will be sending him several volumes of laws—every one that I've promulgated here in Mexico. I must ask Bazaine in person for an explanation as to why Tamaulipas is teeming with bands of Juaristas, and must tell him in writing that I'm thinking of naming him a count or duke of something. The Count of Oaxaca, Blasio? No, better the Duke of Puebla. I must tell my brother Louis Victor that Emperor Moctezuma used to eat fresh fish daily brought in from Veracruz by couriers, and that I am going to reinstate that system. I must write Father Fischer to have him tell them at the Vatican that, with regard to Riche-lieu and the Edict of Nantes, when he reinstated it, it had an amendment that stripped the Protestants of all their political and military rights, and that I can-not do the same in Mexico—least of all if we're going to colonize this country with Confederates! As for Pierron, remind me to ask him to stop comparing my situation to that of Joseph Bonaparte—I don't have Napoleon for a brother advising me to execute my subjects and to rely on galleys, gunpowder, and the gallows as a means of keeping order. Also, I must tell Pierron to remember the words of Julian the Apostate: he who said that a prince is a living law that must temper the excessive rigor of old, defunct laws with kindness. We must tell the Mayor of Cuernavaca to place a commemorative plaque at the Baptismal Font where the first Tlaxcalteca senator to embrace Christianity was baptized. To Saccone and Speed, Blasio, ask that they send us some bottles of saffron, because, as you know, Tüdös likes to use saffron to color the clam chowder . . . To Almonte, send a message asking that he update me as to the progress of his mission to the Tuileries. Send messages to those who are opposing the return of Miramón and Márquez to Mexico to remind them that Miramón participated in the heroic defense of the Military Academy at Chapultepec against the Yankees, and that, for bravery shown in numerous military actions—some of them against foreign invaders—Márquez received the Cross of Texas, the Iron Cross of the Valley of Mexico, the Cross of the Angostura, and the Cross of Ahualulco. And to Don Benito Juárez, who, as you will remember, Blasio, told me in a letter I received on my arrival in Mexico that '*History will be our judge*,' send him a message saying: Yes, you're right Señor Juárez, but if we make peace right now, and you accept the post of my prime minister, History will judge us much more benevolently—take that down, Blasio," and Blasio licked, made notes, licked, wrote; the poor fellow licked his indelible pencil and wrote some new rhymes for Cuernavaca— like *petaca, alpaca, carraca*.

"Enough," I told him. "There are none that work, Blasio, and there are even worse ones like the one I'm thinking of right now . . . but I won't say it to you, God help me, though you can guess what it is, I think, if I tell you, Blasio," and I covered my nose, "if I tell you that . . . *Apesta*! It stinks!"

And Blasio cried with laughter. I know it's not proper to allow a subordinate to laugh like that in front of his emperor, it's not respectful, but that time I let it pass—poor Blasio. He worked so hard on our way to Cuernavaca, and now the tears of laughter ran down his face and mixed with his sweat, and when they got to his lips—by that time his teeth, his palate, his tongue were all stained as well—they picked up the ink and ran down his chin like trickles of purple blood.

"Never again," I told him, "will I let you write with an indelible pencil. And now, finally, take this down, Blasio: We must write to Benito Juárez informing him that a pension has been granted to General Zaragoza's widow. And to Baroness Binzer to tell her that the people who are saying that all the Mexican scientists and intellectuals oppose the Empire, are liars. We have Río de la Loza, Roa Bárcena, García Icazbalceta, and many others on our side. To my brother, Franz Joseph, send thanks for having authorized the formation of the Corps of Austrian Volunteers . . . thousands of them will come, you'll see—they won't abandon their Emperor's brother, I'm sure of it, and lastly—and lastly, take note, Blasio, and with this we'll call an end to our daylong dictation: jot down a great idea that I've been ruminating over—ruminating is the proper word— for several weeks. We should celebrate *comme il faut*, properly, the next 15th of September—and what would be more Mexican, jot this down, Blasio, than having a banquet at the Imperial Palace with, pay attention, the whole menu, from the hors d'oeuvres to the dessert and the digestives, consisting of dishes and beverages that will have . . . try to guess, Blasio . . . only the three colors—green, white, and red—of the Mexican flag; take note, Blasio, I've already memorized the entire menu: first a fruit cocktail on a bed of green grapes, with pieces of white pear and strawberries in the middle; next an avocado mousse with pieces of white cheese and red pimientos; then a spinach soup with some cream in the middle, and on top, chopped sugar beets, the reddest we can find; and for the main courses, on a bed of green *mole*, a truncated cone of white rice crowned with whole radishes, and, on a bed of green asparagus, white fish from Lake Pátzcuaro, the whitest we can find, and on top some kernels of red pomegranate; for salads, take this down Blasio, one of nopal leaves, with the whitest onions and the reddest tomatoes, and another one of lettuce with turnips and red cabbage—don't miss any detail—and then for dessert, green melon filled with cream, and on the cream some cherries, and a jelly of green apple with grated coconut and pieces of red plum, and of course, for ice cream, what else, Blasio, but a *cassata* of pistachio, soursop, and currant; and finally, a slice of watermelon—which already has the three colors in a nothing-less-than-providential order—for everybody. And we will drink lemonade, rice water, hibiscus tea and, as digestives, crème de menthe, and pear and blackberry brandy, and, you know what, Blasio, we'll even use green tablecloths and white napkins and, as a centerpiece, we'll have a big tray filled with crushed ice, bordered all around with red roses and, in its center—you'll never guess, Blasio—a huge imperial Mexican eagle . . . made entirely of caviar!"

I was telling all of this to Blasio, asking him to write it all down while we made our way to Cuernavaca, towards paradise and oblivion.

•

"She was a flower among flowers, Your Honor. A flower as sweet as can be. Her words were nectar. Her lips dark rose honey. I am a humble man, Your Honor. I come from far away, from a steep mountain where, if you look up to the top, you can see toucans drinking the dew from the calyxes of the orchids that dangle from the tops of the tallest trees. Before anything else is said, I want there to be no doubt as to how much I loved Concepción and also how much love I can still give her. How could it be any other way, how could it not be so, Your Honor, if, as I was saying, Concepción was the flower of all flowers? A jasmine when she slept, or a wild violet with sticky leaves that caught, like mosquitoes, all the handsome young men who wanted her for themselves, even though she was mine, my very own, she belonged to my will, to my arms, my little violet poppy. How could I not love Concepción? When I met her, she was almost a child. And I say almost, because, even then, you could see the woman that she would become. Do you know, Sir, those little pink and purple flowers called *cundeamor* that spring up here and there all over the land, and that sway lazily from the living rock? This is how my love for her has spread, from her feet like lilies to her hair washed with Palo Santo soap. Her feet were small, her hair black and radiant. Between her hair and her toes, besides her eyes and her mouth, Concepción had other attributes that I will not describe here, and, with all due respect, Your Honor, you need not concern yourself with them. I am not a very learned man, Sir. There's much in this world I know nothing about. But I'm not a total ignoramus either. Ask me anything that has to do with flowers. Ask me which ones give the cacao tree its shade, and I'll tell you they're called *cacahuananches*; they are small and pink and look like little butterflies. And if you want to find out how to get rid of freckles, I can tell you that nothing works better than the ointment made by crushing the bulbs of the flower called a zephyr lily. If someone who wants to plant daturas in his garden asks me, Sedano, listen here Sedano, tell me when the white trumpets of the datura bloom, I will tell him all year round, just like my Concepción, who, once she bloomed, remained a flower forever. I don't mean to imply that I know your trade, but I'm a gardener by birth, Your Honor. I was born in a poor house full of flowers, and my grandfather, who once was the gardener of a big house in San Cristóbal Ecatepec, taught me the names of all the species and he taught me how to talk to them—he taught me not to touch the mimosa, not even with my fingertips, so as not to suffocate it, and to forgive the *Aristolochia* for its bad smell in case we need to borrow some of its leaves to heal snakebite later on. I learned many other things about flowers and plants, and God knows what twists of fate brought me to the Valley of Cuernavaca. I began working as a gardener's assistant in a large house and then in an even larger one, and then without realizing it I became foreman of gardeners at a still larger house that they call the Borda Villa, where many times during the year the gentleman they call Don Maximiliano came to live, and they say—at least that's what they told me—that he's the King of Mexico. By that time Concepción Sedano and I were living together—she took the name Sedano after we'd gotten married. I, with my own hands, wove her a crown of orange blossoms, and I sewed over a hundred wild daisies into her bridal veil, and irises and arum and white lilies too, though it wasn't with my own hands that I deflowered Concepción Sedano that night. On a trip I was later forced to make and of which I will tell you shortly, I learned about a hummingbird that sucks the honey from the red flower of the xoconostle, and that if it doesn't get stuck in its long thorns it's only because it remains airborne, flapping its invisible wings, holding still in the air while it sucks. I, who don't have wings, Your Honor, got stuck forever on Concepción's thorns. And now tell me, Your Honor, what can a man do if he has a job and a religion and he neither lacks food nor a hammock to rest in on Sunday afternoons—what can he do, except be happy, almost by force? And if we were happy, if we were happy even for one day, we stopped being happy, at first little by little, when Señor Don Maximiliano first arrived at the Borda Villa, and then very suddenly, the day I realized that Don Maximiliano was looking at Concepción, and Concepción was looking at Don Maximiliano, with a kind of look that I'd never seen before, a look that seemed to have been invented between the two of them. I don't want to be in contempt of the law, Your Honor. As I told you, I'm a humble man, but also as I told Concepción so many times, oh Concepción, look at it this way and look at it that way. Look at yourself in the mirror so you won't be surprised by your own beauty, look at your skin. Does Your Honor know those scorpions made out of vanilla branches that people make during Corpus Christi? Well Concepción's skin was just as dark and aromatic and narcotic. The color of her soul was something else—I never told you this, but I should have, it must have been white, back when she was immaculate. When day and night she was my Immaculate Conception. What I mean to say is, as far as her exterior went, that just like those small flowers called *linda tarde* or *guayabillo* are meant to grow wild—anyone can see them, coming down the slopes of the mountains in fall, as if the snow had suddenly started bleeding—just like those flowers are meant to grow wild, I say, the rose called Queen Isabella is meant for the salons, and the proof is that on more than one occasion I was ordered to make a bouquet of those flowers to place in Don Maximiliano's rooms when Queen Carlota was going to stay at La Borda . . . and as everyone knows, just like the elegance of the rose doesn't take away its thorns, the wildness of the *guayabillo* flowers, Your Honor, in no way invalidates their beauty—do you understand? And coming back to Concepción's inner being, Your Honor, whoever saw her, whoever saw her getting up every morning to prepare my chocolate with leaves from the *flor del corazón*, as I had taught her, who saw her—when I would go to work in the big garden—staying home doing her chores all day long, dedicated to her house, to dusting the floor with a broom made of branches and aromatic herbs, who saw her washing and ironing my shirts and my white trousers because the administrator liked to see them looking impeccable (though, as you know, sometimes one gets stained by the wet soil or by the green of the grass, or by the juices of the scarlet creeper), who saw, when I came back in the evening, how she had my pumpkin-flower quesadillas ready, my beans and my tortillas—if anyone were to see her doing all this, whoever that might be, they would be bound to treasure her, as I myself did, as I did more than anyone else in the world. But at night—oh, Concepción, my Concepción, if I'd only known which scorpion bit you, I would have found the sunflower that could have cured you. Your Honor, when *cojón de oro* flowers burst, you should see how the trees get covered, they look like they've been carpeted with cotton balls. And my grandfather would tell me, wisely, that before magnolias bloom, they need to grow for ten or even twenty years, just like women. And just like geraniums can breathe the air better when it's cool, hydrangeas turn blue or pink according to the quality of the soil. And finally, Your Honor, the iris was born from the tears that our mother Eve shed when she left Paradise behind her. I know all of that. I know how to kill worms and weeds, and about fertilizers and manures to make the earth more responsive. But I don't know about other things and never knew about them, never understood how Concepción could suddenly turn into one of those female cats that leave when the sun sets and don't return till the early hours of the morning, wet with saliva, shaking, knocking over the bowl of milk that's waiting for them. What I do know, however, is when all this started, more or less, and it was one afternoon when I was with Concepción in the big garden planting some bulbs that she had in the lap of her skirt, which she'd raised a bit with her hands so as to keep the bulbs from rolling down, and Señor Don Maximiliano came by, accompanied by another foreign gentleman who always had a yellow umbrella and cut plants without asking anyone's permission and caught beetles and lizards by the tail to put them in some flasks that hung by cords from his neck and shoulders. And that gentleman kept telling Don Maximiliano the names of the flowers. But he wouldn't say this is a yellow rockrose and that's a speckled carnation, and still less that that one is *cacomite* and this one is *acocotl*, since I suppose that if that gentleman didn't know Spanish, it was even less likely that he knew any words in the local Indian language. No, he was giving Don Maximiliano the scientific names of the flowers, in Latin, Your Honor, as in the church songs. Then they got to a flower whose name the gentleman did not remember, and Don Maximiliano asked me. I had already taken off my hat and answered; "These are the golden cups, Sir, and the water from their calyxes that must be removed before the flowers can bloom are used as drops for swollen eyes—and because of their hooded shape they are also called Napoleon's Caps, sometimes, too, Busty Ladies." And Don Maximiliano laughed, but not the other gentleman, he seemed upset with me because all he knew about each flower was its Latin name, just one name and nothing else, while I on the other hand know three or four names for each, and sometimes up to ten, depending on if they're planted in Cuernavaca or if they grow in Tomatlán or if once they wilt they lose their leaves in the waters of the Tamesí River. And when no one knows the name of a flower and there's no way to find out, I take some water in my hands and I baptize it: I let the water drip between my fingers and I say, "Flower, because you are white and small and you grow scattered among other blue flowers and you open up when it dawns, I baptize you, flower, as Dawn's Little Foam." And Don Maximiliano, who pretended not to have seen Concepción, kept asking me the names of many more flowers, which I kept giving him, until suddenly he turned to see her, and Concepción, who till then had been looking at the ground, also pretending as though she hadn't seen Don Maximiliano, raised her eyes to him. Don Maximiliano then asked her, "And what's your name?" but before she could answer, I stood up and told him, "Concepción. Concepción Sedano, Sir—she's my wife." I was even tempted to put on my hat so as to tell him that I was the master of that particular flower named Concepción, the flower of all the flowers. I signaled to Concepción to stand up, and Concepción, so as not to spill the bulbs on the ground, got up with her skirt raised, showing her legs just above her knees, without taking her eyes off Don Maximiliano, and I told myself—I told myself the truth many days later—that it hardly mattered now that they'd never seen each other before, since from that moment on it was as though they'd known each other all their lives. In reality, I never saw them together. I never followed Concepción when she would get up at night and leave the room quietly. Well, that's what she thought, Sir, that she was being quiet—but I know a lot about silence. May God forgive me: I never saw Concepción and Don Maximiliano, as I told you. That is to say I never saw them with my eyes open, Your Honor, because I saw them with my eyes closed, and even today, if you let me close my eyes for a moment, I can see them together. Don Maximiliano had a large bed in his room, one of the ones that have a tulle mosquito net made with golden crosspieces. In the corridor, under a huge flowerpot full of ferns that hung from the ceiling next to a birdcage, Don Maximiliano also had a very wide white silk hammock. I saw the two of them there many times, with my eyes closed, trying to imagine what the entire world was already talking about, though they themselves thought it was still a secret. There's a garden wall close to Don Maximiliano's rooms at the Borda Villa that has a door hidden by bellflowers. And if I never saw Concepción go in or out of that door with my own eyes, what I can tell you is that when Concepción would come back at dawn, she still had little lilac and white leaves tangled in her hair. I know all the Borda gardens like the palm of my hand, their paths, their hiding places, their fountains, and their statues. I also know what I used to call the pond of the bougainvilleas because sometimes it would be almost covered with flowers. Though I once removed some wet bougainvillea flowers that had stuck to Concepción's back, I never saw the two of them getting into the pond naked, may God help me, and embrace each other naked among the leaves and the lilies and the little red and gold fish. And when I say the two of them, I don't mean Concepción and Don Maximiliano, Your Honor, but Concepción and the other man, Your Honor, whoever it was. But just in case, just in case it was Don Maximiliano, I assure you that I will not say, like Job: God giveth her to me, God taketh her away from me, Hallowed be the name of the Lord. Because if it was truly God who gave me Concepción, it was a man and not God who took her away from me. And, I think, if a king has a garden and a house as big as those, and in addition he has other, even bigger, palaces and castles and gardens, why would he deprive someone who has nothing of the only thing he has? Because if I have mentioned 'my' house, Your Honor, mine and Concepción's, it was just a manner of speaking, as when I say 'my garden' I'm referring to the one that surrounded 'our' house, because both were only being loaned to us as long as I worked at the Borda Villa, the proof of which is that today I have nothing at all. Though, if you will allow me to say so, to make this judgment, I liked to think that if Don Maximiliano's house was too small for such a big garden, my house, on the contrary, was too big for such a small garden. The following day, Sir, the morning after I imagined them in the bougainvillea pond, I took a bunch of small anise flowers, also called *flores de tierradentro*, which are used to scent children's baths, and I spread them in the water. The next dawn, when Concepción returned, a great smell of anise, Your Honor, the greatest smell of anise that I've ever known, oppressed my soul. As angry and hurt as I was, I never did anything to Concepción, I never touched her except as a man touches a woman. I only cried a bit, I got up, went to the pond, and spread powdered *patol* seed for the fish, but without meaning to kill, only to help them sleep, and perhaps forget what they had seen. Things went on like this until one day when the overseer called me and told me, "Sedano, get your things ready, because you're going to work somewhere else for a while, Señor Don Maximiliano wants you to learn to recognize new plants." I don't know why, but when the overseer told me that, I was sure of two things. The first was that Concepción was not going to go with me, and that she would stay at La Borda, and not even because she had been told to, but of her own free will. The second was that perhaps Señor Don Maximiliano didn't really care whether I stayed or went, and that the overseer was only trying to curry favor with him, and later perhaps they would tell him that I had gone away, leaving my wife abandoned. I told the administrator I wanted to see Don Maximiliano and he answered that he wasn't at the Borda Villa, that he was in Mexico City governing. I told him I could go to Mexico City to see him, and he answered no, Don Maximiliano was always very busy. And then I asked him . . . but it didn't happen that way, Your Honor, I didn't ask for anything else, because I don't like to ask many things of people, only of God. And I asked God, as I am asking you now, to watch over my Concepción while I was away, and to cure her of the scorpion bite she had received, so that on my return to La Borda I would find her as she had been before. They took me far away in a stagecoach, Your Honor, and then in another one and still another one, and then by burro through the sierra until we got to a hacienda where there was a gentleman who had a greenhouse and I worked there and learned many things that I could use when I got back home, Sir, and I was paid well and I was even able to save a bit of money. But I got tired of being there, so far away, waiting for Concepción who would never find me, so one night without telling my boss, and not because of ingratitude but out of fear that I wouldn't be allowed to go if I asked, I left the hacienda without anyone seeing me and I headed toward the Valley of Cuernavaca. So that no one would see me on the road, I returned using detours that I know, even though it was the first time I used those paths, since they aren't paved with stones, but with forget-me-nots—those roads of everlasting flowers that are like yellow bridges between

460

the rainy season and winter, the paths that lead into the blue tunnels created by the cloak of the Virgin when it stretches from one tree to the other in order to dry out—those roads, Your Honor, on which, for those who appreciate them, for those who know the language of flowers, each rose is a compass. And I walked like that for many days and many nights, and during the day the pink flags of the carnations showed me the way, and at night the nocturnal pitahaya flowers would light my path. Then, I walked through sierras, prairies, and gullies with Concepción always in front of me, and though I ran into bad people I had to hide from, I also met good people, as there are everywhere, who would offer me a drop of mezcal, Your Honor, and a dish of hot beans that we would eat together while silently watching the forests burning. At any rate, I never lacked for food, because I know very well when the corollas of the temple flower are ripe, and no one has to tell me when the red clusters of the mother cocoa plant is asking to be eaten. I had plenty of water too, because I'm just as familiar with the orchids whose bulbs are always full, and I know how to suck the stamen of the comb flower so as to sip the nectar that it keeps for travelers. And along the way I baptized several new flowers that I discovered. A little flower that comes in many colors and grows like a cloud on the sides of mountains, I named 'rainbow cloud.' Another white flower that only grows around trees and has narrow red spots I called 'San Sebastián's blood.' And an orchid with long, sharp, and very dark leaves with purple veins, I called 'Satan tongues'—like the tongues, Your Honor, the evil tongues that hurt me so much, first when I still lived at the Borda Villa, and later when I returned to Cuernavaca and they told about the other thing, which I'm going to tell you too, but after I tell you something else—I'm a man, as you can see, Your Honor: I like women and I know how to mount them, if I can put it that way, and no disrespect meant to the court. I like the two roses women have at the tips of their breasts, and I like what they have farther down, the secret flower, as it's known, with its black, pinned butterfly wings spread open. What I'm trying to say to you is that, as a man, I was never cold to Concepción. Does Your Honor know that creeper plant of orange flowers called *llamarada* that climbs through the walls of Taxco and Cuernavaca? Well, just like that, Your Honor, I, full of little flames, would hang from her body, hanging from her mouth with my teeth, hanging from her breasts with my hands, and leaving my male honey in her, to scent her womb with a child. But if Concepción had a child, as I was soon told, it wasn't mine. If one day they came to take Concepción away to La

461

Borda, because her belly was enormous, because she was about to give birth—according to what they told me—well, I couldn't say for certain, God forbid, that the child was Señor Don Maximiliano's, but I can swear before the Virgin and even just counting the months that I'd been away, yes, I can swear, as I was telling you, that the child wasn't mine. "Oh, Concepción!"—I cried to myself, and repeated it a thousand times, as though she could hear me—"You who carry your sin in your name! To think that once you used to be my Immaculate Conception!" I didn't want to believe them, I didn't want to believe that Concepción was no longer at the Borda Villa, so I went to look for her right away, and I knocked at the door, and when someone I'd never seen before asked me who I was, I told him, I am Sedano, I am Señor Sedano—because Your Honor should know that if I'm not a *señor* all the time, like Your Honor is, or like Señor Don Maximiliano, I was when I was chief gardener, and I had Pompilio, or Guadalupe, or Pantaleón to help me, and they called me Señor Sedano—but none of them worked there any more, according to what they told me, or anyway they didn't want to call them to come and identify me, and it was then that I began to shout Concepción, Concepción until my voice grew hoarse and it was then that the police arrived, Your Honor, and brought me here.

Your Honor, I am an honest man. As I told you before, when I talked about the toucans that drink from the flowers, I come from a faraway land, where there are also tiny birds the size of your little finger, emerald in color, and if you put one of them on one end of a scale and put two grams of anything, even angel hair, on the other, the little bird will always be lighter. Your Honor, I promise you that I will go back home and never again show my face in the Valley of Cuernavaca. I promise to take Concepción with me, and if she wants, I'm even willing to take her child along. I don't promise you or anyone else that I shall regard him as my own child, but I do promise to take care of him, to teach him what I know, and promise that he will never lack food. Although with time, who knows? Concepción doesn't have my blood either, and you see how I came to love her. But before that, in order to do all that, in order to keep my promise, and most importantly of all, oh, Your Honor, I need to have my Concepción back. And if you return her to me, oh, Your Honor, if you convince her to come back to me once and for all, I promise you by what is most sacred, I promise you on her name that I will forget everything that's happened and be happy as in those days when she was my Immaculate Conception by day and by night: a sunflower in the mornings, tall and graceful and with her face to the sky; a flamboyant in the late afternoons when the setting sun painted her skin orange; a jasmine when the night skies were strewn with stars and a blooming moon. When I would say to her, "Oh, Concepción, Concepción, with the tallest of the mayflowers I will weave two wreaths: one for the Virgin and another one for your bed. Oh, Concepción, Concepción, with *cielitos de los campos*, with violet sweet peas, and with pansies of three different colors, I will make a rug for our home. Oh, Concepción, Concepción, when the purple rain of the *jacarandas* begins to fall I will invite you to come, naked, and remember that you love me, and I will make you a dress then from little petals drenched in your sweat and mine."

2. The Manatee of Florida

"But that woman is out of her mind! *The Manatee of Florida*! *The Reindeer of Lapland*!"

"No, *Maman*, no. You have to call the cards slower . . . Anyway, yes, that's why they took her away in a straitjacket."

"How horrible, how shameful! *The Manatee of Florida*! In a straitjacket! Drinking dirty water from the fountains!"

"It's yours, Louis."

Louis Napoleon took a silver lune and put it on a manatee with fins like a child's hands.

"*The Reindeer of Lapland*! But how could all of you put up with her?"

Eugénie put a diamond on the Reindeer of Lapland and sighed:

"What else could we do, *Maman*? She wouldn't listen to reason. Ever since she arrived at Saint-Nazaire we told her that Louis was ill, that he had just returned from Vichy . . ."

"And were the thermal baths good for you, Sire? *The Gorilla of Guinea*! Goodness, what an ugly animal!"

Louis Napoleon picked up an iridescent opal and replied:

"Not at all, *Madame la Comtesse*. They didn't help in the least . . ."

He placed the opal on the Gorilla of Guinea.

"Oh, *Maman*, you can't imagine how ill Louis was. Dr. Guillón told him that he had an inflamed prostate, and the day before Charlotte arrived, they had to apply leeches to him, can you imagine it, *Maman*?"

"Oof, awful! *The Cobra of Punjab*! Did you tell Charlotte all that?"

"Of course not, *Maman*. But we insisted she not come here."

"And she ignored us. We suggested that she go to Belgium first. But you see, *Maman la Comtesse*—she took the first train to Paris . . ."

"How rude. *The Llama of Peru!*"

"I was so patient, *Maman*, so patient!"

"Because you're an angel, my daughter. *The Llama of Peru!* Oh, if only your sister Paca were still living!"

Louis Napoleon loved parlor games. Sometimes he played *Gioco dell'Oca*, a game that Philip II had made popular in Spain, with the little imperial prince. He also played Parcheesi or Chinese checkers with Eugénie.

"Can you imagine, *Maman la Comtesse*, what it was like to have that woman here?"

"Not here, but at Saint-Cloud . . ."

"It amounts to the same thing. I was saying . . . to have that demented woman here, screaming at us in front of our ministers?"

"Oof, how awful! *The Buffalo of Malaysia!*"

"Having the nerve to say that she came to talk about a problem that was as much ours as hers?"

"Shocking! *The Crocodile of the Nile!*"

Eugénie put a black onyx bead on the crocodile and said:

"She scolded us for not putting her up at the Tuileries. She complained that no one had notified the Mayor of Saint-Nazaire of her arrival. That the Mayor displayed the flag of Peru . . ."

"How terrible. *The Bison of Canada!* And why of Peru?"

"Because everything went wrong, *Maman*. When she arrived in Paris she got off at one station and our delegates were waiting for her at another!"

"How unfortunate . . . Poor woman!"

Sometimes all three—he, Eugénie, and Loulou—would play a game called *Le Jeu des Bons Enfants*, or else the game of garden mazes, or another called Travels in Mysterious China, and whenever possible, they tried to cheat so as to allow Loulou to win. It made him so happy. About Parcheesi, Louis Napoleon had told his wife and son that Emperor Akbar Jalaluddin, Hindustan's greatest monarch, liked the game so much that he had a patio paved with the board's design so that he and his viziers and courtiers could play from their balconies, using sixteen odalisques from the harem, four in yellow, four in green, four in red, and four in blue. Loulou couldn't believe it.

"She isn't a poor woman, *Maman*. Do you realize that she called us murderers? She said we were trying to poison her!"

"Oh, yes, with a glass of orangeade, wasn't it? *The Camel!*"

"Yes, with a glass of orangeade . . ."

"*The Camel of Kurdistan!* When I heard that part in Spain, I couldn't believe it . . . You have the Camel, Sire."

"Oh, Louis, always so absentminded. You have the Camel of Kurdistan. Tell me, Louis, is something hurting you?"

"No, no, no . . . I was just thinking . . ."

"That's natural, Sire, very natural. Who wouldn't be absentminded with so many problems?"

Louis Napoleon chose a green iridescent lune for the Camel of Kurdistan.

"Quite so, *Maman la Comtesse*. Did you know that the Prussians have mobilized nearly one million troops . . ."

"Oof, how dangerous! *The Tiger of Bengal!*"

"And as I told Charlotte, I don't want to have a war with the United States. It's enough that I can't stomach the American ambassador."

One time, only once, they'd played the game invented by Mr. John Wallis called World History and Chronology. Loulou had been highly amused but Louis Napoleon didn't like it at all, since it was history from the point of view of the English, starting out with Adam and Eve, to be sure, but ending with Queen Victoria and Prince Albert at the center of the board and crowned with angels and laurel wreaths.

"I would be willing to bet that she was faking. *The Toucan of Pernambuco!*"

"Faking, *Maman?*"

"Yes, faking."

"And was she faking madness when she put her fingers into His Holiness's hot cocoa?"

"Oh, how droll . . . *The Monkey* . . . !"

"And when she put her arm into a pot of boiling water at the convent?"

"Oof, how dreadful! *The Spider Monkey of Guatemala!*"

"And when she stayed to sleep in the Vatican library?"

"Oof, what sacrilege!"

"That's not faking, *Maman*. Charlotte is demented."

"Oh yes. Out of her mind."

No, he ought to make up his own game, which would certainly start with Adam and Eve, who belonged to the whole world, but would end with him, with them, with Louis Napoleon and Eugénie, and the little imperial prince, all crowned in glory. And it should include all the important dates and places in French history, and in particular those of his dynasty: 18 Brumaire, Austerlitz . . .

"*The Raccoon of Darien!*"

. . . Wagram, Marengo . . .

"*The Anteater—*"

. . . Magenta and Solferino . . .

"*. . . of the Rocky Mountains!*"

. . . Sebastopol, the taking of Puebla and Oaxaca, Kabylia. Napoleon I surely would have approved of such a game, since he—among other things—had had a china service embossed with the Napoleonic Code in order to educate the King of Rome.

"And why didn't you put her up at the Tuileries, in fact?"

"Oh, *Maman*, because we were at Saint-Cloud . . . By the way, she arrived with two Mexican ladies-in-waiting, Señora del Barrio and another one whose name escapes me. To say that they were very peculiar is an understatement. Both were very short and dark-complexioned. Prosper Mérimée said that . . . what was it, Louis?"

"That they looked like monkeys . . ."

"Yes, monkeys in crinolines . . . But I'll tell you this, *Maman*. Charlotte was received with all imperial honors . . . When she arrived at Saint-Cloud, Loulou met her with the Mexican Eagle around his neck . . ."

"Oh yes, how I wish I could have seen him. *The Hippopotamus of the Niger!* Oof, what a fat animal!"

"But she didn't show the least bit of compassion. Louis could hardly walk that day because of his cystitis . . ."

"His what?"

"Cystitis . . ."

"Difficulty urinating, *Madame la Comtesse*, a terrible burning . . . I think I have kidney stones . . ."

"Oh, poor Emperor! What else did you say was wrong with him?"

"An inflamed prostate, *Maman* . . ."

"And, if all that weren't enough, my gout won't leave me alone, *Maman la Comtesse.*"

"Oh, they say that gout is one of the most painful things ever!"

"And she also called me the Mephistopheles of Europe!"

"Who, Charlotte?"

"Well, who else, *Maman*. She said that Louis was the source of all of Europe's troubles!"

"Oh, I can hardly believe it!"

"And she said that the court was hell itself!"

"Don't say that, Sire!"

"I am saying it, *Maman la Comtesse!*"

"And she talked about the Apocalypse."

"Of the Four Horsemen, *Maman*, and the Red Beast."

"Oof, how horrible!"

"And, *Maman la Comtesse*, she suddenly started to talk about Algeria."

"And what does Algeria have to do with Mexico?"

"That's what I asked. But she tried to throw in our faces that it was her grandfather Louis Philippe who had conquered Algeria for the glory of France . . ."

"After Louis was left with the whole burden of subduing Kabylia!"

"And she spoke of her uncle Aumale as the great hero of the war!"

"And as I asked her, *Maman la Comtesse*, what about Lamoricière, Cavaignac, Mac-Mahon . . . and especially Bugeaud and Saint-Arnaud . . ."

"Also Bazaine, Louis . . ."

"Of course. It was Bazaine and not Aumale who defeated Abd al-Qadir. Later they reenacted the surrender so that Aumale would get the honors . . ."

"Are you tired of calling the cards, *Maman*?"

"No, no, no. Of course not. *The Giraffe of the Cape! The Ocelot . . .*"

"Slower, *Maman . . .*"

"Yes, yes. I'm sorry. I'm nervous . . . *The Giraffe of the Cape!*"

The Giraffe of the Cape, the Rhinoceros of Uganda, the Giant Crab of Japan. Loulou had been delighted with this educational bingo, which had been Eugénie's idea, and which they decided to put together before the game on the history of France. After a few days the little prince could identify all the animals and he was driving his tutors crazy asking about all of them: what part of the world each of them came from, what they ate, did they bite or sting, did they lay eggs, did they sing or roar, what their claws, feathers, fur, or beak looked like, and how large their horns or fangs were.

"*The Ocelot of Paraguay!*"

"How could I muster the strength to talk about Mexico? Don't you agree, *Maman la Comtesse*?"

"And especially, *Maman*, when in those days they were saying that Prussia had made several secret pacts against France with Württemberg, Baden, and Bavaria . . ."

"Prussia wants war, *Madame la Comtesse* . . . it's looking for it."

"And it's going to find it, *Maman*."

"Oh my Lord, no, please!"

"I'm afraid it's an obsession with Bismarck . . ."

"Oh, that man is the devil himself!"

"Yes, *Madame la Comtesse*. A devil with Krupp artillery."

"Oh, poor man!"

"Bismarck, a poor man?"

"No, no, no—Maximilian. A poor man, with that wife of his!"

"Yes, I'll grant you that, but the truth is that he's become so rude and demanding . . ."

"*The Quetzal of Yucatán!*"

"You have it, Eugénie . . ."

"Oh, how I would love to have a fan made of quetzal feathers!" said Eugénie as she put a tourmaline on the tail of the Quetzal of Yucatán.

"I regret, I now regret deeply having agreed to allow Prussian officers to act as observers of the Mexican campaign . . ." said the Emperor.

"Oh yes," Eugénie seconded. "That was a mistake!"

"And tell me. Charlotte said all of this in front of Monsieur Fould and Marshal Randon?"

"And worse things, too, *Maman*. She took out the letter Louis had sent Maximilian at Miramare in their presence . . ."

"No, no, no Eugénie. That happened when we were alone with her . . ."

"As you say, Louis. It's almost the same. I was telling you, *Maman*, about the letter in which Louis asked Maximilian what he would think of Louis if the Emperor of the French failed to keep his word . . ."

"But his Majesty never failed to keep his word . . ."

"Of course not, *Maman*. It was the force of circumstances . . ."

"*The Platy . . . The Platypus*, what a difficult name! *The Platypus of Tasmania!*"

"And she tried to read us many other letters. Imagine, she had a valise filled with letters, from Louis, from me, from Gutiérrez Estrada, from Hidalgo, from

Franz Joseph . . . from the whole world! But the worst thing was that she accused us of not having kept our word of honor!"

"How terrible!"

"And yes, by the way, she did, Louis," Eugénie said, this time choosing a red metallic stone in the shape of a half moon to cover the Platypus of Tasmania.

"She did what?"

"She did say it in Randon's presence . . ."

"No woman, she did not. That happened the last time she was at Saint-Cloud."

"But then, Sire, you've seen her more than once?"

"Oh yes, *Maman*. She burst into our chambers uninvited several times, without warning, unannounced. She screamed, her face all red, and cried. It was awful, *Maman*, just awful. I'll never forget it!"

"How shocking! How shocking!"

And since Eugénie loved to collect little boxes and save precious and semi-precious stones and other knickknacks in them, the Exotic Animals Educational Bingo was a great success. One of the little boxes was for snuff, made of mother-of-pearl, and had belonged to Josephine. Eugénie kept little bits of coral in it. Napoleon the Great's first wife loved coral. In another, a German box, whose lid held a cameo of Leda and the Swan, Eugénie used to keep ivory beads and tourmalines. It was such a success that they often played without the little prince, as indeed they were that afternoon, when Loulou had gone to his riding class and Eugénie's mother, the Countess of Montijo, was visiting Paris, and had been elected to call out the animals.

"*The Tapir of Sumatra*! . . . And how was it that she dared come unannounced?"

From a small gold box with a portrait in enamel of Madame de Maintenon, Eugénie took out a ruby spinel and put it on the Tapir of Sumatra.

"But she even did it to the Pope, *Maman*!"

"What! Him too?"

"Yes, that day that she put her hand in his cocoa, she had burst into the Vatican, *Maman*. She yelled at the Swiss Guard. She raised such a ruckus that the Pope naturally had no recourse but to see her."

"Oh, His Poor Holiness! *The Orangutan of Borneo*!" intoned *Madame la Comtesse*. Louis Napoleon smiled.

"What are you laughing at, Louis?"

"It's nothing, nothing. I suddenly imagined an orangutan dressed like the Pope . . ."

"Ah, Monsieur Emperor, always coming up with something amusing . . . But didn't you explain to Charlotte that you could no longer help her?"

"Oh, *Maman*, until we were worn out! First I went to see her at the Grand Hotel . . . By the way, did you know that when she was in Rome she was keeping several hens with her in the imperial suite of the Albergo di Roma?"

"You mean, live hens?"

"Yes, live hens because she would only eat eggs that she herself had watched being laid, besides the roasted chestnuts she bought in the street . . ."

"Unbelievable! *The Lion of Arabia Petraea!*"

"How I love those old names," said Louis Napoleon once again. "*Arabia Petraea, Arabia Felix* . . ." as he opened a gold filigreed Fabergé egg and took out an amethyst to put on the lion of *Arabia Petraea*.

•

Any type of stone could come out of the little boxes Eugénie collected. There were brilliants of a cinnamon-rose color that resembled those famous diamonds of the Russian royal jewels; rubies of Burma; chrysoberyls; topazes that changed color; and in a vinaigrette—one of those little boxes in which ladies carried a perfume-soaked sponge to put up to their noses when passing through certain streets—there were some chips that (Eugénie had been assured) came from the great diamond known as the Nizam of Hyderabad—from the King of Golkonda—that had been shattered during the Indian Mutiny.

"As I was telling you, I went to see her at the Grand Hotel, along with Drouyn de Lhuys, Fould and Randon . . . They gave her numbers, they showed her budgets. At Saint-Cloud we also discussed France's finances and the Mexican Empire's . . . she refused to listen to reason. Before the episode with the glass of orangeade, moreover, she seemed so lucid that she dazzled that idiot Fould describing Mexico's resources . . . Go on calling the bingo, *Maman* . . ."

"Yes, yes, it's just that I can't believe it . . . *The Cockatoo of Malay!* And with poor Louis so ill . . ."

"Oh yes, *Madame la Comtesse* . . . Eugénie, you have the cockatoo . . . You should have seen what a spectacle she made—she kept interrupting me, she spoke of the greatness of France and wondered how it could be possible for such a powerful nation to abandon her and Maximilian. She called us misers. She said that Maximilian was ready to abandon the Mexican liberals and to

Gallicize—her word—his government. I told her that I could make no decision until the Ministerial Council was called together, and after the Council met, and agreeing with its conclusion, I informed Charlotte once and for all that France was unable to send to Mexico one more man or one more centime . . ."

"Logical, very logical, Your Majesty . . ."

"She aggravated me so much that I was forced to tell her that the Mexican Empire's finances were disastrous . . . Imagine, *Maman la Comtesse* . . . I can even quote you a few figures, in round numbers, from the many that Monsieur Fould presented to Charlotte: the Mexican ports on the Gulf yield some forty-three million francs per year. Those on the Pacific, fifteen. That is a total of fifty-eight million. But from that we must deduct God knows how many things: the municipal taxes, the railroad subsidies, the interest on the English and Spanish loans, so that in total around thirty-four million remain . . . and to sustain an army of twenty thousand men in Mexico costs us sixty-four. So that we have an annual deficit of almost thirty million francs . . . and moreover, to say that the ports produce so much revenue is misleading, since both Matamoros and Tabasco have fallen into the hands of Juaristas . . . And Charlotte still had the nerve to remind me that I had said that the Foreign Legion would remain in Mexico eight years after we recalled the other French troops. Perhaps Langlais could have brought some order to that chaos . . . but, as you know, the poor man died in Mexico . . ."

"Oh yes, poor Monsieur Langlais . . ."

"And then you know what she said, *Maman*? That Langlais had been poisoned and Palmerston too! And her father Leopold and Prince Albert!"

"Oh, but that's not possible . . . that's inconceivable . . . *The Penguin of the Falkland Islands!*"

Louis Napoleon stared fixedly at the Penguin of the Falkland Islands. For the penguin, a black pearl.

"Inconceivable indeed, *Maman*, but that's what happened. You know, sometimes I have nightmares, dreams of Charlotte. I see her again in that black frock, that black shawl that she crumpled and chewed on constantly, looking so thin and pale and wearing that enormous white hat that looked like a bird perching on her head, like a seagull, I guess . . . It's frightful. I dream that what she really wants is to poison *us* . . . and in a sense, *Maman*, that's exactly what she did. She poisoned it all, she ruined everything. She and her terrible ambition . . ."

Louis Napoleon kept staring at the Penguin of the Falkland Islands. Eugénie dried her eyes with a handkerchief. *Maman*, the Countess of Montijo, went on calling the bingo animals in a decidedly lower voice.

"*The Vicuña of Bolivia . . .*"

"*The Ounce of Baluchistan . . .*"

"*The Whale of Greenland . . .*"

"What hurt me the most, *Maman*, is that Loulou was so happy . . . He was so excited to put the Mexican Eagle around his neck. When Charlotte arrived, you should have seen how elegant and poised he was, going down the staircase at Saint-Cloud to greet her. And he kissed her hand and offered her his arm . . . she wasn't worthy of that . . . the people cheered her in the streets of Paris . . . But she was deaf and blind. Insane, *Maman*, in a word!"

"If you would like . . . if it would please Your Majesty, we could stroll around the garden a bit, so that you can forget . . ."

"Some things, *Madame la Comtesse*, must not be forgotten, no matter how unpleasant they may be . . ."

"Besides, *Maman*, I told you that my poor Louis has difficulty walking because of the stones . . ."

"We would not walk on stones . . ."

"*Maman, Maman*, I mean the stones Louis has in his bladder . . ."

"My kidneys . . ."

"Oh, I beg your pardon! But seriously, His Majesty has stones?"

"The truth, *Maman*, is that the doctors have found nothing . . ."

"Oh, no one believes me, but you'll see. I'm positive that I have so many stones I could fill one of those little cases," Louis Napoleon retorted, pointing at a little black lacquer box encrusted with jade, and he added, "When I pass them all, we shall be able to play bingo with them . . ."

"Oh Louis, you are so . . . so . . . I don't know what to say . . . so inconsiderate . . . But let's keep on playing . . ."

"*The Alpaca of* . . . Ah, Eugénie, your father was very partial to garments made of alpaca . . . The *Alpaca of Arequipa*! . . . Tell me, Eugénie, what happened with the glass of orangeade? It was never clear to me."

"Oh *Maman*, it was a very hot day and so Madame Carette had a bright idea to serve us glasses of iced orangeade. When Charlotte saw them she said she wasn't going to drink it, because it was poisoned—can you believe it?"

"How absurd! *The Rhinoceros of Uganda!*"

"And she kept on insisting. She accused everyone of wanting to poison her—even her own companions like Señora del Barrio, Doctor Bohuslavek, the Count of the Valley of Orizaba . . . They tell me that she's even rejected communion hosts because she thinks they're all poisoned . . ."

"Oh, she's going to be damned! Poor unfortunate Charlotte. You have to forgive her, my daughter, she's lost her mind!"

"I? Forgive her, *Maman*? Never! She said so many terrible things . . . Even about you! How can I forgive her?"

"About me? About me? I can't believe that! *The Piraña of the Orinoco!*"

"Yes *Maman*, about you!"

"What did she say? What did she say?"

"Oh, *Maman*, I shouldn't have mentioned this . . . no, I can't tell you, it is such a terrible lie . . . "

"Yes, tell me!"

"No, *Maman*, I can't. Not in front of Louis . . ."

"But if she said it in the Emperor's presence . . ."

"Oh, *Maman*. Do you know what she said? Do you know what she had the nerve to say?"

"What? What?"

"That you had had an affair with Hidalgo! Imagine!"

"Me? And Hidalgo? That . . . boy? That poor fool? Never! Never! Remember, Eugénie, when he got on all fours and we rode him? That's all he was good for! Good Heavens, what evil some tongues are capable of! *The Tortoise of the Galapagos!*"

"Yes, Mama, I remember. Paca used to ride him as well . . ."

"Oh, Paca, Paca, why did you leave us? *The Ostrich of the Sahara!* . . . You have it, daughter."

Eugénie took a small oriental sapphire from a little silver filigreed box and laid it on the Ostrich of the Sahara.

"And then, she had terrible things to say about my mother, can you believe it?" said Louis. "About my mother, Queen Hortense, may she rest in peace!"

"How dreadful! She even had the nerve to talk about Your Majesty's mother?"

"Yes, yes, *Maman la Comtesse*. Tell her, Eugénie."

"Oh, no! I'm too embarrassed . . ."

"Tell your mother, tell her, Eugénie . . ."

"Well, *Maman* . . . Oh, I just can't."

"Yes you can, Eugénie."

"Well, you see . . . Oh, this is so difficult, My God. He called Louis a bastard . . ."

"Oh!"

"She said that all the Bonapartes were parvenus, that she didn't know how she, a princess in whose veins ran the blood of the Bourbons and the Orléans, could ever have knelt before a Bonaparte . . ."

"Oh!"

"And then she said that her father, Leopold . . . But what she said then is so scandalous that I simply can't repeat it . . ."

"What did she say? What did she say? Sometimes it's good to unburden yourself by telling others, daughter . . . I'm the most discreet person in the world, as Your Imperial Majesty knows very well . . ."

"Keep calling the cards, *Maman* . . ."

"As you wish . . . *The Panda of the Himalayas*! Oh, what an adorable animal!"

"She said that her father Leopold had had relations with my mother, Queen Hortense . . ."

"How can that be possible?"

"Yes, *Maman*, that's what the madwoman said. When Leopold came to France with the Russian forces, as a lieutenant of Maria Feodorovna's cuirassiers, Queen Hortense had seduced him . . ."

"Oh! How is that possible?"

"Insinuating that Leopold could be my father, imagine that! But I was already five years old when Leopold came with the Russians, and when he was in Paris before that, I hadn't even been born yet. And at that time the only thing he did was nag my uncle Napoleon to expand the Duchy of Coburg . . ."

"Go on, *Maman*, go on, please . . ."

"Yes, yes. *The Ai* . . . Ai what?"

"*The Ai of Madagascar, Maman* . . ."

"It's like a monkey, isn't it?"

"You have it, Louis . . . And of course for a moment I fainted, *Maman* . . ."

"Of course, of course. That's only natural, poor thing . . . *The Gazelle of Persia*! . . . Oh, that's what I would like to be, if I could be reborn as an animal—a gazelle. They're so beautiful, so agile . . . And what about you, Eugénie?"

"I've never really thought about it . . ."

"Well, *Maman la Comtesse*," chimed in Louis Napoleon, "I would like to be a seal, but one in a zoo . . ."

"Oof, Your Majesty is so amusing!"

"Oh, for Heaven's sake, Louis, you're not serious . . ."

"Very serious. I know of no other animal happier than the seals at the zoo. They swim, they eat all day long, they clap, they bark . . ."

"Your Majesty never loses his sense of humor . . . Is there a seal in this game?"

"Yes *Maman la Comtesse*, I have it—*The Seal of Nova Scotia.*"

"Well I hope it turns up soon . . . *The Zebra of Abyssinia*!"

"In any case, the zebra is mine," said Louis Napoleon. He took a tear-shaped silver sequin and laid it on the Zebra of Abyssinia.

"And does Your Majesty have any idea what might have caused the woman's madness?"

"Well, some people say, *Maman*, that she was given *toloache* in Mexico . . ."

"They gave her what?"

"*Toloache*. It's an herb that makes you go insane."

"Oof, what an outrage! What evil people!"

"Others say, *Maman*, that Charlotte went mad because she was going to have a child . . ."

"No one goes crazy because of that . . ."

"A bastard child, *Maman* . . ."

"You can't be serious! A bastard child? Whose?"

"Well, either a Mexican man's they say is quite handsome, Colonel Feliciano Rodríguez, or else Colonel Van der Smissen's, the commander of the Belgian volunteers."

"How could that be? But that still wouldn't really be cause for madness . . . She could just say it's Maximilian's child . . ."

"No, *Maman*, she couldn't."

"Why not? Is Maximilian impotent? Or infertile? Maybe he needs an operation, like Louis XVI?"

"No one knows, *Maman*. The fact is that Charlotte and Maximilian do not have conjugal relations—that's what they call a well-known secret . . . Can you imagine Charlotte's fear, if she were to have an illegitimate child under those circumstances? The shame for the Coburgs and the Habsburgs? Can you imagine?"

"Oh, so they don't sleep together . . . but why? Didn't they love each other very much?"

"Well, some people say that they do love each other but that Maximilian is impotent . . ."

"And, *Maman la Comtesse*, others say that what happened is that Maximilian got an unmentionable disease during his trip to Brazil . . ."

"Oof, how disgusting! *The Anaconda of Itaparica*! . . . Oh, what a coincidence!"

"I have the anaconda and I only need three more to win. Louis, you need five . . ." Eugénie said, and took a rose pearl of Bermuda from a small tortoiseshell case, placing it happily on the giant anaconda of Itaparica. "There are those who say that Charlotte, being raised as such a devout Catholic, is actually afraid of physical relations . . ."

"Then she wouldn't have taken lovers. That would be a contradiction."

"That's true, *Maman*. Finally, others say that what's happening is that Maximilian, who is fastidiously clean, you know, and takes baths every day in Lake Chapultepec . . ."

"Every day? That's too much! His skin must be diseased . . ."

"I was saying that there is another rumor that Maximilian rejected Charlotte because she's so unclean . . ."

"Oh, that must have been it: a dirty mind in a dirty body . . . *The Tepez* . . . no, *The Tepeizcuinte of Tas* . . . Oh, I can't pronounce that!"

"*The Tepeizcuinte of Tlaxcala, Maman* . . ."

"A Mexican stone for a Mexican animal," said Louis Napoleon, placing an onyx of Puebla on the Tepeizcuinte of Tlaxcala. "I have only four to go."

"How is it that you know all these difficult names, daughter?"

"Because we play this game all the time. Loulou knows them by heart . . ."

"Oh, tomorrow I will ask him to recite them . . . And tell me, was it obvious that she was expecting when she came to Saint-Cloud?"

"No *Maman*, no. But you know, they've kept her under lock and key for several months at Miramare now, out of everyone's sight . . ."

"Oh, then it's certain that she's expecting . . . that hypocritical harlot, pardon the expression. And she dares accuse me, the Empress's mother, of having illicit affairs! Good Lord, what a world we live in!"

"And as you can well imagine, *Maman*, when someone says such things to you, you can lose control. I told her a thing or two myself!"

"Really? Really? Like what? Like what exactly? *The Seal of Nova Scotia*! Ah, I congratulate you. Your Majesty! . . . You have only three to go, now!"

"Ah, we're tied! Well, as I was saying, *Maman*, when she said the Bonapartes were parvenus and that we were descendants of a wine merchant . . ."

"But my father was of Scottish nobility. Everyone knows that!"

"Of course, *Maman* . . . but I asked her who she thought she was. The Orléans were also parvenus and her father Leopold had spent his entire youth hustling for thrones. He had been nothing more or less than Europe's matchmaker, and a miserly old man to boot . . ."

"Good God, you said all that to her? *The Black Panther of Java*!"

"Oh, Louis, you have it. You're going to beat me!"

Louis Napoleon found another stone—a large, round pink one spotted with gold dust, for the Black Panther of Java.

"I told her all that and more, *Maman*. I told her that her father came to Paris looking for prostitutes—he colored his eyebrows and wore make-up to look younger . . . no, not younger, just less old . . . I don't know how I had the nerve . . . but she still went on with her lies. She accused Louis of being unfaithful to me . . ."

"How can that be, Dear Lord! *The Kangaroo of New Guinea*! You have it, Eugénie!"

"I have two to go, Louis, two to go!"

"But she said nothing about your own conduct . . ."

"She didn't dare, but she still offended me so deeply, *Maman* . . . She told me that I spent all my time dressing up because I've not been able to enjoy any of the things one does without her clothes . . ."

"Oh, dear, I'm going to faint . . ."

"Please *Maman la Comtesse*, calm yourself. All this is ancient history."

"Yes, yes Your Majesty . . . I'm calming down, I'm calming down . . ."

"She said even more, *Maman*."

"More still? *The Condor of the Andes*! It's yours, Sire!"

"Ah, tied once again . . . How exciting! Yes, she said—imagine this—that Maximilian was the real Napoleon III, because he was the son of the King of Rome. That's why Louis had been in such a hurry to be rid of him. But she said that Maximilian would return one day to claim the French throne for the Mexican Empire . . ."

"How absurd! That woman has lost all sense of proportion . . . And after denigrating the Bonapartes, she now says that Maximilian has Bonaparte blood? That's ludicrous . . ."

"Very true, *Maman la Comtesse*, very true . . ."

"So, *Maman*, let me blow on the cards to bring myself good luck . . ."

"Although I have no doubt that Sophie was unfaithful to her husband, who was an imbecile, just as Elisabeth now cheats on Franz Joseph . . . There's so much corruption in Vienna . . ."

"Yes, *Maman* but, please, we can't give credence to such gossip."

"I suppose not . . . *The Rhea of Patagonia*! . . . Your Majesty!"

"Oh Louis, you're going to win . . . Go on, go on, *Maman*."

"*The Armadillo of Chiapas* . . . This animal is so . . ."

"I have it! I have it! We're tied again. How thrilling! . . . Please, *Maman*, turn the cards very slowly, very slowly . . ."

"*The Polar Bear* . . ."

". . . *of Alaska*! Of Alaska! I won, I won!" shouted Eugénie, getting up and putting her arms around the Emperor. "Oh, my poor Louis. I always beat him. Here, let me kiss you as a consolation prize."

She gave him a resounding kiss on the cheek, went back to her chair, opened a Murano glass box and took out an emerald.

"For the Polar Bear of Alaska, my favorite stone," she said, "and I propose that we change the subject and forget about Charlotte. Louis, why don't you tell *Maman* about the World's Fair?" Eugénie started putting away the stones, lunes, gems and pearls, each one in its proper box.

"Oh yes, Your Majesty, tell me!"

The emerald went back here, the blood-colored opals there.

"Oh, I could spend days talking about the World's Fair, *Madame la Comtesse*," said the Emperor, twirling his mustache, "but one thing I can tell you right away is that no one, not even the British, have ever put on such a grand exposition . . ."

The coral Mandarin buttons there, Madame Du Barry's diamonds here.

". . . and the world will be amazed at the industrial, scientific, and artistic marvels of France . . ."

The garnets in their silver box, the lapis lazuli in the small, lacquered, candy box.

"And French colonies, Louis . . ."

The turquoises of Kishapur there.

"Yes, we will bring raw materials from the colonies, *Maman la Comtesse*. From Martinique we will get a million gallons of rum . . ."

"Oof, what a drinking spree!"

"And we'll be getting rice from Cochin China, indigo from Madagascar, sandalwood from New Caledonia, sugar from Senegal and who knows what else . . ."

"And the carriage of the Egyptian Pasha . . ."

"But something that everyone will like are the two models that I had made, *Madame la Comtesse*—don't you think so, Eugénie?—one of the Mount Cenis tunnel and the other of the Suez Canal!"

"My, how marvelous!"

And the sapphire, a gift from the King of Siam, here.

3. *Un Pericolo di Vita*

What Maximilian didn't know while on his way to paradise and oblivion:

That the corps of four thousand Austrian volunteers promised by his brother Franz Joseph would never get to Mexico, because after such a detachment was formed, the American Secretary of State, Seward, would give instructions to his Ambassador in Vienna, Mr. Motley, to request his passport as soon as the first ship with volunteers left for Mexico, and to declare that from that moment on the United States would consider itself at war with Austria. Maximilian's envoy in Vienna, Barandiarán, could protest all he wished; Austria would withdraw, since it didn't want a war with the Americans. The threat from Prussia was bad enough. Bismarck was trying to decide who was going to rule in Germany, and some months later would provoke a conflict in Schleswig-Holstein, where, after the Battle of Sadowa, also known as the Battle of Königgrätz, the balance of power was destined to tilt towards the Prussians for many years to come. Two weeks and a few days later Austria, also at war with Italy, would obtain an ephemeral victory near the Isle of Lissa, in the Gulf of Venice: In what was to become history's first battle between two armor-plated fleets, the flag ship *Re d'Italia* would be sunk by the Austrian flagship *Erzherzog Ferdinand Max*, and the happy Emperor of Mexico would remember his "beloved Dalmatian and Istrian sailors," formerly under his command, and he would say that his only regret was not to have baptized the flag of the corvette that bore his name in blood. However before the year 1866 was over—and Maximilian didn't know this either—Austria would forever lose Venice.

Maximilian was also unaware that, after the Prussian victory over the Austrians, due perhaps to General von Moltke's talents more than the effectiveness of the new rifles with firing pins, Randon, the French War Minister, would exclaim, "It was we who lost at Sadowa!" And, whether or not this allegory pleased Louis Napoleon, the fact was that on one side the Thiers Party would only grow larger in the French parliament, and on the other, Prussia would only become more arrogant. When Benedetti, Napoleon's ambassador to Berlin, presented France's request to Bismarck for the ceding of the territories of Saarbrücken, Saarlouis, the Bavarian Palatinate, and Maguncia, among others, as a reward for allowing the expansion of Prussia, Bismarck didn't even favor him with a reply—and it was snubs like that, as well as Prussia's approaching the Russians in search of an alliance, that would end up convincing Louis Napoleon of the need to withdraw his troops from Mexico. Furthermore, the Emperor would have to consider withdrawing the French contingent in Rome as well, in spite of Pious IX's fear that the emerging unified Italian state would annex the Eternal City—as would prove to be the case.

What Max *did* know, but preferred to ignore as much as possible:

That the internecine war was still costing the Mexican Empire sixty million francs a year, and that without France's help there wouldn't be enough money to continue (shortly before his death, Langlais had received the order from Fould, Louis Napoleon's Secretary of the Treasury, to stop all payments to the Mexican army).

That Almonte's mission in Paris to negotiate a new secret treaty to replace the Miramare one had failed, as had Father Fischer's attempts to reach an "underwater" agreement with the Vatican, along with the more or less "above-water" ones made by the three official representatives of Mexico at the Vatican. Pius IX had exclaimed, "Oh, that Mexican triumvirate—one is a child, another is a fool, and the third a schemer!"

That Alice Iturbide—to make matters worse—hadn't ceased her shrill attempts to have little Agustín returned to her by the United States, and that she would succeed if she continued to insist.

Also that, if there was another Frenchman besides Langlais in whom Maximiliam could have put his trust, it was his good friend and faithful Navy Undersecretary Monsieur Léonce Détroyat—but, because he was forthcoming with the Emperor (and one could hardly be honest with Maximilian without betraying France's interests), Marshal Bazaine requested that Louis Napoleon recommission Détroyat to active duty in the French navy.

And what Maximilian did not know but would soon find out, was that Louis Napoleon, in his inaugural speech to the new session of the French parliament, would himself eliminate any possibility of overturning the decision to announce the withdrawal of French troops from Mexico.

Monsieur Détroyat would advise Maximilian to abdicate.

As would his friend Herzfeld.

And Maximilian told himself more or less the same thing on a number of occasions.

But what Max also didn't know was that his beloved, *carissima* Carla would never share this opinion, and that one morning soon, or perhaps one morning and one afternoon or perhaps a whole day and night, Carlota Amélie would sit down and write a longwinded "Memorandum," addressing it to her imperial spouse, telling him that abdication meant condemning himself, and giving himself a certificate of unreliability. Carlota cited the example of Charles X of France and of her own grandfather, Louis Philippe, who were ruined, she said to Max, because they abdicated. In her "Memorandum," Carlota also quoted a saying of Louis the Great: "Rulers must never surrender like prisoners after a defeat." She added that, if a military position must never be given up to the enemy, why should a throne? And she stated that, as long as there was an Emperor in Mexico, there would be an Empire, even if he only possessed six feet of soil . . .

Carlota determined to do one more thing—she went to Europe to visit first Louis Napoleon and then Pius IX. The Empress of Mexico, daughter of the noble houses of Saxony and Bourbon, would be able to put her case before the Emperor of the French and the Pontiff, and she would succeed in convincing them that it was indispensable, not only for Mexico's good but also for France and the Catholic Church, to save her spouse's teetering empire.

The Empress's entourage consisted of the Secretary of the Exterior, Castillo, the Count de Bombelles, Señor Velázquez de Léon, the Count del Valle, and Señora del Barrio and her loyal chambermaid, Mathilde Doblinger. Two days before departing, on July 7th, Carlota wore her imperial tiara for the last time to a *Te Deum* Mass at the cathedral honoring Maximilian's Saint's Day. After the ceremony, Señora Pacheco asked for permission to embrace her. Her other ladies followed suit, their eyes filled with tears.

To finance her journey, in part, as Émile Ollivier states, Carlota took sixty thousand piasters from the funds allocated to protect Mexico City from floods.

On June 9, 1866, early in the morning, the Empress set off. It was raining and some roads were impassable. Maximilian accompanied her to Ayotla, a small village on the way to Puebla in one of the foothills of the Sierra Nevada, known at the time for its sweet oranges. There, perhaps under the shadow of the orange trees, Maximilian kissed Carlota for the last time: they would never see each other again.

And Maximilian didn't know that either.

•

Theories and legends abound on the causes of Carlota's madness. Some authors, like Adrien Marx—in *Révélations sur la vie intime de Maximilien*—clearly don't know what they're talking about: Marx says that Carlota was the victim of "*vaudou*," meaning voodoo, a cult that spread in Haiti and other regions that have Negro populations on the American continent, but that never reached Mexico. Others maintain that Carlota was given an herb in Mexico that drove her insane. It's certainly not improbable that someone might have wanted to or even attempted to poison Carlota or Maximilian. It seems that at times it was believed that the nearly chronic dysentery and other ailments the Emperor suffered were the result of a poisoned beverage that had been used in multiple attempts to kill him. There was talk of the possible revenge of the husband or the father of the *belle jardinière* at the Borda Villa. Even Colonel Blanchot states that Maximilian stopped going to the Imperial Villa at Cuernavaca, the Mexican "Petit Trianon," because he didn't want to run the risk of being feted with another *mauvais café*: another poisoned coffee. But possibly there were other reasons why the Emperor stopped frequenting his villa. For example, there was Concepción Sedano's pregnancy, as everyone speculated, with Maximilian's child. Later, the Emperor stopped visiting because he was simply too far away, in Orizaba, and finally, he heard the sad news that the Republican troops had entered Cuernavaca and looted the Borda Villa. He had worse problems at this point than the matter of regaining the Imperial country home.

As for Carlota, it was said that she was poisoned shortly before sailing to Europe, since the first signs of madness became visible then, on the way from Mexico City to Veracruz. Carlota was to sleep in the city of Puebla, but she suddenly awakened her escorts in the dead of night, got dressed, and demanded to be taken to Mr. Esteva, the former city prefect. Although Esteva was no longer in Puebla, his house nevertheless had to be opened for the Empress, who went silently and very agitatedly from one empty room to another. When she reached the dining hall she remarked that a banquet had been held there for her, and saying nothing more, she returned to her lodgings.

The herb that has been mentioned most frequently, in relation to the Empress of Mexico's alleged poisoning, has been *toloache*, which is nothing but stramonium—of the genus *Datura stramonium*. It has a terrible stench, used for the treatment of asthma, and apparently produces a temporary form of insanity, which can be permanent if the herb is administered on a regular basis. Given this last condition, it's difficult to blame *toloache* for Carlota's madness.

The episode on the mail steamboat *Impératrice Eugénie* is regarded as proof that something wasn't right in Carlota's brain even before she left the Mexican coast. But one must also take into account her excited state after so long and uncomfortable a journey, during which an incident occurred that no doubt brought back some disagreeable memories: the terrible condition of the road caused her carriage's wheels to fall apart. The same thing had happened to her and Maximilian on their journey from Veracruz to Puebla when they were newly arrived in Mexico. The first time they had continued aboard a Republican stagecoach—the second, Carlota was determined not to waste a single minute, and she continued on horseback.

Moreover, on the way to Veracruz, near El Macho Pass—it was said—the Empress had heard some Juarist guerrillas singing a song attributed to a distinguished Republican, Vicente Riva Palacio, which had spread all over Mexico when the news broke that the Empress was leaving for Europe:

Bye-bye, Mamá Carlota

(the song went)

Good-bye my tender love . . .
The French are taking off . . .
And the Emperor has had enough.

Egon Erwin Kisch lists a series of herbs that could have caused the Empress's madness in an article, though it should be noted that he eliminates marijuana as a probable cause. Others are not so easily ruled out: there is, for instance, *ololiuque*, the "eye-popping" herb that, according to Father Sahagún, produces "visions of frightful things" in those who ingest it.

What Carlota saw on her arrival in Veracruz, however, was not a terrible sight, but the French flag waving, according to several authors, on the mast of the mail steamship *Impératrice Eugénie*. This was the ship that was to take her to Europe. An indignant Carlota refused to board until a Mexican flag was raised instead. Corti ignores this episode as does the Countess de Reinach-Foussemagne. Other historians say that Cloué, the French Naval Division commander at Veracruz, finally acceded and the flag was replaced. Castelot leaves the issue unclear and other authors—Blanchot among the older sources and Gene Smith among the contemporary—say that the French flag Carlota wanted lowered was the one flying on the barge or ferry that was to take her to the steamship, and that she said nothing later about that other French flag, flying on the mast of the *Impératrice Eugénie* during the entire crossing.

As to what followed, all biographers and historians are in agreement: that Carlota once more became furious and it was necessary to calm her down, all because the steamship blew its horn as if to rush the Empress and her entourage into embarking. Once on board, Carlota complained of the engine noise, so it became necessary to place some mattresses on the stateroom floor, and nail others to the walls. In any case, from that moment on, Carlota was oblivious to the flag that flew over the *Impératrice Eugénie*, for she remained locked up in her room the entire voyage—even refusing to disembark during a two-day stop the steamship made in Havana—suffering from seasickness and migraines. One might imagine that, if the mattresses were somewhat successful in muffling the noise of the engines, perhaps they were not so successful in keeping Carlota from continuing to hear the mocking lyrics of "Mamá Carlota":

Happily the sailor
Sings with trembling voice
And raises now the anchor
With a clanking noise.
The ship goes out to ocean
On waves that heave and shove:
Bye-bye, Mamá Carlota,
Bye-bye my tender love!

But crazy or not before she left Mexico, or during her long confinement in her stateroom, where Carlota felt like she must have been dying, not only from the migraines but from the merciless heat, from fate, and from the bad luck that plagued all the emperors of Mexico, there were certainly enough reasons for her to begin feeling a little irascible, and probably for precipitating her increasing alienation. It was just more bad luck, for instance, when she arrived at Saint-Nazaire, that the only important personage to be awaiting her was Almonte, and that the mayor was an oblivious man who'd never even heard of Carlota before, and so got hold of a Peruvian flag to greet this unexpected Empress from the other side of the Atlantic—it was probably very difficult for a provincial functionary to distinguish between one or another of the exotic American nations—but it couldn't have helped matters much.

It was bad luck as well that the delegates and the imperial carriages in Paris were waiting for Carlota at the Gare d'Orléans when she was due to arrive at the Gare Montparnasse. She could have interpreted this as another calculated gesture to humiliate her.

But what was indeed a premeditated insult and not bad luck was Louis Napoleon's refusal to receive her, and this was nothing if not explicit, as was made evident by the telegram that the prefect of the Lower Loire Valley handed to Carlota at Nantes, in which the Emperor of the French had the nerve to suggest that she stop off in Belgium first and look in on her siblings. It was likewise quite intentional that, instead of being offered lodging at the Tuileries Palace, Carlota was put up in a hotel. Nor were these humiliations compensated for by the fact that, in the end, Louis Napoleon would indeed consent to receive Carlota at Saint-Cloud with all the necessary honors, and that the imperial princeling, wearing the Order of the Aztec Eagle around his neck, would be waiting for her at the foot of the steps to lead her, gently, by the hand. If the Emperor received her at all, it was because Carlota had made it perfectly clear to Eugénie that, if Louis Napoleon refused to see her, she would force her way into Saint-Cloud: *Je ferai irruption.*

Among the historians who think that Maximilian's many avowals of love for Carlota were hypocritical and superficial, and that Carlota was aware of this, there are some who imagine that the Empress might have caused her own madness by resorting to an herbal formula with the idea of curing her supposed sterility—in order, that is, to bear a child who would ensure her husband's devotion. This is contradicted by the near-certain fact that there was a total absence of marital relations between them. But, nonetheless, it remains a remote possibility, and it's also been said—though it might just be another legend—that, with her face hidden by a thick veil, Carlota once visited an herbalist, who, however, recognized her, and, being a Juárez supporter, she gave her a mushroom called *teoxihuitl*, the "flesh of the gods," which according to Fernando Ocaranza in his *Historia de la medicina en México*, produces a permanent mental derangement, without causing death.

Apparently, those poisoned with the "flesh of the gods" become very aggressive, which could explain Carlota's behavior at Saint-Cloud, as related by Erwin Kisch. It's difficult to know the true extent of the Empress of Mexico's aggressiveness during her several meetings with Louis Napoleon, Eugénie, and their ministers, however. It is doubtful, for example, that she really did shout to Louis Napoleon that she, a Princess in whose veins coursed the noble blood of the Bourbons and Saxony, would never kowtow to a foreign adventurer such as he—a parvenu. But once again one must accept this as a possibility. In the first place, all historians agree that Carlota's conversations with Louis Napoleon and Eugénie were, on the whole, violent, partially incoherent, and above all, humiliating for the Emperor and the Empress of the French. It's not only possible but also quite probable that Louis Napoleon wept more than once before Carlota, and that Eugénie fainted and had to be given smelling salts and have her shoes removed so that her feet and ankles might be rubbed with eau de cologne. Louis Napoleon was indeed very ill, and a great portion of the blame for the failure of the Mexican enterprise had begun to weigh heavily on Eugénie's shoulders.

On the other hand, some phrases are well documented, for example the oft-quoted *Je ferai irruption*, "I shall force my way in," along with others that the majority of historians attribute to Carlota. "Sire, I have come to salvage a venture that is yours," appears to have been one of the initial statements Carlota made to Louis Napoleon on the first day she saw him at Saint-Cloud, which was August 11th of that year, 1866. Two days later, another famous scene took place. Of the many letters Carlota took with her to Europe—aside from the very lengthy memorial that she and Maximilian had written, and that Louis Napoleon could only regard as consisting of a series of impertinent statements—Carlota took out, of all things, the original letter that Louis Napoleon had sent Maximilian to Miramare in March 1864, after the Archduke had announced that he could no longer accept the throne of Mexico. In this letter Napoleon asked Maximilian: "What would you think of me, if once Your

Royal Highness were in Mexico, I should suddenly tell you I couldn't fulfill the obligations to which we have agreed?" This was already too much for Louis Napoleon. Three days later, on the 14th, at his orders, a Council of Ministers was convened which resolved to abandon the venture. The War Minister, Marshal Randon, was the one appointed to break the news to Carlota. On August 18th, Louis Napoleon himself called on the Empress of Mexico at the Grand Hotel. Corti relates that, after a long conversation, Louis Napoleon told Carlota that she could expect nothing and that she should have no illusions of any kind. Carlota, in a fit of rage, replied that the venture concerned Louis Napoleon more than anyone else and that he should have no illusions either. It seems that the Emperor rose silently, nodded slightly, and left the suite.

Carlota realized that there was nothing to be done in Paris. Some historians have speculated that Carlota went mad simply because her empire, and her world along with it, began to crumble at her feet. But when she left France, and despite Louis Napoleon's refusal to continue supporting Maximilian, things still didn't seem entirely hopeless. Louis Napoleon had not yet determined to withdraw the Foreign Legion from Mexico, for instance. And during the first part of her stay in Paris, Carlota still had reasons to entertain hope. After the initial visit Eugénie made to her hotel, accompanied by Princess Essling, Madame Carette, and some court officials (among them the Chamberlain Count de Cossé-Brissac), during which she tried, without much success, to direct the conversation toward trivial topics—soirees at Chapultepec, trips to Cuernavaca, the Floating Gardens at Xochimilco—Carlota was visited by some ministers of Louis Napoleon who seemed to understand and support her. Austria's ambassador to Paris, Richard Metternich, was the only one who warned her that there was nothing to be expected from France, but Louis Napoleon's officials, perhaps afraid of provoking a furious reaction on Carlota's part, showed themselves to be hypocrites. Carlota spoke at length with them—about finances, the customs offices, the Mexican Church, the organization of the Mexican armed forces, the withdrawal of French troops, and Marshal Bazaine—who, it seems, she attacked mercilessly. Randon, the Minister of War, outwardly appeared convinced of all Carlota's allegations, but he himself believed the opposite. Fould, the Minister of Finance, heard her out, paying close attention, and in fact his eyes brightened when Carlota referred to the great resources of Mexico, and he responded that, if he were young, he would also have gone there. But Fould was determined to recommend—as indeed he did—that Carlota be given nothing, since that would be the only way, he thought, that Maximilian's abdication could be brought about. Finally, Lhuys, the Minister of the Exterior, also made a show of keen interest in all of Carlota's allegations, to such a degree that she thought he was on her side, as she later wrote Maximilian. But what the Empress of Mexico did not know was that Lhuys was carrying his resignation in his pocket, the very one that would be accepted by Louis Napoleon at the beginning of September. To add insult to injury, Carlota also received an unexpected and not very welcome visit at her suite in the Grand Hotel de Paris from Alice Iturbide. Count Corti doesn't mention this episode, but there are some who do state that Carlota agreed to return the boy on the sole condition that the Iturbides reimburse the Mexican Empire all the money they had been given. In any case, by that time, Maximilian had resigned himself to losing the little Iturbide boy.

If the first sign of Carlota's insanity hadn't appeared at Saint-Cloud, but at the Vatican, when Pius IX told her that the Church could do nothing—invoking in no uncertain terms the well-known principle of *non possumus*, "we cannot," that proverbial formula used by popes to reject requests that contravene church tradition or interests—perhaps then we would have more reason to believe that, indeed, Carlota went mad on realizing that France, the Vatican, all of Europe, were abandoning the Mexican Empire.

But such was not the case, as the orangeade episode occurred at the beginning of her visit to Paris. Of course, it's also impossible to know for certain whether Carlota really exclaimed, "Sire, they're trying to poison me!" when in one of her meetings at Saint-Cloud with Louis Napoleon and Eugénie, Madame Carette came in with a pitcher of orangeade and offered the Empress of Mexico a glass. André Castelot, a historian, has dramatized the scene to the point of putting much more violent words in Carlota's mouth: "*Assassins! Laissez-moi! . . . Remportez votre boisson empoisonnée!*" ("Murderers, leave me alone! Take away your poisonous drink!")—which would have constituted an open and direct accusation of the Emperor and the Empress of the French. It could have happened that way, or perhaps, as other historians contend, Carlota limited herself to rejecting the drink, and it was only later, during her trip from France to Italy on the imperial train put at her disposal by Louis Napoleon, that she said that at the Palace of Saint-Cloud they had tried to kill her with a glass of poisoned orangeade. There are no grounds, on the other hand, for assuming that she did not in fact tell this story to the Pope, and with a bit of imagination, one can picture her, as Berta Harding has, exclaiming to the astonished and incredulous Pius IX, "*Santissimo Padre, ho paura! Questo Luigi Napoleone e la sua Eugénie mi hanno avvelenato!*" "Holy Father, I am so afraid. Louis Napoleon and Eugene have poisoned me!"

This would have happened during their first audience, that is, the day before the hot chocolate incident. Another version, from the historian Count Egon Corti, referring to that second audience that the Pope granted Carlota—albeit against his will, after the Empress burst into the Vatican early in the morning, dressed in black from head to toe—does not mention her putting her hand in the Pope's cup of chocolate. The Count merely tells us that the Empress refused a first cup that was offered to her and that, when she was brought a second cup, she drank from the first. Other historians, however, go so far as to tell us that she only stuck three fingers (the index, the middle, and the ring finger?) into the chocolate, and then only sucked them; these, however, do not specify whether Carlota burned her fingers in the process—though what many authors do agree on is that the Empress of Mexico did indeed burn her arm the next day, when she plunged it into a large kettle of boiling stew at the St. Vincent de Paul Orphanage kitchen, and that poor Carlota passed out from the intense pain. It appears that that is when her handlers saw the chance to carry her back to the imperial hotel suite bound in a straitjacket.

Some modern researchers reject the theory that Carlota was poisoned with an herb that drove her mad, since her symptoms—or what's known of them—don't match those produced by any known herbs. Another theory goes as follows: Carlota was expecting a child, and, certainly, not Maximilian's. A Mexican colonel, Feliciano Rodríguez, is mentioned as the possible father of the child, but other, later events make it possible to guess that if Carlota was indeed pregnant, the father could as well have been the commander of the Belgian Legion, Colonel Van der Smissen. The fear of the great scandal that Carlota knew very well would ensue—if this theory stands—when it was discovered that she was carrying a bastard child, might well have been sufficient to push her towards insanity. The pregnancy theory is bolstered by the fact that the Empress, taken from Rome to Trieste by her brother, the Count of Flanders—who journeyed to Italy to retrieve her—spent several months locked up in the *Gartenhaus* at Miramare, without anyone being allowed to see her, except doctors and some attendant ladies. Some even claim that Carlota bore a child before reaching Miramare: that she gave birth on the night she spent at the Vatican. Nevertheless, one may suppose that a pregnancy would have been noticed when she arrived in Paris or Rome, and there is no indication that such was the case. Moreover, the clothing she wore in France and Italy do not seem to have been the kind that would have been appropriate for concealing an advanced pregnancy.

It's true that Carlota spent a night at the Vatican, but there is also a certain confusion about how this occurred, and where in the palace she slept. Some historians say that, after breakfast, the Pope led the Empress to the library, where the Pontiff took advantage of Carlota's being distracted to disappear. They add that the Empress refused to leave the room, so a bed had to be brought a few hours later for her to spend the night there. The next day, with the lure of a visit to the orphanage, they managed to get her out of the Holy See. Corti tells the story like this in *Maximilian und Charlotte von Mexiko*: After breakfast, the Pope asked Bossi, a colonel in the Swiss Guard, to escort the Empress to the library. Later, Carlota asked to be taken to the Vatican gardens where she drank from a fountain, and then agreed to have lunch with Cardinal Antonelli, but only on one condition—she and Señora del Barrio would eat at the same time, from the same dish. At nightfall, they tried to convince her to return to her hotel, but the Empress said that she would be surrounded by assassins there and refused to leave the Vatican. Corti says that a woman had never been received at night in the Holy See, but that Carlota's screams were so heartrending that the Pope gave his consent for her to sleep in the library.

Corti published *Maximilian und Charlotte von Mexiko* in 1924. Nine years later, an abbreviated and revised edition entitled *Die Tragödie eines Kaiser* turned up in Leipzig. This book may be abridged, but it's still quite voluminous, and a valuable source of information—though, in the second version, Corti eliminated some episodes or scenes that constitute rather precious material for both history and literature alike. For example, in *Die Tragödie eines Kaiser*, Corti omitted the scene at the orphanage that he described with such rich detail in his first version: Before plunging her arm into the boiling stew-pot, the Empress was given a spoon to taste the dish. Noticing that it was dirty, says Corti, she shouted, "This spoon is poisoned!" It was then that she put her whole arm into the stew and fainted from the pain. Back at the hotel, Carlota, by then conscious, refused to step out of her coach, and she had to be dragged to her suite. Not only is this episode eliminated from the abbreviated version of Corti's work, but the historical facts are changed. It says that the day after Carlota spent the night at the Vatican, the Empress calmed down after dictating several letters and let herself be taken to the hotel. *Die Tragödie eines Kaiser*, moreover, does not say, as in the first version, that Carlota stayed at the Vatican after breakfast with the Pope, and that she remained there until the next day, but asserts rather that Colonel Bossi convinced her to return to the hotel around eight in the evening and that the Empress left the hotel again at ten and headed back to the Vatican, shouting while begging for asylum. It was then, we read, that Monsignor Pacca, the man who received her, ordered that one of the rooms be made ready so that the Empress of Mexico could sleep there. In other words, the Vatican Library as temporary quarters for Carlota disappears from the abbreviated version, along with other details: the candelabra and the magnificent furnishings (including a bed for Carlota and one for Señora del Barrio) that, according to Corti in *Maximilian und Charlotte von Mexiko*, the Pope had ordered be placed in the library. To these details one could add (although it isn't mentioned by Corti, or any other historian—but one may suppose that a Pontiff would never omit such a significant detail) two chamber pots: one for Carlota and one for Señora del Barrio.

Whatever the criterion that Corti applied in order to abridge, eliminate, or make changes in the second version—some of which, perhaps, stem from later doubts, or the discovery of new documents or testimonies—it appears that almost every biographer or historian who followed Corti consulted either one version or the other, but very few read both. Nevertheless, all indications are that the first version was the most consulted, so that some of its more grotesque images—Carlota submerging her arm up to the elbow in a boiling kettle of stew; Carlota being dragged up the steps of the Albergo di Roma; Carlota lying on a bed by candlelight, surrounded by the books and manuscripts of the Vatican Library—survived Corti's revisions and passed into historical lore.

But other elements, like the letters, the glass, and the cat, appear in both versions. Carlota wrote these letters at the Holy See, after having slept there. The letter to Maximilian, to her "dearly beloved treasure," was in fact a farewell letter. Carlota told him that she would die soon, of poisoning, that she willed her entire fortune and jewels to Maximilian, that she did not want an autopsy done on her, and that she wanted to be buried in St. Peter's Basilica, as close as possible to the Apostle.

The glass in question was one that Carlota stole from the Vatican, to drink from the fountains of Rome. It's mentioned in a missive that Pius IX sent to the Empress before she left Rome, where along with his prayers for her to recover her peace of mind, the Pontiff invited her to keep the glass. Finally, the cat was taken to Carlota's hotel suite following the Empress's direct orders: it was meant to taste all of her food for her. The hen, however, that other authors claim was brought to the suite as well—so that Carlota would be able to eat only those eggs she'd watched being laid with her own eyes—appears in neither of Corti's books; though he does say that from the time of her arrival in Rome, the Empress limited herself almost exclusively to eating oranges and nuts that she'd bought herself from street vendors, after carefully examining the peels and shells to make sure that no substance had been injected into them. Afterward, Carlota even went so far as to refuse to have her hair combed, because she believed that the comb's teeth might be poisoned. This obsessive belief that all the objects surrounding her contained poison only grew more intense as the days passed, so that by the time her brother, the Count of Flanders, turned up in Rome to take her to Miramare, Carlota was seeing poisoned spoons and forks everywhere. Even on the quill that she was using to write a message, the dry ink, to the Empress, had become strychnine.

Of course, this quill could have been invented by a historian. And perhaps the cat as well. The important thing is that—whether we want to accept these other details or not—it would have been quite sufficient for Carlota to drink, for example, from a single fountain, for us to know that she had gone mad. As has already been mentioned, we are told that Carlota used the glass she stole from the Vatican to drink from the fountains of Rome. Rome is a city of many fountains, so, if it's true, as several authors claim, that the Empress of Mexico insisted on drinking from a different one every day, we can suppose that one morning she drank from Bernini's Fountain of the Rivers and another from the Fountain of the Moor; that one afternoon she went to the Neptune Fountain and another to the Fountain of the Turtles or to the Barge Fountain—a fascinating conjecture, but it hardly matters. She had only to drink from one fountain, the first one, the Trevi, on the morning that—on her way to the Vatican, accompanied by Señora del Barrio—she ordered the driver to go to the Piazza di Trevi, and there, not from a glass but from her cupped hands, before the Palace of the Dukes of Polo, before the majestic god Oceanus who rises from the sea in a carriage pulled by two white seahorses, driven by Triton, dying of thirst, she drank the refreshing, clear, cool water that wells up from the eternal and polished, white marble rocks; yes, you would only have had to see her this once, on her knees and dressed in black next to the most beautiful fountain in the world, to know that the Empress of Mexico, Charlotte Amélie of Belgium, had gone mad in Europe.

Maximilian found out about Carlota's madness a few weeks later. Carlota woke up among the Vatican's incunabula on October 2, 1866. That same day the *Empire Daily* published a news item, albeit a somewhat brief one, that the Empress had fulfilled her mission in Europe. On the 18th of the same month, Maximilian received two telegrams, one from Rome and one from Miramare, informing him that Carlota was ill and that Dr. Riedel had been summoned to Trieste. Maximilian was with Dr. Samuel Basch, the military doctor to the court, who had arrived that year, 1866, and asked him if he had heard of Dr. Riedel. Unaware of the reasons for Maximilian's query, Basch replied that Riedel was the director of the Vienna mental asylum.

This revelation, as could be expected, was rather shocking, and from then on, it became one more of the many anxieties plaguing Maximilian. The Emperor then decided to go to Orizaba. His journey started all kinds of rumors. If on the one hand there was speculation that Carlota was returning from Europe and that Maximilian's journey to Orizaba was to meet her halfway between Mexico City and the Port of Veracruz, on the other, it became known that Maximilian had ordered all his personal effects and records packed up, sent to Veracruz, and loaded onto the Austrian corvette *Dandolo*, which was anchored there. Colonel Blanchot states in his memoirs, however, that Maximilian had begun sending furnishings and objets d'art, many of which he'd acquired in Mexico, several months earlier. Moreover, Blanchot states that Maximilian managed to "extract" a large number of paintings by old masters from museums in provincial cities, all of which then "took the road to Miramare." According to the Colonel's report, furnishings that belonged to the Chapultepec Castle as well as to the Borda Villa—before it was looted—were gathered up at the Imperial Palace, and from there packed into sixty large crates along with all the other objects being shipped; they were taken out one morning, escorted by an Austrian detachment. At the same time, Maximilian asked Herzfeld to write Rességuier in the United States, asking him to charter a schooner to go to Veracruz and take the Emperor to Europe, along with an entourage of fifteen or twenty men, in case the captain of the *Dandolo* should refuse to take him. Rességuier complied and a few days later a ship named *María* was ready to sail for Veracruz. Finally, Colonel Kodolitsch received instructions to sell the Austrian artillery that was Maximilian's private property.

Maximilian's journey to Orizaba coincided with the arrival in Mexico of an envoy from Louis Napoleon, General Castelnau, whose path crossed the Emperor's in Ayotla, the same town in which he had bid the Empress goodbye. Maximilian refused to give Castelnau an audience and proceeded on to Orizaba. Relations between the Emperor and the French thus worsened day by day. When Marshal Bazaine left for San Luis to speed up the troop concentration, Maximilian refused him an audience as well, claiming illness. The fact that the Marshal and Maximilian had a unique personal connection (Max and Carlota were the godparents of Bazaine and Pepita Peña's oldest child) did not help improve their relationship, so it seems. The French were also offended because Maximilian always referred to the French army as an "auxiliary army," and because, during the most recent celebration of Mexico's Independence, September 16, 1865, Maximilian hadn't deigned to make a single reference to the French troops. The Emperor never visited the French army hospitals and, though he attended Baron d'Huart's funeral—Leopold II of Belgium's friend who had been murdered at Río Frío by Juarist guerrillas—he was absent from Langlais's.

The relations between the French and the Austrian and Belgian legions had also deteriorated, to the point that Thun, the Austrian commander, refused to obey Bazaine's order to head toward Tulancingo, and so remained in Puebla with his men. Also in Puebla were the Belgian youths who formed the Empress's Guard. Blanchot writes that it was natural for Maximilian to want to have his most loyal troops with him on the way to Veracruz.

The mission assigned to Castelnau, who had been invested with sufficient authority to take over the command of all the troops in Mexico—even over Bazaine's head, if he deemed it necessary—had two objectives: first, to speed up the withdrawal of French troops, and second, to persuade Maximilian to abdicate. By then it was evident that Louis Napoleon had had enough of Mexico, and he made it quite explicit in a letter he sent Maximilian. France, he said, could not provide a single coin or man more—"*ni un écu ni un homme de plus*"—and since the United States's attitude had become more and more threatening, a systematic evacuation of the forts was begun. Monterrey was abandoned once more—for the fourth time—as were the states of Sonora and Sinaloa, which meant the loss to the Empire of the important ports of Guaymas and Mazatlán. For his part, General Douay was forced to leave Tampico against his will—and the first thing that the Juaristas did, on retaking that city, was erect a scaffold in the main square to hang the imperial governor.

It shouldn't have been difficult for Castelnau to persuade Maximilian to leave the country, since his decision to flee already seemed evident, based on his decision to leave the capital and have his personal effects and archives put on a ship. Still, in this crisis as in all others, Maximilian again revealed his weakness of character.

He made a proclamation about his motives to the Mexican people that never reached the press. Besides, word was that Franz Joseph wouldn't even allow Maximilian to enter Austria or its territories: according to Pierron, the new Austrian ambassador, the Emperor would simply not be welcome—not even at Miramare or the Isle of Lacroma. This measure is less surprising if one considers a letter that Eloin wrote Maximilian from Vienna in July of that same year. In it Eloin not only made it clear that the Austrian archdukes had the intention of placing their palaces under the protection of the Mexican flag in order to save them from the Prussians, but he also mentioned that on one occasion, as Franz Joseph was passing by, on his way to Schönbrunn after the defeat at Sadowa, the crowd had maintained a sullen silence, interrupted by a single cry of "Long live Maximilian!"

It appears that Max soon regretted snubbing Bazaine and tried once more to ingratiate himself to the French. He considered offering France the concession of building a railroad and a canal in the Isthmus of Tehuantepec, and he added two Frenchmen to his cabinet, appointing General Osmont Minister of War and Lieutenant General Friant Minister of the Interior. Both had Maximilian's complete trust. "With them," said the Emperor, "I shall accomplish in three weeks what Bazaine has not been willing or able to do in three years." But Louis Napoleon realized that Maximilian was using this maneuver to implicate France more directly in future financial responsibilities and military operations, and Osmont and Friant remained in office only two months, after which they were forced to choose between giving up their ministries or the French army.

Maximilian also got rid of a good friend at this point—Herzfeld, one of the more insistent proponents of abdication—whom he sent to Europe to announce the Emperor's return. At the same time, he rid himself of the head of the Secretariat, Pierron, whom he had left in Mexico City when he left for Orizaba. Soon there were no Frenchmen close to Maximilian, as Carlota had advised in one of her letters—but as to be expected, the Emperor didn't seek support (because he simply wasn't able to, among other reasons) from the "indigenous element"—another of his wife's recommendations, but instead, as Corti says, he capitulated entirely, throwing himself into the arms of the ultra-conservatives, thus renouncing his political convictions. Teodosio Lares, the man who had presided over the famous Assembly of Notables that "elected" Maximilian in the first place, was named head of a new cabinet, and Father Fischer, having returned from Rome without the promised concordat in his pocket, was beginning to have a greater influence on Max. That "passionate, ridiculous Mazarin," as Blanchot refers to Fischer, went so far as to install himself in Carlota's apartments when she left for Europe, in order to be in constant contact with Max.

Along with Lares, Fischer, Dr. Basch, the learned Bilimek, and several written and rewritten drafts of abdication resolutions stuffed in his pocket, the Emperor left Mexico City at four o'clock, on the morning of October 31, 1866, escorted by more than three hundred hussars under Colonel Kodolitsch's command. In his book, *Recollections of Mexico*, Dr. Samuel Basch quotes Maximilian: "I shall no longer hesitate. My wife is insane. These people are killing me slowly. I am leaving." Around this time there was word of a conspiracy to assassinate Maximilian. The Mexican general Tomás O'Horan informed the Emperor of this and told him that he had already had the chief instigator and eleven of his conspirators hanged. Dr. Basch speculates that this was all a fabrication by O'Horan. In any case, Maximilian received what Basch calls a "memento mori": the rifle that, according to the Mexican general, the assassin was going to use. Maximilian almost abdicated on the way to Orizaba, in the Hacienda de Zoquiapan, but reconsidered, because he felt he was in too insignificant a place for such a historic act, and besides, Fischer and his friends—whom Max called "bigwigs and mandarins"—dissuaded him once again. Basch says that Maximilian asked Fischer: "Should I abdicate? Should I leave the country without abdicating?" and the former prospector proposed that Max resign in favor of Napoleon III—an idea that seemed positively Machiavellian to the Emperor. Apart from all that, and despite the enthusiastic welcome that was planned for the Emperor in Orizaba, the trip was slow and uncomfortable, with many unpleasant incidents. Maximilian suffered from insomnia, diarrhea, and intermittent fever. More than once he was forced to sleep in freezing rooms, and in a place called Molino del Puente he spent an almost sleepless night because of the racket made by the horses, cows, and sheep in some nearby stables. It was in Acultzingo, however, that the most despicable incident occurred—for it was there that someone stole the six white mules belonging to the Emperor's carriage.

Once he had reached Orizaba, Maximilian calmed down a little, as usually happened to him out in the country, away from the capital—and, among other things, he turned his attention towards gathering herbs and, among the yuccas and the coffee bushes, in Bilimek's company, to chasing butterflies, iridescent beetles, and other insects, as well as to planning new projects such as increasing the funds assigned to public education by means of the creation of a national lottery with twelve annual drawings and five- and ten-peso tickets. At Orizaba too, as he had mentioned previously to Marshal Bazaine, he resolved to cancel the "black decree" of October 3rd. Contradictory as usual, he also wrote a series of farewell letters to Mexican functionaries and friends: he began each of them with the same words—"In the moments that I take leave of my beloved Nation . . ."—and then left them all in a drawer.

The Mexican historian Justo Sierra says that Maximilian—who at this point in his life would often recall the story of Hernán Cortés's night sitting at the foot of a tree in Tacuba, crying after a defeat; and Max would ask himself if he would ever be able to find his own "Tree of the Night of Sorrows" to ease his bitterness at all his failures—that Maximilian was an imprisoned prince in Orizaba, though imprisoned by himself. There is some—or perhaps much—truth to this statement. In any case, all the people who were opposed to his abdication did their best to contribute to Maximilian's isolation and indecisiveness. And not just Father Fischer: Arroyo, the Minister of the Imperial House, began pressuring Maximilian to return to Mexico City. Don Teodosio Lares helped Max see the danger his supporters in the capital were being exposed to, now that he'd abandoned them, and he took the liberty of reminding Max of the oath he'd made on the Gospels at Miramare. Dr. Basch tells us that Lacunza, the new Finance Minister, spoke to Maximilian of the honor of the Habsburgs. Moreover, the imminent withdrawal of the French could still have been perceived at this stage in two different, and opposed, ways: on one hand, it was obviously a risk, but on the other, perhaps, a relief—and perhaps the recognition of the Empire by the United States might follow, since, as Montholon had written to Maximilian, the Monroe Doctrine opposed the presence of a European occupation force in Mexico, but it had no reason to oppose a monarchy sustained by a national army. Carlota was of the same mind. Of course, you couldn't really trust either the French or the North Americans. Hadn't Maximilian been told that Montholon and his wife had attended a party in Washington that Seward had held in honor of Margarita Juárez, attended by President Johnson himself? Was it not a badly kept secret that Seward had gone to the Island of St. Thomas to meet with Santa Anna during a tour of the Caribbean? So, in the end, whom did the United States support? Juárez or Santa Anna? The old general wasn't giving up. He had told all his plans and ambitions to a French lieutenant named Béarn who had also visited St. Thomas and fooled the General into thinking he was a German. As to the aid that the Empire could expect from other nations—England, for example—there were reasons to be optimistic. It was true that the death of King Leopold, who, being Queen Victoria's uncle, had always had influence at the Court of St. James's, and likewise the death of Palmerston, considered by many something of a "champion of liberal monarchs," could both mean that England's support of Maximilian would diminish . . . but it was also true that the new British consul was friendly toward him. What's more, Sir Peter Campbell, in Orizaba on his way to Veracruz, said he shared the Emperor's opinion that he shouldn't leave the country until a National Assembly decided the issue for him. Maximilian not only approved of the idea of obeying the mandate of a National Assembly formed for this purpose, but, it seems, he said that if the Assembly decided to declare Mexico a republic, he would be the first to congratulate its new president.

Around that time, another scandal further endangered Maximilian's status in Vienna. In another one of his letters, Eloin once again mentioned Maximilian's popularity in his native land. In Austria, the Belgian said, sympathy for Max was spreading, while at the same time the people were demanding Franz Joseph's abdication. In Venice, an entire political party had acclaimed its former governor. Eloin sent his letter from Brussels, including painful details of Napoleon III's illness, in a double-thickness envelope addressed to "*le Consul du Mexique à New York.*" Eloin forgot that the only consul recognized by the United States with an office in that city happened to represent Juárez's government, and it was he who received the letter. The Consul opened and read it, and before sending it to the so-called imperial consul, he had it copied and sent the copies to the American press.

In that letter, the contents of which became public knowledge, Maximilian could find numerous reasons for returning to Vienna—in the purely hypothetical case that his brother would have allowed him to enter Austria or its dominions. Did he not carry Habsburg blood in his veins? Was he not by rights the second in line to the Austro-Hungarian crown? And, finally, had he not been told that Louis Napoleon would propose that Franz Joseph and he name Maximilian the Governor of Venice, and thus make the loss of that province less painful for Austria? Trading Mexico for Venice would have helped everyone involved avoid disgrace—and this was so obvious that neither Eloin nor anyone else had to point this out. Max and Carlota, who would no longer represent the Austrian yoke, would end up being beloved and respected by the Venetians.

However, besides a letter from Gutiérrez Estrada—in which the Mexican also invoked the honor of the Habsburgs, and, says Corti, which was "adapted in a diabolical manner to the Emperor's state of mind," and therefore had a profound impact—there was apparently one more letter of note sent at this time . . . though no evidence of it remains. Corti says that Émile Ollivier, in *L'Expédition du Mexique*, attributes Maximilian's final decision to his mother, Archduchess Sophie—but Ollivier never laid eyes on the supposed message from the Archduchess, and based his information solely on the testimony of Baron Lago, who told Alphonse Danó, the French ambassador to Mexico, that he had found out its contents. Indeed, Ollivier considers the existence of this letter an indisputable fact, and he points out that Kératry was the only historian of the time to realize the importance of the presumed missive. It is speculated that the Archduchess told Maximilian in this letter that he would find himself in a ridiculous and humiliating situation in Austria—in the unlikely event that Franz Joseph were to allow him back—and that for this reason alone Maximilian should stay in Mexico and face up to all the dangers awaiting him there. Corti doubts that this letter was ever written and he refers readers to another letter from the same Archduchess Sophie, written to Max several weeks later, to celebrate the Christmas holidays, in which Sophie writes that she approves *completely*—Corti's emphasis—of Max's resolution to stay in Mexico, and indeed later on expresses her desire for him to remain in his adoptive country "as long as possible, and that he may do so with honor." As Corti himself points out, the Archduchess says nothing in this letter (which was found in the National Archives in Vienna) about Max's not being well received in Austria, and nothing about there being the threat of ridicule were he to return.

There was, nevertheless, another, more persuasive reason for Maximilian to stay in Mexico: Carlota's madness. It's likely that, when Dr. Basch revealed Dr. Riedel's position in Vienna, Maximilian surmised that his wife was no longer stable. Among the many letters that Egon Corti uncovered in the National Archives in Vienna, and in the possession of Count Rudolf Rességuier, he published several that Carlota addressed to Maximilian—some in German and others in French, first from Paris and then from different legs of her journey from Paris to Miramare and then from Miramare to Rome. There are long sections of these letters that are not only lucid, but, in fact, it's hard to imagine that such beautiful, delicate, and loving things could have been written by someone not in her right mind. No doubt, the warm reception Carlota had enjoyed in Italy contributed to this. For example, at the Villa d'Este, by the edge of Lake Como—the lake, she tells Max, "you loved so dearly"—Carlota found a portrait of Maximilian with the inscription *Governatore Generale del Regno Lombardo Veneto* in her room. At Desenzano she was received by Garibaldi's troops in their red shirts; the Mexican flag had been embroidered by the ladies of Bari flying next to the Italian; and General Hany paid his respects to the Empress in the name of the hero of the *Risorgimento*—Garibaldi was indisposed—and assured her that Emperor Maximilian would gain all of Europe's support: "*Oh, oui, l'Empereur Maximilien entraînerait toute l'Europe avec lui.*" And one of the most remarkable things was that the King of Italy traveled from Rovigo to Padua to greet the Empress of Mexico personally, despite the fact that a few weeks before—as we mentioned earlier—the ship called *Re d'Italia* (King of Italy) had been sunk at Lissa by the *Erzherzog Ferdinand Max*, named after the consort of the woman whom the reborn Italian nation was now honoring.

The Battle of Lissa and the Castle of Miramare—Carlota wrote Max—were the two achievements of the "absent prince" that astonished everyone. Carlota told him from Miramare that its ivy-covered pergola had become a marvel; that the cedars in the garden had grown tall; and that the arms of Mexico had been added to the Imperial Crown in the castle dining hall—although Jilek, their former personal physician, had suggested surrounding the crown with thorns. She also told him that she had celebrated Mexico's independence—September 16, 1866—at Miramare. As for Lissa, Carlota told her "beloved, adored Max" that the victorious squadron would sail past the castle in the same pattern as in the battle, with Tegetthoff, Maximilian's triumphant admiral and friend, at the head of the fleet on the *Ferdinand Max*. "*Moriture te salutant,*" wrote Carlota, and at the end of her letter: "*Plus Ultra* was your ancestors' motto. Charles V showed the way. You have followed him. Do not regret it. God is with you."

All of that was fine, of course. It was fine that in Verona and Peschiera, the old and new Europe both—as Carlota described them—had vied to pay tribute to the Empress of Mexico, and that at Reggio all the city dignitaries had come out to greet her in dress uniform, and that in Mantua she was given a one-hundred-and-one gun salute, and, finally, that Carlota wanted to show Max in her letters that she was adored, they both were adored, all over Italy. All of that, certainly, must have been encouraging to Maximilian. But not the discovery here and there, of strange intercalated statements such as, "The Republic is a stepmother like Protestantism"; "You have the most beautiful empire in the world"; "A monarch is the Good Shepherd, a President is a mercenary"; "Austria shall lose all of its possessions . . . Mexico shall inherit the power . . . and none of these nations—Germany, Constantinople, Italy, or Spain—shall attain what Mexico will if *you* alone work for your Empire," woven into the text. These incoherent statements could only have come from a disturbed mind, and Maximilian must have realized this in the very first letters that Carlota had sent him from Paris in August—which, besides saying that the atmosphere in Europe was repulsive and depressing, included the information that Louis Napoleon was *the source of evil in the world and the devil incarnate*, that Bismarck and Prim were his agents, and that the Babylon called Europe reminded her everywhere of the Four Horsemen of the Apocalypse. Corti tells us that King Leopold owned a copy of Dürer's famous engraving, which shows how, after the Lamb of God undoes the first four seals of the Book of Revelations, the Four Horsemen—Famine, Plague, Death, and War—will fling themselves upon the world to destroy the human race, and this engraving, he goes on, seems to have had a profound effect on Carlota, ever since she'd seen it as a child.

No, it wasn't difficult to recognize Carlota's increasing madness through her letters, so, as we were saying, perhaps this is why Maximilian decided to stay in Mexico. But this is still only conjecture. Although Blasio, sent by Max, traveled to Miramare, where Eloin was also staying, it's probable that neither one of them—nor anyone else—had written or spoken to Maximilian about some of the more grotesque details of the scenes caused by Carlota's sudden paranoia. So that, if the Emperor never heard about the orangeade, hot chocolate, or boiling kettle episodes, if he was never told about the cat and the hen, if no one ever mentioned having seen Carlota on her knees drinking from the Trevi Fountain, if Max hadn't been informed that at Bolzano Carlota claimed to have seen Colonel Paulino de la Madrid disguised as an organ grinder—who had apparently traveled to Europe in order to poison her—and that at the Villa d'Este she had pointed to a peasant and said he was General Almonte who was trying to shoot her, and that in Rome the Count del Valle, Madame Kuhacsevich, and Dr. Bohuslavek had all had to hide, because Carlota had ordered their arrest for trying to poison her, and that, finally, the Empress now believed that everyone around her, including Radonetz, the Miramare superintendent, and José Luis Blasio, were trying to poison her, and that she even believed that her treasured husband, her dearly beloved Max, also wanted to get rid of her—if Maximilian never found any of this out (and there are many reasons to think that he was spared the pain), he might, on the other hand, never have lost hope on this score. And in that case we may suppose that he remained in Mexico primarily to save the honor of the Habsburgs.

On October 7th, the Count of Flanders arrived in Rome. The following day Carlota gave orders for the purchase of a gold heart and engraved it with "*A Maria Santissima in riconoscenza di esser stata liberata de un pericolo di vita il 28–7–1866. Carlota Imperatrice del Messico*" (To Holy Mary, in thanks for having saved her life on July 28, 1866. Carlota, Empress of Mexico). She then ordered the ex-voto delivered to the Church of San Carlo. On October 9th she left with her brother for Miramare Castle.

XVII
BOUCHOUT CASTLE
1927

They've invented the bicycle, Maximilian. The messenger arrived a few days ago. He was disguised as Count Zichy, and dressed as a magician. He brought me a bicycle made of sterling silver. My ladies-in-waiting wove tricolor crepe paper through its wheels. They covered the seat with imperial purple and trimmed the handlebars with ermine. They capped it with a white silk, gold-fringed parasol. I ride it, Max, through the castle halls, my skirts hiked up to shock all the slack-jawed kings and queens who stare down at me from their portraits. A few days ago I rode it in Paris, alongside Señora del Barrio and Princess Metternich. Pauline took us to lunch at the Leisure Gardens in Mont-souris. Later, I treated them to cafés-au-lait at the Pré Catalan in the Bois de Boulogne. From our bicycles we scattered breadcrumbs for the ducks in the ponds. We threw candy to the velvet-clad children in silk-tasseled hats who played with yellow hoops. At Montparnasse we met Barbey D'Aurevilly who offered me the live lobster he takes out for walks on a blue silk leash every afternoon. How I wish you and I could ride bikes all over Paris, Maximilian. You could take a picture at M. Nadar's studio with a painting of Chapultepec Castle in the background. We could throw coins to the children chained to the coal wagons that are towed on the Île Saint-Louis, and to old hags who sell tiny baskets of dirt from the Suez Canal. We could sprinkle confetti at the beggars and the junk peddlers who chase the dragon-shaped sled of the Duke de Morny through snow-covered Paris streets. We could go to the Bouffes Parisiens to see *Ba-Ta-Clan*. Or in Vienna, we could ride through the Prater or in London though Hyde Park and give our regards to Big Ben. We could both ride our bicycles, mine of silver, its wheels sporting the Mexican tricolor, yours of gold with the imperial coat of arms. We could go to Mexico, down the Tlalpan Causeway, to Cuernavaca, and on to Tepozotlán Chapel. We could go, Maximilian, to hear Mass at the Metropolitan Cathedral, followed by our generals on their feather-decorated bicycles.

They've invented the bicycle, Maximilian, and on my bicycle I've gone once again to Paris, to the World's Fair. This time I went alone, to look for you. Of course I saw everyone there. I'm so used to being alone that the lights and the noises overwhelmed me. I closed my eyes as I did as a child, when Brother Leopold described Breughel's *The Massacre of the Innocents* to me. He told me that those wretches were none other than the thousands of Flemish subjects massacred by the Duke of Alba's Court of Blood. Just like when the messenger came to tell me about the ten days at Yser when more than sixty thousand Belgians lost their lives at the hands of the 4th German army. I should have closed my eyes, but never did, every time I saw Dürer's etchings of the Four Horsemen of the Apocalypse at the Palace in Laeken. I should have closed them, but refused, when I heard from all the court gossips that you had fathered a child with Concepción Serrano. I closed my eyes tight; I squeezed them shut until I saw multicolored lights, until I saw you on your horse Orispelo, riding through the storm clouds. I covered my ears; I cupped them until I began to hear Concha Méndez's "La Paloma" once more—until I heard your voice. I told them, I shouted to all of them that you were there, very much alive, at the World's Fair in Paris. Then I opened my eyes and dropped my hands from my ears. I took a deep breath and felt that I was choking on the fragrance of molasses from Guadeloupe; on the aroma of the verbena from Valencia that Princess Radziwill dabbed on her temples; the pungency of cachou vinegar. I mentioned this to my former governess, Madame de Beauvais. I told it to Giuseppe Garibaldi, who was hiding behind his alabaster bust, clad in a red shirt from the thieves' market in Buenos Aires. I felt that the noise was driving me crazy: the voices of blue-eyed *Mädchen* who served Viennese sausages and sauerkraut; the clanging of the four swords worn by Prince Tou Kougavva's—the Shogun of Japan's—brother, and the carillons from the Leroy and Son clocks that chimed the hour in two countries simultaneously; the clamor from Pleyel Hall where one hundred pianists were playing in unison. I told Louis Napoleon III, who was playing the "Queen Hortense Hymn" for Franz Liszt, that you were alive. I shouted to him that my grandfather, Louis Philippe, had conquered not only Algiers but also the Ivory and Gold Coasts, Gabon, and the Marquesas Islands, for France. I reminded him of all that. I said so to my sister-in-law, Marie Henriette, who claimed to be all alone at the

Hotel du Midi in Spa, with her daughters Stephanie and Clementine and her two parrots Caro and Mucho, her horse Cocotte and a llama that spits in her guests' faces; all alone, dancing with the maître d'hôtel. I said so to my nephew Albert, the Gentleman King; to Cavour who looked at me from glasses thick as bottle bottoms; to Don Martín del Castillo, to Barandiarán's Peruvian wife. It was so hot that Prince Leopold von Hohenzollern-Sigmaringen fanned himself with a telegram from Ems. Venustiano Carranza used a telegram from Zimmerman. But the telegram that I was intent on tearing up before its contents were made public had arrived at the Quai d'Orsay that morning and been handed to Louis Napoleon and Eugénie just as they were about to award the prizes—nine hundred gold medals, four thousand silver, and an infinite number of bronze. I tried to snatch that telegram away from them, but it flew away like the dove in Concha Méndez's song. It wafted from pavilion to pavilion, from the German to the Spanish. It hid behind the damask curtains. It flew from the Norwegian to the Egyptian exhibit; it crawled into M. Pasteur's bottles of preserved wine. It floated into the pavilion from the principalities of the Danube. Czar Alexander II shouted at me that the telegram had come from Washington as he wiped off the horse's blood that had bonded him to Louis Napoleon that morning, after a Polish patriot fired at them on their return from Longchamp. Still drifting, it flew into the leather cornucopias from the Sudan. Count Gontaut-Biron shouted the news at me, as did Captain Groeller from the S.S. *Elizabeth*, which had anchored at Veracruz. I refused to listen to them. I said they were liars, because the truth was that you were alive, sitting atop the pyramid at Xochicalco, on a copper throne from the Tinto River, holding a vase brimming with glycerin-preserved orchids from Guerrero, and a talking doll from Théroud that said "Mamá, Mamá Carlota!" You were alive in your kangaroo-hide boots from Australia, a crown made of swallows' nests from Reunion Island on your head. I said so to my brother Leopold, who had put his penis in a centrifugal beet-slicer from Champonnois; to your nephew, the Czar of Bulgaria, who wore one of those chamber pots on his head that play music when you sit on them. Maximilian, I'm going to buy you a silver chamber pot that will play "La Paloma" by Concha Méndez when you become lovesick and want to see me; a steel pot that will play the "Radetzky March" when you get diarrhea in your field tent; a gilded porcelain pot, painted with roses and violets, that will play the "Remembrance Waltz" if you get another attack of dysentery and homesickness in Cuernavaca. I told Francisco de Asís that you were alive, Francisco who was called "Paquita" after he jumped out of a bubble machine wearing a lace gown, followed by a pack of dogs named for all the men who were the lovers of his wife, Isabella II of Spain. Those rabid dogs came after me, barking and foaming at the mouth: General Serrano y Arana, the Marquis de Redmar y Marfori, McKeon y Puig Montejo the dentist, and Colonel Gádara. A whole menagerie followed me to the exposition—goats from Egypt, greyhounds from Siberia, cows from England. I rode a gazelle from Tunis; I tied some strings to the feet of Chinese birds and to the wings of Bombix butterflies. I said the same to General Victoriano Huerta, who was drunk as a skunk; to Countess Lustow, Gutiérrez Estrada's mother-in-law; to Plon-Plon, Napoleon III's cousin, and to his poor wife Chichina. I told Nero, Louis Napoleon's favorite dog, so he'd fly with the birds and the butterflies up to the velarium of the Palace of Industry, covered with stars. I told General Fierro you were alive, who drowned, weighed down with gold, in the swamps of Guzmán Lagoon. But the telegram evaded me, fluttering about the waving flags of all the nations. It landed and was picked up. I screamed for them not to read it. I ran in to take it away from them. It was so hot, it was so crowded, my God, and I elbowed my way through them all. Then the telegram flew away again, away among the diplomats who were receiving Fine Arts and Liberal Arts awards, as well as trophies in Technology, Furniture, and Design. It brushed the British ambassador's scarlet frockcoat; it stained the pristine white uniform of the Austrian minister, who ran out of the exposition to send your brother a new telegram; it brushed the Prussians' blue elbow patches and the Russians' green ones. When I saw Eugénie and saw her hands tremble, when I knew that even if the telegram hadn't reached her, there was nothing—not the fountains, not the interior gardens of the exposition palace, not the cages with macaws and quetzal birds, not the aquaria with tropical fish, and not the rubber newspaper I bought you so that you could read it while bathing in orange-blossom water in your alabaster tub—there was nothing to stop the tears that Eugénie shed that morning in the golden carriage borrowed from the Trianon Museum—the one that, wearing white and a diamond tiara, she had used to go from the Tuileries to the Champ de Mars, those broad avenues built by Baron Haussmann who came out of a Paris sewer covered in bloody rags and shouted at me that it was true, that you weren't at the exposition, alive and sitting on your buffalo-horn throne, with wax fruit from the Island of Mauritius in your right hand, and a shower of ribbons from Coventry on your head, and a postage stamp with your face, your name, and Mexico on your lips. Alive! I shouted at the bust of my great-grandfather Philippe Égalité, who was floating on a bed of oysters. Nothing could hold back those tears that Eugénie shed when the people of Paris cheered and all gave their blessing as the imperial carriage rolled by down those avenues that Haussman had ordered built not only to beautify and modernize Paris, for its dandies and cocottes to stroll in—Viollet-le-Duc and Garnier and the Duke de Morny in his lemon-yellow gloves—or courtesans such as La Païva, who invited me to see the onyx stairway in her palace, but also so that *Chasseurs d'Afrique* could gallop down them at full speed, blades unsheathed, and charge into the beggars and the downtrodden of the City of Light, the cripples and the blind at the Court of Miracles. I shouted it at Louis Napoleon, and at Marshall Randon, at the hundred guards in their sky-blue tunics, at the courtesans who carved love messages on mirrors and on the guards' cuirasses. I shouted it at Nini de Castiglione, who died old and sad, locked away in her Place Vendôme apartment. I shouted it at Baron Puck and General Boum, who fired his pistol into the air just to enjoy the smell of gunpowder, at Emperor Soulouque and the Duke of Lemonade, at Octave Feuillet and Honoré Daumier, because neither "Pesaro's Swan"—the hymn composed by Rossini in honor of Louis Napoleon and his brave people, and that Rossini himself conducted in the concert hall at the exposition—nor the landscapes made of cork from Gerona, nor the Turkish rugs and the jewels of Fontenay and Boucheron, nor the Chassepot rifles, nor Rose Bonheur's paintings of horses, were able to keep those tears from falling. They had run down Eugénie's cheeks that morning as she arrived secretly at the Church of Saint Roch accompanied by a court lady, dressed in mourning, her face behind a thick veil. She kneeled before the altar for more than an hour, alone with God and her conscience, a conscience that her tears could not cleanse because she did not shed them for you, Maximilian, but for the humiliation that a common Indian had been inflicted on France. I elbowed my way through the crowd but the telegram kept slipping out of my fingers. I couldn't get hold of it. It landed on my cousin Victoria's bonnet as she complained about all the blows to the head she had received as she strolled through Hyde Park. It nestled in the paralyzed armpit of the Prussian Kaiser who exhorted the Italian troops to massacre their enemy as Attila and his Huns had done; it flew into the cleavage of Alice Keppel who kissed Edward VII, Victoria's son, while Queen Alexandra cheered them on. But the Queen couldn't hear her own applause, couldn't hear what I was telling her, since she was becoming deafer and deafer. I shouted it at La Bella Otero, who danced a polonaise with Menelik, the Ethiopian Emperor, shortly after he defeated the Italian troops at Adua; to Victor Emmanuel, the King of Italy, who took walks with his six hundred bastard children; to Elena Vacaresco, who told me that my nephew Prince Baldwin was Lohengrin resurrected and then dead again. I argued that, if they hadn't seen you yet, they soon would, because you were going to fly through the Paris skies in an airship that would look like the whales that had churned up the water frolicking nearby as your boat *Fantaisie* sailed through the Tropic of Cancer. I said that this airship would have a glass skin and a rib cage of iridium tubes from which hourglasses filled with rainbow-colored sand would dangle. I told Archduke Franz Ferdinand, who was napping in the rose garden of his Castle of Konopitsch; I told Count Mensdorff-Pouilly, who was wearing my wedding gown; my sister-in-law Sisi, who complained because Sophie wouldn't let her eat without gloves; Viscount Conway and Baron Saillard; Colonel Van der Smissen, who had fallen into the water at Saint-Nazaire; I told Eloin who went after him with a pistol. I told Marshal Bazaine, who walked very proud arm-in-arm with my son Weygand and wore the Military Order of Savoy that he received from the King of Piedmont. I pulled his ear so he could see how Duke Malakoff was making love to his first wife, Soledad, under the piano sent from Istanbul to the Marmara Sea, and I told him that the tail of your airship would be made of copper trimmed with water-filled doe eyes and would have the shape, I said to the Duke of Peñaranda, of a hypodermic needle with a propeller on its tip that looked like an orchid. I told my niece, Kronprinzessin Victoria. And from the belly of the ship hang six pairs of brooms that will serve as its legs when it lands on the snows of Popocatépetl, and which during the flight serve to sweep the rivers of blue hail that run through the heavens. It has, besides, an infinite number of wings covered with mirrors that reflect the northern constellations and your disfigured face; they reflect fragments of Schönbrunn Palace and Miramare Castle—I told Baron Beust—and pieces of your portrait in a sailor's uniform, and of Manet's painting of your execution. Other wings are like giant ferns. When they writhe, snakelike, a burst of dew cools the airship's engines, I told everyone. Other wings are like the sails of the *Niña* and the *Santa María*, and others are like the wings of angels of all different sizes and ages. My ladies-in-waiting comb these wings to remove the horseflies that gather in their feathers. The giant rudder is a bamboo wing, and it's covered with the nests of varicolored hungry birds that flutter frantically and slam against the ship's frame and devour each other in desperation. Their blood falls into a funnel so that it—and not your blood, nor the blood that trickled down the stairs of the Pyramid of Xochicalco—I told them, I shouted to them, so that it, this blood, fuels the King of the World's airship, so that his airship is fueled by the blood of all the birds in Mexico, the blood of the vultures that greeted us at Veracruz, of the eagle devouring a serpent; and when I saw the stone serpents dripping with your blood, I told them, Maximilian is not dead, and forced my way through the crowd visiting the World's Fair in Paris that day. I stumbled on my brother Philippe who had just turned down the thrones of Greece and Romania. I elbowed my way through the French lancers and the grenadiers in bearskin shakos, the cuirassiers, the Zouaves in turbans and loose pantaloons, the green-plumed *Chasseurs d'Afrique* and the riflemen in yellow tunics. And the telegram eluded me again. It hid in a barrel of cod-liver oil, in a pineapple wine cask from Natal, in a Bohemian crystal chalice, under the carpets of the Ottoman Empire Pavilion's mosque. I told Count Palikao and Count von Moltke, and Count Thun and the Duke of Isly, that if anyone was to be sacrificed that day on top of a pyramid it should be me, Empress Carlota, whose belly would be cut with an obsidian knife so that she could give birth to the New World's Caesar. I said that Eugénie could save her crocodile tears, as could her evil, two-faced husband. I also told Charles V's salt statue, whose eyes were weeping from the heat. I told the salt horse he rode, as it shed huge saltwater tears, but I began to get tired. I plunged through the bottles of Dr. Brunetti of Padua, who had preserved human parts—arms, legs, hearts, and lungs that I wished could have belonged to Salm-Salm, Juárez, Eugénie and Colonel López—and I rode the lift invented by M. Edoux, an aerostatic balloon that went up and down pulling a tall and narrow, honeysuckle-covered cage. I got down on my knees in front of the Pyramid of Xochicalco. When I tried to wet my lips with your blood, I realized, Maximilian, that those red trickles dripping down the stone steps were not your blood at all, but the rivers of beetles that had devoured you in Mexico and in Querétaro and left you, dead and bloodless, terribly pale atop the pyramid, all alone, your heart hollow and empty. I began to eat them alive. Do you remember, Maximilian, do you remember those *jumiles*, the nauseating live beetles the Indians in Cuernavaca ate, and which crawled out of their mouths onto their faces? So when I left the exposition holding the telegram that said Maximilian is dead, those insects crawled out of my mouth, up and down my cheeks and my neck. They crept out of my nose, around my eyes. I thought then that I must be imagining things, because the whole world was present at the exposition—I ran from the Austrian Pavilion to the Bahamian Pavilion, to the Belgian Pavilion and the North American Pavilion and the Dutch Pavilion—and I believed, or wanted to believe, that if you were really dead, the whole world would be crying for you. But out on the street, outside the Café Tortoni, I collided with a flower girl who was selling those white violets that your father, the King of Rome, loved so much. When I held out the telegram to her and said that Maximilian, my beloved Maximilian, the King of the Universe, had died, she asked in puzzlement, Maximilian? Maximilian who? So I realized that if I did not tell the world who you are, Maximilian, the world will never know who you were.

•

To do this, Maximilian, I must escape my dreams. The price I must pay is to die like this—a muzzled prisoner. This has been my punishment, but not because I left Mexico, or because I escaped reality to live in a dream. If there's a difference between you and me, Maximilian, or between me, Marie Charlotte of Belgium, and the rest of humanity, it's that I chose to dream and to remain in my dreams. But because of my dreams, ah, my dreams, I paid a very high price. I've paid by being alive and dead at the same time. And do you know why? Because neither day nor night exists in our dreams. Not even the first light can tell us how dreams rise from their ashes. Twilight can't tell us how flames consume dreams. In dreams there is no time. Neither the sun nor the stars exist for them. The sands from an hourglass can't tell us how dreams crumble and give way to new dreams. The clepsydras's slow tears can't tell us how dreams drown in their own dirges, in their own laughter, in their madness and their sanity, in their own dreams as in the shadows and the brightness of a noon and night that have no beginning and no end—that dance, make love, and are conjoined in order to celebrate the eternal marriage of light and darkness. Sometimes I am able to escape. The other day I got out and was lying at the bottom of the moat at Bouchout. It was winter and I watched the skaters above me through the ice that covered the surface. Some fishermen made holes in the ice and lowered their lines but, instead of hooks, they used blue, crystallized roses to tempt their Empress. Spring came and the ice melted. I saw the bottoms of the boats that cast silver anchors covered with butterflies. I watched the swimmers, their hairless legs, their shining torsos; I watched the ducks' and the swans' bellies as they dipped their necks into the water to watch me back. I watched my washerwomen as they washed my first communion gown on the banks of the moat. Their veins shed blood that turned into threads of coral. Autumn came and the castle servants tied pebbles to dead leaves to sink them to the bottom. The leaves came down, little by little, like a rain of canary wings, down through the waters of the Bouchout moat, among the grape clusters tied to the paperweights from the Tuileries, like a cloud of seahorses descending with tiny parachutes. This vision, however, lasted only a moment. I was back in my room at Bouchout, sitting all alone, as I have been the last sixty years.

To do this, Maximilian, to tell the world who you were, my veins and bones would need to be made of glass, and my soul made of water. I wish that my soul would seep, little by little, out of my mouth, and that the world, Maximilian, would drink it. That the world would thirst for my words. I wish my words were a river. That as it flowed the river would give each object it touched its proper name. That it would name a stone a stone, give sand its name, name the stone's song "song," and the sea's laughter "foam." I wish my words were rain, a gentle, fine drizzle; that, as they fell, my words would name what they touched from the clouds to the ground, from the top of the rainbow to the buried crystals of salt, from the highest moonbeam to the lowest blade of grass and dew-covered beetle.

Tell me, Maximilian, can't you hear my soul dripping like rain? Don't you hear it beating with its thousand watery fingers on the door of your breast, giving a name to your desires? Don't you hear it drumming on your skin, to filter into your pores? Formed into words my soul tears its gown of water. With watery streamers it wraps around your fingers and around the egrets' necks. Its flowing lariat lashes itself to your eyelids and the hollows of the mountains. Listen, Maximilian, has anyone told you that my soul, which will change into your own tears, could rain on your face? Would you dare to drink my soul? Would you dare, tell me, turn your face toward the sky so that my words could rain on it, so that through them I could name your eyes and describe the way they shine? Would you dare—answer me—open your mouth, so that my soul could enter to bathe your own soul with words, to saturate your heart, to bind it in a cool embrace?

I made the water my sign. I, who could perceive the whole world in a drop of water, which itself held all the waters of the world. I, who went to Castle Schwetzingen not to drink from the Fountain of Nicholas de Pigage; to Versailles not to quench my thirst in the Dragon Fountain; I, who ran up and down the streets of Rome like a madwoman, but I swear it, not to drink from the fountains of the Piazza della Pilotta; I, who played into the sacred pools, but not to absorb, face down, the Mayan princesses' liquefied souls; I made my dreams out of water and turned them into the birds of Schwetzingen Fountain. When you go there, Maximilian, you will see how my soul bursts like a stream from the birds' beaks. When you go to Versailles, you will see my soul pour out to give the sun its name, and scatter itself in the wind to give the wind its name. When you go to Yucatán, Maximilian, and visit its sacred pools—if you want to—you'll be able to see your face reflected in my soul, still and deep. But I'm warning you—all you'll see of my love will be a watery mirror. If you break it, all you'll be able to hear will be the silent echo of your enchanted voice turned to water.

I will make my memories out of water, and my memories out of words: Princess Charlotte wants to transport her bathtub to the Tuileries so that Queen Marie Amélie can bathe her. I will create a kind of water that is in love with itself: Princess Charlotte wants to wash her hair in Actaeon's waterfall as Diana's hounds pursue him. I will invent a circular water that can eat its own transparency, like a crystal serpent: Princess Charlotte, her face hidden by a veil, wants to touch the water in the baptismal font at Santa Maria Maggiore. I shall create a water that will confine me in a world of reflections: Princess Charlotte lives motionless, in a castle of round water, surrounded by white ladies, by blue ladies, by violet ladies, by ten Maximilians in their sweet little sailor outfits. I shall give form to that castle. By wishing, only by wishing, I will make my love and my memories—liquid as springs—rise like symmetrical crystal columns to carve out their own architecture in arabesques and spume: their arches and cloisters, their ogees. Princess Charlotte wants to do her schoolwork in the notebook that her uncle, Prince Joinville, brought her. She will do it in the invisible ink the Magi brought her. Princess Charlotte wants to write the history of the wars against the Moors in water, as told by her brother, Prince Leopold. Princess Charlotte wants to describe her afternoons at Claremont Castle in water, where on Sunday Grandpapa Louis Philippe awaited her, a cluster of berries in his hands, a cluster of kisses in his mouth. Princess Charlotte wants to write her life in water; she wants to write it in air, in nothingness. Princess Charlotte wants to invent nothingness, the clearest, purest, most diaphanous, most transparent nothingness of all, and to drink from it.

But if you want to write, they said to me, you have to write the word "Mama" ten times. I wrote the word "water" one hundred times. They ordered me to write the word "Papa" twenty times. One thousand times I wrote the word "water." Mama and Papa were made of water. The ink was made of water and the water's blue color became lighter and lighter, as I wrote without stopping, without dipping my pen in the inkwell. My thoughts also turned lighter and lighter—from dark-blue they turned to sky-blue, from sky-blue to an invisible blue. Writing like that, in a stream, running all my words together into one, I made a river that undulated in its *Ms*, curled in its *Os*, zigzagged in its *Zs*. To write everything in a single line, with no spaces or breaks, was to live what I was writing. You must separate your words, they told me. As though I could separate each moment of my life, each drop of water of that childhood—sailing through my mother's caresses, the lilacs at Laeken, *The Life of Saint Louis*, chestnut purée, Uncle Joinville's drawings—open and tranquil, like a bankless river, flowing toward an immense ocean that with each wave left an avalanche of promises and that with each ebbing of the tide washed away the huddled, sleeping dreams that were carved in the sand. As though it were possible to separate each trickle of that waterfall, the luminous waterfall that was my childhood when you arrived in Brussels, when my soul thrashed in the void and in your eyes, thrashed in the lunacy of a bottomless love. As though it were possible, today, to separate those frozen drops of water that encase, that freeze my heart.

What I mean to tell you by saying all of this is what I have always tried to tell you and failed, Maximilian. I invented the invisible ink the Magi brought me: from an inkwell that everyone thought was empty, everyone but me, I drew out the air, the nothingness that wet my pen. I wrote in notebooks that everyone but me thought were blank; I wrote words that only I could read. On those blank pages I wrote the story of my life. Although I was only eight or nine then, my life was as long or as short, as beautiful or as sad, as dull or amusing, as I wanted it to be. My life changed completely every time I reread those pages. Whoever might have seen me staring at those blank pages must have thought I was mad. But no one did. Or rather, they all saw me, yes, they spoke to me, but only from those pages that I had filled with music and color. My imagination was the river that ran through those pages and gave things a name—pillow, trees, stars—and gave my loved ones their names—Marie Louise, Leopold, Philippe. My imagination gave the pillow its softness, the trees their leaves, the stars their twinkle. It was what gave my father the color of his hair, my brother his smile, and my mother the blue of her eyes. I lived inside my imagination and only inside it that I could breathe. Outside I felt like I was suffocating. I lived the double life of water, born to be pure—sometimes still, sometimes turbulent, but always clear. When it was still, my imagination would be a frozen palace. It was Laeken. In Laeken there lived a princess. The princess was Sleeping Beauty. Sleeping Beauty dreamed of a prince, dressed in blue, who would come to awaken her. When it was violent, the water could crash onto the imaginary rocks that it had invented, break up and fly into the air, smashed into a thousand pieces, into a thousand shattered dreams, but always reassuming its original shape, later, never lacking a single drop. Because water doesn't break. Because water, in real life, never gets hurt.

I don't know exactly when I forgot what I had written in my diaries. In my dozens of diaries. I don't know when I lost the ability to read what had taken so much love and was so difficult to write. I only know that for a long time, the pages became as blank for me as they were for others. When I became aware of that, I was enraged. I felt so despondent that I tore out each page, one by one. My room was covered with sheets of paper, which reminded me of José Luis Blasio, your faithful Blasio, who in your office in Chapultepec Castle would spread your letters out on the parquet floors and the rugs to dry the ink. I could have twisted my diary pages and bound them together into a rope to escape from a Bouchout balcony. But I didn't want for people to say some day that I had run away, clinging to my own nothingness. I could also have used my gray hair to stitch the sheets of paper together into a shroud for you. But I didn't want people to say some day that I had buried you with my silence. I gathered the pages again, one by one, as I knelt on the floor. I made a pile and I swore that even if I had to live, to suffer, and to die all over again, I would write in those pages what I've always wanted to say to you. I remembered your son, Sedano y Leguizano, who gave himself away because the letters he wrote the Germans in invisible ink were all blank. The idiot never thought to put his secret messages between the lines of an ordinary letter. I will not have that happen to me. I have written, in real ink, in the purple ink of the pink amapa that Blasio brought me from Mexico, the trite history of my madness and isolation, the empty memories of sixty years of oblivion, the dark diary of 22,000 days that turned into 22,000 nights. This is the story nobody cares about. No matter how much effort I put into retelling the most beautiful parts of my childhood and our love story. No matter how hard I try to make sure that I've told the most tragic parts of our adventure and your death in Mexico. Or perhaps because I've told it all too many times. Between the lines, Maximilian, between those lines where I can only write about the flowering limes in the Tuileries or the bullet that took your life on Las Campanas Hill, between those lines, using the holy water that the messenger, dressed as the Archangel Michael, brought me the other day, I shall write endlessly, though at times it may seem I'm frozen dead, that the day I played "freeze" with my brothers at Laeken Gardens I became a statue for all eternity. I shall write, yes, without stopping, my words flowing like a river that never reaches the horizon, like a torrent that plunges toward infinity, and at the same time I will sit still, very still, even though it may seem that since the night I dreamed my mother was dead, and I woke with a start, and ran to her room, and opened the door, and saw that I was in a very large hall, and I ran to the end and found a stairway and I went downstairs and found another door . . . even though it may seem, I say, that I do nothing but run around the world opening doors and going downstairs in search not of my dead mother nor my living mother, but in search of myself, I will be still, and my words will be like the deep water of a pond. My words will be a pool of stagnant water. When they call the lily a lily, the lily will plunge into the pool of my words and will be a lily twice over. And when the bird is called a bird, it will be born from my words, it will fly with wet wings in the sky and it will be a thousand times a bird. Only then will I begin to tell you, finally, what I never thought I could say to you, and which I'm telling you now.

At that time, Maximilian, you and everyone else who wants to understand me will have to learn to read again. You will have to find out for yourself what I'm saying to you between the lines. You and every Mexican will have to understand that when I speak of my anger toward you and toward them I am really only speaking of affection. That when I talk of hate I can be writing, in reality, of my love for you, my love for Mexico, for what you were, for what my Empire will be. My Empire, Maximilian, will only rise from forgetting. We need to forget what they did to us. They, the Mexicans, need to forget what we did to them. The other day Napoleon III came to see me. He offered me a glass of orange juice so that I could write my memoirs with it. He swore that it might well have been the very same juice from the very same orange trees found at the Alhambra, under which you pondered the former glories of the House of Austria. It could have even been the sweet juice of the oranges from the Ayotla trees in whose shade—do I still need to remind you? do I still need to keep telling the world?— we said good-bye forever. I knew that it wasn't with perfume or amber or golden liqueurs that I needed to write what I will write to you—even if they swore to me that they'd brought me the juice from the fruit of the same orange trees that had provided the blossoms for my wedding wreath. Then the messenger came disguised as Pius IX and he brought me a mug of cocoa. I realized that the dark fragrance, the burning foam of that sumptuous concoction I drank one afternoon at Hecelchakán, and again at Ticul, at Hunucmá, at Calkiní and Halachó, was also not what I should be using as ink to write you. Besides, Maximilian, can you imagine how sick I got when I mistook the orange juice for my urine and the chocolate for my excrement? Can you imagine how sick I felt when I remembered Dr. Jilek standing by my bedroom window, holding a jar of urine up to the light? To test for what, Maximilian? To find out whether, as well as insane, I might also be diabetic? To find how much sweetness I've built up over all these years—so much sweet love for you and for Mexico, and with no one to give it to, because no one wants to hear me? A sweetness that chokes me, that makes my heart want to burst, that saturates my blood, pours out of my pores, shows up in my spit and my urine? You should see how nauseated I felt when I remembered Dr. Bohuslavek examining a sample of my excrement in a bowl. To find out what, Maximilian? To look for a badly digested rose petal from the Bouchout Gardens or a scrap of your admiral's uniform? Or to find out if I'm riddled with parasites and that it is they—not Colonel Van der Smissen's child—that bloat up my belly like a balloon? If you could see, Maximilian, how much it hurts to see those disgusting liquids and be reminded that I'm alive. Yes, I'm alive but so very old. As a child I was proud and very clean, so I learned very quickly to answer nature's calls in a porcelain chamber pot that was a gift from Grandmother Marie Amélie. But I can't even do that anymore. Every night I wet my bed. Sometimes I dream that I am rotting alive, waking up in a pool of my own stinking foulness. And then I start to cry.

Oh, Maximilian, Maximilian. Did they tell you that they saw me cup my hands to drink the water from a Villa Medici fountain? Did they tell you that I left Miramare barefoot to drink from the fountain that has a sculpture of a boy strangling an egret? Have they told you that they're quite sure they've seen Empress Carlota drinking water from the Tlaxpana Fountain in an earthenware jug, and bathing in Niagara Falls fully clothed, and then nude in Trafalgar Fountain? Did they tell you that they saw me washing myself with water from the blue grotto at Linderhof, or gargling with water from the Churubusco River? Did they tell you, Maximilian, that they saw me kneeling at the Trevi Fountain drinking out of the Murano glass goblet the Pope gave me? I feel sorry for you, Maximilian, if you believe everything they tell you. Listen, it's not between my legs, through my vagina, that I want, that I've always wanted to be impregnated. In any case no one, not even you, could penetrate me there today, because the black widow spiders that the messenger brought me have all crawled down from my wig to nest in my pubis, and have spun an iridescent web of steel threads there between my labia. And it's a lie that I made myself a chastity belt out of roses. I used thorns instead. No, it's through my mouth, I'm telling you—and not with your penis, Maximilian, not with your sperm but with water—that I want to impregnate myself. With the water that I have yearned to drink since I first began to die of thirst. But Maximilian, I, Marie Charlotte of Belgium, the madwoman of the house, the Empress of Mexico and of America, must never drink from the fountains where the beggars drink, where children splash and lepers wash their wounds. My thirst is different. I am a child and I shall remain a child, but not because I haven't grown up: my purity and innocence are as lofty as a Gothic cathedral. I am now and will always be a beggar, but what I beg for are the signs of dawn; what I search for, in the trash, is the rind of the moon. I am ill, sick from dried roses, because of the rainbows piercing my chest, from the stars and sunrises that get into my eyes to light up my delirium. I shall drink, yes, but from the same springs that Heine and Rilke and Mozart drank. One day I will drink from those springs, if God allows it. If God and my imagination bathe me with their grace—so that I may regain my transparency.

XVIII
QUERÉTARO
1866–67

1. In the Mousetrap

During the whole of 1866 the European nations were kept very busy by a series of outbreaks, revolutions, and wars. The Parisian newspaper *La Patrie* stated that the insurrections in Palermo, the rebellions in Crete, the disturbances in the Ottoman Empire, the unrest in Greece, and the victories achieved by Juárez and his troops in Mexico were all events that formed part of a vast international conspiracy forged in anticipation of the imminent war with Germany and a general conflagration in Europe. Faced with the Prussian menace and pressure from the United States, France had more than enough to worry about without Mexico, and thus Maximilian could expect nothing more from Louis Napoleon. Carlota had summed Europe up in three words: All is futile. Of course England and Spain—those two other nations that had originally taken part in the tripartite agreement and invasion—were now even less inclined to reinvest in Mexico and its Emperor: In the course of '66, the English, for example, had to face, on the one hand, a rebellion from the African population in Jamaica and, on the other, some troubles much closer to their own land and conscience: after the Civil War in the United States, all the Fenians who had taken part in the fight had now returned to Ireland to fight clandestinely as terrorists for the emancipation of their homeland from the United Kingdom. Spain, for its part, after more than forty years of refusing to recognize Peru's independence, was now at war with this South American nation. In 1864, Admiral Pinzón had occupied the Chincha or Guano Islands, and in 1866 the Spanish Armada bombarded the Port of Callao and—because Chile was Peru's ally against Spain—the Chilean port of Valparaíso.

As to Juárez's victories, cited in *La Patrie*, these were many and frequent during 1866, a year that had been unkind to the increasingly unstable Mexican

Empire practically from its very first days. On January 5, nearly a thousand black American soldiers under the command of Colonel Reed and General Crawford invaded the border port of Bagdad, Tamaulipas, which at the time was under the control of imperialist forces, and looted it mercilessly. Soon after, three hundred Foreign Legion soldiers at the Hacienda Santa Isabel, near the city of Parras, suffered a scandalous defeat, reminiscent of the disaster at Camarón. When, some days later, General Douay tried to lead a punitive assault on the victors, they simply vanished into Mapimí Desert.

Another debacle suffered by the Franco-Mexican troops was at Santa Gertrudis, in March, and this was the prelude to Matamoros falling into the hands of Juárez's army. In his memoirs, Colonel Blanchot recalls the famous statement by a French queen who, when told that the Parisian commoners had no bread to eat, retorted, "If they have no bread, let them eat cake!" Blanchot wonders—not quite jokingly—why General Olvera didn't bear this story in mind, and simply bid his soldiers, who had no water, to drink wine. Olvera's column had gone more than forty-eight hours without water when they were wiped out by the forces of the Juarist general, Mariano Escobedo. The convoy escorted by the column, however, was carrying no less than forty thousand bottles of Bordeaux wine. If General Olvera had just been a little more imaginative . . . one bottle of Château Margaux per head, says Blanchot, would have clinched his victory.

With or without wine, however, the Juarists won the battle, and Santa Gertrudis and Santa Isabel were added over the following months to other Republican victories that, when considered in the light of the gradual French withdrawal from the fortified towns, made Maximilian's decision all the more urgent. He would either have to abdicate and sail back to Europe, or to reestablish himself on the throne and return immediately to the capital of the Empire. Rumors had it that Porfirio Díaz was approaching Orizaba. And, if there might still have been doubt as to this immediate danger, it was certainly true that the Mexican general's forces had destroyed a column of the Austrian Legion at La Carbonera—a column led by Karl Krickl, the officer who, in a letter to his brother Julius in Vienna, had commented that Maximilian was in Orizaba, "surrounded by adventurers and charlatans."

Something similar had happened to the Belgian Legion commander, Van der Smissen, who not long before had proposed to Maximilian that he organize a division and put himself, the Emperor, at its head, and suggested too, among other measures, the creation of an Austro-Belgian brigade that he, Van der Smissen, would command, as well as another one under Colonel Miguel López (another of Maximilian's inner circle). General Mejía would be given the position of Chief of Staff.

Less than a month later, Van der Smissen was defeated at Ixmiquilpan, having been deceived—as he says in his *Souvenirs de Mexique*—about the number of Liberals that he had to face. Corti writes that the Mexican soldiers in the Austrian Legion ran off when they spotted the enemy. The same thing happened to Van der Smissen towards the end of the same year—and he also relates this in his memoirs—when on pulling out of Tulancingo the Sixth Cavalry left at a gallop to join the enemy. But Mexicans weren't the only ones abandoning the Imperial ranks—French, Belgians, Austrians, and the Nubians of the Egyptian battalion deserted as well, especially the men of the Foreign Legion, and Blanchot himself tells us that once, when they were near the border, eighty-nine legionnaires ran off into the U.S. all at once.

Long-time supporters were deserting the cause as well, and it was widely known that several distinguished families were already packing their bags to flee, protected by the French contingent, for Veracruz and Europe. Even old friends were leaving the Emperor, such as Hidalgo y Esnaurrízar. Maximilian had summoned him to Mexico to give him a post as State Counselor after replacing him as ambassador to Paris with General Juan Nepomuceno Almonte. Hidalgo did get to Mexico, but in a constant panic, and overcome by fear he took the first opportunity to sneak off back to Europe.

But, though some were deserting Maximilian, others, such as Generals Miramón and Márquez, were arriving in Mexico to take up the Imperial cause. Their unexpected return infuriated General Tavera, the War Secretary, since they had both deserted their respective posts. Tavera didn't dare have them arrested, however—and in fact he never managed this—without first consulting the Emperor—and Maximilian himself had practically been sequestered at Hacienda Xalapilla, near Orizaba, by Father Agustín Fischer. Colonel Blanchot, who named himself Interim Vice Secretary of War, says in Volume 3 of his memoirs that a congress charged with deciding between Maximilian's abdication or persistence was constituted in Orizaba on November 26th and attended by only eighteen members, four of whom were Imperial Cabinet ministers. The absence of the other members was due to the fact that many simply weren't prepared to confront the dangers of a sixty-league journey for such a meeting, nor to travel through areas increasingly riddled with Juarist guerrillas. Blanchot says that the four ministers' votes were part of a ten-vote majority in favor of maintaining the Empire. Other writers, Corti among them, don't mention a "congress," but a Council of Ministers, that should in fact have included Bazaine, but that the Marshal had snubbed. Corti states that eleven ministers were in favor of abdication, while "another group was opposed, and the rest wished to postpone the decision until the interests of the Empire's supporters were assured." Scarlett, the British minister, offered another opinion, informing London that the Council had cast nineteen votes in favor of prolonging the Empire, with only two votes against. One way or the other, on the morning of November 28th, Maximilian seemed to have once again made up his mind to leave, and he dictated several farewell letters to the European ambassadors in Mexico. But, then, that same afternoon, he changed his mind and announced that he would not abdicate.

That same day, the paddle-steamer *Susquehanna* arrived in Veracruz from New York and Havana. On board were the renowned General William Sherman and Mr. Lewis Campbell, the new American minister recognized by the Juárez government. It later became known that General Sherman was standing in for General Ulysses S. Grant, who had refused to accompany Campbell to Mexico, but what we still don't know for certain was what the eccentric ambassador was doing in Veracruz when Juárez was in Chihuahua, 1,200 miles away. It appears that both Yankees intended to disembark the moment Maximilian announced his abdication. Since this didn't happen, the *Susquehanna* sailed back to New Orleans, and the emissaries that Maximilian had sent to Veracruz—on learning that the Americans were there—found themselves unable to contact them.

In a letter to the President of the Council of Ministers, Teodosio Lares, Maximilian said that he had been deeply moved by the show of "loyalty and love" on the part of the members of his cabinet, and he vowed to be ready for "any type of sacrifice." He specified, among other conditions for his remaining in Mexico, that conscription laws be passed, that all ties with the French be cut, that the Decree of October 3rd be annulled, that the Empire continue to seek an agreement with the United States, and, finally, that court-martial be invoked only for common criminals. December 10th was the date selected to announce to the Mexican nation that Maximilian would hold tight to the reins of the Empire.

Maximilian left Orizaba December 12, 1866, the date of the celebration of Our Lady of Guadalupe, patron saint of Mexico and America. The night before, his ministers had celebrated his departure with liters of champagne, and Father Fischer had drunk so much that he was unable to escort the Emperor on the first leg of his journey. The group passed Ojo de Agua and stopped at the country villa of the Archbishop of Puebla, the Hacienda de Xonaca, where, as Montgomery Hyde relates in his book *Mexican Empire*, Maximilian continued his botanical and entomological expeditions. Dr. Basch tells us that the Emperor also amused himself by sketching Miramare Castle and Lacroma Abbey from memory, and that he engaged in target practice with pistols after lunch, but that this caused Bilimek to withdraw, as he couldn't bear the loud noise. It was in the Hacienda de Xonaca that the Emperor finally agreed to give General Castelnau an audience, after the latter arrived with the French minister in Mexico, Alphonse Danó.

General Castelnau was frank with Louis Napoleon concerning his opinion on Maximilian. Montgomery Hyde cites the August 27th *Revue de Paris*, where fragments of a letter from the General to the French Emperor were printed. What was needed in Mexico, said Castelnau, "[was] a man with common sense and energy." And Maximilian, he added, had neither of these. For Castelnau, Maximilian was, if anything "a dilettante" who had added to his extant faults a "very Mexican sense of malice that helped him conceal his intentions." By this time everyone knew about the telegram that the profoundly angry French Emperor had sent to his aide-de-camp when he found out about Maximilian's decision to stay in Mexico, and in which Louis Napoleon ordered Castelnau to proceed with the immediate repatriation of any French citizen who wanted to return home. Another consequence of that telegram was the dissolution of the Austrian and Belgian volunteer corps.

Castelnau and Danó's mission was to bring about Maximilian's abdication at all costs, and to do this they painted his situation to him in the darkest possible colors. But we must remember that Maximilian was surrounded by people who were trying to convince him to remain in Mexico, and whose arguments, after all, were decisive. Further, it was evident by then that Bazaine himself was very ambivalent on the subject. When Danó and Castelnau told Maximilian that his only way out was abdication, and that the French Emperor himself held this view, Maximilian pointed to a telegram on his desk. It was dated the day before, and in it the Marshal urged Maximilian to preserve his crown, promising every effort to support the Empire. Nothing could have been more contradictory to Louis Napoleon's instructions.

According to Blanchot, Father Fischer had forged this telegram. But in any case, Bazaine's conduct still raised many suspicions. Some historians theorize that the Marshal wanted to stay in Mexico because that was what Pepita Peña wanted. It has also been said that at some point Bazaine had developed aspirations to become Mexico's Bernadotte and, once the Archduke was gone, to establish a Mexican dynasty as brilliant and lasting as that of Karl XIV of Sweden. Émile Ollivier tells us that Maximilian, amused by Danó's and Castelnau's astonishment, told them that he was well aware of the Marshal's duplicity, and that he was aware that on the same day he sent it, Bazaine had made all kinds of promises to Miramón and Márquez, and had invited Porfirio Díaz to lunch. General Díaz would later say that Bazaine had offered to sell him, through an intermediary, six thousand rifles and four million shells, plus cannons and gunpowder, with the understanding that the sale would only go through if Díaz took over as Mexico's political and military leader. Nevertheless, Ollivier points out that no military chief could have made that offer without previous authorization from his minister, under the penalty of being court-martialed.

In any event, Danó and Castelnau needed no help to fuel their resentment for Bazaine. At that time all the French leaders in Mexico were attacking each other either openly or covertly, and Bazaine was the main target of criticism, in particular by the machinations of General Douay, whose correspondence with his wife in Paris was quite explicit as to his low opinion of the Marshal. Douay knew well enough that his letters would end up in Louis Napoleon's hands, since his wife was the daughter of General Lebreton, the military commander of the Tuileries Palace. Bazaine himself, says Corti, managed to obtain a draft of one of Castelnau's reports to the French Emperor, and, indignant at the accusations against him in the report, he wrote to Paris and asked to be relieved. Marshal Niel, Louis Napoleon's new Secretary of War, tried to placate him.

Upon his return to Mexico City, Maximilian did not immediately take up lodging in the Imperial Palace or Chapultepec Castle. It was likely that both palaces were half empty, not only because the Emperor had shipped off most of his personal effects to Veracruz, but also because, in his absence, anything could have happened, and not just looting, but all kinds of sales or auctions. Castelot tells us, for example, that when Maximilian and his entourage left Chapultepec Castle, the gates were left open, and that since the Emperor had neglected to pay the castle chef his salary, this forced the latter to sell all the kitchen equipment and provisions belonging to the household. Maximilian settled instead into the Hacienda de la Teja, a few kilometers away from the capital, where his former liberal ministers—Ramírez, Robles, and Escudero—all arrived to bid him farewell. Miramón and Márquez had rejoined the Emperor at the estate, as had General Mejía. These officers agreed that the situation was surely difficult but not hopeless. Supporters of the three officers joined them. Colonel Khevenhüller assumed the task of forming a regiment of Mexican hussars, Lieutenant Colonel Baron Hammerstein an infantry battalion, and Count Wickenburg took it upon himself to organize the military police. Then, Tomás Murphy, former Mexican Ambassador to Austria, presented a plan for organizing an army, stating that the three branches would have 1,913 officers, 29,663 men, 6,691 horses, and ten and a half artillery batteries. As Corti points out, the object of this report was to make Maximilian believe that he would soon have a considerable military force at his disposal, and that if, according to Murphy himself, the opposition added up to approximately thirty-four thousand, there would be a relative equality of forces. But none of this was true then, nor would it ever be.

Around that time, Maximilian received a communiqué from Vienna informing him that the Empress Carlota had enjoyed a complete physical and mental recovery. That was also untrue, and another telegram, sent immediately thereafter, refuted the first. In any case, the die had been cast, and nothing and nobody appeared able to dissuade Maximilian, who then resolved to take another vote. This time, Marshal Bazaine did attend the meeting, although he appeared to regret it later on, deeming it a farce, since it was clear that Maximilian had already decided to stay in Mexico.

This much can be demonstrated by the fact that Maximilian, aware of the impossibility of calling together a real National Assembly, agreed that a "council" made up of his cabinet and a few prominent Mexican conservatives should determine the Empire's fate. Secondly, he accepted the decision of the council without any comment on the actual results of the vote, despite the fact that the Empire won over abdication by only one vote. (The numbers issue still seems to be disputed, however, since Hanna and Hanna, in their book *Napoleon III and Mexico*, mention thirty-five participants, of which—these U.S. historians claim—twenty-four voted in favor of the Empire, six against, and five abstained; and those who abstained, the Hannas say, were members of the clergy, who determined that politics were outside their province . . . But other historians, who cite different numbers, say that Fischer was given the right to participate, and that his "aye" was the determining vote. If this was indeed the case, we could say that the fates of both the Mexican Empire and of Ferdinand Maximilian of Habsburg were determined on that day by one former German Protestant pastor.)

Whatever the truth may be, the fact is that Maximilian accepted the council's decision and remained in Mexico.

The French, on the other hand, left—to the tune of the following song:

> The French are taking off
> toward San Juan de Ulúa
> to pick *jujurifirifiró*
> and to drink sherry *vino*
> whistles and drummmy-drum-drums
> in crystalleee goblet-de-dums . . .

Along with "Bye-bye Mamá Carlota," this song became part of the Mexican folklore on the French Intervention.

But before the final departure, there was a total breakdown in relations between Maximilian and Bazaine, as a result of an article in the newspaper *La Patrie* that was insulting to the French—or at least that's how the French interpreted it. Bazaine had the paper shut down and the author arrested. Around that time, Márquez ordered the imprisonment of a Mexican citizen, Pedro Garay, who Corti claims was in Bazaine's service. The French commander Maussion demanded Garay's release. When his orders fell on deaf ears, he had General Ugarte, the Mexican chief of police, arrested. Maximilian considered this to be unacceptable interference. Lastly, Bazaine received a letter in which Teodosio Lares, among other things, contended that the French had given no support to the Mexican Imperial troops during a raid against the town of Texcoco. The Marshal replied that, because of the letter's tone, he would no longer be in communication with Lares's office. He imparted this to Maximilian in another letter that came back the same day, with an attachment signed by Fischer stating that His Majesty wished to have no further direct contact with Bazaine, unless the Marshal took back his words.

That was the end of it. Maximilian never saw Bazaine again, since he refused the audience the Marshal requested to bid him farewell. On February 5, 1867, Maximilian, from behind a half-opened curtain on an Imperial Palace window, watched the withdrawal of the French army. The column crossed Alameda Park at nine A.M., it continued through San Francisco and Plateros Streets, it arrived at the Plaza Mayor, and it paraded before the Palace.

An escort of spahis or Turkish cavalrymen preceded Marshal Bazaine. After them came the following, in this order: General Castelnau, the Chiefs of Staff, an escort and a squadron of French *Chasseurs*, a group of *Chasseurs* from Vincennes, General Castagny, the 7th and 95th troops of the line, the artillery units, a battalion of Zouaves from the 3rd, the beasts of burden, and another Zouave squadron from the 3rd to bring up the rear. The column proceeded to the San Antonio watchtower.

They say that Maximilian then spoke these words: "I'm free at last," a phrase reminiscent of Eugénie's comment when Spanish and British forces left Veracruz: "Thanks be to God, we've lost our allies!"

Before leaving Mexico, the French destroyed all the weapons and ammunition that they couldn't take with them. Léonce Détroyat cites a publication, *Nord*, that asked, in shock, how it was possible that—at the time of the evacuation—Bazaine could have had fourteen million cartridges cast into the ocean instead of leaving them for Maximilian. Still, Bazaine subsequently began to pity the Archduke, despite all the misunderstandings between the two. Therefore, he telegraphed the French minister Danó from Acultzingo, asking him to inform the Emperor that he could still help him leave Mexico and make it back to Europe. Of course Max ignored the offer. The Marshal prolonged his stay in Orizaba, in the vain hope that the Emperor would change his mind.

Through a tacit agreement, French troops did not meet with hostility from Juarist forces as they left Mexico, though the Juarists followed at a distance and occupied each fortified site the French left behind, one after the other.

Marshal Bazaine was the last of the French occupying force to leave Mexican soil.

On March 12, 1867, Colonel Blanchot reports, there was a very significant event. After the *Souverain*, the ship on which the Marshal was sailing, weighed anchor, the packet steamer *France* was sighted carrying the mail from Saint-Nazaire. Everyone thought that Bazaine would give orders for the boat to stop and send a dinghy to the flagship with any correspondence directed to the chiefs and officers—it could have included important dispatches from the Tuileries, messages from the Quai d'Orsay, letters from friends and spouses, etc. . . . However, Bazaine showed no interest in doing this. Perhaps his head was still ringing then with the phrase spoken by Señor Araujo y Escandón at the Council of Ministers—the same words that a Pope had thought the Duke de Guise had deserved: "Leave. It is of no consequence. You have done little for your sovereign, less for the Church, and absolutely nothing for your honor."

The packet boat continued straight ahead until it was hidden by the shadow of Fort San Juan de Ulúa, and the *Souverain* and its convoy of ships disappeared into the sunset, toward Toulon, through the Florida Canal and Gibraltar.

Bazaine was received in France without the ceremony appropriate for a Marshal. A scapegoat was needed for the Mexican fiasco. Five years before, de la Gravière had said that with just six thousand men, he was the master of Mexico. In fact, forty thousand had not been enough, and in the end, Eugénie had decided that they just might have been able to conquer that vast country with three hundred thousand. Louis Philippe, Carlota's grandfather, had needed one hundred thousand to subdue Algeria, a country ten or fifteen times smaller than Mexico.

For a few days, Maximilian had cause to be optimistic, thanks to a spectacular victory by Miramón. Benito Juárez was approaching the central region as the French troops withdrew. When he crossed Durango, the enthusiastic reception he received from people who had so much admired Maximilian caused him to exclaim: "A Viceroy gone, a Viceroy come"—something like, "The King is dead, long live the King!" Juárez got to know his countrymen a little better that day, and learned that they were like any other people in the world. From Durango, he went down to Zacatecas, where, as we're told by the Mexican historian Valadez, the President, for some reason, felt a little like a soldier, and determined to inspect the city's lines of defense personally. Miramón attacked by surprise, and Juárez got on a horse and galloped off. They say that Miramón thought Juárez was fleeing in his carriage, which he sent men after in vain, and that this is how Juárez slipped between his fingers. Juárez took refuge in Jerez, but his baggage remained in Miramón's possession, except—thanks be to God—for his beautiful, expensive cane, valued at two thousand pesos.

The Imperialists remembered another time that they had forced President Juárez to take off on horseback—in November of '65, when Bazaine attacked Chihuahua—and they joked that the Zapotec Indian would soon be an expert at something he hadn't managed to teach himself over half a century—that is, to become a good horseman—from having to escape so many times with the

Imperialists treading on his coattails. The Emperor, delighted with the news, wrote Miramón instructing him to try Juárez and his ministers on the spot, if they were captured. He did not, however, want them sentenced without prior approval. These instructions fell into the hands of Juarists, and a few days later, the Republican General Mariano Escobedo—whose forces had flanked Miramón on his march toward Zacatecas—attacked and defeated Miramón at the Hacienda San Jacinto. Miramón lost the imperial cash box and twenty-two cannons, while fifteen hundred of his men were imprisoned. Of these, nearly one hundred Europeans, mostly French, were executed. Benito Juárez declared that after Louis Napoleon's army had withdrawn, any Frenchman in Mexico found bearing arms for the Imperial army had to be considered a filibuster. Miramón's brother was also captured, and was executed. It was a known fact that he was carried to the wall in a chair, since his feet had already almost been blown off, and that he was shot by candlelight.

It was around this time that Maximilian must have received the letter from his mother, cited by Corti and now to be found in the State Archives in Vienna, a letter in which—besides approving of Maximilian's decision to remain in Mexico—the Archduchess described how the family had celebrated an intimate Christmas on December 26th, after the official celebrations of the previous day; how her grandchildren, Gisela and Rudolf, had played happily with their little cousins; how Emperor Franz Joseph had pulled chubby little Otto on a sled; and how, finally, the following Sunday, as they were all having breakfast, Max's clock from Olmütz had chimed, and the Archduchess Sophie's eyes filled with tears. "I became all teary-eyed," she wrote, "and I felt that you were sending us greetings from so far away." Mother Sophie also wrote Max that Gustav Sachsen-Weimar had said during a luncheon they'd shared that he had bet a large sum that the Emperor would still be in Mexico come May.

Maximilian was indeed still in Mexico in May of 1867, but not in the capital. He was in the city of Querétaro, besieged by thirty thousand Republican troops.

Many historians assert that Maximilian had put himself into a mousetrap, since that's the only way Querétaro could be described. Others are of the opinion that his decision to leave Mexico City to face the Republican forces was a logical one. The Juarist generals, Escobedo, Corona, and Riva Palacio, were converging on the capital from diverse areas of the Republic with a total number of troops estimated at twenty-seven thousand men, and Querétaro, as the point of intersection of various roads from the north and the west, was an excellent position to take up. Moreover, Teodosio Lares was in favor of saving the capital from what he called "the calamities and horrors" of a siege and invasion at all costs.

The Sierra Gorda foothills reach all the way to the valleys of Querétaro and San Juan del Río, where—it was said—the Imperialist General Tomás Mejía had a great number of followers, and the same was true of General Olvera, who could command two or three thousand "mountain Indians"—which were two more reasons for Maximilian to go to Querétaro. The Mexican historian Justo Sierra says that, militarily, Lares's plan was perfectly sensible, since the Imperialists could conceivably have defeated General Corona in about a week. But a total inertia, caused by indecisiveness, doomed Maximilian's men, and when Escobedo's troops were able to link up with Corona's, victory became impossible. To be clear, this is *not* what Justo Sierra says, but Carlos Pereyra, the Mexican historian who wrote the last two chapters—entitled "Querétaro" and "Richmond"—of Sierra's book on Juárez. Sierra was so busy in his post as Minister of Public Education that, when the book was released, he neglected to give Pereyra the necessary credit. Juárez himself had a hunch that, if the Archduke were kept captive in Querétaro, the passage of time would suffice in itself to defeat him, and he said as much in a letter to his son-in-law Santacilia. It's worth noting, however, that some historians don't blame the Emperor's eventual defeat entirely on his indecision, but also on the people of Querétaro: apparently, as the Imperial army tried to move out to confront the Republicans, the citizens begged Maximilian not to leave the town and fortress unprotected, and the Emperor yielded.

"How beautiful and full of majesty was that noble descendant of the Caesars and the Germans!" Albert Hans says, or rather exclaims, in his book *Querétaro: Memorias de un Oficial del Emperador Maximiliano*. And maybe Hans was right, and Maximilian, who had taken charge of the supreme command of his troops, dressed as a Mexican general, with his long, golden beard parted in two, and his large, white felt hat, and the grand Order of the Mexican Eagle around his neck, seated on his frisky horse Orispelo, did indeed resemble a "New World" Jason, or perhaps a "New World" Don Quixote—who, to make a Sancho Panza of his secretary Blasio, asked him to dismount while on the way to Querétaro. "Secretaries are men of letters and not of the sword," he said, and told Blasio to ride a tame mule so that, as they trotted along, the Emperor could dictate some notes to him. Blasio obeyed and probably wrote using his customary indelible pencil.

Maximilian left Mexico City at five A.M. on February 13, 1867, with fifteen hundred men and fifty thousand pesos. No one knows why it was that, being (as it was said—and as he himself said) so superstitious, the Emperor chose the 13th to leave the capital . . . but, then, Carlota had also departed for Europe on a 13th. Neither Agustín Fischer, the cabinet secretary, nor the learned Bilimek accompanied the Emperor on that mission to Querétaro. But, besides Blasio, others such as Pradillo, his field officer, Anton Grill, his Austrian valet, and his Hungarian chef, Josef Tüdös, formed Maximilian's entourage. He was also accompanied by the Mexican generals Vidaurri and Del Castillo, and Prince Felix Salm-Salm, a member of one of the great German princely dynasties. A Salm-Salm, in fact, had been a candidate for the Belgian throne a short time before Leopold ascended. This Salm-Salm, however, up to his eyes in debt in his native land, was an adventurer who had taken part in the war over Holstein—the Prussian King rewarded him with a "sword of honor"—and later in the American Civil War when he attained the post of Civil and Military Governor of North Georgia. It seems that he wasn't well-liked by Maximilian at first, but in time he gained the Emperor's full confidence. Salm-Salm, a career soldier, thought Querétaro the worst possible site to protect since every house—he pointed out—was within rifle range of the hills surrounding a city of thirty thousand inhabitants, and which was called the "Levitical City" because of its many churches and convents, some of which were veritable fortresses.

"Majestät sind nicht allein"—"His Majesty is not alone"—Harding quotes Salm-Salm, speaking to Maximilian—and undeniably, Maximilian had not been totally abandoned. Generals Márquez, Miramón, Mejía, and Méndez marched along with him. The coincidence that their surnames all began with the same letter started a legend about the dire significance the letter *M* had for the Emperor: there were the *M*s of his four generals, the *M* beginning his own first name, the *M*s in Miramare and Mexico, and, lastly the *M* in mortality . . . But, then, there's also the *M* in the first name of the "friend" who would betray him in Querétaro—Colonel Miguel López, that blond, blue-eyed, slender, distinguished head of the Empress's regiment, who rode by her side looking quite elegant in his red hussar's waistcoat, trimmed with black frog loops, and the cross of the Legion of Honor.

On the way to Querétaro Orispelo, the Emperor's mount, stumbled. And if this ill omen wasn't enough, the column was attacked by a band of Liberals at Lechería and a bugler fell wounded at Maximilian's feet. Later, at Calpulal-pan, the group spotted an Imperialist soldier hanging head-first from a tree, his body hacked into by numerous machetes, though the body was almost obscured by the enormous number of butterflies hovering around it—white and yellow, yellow and black, orange—and not green flies. Also, Tüdös, the Hungarian chef, was grazed by a bullet at Calpulalpan—it passed by his cheek, and he spat out several shattered teeth.

But Querétaro was such a beautiful city . . . There were the tall, red gran-ite arches of its aqueduct, built 130 years earlier in order to pour out a con-stant stream of clear and fresh water from La Cañada. There was the wide and bucolic and fertile valley that surrounded the city. There were its grand churches and convents, abounding with marvelous examples of colonial, ro-coco, and Churrigueresque art—like the churches of Santa Rosa and Santa Clara: Santa Rosa of Viterbo with its tower and angular buttresses, its almost-oriental curves and carvings; Santa Clara with its majestic portico and the monumental gold filigree of its pulpit. And, too, there were the clear and luminous, sun-splashed streets of Querétaro, its blue skies, the astonishing façades and interiors of some of its most notable houses, like the residence of the Marquesa del Villar with its shady patios of lobular arches, or Ecala House, with its awe-inspiring iron work; and there was the elegant Neptune Fountain built by the brilliant architect of Guanajuato, Tres Guerras, who also designed the Teresitas church and convent . . . Because of all this, and its innumerable other beauties, Querétaro was certainly worth not only a High Mass, but a battle, or a thousand battles, for that matter—it was a heroic site, well worth a victory or rout. Querétaro—site of the Great Rock: its name having come from the words "*queréndaro*" and "*querenda*," which in the Tar-ascan language mean "place with a great stone"—was a city made for attain-ing glory in, dead or alive.

This is what the Emperor of Mexico understood or decided when a great number of citizens greeted him on the so-called Chinese Hill. But during his first days there, Maximilian couldn't find lodgings inside the city and so camped out on the outskirts, on a hill called *Las Campanas* (The Bells), be-cause, it was said, there were stones or rocks there that tolled like bells when struck. There on that hill, topped by the ruins of a viceregal fortress that over-looked the entire valley—vast plains dotted by tiny but thick groves, and the roads leading to San Luis, to Celaya, and to Mexico City—Maximilian spent several nights, sometimes in a tent, others al fresco wrapped in serapes and Scottish coverlets. But, when the Republican troops began closing in, Maximilian moved his quarters to La Cruz Convent. The date selected was another 13th—March 13, 1867. Two days earlier, Republican troops had destroyed part of the tall red aqueduct to prevent water from reaching Querétaro. But the city had wells and cisterns that could provide the inhabitants, the army, and the cavalry with water for at least a few weeks. Also, there was a river that ran through part of the city, though its waters would soon be fouled by rotting corpses.

Castelot, who referred to La Cruz Convent as a "somewhat heteroclite combination of patios, cloisters, vaulted passages, chapels, and nooks, connected by stairways and innumerable corridors," says that the convent was given that name because the Indians, when surrendering to the conquistadors on that spot, had seen a cross drawn across the sky. The convent, clearly, was a place to surrender, because it had also been the last bastion of the Spanish troops that capitulated to the Insurgents on June 28, 1821—the year that Mexican independence was achieved.

On March 13th, the same day that Maximilian moved into La Cruz, Republican artillery opened fire on the convent. The Emperor, in a small cell furnished with an army cot, an iron-legged table with a silver washbasin and his personal grooming kit, an armchair and two pictures on the wall—one portraying Ferdinand VII and the other the city of Santiago de Compostela—had by then fully assumed his duties as Supreme Commander of the Mexican Imperial Army. He had nine thousand men, concentrated in Querétaro (twenty thousand fewer than estimated by Murphy), and forty pieces of artillery. Leonardo Márquez was his Chief of Staff. Miramón commanded the infantry. Mejía, the cavalry. General Méndez, the reserves. Reyes headed the corps of engineers and Salm-Salm led the sapper battalion.

Although some writers gloss over the siege at Querétaro—perhaps impatient to get right to the tragic, grotesque denouement of Maximilian's story—historians would have a plethora of material at their disposal if they wanted to expound on it at greater length. There are the many diaries, memoirs, chronicles, reports, and chronologies authored by the people who lived through the siege and survived it, including—among the Republicans—the Generals Sóstenes Rocha and Mariano Escobedo, Juan de Dios Arias, and others; and, in the Imperialist camp, likewise among others, Officer Albert Hans, Prince Salm-

Salm, Dr. Samuel Basch, and Maximilian's secretary, José Luis Blasio. To these, one could add the articles written by the *New York Herald*'s correspondent in Querétaro, who by the time of the siege concluded that the Archduke was doomed, and that the war would go on—as he said—until the Austrian Eagle had lost all his feathers, and not a single quill remained with which to sign his will. As there is no space here for a detailed description of what happened between the beginning of the siege on March 10, 1867, to its ending sixty-one days later (on the dawn of May 15th), it's worth concentrating on the primary events, as well as on some conclusions reached because of them, and some of the commentary on these conclusions, with a marginal note to be included up-front to read: During most of the time the siege of Querétaro lasted, all of Maximilian's ailments worsened, in particular his dysentery and malaria. As for General Mejía, he suffered several sharp attacks of rheumatism that kept him bedridden on more than one occasion.

To begin: a victory on the part of Maximilian in Querétaro would not necessarily have assured a final victory for the Empire. But the truth is—or seems to have been—that his troops senselessly squandered numerous opportunities to attack the enemy, and from an advantageous position. This lack of action was caused by a series of orders followed by countermands that resulted from the rivalry and ill will that existed among Maximilian's closest generals. Hence, on March 17th, when Miramón and his men were preparing to depart with the objective of taking San Pablo and San Gregorio Hills, Márquez aborted the plan. Miramón was furious and, after throwing his hat on the ground, teary-eyed and "white with rage"—at least this is how an eyewitness described him—he asked Vidaurri to inform Maximilian that from then on he would limit himself to obeying orders, and that he would never again attend a war council.

It was obvious that Márquez was jealous of Miramón's triumphs, but the reason he gave for quashing Miramón's plan was that La Cruz could not be left without sufficient protection. A few days before, on the 14th, the enemy had attacked La Cruz and forced Márquez himself to give up the convent church, the cemetery, and the garden in turn. Salm-Salm, who couldn't bear the sight of Márquez, wrote in his diary that this setback had occurred because of what he called Márquez's "stupid or traitorous negligence." That same day, March 14th, Salm-Salm single-handedly seized a rifle-barreled cannon that had been set up at San Sebastián Bridge, and that had been causing no end of trouble to the besieged.

On March 20th, Miramón found an opportunity to get even with Márquez by opposing his plan to initiate a "mass sortie" of the Imperial forces. By then, the city was besieged on three sides.

However, Márquez would vanish from the scene soon after. With the pompous title of Imperial Deputy in his knapsack, he left Querétaro the night of the 22nd or 23rd of March, accompanied by twelve hundred cavalry soldiers, charged with bringing reinforcements within twenty days, and attacking Escobedo from the rear. His sally was successful, but Márquez never returned. The Republican General Porfirio Díaz, who had defeated the Imperialists at Tehuitzingo, Tlaxiaco, Lo de Soto, Huajuapan, Nochixtlán, Miahuatlán, La Carbonera, and Oaxaca, added another name to his long list of victories—the city of Puebla.

Porfirio Díaz took Puebla on April 2nd. Márquez, who by way of a forced conscription had increased his total strength to six thousand men—including, it appears, numerous convicts—headed toward Puebla and was defeated by Díaz at San Lorenzo. Some writers—Gene Smith, for example—state that Márquez's troops, during their withdrawal, had to resort to scattering the contents of a wagon full of gold in the middle of the road, so that the Republicans would stop to collect it and wouldn't catch up with them. Márquez fell back to Mexico City, and he remained there until the Empire fell, when he snuck away disguised as a muleteer.

The Tiger of Tacubaya's departure from Querétaro was timely; on the following day, General Vicente Riva Palacio arrived at Chinese Hill with four thousand men to finish sealing off the city. It was March 23rd. On the 24th, at the Battle of Casa Blanca, the Imperialist Colonel Ramírez de Arellano—who that same day was promoted to general—distinguished himself by repelling General Corona's troops. Also on that day—a day when the battlefield was covered with the corpses of two thousand Republicans—Maximilian nearly died when a grenade went off nearby.

On the 26th, a plumber from Querétaro was able to drill a hole in a blocked length of the aqueduct, restoring running water to part of the city. But other things, besides water, had already become scarce, like lead and zinc for cannonballs. General Severo del Castillo—Márquez's replacement as Chief of Staff—ordered that all metal plates from the Iturbide Theater's roof be removed. Castelot says that this gave the Imperialists up to eight hundred kilos of lead per day, at first. Later, they melted down bathtubs, and even printing type.

They also found it necessary to impose forced loans and war taxes, and abuses of these measures were rampant. Castelot himself tells us that the Spanish consul in Querétaro was relieved not only of eight thousand sacks of corn, but also of the rafters of his house, which were used to shore up the parapets on the new ramparts the Emperor had ordered constructed. Castelot adds that Maximilian also established a tax on doors and windows—a piaster a week each, plus another piaster every time they were opened. And General Castillo posted a warning that anyone hoarding supplies of corn and other grains would be executed within twenty-four hours.

On March 30th, Maximilian organized a celebration at La Cruz, and, as a surprise, it was he, himself, the Supreme Commander of the army, who was decorated by his troops on that occasion.

The next day, General Miramón tried to retake San Gregorio Hill, to no avail. Other attempts on his part—such as that on April 11th, when he failed to regain the Mexico Sentry Station—were likewise futile. It was an open secret that there was growing enmity between Méndez and Miramón, and at the same time, that Colonel Miguel López was extremely jealous of Prince Salm-Salm, whom Maximilian had named his aide-de-camp, and who had by now—to his credit—captured more than six enemy cannons.

On April 22nd, Maximilian heard the news of Márquez's defeat, but he kept it from the people and from his army. Severo del Castillo began to pen fake news briefs from the capital, and nonexistent Imperial victories were trumpeted with cheers and fanfares—although everyone knew there was no mail getting in or out of Querétaro, from Mexico City or anywhere else, since any arriving or departing Imperial messengers usually wound up hanging from poles or stakes on the outskirts of the city, wearing signs that read: THE EMPEROR'S MAIL.

Meanwhile, Márquez used similar tactics in Mexico City to keep the population calm. In other words, in Querétaro they said everything was going splendidly in the capital, and in the capital, the word was that everything was going splendidly in Querétaro. The truth, however, was that in both cities—the capital and Querétaro—the Empire was crumbling.

That same April 22nd, a Republican member of parliament entered Querétaro—Corti doesn't mention his name; Castelot says that it was Colonel Rincón Gallardo—to propose that, if the city surrendered, "the Emperor would be allowed to leave with the honors of war." Castelot adds that the parliamentarian stipulated that the principal condition of the deal would be for the Archduke to sail out of Veracruz immediately. Maximilian refused the offer.

Around that time, a yellow carriage, drawn by four mules, was spotted at Chinese Hill heading toward Escobedo's camp. Rumor had it in Querétaro that Juárez had arrived. Later it was revealed that it hadn't been the President, but a woman: Princess Salm-Salm.

By that time Maximilian was regularly exposing himself to the heavy firing in the trenches, hoping to receive a "merciful shot" that would end his life, and with it the siege. He had not only rejected the parliamentarian's offer, but had also quashed several suggestions from other Imperialists to try and break out of the city accompanied by an escort. His honor, he kept arguing, kept him from abandoning his followers. But, as told by E. Masseras in *Un essai d'empire au Mexique*, he finally let himself be convinced, and asked his generals to draft a document that would absolve him from blame in the eyes of history. The date selected was April 27th, a day that the Emperor would try to leave Querétaro at five A.M., with his baggage and an escort, sheltered by a diversionary attack that Miguel Miramón would launch against El Cimatario Hill.

The Battle of El Cimatario was another of the curious episodes from the siege of Querétaro to go down in history, and which, for Maximilian and his troops, represented both a victory and a defeat.

A victory because Miramón's brilliant raid sent ten thousand Republicans into retreat, "possessed by panic," and the Imperialists were able to capture twenty-one pieces of artillery and thousands of rifles, along with food supplies and cattle, mules and goats by the dozens, plus more than six hundred prisoners.

A defeat because the Imperialists—and several historians agree on this point—lost several precious hours congratulating themselves and celebrating their victory afterward, and as a consequence, the Republicans had time to regroup and reoccupy El Cimatario. In his *Memoirs*, Albert Hans tells of his disappointment on ascertaining that a large part of the Imperialist army was made up of "green *chinacas*" a pejorative term used to designate inept and undisciplined troops, as opposed to the "red *chinacas*," all on the Republican side. But this same Hans had the opportunity to confirm that not all the liberals were "red"—though Galeana's riflemen—who in the end were the ones who successfully warded off Miramón's second offensive—were very effective. They were aided in this by two things: sixteen-millimeter American rifles, and a hatred—Hans says—that "was greater than our own." As a result, when the bugle sounded the battle call after a signal from Galeana, it was the Imperialists who started running.

After El Cimatario, no one in Querétaro believed that the Empire would win. The final blow was, perhaps, the so-called Battle of Calleja, on May 10th. The Republicans occupied a hacienda of this name, and the Imperialist troops were ordered to drive them out. The task of heading the detachment was assigned to Colonel Joaquín Rodríguez, one of Maximilian's favorite officers—golden-haired and blue-eyed, like López. That morning, he told the Emperor, "Your Majesty will make me a general today. If not, it will be because I have died." A bullet to the heart left Colonel Rodríguez on the plains of Querétaro, and he never became a general.

On May 5th the Republicans celebrated the anniversary of the Battle of Puebla with music, cheers, and fireworks.

In Querétaro itself, fires were burning to cremate bodies, many of which had to be pulled out of the river with hooks, in an advanced state of decomposition.

General Ramírez de Arellano, who had given himself the task of setting up one factory to produce salt and another to make gunpowder—for which sulfur and rock salt had to be confiscated from every pharmacy in Querétaro—relates in his book *Ultimas horas del Imperio*, that Maximilian's forces in Querétaro had been reduced to almost half, firstly because Márquez had taken more than one thousand men with him, and secondly because of the great and growing numbers of casualties, prisoners taken, and deserters.

In addition to this, the heat, the precarious sanitary conditions, and the lack of food, were all killing off the wounded at an alarming rate at the makeshift hospitals. Gangrene was rampant and typhus raged. Wounds and amputated limbs were infested with maggots.

As happened in all the contemporaneous sieges, the straw from mattresses was used to feed the army's horses, and when that was gone they began to eat the bark off the trees; finally, the soldiers decided to eat the horses and the mules.

In his diary, Prince Salm-Salm wondered what had happened to all the dog-barks that usually made the nights in Mexico so intolerably noisy.

One didn't need much imagination to deduce one of two things: either the dogs were busy eating the dead, or the living were busy eating the dogs.

López's betrayal took place on the night of May 14–15, 1867. The Colonel arrived in General Escobedo's camp with a white flag and negotiated the terms of the surrender of La Cruz Convent and the Imperial personage himself—

López's close friend. He then led a Republican detachment up to the gates of the convent, which were being watched by his accomplice, Lieutenant Colonel Jablonsky.

Maximilian had lain awake until one-thirty A.M. But a short time after falling asleep, he was awakened by a terrible cramp. Dr. Basch ran to his bedside, sat with him for more than an hour, and then retired again. Then the Emperor slept.

At four-thirty A.M., Colonel López entered the room in La Cruz occupied by Prince Salm-Salm. He awakened the Prince, shouting: "Quick, save the Emperor! The enemy is inside La Cruz!"

The Colonel left Salm-Salm's room. In the meantime, Blasio, also awake, having been alerted by Jablonsky, ran to Maximilian's chamber to warn him. Prince Salm-Salm came in as well, urging the Emperor to leave La Cruz.

Maximilian dressed in civilian clothes and left the convent with four of his closest men. Some Juarist soldiers almost blocked his way, but the Liberal commander, Colonel Rincón Gallardo, said: "Let them pass . . . They're just ordinary people."

The Emperor continued on foot to Las Campanas Hill, and from there, as he saw that there was no chance of escaping unnoticed, he sent an emissary to Escobedo to announce his surrender.

General Echegaray rode to the hill, dismounted, approached Maximilian, and said, "Your Majesty is my prisoner."

It appears that at this point, according to Blasio, Maximilian was riding Anteburro, while a groom was leading Orispelo, but a soldier pulled off the horse's bridle and let him loose.

Count Corti tells us that Maximilian informed Echegaray that he was no longer Emperor, and that his abdication letter was in the hands of the Council of State. He was then led before General Escobedo to whom he handed his sword.

The Mexican general in turn gave it to one of his officers and said: "This sword belongs to the Nation."

2. *Cimex domesticus Queretari*

The pair of scissors and two mirrors—one an oval-shaped table mirror, and the other a round hand mirror with a tortoise-shell handle—were the two best possible presents he could have received at that moment. General Mejía remarked that if they hadn't been allowed to use forks for so long, they certainly wouldn't be able to use scissors. Who did they think they were, anyway—suicidal maniacs who would kill themselves with forks? Or that they would use those forks to attack their guards and dig their way out to the Sierra Gorda?

Well, the main thing was that the forks had returned, that the guards hadn't mentioned the scissors, and that along with the comb and brush Dr. Basch had brought, Maximilian now had a complete grooming kit for his beard.

All this, no doubt, was a result of his talent—Maximilian's, that is—for persuading people around him to do anything he asked them to. For example, Princess Salm-Salm insisted that only the Emperor had been able to tame that cross-eyed, illiterate brute, Colonel Palacios, on whose whim the future of the Empire now rested. Beyond this, in his captivity, there were many people who treated him splendidly. Everyday, Señor Rubio sent many succulent dishes prepared in his hacienda for the Emperor's table. The ladies of Querétaro had provided him with plenty of much-needed underclothing and had brought homemade sweets—pears candied in sugar, fig compote—and oranges. Oranges, he was told, that were related to those from Montemorelos, the sweetest oranges in the world. And Maximilian had thanked them with a smile: "My dear ladies, if I could only tell you . . . If I could only tell you my troubles and my joys, I would tell you that the sweetest oranges that I have eaten in my life, and that perhaps I will be able to eat again some day, are from Ayotla—though the bitterest oranges in the world also come from there."

He didn't clarify this mysterious contradiction. But surely many of those kind Querétaro ladies knew that it was in Ayotla that Maximilian had last laid eyes on his poor wife, his poor *cara, carissima Carla*, now so alone and isolated, so far away, across the ocean . . .

He looked at himself in the mirror that he had set up next to the basin, though it wasn't the same silver basin he'd had in his cell at La Cruz: this had been stolen along with his magnifying glass and other important objects and documents. The Republicans had respected nothing. In fact, they'd even shredded his mattress. Did they think the Emperor was keeping his savings in a mattress? For Heaven's sake!

This one was a modest washbasin, a cheap white porcelain one, with a few hand-painted flowers on it. Another gift from the ladies of Querétaro.

He looked at his reflection in the mirror and covered his long, blond beard with his hands. How would he look without it?

"Me, clean shaven?" he had asked his generals one night, near the end of the siege. "You think, my dear sirs, that I should shave my beard and mustache and sneak away from Querétaro like a thief? For Heaven's sake, gentlemen!"

He took his hands away from his beard, picked up the brush, and began to run it slowly through his long and fine, golden hair . . .

"You're actually suggesting that I shave my long, blond beard in order to leave La Cruz stealthily, at night, disguised—as what, gentlemen? As a notary public? As a priest? As a ruined landowner? Or dressed as a carpenter with a blue apron and a black wig and carrying a plank on my shoulders, like Napoleon III did escaping from Fort Ham?"

He traced a line with the comb and parted his beard down the middle. Then he picked up the brush again.

"For God's sake, General Miramón! For God's sake and for the sake of your brother Joaquín, executed by candlelight while a military band played a polka! We cannot let his sacrifice be in vain!"

He left the brush on the table and smoothed his whiskers with both hands, pulling one half to the right, and the other to the left . . .

"For God's sake," he had said, "for God's sake, for your brother Joaquín Miramón and for those others like Colonel Rodríguez who have died for our cause. What a brave man! Or have you forgotten his courage?" he asked them.

"Have you already forgotten how he lunged forward, to the attack, shouting in his fine French—impeccable, I would say—*En avant, mes Chasseurs!*—Onward, my troops!—as he was felled by the Republican bullet that tore open his heart?"

Maximilian smoothed out his mustache. It was a bit long. The proof was that it was getting wet from his cocoa and his soup. Ah, those soups that poor Tüdös was still taking the trouble to cook for him!

"Gentlemen, I will drink to Colonel Rodríguez—whose body we could not have given a proper Christian burial at La Congregación Church if our intrepid Captain Domet hadn't dragged it back to us, risking his own life in the process . . . Here's to Captain Domet, gentlemen!"

And to Tüdös as well, of course. To all the living and the faithful who continued to stand by him. To those who had never left him. To those who had not betrayed him, as Leonardo Márquez and Colonel López had.

There was a pitcher of sugared water on the table. Dr. Basch had prescribed several glasses a day so Max wouldn't become dehydrated from his constant diarrhea. Max removed the napkin that protected the pitcher from the flies, poured himself a glass, and raised it before the mirror, as if drinking a toast to his own image, as if saying "Cheers!"

"And to Blasio, to Méndez, to del Castillo . . ."

And he sipped the sugared water as though it were wine. He remembered the toasts he had made another time—another night very close to the end of the siege, when everyone was eating dog and rat—after finding a cellar full of fine wines, in the house of a Querétaro merchant.

"To you, Felix . . ." he had said to Salm-Salm.

"And to you too, Miguel," he had said to Miramón, calling him by his Christian name for the first and last time. But Miramón refused the honor until they toasted the Emperor first. Maximilian, however, would not agree to this, and he kept toasting the Mexican general, although the latter's insistence reminded him in turn—now he was remembering having remembered—that glorious day in March when the Plaza de la Cruz was so brightly decorated, and they'd gathered several generals and soldiers for the Emperor to award medals for bravery, when suddenly Miramón had stepped forward and presented the same bronze insignia to Maximilian. "For merit," he'd said, because Maximilian deserved it more than any of the others present . . . And that same day he was given a certificate that read: "No other monarch has ever descended under similar circumstances from the height of his throne to undergo along with his soldiers—as we hereby witness—the greatest dangers, and privations and penury . . . etc., etc."

And that much was true. He tied a white towel around his neck. He had never run away from the risks of battle. He combed his mustache's left side downward. He had even mocked danger itself, as he had mocked so many other things. And he trimmed a few millimeters off his mustache.

"You are my witness, or rather, you all are my witnesses: you all saw that shell, which came through that window . . ." he had told them.

The shell had come through the window of the bell tower at La Cruz.

"That twelve-gauge shell, which hit the wall across the way and made a hole . . ."

It was indeed a twelve-gauge shell that hit the wall across the way, where it made a hole and raised a cloud of dust . . .

"And we were all covered with dust, from head to toe!"

"Including General Miramón, who looked like a miller . . ."

"Who'd come directly from his mill!"

They had all laughed at the Emperor's joke. No war is cause for laughter, but all wars cause extraordinary things to happen. He combed the right side of his mustache downward. For example, the Republicans had sent them an ox that was all skin and bones, with a sign that read, SO YOU CAN HAVE SOMETHING TO EAT. He brought the scissors up and trimmed his mustache. In exchange, his people had sent the enemy a nag, likewise all skin and bones, with a sign that read, SO THAT YOU CAN TRY TO CATCH US WHEN WE BREAK THROUGH YOUR BARRICADE.

One side was slightly shorter than the other . . . the left one. So he brought the scissors up to the right side . . . and, who could deny how funny some skirmishes were? When the Republicans captured La Cruz Cemetery, a number of the Imperial troops lost their rifles because of Captain Echegaray's cleverness. Whenever a rifle barrel barely stuck out of a hole in the cemetery wall, the Captain yanked it in. And he trimmed his mustache. Echegaray collected more than twenty rifles doing that.

As to that twelve-gauge shell that went through the wall and then fell to the ground without exploding, Maximilian had it engraved with the name of all those present to send it to Miramare . . .

"Yes, gentlemen. To the Miramare War Museum where someday we shall keep all our trophies, including of course the cannon from the Saint Sebastián Bridge."

He noticed that he hadn't covered the pitcher holding the sugar water and worried that if he kept trimming his mustache he was going to get hair in it. He covered the pitcher. Then he took off the cloth from around his neck and put it on the table, unfolded.

And he looked at his eyes in the mirror. So what about the bullets that will be used to execute me? What museum will they end up in? Shall I request that they be sent to Miramare as well, in my will? Or to Vienna? Where, Carla? My God, where?

And for a fraction of a second, as he said—or thought—"My God," he directed his gaze toward the silver crucifix on the wall.

Then he picked up his hand mirror to look sideways at his mustache, his long, blond mustache. First the right side. Fine. Then the left. Not bad. Considering that I did it myself, it's not bad. He put the mirror back on the table.

And he smiled again. His brow was unfurrowed and his eyes recovered their brightness.

"*Hombre! Hombre!* Maybe everything will turn out better than you think, old man," he muttered to himself as he remembered—with affection, almost tenderness—the Spanish instructor back at Miramare who had taught him, in the Hall of Seagulls, how to use the word *hombre* as an exclamation of joy, of awe, of anger, of anything at all.

"*Hombre*, of course everything will be fine. *Hombre, Herr* Professor, the Mexican people wouldn't dare execute their Emperor. Is that not true? It would be a crime, *hombre!*"

That's what he would say to that professor, if he ever met him again. If he appeared, miraculously, in Querétaro . . .

He sat on the cot and thought about Agnes Salm-Salm. That evening, if all went well, Colonel Palacios would hand him, Max, the imperial signet ring that the Emperor had given the princess. If that happened, it would mean . . . it would mean that Palacios and Villanueva had accepted the IOUs for one hundred thousand pesos that the House of Austria would repay if the escape were successful . . .

He set his elbows on his knees and put his head in his hands. He closed his eyes. And so, after all those refusals, he would just end up running away? After he had told his generals, in indignation, taking long steps up and down the Gardens of La Cruz, on a golden, stiflingly hot afternoon: "Gentlemen, do you honestly expect *me* to sneak out of Querétaro? *Me* to escape like a common criminal, like a convict? *Me* to flee the country, run away and sail out of Tampico, or Tuxpan, or some other place, in an American sloop lent to me by the Yankees out of pure pity? And leave the country like Iturbide, like Juárez and Santa Anna have done so many times? For God's sake, gentlemen! For God's and Mexico's!"

He opened his eyes and remembered Agnes Salm-Salm's beautiful face. But the Princess—who was not only lovely, but also persuasive—had said, "Your Majesty, it's one thing to flee from justice, and quite another to flee from injustice. Your Majesty's duty is to live, to survive, for your people, for Mexico."

He had smiled. He ran his fingers through his beard, now that he was in his cell at Las Teresitas, as he had done when he rode with the Princess to the Hacienda Hercules, in Señor Rubio's splendid carriage, when the wind had played with it—his long, golden beard, mussing it. Like an echo, his words came back to him: "And, it would be one thing, my Princess, to shave my beard in order to escape without being recognized, and another to leave with a whole beard, would it not? With my beard held high, would it not?"

And he had not only enjoyed his play on words—for in Spanish, "to leave with one's whole beard" means to leave with chin up, proudly—he had also made a decision. If Agnes Salm-Salm, or Baron Basch, or Miramón, or Felix Salm-Salm, if any of them—or more likely, all of them—did manage to convince him to escape from Las Teresitas or Querétaro, it was something that he had to do for the good of the Mexicans and his adoptive nation; he would do it, yes, he would make that sacrifice but:

"I shall never shave off my beautiful beard," he declared to the Prince. The latter assured him that it would not be necessary to do so, only to hide it, to cover it a bit. And for that he had sent him some wax and some thread . . . what nonsense . . .

"Yes, nonsense," he repeated, rising to regard himself in the mirror once more with his beard intact. "I shall never hide it either—I, Ferdinand Maximilian, Emperor of Mexico, have nothing to hide, my dear lady," he had said, turning to Princess Salm-Salm, who was descending from the carriage, offering her his arm, and walking with her through the hacienda's beautiful garden, where, near a pond, General Escobedo awaited them.

And now Maximilian paced in his cell at Las Teresitas after offering his arm to an invisible Princess Salm-Salm—pretending that the room was one hundred meters long, an enormous plaza or a plain . . .

But since the cell was only a few square feet, he almost hit the wall, stumbled over the table, reached another wall, stumbled on the cot, and then found himself, once again, in front of the mirror.

He looked at himself. He winked. He shrugged his shoulders and said:

"*Hombre!*"

"*Hombre*, what can we do for you?"

If there was one thing that really hurt him deeply about his capture and captivity, if there was one thing that he really resented, it was that he had been confined to such a small space, and wasn't allowed to move freely around Querétaro . . .

"Some cities I have known," he had written in his memoirs when he was young, when he was free, "have made me think of particular colors. Rome, for example, is violet and blue." "And what about Venice, Max?" Carla had asked. "Venice? Venice reminds me of dark red marble . . . Cartagena is yellow . . . Granada, green . . . Constantinople is the color of shimmering gold . . ."

"And Querétaro, Your Majesty?" Blasio had asked him one morning as they strolled together in the main plaza.

"Querétaro?" replied Maximilian, stopping to greet some appreciative and admiring local ladies, then resuming: "Querétaro, my dear Blasio, has made me think of white, but not the swan-white of Cádiz, but the blinding white of snow in the sun. And not only because of the many white houses and churches. A city's color comes not so much from its buildings as from its spirit . . ."

Not only did *he* know Querétaro, but the whole city knew its emperor. He would walk around the square with Blasio, yes he would, a Cuban cigar wedged between his lips, and he would ask a surprised stroller for a light; he would dictate some amendments to the *Court Ceremonial* to Blasio; he would bid a good afternoon to the officers on their way to the Hotel Aguila Roja to play monte; or he would smile at those who, accompanied by unchaperoned ladies, were going into the Iturbide Theater to see a naughty vaudeville show; or he would stop to pet his greyhound Bebello, the faithful dog he had been given in Querétaro, and that had miraculously avoided becoming barbecued meat; or he would visit the makeshift hospital in the Casino, arm in arm with General Severo del Castillo, and would chat with the wounded . . .

"For God's sake!" he had exclaimed. "For His sake and that of poor Captain Lubic who not only lost a leg but his life as well, in Querétaro!"

And like Lubic there was Colonel Loaiza whose feet were both amputated and who finally died in Querétaro.

"For God's sake, gentlemen, and for Colonel Loaiza, and for Colonel Farquet who died from a wound to his knee, gentlemen, and left his two children in the care of General Miramón because he was a widower. For the Colonel's children, gentlemen!"

And he almost had to shout into General del Castillo's ear:

"Remind me, general, to ask the ladies of Querétaro for more sheets to make bandages . . ."

"To make appendages, Your Majesty? More appendages?" the deaf old general asked.

"Not appendages, my dear general. Bandages. Ban-da-ges!"

Bandages for wounded Imperialists. But bandages too for wounded Republicans. Even when he became a prisoner, Maximilian had blankets brought for the Juarist guards who slept outside his cell, sprawled on the ground like dogs, just as that generosity had also been demonstrated during the siege toward the Republican wounded who had been picked up on the battlefield. He spoke to them and had kind words for one and all, despite the stench that, in the midst of the stifling heat, lingered in the hospital's halls and wards, like noxious fumes, although he had warmly thanked his men for always managing to incinerate their own dead and the enemy's at a time when the wind would carry the smoke away—and with it the appalling odor of burnt flesh—from the Convento de la Cruz. Also, he had been spotted at the front and on the parapets many times, frequently followed by Colonel López, and he would ask his soldiers if they were well fed and happy . . . He strolled around Querétaro so often that its people and his troops all had to be forbidden to shout "Long live the Emperor!" as he went by, because this would usually be followed by a hail of bullets from the enemy, guided by their voices.

It would definitely be a stray bullet that would take his life and not the townspeople whom he let approach him—beggars for whom he always had some coins; nuns who brought him bread made with flour meant for communion hosts; musicians who played "La Paloma" on their marimbas one evening, in honor of his absent Empress, to drown out the Republicans; who off in the distance, were singing "Bye-bye Mamá Carlota."

He rose and looked at the mirror.

"None of them," he had thought, "not a single one of them would dare lift a hand against his Emperor. No one will take a dagger from a carnation bouquet or a basket of strawberries and plunge it into my breast . . ."

He put his hand around his neck.

"My brother Franz Joseph was very fortunate that a button on his uniform deflected Libényi's knife . . ."

He stroked his beard again. He smiled:

"My beard would save me . . . It's so long!"

He picked up his hand mirror and regarded his profile. Maximilian's beard was so long that the man who had been given the task of sketching his image in profile for use on coins had complained that it was "not very numismatic." He couldn't work the entire beard onto the coin; or, if he was to force it to fit, he would then have to reduce the size of the Emperor's head, which came out too small.

Maximilian turned and looked at his other side. Good—both halves were of equal length. Or if they were uneven, it wasn't obviously noticeable.

He thought he had seen a tiny shadow move on one of the cell walls . . . A spider, perhaps? A cockroach? He shivered and remembered the bedbugs. "I have discovered, here in Querétaro, my dear Bilimek," he had written the wise old entomologist, "a type of bedbug, next to which the ones at the Imperial Palace in Mexico City pale . . . a bedbug, my dear friend, with huge mandibles, with a formidable stinger and breathing apparatus . . . As soon as I can, I will send you some dried specimens. For the time being, I want to inform you that I have already named it '*Cimex domesticus Queretari*,' a minuscule creature that particularly enjoys blue blood. I can assure you of that much, because I have experienced it myself—in the flesh . . ."

"*Cimex domesticus Queretari* . . . What do you think, General Mejía?" he asked the "Little Black Man."

At Querétaro he not only named the bedbug but he also gave his generals nicknames, although no one was aware of this. It was a secret between the Emperor and Salm-Salm. Mejía got the name of "Little Black Man," and, so, the "Little Black Man" replied:

"*Cimex* what, Your Majesty, if you'll excuse me?"

"*Cimex* is the species, like *Cimex lectularius*, the common bedbug, my dear general, of the family *Cimicidae*, is it not, Dr. Basch? *Domesticus* because it is found in homes, along with humans . . . as well as in convents, of course. Finally, *Queretari* because it is native to Querétaro . . ."

"Ah, Your Majesty is so clever," said General Mejía, but Maximilian realized that the General didn't really get his joke. At any rate, the "Little Black Man" was fine at his job—he was a good soldier, a good believer, and a good monarchist. And it would have to be he who would have to guide him from Querétaro to the Sierra Gorda, and from there to the coast. "We will spend the winter in Naples or Brazil, General," Maximilian would say to Mejía to distract him from his rheumatism and his other troubles, and he would describe life at Miramare and Lacroma, but it would do no good. The General appeared indifferent to the six thousand books in the Miramare Library or the blue beauty of the Adriatic. "I'm a simple man," he said to Max. "If you take me to Miramare, I'll just go fishing."

Once again he thought he saw something moving on a wall, but that part of the cell was dark. It was impossible to recognize the pest, if that is what it was. He arrived at the conclusion that it wasn't a bedbug—bedbugs don't crawl on walls, or at least that's what he'd been told—because they are nocturnal creatures, and his cot and frame had been washed with boiling water. Bedbugs couldn't have survived in that part of the convent, or at least not in his cell.

Then he had a simple idea. He approached a sunbeam coming through his window and put his hand mirror into it. With the reflected beam, he lit up the part of the wall where he had seen that tiny shadow move. There was nothing there.

He shone his beam on the other walls, the corners, the floor. Nothing. Then, still standing under the sunbeam, he placed the small mirror against his chest and so, from above, looked at his beard from below. It looked thicker and more golden than ever—a great golden cloud. He took a deep breath, his chest moved, and the mirror with it, and the sun's reflection flashed into his eyes and blinded him.

In that instant, he had a terrible premonition. He had heard the shots of the firing squad at his execution, and saw himself fallen, but still alive, his eyes open, his face toward the sky. The sun poured all its glare and splendor into his eyes, and he asked himself what his mother Sophie was doing at that moment at Schönbrunn Palace.

He stepped toward the table and put the mirror on it. He sat down on his cot. He took off his boots and stretched out. There were orders not to bother him for a few hours. If he was lucky, he would be able to take a nap.

Once again he saw Princess Salm-Salm's face. What an incredible woman. She had managed to get herself seen by everyone: Porfirio Díaz, General Escobedo, President Juárez himself. She saw them all; she spoke to everyone. She was allowed to go anywhere—to San Luis, the Capital, Querétaro, back to San Luis, Tacubaya, Puebla—and she could appear anywhere, when least expected, in her pale yellow coach, with her inseparable companion Margarita, with her dog, Jimmy, on her lap, and on her chest, in the warm etui formed by her two round, white breasts, her likewise inseparable six-shooter. "Oh, my dear Princess," the Emperor had said to her one afternoon as they strolled around the Teresitas patio, "if I ever leave this place a free man, I shall name you my Minister of Foreign Affairs . . . that is to say, my 'Ministress.'" She was capable of everything, and would do anything, to save the lives of her husband and the Emperor.

Of course, the Princess didn't only travel in that old yellow hackney coach. She hadn't been a circus stunt rider for nothing—they had called her the female centaur—and when necessary she would ride a high-spirited animal and gallop off to military posts or leap over trenches, with a white handkerchief tied to the tip of her whip.

Maximilian's experience told him that governing was far easier when one surrounded oneself with educated, sensitive women like Carlota, his mother Sophie, and Agnes Salm-Salm, of course. For with women, one could just as well discuss military strategy as cooking. Usually he couldn't even discuss uniform design with his generals. They were never interested. Although there was that time that General Méndez had pointed out that the red blouses of the soldiers of the Emperor's Battalion are too similar to those worn by the red Juarista rabble. "But, General," Max had replied, "you must also take into account that Garibaldi's troops wear scarlet shirts, and that Abd al-Qadir's regular cavalry's uniforms were red from head to toe . . . And, besides, what red Juarista rabble are you talking about, anyway?" he asked General Méndez, that afternoon, standing on the convent roof with their binoculars, watching the enemy soldiers walk naked at the foot of the hill, holding their rifles while their white uniforms dried, spread out on large rocks—yes, white from head to toe, not red. And not only white but impeccably snow-white from so much laundering—a fact that not only surprised the Emperor, but grieved him. One of the things he missed the most was his morning dip in Chapultepec Lake. In Querétaro there was hardly even any drinking water, yet the Republicans had more than enough. After the aqueduct was drilled into, some clear, tiny waterfalls fell from its high arches. Maximilian had ordered his troops not to shoot at the Juarista soldiers while they were doing their laundry, because he thought it would be wrong to kill a man stripped of the very thing that, more than a weapon, made him an enemy—that is, his uniform. "It's what gives a man dignity, is it not, General Méndez?" But General Méndez didn't seem to know the difference between an enemy who was dressed and one who was naked.

Then he realized that he was getting sleepy—that it would finally be possible to fall asleep, if only for a few minutes. The night before, the convent guards—it wasn't the first time—had screamed at the top of their lungs at regular intervals: "Guard on the alert! Guard on the alert!" and, of course, the Emperor couldn't sleep a wink. To make things worse, he had had a new bout of dysentery and terrible pains that Little Doc Basch's opium pills had not been able to subdue . . .

"Little Doc" is what Basch was called in Querétaro.

He also realized that he had already been sound asleep, because just before opening his eyes, although already awake, he noticed he had been drooling on his pillow. It was spit, no doubt, because it was cold. Blood is not cold, but warm, and that stream that dribbled from his mouth was not warm, but it became blood anyway, because Maximilian fell asleep another few seconds and had the sensation of slowly dying. "Blasio, tell me, did they hurt my face?" he asked his Mexican secretary. Blasio turned around. A thick bloody purple stream was dripping from Max's mouth. "Can you hear me, Blasio?" But Blasio couldn't hear. Maximilian felt a shiver running up and down his body, from his feet to his brow, like a river of red ants . . . But, were they ants or bedbugs?

He hopped out of bed and pulled up the bed sheets. *Cimex domesticus* . . . He felt a wave of nausea, *Cimex domesticus Queretari* . . . the nausea that comes from imagining rows and rows of pale bedbugs, and rows of red ones sated with blood . . . but luckily he didn't really see a single one. Not a single one.

He sat on the cot and cleaned off the drool on his beard with the back of his hand. He rose and looked at himself in the mirror—"With a whole beard," my dear Princess, "with beard held high," my dear Agnes Salm-Salm. Once again, however—the never-ending story—his beard had been rumpled while he slept.

He picked up his brush. He realized that night had fallen and that someone—most likely Grill—had come in to light the candles in the holder also donated by the ladies of Querétaro. Ah, the ladies of Querétaro, who had been so brave during the siege, who had greeted him in such a friendly manner when he left the casino after bowling with his colonels, and who had suffered so much.

"To the ladies of Querétaro," he said, brushing the whole length of the left side of his long beard.

Prince Salm-Salm, playing whist with Major Malburg, had concurred: "To the ladies of Querétaro."

"To the ladies, the gentlemen, and the Hungarian troops who died at El Cimatario!" exclaimed Maximilian, brushing the whole right side of his long beard.

Tüdös had been very touched by the mention of his Hungarian compatriots killed in Querétaro. And naturally, too:

"To my faithful Tüdös who had to spit out three teeth after being hit by a bullet at Calpulalpan!"

Miramón had agreed, not only because a few weeks later and after the fall of Querétaro he himself would likewise take a bullet near the mouth.

"And, gentlemen, here's to General Miramón, wounded in the heroic siege of Querétaro!"

". . . but also to Tüdös's perseverance, to his ingenuity, to his genius at making ragout from horse meat, paté from dog meat, sausages from cat . . ."

And once his beard was smoothed out, he put the towel around his neck, took the scissors . . .

"And to the Algerian volunteers who died at San Pablo, gentlemen, and to the soldiers of the Celaya Battalion who gave their lives for their Emperor on the Plain of Carretas, and to the men of the third corps of engineers decimated at La Cruz Cemetery, and to the women soldiers slain at the foot of the aqueduct, and to the men of the Iturbide Battalion who perished in the battle of Casa Blanca, gentlemen, and to Colonel Santa Cruz, the poor man, who, on the morning of May 15th, was riddled with bullets . . ."

"And of course . . ."

And of course at that moment he remembered General Méndez. Ramón Méndez the man responsible for the deaths of the Republican Generals, Arteaga and Salazar. At Querétaro Maximilian had nicknamed him the "The Intrepid Little One," or something of the sort. And he remembered, as though he were standing there in front of him, the general's swarthy, shiny face, his long and bristly mustache, his bright eyes, and his hair, as smooth and black as coal. Méndez always said that, if the Emperor left Querétaro, he would go with him to the Zitácuaro Mountains, which he knew like the palm of his hand . . . When La Cruz fell, Méndez went into hiding in a house in Querétaro. When he was found, he was taken to the Alameda where he was shot—in the back—for betraying his country.

"And of course, gentlemen, to General Méndez, who died from a shot in the back . . ."

Although it was said that on hearing the commander shout "Fire!" Méndez had had time to turn around and offer his chest to the bullets . . .

The Emperor shook out his beard, wiped it with the towel, shook the hair out of the towel, picked up his brush, and muttered: "Any way you look at it, in the back or in the chest, he was not a traitor. I repeat, gentlemen: to General Méndez!"

He began to brush his beard slowly, and he thought that the Swiss barber Salm-Salm had brought to Querétaro could not have done a better job.

Yes, here's to all of them, to all the dead. He had to preserve his beautiful beard, and in case he was able to escape from Las Teresitas and Querétaro he had to do it not only without shaving but also without hiding the long, blond beard that, as General Miramón had said, it was possible to recognize from two leagues away, in daylight . . . "And in moonlight?" asked Maximilian, who had never lost his sense of humor, either during the siege or during his captivity—and proof of this was in how much he had reveled in Mejía's words, the words of that faithful "Little Black Man" when he had begged him not to expose himself to so much danger: "Can Your Majesty imagine? If, God forbid, you should die, we would all have to fight among ourselves for the presidency!" And Maximilian imagined a battlefield where everyone was fighting everyone else—Mejía against Miramón, against López, against Méndez, against Santa Anna, against Vidaurri, against del Castillo, against Teodosio Lares, against Márquez . . . No no no, it was unimaginable. One could definitely not leave Mexico to its own devices . . .

And if it was necessary to keep one's dignity, to not lose one's honor, on behalf of the dead, it was all the more necessary to do so for the living:

"Here's to all Mexicans . . . today's and the future's . . ."

. . . not losing one's life. And very soon, that same night, in a few hours or a few minutes, he would know whether Princess Salm-Salm's plan would or wouldn't be carried out.

As it turned out, Maximilian found out within seconds.

Someone knocked on his door and shook him out of his reverie. The guard was announcing that Dr. Samuel Basch wished to see the Archduke of Austria.

The doctor didn't look good. He seemed sad. He tried to smile, made a bow, and took Maximilian's signet ring from one of his jacket pockets. Princess Salm-Salm had asked him to return it to His Majesty and to notify him that it had been necessary to abort the plan, that Colonel Palacios had not accepted the promissory notes, and it was very possible that Escobedo now knew of the plot. Yes, it was not just possible but rather probable: Galeana's guardsmen had been replaced that same afternoon. All the guards were new and, moreover, they had been doubled in number . . .

"Doubled?" asked Maximilian as he took the ring and put it on his finger. "Oh, my dear Dr. Basch. They are afraid that their prey will escape; they are trembling because the lion is stirring in his cage . . ."

"That is the case, Your Majesty," replied the doctor.

Maximilian walked toward the mirror and peered at himself. In candlelight, as in sunlight or moonlight or starlight, or the light of the imagination, his beard was and would forever be unmistakably long and golden . . . Many years later, a poet would describe Maximilian as follows:

> . . . Golden-haired, blue-eyed, smooth of
> brow—a blank page undisturbed by dolor—
> Long, parted in two, his flowing beard
> Bathes his breast in golden splendor . . .

He then remembered a walk he had taken with General del Castillo on a sunny, dusty afternoon, in the beginning of May. Maximilian had asked him how Father Miguel Hidalgo—the father of Mexican Independence—had died. He was shot, shot by the Spaniards, the general replied. But it was very difficult to kill him, he added, because the soldiers had poor aim. The priest was seated on a bench—del Castillo didn't know why he was shot sitting down—and the first volley only broke his arm. The second broke a collarbone and his guts popped out. The third hail of bullets only fanned the air, the priest's blindfold slipped down and the firing squad got upset when they saw his tear-filled eyes. It's also said that another volley knocked the priest off the bench into a pool of his own blood, but even then he was still alive, and only by shooting him several times at close range were they able to finish the great man off. Afterwards, imagine, Your Majesty, he was beheaded and his head was taken to the Granaditas Grain Warehouse in Guanajuato, along with those of his three captains. There they displayed, one head in each corner, hanging in iron cages, as a warning to the insurgents . . .

Maximilian was sure that Juárez would never do such a thing, that his head wouldn't end up in an iron cage, nor Márquez's, nor Miramón's, nor Mejía's . . .

But how could one be assured of the firing squad's aim? He would have to insist on it . . . to write Escobedo . . .

"What did Your Majesty say?" asked General del Castillo.

"I said that I shall write to Escobedo or Juárez himself, if necessary, to ensure that all the soldiers are excellent marksmen, so that they kill me with just one volley."

He was still standing in front of the mirror. Basch, in a corner, watched the Emperor quietly.

"And so that my face isn't mutilated, I will ask them to aim at my heart. I will point to it myself . . ."

He pulled apart the two golden sheaves of his thick long, flowing beard, and he pointed to his heart.

"Right here, gentlemen."

3. Seductions (II): "Hold It, Hope . . ."

Hold it, Hope. Take your hand off my armpit. You're tickling me. What? You just realized that I'm ticklish? Don't tell me you're not. Let's see . . . I can tell you're trying not to laugh. You know something? I love my hands to smell of your sweat. Yes, I know you're clean. But a woman has to smell and taste like that, like a woman, not just soap and patchouli. But leave me alone. I already told you that I didn't come for that. I came to see about the Archduke's trial. It's tomorrow, at the Iturbide Theater. No, I don't know if they'll let women in. I know that he won't be there and that he's going to be tried in absentia. I heard he's very sick; he's got dysentery and he sits on the pot all day. I think it's probably from fear. But I'm glad, Hope . . . Leave my hair alone. I didn't put so much oil on it today. I'm glad that he couldn't escape even after sending that Princess, that Salm-Salm woman, to throw herself at Colonel Palacios. He can't escape from jail, and he can't escape from justice. I'm glad too that he ended up getting arrested here, in Querétaro, because, if it had been someplace else, Hope, we couldn't have seen each other for a long time. Let go of me, I'm telling you. Leave my coat buttons alone. No, I'm not hot. He couldn't escape, after he was asked so many times why he came to Mexico—three times, as is the custom, and he answered three times . . . Where did you get that ring? I gave it to you? I don't remember. Three times he said that it was a political matter. In other words, he was ignoring the authority of a war council. Can you imagine the nerve of that Austrian? How can I write if you don't let go of my hand? I have to write lots of notes. As if everyone didn't know that when he was headed for Querétaro, he put himself at the head of his so-called Imperial Army, dressed half as a Mexican *charro* and half as an Austrian general. Yes, woman, you know I've always loved your hands. That long hair on your arms. I love your breasts too. I love all of you. But right now, either I touch you or I write, so I'd better write. I have to be at the Iturbide Theater very early, all rested up. I have to say that I don't really dislike the Archduke, overall. Sometimes I even feel sorry for the guy. But I hate Miramón with all my heart. President of the Republic, hero at Chapultepec and Padierna. What good did all that do after he betrayed his country and gave the order to kill the Tacubaya martyrs? It's getting a bit warm. Okay, go ahead and undo my coat. And the Austrian's cynicism went even further. You won't believe it—he said that the legislation . . . I'm a bit heavier, you say? Well, in the gut, maybe. Probably from sitting still so long and drinking so much pulque to celebrate the fall of the Empire. You already said that yesterday. The legislation by which he's being tried has to take into account the laws dictated by President Juárez on the matter. No, I won't take off my coat. What the Austrian doesn't know is that, hold it, Hope, don't squeeze my legs so hard, move back, you're going to make me slip up. What he doesn't know, because he's not well acquainted with the laws of this nation—he'd have to know Spanish better . . . Hope, my darling, leave me alone . . . is that those laws, as I was saying, consider that a person who remains silent and refuses to defend himself has admitted to the charges against him. That, Hope, is called contumacy. This nail? I broke it yesterday. No, don't bite it off. Bring some scissors. Wait a second. You have beautiful teeth, Hope. Yes, you hurt me, but just a little bit. And that's why the last of the thirteen counts . . . imagine, it would have to be thirteen, since the poor Archduke is so superstitious . . . Don't suck my finger. It makes me nervous. The last count, I was saying, is sedition and contumacy. C-o-n-t-u-m-a-c-y, my love. How can I explain it? It's something like being obstinate. Or stubborn. As you are sometimes, Hope—like today. I'm sure they'll say that the tacit or implicit confession in a refusal to answer is very far from having the weight of an overt confession. They will cite Escriche, I think. Escriche, the Spaniard who wrote the *Diccionario Razonado de Legislación y Jurisprudencia*. Why should my back itch just because you want it to? Quit scratching me. I told you that I came here for quiet, to focus on the Emperor's trial. I mean, the Archduke's. See what you made me say? Under the shoulder blade. The shoulder blade, woman, that bone that sticks out—like that, yes . . . Imagine, how absurd, I called the defendant "Emperor" . . . Not so hard, you're hurting me. My back is still all scratched from yesterday . . . Considering that one of the primary accusations, the main one, I'd say, is of being a usurper. He's accused of coming to Mexico to usurp the legitimate constitutional office, of letting himself be the instrument of the French Intervention that sought to . . . yes, of course. I do remember that dress. I gave it to you the second time I came to Querétaro. How could I forget? It's made of Chinese silk, it's the same green that's on our flag, and it's revealing. I told you, I don't want anyone but me to see you wear it. That sought to disturb the peace, I was saying—Mexico's peace, of course— by means of . . . Why are you hiking up your skirt? I told you I want you to leave me alone right now. Oh, yes, your garters. I remember those too. Listen to me, listen to me, Hope. If you're going to show me everything I've given you, you're going to end up naked. Tell me, did you get the whalebone corset I bought in Mexico City, on San Francisco Street, remember, that I brought you dressed as a muleteer, with a burro blanket on? Remember? To disturb the peace in Mexico, I was saying, by means of . . . Wait, darling. Don't take off your stockings. Yes, yes, I know that the mole on your thigh didn't come from me . . . by means of . . . as I was saying, an unjust war, illegal by nature, disloyal and barbaric in execution . . . I'm going to write this down. It sounds very nice. Did you notice, Hope? You have a long, blonde hair on that mole. Unjust and illegal by nature, what else did I say? Oh, yes, disloyal and barbaric in execution. You have beautiful legs, my dear. If I could just tell you. They're really beautiful. If I could just tell you, I was saying, the many atrocities they've all committed, the French and the Austrians alike. They brought us execution by hanging. All we have to do is remember Cavaignac's crimes in Paris, not to mention that damned Colonel Dupin. Did you know that during the siege of Querétaro, an Austrian, Major Pitner was his name, I think, blew out one of his own soldiers' brains just because he misbehaved a little bit? And then they lecture us on justice, on civil law, on the incompetence of our War Council. How can you say you don't like your knees? They're fine with me, except that they always feel a little cold. Or maybe my hands, as you keep saying, are always too warm. Okay, that's enough. Hope, darling, put on your stockings and cover your legs. You're making me lose my concentration. Bring me a glass of water, will you? After he usurped power and formed an army of foreigners, or rather freebooters and subjects of nations not at war with Mexico . . . this sentence came out nice, didn't it? . . . the Archduke is now saying that we need to clarify formally whether or not he is considered an ex-emperor. If he's not, he can only be tried as an Austrian archduke . . . what do you think about that? . . . In which case he can only be turned over as a prisoner . . . please Hope . . . to his own country. And bring me the water I asked for. Poor devil. I'm telling you, I kind of like that Archduke. But we're going to send him to the gallows. Well, all three of them. Yes, woman, I know that while your knees are always cold, your thighs are always like fire. Tell me about it. I don't need to touch them to know that. What he wants, of course, is to save his skin at all costs, and to go back to his Miramare and ignore what happens to his acolytes and straw men in Mexico. People who carry incense in the churches. Wait a second, no, acolytes, not electrolytes . . . Wait, woman, let me write, let go! You shaved your legs again, didn't you? You know I don't like it. They feel scratchy for days.

And I'm telling you, he had the nerve to send letters and messages to Don Benito, writing that he's unfamiliar with legal Spanish—and he calls him Mr. President! Yes, now you recognize him, don't you, Mr. Archduke? Now that you're stuck in your Teresitas cell, always sitting on the pot, with only a silver crucifix for company. Wait a second. Let me write. How can you come up with such silly questions? Why should I like one of your thighs more than the other? He was finished, yes, from the moment that he decided that his case could ever rise to a plenary. No, that's not right. It was all over from the moment he disembarked from the *Novara* and set foot on the sands of Veracruz. Look, I'm not going to explain every single word to you. Later . . . If I begin explaining "plenary," "interlocutory," or "defense," we'll never finish. Don't get mad, Hope. Yes, sit here, but not so close. Thanks for the water. It's very refreshing. No, sit on this side. How many times do I have to tell you I'm left-handed? Yes, I write with my right hand because I was taught to do that . . . Later, he ordered his own agents, or he agreed for foreign agents, to kill many thousands of Mexicans. Now you've derailed my thoughts. Do you spell derailed with an *A* and an *I*? Then . . . then what, Hope? Well, although I won't do that now, I'd rather have you on my right side so that I can caress you with my left hand. I can do it better with that one. Sit still. Tell me, do you like this sentence? The mendacious remains of the vanquished classes, I mean those defeated in the War of Reform, called on a stranger, hoping to satisfy their greed with his help. What worries me more is the count of treason to the nation. They wanted to charge him with that, but the death penalty can only be imposed on a traitor to the nation in a foreign war. Miramón, Mejía, Márquez, and many others, for example, fit the mold. Yes, I can feel your heartbeat with my hand. But not the Archduke. Let go of it. Since, according to the defense, he can't be charged . . . That is to say, not being Mexican, but Austrian, how can he be charged with . . . You know? You have the roundest, firmest breasts . . . charged with the crime of treason to the nation? In any case, he is a traitor. No, not that. My crotch itches. Traitor to Austria. I need to stretch my legs. Yes, traitor to his own nation, Austria. What stain? I must have dropped some water on my pants. In contrast to those shits Miramón and Mejía. Miramón, you know, has had the gall to say that any military man who speaks against the Republic while serving it betrays it for failing to be faithful as promised, but that a man who has never recognized the Republic, nor served it, might be an enemy, but never a traitor. Imagine, a man who was the President of the Republic saying that. He, the same crook who—as president—had the English legation seals broken to take out funds designated by the constitutional government to pay for the Convention . . . All right, yes, I'll sit down but just for a little while. I've got to leave soon. At any rate, it would be good for me to stop thinking about the Archduke and his trial for a few minutes to tell you how beautiful you are. Come a little closer, will you? You know, I have to confess that of all the things brought by the Austrian and the French, whom I hate so much—the Empress's *swarays*, all their *orrevwahs*, those strange dances, the pâté de *fwagra* here and the champagne there—of all those things, as I was saying, what I did like were the gowns, like the one I gave you, cut so low that you can almost see the nipples. You have goose pimples, Hope. Now what's wrong? What's going on? First you throw yourself at me and now you don't want me to lay a hand on you. Who can figure you out, woman? Fortunately I'm very familiar with my Grotius, and with Wheaton's *International Law*. The defense will no doubt refer to this. Did you know that the Yankee lawyer, a certain Mr. Hall, came in with Wheaton under his arm? They'll quote Vattel, that much is certain . . . I wonder if it's spelled with a *V* or a *W*? Vattel, woman, the one who wrote about international law . . . Let me touch them. Just for a moment, please. I'm telling you, they're so soft and so firm at the same time. No, please, don't uncover them. For God's sake. Do I believe in God? Of course not, it's just an expression. Do you know that they're claiming now that the Archduke's government was recognized de facto? De facto, in practice. And that the real usurper was Napoleon III? Now stop it, Hope. For God's sake or whoever's, cover up or you'll catch cold. Man is a creature of the circumstances that surround him: that's another argument the defense will use. How can we bring Napoleon to Mexico and try him? And that cynic, Mejía, said that in his view the Regency and the so-called Empire were not the work of the French Intervention but of the Mexicans who expressed their consensus by voting and bringing the Archduke here. No, I told you it's just a little itch in my crotch. Vattel says that a powerful party always considers itself entitled to resist a sovereign . . . You're wearing the perfume I gave you today, aren't you? And if that party is able to take arms against the party in power, it is necessary . . . it is necessary . . . Cover up! Why do you think I told you not to wait for me in bed naked, but that I wanted you to be dressed, head to toe, Hope? It's necessary to consider those two parties, thereafter, at least for a time, as two separate bodies. Bodies, yes, but in the sense of nations, of peoples, don't be an ignoramus. Can you conceive of their being two Mexican nations? Hold it, Hope, my uniform is getting wrinkled and it's the only one I have. I have to look very neat and well groomed so that they don't say the Archduke was tried by a bunch of ragtag peasants. When do you think you could press it, woman? I'm telling you I have to go back to the barracks soon to get a few hours' sleep and be alert tomorrow. And they'll cite Hallam and Macaulay. Who are they, my love? Why do you want to know? Some boring men who oppose the death penalty. Careful, you'll get my coat dirty. All right, all right, I'll take it off but just for a little while. I have to go. Someone will certainly bring up Alexander the Great, how he pardoned some Milesians for their bravery. Or the execution of Charles I's rival, so roundly denounced by Pedro of Aragón. No, don't just leave it there. Hang it up properly, please. But tell me if a coward like that poor Archduke deserves mercy, a man who's also going to be charged with having abdicated his false Imperial throne so that his abdication would take effect not immediately but from the moment he was defeated. Leave me alone, let me be, Hope. Or rather, I was saying, for a moment, an abdication, taken not voluntarily . . . No, I'm not trying to kiss you . . . but by force. Of course, Hope, I can change my mind if I feel like it. But, with or without abdicating, he was going to be deprived of his title—which he usurped—as ruler of Mexico. Of course I have gray hairs on my chest. You hadn't noticed before? Let go there. What are you doing? Leave my belt alone, please. Although Mejía hasn't stopped boasting of the fact that he once spared the lives of Generals Escobedo and Treviño. You're going to pull them. What? Hair gets curly with a little spit? What did they do? Please stop touching my nipple. It gets hard for hours and then it chafes with the uniform. What did they do with Arteaga and Salazar? What did they do, I wonder, with all those Juarists that they tortured and killed, with those towns that they razed and burned to the ground, and especially . . . You have an eyelash next to your tear duct. Oh, Hope, what a lovely face you have and how soft it is. Hold on, don't put your leg on me. My pants will get wrinkled. Especially, I was saying, in Michoacán, Sinaloa, Chihuahua, Coahuila. Stop unbuttoning my pants, will you? Nuevo León, Tamaulipas. Why didn't I come in civilian clothes? Haven't you told me a thousand times that you like me better in uniform? And I'm also going to remind them that Vattel wrote only for the European rulers and that in fact he was unfamiliar with the constitutional law of modern republics like ours. Look, if I take off my trousers I'll have to get in bed. You don't think I'll just sit here in my shorts. If I get in bed I'm not going to lie there alone, like an idiot. If you get in bed with me, Hope—what do you think, I'm made of stone . . . ?

•

Hope . . . Hope . . . Are you sleeping? You can't have gone to sleep so soon. You're pretending, aren't you? I told you if I got in bed with you it was on the condition that you would be quiet and not move, that you'd let me think about the Archduke's trial. But I didn't tell you to go to sleep. I like your company. I like you to listen to me. Do you hear me, Hope? Well, it's your loss. I'm getting dressed and leaving. What? Forgive me, I thought you were asleep. No, I'm not biting your neck. It's just a kiss. Why don't you turn toward me? Of course I love your back. I love all of you. No, don't fall asleep, please. I promise you to stop talking about the Archduke. I'm sick of him, and Mejía and Miramón. I'm sick of the Constitution and Escriche and Vattel and Reynoso. Oh, of course they'll cite Reynoso and the situation of defenseless nations . . . well, if you don't want that, turn around . . . submitting to a conqueror according to natural law. Like that, like that. Put your arms around me. And political. And they'll say that the law of October 3rd . . . I prefer to touch your ass when you're turned towards me. What a gorgeous ass you have, Hope. Hold on. Don't touch me. And they'll say, as I was saying, that the law had goals similar to those of the Decree of January 25th and that only came out *ad terrorem*. Don't touch me, I said. You know, I love it when your hipbones hit my groin. These, Hope, are your shoulder blades. Spread your legs, just a little. Please, Hope, come on— don't be difficult. You're wet. Yes, yes I washed my hands, remember? You're trembling again. Wait, don't turn around. You won't feel cold like that. Am I too heavy, darling? Besides, I'd say that the January 25th decree . . . No, don't spread them so far, just a bit. Help me out a little. Wait, wait, you're hurting me with your ring. Like that, like that. Oh, Hope, my darling, you don't know how much I like you, how much I love you, how much . . . As I was saying, the January 25th decree. Juárez . . . Don't get like that. For God's sake, Hope, how can I care more about the Archduke and the trial than about you! Like that, like that, my love. You know I need to think or to talk about other things so I don't climax too fast. Hold on, now you're scratching me with your nails. Not so hard. Oh, Hope, Hope, you move your body so nicely. Like that, like that, more, my love. No, not so much. Don't spread your legs so much. I can't stand it anymore. Mejía, Miramón. Wait: be still for a few minutes. No, just as we are right now. But don't move—let me think about other things. The atrocities they committed. Don't move. They bayoneted them to death. Michoacán, Coahuila, Sinaloa. Are you listening, Hope? Tamaulipas, Nuevo León. Let me start moving, like this, very slowly. But not you, as if you were asleep, you hear me? Nuevo León, Tamaulipas. We're going to kill the Archduke. Like this, my darling, like this, just a little. Are you listening, Hope? Tamaulipas, Nuevo León. Let me start moving like this, just a little. And not you, as if you were asleep, you hear me? Nuevo León, Tamaulipas. We're going to kill the Archduke. Like this, my darling, like this, just a little. No, don't spread them any more. Miramón, Miramón. And Mejía, Márquez and Coahuila. For having come . . . having come . . . Am I hurting you? . . . To kill him. For contumacy, for rebellion. A little more, again. No, not that much . . . Okay, yes like this, like this, Hope, slowly. Very slowly and then, when I tell you, quickly. Oh, you don't know how much I like you, Hope. Coahuila, Juárez, Tamaulipas. You're killing me, Hope. No, I'm not complaining. It's just . . . spread your legs more, now, Hope, all you can. Move, darling, move, Hope. No, hold it. Hold it, for God's sake. Coahuila, Miramón, Mejía, Hope, my God, Márquez, Hope, please, Tamaulipas, Nuevo León, please, I'm coming, Coahuila, Mejía, Miramón, Miramón, Miramón! Miramón! Mira . . . mmm . . . oooohhh . . . !

•

Hope . . . Hope . . . Can you hear me? I fell asleep. I barely have time to get to the trial. Don't worry, I won't be late. Let's see what you think of this: I'll conclude by requesting the death penalty on behalf of the Nation for the above-mentioned accused. The first according to Articles 13 and 24. Look how creased my trousers are, Hope. And the stain hasn't come off. And the other two, as I was saying, according to Article 1, fourth part of section 13, and the first part of number 21 of the Law of January 25th, 1862. Did you see where I left my hat? You didn't press my coat and didn't sew the button back on, after all that. No, woman, I'm not angry. Look, you have a gray hair of mine here, on your chest. You know something? I'm going to buy you another ring. A ring that always reminds you of me. No, no more, Hope. I have to go. Sleep. Get some rest. As soon as the trial is over I'll run back here. Put on the green dress again, will you? No, you'd better wait for me naked. Are you listening? You'll wait for me in the nude, in bed . . . okay, Hope?

But to tell the world who you were, Maximilian, I have to recover from that disease I got from you.

Why do you think Cousin Victoria died of sorrow after she couldn't forgive Prince Albert for having preceded her into the grave by forty years, those years that the ghost of the German Prince, dressed as a Scotsman, the Order of the Garter on his leg, followed by his favorite horses and hounds, haunted her in the halls of Sandringham, the Osborne Gardens, the Buckingham Palace corridors, and her Balmoral apartments where John Brown, Abd el-Krim, the jade figurines stolen from the Peking Summer Palace, or the gold dinnerware of Charles II, failed to make her forget the death of her beloved Albert even for a minute. His ghost whispered in her ear that it was his own son, my nephew Edward VII, who had killed him, not typhoid fever. He had died from the pain of seeing his son having taken Nellie Clifden as a mistress. Neither Victoria's golden jubilee, nor the multicolored feather wreath from the Queen of Hawaii, nor the presence of her favorite daughter-in-law, Princess Alexandra, in her rose tiara, nor the attendance of all the European dynasties—Bourbons, Habsburgs, Romanovs, Hohenzollerns, Coburgs, Savoys, Wittelsbachs, Hesses, Braganzas, and Bernadottes—nor the day she bowed before God at Westminster Abbey to thank Him for letting her rule for half a century and for having given her all those children, could keep her from hearing Albert's ghost at the *Te Deum* service, the hymns he had composed, and the words he whispered in her ear to remind her that Edward, Prince of Wales, who that morning had walked under the Admiralty Arch in his red field marshal's uniform, was an irresponsible sybarite, an unrepentant womanizer, a degenerate who gambled his life away at baccarat in clandestine London casinos, a frivolous man given to dancing the cancan with the Duchess of Manchester, and, in sum, a prince who had revived the resentments and misunderstandings that had existed in the distant past—from the time of George I of England—among rulers and heirs to the crown in the corrupt Hanover dynasty. While Victoria thanked the Lord for giving her half of the Suez Canal, and making her Empress of India, that vast territory where she never set foot, Prince Albert's ghost reminded her that one of her grandsons, the Duke of Clarence, who that morning had paraded in his blue uniform beside his father the Prince of Wales, was a pervert who frequented the pederast brothels so favored by Lord Somerset, a lost soul who at sixteen had taken a sailor for a lover and had contracted syphilis. Perhaps he had also been a murderer, because when he died at the age of twenty-eight, rumor had it that he, the Duke of Clarence, grandson of Queen Victoria of Britain, had been the man who stabbed and quartered London prostitutes, and was known as Jack the Ripper.

Do you know why, Maximilian, do you know why Cousin Victoria died consumed not only by sciatica, cataracts, and old age, but also by sorrow? Because she was immensely sad to die in the arms of someone she detested, her grandson Kaiser Wilhelm II of Germany; hopelessly sad because, on the other side of the Channel, her daughter Vicky, the Kaiser's mother, was riddled with cancer, and would die a few months later, at the precise moment a butterfly entered her bedroom window to take her to heaven, but only her soul, for her nude body, shrouded in the Union Jack, would return to England where her mother was no longer there to weep for her eternally. Do you know that something more painful—infinitely more painful—than cancer prolonged Vicky's agony for years? It wasn't the disdain that her Prussian subjects, who tagged her *Die Engländerin*, showed her, but rather the bitter knowledge of having ruled only a few months, because her husband, Europe's most handsome man, a man who could have been another Frederick the Great of Germany, occupied the throne of the Kaisers for a mere ninety-nine days without uttering a word. He kept this silence, not like your cousin, the mute King Otto of Bavaria, who didn't speak a word because he was as mad as his brother Ludwig, but because Frederick's throat was rotting from cancer, according to some, and according to others because he had contracted syphilis eighteen years earlier from a Spanish Gypsy dancer, and his vocal chords had been removed. Do you know why, Maximilian, when Frederick and Vicky arrived at the *Altes Schloss* on their wedding night, they found it crawling with bedbugs and bats, as we did at the National Palace in Mexico? Can you tell me why all of Vicky's most beloved children died, and the son destined to be the future Wilhelm II of Germany was born to her with an atrophied left arm and grew to hate her always, and after his father's death expelled her from the Friedrichskron, the palace where she had lived with him? Since Wilhelm couldn't take Frederick's memory away from Vicky, he took Frederick's name from the palace. Do you know why that Kaiser, whose good arm supported the pillow on Cousin Victoria's deathbed, a man who tried to be another Napoleon without fighting any battles, tortured so much as a child by my niece Vicky and his riding teacher so that he would learn to ride without falling as the idiot did so many times, became such a poor arrogant devil, a friend of pederasts such as Count von Eulenburg, who tried to be a poet and a soldier, an architect and a painter but failed at everything, who before the fall of the Second Reich and his flight to Holland, his tail between his legs, sawed wood and drank tea while his generals decided on the course of the war? Maximilian, do you know why my nephew Wilhelm never became the new Caesar, destroyer of Gaul, despite swearing to do so to Bismarck on a bust of the great Roman emperor? Do you know why he never became history's new Charlemagne, despite the fact that he promised it to himself as he placed a floral wreath on Saladin's tomb?

For the same reason, Maximilian, that your horse Orispelo tripped on the way to Querétaro.

Maximilian, do you know why Victoria died so infinitely sad as she thanked God for giving her Albert as a husband and at the same time chastised Him for taking her son, Leopold Duke of Albany, the first of her brood, to whom she had transmitted hemophilia, the royal disease, three years prior to her golden jubilee? Do you know, Maximilian, why that sovereign of what would become the greatest empire in the world was a carrier of a malady that condemned sixteen of her male children and grandchildren to a most precarious and fragile life? Why she made them so vulnerable that any anarchist or madman could have assassinated the Duke of Albany, or Victoria's great-grandchildren the Prince of Asturias and his brother Don Gonzalo, without having to resort to a bomb, a dagger, or a firearm, as Orsini, Berezowski, Ravaillac, or Princip had? All they needed was the thorn of a rose.

For the same reason, Maximilian, that you were betrayed by Leonardo Márquez and our friend, López.

And, Maximilian, do you know why Alfonso XIII had a deaf mute, Don Jaime, for a son, besides those two hemophiliacs? Do you know why it did him absolutely no good to have the world handed to him on a gold platter, or to be king from the moment he left his mother's womb and let out his first cry? The messenger has told me that three of his ministers were murdered, that the

Catalonian women dumped the rifles of the men he sent to Morocco into the ocean, and that the men set fire to forty churches in Barcelona. He told me too that Spain lost its last possessions in America, as well as the islands that immortalized Philip II with their name; that Alfonso is a puppet king because General Primo de Rivera is the one really running Spain. Do you know why? Do you know why it did no good for Alfonso to marry the woman who, after Sisi, was the most beautiful queen in Europe, my niece Ena, Cousin Victoria's daughter and goddaughter to Eugénie? Because they were never happy. Alfonso knew it, he must have known it from his wedding day when a bouquet dropped from a balcony on the Calle Mayor in Madrid. Like a sign from the sky, an omen, the floral arrangement exploded in front of his carriage, disemboweling the horses, killing sixteen people, ripping apart Alfonso's medals and uniform, staining poor Ena's silver slippers and her immaculate white gown with the blood of men and beasts. Do you know why it was useless for that libertine pig Alfonso XIII, who deceived my niece Ena so frequently, to have been baptized in the waters of the River Jordan? Do you know why the sun sets every night on the kingdom of Spain?

For the same reason, Maximilian, that you and I were expelled from the Lombardo-Veneto provinces.

Do you know why, Maximilian, Victoria's favorite granddaughter, Alix, married Czar Nicholas II and not only became the Czarina of all the Russias but also went mad, sinking into darkness and fanaticism, collecting tapestries, cabinets, and carpets in her rooms, while her people were massacred on the grounds of the Winter Palace in St. Petersburg, and the crew of the ship Potemkin mutinied, and the Russian fleet was defeated at Tsushima by the children of the Rising Sun? Do you know why, while her empire crumbled, taking with it Nicholas's dreams of annexing Manchuria and conquering Tibet and Korea, Alexandra's soul burned with the prophesies and charms of Grigori Yefimovich Rasputin, a mad, murdering monk, a rustler of horses and souls who promised her that as long as he was at her side her son would not die of a hemorrhage but who did not warn her that two years after he was assassinated by three Russian nobles, the hemophiliac boy and with him his brothers as well as Alexandra and Nicholas themselves would be shot by the Red Guard at Ekaterinburg?

Tell me, do you know why your nephew Karl I of Habsburg and Lorraine was exiled in Madeira to keep from appearing like a fool? Twice he entered Hungary and twice he was thrown out. He dressed as a gardener and covered his face to remain incognito. He used a pencil to sign his abdication to an Austro-Hungarian Empire that no longer existed. He and Zita were kicked out, robbed of their jewels, taken away from Europe on an English packet by way of the Danube. Karl died of consumption and sorrow while Austria begged the world for help and the chamberlains had to work as firefighters, the barons became pianists, colonels did gardening, and the Lipizzaner horses of the Spanish Riding School of Vienna pulled coal wagons. I never slept with you again so you didn't give me the chancres you caught in Brazil. But I got something worse from you, Maximilian. Why do you think that stonemason murdered Sisi? Why do you think that your sister-in-law, the Black Archangel—on that fateful lustrous afternoon, with the sun shining on the crest of Mont Blanc, as she walked arm-in-arm with Countess Sztaray on the banks of Lake Leman, having heard the overture from Tannhäuser from a music box— would die as she was destined to from the stiletto that pierced her breast, her heart overflowing with bitterness from having a bastard daughter she never saw again, and from knowing that it was not she, the Austrian Empress, but Katharina Schratt who would weep for Franz Joseph—the man she so much wanted to love but was unable to—since she herself had put this mistress into her husband's arms to bind his heart with sausages and chorizos in their Felicitas Villa. Why do you imagine that Luccheni never found the Duke of Orléans, whom he intended to assassinate, but did run into that Empress of Loneliness, the Sybil of Corfu, on the banks of the lake, she who dragged from spa to spa, from island to island, from Madeira to Baden-Baden, from Lainz to Ischl, to Malta, to Palermo, to the Convent of Paleocastrizza, the live memory of your nephew, her son Rudolf, who died by his own hand in the hunting lodge at Mayerling? Why do you think that Sisi, dressed in black the last ten years of her life, ran away from your brother, ran away from Vienna, the city of the damned, ran away from life—and neither riding nor walking through the woods until she dropped from exhaustion, nor eating raw meat and drinking bull's blood, nor putting herself in the hands of masseurs, hairdressers, fencing instructors or fox hunters, ever let her forget her son Rudolf's face, with the pink wax that disguised the wound that blew his head apart melting from the candles at the wake? She would never forget that the face she saw in the mirror every morning was no longer that of the most beautiful empress in Europe but the portrait of an old hag into which death carved new furrows daily, and planted in them the flowers of her rotting flesh; it was a face that she tried in vain to hide from others and even from herself behind thick veils and the violet shade of her parasols.

How you would have loved, oh yes, Maximilian, for me to spread my legs once and many times more to satisfy your filthy desires. I didn't do it, so you never poisoned my blood, but it was enough to meet you and to love you for you to poison my life. Why do you think that Rudolf died at Mayerling? You think he died of love because he was the heir to a Catholic throne and so couldn't divorce my niece Stephanie? Do you think that because he couldn't marry Maria Vetsera he shot her with his rifle, covered her with roses, and cried at her death all night—that he shot himself at dawn and fell down embracing the corpse of that little seventeen-year-old whore who had taught him to smoke hashish? If Rudolf was really mad (which was what the Austrian court had to tell the Pope—that he had taken his own life in a moment of insanity—so that the Church would allow him to be buried in consecrated ground) how do you think, Maximilian, it happened? Because of the hashish that the baroness had brought from Cairo? Or from the morphine that he injected every day in order to live, in those burgundy wallpapered and furnished rooms, what he called his "white hours"? Or had he always been mad? You should know that when he was a child he took birds from their nests at the Laxenburg Gardens and killed them by wringing their necks and making their veins burst as revenge for Sisi's absences, since she left him to sing Schubert ballads and declaim Heine poems in the solitude of the Borromeo Islands under the shade of the araucarias and the flowering camphor trees. Or do you think he killed himself because he was in love with her, with his own mother Sisi? Or was it, as they say, because he found out that the baroness was Franz Joseph's illegitimate daughter and he preferred death to incest? Or because he had conspired with his cousin, Archduke Johann Salvador, and his coterie of revolutionaries, to assassinate Franz Joseph and end the monarchy in order to create a socialist republic in Austria, and finally the thought of being an accomplice in his father's death drove him mad? Unless it's true that Bismarck simply had him killed. Or Clemenceau. Unless his own friends took his life because they thought he would reveal the conspiracy to Franz Joseph. Unless it was his own father who had him murdered, Maximilian—and, if so, why did he do it? Because he couldn't bear the fact that the heir to the House of Austria was a madman who wore a gold reliquary filled with poison around his neck, a maniac who proposed suicide pacts to singers and chorus girls? Because he couldn't understand how the boy over whose cradle he had cried with such emotion as he placed the Order of the Golden Fleece on the newborn's breast—barely just learning to breathe the damp Schönbrunn air and the lavender-scented breath of Empress Elisabeth—could have become an anarchist who used pen names to publish antimonarchy articles in the *Wiener Zeitung* and conspired to liberate Hungary from the Habsburg Empire and proclaim himself its ruler? Oh, and don't let anyone tell you now, Maximilian, that Rudolf didn't die, that he fled with La Vetsera, both in disguise, and that to avoid the shame of revealing this to the whole world, the House of Austria borrowed two corpses and dressed them as Rudolf and Maria and buried them under their names, while the genuine articles buried themselves alive in anonymity among the rivers and mountains of a South American jungle. No, your nephew Rudolf and Baroness Maria Vetsera died at Mayerling because it was their destiny and they knew it, or certainly must have guessed it—and not just because a few hours after Rudolf's death a gigantic crystal chandelier fell and smashed to pieces on the floor of the Ceremonial Hall at Schönbrunn, or because, as rumored, Rudolf once killed a white stag in the Helenental. But he must have known it from the moment when he gave Maria Vetsera the ring that said "United in love until death," or when he said good-bye to Mitzi Kaspar, the chanteuse who refused to join him on his journey to the other world and who denounced him to the Viennese secret police, or when he said good-bye to Sisi in a letter, or to his friends, or the Archduke Johann Salvador, or Michel de Braganza, or when he patted Probus, his trained crow, for the last time, and climbed into his carriage and told Bratfisch to take him to Mayerling, and on the road that dark, starless night while it snowed and Bratfisch whistled and hummed Tyrolean songs, he, Rudolf, must have known that he and Maria both had to die there, as indeed they did—die in the hunting lodge covered with snow, and with its interior covered in turn with glass-eyed heads of all the deer, gazelles, wild boars, chamois, and moose that Rudolf had killed in his life, his "blood wedding" bed covered first with roses and then Rudolf's blood, which spattered his bride's lifeless porcelain face and her slippers filled with swan's neck down, as the roses were covered first in tears and then spattered with the brains of the heir to the Austrian throne, likewise Maria's sealskin cape, the lace of the sheets, the rosewood furniture. Maria Vetsera's body was hidden in a clothes hamper, and when her uncles Stokau and Baltazzi arrived to take her down the stairs on foot, held by her armpits, so that the servants at Mayerling would think she was alive, they had to tie a stick onto her back and her neck to the stick because Rudolf's gunshot had broken her spine and her head was like a cloth doll's. Maximilian, they also had to put back an eye in its socket that had popped out and hung from its optic nerve—the eye that Rudolf had placed on a rose on Maria Vetsera's cheek, his beloved who was expecting a child, soon buried alive in that double tomb, at night, under cover, at Heiligenkreutz Cemetery.

That is how they died and that is how they were meant to die. You know why, Maximilian? The same reason that your cook Tüdös lost his teeth from a gunshot on the way to Querétaro.

And do you know why your brother was never spared any sorrow in his life, as he said himself when he learned of Sisi's death? Do you know why Franz Joseph died so alone, without having even Katharina Schratt by his side, after your cousin Prince Montenuovo had locked the secret door that led to his bedchamber, leaving her unable to get in to console the dying man, so tormented by remorse from all the sins he had committed: raping a basket weaver who was almost a child in the gardens of his Hietzig Villa, and from whom he also had a bastard daughter; rejecting his only son and heir to the House of Habsburg; and also tormented because Austria, brought to shame by Louis Napoleon at Solferino and by Bismarck in Königgrätz, and then humbled by Mexico in your person and through your martyrdom, shamed further by the loss of Lombardy and Venice, and having lost its power in the German world forever, had become just a satellite of Prussia. The Empire to which Napoleon I had struck the first mortal blow when he created the First Confederation of the Rhine, the vast kingdom that had protected so many of the world's nations under the aegis of the two-headed eagle, the Empire founded by the descendants of Guntram the Rich and Maximilian I, by the Landgraves from Alsace and the Counts of Zurich, by Caesar, by Aeneas and the Trojans, by Cham, by Osiris and Noah, was crumbling under its feet. The Empire was bleeding to death in Bosnia and Serbia, in the fields of Rava Russkaya, in the waters of the Drina and the Kolubara, because of a war that Austria itself had initiated when the heir to the throne, Archduke Franz Ferdinand and his wife Sophie Chotek, were felled by Gavrilo Princip's bullets in the streets of Sarajevo. And do you know why?

For the same reason, Maximilian, that those bedbugs ate you alive in Querétaro.

Your brother must have known it from the moment the Berlin Congress offered Austria a poisoned gift—the protectorate of Bosnia-Herzegovina. He must have seen it when Queen Draga of Serbia was assassinated along with her husband and her siblings, or when, a few years later, he determined that Austria should take forceful possession of those two regions. And those unfortunates—the Archduke Franz Ferdinand, a despot who grew exotic roses, who hated democrats, socialists, Magyars, and Jews alike, and that plebeian outsider, Duchess Sophie Chotek, Princess of Hohenberg, detested by Franz Joseph, who forbade his friends and closest relatives from attending their funerals, and who ordered a black fan and white gloves placed on her casket, as was customary for ladies-in-waiting, to humiliate her more in death than in life—probably knew it too. The Chotek woman must have known it when she determined that the visit to Bosnia-Herzegovina would include Sarajevo. Did she not consider the incident a few days earlier when three young Serbian patriots, not even twenty years old, had come together at the Serbian border in an all-black room—black walls, black masks hiding the faces of the organization's leaders, a black cloth covering the table on which there were two burning candles, a crucifix, and a skull—where Princip, Grabez, and Cabrinovic swore their allegiance to the Black Hand, to assassinate the heir to the Austro-Hungarian throne, and then, armed with bombs and grenades, pistols, and cyanide pills to take their own lives so that they wouldn't fall into the hands of the Austrian police, crossed the border toward the capital, where besides them Popovic and other potential assassins wandered the streets on the day that the Archduke and Archduchess were to ride in their automobile to the city's museum. It did them no good that Cabrinovic's grenade bounced off the roof of the imperial carriage and went off several meters away. It did them no good to come out of *that* attack unharmed, nor that Grabez was too paralyzed with fear to make his move, nor that Popovic ran off and hid his bomb. It did them no good that Cabrinovic took his cyanide pill (it had no effect), nor that he jumped into the river (the police fished him out alive and kicking). No, Sophie Chotek must have known it when their route was changed at the last minute without General Potiorek's knowledge, since he shouted to the driver to go by the Appel Quay and the car backed up and stopped right before Gavrilo Princip, who had thought he'd missed his only chance and was standing in front of the Schiller Department Store, on the sidewalk where his footprints would be set in concrete, to remind the world forever that he, the patriot Gavrilo Princip, had fired the pistol that took Franz Ferdinand and Sophie Chotek's lives, so that if they died then and there, on June 28, 1914, and a month and four days later the whole of Europe was at war, it was because they had to die, there and in that way—he with a bullet in the throat, she with one in the stomach—just like the half a million men at the banks of the Marne, the million at Verdun, and the 400,000 in the mud of Passchendaele also had to die, and would.

You know what I'm talking about, Maximilian. You know that those times I went to meet you in Cuernavaca, it wasn't because of exhaustion that I stayed in my rooms or that you never surprised me lying in bed, even though I couldn't rest but was wide awake, knowing that you wouldn't come, that you wouldn't even try, that your hands wouldn't become wet with the sweat that covered my skin those star-filled nights, those nights perfumed with begonias, those Cuernavaca nights. You know it, as you always knew that I didn't start to go mad on the return trip to Europe when I ran through the deserted halls of the Municipal Palace in Puebla, talking to myself. Nor when I had the French flag replaced with the Mexican flag on the packet steamer that took me to the *Impératrice Eugénie* in Veracruz. Nor when I ordered mattresses tacked to the walls of my stateroom because I thought my head would explode from the infernal noise of the ship's engines. Nor when I refused to leave the ship in Havana. No, I didn't start to go mad when I was alone in my chamber and sweat oozed from my pores in tiny drops that those clear, warm Cuernavaca nights also traced luminously onto my breasts, my thighs, my belly—the pattern of the constellations that, had I desired it, you could have extinguished with your body.

If I didn't allow this it wasn't because I truly believed that a Brazilian Negress had given you chancres. That almost didn't matter to me. In any case, you never had the opportunity to afflict me with any venereal diseases because I decided never to give myself to you, as revenge for all your absences and your infidelities. I swore to myself that, just as I had spent so many nights alone in Miramare, Madeira, Cuernavaca, Chapultepec, and Puebla, thinking of you, seeing you, my eyes open or closed, taking off your Neumark Dragoon uniform to bed a Viennese chorus girl, removing your blue serge *charro* suit to make love to the first of my ladies-in-waiting to volunteer to give herself to you, getting out of your white linen suit to tumble with Concepción Sedano in the grass at Borda Gardens, I swore to myself that—even if many years went by—no matter how much I loved you and wanted you alive, next to me—no matter that my own life's breath was yours—I swore to myself that the night would come, though it might be far away, that I would see you taking off your skin, leaving naked bone, and then taking off your bones, to become dust, and lying down, Maximilian, at last, with your own death.

At the time—poor me, poor you—I didn't know you would die so soon. I didn't realize that you had a much more serious disease, and that you had given it to me. Do you know why, Maximilian, we were met by vultures in Mexico? Do you know why our carriage wheel came off on our way to Córdoba? Why you were betrayed by Colonel Miguel López? For the same reason, Maximilian, that Hartmann, your ancestor Rudolf I of Habsburg's son, drowned in the Rhine. Do you know why Napoleon III betrayed you, Maximilian? Why the *Novara* ran out of coal on our way to Martinique? Do you know why your coffin was too short? For the same reason, Maximilian, that Rudolf's other son, Albert I, was stabbed to death by his nephew, John the Parricide. Do you know, tell me, do you know why everyone abandoned you, why even the Nubian slaves the Egyptian Viceroy had sent us deserted your army? Why the Foreign Legion soldiers crossed over, when they were able, to the United States? Do you know why the kitchen cookware was stolen from Chapultepec Castle when you went to Orizaba? Do you know, Maximilian, why you had to receive a coup de grâce? For the same reason that the children of Albert I became obsessed with exterminating the descendants of John the Parricide—for the same reason that General Prim died of the gunshots fired by an assassin on the streets of Madrid, that our friend López died of a rabid dog's bite, and that Napoleon I, forgotten by France, died on the Island of Saint Helena.

For the same reason that Loulou, the Imperial Prince, never became Napoleon IV. Why do you think that the four-leaf clover Eugénie sent to Saarbrücken, where Loulou got his baptism by fire as a shell landed next to his horse Kaled, was useless in changing his bad luck and bringing about his father's dream of consolidating, in the not-too-distant future, the Bonaparte dynasty in France, as the Capets had done eight centuries before? And if they tell you that the savaged and unrecognizable body Loulou's faithful servant Ulhman took to England was not his, if they tell you that the real Imperial Prince became the man in the iron mask, tell them that it is a lie. Loulou had to die like that, as he did, betrayed by Lieutenant Carey, abandoned by his countrymen to the rage of the Zulus, pierced by seventeen spears, on the same day that a violet flew out of Princess Pilar of Spain's prayer book and fell apart on her lap. For the same reason that she would die a few weeks later of a broken heart, perhaps because she loved Loulou so fiercely, or of rage, perhaps, because she would never become empress of the French.

And do you know why, Maximilian? For the same reason that you were executed in Querétaro.

My brother Leopold told me one day. He told me about the young maiden who, a thousand years ago, was raped in the woods of the Habichtsburg, the Falcon Castle, and who died after giving birth to a stillborn child. Mother and baby are buried there, together. That is how, he told me, the legend was born. That is also why Joanna of Castile went mad and fell in love with a ghost. And Don Carlos of Austria went crazy and bit off the heads of turtles, which is why his father, Philip II, had him locked up until he starved to death and why all the gold in the world and indeed the greatest empire in the world failed to make Philip II happy. He became a living corpse. Leopold told me that he liked to put his crown on a skull to see himself in the mirror of death. They're all there, some in the Escorial burial chambers, others in the Capuchin Crypt in Vienna—the most unfortunate monarchs in the history of the world. Then, of course, although I listened in awe, Leopold acted as though he weren't taking it all very seriously. He didn't know that he, and I, and one of his daughters, would each marry Habsburgs. He married your cousin Marie Henriette, the daughter of Hungary's Count Palatine. I married you and Stephanie your nephew Rudolf. The days were still far off when my brother would cry like a baby on the death of his son the Duke of Brabant, and banish and lock up his other daughter Louise in a madhouse. His own death too, in a greenhouse where he ordered his bed set up so that he could be drunk with the scent of the tropics and forget that his rotting soul was leaking out of his pores. To see if that dense sweet fragrance would let him forget the atrocities that my Belgian countrymen had committed in the Congo in the name of civilization and rubber. Leopold didn't tell me that. No one did. I saw it myself, I always knew it. I saw the towns reduced to ashes by my brother Leopold's orders. Children chained as hostages. I saw the black men who didn't work as hard as the foremen wanted and so had a hand chopped off. Just as, the afternoon that Grandfather Louis Philippe told me about Uncle Aumale's adventures in Algiers, I saw Abd al-Qadir's camels loaded with bags filled with the heads of his enemies, as a warning for the infidels—and as, on another day, when Prince de

Ligne told me about all the wealth that I possessed, I closed my eyes and I saw my brother's foremen going from town to town in the Congo, carrying baskets full of dismembered hands to motivate the shiftless.

So, Brother Leopold had to die that way, turned into human garbage. His daughter Louise had to wreck her life, after running away from the sanitarium at Purkersdorf, into the arms of her Count Mattacic. The Duke of Brabant had to die. Eugénie had to die, full of sorrow, because the city of Paris had borrowed the little Imperial Prince's crib and never returned it. General Leonardo Márquez had to die in Havana, at ninety-three, in abject poverty. José Manuel Hidalgo y Esnaurrízar had to die in Paris, forgotten by all. A million men had to die in the Mexican Revolution; the Russians had to cross the Danube; the Turks had to massacre the Bulgarians. My niece, María de las Mercedes, Alfonso XII's first wife, had to die poisoned by Princess Isabella. Your nephew, the Archduke Otto, who humiliated your brother by jumping his horse over the coffins in funeral processions and riding nude around the Prater, had to die from the ravaging effects of a mysterious illness, his face disfigured. Your other nephew, Archduke Johann Salvador, had to die deprived of all his titles and his Austrian nationality, swallowed by the sea or by Buenos Aires, because he disappeared without a trace. All of them had to die, one by one. And I had to be left alone more and more to realize what Leopold meant when he talked about the falcons that dwelled in the Habichtsburg and all the other palaces and castles of the Habsburgs—Laxen, Schönbrunn, the Hofburg, Ischl, Gödöllő—where they were used to catch rats. Only then did I begin to understand, did I begin to remember that my brother Leopold had told me that, according to the legend, when the falcons left the Habsburg possessions, when the last of the falcons took flight from the last of their castles, it would carry the curse of the Habsburgs on its wings. I also understood that on that day I would recover my innocence and purity of soul. I would be a child again.

No, what I contracted from you wasn't a venereal disease. Syphilis didn't prevent Maximilian I from realizing his dream of becoming pope. Epilepsy didn't cause Joseph II of Austria to fail at everything he tried to do. No, all of them, you, all of your relations, all these imbeciles, madmen, tyrants, and degenerates, all of them suffered from the same disease I contracted from you the night we danced together for the first time, and the day that onboard the *Reine Hortense*, when you showed me the navigation instruments and took my hand in yours—remember?—and in that double reflection of your blue eyes I saw myself looking more beautiful than ever because I was in love, and your love was what made me so beautiful, as did the certainty that your entire being had entered into my eyes forever. What I contracted from you, Max, what everyone contracted from you, was your bad luck. Your terrible, awful, goddamn bad luck.

Why do you think, Maximilian, that your ancestor Rudolf II went mad and locked himself up in the Prague Hadreschin, surrounded by dwarves, monsters, and silver-nosed astronomers? Or why your father was a poor mental defective and his brother, Emperor Ferdinand, an imbecile, an idiot who only liked to walk among his apes or to stand at a palace window all day long counting the fiacres that passed on the way to Schönbrunn, or to catch live flies to feed his frogs? And if your father wasn't Franz but the King of Rome, do you know why the Eaglet ruled for only ten days and never paraded under the colossal triumphal arch that his father had built but never finished, without a great star on it, without a huge eagle, without the elephant of the Bastille, without the statue of the emperor standing atop the earth, all those things crowning the arch for the glory of his dynasty and of France? Tell me Maximilian, why you think that the King of Rome died of melancholia and tuberculosis at twenty-five, never returning the love of the beautiful Countess Camerata who kissed his hand in a Schönbrunn corridor dressed as a man, leaving your mother Sophie a widow of love and married to solitude, love's widow and solitude's wife, to inherit from your father not an Empire, not even the house in Ajaccio and the fifty-thousand lire pension he left in his will, but only his memory and the curved saber that Napoleon took to the pyramids. Why do you think they took away the Eaglet's toys, that they hid his Legion of Honor medal from him, that they refused him the Order of the Golden Fleece, and that they used yellow and black on his shroud (the colors of his father's enemies) instead of those of the flag that triumphed at Austerlitz and Wagram? Tell me, why do you think that commoners executed Jecker the banker and that Colonel Van der Smissen committed suicide, that Prince Salm-Salm and General Douay outlived you only to die later in the disastrous war France was dragged into by Napoleon and Eugénie? Why do you think that Louis Napoleon became the coward of Sedan and posters that showed him licking Bismarck's boots were put up all around Paris? Why do you think Bazaine turned traitor when he surrendered at Metz with the one hundred and seventy thousand men of the Army of the Rhine? Why do you think, Maximilian, that the Prussian army

575

paraded under that same triumphal arch whose shadow your father never approached, to the shame of Ollivier who claimed to accept the responsibility for the war with a happy heart; to the shame of Favre who'd sworn that the French wouldn't give up an inch of land, nor a single stone from their forts, to the disgrace of France? And why Paris then decided to inflict an even more humiliating and cruel defeat upon itself than that brought by the Iron Chancellor, as a punishment for its stupidity and pride? Why do you think the Parisians knocked down the Place Vendôme Column and reduced the toga-clad statue of the great emperor there to dust? Why do you think that the Strasbourg monument in the Place de la Concorde ended up under a black cloth and the mob tore the name plaques off the Avenue of the Empress, the Avenue of Queen Hortense, and Duke de Morny Street, that it stoned and toppled the eagles at the Tuileries, that it set fire to the palace itself so that it was reduced to ashes: all of Eugénie's lace crinolines, her silk parasols trimmed with ostrich feathers, and the jewelry she couldn't take with her to exile. Why do you think, Maximilian, that thousands of beggars and women and children, thousands of Communards were killed by Thiers's and Mac-Mahon's Versaillais henchmen, their bodies thrown into the Seine and into Baron Haussmann's sewers and drains and turned into rat food?

For the same reason, Maximilian, that your blood was shed in Querétaro, and, what's more, for the same reason that you lost every drop of it. Do you remember, Maximilian, the speech you gave before the firing squad took aim, asking for your blood to be the last shed in Mexico? Certainly more than enough Mexican blood had already been shed on our account, but, nevertheless, much more was still to be shed—Sóstenes Rocha shed it at the Ciudadela, Pancho Villa shed it in Celaya and Trinidad; Porfirio Díaz shed it when, in the heat of the moment, he gave the order to kill the crews of the gunboats *Independencia* and *Libertad*. But the bones of all those dead Mexicans returned to the dust whence they had come, and their blood tinged the same earth that had fed their flesh, fertilizing a barbarous history of betrayals and lies, a beautiful history of triumphs and heroic deeds, a sad history of humiliations and failures; but, in the end, their own history, the history of a people who were never yours nor mine no matter how much you wanted it, how much I wanted it, no matter how long I was doomed to roam Mixcalco Square—every night of my life—barefoot, my hair loose, in a madwoman's gown, calling out for my children, my Mexican children, felled by imperial bullets every dawn of every day and every month and year of all the years we were in Mexico. That is my fate for having outlived you for so many years carrying those deaths on my conscience. Oh, Maximilian, do you remember in your memoirs how you describe the days when you were still a young prince, your eyes and heart open to the world, especially in those pages that you dedicated to the Alhambra, to its enchanted fountains and its Damask roses, to the Garden of Lindaraja and the court with the wrought-iron grille where Zoraya, the most beautiful of the Sultan's wives, the one who had Joanna the Mad as her jailer, went to get fresh air? Do you remember in your memoirs how you described the blood of that great warrior Wallenstein that stained the floors of the Municipal Palace in Eger where he was assassinated? Do you remember writing that on the interior tiles of the Fountain of Lions at the Alhambra, you saw the bloodstains of the Abencerages decapitated at the orders of King Abu-Abdallah, bloodstains that four centuries' worth of the water from Granada couldn't wash away? Oh Maximilian, if you could come to Querétaro you could see that there isn't a trace left of your blood, the blood you wanted to be the last shed in your new nation, not even a hint of it in the dust or on the rocks. Your blood didn't nourish anything in the eternal shadow of Benito Juárez, at the foot of Las Campanas Hill. It's gone with the wind, swept away by history, forgotten by Mexico.

XX

LAS CAMPANAS HILL

1867

1. The Traitorous Friend and the Princess on Her Knees

Maximilian had a notebook, later known as *El libro Secreto de Maximiliano*, Maximilian's Secret Book, in which he kept a list of the members of his court, almost all Mexicans, along with brief descriptions of their ancestors and various character traits assigned them by the Emperor's various informants, almost all of them foreign. For instance, the book reports that Almonte was "cold, miserly, and vindictive." About Miramón it says that he was intelligent but "passionately fond of gambling," and a poor loser. The book points out that Miramón had threatened a man at saber-point who had won a large amount from him in Toluca, making the winner return everything, to the last penny. Of Archbishop Labastida, the book tells us that, while being both intelligent and a scholar, he was also an impassioned fanatic. And the rest of the entries are of a similar nature. The informants were, among others, Jeanningros, Aymard, Castagny, Kodolisch, Eloin . . . and even Colonel Dupin himself!

The paragraph about Colonel López says:

"López, Miguel: He served in the counterinsurgency organized by the Americans in 1847. After Santa Anna protected him, he declared him an outlaw for betraying his country. He is very brave, but there are serious questions about his honesty."

It's difficult to explain how, knowing this history, Maximilian agreed to sponsor the baptism of Miguel López's son.

On the other hand, it's easy enough to understand the treachery of the colonel: Once a traitor, always a traitor.

But . . . was López really a traitor?

There are certain "traitorous acts" in history that have always seemed clear enough, so to speak. But then there are others that we'll never truly know about—whether they were, or were not, actual betrayals. For instance, nobody in Querétaro had any doubt that Márquez had betrayed Maximilian, because he didn't return to the city as promised. However, some historians say that Leonardo Márquez—who, in spite of being considered a scoundrel, was always a good soldier—calculated that if Porfirio Díaz took Puebla, the Republican general would be free to advance on the capital in order to stop the Imperialists from sending any reinforcements to Querétaro. Therefore, Márquez's decision to attack Díaz's troops, according to those historians, was the correct one. The defeat that the Tigre de Tacubaya, as Márquez was known, suffered in San Lorenzo at the hands of the Oaxacan, stopped him from marching on to Querétaro. This, then, was no betrayal.

So, what about López? Well, if López *did* betray Maximilian, as many insist, his wife, that is, the wife of López himself—among others—was right: According to Baron Magnus, when the Colonel returned to his house in Puebla, his wife shouted at him: "Oh, Miguel! What did you do to our child's godfather? If you don't bring him back alive, I'll never speak to you again!" And if she was right, if Miguel López really surrendered the Convent of La Cruz and Maximilian with it for a predetermined sum of money at dawn on May 15, 1867, then the Emperor's dog, Bebello, was also right, because he always wagged his tail at all the Emperor's generals and officers, except at Miguel López. He would growl at him, and if possible try to bite his heel. The authors who dwell on the animosity that the Emperor's dog had for the Commander of the Empress's Dragoons tell us that he was so vile, smelled so much like a traitor, that Bebello must obviously have sensed it, since the dog could hardly have known that López's record in the Mexican Army was hardly unblemished.

When people found out that López was being considered as a candidate for brigadier-general, those in the know about the shameful events at Tehuacán requested an audience with the Emperor and explained to him why they thought his friend didn't deserve such a promotion. During that meeting, one of two things happened: either Maximilian told his generals that he was aware of López's actions and that, yes, they were right, or else Maximilian acted as if he didn't know anything about López's previous betrayal and pretended to be surprised it was revealed to him. In either case, the Emperor changed his mind and did not in fact bestow the green sash of a general to the father of his godson, and it was because of this, some say, that López, consumed by anger, resentment, and envy, betrayed him.

According to the accounts of Albert Hans, Prince Salm-Salm, and Dr. Basch, among others, at two in the morning on May 15th, Colonel López appeared before the officer in charge of one of the several artillery platforms at the Convent of La Cruz and ordered him to pull a cannon back from its embrasure and "tilt it to the left." The night before, this same López had replaced the municipal guard's platoon assigned to that platform with an irregular troop of scouts under the command of a so-called Lieutenant Yablouski, or Jablonsky, who, they say, was his accomplice, and wouldn't challenge his orders. Immediately after the cannon's position was changed, the infantry platoon commanded by López lined up nearby. At that moment, Hans realized his sword was gone—other soldiers were complaining that their muskets had been stolen—and when he recognized the Republican soldiers of the Battalion of the Supreme Powers by their gray cloth uniforms with yellow stripes and black shakos, he realized that the Convent of La Cruz was in enemy hands. The artillery lieutenant adds that he asked the officer in charge of the troop of the Supreme Powers if it was Colonel López who had let them into the convent, and the officer's answer was affirmative.

Corti tells us that López had already been making contact with Juárez's troops since the night of May 13th, visiting the enemy camp—General Escobedo's—more than once, to continue negotiations. Corti also refers to a statement Maximilian made to Baron Lago, to the effect that "López had offered his services" four days before the fall of Querétaro, for the sum of two thousand ounces of gold—though it appears he only received seven thousand pesos, in the end. "The Emperor even calculated that López had sold him and his troops for about eleven *reales* apiece." But this same Corti points out that about eleven in the evening of May 14th, López had a secret conversation with Maximilian, who decorated him with the medal of valor during the interview and asked him—Dr. Basch says Maximilian himself told him this later—to shoot him, the Emperor, dead, in case he was wounded during the escape they had planned, and consequently unable to avoid being taken prisoner by the Juaristas. Some historians feel that this sudden decoration, at such an unusual hour, was a prize Maximilian gave López for his sacrifice—that is, the sacrifice of appearing to history as a traitor. Shortly before narrating the fall of Querétaro, and in reference to Maximilian and his insistence on accusing Márquez of betrayal, the Mexican historian, Carlos Pereyra, refers to the Archduke's often-noted and spontaneous perversity, and states that Maximilian simply wanted there to be a responsible party in his downfall: a traitor. "He could find no other explanation for the unfortunate events than treasonable acts committed against his sacrosanct person," states Pereyra, and who then goes on to tell the story of the events of the evening of May 14th, continuing into May 15th. Without saying so explicitly, Pereyra informs us that besides Márquez, Maximilian decided he needed another traitor as well, and the chosen one was his friend Miguel López. The sacrifice asked of the latter, and for which he was being compensated, was the greater.

Those who insist on López's treason, however, cite over and again the accounts of the survivors of the siege, who tell how during that entire night, till dawn, and during the course of the following day, they saw Colonel López on horseback, wearing a flashy uniform with silver embroidery, guiding the Republican troops and going from one end of the city to the other without being molested by the enemy. Lieutenant Hans adds another detail that contradicts several of the eyewitnesses like Prince Salm-Salm: The Prince states that it was the Republican Colonel Rincón Gallardo who, on meeting Maximilian, Pradillo, del Castillo, Blasio, and Salm-Salm himself sneaking out of the Convent to Las Campanas Hill, said, "Let them through, they're civilians," and adds that López was seen next to the Republican officer when this occurred; but, according to Hans, who doesn't mention Rincón Gallardo at all, it was López himself who said this. Salm-Salm says that he, Felix, was in uniform, so it's incomprehensible that Juárez's troops would take him for a civilian. And though some historians suggest that Maximilian's overcoat hid his general's uniform, these don't say how del Castillo was dressed; if, as expected, del Castillo too was in uniform—and Joan Haslip says he was—it is likewise incomprehensible how Rincón Gallardo could say that he was a civilian. The whole affair gets even more complex when we find that not everyone agrees that Maximilian's overcoat hid his uniform at all, and there are even authors who describe what he was wearing—besides the "white, wide-brimmed hat with a thin golden ribbon, mesh-knit riding breeches, and riding boots"—there was a blue military frockcoat with loose lapels. And then, of course, the sword he wore "clinging to his belt," under the skirts of his frockcoat.

Though many of them are insignificant, inaccuracies and contradictions like these abound in accounts of the siege. For instance, Maximilian's dog, named "Bebello" by some, changes name and sex and becomes Baby, a bitch, in Salm-Salm's account, which tells us that "Baby" followed her master to Las

Campanas Hill, got lost, and reappeared later as the dog of a so-called Colonel Cervantes, who had given her the name of Empress and refused to sell her to Prince Salm-Salm, who wanted to take the animal to Vienna and offer it as a present to Archduchess Sophie. At any rate, though one may ask whether "Bebello" and "Baby" might have been two different dogs, there's also a third, "Patschuka," featured in the Prince's *Memoirs*. Historians will probably never clear up this point.

Now, if these inaccuracies are relatively unimportant on the subject of dogs, it doesn't necessarily follow that they are the opposite—that is, important—when we speak of Colonel Miguel López, who has long been considered something less than a dog. In other words, it hardly matters whether or not he was the one who said, "They're civilians," nor does it really matter if he was a free man or a prisoner on May 15th and the days that followed, because neither one of these events in themselves proves him guilty or innocent of his alleged betrayal.

Hans, Basch, Salm-Salm, and other contemporary eye-witnesses wrote and published their memoirs and chronicles a very short time after the events at Querétaro, and for all of them López was a traitor, without a doubt, as he appears to have been in the eyes of his wife, who kept her promise: she didn't speak to the Colonel again, and soon left him for ever. But twenty-one years later, López again proclaimed his innocence—he had already done so in July 1867, in a declaration to the citizens of Mexico and the world—and he published a letter in the daily paper *El Globo* in which he asked General Escobedo to reveal "the historical truth." Escobedo yielded to López's petition, and in a report dated July 8, 1888, addressed to the President of the Republic, General Porfirio Díaz declared that the "Imperialist Colonel Miguel López," whom he describes as the "Archduke's Chief Commissioner," had only been an intermediary between himself and Maximilian who could not and would not continue defending the fortress. "López," Escobedo says, "though indifferent towards the nation, did not betray the Austrian Archduke Maximilian, nor did he violate his oaths as a soldier in exchange for money." López told Escobedo that Maximilian was ready to surrender Querétaro if he was allowed to leave the country, and he promised never to set foot on Mexican soil again. Escobedo answered that his orders from the Supreme Government were not to accept any arrangement other than the unconditional surrender of the fortress. Some authors say that Escobedo probably promised López in secret that Maximilian would indeed be allowed to escape. According to these historians,

Escobedo might have been of the opinion that having the Archduke as a prisoner of war could cause Juárez more headaches than satisfaction, and that it was because of this that, following Escobedo's instructions, Colonel Rincón Gallardo allowed Maximilian to get through when he left La Cruz. By the way, with regard to the question of whether it was López or Rincón Gallardo who spoke the famous "they're civilians" line, Count Corti chooses to put it in both their mouths at the same time. Nevertheless, Gustave Niox, in his *Expédition du Mexique: Récit politique et militaire*, leads the reader to believe that Rincón Gallardo's response wasn't due to any specific order, but to other reasons. According to Niox, the Colonel's father, the Marquis of Guadalupe, had accepted a position in Maximilian's court. But, again, there is some doubt: was it Rincón Gallardo's father or his sisters? On the list of Carlota's "palace ladies-in-waiting," Harding mentions two with the same last name: Ana Rosa de Rincón Gallardo and Luisa Quijano de Rincón Gallardo. By the way, the *New York Herald* refers to another incident, cited by many historians, in the relationship between López and Rincón Gallardo, in which the alleged traitor asked Gallardo to recommend him for "a position" in the Liberal army, and Don Pepe answered him, "If I recommended you for a position, Colonel López, it would be a position on a tree, with a rope around your neck."

However, General Escobedo says in his report about López, that instead of leaving when his offer to surrender the fortress in exchange for the safe-conduct of the Archduke was rejected, he insisted that Maximilian didn't want to prolong the horrors of war any longer, and that his orders were, at all costs, to negotiate an agreement for the surrender—unconditional, if necessary—of the city and the convent. "López," Escobedo adds, "left for the fortress carrying a message to the Archduke that at three in the morning La Cruz would be occupied whether there was resistance or not." Later, the Mexican general says that after the fall of Querétaro, López came before him again and showed him a letter "Whose exact words are," as Escobedo says: "My dear Colonel López, we recommend you keep a profound secrecy about the commission we gave you for General Escobedo, for if it becomes known, our honor will be sullied. Yours Truly, Maximilian."

López asked Escobedo if he had any problem with keeping the secret. Escobedo answered that he would reserve the option to divulge it whenever it appeared necessary. Next, the General's report describes a private conversation he had a short time later with Archduke Maximilian in his cell at the Capuchin

Convent. During this conversation—according to the General—Maximilian himself asked him not to reveal anything. Escobedo then told him he believed the Archduke should talk to Miguel López instead, "who was the one who was morally damaged by these events." Maximilian replied that López would not talk as long as Escobedo kept quiet, and that he was only asking him to keep the secret for a *very short time*: "until the death of Princess Carlota, whose life would ebb away upon learning of her husband's execution."

At that time Maximilian had reason to believe that Carlota could die soon, and as a matter of fact there were several rumors already going around about the demise of the Archduchess. As we know, however, Carlota lived many more years, and when he made it at last, Escobedo probably thought his revelation couldn't do much harm to her, not only because twenty years had already gone by, but also, above all, because the Empress had not regained her sanity in all that time, and there were no indications that she ever would. Ten years later—that, is thirty years after the fall of Querétaro, Gustave Gostkowski, author of *Los últimos momentos de la vida de Maximiliano*, had the opportunity to travel with General Escobedo for several hours—or at least he says so in his book—and when he asked if López had been the Judas that he's made out to be, the old general answered with an emphatic no, that the situation of those under siege in Querétaro was desperate, that they were decimated by typhus and hunger, and that Maximilian decided to send López secretly to offer the surrender of the city. Anyone might assume that what Escobedo told Gostkowski confirmed, in all details, what the same general had said ten years earlier, particularly if we are willing to believe that Escobedo had "a prodigious memory," as the author assures us. But this is not the case, because in his report to General Díaz, Escobedo says that the first—and only—time he spoke with López was the night of May 14th, but in his conversations with Gostkowski, he talks about *three* visits López made to the Republican camp. The first, to propose the surrender of the fortress with the condition that the Archduke be allowed to leave the country. The second, "armed with a document accrediting him without doubt as Maximilian's envoy," to be given the answer. The third, to inform Escobedo that, in any case, Maximilian was giving up the fight. Either Escobedo's memory wasn't as prodigious as Gostkowski claimed, or his own was very weak, or he was prone to fantasy. However, all indications are that Corti gave him and Baron Lago—among others—more credit than Escobedo's official report. Moreover, the document that Escobedo refers to in his report as well as in his alleged conversation with Gostkowski—the letter from Maximilian to López—also showed up twenty years later in the hands of the alleged traitor. As expected, its authenticity was immediately questioned, and as Émile Ollivier points out, Doctor Kaska, "a friend of Maximilian," declared it false, basing his statement on the opinions of four painters he had examine the handwriting. Ollivier refers to the book by the Mexican historian and politician José María Iglesias, *Rectificaciones históricas*, wherein the latter points out that these opinions can hardly be taken seriously. Setién y Llata, on the other hand, reminds us that Iglesias believed that a very bad forgery served the interests of Maximilian admirably by giving his accomplice, "instead of a real safeguard, a ridiculous document that could easily be labeled as false." In other words, Maximilian might very well have done his best to make the document appear false. Ollivier adds that Iglesias, thanks to his sagacity as well as to the lucidity of his arguments, "destroyed the legend of López's treachery forever."

But Ollivier was wrong. From that time on, there have been an abundance of essays, articles, and even whole books—for instance A. Monroy's, *López no fue traidor* (López was not a traitor), and Alfonso Junco's, *La traición de Querétaro, ¿Maximiliano o López?* (The treason at Querétaro: Maximilian or López?)—produced, making a case for or against the Mexican colonel, in which the tiniest and most trivial details are analyzed, in an attempt—or rather in numerous attempts—to prove one theory or the other. For instance, they tell us that on May 14, 1867, the sunset in Mexico City occurred at six-twenty in the evening—the source is the *Galván Almanac*—and therefore it set a few minutes later in Querétaro. But the twilight—in other words, the last light of day—lasts half an hour past sunset. Therefore, when Colonel López says, as he did in his statement, that "on the *night* of May 14th, that unfortunate Prince [Maximilian]" had asked him to get in touch with Escobedo, López is lying. He's lying because the Mexican general informs us that it was seven o'clock in the evening on May 14th when an aide informed him that López was at Colonel Cervantes's tent and that he wished to see him on behalf of Maximilian. So that, in order to be at the Republican camp at seven in the evening, López *had* to leave La Cruz and Querétaro during daylight, and he could not have done this unnoticed.

But, what if López wasn't lying? Did Escobedo lie, then? Or did he only make a mistake about the time? These and many other questions, none of which seem to have definitive answers, have been appended to arguments new and old, and will continue to haunt future treatises on the subject as well. Here's another: Basch tells us that when Maximilian was already a prisoner, he had told the enemy officers several times: "If you were to put López and Márquez in my power, I would set López, a man with a wicked and traitorous nature, free, but I would hang Márquez, who is a traitor in cold blood, and with premeditation." Was this strange attitude provoked by remorse, perhaps? It seems certain as well that López lived most of the rest of his days in near-poverty. What happened to the money he supposedly received for his treachery? Or could the rumor's cited by Ollivier, to the effect that López lost two hundred thousand francs gambling, be true? And, why did Maximilian ask Escobedo to keep the secret not when he gave up his sword on May 15th, but two weeks later when the "secret" would already have been common knowledge? And why haven't the writers who accuse López of forging—and so clumsily—the letter that the Archduke allegedly gave him ever stopped to think that López had twenty years to learn how to copy Maximilian's handwriting and signature? But isn't the letter itself absurd? Why would Maximilian put into writing something he had already asked López in person? And in writing a letter asking that a secret be kept, wasn't Maximilian running the even greater risk that it might be divulged simply through his own acknowledgement that such a secret existed? And whether absurd or not, true or false, why did Miguel López endure twenty-one years of misery before flaunting the letter to the world instead of showing it to people as soon as Maximilian died at Las Campanas Hill? And also, why did Escobedo wait so long to tell the truth himself? The day of the fall of Querétaro, Juárez, who ignored the details of the López affair, beaming with enthusiasm, wrote General Berriozábal: "Long live the Nation! This morning at eight, Querétaro was taken by force." It was said then that López's betrayal detracted from the prestige of the Republican victory, because the city had been handed over, and in no way *taken by force*. But if Maximilian didn't try to escape, how would this make the Juarist victory any more or less impressive? And at any rate, after twenty-one years of being a live Mexican hero, why would General Escobedo decide to cook this story up, if he was lying? Did he think that his revelation neither diminished the heroism of those who had resisted the longest siege in Mexican history, nor deprived the Republic and its generals of their triumph?

And finally: if people exonerate López, does that make Maximilian guilty? Ollivier, with all the support he shows for Juárez's cause, thinks that destroying the legend of López's betrayal doesn't require replacing it with Maximilian's betraying his generals, because all the Archduke wanted to do in that situation was to avoid "a useless and frightful holocaust." If we assume that was the case, then of course Maximilian's silence did *not* betray López. But it did hurt him nonetheless, and it hurt him badly. So much so, in fact, that it should have been Carlota who demanded of her husband: "Oh, Maximilian! What have you done to our friend López?" As far as the generals, the officers, the troops, the volunteers, the dead, and the wounded are concerned, weren't they betrayed when Maximilian balked at an honorable surrender and provoked a humiliating handover of the city? Wasn't it a betrayal of their faith, their courage, their loyalty, their sacrifices? There may not be any answers as definitive and direct as a yes or a no to such questions. The fact is that if Escobedo is telling the truth and Maximilian asked him not to divulge the secret until after Carlota's death, the Archduke must have left this world with a somewhat clearer conscience—though with a heavier heart—because on June 15th, four days before his execution, Mejía informed him that, according to news from Europe, the Empress had passed away.

Given the impossibility of reaching a firm conclusion on these matters, one might have thought that the authors who have written about the melodrama of Querétaro, many years after the fact—thirty, fifty, or even a century later— would have informed their readers of all the uncertainties and polemics on the subject. But, curiously, this has not always been the case. Corti implies that such questions exist, but in spite of calling Émile Ollivier's work "magisterial," he silently disagrees with his assessment of López, and even though he includes Iglesias's books in his bibliography, he doesn't cite him in the text. Furthermore, in his *Die Tragödie eines Kaisers*—that is, in his revised and abridged version of *Maximilian und Charlotte von Mexiko*, Corti adds a reference to the "eleven *reales* a head," the alleged price for which López had sold Maximilian and his troops. It would seem then that Corti prefers not to doubt López's treachery, and this also appears to be the position of those authors who sympathize with Maximilian and for whom having a traitor is more convenient and perhaps even more romantic a climax to his story. And if the traitor was a Mexican, so much the better—it was even convenient for Louis Napoleon himself, who, in his letter of condolence to Franz Joseph, dated August 2, 1867, claimed to be "inconsolable" for a man who had fought alone against "a party that had triumphed only by treachery," as the Emperor of the French put it.

And if we say, "if the traitor was a Mexican, so much the better," it's because almost all the authors who have decided that their readers should be encouraged to believe that Miguel López was a traitor, are *not* Mexicans, but Europeans. At one extreme is Corti, whose honesty didn't allow him to ignore Ollivier's and Iglesias's allegations, but who doesn't put any stock in them, and says so emphatically. We find writers like Gene Smith, Castelot, or Haslip in the middle, who don't bother going into any detail about the existing doubts. At the other extreme we find the fanatical authors who manifest a visceral hate for all Mexicans—López as much as Juárez, Santa Anna, and Almonte—and they insist it was they, the Mexicans, who caused the downfall of the Archduke, and not he who caused his own. And then, there are those other writers, who in order to dramatize the alleged treachery, narrate things that never happened: some perhaps because they've misinterpreted some existing information, and others simply because they had the urge to try their hands at fiction. Thus, we see how Dr. J. P. des Vaulx, in his book *Maximilien—Empereur du Mexique ou Le Martyr de Querétaro*, tells the reader that at Las Campanas Hill, Maximilian exclaimed: "Tell López I forgive his treachery. Tell all of Mexico that I forgive their crime." And immediately, Des Vaulx adds, "His Majesty shook the hand of Abbot Fischer." Maximilian said no such thing before dying, and of course Fischer was not present at the execution. The man who consoled the Emperor in his last minutes—or, rather, the one whom the Emperor had to console in his last minutes—was, as is now known, Father Soria.

Apropos of Soria, and to close this chapter on the traitorous friend, it's worthwhile to call attention to a statement of this priest cited by Ollivier, and ignored by the great majority of writers on the subject of Maxmilian. "Lopez," said Soria, "did only as he was ordered." Whether Maximilian sympathizers like it or not, the most logical interpretation of these words would be: bound by the secret of confession, Soria could not reveal openly what Maximilian might have been able or might have wanted to tell about the night of May 14th to 15th. But what he could indeed have done was to insinuate, with a statement such as the above, that he knew the truth. And why should he bother doing this? Perhaps because his conscience told him that if he couldn't do anything more to save the soul of the deceased godfather, Maximilian, there was still something he could do to save the honor of the living friend, Miguel López.

•

There are also doubts and contradictions about other episodes of the siege and its aftermath, like the scene that's said to have taken place between Colonel Palacios and Princess Salm-Salm in her private quarters. In the part dedicated to Querétaro in her book, *Ten Years of my Life*, the Princess omits it; but her forgetfulness is more than understandable if, in effect, as people say, seeing everything lost, the Princess couldn't think of anything else she could do to convince the Mexican colonel to allow Maximilian and her husband to escape but to invite the military man to the hotel where she was staying, lock the door, and start to unbutton her bra. It seems Palacios, terrified, threatened to jump out the window, and the Princess had no other choice but to unlock the door, through which the flustered colonel made a hasty escape.

But if the Princess wasn't the one who told this story, and there wasn't a single witness to the incident, how do we know about it? Who started the legend? Palacios? Hardly. A colonel in the Mexican army—who we can assume boasted of being a tough and courageous man—wasn't about to tell his comrades, pals, and subordinates that he was ready to jump off a balcony because a beautiful foreign princess, the beautiful Yankee known to everyone, had offered him her splendid body. Fuentes Mares solves the problem, citing several witnesses, and he tells us that the night Escobedo ordered the Princess and all other foreign representatives to be expelled from Querétaro, Agnes Salm-Salm—in a sudden impulse, befitting her temperament—began undressing in front of the officers who went to apprehend her, and offered herself to whomever helped her save the Emperor. She didn't find any takers.

Balconies and corsets aside, there isn't the slightest doubt the Princess did something else in order to save the life of Ferdinand Maximilian, and that was to kneel down before Benito Juárez to beg his mercy. This episode took place at the Government Palace in San Luis Potosí, where the Republican regime had set up its headquarters, and in the prologue to the Spanish edition of Salm-Salm's memoirs, Daniel Moreno reminds us that this moment was immortalized in a painting by a well-known Mexican artist, and that the scene includes "the . . . figure of the lawyer Sebastián Lerdo de Tejada, who, with a Mephisthophelean look, is standing behind the President denying the pardon."

Before getting to Mexico and Querétaro, the Princess's memoirs begin with the several trips she made through the American Union, and she talks about the spiritualist fever that got hold of the Yankees during that time, of the professional embalmers who followed the American armies during the Civil War, and of the floating hospitals that sailed white and silent down the Mississippi. Her lapdog Jimmy, who seems to have developed a noise phobia in Querétaro due to the sounds of bullets and drums, already appears in these early pages. Jimmy fell in love with the sofa President Benito Juárez had in his San Luis Potosí office, and would sprawl there every time the Princess went to ask something of the President. (This is the fourth dog in this chapter.) In Agnes's memoirs, we also read that on a trip from Nashville to Bridgeport, Jimmy jumped off the train during a stop in the middle of the countryside: the train began to move, the Princess pulled the alarm cord, the train stopped, panicking its passengers and crew, and Jimmy, running wildly behind the caboose, jumped onto the train again, and into his mistress's lap. She scolded him, and the conductor arrived to scold the Princess, but she shouted at the man, gave him a piece of her mind, accusing him of being inhumane and unimportant, and the conductor ended up feeling so ashamed that he begged her pardon. A woman capable of doing this, of following her husband to Mexico in order to save an Empire, of jumping over trenches at a gallop holding her yellow parasol while bullets whistled around her loose black hair, capable of facing Leonardo Márquez in Mexico and Porfirio Díaz in Puebla—and when the Oaxacan general ordered her to leave the country, capable of answering him that he would have to put her in chains or shoot her before she would leave the country without seeing Escobedo, whom she also confronted in his campaign tent outside of Querétaro . . . of course a woman like that was capable of undressing in front of a Colonel or kneeling down before a President, and capable too of planning, as she did, Maximilian's escape, and his prospective departure from Mexico, down to the last detail.

In reality, however, there weren't so many details involved in this escape, nor were they particularly complex. At Agnes Salm-Salm's insistence, Maximilian acquiesced to having Prussia's representative, Baron Magnus, come to Querétaro. It was expected—though they would have been there merely for appearances' sake—that the other European diplomats who had once represented their respective countries in the Empire would join Magnus on this visit. Soon the Austrian Lago, Hoorickx the Belgian, and Curtopassi the Italian joined the Prussian. Forest, the special envoy of the French ministry, arrived a short time later. The Princess wanted to count on the involvement of some or all of them: either to put concerted pressure on the Juárez government, or else to organize the escape. One of Agnes's ideas was to have the foreign powers agree to pay a ransom for Maximilian, or else guarantee the payment of the Mexican war debt if the Archduke's life was spared. The Princess was sure she could count on the support of those faraway countries on the other side of the Atlantic, since Maximilian was supposed to be considered something like "Europe's Cousin" at the time. The idea fell through, because there was no way the Republican government would accept that sort of offer. Escape, then, was the only solution left for Maximilian, as Colonel Villanueva assured Agnes.

Baron Magnus considered escape to be madness, and he said so to the Princess, who soon realized the conduct of the foreign representatives in Querétaro was only helping to hasten the catastrophe. Because she was an American, Agnes tells us, and therefore "not familiar with European ideas," she understood the Mexicans much better than the ministers. Furthermore, Agnes underscores that as Europeans they did not believe that the government of Benito Juárez would actually dare to take Maximilian's life, because it would be an act that "all the European powers would try to avenge." But the Princess knew very well that Europe was no worry for Juárez and his cabinet, and that if the Archduke were condemned to die—as indeed he would be—the sentence would be carried out. Agnes Salm-Salm would have confirmed her opinion, if she had known the statements made by Juárez's representative in Washington: "No one in Europe would give us credit for our magnanimity," said Matías Romero, "because weak nations are not supposed to be magnanimous . . ."

The first escape attempt was set for the night of June 3rd, but the day before, a telegram was received in Querétaro announcing the arrival of Baron Magnus and Maximilian's two defenders, de la Torre and Riva Palacio. Though Prince and Princess Salm-Salm didn't see this as sufficient reason, Maximilian asked that the plan be scrapped. Did Maximilian really want to escape? We're told that once he was a prisoner at Las Teresitas, he would talk openly with his friends about the different possibilities of flight, and that even in his last days he imagined himself on board the Austrian corvette *Elizabeth* anchored in Veracruz at that time under the command of Captain Groeller. He made plans for the future with his secretary Blasio: he wanted to go to London first, and then to Miramare to write the history of his reign. He also made plans for trips to Greece, Naples, and Turkey. But a few minutes later he would come back to reality and begin talking about the embalming of his body or about his will. It was then that he accepted the fact that someone else would be the one to write his history. "You are the only one who has the possibility of returning to Europe," he told Dr. Basch one day, "so you write that history and do me justice. I suggest you title it: *The Hundred Days of the Mexican Empire.*"

Be that as it may, Agnes Salm-Salm *did* know what she wanted, and she wasn't about to let anything stop her, much less the ineptitude or fear of the European ministers. They would serve to guarantee the promissory notes. It was lack of money that made her seize on this plan. If, during the siege, Maximilian had already complained about his lack of cash, and had said that in the future he "would only keep one servant and would sell his horse and go on foot to save money," now that he was defeated and a prisoner, he certainly didn't have a single tlaco, and it would be impossible for him to deposit one hundred thousand pesos in Señor Rubio's bank, as Agnes had first suggested. But what could still be done was to create some bills of exchange or promissory notes signed by Maximilian and endorsed by the foreign ministers. Maximilian agreed, but not the ministers. In the final analysis the Emperor signed two promissory notes, each for one hundred thousand pesos, that would be paid by the House of Austria, though only if the escape succeeded. During the first days of Maximilian's imprisonment some Republican officers had asked for money to allow the Archduke to escape, but none of them had had the ability to actually organize a getaway, and they were the ones who made escapes, with money in their pockets. But these had only been small quantities: five hundred pesos here, two thousand there. Now it was a matter of bribing, and with substantial amounts, the two men who truly had the power and the means to allow the Archduke to escape: Colonel Palacios, who was "supreme commander of the prison," and Colonel Villanueva, "commander of all guards in the city." Each one of them would receive one hundred thousand pesos, an amount that for those poor devils—Agnes Salm-Salm tells us, for instance, that Palacios was an Indian who could hardly read and write—must have seemed an immense fortune.

Baron Lago, the Austrian representative, was the only one to put his signature on the promissory notes, but his signature disappeared very quickly. Once the foreign representatives met, they convinced him to take it off, and one of them took a pair of scissors and simply cut it out. At any rate, Colonel Palacios wasn't about to be seduced by some pieces of paper with unintelligible scribbles, and not because he was ignorant as Agnes Salm-Salm says. Given the circumstances, and as Agnes herself says, a pocketful of gold would have spoken a more persuasive language, not only to a semi-illiterate Indian—if Palacios really was one—but to any knowledgeable officer willing to risk his honor and his neck to save the life of a foreign invader who had already fallen from grace and had been abandoned by nearly everyone. Palacios returned the promissory note to Agnes who then gave him the Emperor's signet ring and begged him to give it to Max in his cell. This was the agreed-upon sign in case the plans for an escape failed. But Palacios wasn't willing to do the Princess this favor either, and after trying on the ring, he returned it to her. Agnes then gave the ring to Doctor Basch so he could give it to the Emperor. It was June 13, 1867. That night Baron Lago and Monsieur Hoorickx fled Querétaro leaving behind their luggage and unwittingly anticipating the wishes of Escobedo, who decided to order the expulsion from Querétaro of all foreign representatives implicated in the escape attempt. Escobedo also summoned the Princess to advise her she would be leaving the city in a few hours. And so it was. That same night Agnes Salm-Salm left on a stagecoach bound for San Luis Potosí with her chambermaid Margarita, her lapdog Jimmy, and her six-shooter.

The trial of "Fernando Maximiliano" and his two generals, Miguel Miramón and Tomás Mejía, had begun the previous day at the Iturbide Theater. The Mexican historian, José Fuentes Mares, toward the end of his book *Juárez y el Imperio*, becomes a bit of a novelist, creating and imagining situations and dialogues. He describes a scene between the Emperor and the Frenchman Forest in which Maximilian categorically refuses to attend the trial: "I shall be judged tomorrow, is that not so?" he asks the French representative, "Well, I'm not going to appear before that tribunal. Never, listen to me, Forest! I will run any risk before doing that. I will not sit on the bench for criminals. Never, listen well!" And though Forest took care to remind his Majesty that the bench for the accused had been a "pedestal" for Louis XVI and Marie Antoinette, Maximilian got his way and he was judged *in absentia*: the Chief Medical Officer of the Republican Army, Doctor Rivadeneira, certified that his health would not allow him to attend. And after all, it was not a lie: Maximilian was very ill.

Those who at all costs want to prove that Maximilian was murdered in Querétaro have found proofs in many of the colorful or unpleasant details surrounding the trial that, according to them, substantiate their claims. First of all, they say it is scandalous that the trial was held in a theater. But Querétaro was a small city, a trial of such enormous importance had never before been held there—never once during the entire history of Mexico—and it is probable, given its size, that the most appropriate place was the theater. That the hall was named after the first emperor of Mexico and that he was shot dead by his fellow countrymen was just one of the many ironies that plagued Maximilian throughout his life. But the Juaristas had nothing to do with the name of the theater.

However, given that it *was* a theater, "the auditorium was brightly lit as if for a play," wrote Forest to Alphonse Danó. Many wanted exactly that from the trial: the staging of a memorized drama, a bloody farce in which the counselors, the prosecutor, the judge, and the audience, the members of the jury and the accused himself, were accomplices and actors: they all knew what the ending would be, tragic and inevitable.

The ending was in effect, foreseen, and not because the drama took place in Mexico and Mexico was a country of savages, but because in any European country—or in any country at all, at that time (and even in ours)—the outcome would have been the same: Maximilian was a foreign usurper of an established government—and a constitutional government to boot—and had been the main instrument of a foreign invasion that supported him in establishing a second and illegal regime. Of course, Europe certainly didn't consider this outcome civilized. As a matter of fact, most of the foreigners who participated in the adventure weren't willing to recognize anything in Mexico, or Juárez and his government, as deserving of that particular adjective. For instance, in his memoirs, Prince Salm-Salm is surprised that Escobedo didn't carry out his "sinister promises" against him, Felix, after he had participated in a second attempt to allow Maximilian to escape, and adds that this—not fulfilling the threat of a particular punishment—would not have happened in a more civilized country—thus proving Matías Romero right.

What's astonishing is that, in spite of everything, Maximilian almost came out of the adventure alive, once he was declared guilty,—though three jury members voted for the death penalty, the other three voted for exile in perpetuity. This tie, which was resolved with the vote of Colonel Platón Sánchez, the presiding judge, shows that its members were not as biased as some may have thought, and that the Juárez government didn't need to grease the palms of the jury members—as des Vaulx says it did—so that they would condemn Maximilian to death.

In an entry dated June 13th, Dr. Basch quotes Maximilian in his diary, referring to the jury, saying: "May God forgive me, but it seems to me they've just selected men who had better-looking uniforms, so that at least they're decent to look at." It is impossible to ascertain, at this time, the backgrounds of all the members of the tribunal. But we do have some information about the presiding judge and the prosecutor. The latter, Manuel Aspiros, had distinguished himself as a lawyer and politician in his native state of Puebla, and after 1867 and until his death held several diplomatic positions when he was Mexico's Ambassador in Washington. There is nothing to indicate he wasn't capable of being a prosecutor.

Colonel Platón Sánchez, described by some authors as "a man in an elegant uniform with kid gloves," died a few months after the trial in a place called Rancho de Lobos, murdered by some soldiers of the Empress's Regiment who had joined the Republican Army and were under the command of Miguel López. He didn't have the time, therefore, to make himself better known, after having secured a place in Mexico's history by the mere fact of being the presiding judge at Maximilian's trial. But there are aspects of Colonel Sánchez's background that appear in the diary General Francisco P. Troncoso wrote about the siege of Puebla in 1863. Troncoso could not at the time have imagined the sort of immortality reserved for Platón Sánchez, beyond pointing out, "the boundless courage" of the then-captain, referring to him as a man of extraordinary generosity.

On the other hand, Maximilian's defense was in the hands of two of the most prestigious lawyers in Mexico at that time. One was Mariano Riva Palacio—father of the Republican general who authored "Bye-bye, Mamá Carlota"—and to whom Maximilian had at one time offered the position of Minister of the Interior. The other one was Rafael Martínez de la Torre, who turned down his honorarium for the defense, and because of this, Emperor Franz Joseph sent him a silver dinner service as a gift. Together they left Eulalio Ortega and Jesús María Vázquez in charge of preparing the "details of the legal defense" in Querétaro while they traveled to San Luis Potosí to see President Juárez. Their goals were: one, to ask for more time to prepare the defense; two, to ask the president for Maximilian's pardon.

Riva Palacio and Martínez de la Torre complained bitterly about the short time they'd been given to prepare the defense, and seeking more, they lost precious time. They wanted a month, and Juárez only allowed a three-day extension. Nevertheless, the trial did begin a month after the fall of Querétaro, and everyone knew from the beginning that Maximilian would be tried—just as they knew what the charges against him would be, and what the jury's most likely verdict would be, since Maximilian had signed his own death penalty warrant when he issued the Decree of October 3rd. The fact is, just before the trial was to begin, Maximilian's counselors sent a long and moving letter to President Juárez attacking what they described as the terrible and monstrous Law of January 25th, but President Juárez reminded them that the law had been passed before the Archduke traveled to Mexico, and that, besides, an envoy of the Republican Government, Don Jesús Terán, had visited the Archduke at his castle in Miramare to warn him about the risks and dangers of his venture.

With regard to the pardon, Maximilian's defenders made an error. They asked for it before the verdict, and the government naturally responded that a sentence that hasn't been pronounced can't be nullified. After the trial, when the defense pressed again for a presidential pardon, Juárez answered that the "law and the sentence" were at that moment "inexorable" because the "public welfare" demanded it. This same public welfare, the president added, "could also advise us to spill less blood in future, and this will be the greatest pleasure of my life." We must note here that, after the fall of Querétaro and the Empire, very few people were actually executed: Maximilian, Mejía, Miramón, Méndez, O'Horan, and Vidaurri, among them.

A careful reading of the so-called *Case of Ferdinand Maximilian of Habsburg Who Has Titled Himself Emperor of Mexico and of His so-called Generals Miguel Miramón and Tomás Mejía, His Accomplices in Crimes against the Independence and Security of the Nation, Law and Order, International Law, and Individual Rights*, a book of over six hundred pages crowded with text, can help dispel doubts about the legal and moral qualifications of the prosecutor and Maximilian's attorneys. The manuscript was lost for eleven years. In 1878, a general by the name of Tolentino—warned of contraband cacao and cinnamon being smuggled into Guadalajara in a shipment of army supplies—ordered a thorough search: the contraband was found, and there too, yellowish and brittle and smelling of cinnamon and chocolate, the manuscript appeared. "Not even air should touch this!" shouted the overjoyed General Tolentino. Thanks to this incredible find, and to the fact that, indeed, it had been preserved so well, away from the air, a document of enormous historical value was recovered, one in which a reader can appreciate all the efforts of the defense attorneys to save the Archduke, and also of the prosecutor to dignify the trial as a whole. Also, we can see the legal subtleties to which the Emperor and his lawyers resorted: one, a challenge to the legality of the tribunal, because the charges against Maximilian were "political in nature"; two, an emphasis on the *retroactive abdication* that would have taken place at the moment he was defeated and arrested; three, the insistence on Maximilian's pure intentions and good faith. The verdict of the jury was unanimous, and the Emperor and his two generals were found guilty. There were thirteen charges against Maximilian—again, that unlucky number—and in his case, as has been pointed out, the sentence of death was decided by the vote of the presiding judge.

Querétaro's Iturbide Theater, a smaller replica of the Gran Teatro Nacional in Mexico City, and on whose ceiling, among clouds and golden auras, seven Mexican playwrights and two Spaniards were portrayed—one of the latter being Maximilian's friend, José Zorrilla—had a seating capacity of two thousand, and, as Foster pointed out, it's probable that "the auditorium was illuminated as if for a play," since there was no reason to conduct a trial in dim light. Moreover, it's possible that tickets were sold to the public, as some authors claim, but in any case this must have been done by some cunning devil acting on his own behalf, not for the government's; and it's also possible that some people were eating during the trial, though this would hardly be a characteristic unique to the Mexican people. In France, during the Terror, there were women knitting and eating while the heads of those condemned by the Revolution were falling into a basket a few meters away. Details here would be superfluous—Harding says that those in attendance at Maximilian's trial were eating cherimoyas and pine nuts—it makes little difference whether the French women in question were eating oranges or roasted chestnuts next to the gate to the other world, which according to some was invented by Dr. Joseph-Ignace Guillotin, and according to others by Dr. Antoine Louis.

On June 15th, as we've mentioned, General Mejía went into Maximilian's cell and said he had news of Carlota's demise in Europe. It appears this was a lie concocted by Mejía and Miramón to ease Maximilian's passage into the other world. Basch tells us that though this was a terrible blow to the Emperor, at the same time it made it "less painful for him to die." With the Empress "among the angels," Maximilian had one less link to this world, or so he said. Basch tells us that at twelve o'clock in the afternoon, on June 16th, the "new Prosecutor González" showed up at the Teresitas Convent and, standing at the threshold of Maximilian's cell, read the sentence. Dr. Basch states that Maximilian listened to the announcement "pale but smiling," and then turned to his doctor and friend and said: "The appointed hour is three—you have more than three hours to do whatever you need to do, so you won't be rushed." He then dictated a letter to Blasio addressed to Don Carlos Rubio, in which he asked him for a loan for the embalming and transportation of his body. The three condemned men heard Mass and received the Holy Communion in Miramón's cell. Just before three, Maximilian took off his wedding ring and gave it to Basch. "Tell my mother," the Emperor implored him, "that I have fulfilled my duty as a soldier and that I die a Christian." He gave Blasio his tiepin and his cuff links and Prince Salm-Salm his hair brushes and other personal items. "But the clock sounded three," Basch tells us, "and no one showed up to take the Emperor and the generals. In fact, no one was going to take them that day, and the wedding ring returned to Maximilian's finger, because in San Luis Potosí, Prussia's representative, Baron Magnus, had managed to get Juárez to postpone the execution to the 19th of June at seven A.M.

And it is here that Princess Salm-Salm reappears with her chambermaid Margarita and her lapdog Jimmy to earn an everlasting place in Mexico's history as the beautiful foreign lady who fell to her knees before President Benito Juárez and begged him to save Maximilian's life.

As was to be expected, other foreigners intervened with the same objective. Garibaldi sent Juárez a message in which he asked for clemency. Victor Hugo did the same, though it is said his letter arrived after the execution. At any rate, one cannot suppose that it would have influenced Juárez's decision. As far as Agnes Salm-Salm is concerned, the first thing she did was to exhort Johnson, the American president, to ask at least for a new suspension of the sentence. Juárez, however, was sorry he had postponed the execution date. Foreign journalists had said that the only thing the heartless Indian, "thirsting for blood," had wanted to do was to "prolong the suffering of the Archduke." And the American president was powerless: Wydenbruck, the Austrian minister in Washington, had asked Secretary of State Seward for his government's intervention, and Johnson had wired Campbell, the new American representative to the Juárez government, ordering him to move immediately from New Orleans—where he had taken refuge—to San Luis Potosí to intercede for the life of the Archduke. But Campbell, like Baron Lago, was deathly afraid, and he preferred resigning his position to actually traveling to Mexico.

On the day before the execution, at eight o'clock in the evening, Agnes Salm-Salm asked for an audience with Benito Juárez, who saw her immediately. The President, the Princess tells us, "looked pale and suffering himself." Agnes dropped to her knees before Juárez and asked him to pardon Maximiliano. The President tried to help her get up, but the Princess clung to his legs. Juárez, writes Agnes, his eyes wet, said the following:

"I am grieved, madame, to see you thus on your knees before me; but if all the kings and all the queens of the world were in your place I could not spare that life. It is not I who take it, it is the people and the law, and if I should not do its will the people would take it and mine also."

Even though Juárez—who always seemed sure of what he said, at least about himself—once asserted, "Revenge is not my forte," some European historians do not believe him, and preferred to see in his inflexibility—"Never before had an attempt against the Principle of Nationalities been punished so quickly and horribly," wrote Émile Ollivier—an act of revenge at the individual and conscious level as well as at the collective and unconscious: Moctezuma was finally getting even with Cortés. However, the Mexican Fuentes Mares holds that it was a matter of settling another, almost as ancient, dispute once and for all: the endless struggle between liberals and conservatives. Almost a half-century of civil war, says Fuentes Mares, demanded this blood. According to the Mexican, the death of the Archduke was therefore an internal political necessity of the Benito Juárez government.

On Agnes's way out of the presidential office, she found "more than two hundred ladies of San Luis assembled, who came also to pray for the lives of the three condemned" in the antechamber. A short time later, Juárez saw Miramón's wife, who came with her children and who fainted when the President told her there was nothing to be done. Baron Magnus also realized the futility of these actions, and he soon left for Querétaro with Dr. Szänger—who, in accordance with the Prussian minister's wishes, could take part in the embalming of the body of the Emperor.

Ferdinand Maximilian, besides writing individual messages to his lawyers thanking them for their "vigorous and valiant defense," also sent a letter to Benito Juárez. José Fuentes Mares tells us that though the letter was written on June 18th, Maximilian dated it the 19th so that it would bear the date of his death. In it the Archduke declared: "If this sacrifice of mine can contribute to the peace and prosperity of my new homeland, I gladly face the loss of my life," and he asked clemency for Miramón, for Mejía, and for all the rest: "I entreat you most solemnly, and with the sincerity appropriate to the moment in which I find myself, that my blood be the last to be spilled . . ."

The answer to Maximilian's request arrived in Querétaro at five o'clock in the afternoon of the 18th, according to Dr. Basch: there would be no pardon for his generals. At eight, the Emperor went to bed and Dr. Basch stayed by his side. The Emperor's doctor relates that, around eleven-thirty at night, Dr. Rivadeneira and General Escobedo showed up. Basch left them alone with Maximilian, and when Escobedo left with an autographed picture of the Emperor, Maximilian told his doctor: "What Escobedo wanted was to say goodbye to me. I would rather have kept on sleeping."

And he did: the Emperor went back to sleep, but only for a few hours. He woke up at three-thirty in the morning. It was June 19th. Father Soria arrived at four o'clock. Basch tells us that at five Maximilian heard Mass with his two generals, and had breakfast at a quarter after six: meat, coffee, half a bottle of red wine, and bread.

Maximilian gave his wedding ring back to Basch and also a scapular he took out of his vest pocket asking him to give them to his mother. Other chronicles, however, say that the scapular Basch took to Vienna was pierced by one of the bullets fired at Las Campanas Hill, and if it did happen that way, Maximilian, of course, never gave it to Basch, and it was he who took it from the dead body. Be that as it may, the fact is that Dr. Basch carried a number of objects the Emperor gave him back to Miramare and Austria, and, according to accounts, among them were the scapular, with or without bullet holes, and the ring destined for Max's mother. Basch brought back the Knight's Cross of the Order of the Eagle and a gold medal with the image of the Virgin Mary for the Emperor of Austria. Maximilian's sister-in-law, the Empress Elisabeth, received a fan. It seems Max's mother, Sophie, also received a picture of Maximilian embroidered by the ladies of Querétaro. Archduke Charles Louis got the signet ring, and his brother Louis Victor a silver medal with another image of the Virgin. Victoria, Queen of England, was given a medallion containing a lock of Empress Carlota's hair. Queen Caroline Augusta received a rosary. To Dr. Zelley, chief medical officer of the Imperial House, went Max's copy of César Cantú's *History of the Italians*. To Leopold II of Belgium the Order of Guadalupe that Maximilian had around the neck when he entered Querétaro, and to his brother, the Count of Flanders, his watch and chain. To Radouch, a ship's captain, a small hand mirror used by the Emperor. To Princess Maria Auersperg, former lady-in-waiting to Carlota, a fan made of palm leaves. To Count Hadik de Futak, who had been Maximilian's Grand Chamberlain when he was an archduke, a pair of shirt studs, and to Marquis de Corio, some gold spurs. Basch also brought the Grand Chamberlain the hat that Maximilian had worn during his incarceration in Querétaro, and that he'd given to Tüdös when he arrived at Las Campanas Hill to be shot. Maximilian had asked that it be taken to the museum at Miramare.

At six o'clock in the morning, four thousand men, under the orders of General Jesús Díaz de León, lined up in a square at the foot of the hill, waiting for the Archduke and his generals. At six-thirty Colonel Palacios showed up at Maximilian's cell with the escort. Outside of the convent there were three hired cars numbered ten, thirteen, and sixteen. This time at least, Maximilian avoided the unlucky number: he climbed aboard the first car with Father Soria. Mejía and Father Ochoa were in the second one, and Miramón with Father Ladrón de Guevara went into the third.

The men in charge of escorting them to the Las Campanas Hill were from the Battalion of Supreme Powers and from the Galeana Light Infantry. According to contemporary accounts, a squadron of lancers was at the head of the procession. An infantry battalion marched at the sides of the condemned men in two rows of four soldiers each. A group of Franciscans followed the carriages with lit candles and holy water. At the rear there were some men carrying three black coffins and three crosses, also black.

The streets of Querétaro were empty, and all the windows and doors of the city remained closed.

2. Ballad of the Coup de Grâce

It was in sixty-seven
It seems just like today
In the City of Querétaro
Our Emp'ror passed away.

A nineteenth day of June
That the world never forgot
We carried out the sentence:
Our President had him shot.

Carlota was nowhere near:
Of the execution unaware;
And being quite insane
Nothing of it did she hear.

1867, how can I forget that year. If it seems like I was only born for that, to live in that year, that 19th day of June, with a rifle in my hands and a bullet in it—if it seems like the only reason I became a heretic and then a soldier, that I learned to aim a gun and squeeze a trigger, to shoot the heads off the statues on churches, was to be able to participate in that day—I have to wonder now why I didn't have this revelation earlier, why the Lord didn't warn me about my purpose back when I first joined up with the Red Chinaca, stealing snatches of brocade rags from all the Saint Josephs, not just because the general had ordered us to—so that he could have the pleasure of covering his horse with saints' vestments and trimming his velvet slippers with the pearls that I stole with my own hands from a statue of the Christ of the Three Powers—but also because I liked doing it, because what could be better than undressing virgins and tearing the silk tunics off Archangel Michaels? 1867, how can I forget that year, any more than I can forget the city of Querétaro with its white churches and houses that I saw for the first time from Cimatario Hill when I arrived with General Escobedo's troops to begin the siege. The rifle burned in my hands and I felt my index finger itching to shoot and kill those sanctimonious traitors to our nation, as I called them, to kill the Usurper, as I called him. And I fired my rifle one more time, the last time, on Las Campanas Hill.

Very early in the morning
The Emperor was awake
And his confidant the priest
His confession heard him make.

And as he left the convent
He bid everyone good-bye
And said, "How glad I am
On so bright a day to die."

The cortege made its way.
Towards Las Campanas Hill
And arriving there they found
A squad prepared to kill.

And if I could forget. If I could possibly forget that year and that day. If by some miracle my memory went blank, I'm sure that my guilty conscience would force me to make it up all over again from scratch, with all its details exact, and that I would end up believing it was all true, that it really happened that way. I would imagine a clear, sunny morning in June. I would imagine that at the time I was getting up, at the sound of reveille, the Emperor was confessing to Father Soria. That while I answered the call of nature behind some magueys, the Emperor, in his black frockcoat, heard Mass with Miramón and Mejía in the Teresitas Convent chapel. That while I breakfasted on a cup of coffee and a cigarette, sitting on a gun carriage, the Emperor was leaving the convent where he had been imprisoned since he had been sentenced as a traitor to the nation and the Constitution, and he looked at the completely cloudless sky, a sky that promised a hot day, and was saying, "I, Maximilian, always wanted to die on such a morning." And overhead, some green ducks flew by quacking. And I would convince myself that all of that was true: the three black coaches sent by the President of the Republic awaiting Maximilian, along with Miramón and Mejía. The cortege that passed through the streets of Querétaro in total silence—at the time that I was handed my weapon—escorted by an infantry battalion and a cavalry squadron. The cortege that reached the outskirts of the city at the time I finished polishing my rifle barrel. General Mejía's wife who ran weeping after the black carriages, holding a baby in her arms. I would imagine that, around ten minutes before seven on such a clear, blue morning, the cortege arrived at the foot of Las Campanas Hill, and that the squad was already waiting there, the men selected from the Nuevo León Battalion to carry out the execution. I would imagine that I was one of them. Afterwards, I would make all of this up, dragging my sorrow behind me for years . . .

On the black coach that he rode
One of the doors became stuck
So, having made his decision
Out the window the Emperor snuck

Like Jesus Christ at Calvary
The Emperor seemed there:
Juárez his Pontius Pilate
And López Judas, in despair.

To his right side there was Mejía
Miramón the left side had
Like Jesus 'tween the two thieves:
A good one and a bad.

Please don't aim at my face,
He begged the riflemen;
And then he handed out coins:
A gold piece for each hand.

But if they say to me then, "And you, sir, why do you make up so many stories? Why so many lies and deceptions? Who do you think will believe that you were one of the men chosen for the firing squad that killed Ferdinand Maximilian of Habsburg?" The fiacre door wouldn't open so Maximilian had to get out through the window. "And what about the stories we hear, like the one about the ounce of gold that Emperor Maximilian himself supposedly gave you all to aim well and not hit his face?" They stood them with their backs to an adobe wall that had been used as a Republican redoubt. "So why these malicious stories? Where do you get all this nonsense?" Maximilian handed his gold watch to Father Soria, in which he kept Carlota's portrait, to give to the Empress, who had gone mad at Miramare (did he know she was still alive?). "And at what time, on what day, in what year did you see the three condemned men kneeling in front of three priests for absolution—be specific!" He handed his kerchief to his Hungarian cook. "And who do you think will swallow this idiocy—that you, a confirmed blasphemer for so many years, who liked to yank off the saints' wire haloes to play horseshoes with them over the necks of liquor bottles, suddenly started to pray that morning of June 19, 1867?" He sent his rosary to his brother, Archduke Karl. "Praying for what, after so many years without praying—since you were a child, as you said, when you stopped being a saint like your mother to become a nonbeliever like your father and join up to fight against religion and the clergy?" He sent his scapular to his mother. "To which saints did you pray, or which virgins? You who took such pleasure in telling us how, after you left off clinging to your mother's skirts, you went after the priests' instead, since you liked nothing better than to lift the priests' skirts and make them march to the rhythm of the Red Chinaca drums as you whipped them." And he gave me this gold coin; with it I made a medal; with the medal I made a heart-shaped ex-voto. "To what apostles did you pray, since you told us that after you stopped clinging to your mother's skirts and had finished with the priests', you went after the stone virgins' skirts, since you liked nothing better—and not just because of the general's orders!—than to lift up the petticoats of the holy effigies, to show people that, if they were virgins, it was because they never had the apparatus to become anything else . . ." And when he gave me the coin he said, "Don't aim at my face." "Who'll believe all those tales?" If they ask me all that, if they turn me this way and that. If they question everything I tell them, from the blue sky of that morning down to the make of the American percussion rifles we used, from the black fiacre carrying the Emperor down to the heart-shaped ex-voto that I made and then later melted down to gold-plate this bullet that I have in my pistol, I'll tell them, "All right," that's fine; I won't contradict them; I'll play along and I'll tell them it's true. That is, I'll tell them I was lying.

> Then he turned to face them,
> Ceding the place of honor
> To his general, Miramón
> Recognizing his great valor.
>
> Then he parted his whiskers
> Leaving his breast exposed,
> And for all those who there gathered read
> A short speech he'd composed.
>
> He asked them to forgive him
> And said, "I'll do the same
> I came for Mexico's welfare,
> And not for gold or fame.
>
> I came because they called me
> To be your Emperor.
> You were the ones who crowned me:
> I did not usurp your power."

Yes, it's all a lie. It's wasn't me, gentlemen, I swear. When I was born, I wasn't born. My mother wasn't my mother—I swear by her memory! When I was a saint, I wasn't a saint. Then, when I stopped being one, I did not stop. When

I violated the churches and the altars, I was not violating them. When I saw that Maximilian at Las Campanas Hill was like another Christ being crucified, I didn't see it. When I understood that Maximilian had chosen not only the time, the day, and the place of His sacrifice, but that He had also chosen me myself to carry it out, I did not understand it. Many years had to pass. And when I prayed before Him, begging—who knows who, exactly, I prayed to, as you've pointed out: whether it was that God whose existence I'd denied so many times, or those virgins I had so abused, or perhaps He Himself, He who was only a few steps away from me, His head held high, making that morning bluer with His blue eyes, His long blond beard pulled apart to leave His chest exposed—begging, yes, me, begging all the saints and angels in paradise, kneeling in my heart because one's duty as a soldier was to stand, very firm, American rifle in hand, begging Him, Maximilian, that new Christ who came to Mexico to redeem our sins, beseeching Him in the name of all those figures I had destroyed with my machete so that their feet and their hands could serve as wood for our bivouac fires, begging Him for that blank that they always put in one of the firing squad rifles so that each man can believe, if he so wishes, that he wasn't the one who killed the condemned man, imploring Him, yes, for that blank to be in my rifle, so that I could save my soul with it, so that I would not have to bear the guilt for the rest of my days of having killed the Son of God, Maximilian. For, in those moments, as I was saying, I was not praying, because I was not myself.

The captain said, "Get ready!"
And the Emperor, he smiled:
"May no more blood be shed,
I beg of you, by God."

The captain thus said, "Aim!"
And the Emperor loudly cried:
"I want to be the last
For Mexico to have died!"

Thus he spoke and hoarsely
Shouted "Long live Mexico!"
The captain then said, "Fire!"
And the firing squad let go.

So then, who was praying? Who recited Our Father who art in heaven? Mexicans, the Emperor exclaimed. Hallowed be Thy name? I want all of you to know. Thy kingdom come? That the men who have a divine right to rule. Our Father who art in Mexico? Were born to serve the people. Thy will be done? Or to become martyrs. On earth as it is in heaven? And I want to be the last. Will you give me the bullet, Lord, the blank bullet? Whose blood is shed. Hallowed be Thy Name? In the Nation. The blank bullet, Lord, will you give me the blank bullet to save my soul? As on the Hill. Can You hear me, oh Lord. And I want everyone to know. Our daily bread? The blank, Lord. That I grant them all forgiveness? Give us it this day. And I begged them for it. And forgive us our trespasses. The captain said, "Get ready!" I beg the Mexican people. In the name of God the Father? To forgive me. In the name of the Son? As we forgive those who trespass against us. Did I hear the Captain? Did I hear the first bell at seven in the morning? For if I came to Mexico, said the Emperor. In the name of the Holy Spirit? It was to serve the Nation. Did I hear the second bell, or the captain's voice saying "Aim!"? May God be my witness. The third one? I did not come, gentlemen. Lead us not into temptation? For personal gain. And deliver us, oh Lord? But deliver me, oh Lord, from causing Your death. Who was praying like that? Give me the blank. Who said, at the time, "Mexicans, long live Mexico!"? Who heard the captain's voice saying "Fire!"? Deliver us from what? From all evil, amen? Who heard the volley and the seventh bell at seven A.M., the sounds that rebounded from hill to hill, from Las Campanas Hill to the top of Cimatario, to the foot of La Cañada, to the summit of San Gregorio. And who, above all, remained so still, unmoved, despite having held his American rifle steady, of having aimed well and calmly, of having pulled the trigger on hearing "fire!" as placidly as though he was taking communion, when he was blessed, still clinging to his mother's skirts, as at peace with himself then as in his rebellious years when he lassoed the stone virgins in the churches, dragged them out and hung them from trees to make them all the more miraculous, body and soul, between heaven and earth. Well, it was I, gentlemen. Who else could it be? Who else but me, a sinner repenting of all his transgressions, whom the Lord privileged with a great revelation on that morning of June 19, 1867—a day that seems so like today—when He deigned to reveal to my eyes, to my eyes only, the fact that Christ on the Cross and Maximilian were one and the same person? Who else would have been given a blank to save his soul? I, gentlemen. At least that's what I believed during those moments when the Emperor—and along with him Generals Miramón and Mejía—was toppled on Las Campanas Hill.

When the shots were heard
The Emperor went down
And his hand did tremble
As he lay on the ground.

That he was barely alive
The captain saw with a start.
With the tip of his sword
He pointed toward the heart.

A soldier with his rifle
Fired at that spot.
Since it was point blank
His vest beneath burned hot.

Yes, I did get the blank. No, I did *not* get the blank. You can believe whatever you like, it's all the same to me. That Maximilian never came to Mexico, he stayed in his castle at Miramare writing poetry while Carlota played the harp. That Maximilian did come, on board the *Novara*. You can believe some things and not others. Maximilian never ruled in Mexico. Maximilian in Chapulte-pec Castle drew up decrees and had museums built. Or you can believe, if you like, that half of the things I say are lies and the other half are true. But you go and figure out for yourselves which are which. The city of Querétaro was never under siege. When Querétaro fell, the Emperor was arrested. Maximilian was never put on trial. Maximilian was sentenced to death. Maximilian was never executed at Las Campanas Hill. When Maximilian arrived at Las Campanas Hill, the firing squad was waiting for him. Maximilian arrived alone. Miramón and Mejía accompanied the Emperor. Maximilian never gave me a gold coin so that I wouldn't aim at his face. The coin burned my hands, and when I made a medal and hung it around my neck, it burned my chest. The captain did not say "Get ready!" I gripped my American rifle. The captain did not say "Aim!" I aimed. The captain did not say "Fire!" I fired. Maximilian did not keel over. Maximilian fell to the ground. Maximilian was not Christ. Maximilian was the Son of God. The captain did not gesture to me to advance. I stepped forward a few paces. The captain didn't point to the Emperor's heart with the tip of his sword. I placed my rifle barrel almost directly on Maximilian's chest, as he lay there, bathed in blood, with hands trembling, his face contorted in something like a laugh, a laugh of pain and fury, and his eyes half open. The captain didn't give me another order to shoot. I pulled the trigger. The shot did not come out and Maximilian's coat did not catch fire. The shot did come out and the Emperor's coat burst into flames. The shot did not kill him because Maximilian was already dead. The shot did kill him because Maximilian was still alive.

Afterwards they picked him up
To take away and bury his body:
They put him in a pine coffin
That the president had ready.

Since he was quite lanky,
Something no one suspected,
From one end of his casket
Both of his feet projected.

Before he was enshrouded
And sent back to his nation,
In a large vat of alcohol
He was steeped for preservation.

When they opened up his chest
His heart was chopped to bits
And the bloody, little fragments
Sold retail, by the piece.

His eyes were a shade of blue
The doctor could not get.
So, instead, he placed in their sockets
A saint's eyes, black as jet.

I would go on to tell myself the story about how Maximilian's Hungarian cook then put out the fire and that after the doctors certified the Emperor's death, they wrapped him in a sheet that looked like sackcloth, and they put him in a rough pine box that cost around twenty *reales*. Since the Emperor was very tall and the carpenter had not been given measurements, the Emperor's feet stuck out from the box. I would then imagine that the box was taken to the chapel of the Capuchin Convent and then to Dr. Rivadeneira for embalming, and that Dr. Licea first made a death mask with plaster of Paris and then cut Maximilian's beard and hair to sell. That Colonel Palacios crowned the Emperor with his own intestines and said, "You liked crowns, didn't you? Well, this is your crown now." That another officer exclaimed, "What's all the fuss about? A dog more, a dog less, what's it matter?" That the Emperor was embalmed like they used to embalm the mummies in Egypt. That the bullet that was the coup de grâce, although it had killed him and remained embedded in his spine, had not touched his heart, and so the doctors cut his heart into little pieces and put them in alcohol-filled jars to be sold. That Dr. Licea sent one of those pieces to Prince Salm-Salm. That the liver and the entrails were thrown into a bucket and were dumped into a sewer. That, since they couldn't find blue glass eyes in Querétaro, they tore the black eyes from a Saint Ursula statue at the hospital and they put them on the Emperor. That they placed him into a triple coffin, made of rosewood, zinc, and carved cedar, and took him to the Capital, and that it was there that the Emperor's corpse began to decompose because he had not been embalmed properly, and his skin turned black and the little hair he had left fell out. That then they undressed the body and hung it upside down to let out all the dark liquids and that then, newly injected with embalming fluid and laid out on a table, dressed in black on black velvet cushions, the corpse was visited by President Juárez, who, after a few moments of silence, said that the Emperor was very tall. Yes, I would make all that up if I had enough imagination, if I dared. I would make it up to make more lies, so that they won't believe me, so that they'll ask "How can you come up with so much exaggerated nonsense? Where do you get all these inflated, extravagant details? Those things only happen, when they happen at all, in novels!"

Now that he's in Heaven
At the right hand of the Lord
All his wounds have healed
And he's an Emperor once more.

Carlota is in her castle
Insane and full of hate.
And some evil bandits murdered
The judge who sealed his fate.

López died of anger
Napoleon of his bile;
Juárez died of very old age,
Clutching the Constitution all the while.

Márquez died a pauper,
And Bazaine a traitorous chief:
I was left, ladies and gentlemen,
Consumed by heavy grief:

For I fired the coup de grâce
That killed our Emperor.
It was I, to my disgrace,
Who fired it, in the war.

I'll say good-bye with these verses. I'll leave you with lies and truth, ladies and gentlemen. I'll leave you the Emperor's remains so you can dispose of them as you will, and the crown of thorns he wore in life. I'm leaving you the black fiacre with the jammed door. My American percussion rifle. The watch with Carlota's portrait. The adobe wall. The ringing of the bells at seven A.M. The cavalry detachment and the infantry battalion that accompanied the cortege. I leave you the city of Querétaro with its white houses and churches, and Saint Ursula's black glass eyes, and the silver crucifix that the Emperor had in his cell. The cigarette I smoked that morning. The Emperor's last words. The communion hosts I stole to use as chips in card games. The sounding of reveille. The rosary the Emperor sent his brother, Archduke Karl. I'll leave you the blank that did not blank out my sins. The paradise I envisioned when I had my revelation, the hell in which I've lived since then, when I knew that He had chosen me to carry out the sacrifice, as punishment for my many sins, heretical and sacrilegious. I'll leave you a morning sunny and blue. The glass of wine and chicken drumstick that the Emperor had for breakfast that morning. I'll leave you the insane Carlota. The assassins of Colonel Platón Sánchez, the judge who sentenced Maximilian. The rabid dog that bit Miguel López, the traitor. I'll leave you Bazaine's marshal's baton. I'll leave you Benito Juárez and his Constitution. I'll leave you Márquez's scar. I'll leave it all to you so you can make whatever you want of it: a history book, a tale, the chronicle of June 19,

1867, a novel, a song, a ballad—it's all the same to me. I'll leave it all to you so that you can decide, as you like, what was true and what was false, so that you can arrange it all however you want it, so that you can tell people, if you want to, that the Emperor had to jump, not out of his coach, but out of his coffin. That Maximilian sent Carlota his watch but not with the Empress's portrait inside it, but a piece of his heart. That at the command to fire the firing squad raised its rifles and aimed at the flock of green ducks crossing the sky, quacking, on that clear, sunny morning. It's all the same to me because I'm satisfied enough being the only one who knows the truth. The only thing I won't leave you is the bullet that I had plated with the gold from the heart-shaped ex-voto that I made from the coin that I got, didn't get, yes, did get from Maximilian that June morning on Las Campanas Hill, so I wouldn't aim at his face.

I'll leave you with these lines
Writ' neath a lemon tree
With another coup de grâce
That shall rebound to me.
I'll finish this sad ballad
Of the tragic Emperor
And of the profound anguish
Of his killer—evermore.

3. Saint Ursula's Black Eyes

The story of Saint Ursula's black eyes—or rather, the eyes made of paste or glass that were gouged out of a life-sized image of Saint Ursula at the hospital in Querétaro to be plugged into the empty eye sockets of Ferdinand Maximilian's newly-embalmed corpse—belongs to that collection of anecdotes and tales—some grotesque, others unbelievable, many of them horrifying—that gave the Querétaro tragedy an even greater dimension of melodrama.

There seems to be no doubt as to the truthfulness of some of those events. It was customary, when embalming a corpse, to substitute artificial eyes of the same color for the corpse's originals. Moreover, it was quite improbable that in a small city like Querétaro there would have been any *real* blue eyes—out of the question—let alone blue paste or blue glass eyes or indeed paste or glass eyes of any color to replace the Archduke's, and so the idea of taking some from a statue sounds plausible. Photographs of Maximilian's embalmed corpse show it with large, black, open eyes—Saint Ursula's own.

There also seems to be no doubt that the carpenter who built the three coffins taken to Las Campanas Hill—pine boxes that cost twenty *reales* each—had not been made aware of Maximilian's stature (1.85 meters), so that the Emperor's feet protruded from the coffin. Some writers claim that the coffin bore a cross on top. Montgomery Hyde, who saw the coffin in the Museum of Querétaro many years later—his book was published in 1946—stated that it still contained traces of blood.

If the corpse's false eyes weren't blue, then what *was* definitely blue—a blue as clear and limpid as the Emperor's gaze—was the morning on which he left the Teresitas Convent for the place of execution. Hence, a wish he had expressed once of dying on a beautiful day such as that one, came true. It was also true that in some bad poems Maximilian had written when he was a young admiral, smitten by sargassum, astrolabes, giant fireflies in Bahia, and the oleander that bloomed off the coasts of the foaming Gulf of Lepanto—all this found in his memoirs—he had described another wish that did indeed come true: dying on a sun-drenched hilltop.

On the other hand, it's a bit more difficult to believe, as several historians state, that upon arriving at the place of execution, Maximilian had to descend from his coach by jumping out the window, for even if the door was stuck, he could have used the other door. Nevertheless, Father Soria tells us in his memoirs that upon reaching the hill Maximilian tried to open the carriage door, and since he was unsuccessful, he climbed out of the coach without opening it. "This surprised me because he was very tall, and soon he was climbing the hill so fast that I could not keep up with him." Some historians say that Maximilian wore a white felt hat that morning. But Soria states that the hat Maximilian threw on the coach seat before getting out and saying "Alas, I won't need this anymore!" was "dark purple, made of plush, with a low crown." It's also true that Soria—described as a mild-mannered Otomi Indian, short, swarthy and shy, with a sweet nature—almost fainted at the execution site and that Maximilian himself took a small silver vial with English smelling salts from his jacket pocket and put it up to the priest's nose. The latter describes in his memoirs that the vial contained alkali and adds that afterwards, the Emperor handed it to him, along with a crucifix and a rosary, for the Archduchess Sophie. Father Soria, who suffered stomach disorders for several days after the execution, says that later a German tried to buy the crucifix for 500 pesos, but that he refused to sell it.

It was also true that the Emperor ceded the place of honor, the center, to General Miramón, and that he gave each man in the firing squad an ounce of gold—at that time equivalent to twenty-four francs—asking them not to aim at his face. Each of the coins was a gold "Maximilian" and bore the Emperor's profile. Later, to console General Mejía, he assured him that a man who did not get his just reward on Earth always received it in Heaven. It appeared that Mejía was the palest of the three, which was attributed to the fact that he had a newborn child. Still, shortly before the execution, Mejía showed that he hadn't lost his sense of humor. When Maximilian heard a trumpet at the convent and asked him if that was the signal to go to their deaths, "El Negrito" replied: "I don't know, Your Majesty. This is my first time being executed." Mejía's wife, with baby in arms, followed the coach from Querétaro to the hill. Also following the group was the Hungarian chef Tüdös, who, according to Harding, wept and screamed in Magyar, his native tongue: "*Boldog Istenem!*"—"Good Lord!" When they arrived at the Hill, Maximilian asked him, "Do you believe now that I am going to be shot, Tüdös?" recalling that when he was imprisoned, Tüdös had said that they would never dare. It was also the loyal chef who threw himself on the Emperor's body to stifle the flames when Maximilian's waistcoat—or in any case his jacket—actually caught fire after the coup de grâce. Had it not been for Tüdös, the Emperor's body would have become a bonfire.

At that time, as ever, it wasn't unusual to compare a common martyr's death with the Calvary. If the man who could have been Maximilian's birth father, the Duke of Reichstadt, who died in his bed, was described by Catulle Mendès as "the little Jesus from the Tuileries who became the Christ of Schönbrunn," it's easy to understand how the public's imagination would be captured by the execution of a European prince before whose portrait Mexican Indians still made the sign of the cross. General Mejía contributed to this by saying to Maximilian at the time of execution that he did not wish to be at his left because at Golgotha the damned thief had been to the left of the Savior. The Emperor smiled, called Mejía a "little fool," and said that he would place himself at the left of General Miramón because he was the worst sinner of the three. Carlota herself, during one of her rare lucid moments, having been apprised

of Maximilian's death, wrote Countess d'Hulst in January of 1868: "It is difficult for me to imagine a more noble and Christian end. It could be compared
to the sacrifice offered at Calvary." And yes, Maximilian's death was indeed
Christian, and noble no doubt not only because of his incredible integrity and
noble state of mind that did not waver at any time, but also because his final
words, albeit naïve and maybe even simple, served to dignify his last moments.
The Emperor, in fact, made a small speech seconds before the volley, and most
chroniclers and historians agree more or less on the general gist of how this
speech ended: "I shall die for a just cause—the cause of the Independence and
the Freedom of Mexico. May my blood put an end to the misfortunes of my
adopted Nation. Long Live Mexico!" Mejía, it is said, murmured a few words
himself, and Miramón asked that he not be considered a traitor. Nevertheless Maximilian said something besides "¡*Viva Mexico!*" before dying, for the
eyewitnesses of the drama on the hill state that, after the discharge, as he lay
on the ground, the Emperor said, "¡*Hombre, hombre!*" while he himself tore
off a button from his frockcoat with contorted fingers. Of course, this wasn't
the same coat later used to dress the embalmed corpse, described as a blue
dress coat with gold buttons. The body's ensemble was completed with black
trousers, military boots, black cravat, and black kid gloves.

It was also true that Maximilian refused a blindfold and that before the volley, he pulled apart his beard with his hands to point to his heart—although
this gesture, as stated by the novelist Juan A. Mateos, was probably done to
prevent his beard from catching fire. In his *Recollections of Mexico*, Dr. Samuel
Basch states that General Díaz de León had already given the order not to
aim at the Emperor's head, but at his chest, and that the soldiers fired from a
very short distance so that, says Basch, the autopsy did not turn up a single
one of the six bullets that went through the body. "The three chest wounds,"
Basch continues, as we quote verbatim from the original translation of 1870,
by Peredo, "were fatal in themselves. The first pierced the heart from right to
left; the second, piercing a ventricle, severed the large veins; the third, finally,
pierced the right lung. The nature of these three wounds, therefore, leads one
to believe that the Emperor's struggle was extremely brief, and that his hand
movements, which someone's cruel imagination interpreted as an order to
repeat the shots, were only convulsions." Nevertheless, Mexican doctors said
they found a bullet embedded in Maximilian's spine and, in his memoirs, Felix
Salm-Salm supposes that perhaps it was the one aimed at his heart when he

was on the ground. Moreover, one must remember that Basch was not present at the execution, and could not state with any certainty whether Maximilian had required a coup de grâce or not. Bertha Harding says that a bullet had grazed and gashed the Emperor's eyebrow and temple but there was no evidence of this on the plaster of Paris death mask made by Dr. Licea.

Truth be told, the eyewitnesses to the Las Campanas Hill tragedy were few, since the execution was closed to the public. Manet's famous painting of the shooting is nothing but an allegory—there was no wall behind the accused with spectators looking over it. Maximilian was not wearing a hat; he was not in the center; the soldiers were not as well-attired or uniform in height as the French painter depicted them, or indeed as Maximilian himself would have liked. The eight men, including the officer who issued the order, came in all shades and sizes. Manet's painting aside, the most absurd portrayals of Maximilian's execution abounded at the 1868 Paris Salon, since the artists let their imagination run wild. All this iconography was added to the better-documented paintings and canvases on the Intervention and the Empire, executed by artists such as Jean-Adolphe Beaucé, Félix Philippoteaux, Charles Dominique Lahalle, and many others, which were added in turn to the photographic materials, and then the other graphical documents of, for instance, the Pastry War of '38, and the taking of San Juan de Ulúa. During this time too, all the Europeans and North Americans who had been in Mexico around that time (or least a large number of them) published memoirs, among them not only those already mentioned—Basch, Hans, the Salm-Salms, and Van der Smissen—but also Frederick Hall, an attorney from the United States who arrived in Querétaro after Maximilian had fallen, Sara York Stevenson, an American woman who lived in the capital during the Empire, and the Countess von Kollonitz, who had accompanied Carlota to Mexico. To these were added the works of Du Barail, Gaulot, Blanchot, Niox, Détroyat, and many others. The bibliography on Maximilian and Carlota's adventure in Mexico and the French Intervention is endless. Elsewhere, Emperor Franz Joseph ordered the immediate compilation of his brother's memoirs, along with his aphorisms, which were soon translated into other languages and published. Maximilian's memoirs, however, had been interrupted, and were left unfinished before his journey to Mexico. In them one perceives a refined, cultured spirit, with an acute sense of observation—but also the Archduke's deep-rooted racial prejudice, and especially the profound disdain he had for the Negro race.

One more thing stands out in his memoirs, and this is the mixture of revulsion and fascination that Maximilian felt for the operations involved in the embalming of cadavers. Thus, at Santa Ursula in Tenerife—it had to be Saint Ursula—when he was shown the mummies of four Guanche kings wrapped in goatskins, Maximilian was reminded, with a shudder, of the terrible figures of the *Frati secchi* at Parma, and he refers to the substance used in embalming them—a combination of salt water and dragon's blood. He then tells how the dead were embalmed in the Canary Islands—first washed several times with aromatic herbs, cut open with knives made of a type of obsidian, and, after being disemboweled, stuffed with herbs and sawdust and left in the sun to dry. This morbidity eventually turned into a braver—or more eccentric—act on Maximilian's part, for we are told that he later decided to dictate the procedure to be followed in the embalming of his own body, and communicated the details to General Escobedo. Someone pointed out that, in doing this, Maximilian acted in a similar manner to that of his illustrious predecessor, Empress Maria Theresa, who delighted during her last hours in planning the construction of a beautiful rococo tomb for herself. It's worth noting that another of Maximilian's ancestors, the renowned Emperor Charles V of Germany and I of Spain, having retired to a Hieronymite Monastery at Yuste, constantly gazed upon the coffin that eventually would bear his mortal remains.

Bertha Harding states that, not succeeding at finding naphtha in Querétaro, the doctors present opted for injecting the corpse with zinc chloride, although one of the European doctors located in the city said that, due to the perforations caused by the bullets in the thorax and abdomen, it was not possible to embalm Maximilian's body by injection. Instead, the Egyptian method was employed—as Masseras states, not giving further details on the process—although we can assume that the Emperor himself knew of it and would have approved. The embalming process apparently abounded in grotesque and gruesome episodes. To begin with, Maximilian was shorn in minutes, and the locks and curls of his golden hair were sold as souvenirs. The guilty party here was the Mexican Dr. Licea, who himself took the scissors to the Emperor only after, no doubt, casting his death mask: the latter has its beard intact, as one can see at the Maximilian von Mexico Museum in Hardegg. We are told that Licea took a scalpel and made the first incision on Maximilian's skin, exclaiming: "What a delight to wash one's hands in the blood of an Emperor." Some authors relate that Colonel Palacios pointed to the corpse and said: "Behold what France has wrought!" Later, a false beard was placed on the Emperor. It's worth remembering that this type of vandalism—as perpetrated on Maximilian's beard and hair—had many precedents in history. E. M. Oddie says in a biography of the Duke of Reichstadt that only minutes after his death, the poor King of Rome had been completely shorn, and that locks of his blond hair were distributed into many different lockets. More sinister, apparently, was the fate of Maximilian's heart—the heart that, according to the wishes he expressed when he thought Carlota was dead, was to be buried in the same tomb as that of the Empress of Mexico—for it's said that after being left sitting on a chapel bench a whole day (according to Hyde), it was chopped into pieces and these were placed in small alcohol- or formaldehyde-filled vials to be sold as well. Prince Salm-Salm, for example, states that Dr. Licea sent him one of these pieces, in a jar, along with one of the bullets that had pierced Maximilian's body. His wife Agnes, moreover, tells us in her diary that Dr. Licea, "a repulsively ugly man," turned up soon after the execution offering to sell her "the Emperor's garments and other relics," and that he made her a gift of "part of His Majesty's beard and a red silk sash steeped in his blood." Licea asked thirty thousand pesos for the "souvenirs" and the Princess asked him if he had the Archduke's death mask in his possession, to which Licea answered in the affirmative, but that he had already been offered fifteen thousand pesos for it. The Princess turned up several days later at Dr. Licea's house, accompanied by a witness, Colonel Gagern, and the doctor showed her the mask. Agnes Salm-Salm consulted Admiral Tegetthoff, who told her that those objects had to be acquired and burned as they would not be "an appropriate gift for the bereaved mother"—that is, Maximilian's.

Agnes Salm-Salm tells us that she then called on Juárez and denounced Licea. Juárez became indignant and soon after Licea was taken to court and sentenced to two years in prison.

No one knows what happened to those two blue eyes, Maximilian's real ones, but, as to the disposition of his organs, which included the intestines and the stomach with its partially digested contents of wine, chicken—or beef, depending on your source—and bread, Montgomery Hyde states that they ended up in a sewer, mixed with tannin and bile.

Bad luck continued to plague Maximilian even beyond his death. For some unknown reason, the embalming was not effective, and so, when the body was moved from Querétaro to the capital to be placed in the Chapel at San Andrés Hospital, signs of decomposition began to appear, of which the most obvious were a terrible odor and a darkening of the corpse's skin. The government of the Republic ordered that a second embalming be done. It was necessary, therefore, to drain the liquids already contained in the body, and so it was undressed and bathed in an arsenic solution, new incisions in the appropriate veins and arteries were made, the arms were tied to its sides, and the body was hung by its feet from a lamp chain that was lowered from the very center of the dome at San Andrés Chapel. For seven days the blackened, nauseating body of the Prince someone had once called "a handsome plaything of the European courts" remained hanging there, like an apparition. Seven days and seven nights, bathed by torchlight or the sunlight that streamed from the chapel windows, dressing it in a luminous, dusty nimbus. Under the body a vessel was placed to catch its dripping liquids. It seemed, however, that the container was smaller than required, judging by the stains some visitors saw on the tile. The new casket, of *granadillo* with a bas-relief cross on the lid, and an interior lined with cedar, replaced the one in which Maximilian had been transported from Querétaro to Mexico City, and that consisted of a box made of wood, lined with zinc on the inside and with black velvet on the outside, and with two lids: the inner lid was made of three bonded sheets of glass and—according to Basch—"bearing a golden *M* in the middle sheet." The Carmelite nuns made a pillow of black velvet trimmed with golden borders and bells for the Emperor's head, and another group of pious ladies made a cloak, also of black velvet, with trimmings of gold-threaded lace.

Other reports, however, lead one to believe that Maximilian's body did arrive in Vienna—if not with organs intact, then at least in their entirety—after all. In 1885, the Mexican government printed a booklet entitled *Juárez y César Cantú*, in which some of the Italian historian's "favorite accusations" against Benito Juárez were refuted. The booklet includes a report, dated November 11, 1867, and addressed to the Mexican Secretaries of State and of the Interior, by Drs. Rafael Montaño, Ignacio Alvarado, and Agustín Andrade—those charged with the Archduke's second embalming. The doctors' report states that they had placed the body on a Gaudl dissection table installed in the Chapel of San Andrés, and carried out the necessary procedures to achieve a satisfactory preservation. They add that the organs were found in two lead boxes and that these were taken out and put in a liquid to preserve them while they proceeded with the embalming. The report does not describe the state of the organs when they arrived in Mexico City, but it does say that the doctors then decided to place them back into their natural cavities, "stuffed with floss coated with the powder recommended by Souberain," following this by making a hole in the Archduke's cranium and inserting the varying-sized pieces into which the brain had been cut, along with the cerebellum and a section of the medulla oblongata. In the same way, the doctors placed the heart, the lungs, the esophagus, the thoracic aorta, the liver, the stomach, the intestines, the gallbladder, and the kidneys back into the chest and abdomen. Then they bandaged the body in a fine linen, covered with a veneer of gutta-percha, and proceeded to dress him—the report goes on—in the garments "brought in by Mr. Davidson," with the exception of two pieces of underclothing that it was necessary to purchase, as they were not in Mr. Davidson's possession. The doctors say that they burned all the objects used in the re-embalming, along with the caskets, bandages, and clothing brought from Querétaro, at Santa Paula Cemetery, and they note that all of these procedures were carried out in the presence of the police inspector—to whom the body was officially turned over in its new coffin—as well as of other government functionaries. Moreover, in his *Recollections of Mexico*, Dr. Basch refers to another set of Maximilian's garments—perhaps those he wore in Querétaro—which he said he had handed over to the Secretary of the Austrian Legion, Herr Schmidt, who took them to Europe.

It is known that the instruments used were transferred to the chapel after the Sisters at San Andrés had been asked to move out, taking with them the Holy Host, the sacred vessels, the altars, the altar cloths, and the rest of the paraments and other ritual objects. One may speculate, therefore, that the Gaudl dissection table mentioned by the doctors was also taken there. But it seems that the Archduke's body was later laid upon a long table dating back to the end of the sixteenth century or the beginning of the seventeenth, around which the Mexican arm of the Holy Inquisition had gathered to pass its sentences. This table was acquired later by the Grand Lodge of the State of Mexico.

After the second procedure to preserve the body was completed, and, as speculated, before it was dressed, the President visited San Andrés Chapel. Benito Juárez showed up at midnight, accompanied by his minister, Sebastián Lerdo de Tejada. Lighted torches surrounded the nude body. As the photographs of the Archduke's corpse that the Mexican government allowed taken show him with his eyes open, one can surmise that on that night he still had them—that is to say, Saint Ursula's, not his own. The various versions of Juárez's visit to the chapel and what he said there diverge very little. The Mexican playwright Rodolfo Usigli, in the prologue to his historical melodrama *Corona de Sombra* (Crown of Shadows), notes the fact that the President's observations were of a "physiognomical and anthropometrical nature." That is—Usigli is saying—it was a replay of Henry III's visit to the cadaver of the Duke de Guise, spurring the same reaction—"He's taller dead than alive"—as well as the reiteration of the phrase "An enemy's dead body is always a pleasant thing to see." Moreover, the playwright adds, "it is evident that this lack of originality, that this adherence by Juárez to the lessons of history constituted his strength, just as Maximilian's very originality determined his fall." Of course, these are arguable statements, but they are based on what, according to all sources, was indeed factual: that is to say, that President Juárez commented on how tall Maximilian was, or, in any case, had been while alive. Other writers say that Don Benito added: "He had no talent. So, although his forehead appears broad, this is simply because of his baldness." The President and his minister sat on a bench and chatted in low voices for around thirty minutes. The next day the corpse was dressed again and some visitors were allowed to view the Archduke's mortal remains.

The chapel at San Andrés Hospital is gone. On June 19, 1868, the first anniversary of Maximilian's death, a religious memorial service for the Archduke was held there, with Father Mario Cavalieri giving the homily. The Italian Jesuit not only greatly lauded Maximilian but he also launched a violent diatribe against Juárez and his government. As a result, the President ordered the mayor of Mexico City, Juan José Baz, to demolish the chapel. After talking to several architects who would not commit themselves to tearing down the church as rapidly as was desired, Mayor Baz applied a method of his own devising. On the night of June 28th, he arrived at the chapel followed by a contingent of stonemasons who carried wood beams soaked in turpentine. The masons started by inserting beams at the four cardinal points of the circular base that supported the dome, then eight and sixteen consecutively, until the whole dome rested on the beams. Then they set fire to them, and, as they turned to ashes, the entire dome came tumbling down. When the sun rose, instead of a chapel there was nothing but a pile of rubble. Soon after, Juárez ordered that a street be opened through that site. Only on Las Campanas Hill, many years later, was permission given for a small oratory to be built in memory of Maximilian, Miramón, and Mejía. Inside the oratory—in Neo-Romanesque style—there are three crosses. Maximilian's, made of wood from the frigate *Novara*, was sent to Mexico by Emperor Franz Joseph. At the top of the hill is a giant statue of Benito Juárez.

June 19th was also the last day that the *Empire Daily* appeared at the capital. This paper had been systematically printing concocted news. On Saturday, June 15th, the paper was still stating that "His Majesty the Emperor's arrival is imminent, in command of his undefeated, heroic army." On Wednesday the 19th, under the headline "Military Operations in the Capital," the paper reported: "No event of importance has occurred until the present time, nine A.M." On the inside pages there was a long article on the healthfulness and enjoyment of horsemeat as food. And, at the end of the last column of the last page, an advertisement reading: "Funeral Coach. There is a quite good one at the Hospice for the Poor. Those who need it to transport the dead may go to the above-mentioned establishment. You can also find wax candles and all other essentials for the service." Mexico City fell two days later and Márquez fled. Some say that he spent several days hiding in a tomb and that he later left the city disguised as a coal vendor, to end up in Havana. Juárez's triumphant entrance into the capital took place on July 15th.

The European press of the time severely criticized Juárez's refusals and delays in handing over Maximilian's body—and historians have done so until the present day. But the Austrian government and its representative, Admiral Tegetthoff, who was already in the city at the first part of September '67, shared the blame. The admiral claimed that his was not an official mission, as he was merely carrying out a private errand for the Archduke's mother, and his brother, His Majesty the Emperor of Austria. Tegetthoff added that he brought no documents or letters with him since he had been given his assignment orally. Faced with the absence of a formal, written petition, whether from the Austrian government or Maximilian's family, Benito Juárez refused to hand over the corpse. Previously, Baron Magnus as well as Dr. Basch had also requested the body, with the same results. Tegetthoff had no choice but to cable Vienna to have the petition sent to Mexico. On the first part of November, the official letter, signed by the Austrian Chancellor, Baron von Beust, was finally received. The Mexican government thereupon turned over the Archduke's remains, which the admiral took to Veracruz on the 9th of that month, accompanied, among others, by Basch and Tüdös, and with an escort of three hundred dragoons. The frigate *Novara* awaited Maximilian, and a funeral chapel was installed in the stateroom that replicated his office at Miramare. When the *Novara* left Mexican waters, one hundred and one cannon shots were fired. It was November 28, 1867. The *Novara* arrived in Trieste in the third week of January 1868. It dropped anchor in the blue waters of the Adriatic, and the body was carried to land on a barge that, according to José Luis Blasio's description, was draped in black velvet, and at whose center lay a catafalque that held the coffin in the shadow of an angel with outspread wings, wearing a laurel wreath. The coffin was covered with the Austrian war banner. That same day a special train carried the mortal remains to Vienna. It was snowing in the capital of the Austrian Empire. Archduchess Sophie awaited the remains at the Hofburg gates. When they arrived she looked at her son's embalmed face beneath the snow and the glass lid and threw herself weeping on the coffin. It was January 18. Maximilian's remains were left in the palace chapel one day, in the glow of two hundred tapers in silver candlesticks. Hundreds of Viennese subjects went by the chapel to pay their last respects. With the sole exception of Blasio, none of the Mexicans in Europe who owed so much to Maximilian—namely Almonte, Hidalgo, Francisco Arrangóiz, José Fernández Ramírez, and Velázquez de León, among others—was present at the funeral. Gutiérrez Estrada, the old Yucatán landowner who died in March of 1867, was spared witnessing the fall of the Mexican Empire and along with it, his most cherished dream. Maximilian's body was then transferred to the Capuchin Chapel. Following tradition, the friar who was guarding the entrance to the crypt would ask the name of the deceased; the response would add all his titles to his name, that of Emperor of Mexico as well as those that the Family Pact had taken away: Archduke of Austria, Count of Habsburg, Prince of Lorraine. The Capuchin would repeat the question and the answer would be the same. One more time, the third, the crypt guard would ask the name of the deceased, and the answer, this time, would be limited to his Christian names: Ferdinand Maximilian Joseph, Servant of the Lord, with no titles mentioned. Only then would access to the crypt and to glory be granted. Maximilian's casket was placed next to the mortal remains of the Duke of Reichstadt, the King of Rome. After the funeral, a commission was charged to identify the body officially, and the corresponding document certified having found "an embalmed body, in a well-preserved state, that the undersigned have recognized to be that of H.M. the deceased Emperor of Mexico, Ferdinand Maximilian." The coffin lid was closed and the palace official handed the key to the secretary to deposit in the Crown's Treasury. On the coffin lid was left the bouquet of dried immortelles tied to a palm leaf, that had been given to Maximilian by the people of the town of Xocotitlán, with a message written in the Nahuatl language: "*Nomahuistililoni tlahtocatziné nican tiquimopielia moicnomasehualconetzihuan, ca san ye ohualahque o mitzmotlahpalhuilitzinoto. Ihuan ica tiquimomachtis ca huel senca techyolpaquimo . . .*" ("Our dear Honorable Emperor, here are your humble children, these Indians who have come to greet you . . ."). The news of the execution at Las Campanas Hill, as it turned out, arrived in Paris on the day of the awarding of prizes at the World's Fair of 1867, held in a huge, elliptical palace built on the Champ de Mars, in an area that extended from the École Militaire to the banks of the Seine. There the 42,237 participants who had flocked from the four corners of the Earth exhibited in pavilions, tents, kiosks, and booths all the marvels, raw materials, merchandise, products, and contraptions discovered or invented to that time. The bad news was given to Louis Napoleon and Eugénie that morning, but the Emperor chose not to make it known until after the ceremony. "The principles of morality and justice are the only ones that can consolidate thrones, lift up nations, and ennoble humanity," Louis Napoleon had said at the opening of the exposition. "France," the Emperor added, "was proud to show itself to the world as it was—grand, prosperous, and free, hardworking and peaceful, and always brimming with generous ideas." Sixteen years before, on becoming Emperor, Louis Napoleon had said, "*L'Empire, c'est la paix*" ("The Empire is peace"). But since Magenta and Solferino, and then the endless series of wars and skirmishes, interventions, and punitive expeditions that culminated in the disasters at Metz and Sedan, would all serve to demonstrate that Louis Napoleon's reign had more to do with war than with peace: "*L'Empire, c'est l'épée*" ("The Empire is the sword"), a German publication had declared. Nevertheless, France was no longer the same, said Napoleon III in his speech. It was not "that France, so restless in the past, had been able to cause unrest outside its borders." Of course, the Emperor neglected to mention the names of those nations—Indochina, Algeria, Mexico—to which France had exported its turbulence in the name of civilization, though those nations were represented at the Paris World's Fair by, among other things, sandalwood boxes from Battambang, onyx from Ain-Sefra, and a scale reproduction of the temple of Xochicalco atop which, as the exposition guide stated, ancient Mexicans sacrificed propitiatory victims to the sun by cutting out their steaming hearts with an obsidian knife.

The ceremony took place just as planned: the Imperial family arrived at the Champ de Mars in a golden carriage from the Trianon Museum with Louis Napoleon dressed as a civilian and Eugénie all in white with a diamond-studded tiara, and Prince Loulou assigned to award the important prizes. However, the absence of the Count and Countess of Flanders was conspicuous, as was the withdrawal, sudden but discreet in mid-ceremony, of the Austrian ambassador in Paris, Prince Richard Metternich.

Having foreseen Maximilian's execution in Mexico for some time, Louis Napoleon was more worried about Vienna's reaction. But Emperor Franz Joseph replied with kind words to the telegram that delivered Napoleon's condolences to the Austrian court. This greatly relieved the Emperor and Eugénie and made manifest a political reality: that neither France nor Austria wished, at that point, to do or say anything that might disturb their relations. Consequently, the French Emperor and Empress planned a journey to Vienna to convey their condolences to Maximilian's family in person. Archduchess Sophie, however, claimed that she was in no condition to receive them, and Eugénie, who feared being the object of hostile demonstrations in Vienna, proposed a meeting in Salzburg. Franz Joseph agreed to this. It was a clear, sunny day, August 18, 1867, as Corti tells us on the last page of his book. He also states that Eugénie showed up in the simplest attire, "making a great effort," as von Beust relates, "to efface herself" before the dazzling beauty of Empress Elisabeth." Napoleon, for his part, appeared good-humored and healthy, at least for the time being. "At first," Count Corti tells us, "they talked of Maximilian and the sorrow caused by his death. But soon political matters took priority over the painful recollections." They talked about Germany, Crete, and, as was to be expected, of the eternal crisis in the East, "that Balkan hornets' nest." A few days later, Georges Clemenceau sent a letter to a lady friend in New York that would become well known for the implacable, anger-filled opinion expressed therein on Maximilian and Carlota by the French politician: "Those whom he wanted to slay have slain him; that makes me infinitely happy," said the "Tiger." "His wife is insane. Nothing fairer than that . . . It was that woman's ambition that pushed that imbecile forward . . ."

Carlota wasn't told of Maximilian's death until January 1868, during one of her rare moments of lucidity. But before that, she was moved to Brussels and, in the meantime, the Miramare staff was forbidden to dress in mourning. Early in July 1868, Marie Henriette, the Belgian queen, left for Trieste accompanied by Countess Marie d'Yve de Bavay, Colonel Goffinet, Baron Prisse, and Dr. Bulkens, director of the Gheel Mental Hospital. The Queen found an unrecognizable Carlota, frightfully emaciated and pale, with an expressionless stare. The journey to Brussels was set for July 29, and it is said that on that morning Carlota looked from the castle terrace onto the blue waters of the Adriatic for the last time and murmured, referring to her husband, "I shall wait for him for sixty years . . ."

Carlota was first put up at Laeken and soon after moved to the Castle, or Villa, of Terveuren. She asked frequently whether Maximilian had arrived in Europe and for several months she was told that the Gotha Almanac had not come out. Marie Henriette was eventually able to secure several issues of the well-known catalogue of European nobility with the reference to Maximilian's death in Querétaro edited out. But in the end the Belgian royal family determined that what had happened could no longer be kept from the Empress and the task of speaking to Carlota was assigned to the former chargé d'affaires in Mexico, Frederick Hoorickx. When the latter finished his account, Carlota rose, left the Terveuren château, and ran into the garden with heartrending screams.

It is very probable that we will never know whether or not Carlota gave birth during her stay at the Gartenhaus of Miramare, but one cannot dismiss the fact that she did indeed have a son, whose father was very likely Colonel Van der Smissen, and who was baptized Maxime Weygand. In any event, the likelihood is seriously considered whenever the noted French general—born in Belgium to unknown parents, brought up as a prince; a graduate of the prestigious Saint-Cyr Military Academy—is mentioned. Among other things, he was Marshal Foch's Chief of Staff in World War I, and in 1920 reorganized the Polish army and fought beside Piłsudski against the Bolsheviks.

Weygand had been given that name because, some speculated, he had been born "on the way to Ghent" or *Way-Gand*; but this was no doubt another of the many fanciful notions that have been bandied about because of his mysterious origins—in any case, one of the more innocuous. But . . . why was he given a Christian name so similar to Maximilian's (Maxime) if his father was not the Archduke? Among the few known facts on the matter of Carlota's child is that the Belgian doctor and obstetrician Louis Laussédat declared that on January 21, 1867, a child of unknown parents had been born in Brussels, at

59 Waterloo Boulevard. Castelot points to a connection between Laussédat and the Belgian royal family when he tells us that it was Henri Laussédat, the doctor's nephew, and also a doctor, who was responsible for the care of Leopold II during his final years. Castelot adds that Weygand was raised by a David de León Cohen, who, later on, "had him recognized by his own accountant," a Frenchman named François Joseph Weygand, and that "recognition" was what allowed Weygand to enter Saint-Cyr Military Academy. Weygand's son relates that his father received several announcements when Carlota died saying, "Your mother has died." But Weygand responded to none of these messages, nor did he attend the Empress's funeral. Castelot adds that Baron Auguste Goffinet, Empress Carlota's Grand Master and administrator of Leopold II's personal estate, acquired the house where Weygand was supposedly born, and that later became the "Taverne Waterloo," in 1904. Lastly, André Castelot quotes Albert Duchesne, who said that the daughter of one of Carlota's physicians affirmed that every time General Weygand went to Brussels, he visited Bouchout Castle and sometimes dined with Baron Goffinet himself. Some descendants of the man who was undersecretary in Maximilian's navy, Léonce Détroyat—one of Carlota's favorite officials—said that Détroyat had been the father of the Empress's child, but the truth is that the resemblance between Van der Smissen and Weygand is "remarkable." Seen side by side, as they appear in Castelot's book, a photograph of the Belgian commander at around age fifty—*Musée de la Dynastie, Bruxelles*—and one of Weygand when he had reached more or less the same age—*Roger Viollet*—there can be no doubt at all that, if we'll never really known if he was Carlota's son, one can be sure that he was Van der Smissen's. The photographs appear to be of twin brothers. This extraordinary resemblance at the same time eliminates the possibility that Weygand was a bastard son of Leopold II—as has also been suggested—who never tried to hide any of his many bastard children.

On the other hand, the pretensions of a London fishmonger by the name of William Brightwell may be characterized as folklore—Cockney folklore of the kind rampant in English markets. In 1922, Brightwell told the British press that he was Carlota's son, that his true name was "Rudolf Franz Maximilian Habsburg," and that he had been born on the night that the Empress of Mexico had slept at the Vatican. For several years Mr. Brightwell kept promoting his story. Among other things, says Richard O'Connor in *The Cactus Throne*, Brightwell laid claim to some of Maximilian's and Carlota's relics and jewels, supposedly lost in a shipwreck while being transported by Porfirio Díaz's supporters as they fled Mexico in 1911. Harding says, regarding this event, that the cruiser *Mérida* sank at Cape Hatteras, off the North Carolina coast, after being rammed by the steamship *Admiral Farragut* of the United Fruit Company and that with it sank some valuable jewelry that a Count Herrmann, a Habsburg adventurer, had stolen from a Burmese temple, and that along with these were lost some precious emeralds that had come from the Temple of Quetzalcóatl. Another version of the final fate of those Burmese jewels appears in the book *Jewels of Romance and Renown*, in which the author, Mary Abbot, claims that Carlota took some rubies to Mexico that ended up in the family of the Mexican Revolutionary Francisco Madero, and which were later shipped to Europe, only to be shipwrecked in Chesapeake Bay.

With regard to the son that, it's said, Maximilian had with Concepción Sedano, several writers assert that he was also taken to Paris to grow up. True or not, the fact is that a man who called himself Julio Sedano y Leguizano, who put on the airs of a gentleman and wore a long beard in the style of Maximilian—in his case the beard was black, not resembling the Emperor's at all—made a name for himself in Parisian circles by insisting that he was the son of Ferdinand Maximilian of Habsburg and Concepción, his paramour in Cuernavaca. If no one ever knew for certain where Sedano came from, how he ended up did become fairly well known: during World War I, the Germans who found him penniless in Barcelona hired him to spy for them. H. Montgomery Hyde tells us that, on returning to Paris, Sedano's job was to send military secrets written in invisible ink by means of letters addressed to a Swiss intermediary. But instead of writing the information between the lines of dummy letters, he did it on blank pages, thus awakening suspicions in the French censor. Sedano, Hyde tells us in *The Mexican Empire*, was spotted by the police and detained as he was mailing the letters on the Boulevard des Italiens, and he was arrested. The morning of October 10, 1917, he was taken from his cell in La Santé Prison in Paris to the wall at Vincennes. It is rumored that the official who led the firing squad said, "Sedano y Leguizano, son of the Emperor of Mexico, you are about to be executed as a traitor."

At five o'clock in the morning of March 3, 1879, a fire started that reduced the château built by the Prince of Orange in the beginning of the 19th century—on the road to Louvain, at the edge of the Soignies Woods, that Carlota's brother had purchased for her from Count Beaufort—to ashes. It is rumored that Carlota herself set fire to Terveuren, but like many other allegations, this will never be proven. It's also been said that the Empress, standing in the villa's garden, watched the flames and praised their beauty.

The Belgian Royal Family then decided to transfer Carlota to Bouchout Castle, situated a few kilometers from Laeken. This is a veritable fortress, built during the twelfth century, bristling with turrets and barbicans, and surrounded by a pond—previously a moat—teeming with swans and, at that time, equipped with a barge. As the years went by, the Empress's lucid periods were increasingly rare and brief. It's said that she would occasionally take to breaking mirrors and crockery, destroying photographs and oil paintings, but she never touched any of the objects or clothing that had belonged to Maximilian, nor the canvases and daguerreotypes in which he appeared, nor his letters or papers.

For Carlota, Maximilian was alive while she was mad, and dead when insanity abandoned her for a few minutes or hours. Maximilian would thus go from being Lord of the Earth and King of the Universe, as the Empress called him, to just being a good shepherd who had given up his life for his flock. These were the moments when Carlota's servants heard her speaking with no one else present, saying "Pay no mind, milord, if one's mind wanders—one is a fool, a madwoman . . . The madwoman never dies, milord, and you are in the house of the madwoman . . ." Or she would be playing the piano or the harp and could be heard murmuring: "At one time one had a husband, milord, a husband who was an Emperor or King. Oh, yes, it was a grand marriage, milord. And then came the madness . . ." Louis Napoleon appeared frequently in her delirium, always as a demon and a crook, and she never quite got over the fear that someone was trying to poison her. Nor did she ever stop demanding the deference due an Empress, and it's said that when Archduchess Zita, the future Empress of Austria, visited her in Bouchout, she was told, in the antechamber outside of Carlota's closed door, that she must make the three required bows . . . The Mexican Empress, they warned, would be looking through the keyhole to ensure that protocol was followed. Carlota, they tell us, became one of the richest women in the world. Gene Smith relates that when the Prince de Ligne was charged with administering the Empress's fortune, on his visits to give her his accounts, Carlota invariably received him in a hall where twenty or more chairs had been placed, all in a row, and that the Empress bowed before each one as though it held a visitor. The Prince de Ligne, however, was always under the impression that Carlota understood everything he told her about the state of her finances.

Some biographers of the Empress report that she managed to obtain a life-sized mannequin that she dressed in Maximilian's clothes and that she spoke to it for hours on end. And they say that every first day of the month, Carlota went down to the pond at Bouchout and got on the barge. Each time the madwoman repeated this strange ceremony, she would say, "We are leaving for Mexico today."

Many modern psychiatrists have offered differing opinions on the specific variety of madness that afflicted Carlota. One of them, interviewed by Suzanne Desternes and quoted by Castelot, was Dr. Pierre Loo. In his view, Carlota already showed the symptoms of her illness from childhood: hypersensitivity in relation to certain external incidents, sudden onsets of dejection and periods of depression, followed by "optimism and self-esteem." In other words, she had a type of cyclothymia, a manic-depressive psychosis in which euphoria and melancholy take turns. When reality becomes unacceptable, Dr. Loo adds, an artificial compensation takes over, characterized by periods of joviality, "combined with mystical themes, persecution fears, and at times erotic fantasies . . ." Paranoia? Schizophrenia? Both?

"*Miserere mei, Deus*! I shall die as well. Have mercy upon me, Lord," the madwoman of Bouchout would scream.

But the Lord did not have mercy on Carlota until sixty years after Maximilian began to see the world with the eyes of Saint Ursula.

XXI
BOUCHOUT CASTLE
1927

And to tell the world who you were, I must first tell you. Abdallah el-Zaquir wept like a woman when he lost Granada. Abd al-Qadir wept when he couldn't fight like a man after he was defeated at the Battle of Algiers. Hernán Cortés wept under the Tree of the Night of Sorrow when he thought he would never conquer the great city of Tenochtitlán. But you did not weep, Maximilian, when you lost all of Mexico along with Querétaro. You were Maximilian, the Unshakable. You were also Maximilian, the Honorable. My grandfather fled the Tuileries hiding behind dark glasses, his sideburns shaved off, but you kept your blond beard. Napoleon the Great fled France toward the Island of Elba, first dressed as a cab driver, later as an Austrian officer, and then a Russian commissar. You never donned the red uniform of the Chinaco army. Napoleon's nephew, Little Napoleon, fled Fort Ham disguised as a stonemason. You didn't pass yourself off as a muleteer. Don Carlos, the aspirant to the throne of Spain, fled to England, after dyeing his hair. You never dyed your hair, Maximilian. Instead, you stayed in Querétaro. Maximilian—you weren't another Pedro the Cruel of Aragón. There were no Sicilian Vespers in Mexico. You were Maximilian the Just. Remember García Cano? You were not another Richard III, nor a Peter I of Russia. You never took—would have never taken—his life from someone in whose veins your own blood flowed, as Richard of Gloucester did with his nephews, as Peter I did when he assassinated his son, Alexis. You were Maximilian the Merciful. Remember García Cano, the Mexican accused of conspiring to take your life? No, you were not another Ferdinand II of Austria, under whose reign Tilly's troops caused such a massacre at Magdeburg that it could only be compared to the crusade against the Albigensians. Neither were you an Ivan the Terrible: unlike what happened at Novgorod, no one was butchered or roasted alive in the streets of Mexico. You were Maximilian the Good-hearted. Do you remember García Cano being executed after you refused him a pardon? Do you remember his wife groveling at your feet in Chapultepec Castle, and you refusing to listen and having her expelled? Did you think of her, tell me, when you stood before the firing squad at Las Campanas Hill? Did you think of Princess Salm-Salm who begged Juárez to spare you? Do you remember, Maximilian, running into García Cano's wife on Empress Avenue and ordering that your carriage turn away from her? Do you remember her running after it screaming for mercy? And did you remember García Cano's wife when you heard the moaning and sobbing of Mejía's wife as she ran after the carriage that was taking him to Las Campanas? No, because no matter how many times you try to douse yourself in purity, you must know that you were also Maximilian the Deaf, Maximilian the Merciless. Just as Napoleon the Great refused Josephine a pardon for the Duke of Enghien, as Louis Napoleon refused Eugénie her request to spare Orsini— Enghien was later executed and Orsini died at the guillotine—and as your brother Franz Joseph refused a pardon for the rebellious Count Louis Batthyány, despite his wife's begging on her knees (in fact, he slashed his wrists the eve of his execution), as they all did, you were incapable of pardoning those who made attempts on your life or your empire. You were Maximilian the Inflexible, Maximilian the Resentful. And because you didn't pardon García Cano, the Mexicans will never forgive you. You were also Maximilian the Fool, because you wrote Marshal Bazaine on pink stationery to congratulate him on his wedding. And Maximilian the Incredulous, because you ignored Détroyat when he warned you that everyone would forsake you. You were Maximilian the Oblivious, Maximilian the Orphan, Maximilian the Blind. You wrote Napoleon that there were only three types of men in Mexico: stubborn old men, ignorant youths, and mediocre foreigners and adventurers with no future in Europe. You could never see that you were all three rolled into one. You were also Maximilian the False, because, in San Martín Texmelucan, you cried on my shoulder at my father Leopold's death after I returned from Yucatán, and you were furious at Archbishop Labastida when he refused to conduct a funeral service for his soul, arguing that Leopold had been a Lutheran. This, Maximilian, after you had maintained a vendetta against my beloved father, and had sworn to a love that you never felt for me, always talking about us behind our backs. You had accused my father of an "invincible rapaciousness," and you called him a greedy miser and said that you were glad to have deprived him of a very small part of what he held most dear in the world. What you neglected to see was that I was his sweet Marie Charlotte, his little brown-eyed princess, the one he had told everyone was his most beloved being on earth. In a letter to my aunt Countess Nemours, he had called me the flower of his heart. He had said it to me and predicted that I would be one of the most beautiful princesses in Europe. He had hoped to make me happy by telling me this, swearing that he loved me more than anything else in the world, more than my trousseau, the jewelry, the silver, and the 100,000 florins of my dowry that you took from my father, or the 308,000 francs that Count Zichy deposited in Vienna to secure our marriage. Maximilian, you lied as well when you told Franz Joseph that you would have to make an enormous, inconceivable sacrifice to renounce all your rights to the House of Austria, since you had given your word to nine million souls who had turned their eyes toward you. You lied because what mattered to you most at the time wasn't those people who had never summoned you, who didn't even know you existed. The only thing you wanted was for your empire not to be stillborn. You hoped not to lose the crown before it was placed on your fair head. You lied in the same way when you wrote to your mother Archduchess Sophie from Milan that were it not for your religious principles, you would have abandoned the government of the Lombardy and Veneto Provinces. More than God, the Church, and religion, what mattered to you was holding on by your fingernails to the miserable scrap of the Austrian Empire that your brother gave us, like a bone thrown to some dog. For that, God, the Church, and your subjects from Lombardo-Veneto will never forgive you—just as the Italians and the Hungarians will never forgive that prince in Naples who had been so moved by the scarlet-clad prisoners, laden with heavy chains, who were repairing the fortress walls; the prince who, in Gibraltar, had felt such compassion for the prisoners that the English had forced to pick up enormous iron balls, walk with them, and then place them on the ground, only to lift them up again and put them back where they were; the man who had kept his mouth shut when General Haynau had the Hungarian rebels asphyxiated in '49, and when the Austrian soldiers massacred the martyrs of Belfiore. The Prince was—you were, Maximilian—more interested in sending corsages to countesses and prancing around on Lipizzaner horses at the Vienna Spanish Riding School than in the hunger of those ruled by the Habsburgs to be free. You were many other things as well, and I must tell the world, and you, what they were. In your Teresitas

Convent cell you read César Cantú's *History of the Italians* and Heine's ballads. You were Maximilian the Enlightened. Maximilian the Understanding, who forgave Father Fischer the many bastard children he had scattered around the world. And because you planned to send Prince Salm-Salm to the United States with a million dollars to buy the support of that nation, Maximilian, you were Maximilian the Dreamer. You were Maximilian the Proud when you refused Colonel López's offer to hide you in Señor Rubio's house. Maximilian the Hypocrite, because you asked Salm-Salm to kill you if you were captured, but you knew that the Prince would never dare execute the order. Maximilian the Philosopher who, a few years before, had written in his aphorisms that he who does not fear death has made great progress in the art of living. Maximilian the Artist, the expert in the art of living, who on June 16, 1867, exclaimed that dying was easier than you thought. Maximilian the Heroic who, during a siege, during the most intense attacks, scanned the horizon through a sailor's telescope from the trenches, as if you were on a ship's forecastle. Maximilian the Ingenuous, the prisoner who amused himself smuggling messages to Salm-Salm in bread chunks, and who received secret messages in cigarettes from the military chaplain, Aguirre. Again you were Maximilian the Deceitful, because you wrote the Prefect of Miramare that you had "only Mexicans" among those closest to you, when you were ignoring Salm-Salm, Basch, the head horseman Malburg, the officers Swoboda and Fürstenwärther, Major Pitner, Captain Curié, Major Görwitz, Artillery Lieutenant Hans, Count Patcha, General Morett, Tüdös, Grill, Schaffer, Günner, Khevenhüller, Hammerstein, and Wickenburg. You were also Maximilian the Sportsman, because you bowled and played billiards at the Querétaro Casino. Maximilian the Lucky, to whom the ladies of Querétaro, you claimed, had surrendered more undergarments than you had ever owned yourself or indeed seen in your entire life. Of course these were none other than the wives of your own soldiers. Maximilian the Generous, because you filled beggars' hands with little silver and copper coins as they crowded around you outside the casino. You were Maximilian the Romantic, because you arrived in Querétaro and installed a secret office in a cave at the foot of Las Campanas Hill from where a pair of frightened lovers had emerged. You were Maximilian the Patient, because you indulged your officers by playing dominoes, although the game bored you to tears. Again, you were Maximilian the Magnanimous, because you tore up a list of names of those of your officers who were planning to desert or to betray you during the siege. You were Maximilian the Grateful, because you awarded Agnes Salm-Salm the Medal of the Order of Saint Charles, although you were unable to give it to her as you didn't actually have the award with you in Querétaro. However, you described it to the equestrian princess in detail: a small, white lacquered cross, green on the inside, with the legend *Humilitas* on the front and a San Carlos on the back, hanging from a red ribbon. Finally, you were Maximilian the Learned, because you could describe in detail the lovely baptismal font at the Temple of Santa Rosa to General Castillo, and could lecture Blasio on the Medusa-headed gargoyles at the Casa de los Perros, and expound to General Méndes—Maximilian the Rememberer—that you could with your eyes closed describe Querétaro and all its surroundings: San Gregorio and San Pablo to the north; to the south the Cuesta China and the ravine; in the hinterlands, the Cimatario; to the west, Las Campanas Hill. Tell me, Maximilian, how is it possible that the Mexicans have forgotten who you were? How is it possible that they've failed to see how noble and generous you were? When did that country of savages ever have another ruler like you, so concerned about the arts and letters, about the glory of its heroes? When did anyone else ever love those poor Indians, forgotten even by Juárez, more than you did? When did those people ever have an emperor with eyes as blue as the sky who suffered hunger, fever, dysentery, who was ready to shed his blood, to give his life, as you did, for them, for their freedom, their sovereignty, for the greatness of that land that you made your own? When did the Mexicans ever dream that they would have a queen with the blood of Saint Louis, King of France, the most important Catholic monarch in history, leader of two crusades against the infidel, flowing through her veins? A queen with the blood of the French, Spanish, and Italian Bourbons, the same blood that flowed through the veins of Louis XIII and Henri IV of France; of Philippe Égalité, founder of a monarchy based on the will of the people; of the Duke of Orléans, the Enlightened, murdered by John the Fearless; of the poet Charles of Orléans, imprisoned by the English after the Battle of Agincourt? Tell me, when did they ever suppose that in the veins of their Empress, with skin as white as a lotus, kneeling on the ground to lay the foundations for their schools, ran the blood of Isabel Farnese and the Sun King, of Eleanor of Aquitaine, of Maria Theresa of Austria, and of Blanca of Castile? Their Empress. When, tell me, did the Mexicans realize that when I married you I had an immense fortune of more than two million eight hundred thousand francs in Belgian, U.S., English,

Prussian, French, and Russian bonds? And that I took to Miramare from Brussels twenty-three necklaces, one of which was worth more than two hundred thousand francs; thirty-four bracelets, one of which bore my father's portrait surrounded by diamonds— my father, Leopold, the wise King of Belgium, whom Napoleon the Great described from St. Helena Island as the most handsome officer ever to set foot in the Tuileries; I also took fifty-one brooches, eleven rings, three hundred and sixty blouses, seventy-two nightcaps, seventy-seven dressing gowns, eighty-one shawls, four hundred and eighty pairs of gloves, two hundred and fifteen handkerchiefs, two hundred and eighty-eight pairs of stockings, and one hundred pairs of shoes, along with a pair from when I was five years old. All of that I left in Mexico, along with the rubies from Burma and the large brooch your brother gave me that I never saw again. When had those Indians ever seen a golden imperial carriage pass through those roads bordered with cacti and agave? When did Titian or Velázquez ever paint one of their presidents? When did those starving bandits ever have a leader like the French Marshal in his white-plumed bicorne? When, tell me, did those miserable wretches ever see a Hussar halving coconuts with the same saber he had used to behead a Turk? When did they even imagine the grandeur, the splendor of a European empire? When did they have a court chamberlain, a Kapellmeister, one hundred of the Empress's dragoons? When did they ever see a lackey in a royal purple velvet frockcoat buying phalaropes at the Santa Anita market? Tell me, when did they imagine that the Prince who cleaned up the Venetian lagoons of Lombardo-Veneto, who drained the swamps to arrest the spread of malaria, who broadened the avenues in Milan, who built a new square between La Scala and the Marine Palace, who restored the Ambrosian Library, who irrigated the Frioul plains with the waters of the Ledra, tell me, when did they dream that the same prince, Maximilian the Wise, Maximilian the Liberal, Maximilian the Maecenas, Maximilian the Heir to the Holy Roman Empire, Maximilian the descendant of the greatest, most important dynasty in history—the Naples Bourbons and the Hohenstaufens each had four monarchs, the Bonapartes five, the Tudors six, the French Bourbons seven, the Hohenzollerns nine, the Stuarts and the Spanish Bourbons ten, the Hanover-Windsors eleven, the Savoys twelve, the Valois thirteen, the Plantagenets fourteen, the Braganzas and the Capets fifteen, and the Romanovs eighteen; the House of Austria, the Habsburgs, your house, Maximilian, the only one that gave the world twenty-six monarchs, twenty-two of them emperors and four kings of the Spanish branch of the Habsburgs, besides four European queens—when did they realize, those Mexicans, that one of those emperors was the very same one they had before them, a blond-bearded Emperor who lay in a hammock in the burning shade of the flowering flamboyants, who drank sherry all afternoon, and Rhine wine from Bohemian crystal goblets; Maximilian the Sybarite, the one who dined on Limoges china, Maximilian the Elegant, strolling, arm in arm with Commodore Maury under the chandeliers brought from Austria and gazing at the tapestries with illustrations from La Fontaine's fables in the conservatory of Chapultepec Castle; Maximilian the Thinker, who meditated in a Louis Quinze chair, next to the stained glass figures of Ceres and Pomona, Flora and Diana, which you had made to bathe the castle hallways in the light of Greek mythology. When, tell me, did they realize that one of those Habsburg emperors was the same man who knocked on bakery doors at night in Mexico City—Maximilian the Incognito, the one who rode across the Jamapa River, with water up to his waist—Maximilian the Daring—and atop the Pyramid of the Sun decided to become a new Justinian, the new Solon of America—Maximilian the Ambitious? Oh, Maximilian, sometimes I think that I shall never forgive the Mexicans.

You were also Maximilian the Failure, because you dreamed about being a new Maximilian I of Habsburg, another Joseph II of Austria. But Joseph II abolished slavery and colonized Galicia—you tried to restore it in Mexico, and couldn't even annex the Belize territory to your Empire. Maximilian I reclaimed the Hungarian territories for the House of Austria, along with the silver from the Tyrolean mines. But what did you do, tell me, with the Mexican silver, but fill the pockets and the bellies of the French military, fill their rifles with gunpowder, their cannons with fodder? You were, therefore, a traitor to your new Motherland. And for that reason Mexico will never forgive you. For that reason, Mexico will always despise you. You are, you were, Maximilian the Despised, the Forgotten. Archduke Karl and Prince Eugene of Savoy were immortalized on their equestrian bronze statues, at the Hofburg's Heroes' Square. But you're not there, Maximilian. Archduke Karl defeated Napoleon at Aspern, and Eugene of Savoy annihilated Mustapha II's Turkish troops at Zenta. But you didn't win the Battle of Mexico and for that, Maximilian, your own people, the Austrians, will never forgive you.

•

For all those reasons, Maximilian, I know now that transparency and purity are not enough to help me rewrite your story, that I am damned to live and die like this, with my guts on fire. I knew it the moment that the water mirror where I looked at my face clouded over. I knew it when the water in which I was floating in a state of confusion became cloudy with putrid liquids, when it began turning red. When I realized that I would have to write your story and mine, at least for now, at least for those years, those days, those minutes I have left to live, with that polluted liquid that runs through my veins. With the same liquid that stained the back of my cousin Minette's wooden horse; the same that my mother swore was blue and immaculate, but—I found out later—was really black, illegitimate, and cloudy: my blood. Yours too, Maximilian, and that of many others. A few days ago the messenger came disguised as Benito Juárez and he was carrying the lid of a skull brimming with blood. It was the blood, he said, of every Mexican who had died during the Intervention and the Empire. He said that if the Mexicans had wanted to stretch out a red carpet from the National Palace to the Grand Altar of the Cathedral the day that you and I walked there to give thanks to God, the bodies of all my Mexicans killed by French troops, by *Chasseurs d'Afrique*, by legionnaires and by counter-guerrillas from Tamaulipas, along with the blood shed by the Austrian and Belgian volunteers, the limbs lost by Mexicans at Puebla and Tampico, the ears that Egyptian soldiers cut off, the ones shot or hanged after you signed the Decree of October 3rd—those corpses would cover one hundred times the distance. And the Indian said more. He told me that even though you had to be embalmed twice, at least you were returned to your homeland, filled with Egyptian perfume, under an angel's wings. And so, there you are now, in Vienna, where the descendants of those Mexicans who took you to Mexico can worship all of your bones. But where—Juárez asked me, and I ask you—where are the remains of the soldiers from Zacapoaxtla who were left under the mud of the Puebla plains? Where are the bones of the guerrillas that Colonel Dupin threw into the waters of the Tamesí River weighed down with stones hanging from their necks? Where are the bones of those felled by firing squads in Mexico City and dumped into common graves at Campo Florido Cemetery? Where are the ones whose bodies were devoured by sharks in Guaymas Bay? Then, Maximilian, I took off my clothes. I got naked, Maximilian, in front of Juárez, not to give myself to him but to write our story on my flesh, with my flesh, with my blood and Mexico's. I dipped my middle finger in the blood and traced a cross on my brow. I drew a circle on my abdomen. With my finger and the blood of Mexicans shed at the Battle of Santa Gertrudis, at the Battles of

Pinoteca and San Lorenzo, on the coasts of Tamaulipas, at the siege of Querétaro, in the deserts of Sinaloa, in the Street of Fools in Puebla, under horses'
hooves, devoured by dogs, dead from typhus and gangrene, of thirst, with
broken skulls, in the Hidalgo ravines, in the Battle of Calleja, Maximilian, I
tattooed my entire body. It is there, on my skin, where all of this is written, not
in the thousands of blank pieces of paper I've torn out of my diaries and scattered around my rooms, stacked into piles and then scattered again, becoming
frustrated once more because I've still failed to tell your story. But then I am
happy again because, after all, I have been given the opportunity to start from
the beginning. Oh Maximilian, sometimes I think that the pages from the
notebook where you wrote your aphorisms and the rules of conduct that you
followed all your life, the pages from the Bible that Monseigneur Rechich and
Abbott Gómez presented to you at Miramare so that you could be sworn in
as the monarch of your new nation, and the pages from your secret diary, the
memoirs from your travels through Albania, Algiers, and South America, the
Family Pact in which you renounced all your rights to the Habsburg Throne,
the letters Kuhacsevich's wife wrote to Radonetz to complain that she had to
play every type of role in the Mexican court—chief steward, lady-in-waiting,
reader, secretary, equerry, parlormaid, nurse, stable maid—along with the letters from Colonel Loizillon and Bazaine and the Countess von Kollonitz, the
letters Santa Anna wrote you from Saint Thomas, offering you his support
for the Empire, and those you sent Baroness Binzer to describe the charms of
the Borda Gardens, the endless reports that Fischer sent you from the Vatican—with all of that, Maximilian, and the speeches to the Mexican Senate
that you first wrote in German to be translated into Latin, the menus from
the Mexican Court banquets that you sent to Europe so that everyone would
see how well you served your imperial guests, the letters from Eloin where he
told you that all of Vienna lamented that their Max was so far away, and then
those you wrote back to inform him that everything was fine in Mexico thanks
to Bazaine's apathy and the indifference of the French, the letters where you
told Count Hadik that you had ordered five hundred and ninety flowering ash
trees to be planted in Mexico City and that the necessary funds had come out
of your own pocket to care for the almost unique *árbol de manitas* that grew
in the interior garden of the National Palace and that had so been admired
by Humboldt and Bonpland, and too the letters from my father Leopold in
which he advised us not to lose the Indians' affection, the memoir of Pierren

in which he compared you to Pepe Botella, the King of Spain, and the letters written by Leonardo Márquez from the Palace of el-Woska in Alexandria, and the farewell letters you wrote the people and your ministers from Orizaba when you decided to leave Mexico and then to stay, the edicts that you signed to stimulate the pearl industry and the breeding of leeches, the pages from the books by Blanchot and Niox, Détroyat and Hans, Blasio and Dr. Basch, those from the official Imperial journal that published the news of the military triumphs of Douay and Castagny, and the Empress's Monday socials, and the five hundred pages of the Court Protocol, all that, Maximilian, and the thousand and one folios of your trial and sentencing, could make up a carpet that would cover the road from Vienna to Querétaro, from your blue room with the stuffed nightingale at Schönbrunn to your cell at the Teresitas Convent, from the Hofburg gate with its golden eagles to the dirty adobe of the makeshift wall at Las Campanas Hill. But all of that would not be sufficient, Maximilian, to cover our dishonor and misfortune.

Because, in the final analysis, tell me, what good were all the riches of Mexico? What good were all its precious woods, when you ended up in a pine box that was too small for you? What good were they if you couldn't build a scaffold for Bazaine or Escobedo from the National Palace oak beams? Tell me, what did you gain from all the silver from Sonoran mines when you couldn't even bribe your jailers and henchmen?

With all the scorpions of Mexico, Maximilian, we could carpet Saint-Cloud Palace, but we would not have enough snake skins to cover up its traitors, those who left you, Maximilian—our Little Napoleon, Hidalgo y Esnaurrízar, Márquez, López and so many others—who fled like rats from a sinking ship. Or your own mother who told you to stay in Mexico, away from Austria forever. And the medals and prizes, oh Max, my dear, innocent Max, who but you would have thought of casting them out like pearls to swine? The medals you threw at the crowds of beggars who flashed you with their sores and their stumps in the Street of Red Bridges in Naples, in Madeira at the boys who swam around your ship, at the Mexican peasants and beggars when you became godfather to your *compadre*'s son? Oh, Maximilian, we could cover your tomb with all the medals, the ribbons and the crosses that you awarded in Mexico; we could bury you in a pyramid of gold and silver, of bronze and silk. Tell me, Max, why didn't you award the great medallion of the Order of Crime to Colonel Platón Sánchez? Why didn't you pin the Order of Cowardice on

Baron Lago and all the other European consuls who suddenly fled Querétaro? Why didn't you name your brother Franz Joseph to the Order of Perfidy? Why, tell me, didn't you award Juárez the Order of Mercy in order to get a pardon from him? You, Max, my dear Max, as a child, played at making medals and awards with colored paper, silver foil, ribbons, tassels and curtain fringe, and demanded that your brother Ludwig Karl name you Grand Master of the Orders of the Iron Crown and the Red Eagle, of the Golden Fleece, in Napoleon Hall at Schönbrunn; in the Hall of Mirrors where Mozart played as a child, you were knighted in the Order of the Bath and the Order of Philip the Merciful; in the shade of the garden statues of Euridice, Jason, and Hannibal you were dubbed Commander of the Order of the North Star. Listen to me. I have here with me the Order of Saint Olaf, with its gold Maltese cross and the Norwegian lion that Haakon VII brought me to deliver to you in Mexico. I have the great medallion of the Order of Charles III, with the golden fleurs-de-lis of the Bourbons that Alfonso XIII sent to put around your neck next time I see you. I also have the Order of Saint Hubert of Bavaria that your cousin Ludwig sent for your next birthday, and the Order of the Garter sent by Cousin Victoria. The Order of Leopold of Belgium sent by Papa Leopich, and the Order of the Southern Cross of Brazil that Pedro wants you to wear on the anniversary of your Empire. I also have the Order of the Congo Star sent by my brother Leopold; the Order of Nichan-el-Anour that President Poincaré wants to award to you on your saint's day; the Order of Saint Seraphim with its three Swedish crowns and the three nails from the Holy Cross sent by Oskar II; and the Order of Saint Gregory that Pius X asked me to bring to you as a Twelfth Night gift in Mexico. But I will give you nothing. Maximilian—tell me why, when the French troops deserted you in Mexico and Bazaine threw millions of cartridges that landed among rocks and weeds to the bottom of the Viga Canal rather than leave you the ammunition that ended up then with the lost jewels from Cuauhtémoc's treasure and with the idols and figurines, the offerings that the Indians tossed into the river to calm the wrath of the god Tlaloc, begging him to spare the Aztec city from flooding; when you found out in Orizaba that the Republicans had looted your beloved Borda Villa in Cuernavaca, when on the way to Querétaro your horse Orispelo tripped up and a bugler fell dead at your feet; why was it that when in the Religious City Escobedo's forces blocked the escape routes and when Galeana's riflemen finished off the Imperial troops who were left lying on Carretas Plain with their swords, and when the victory at Cimatario turned not only into a rout but a total fiasco—everyone knew that after Cimatario your empire was condemned to disappear—why, tell me, when a cannonball brought down the statue of the Goddess of Liberty in Querétaro, and when your generals ate mule meat marinated in vinegar, and you offered one dollar for every bullet in good condition, and the Querétaro air was fetid from the charred flesh of the piles of dead bodies that there was no time to bury, and the rotting smell of gangrene, and when almost every day you found one of your men hanging from a tree, and when you had to turn the casino into a hospital for amputees, and when you still had the strength to dream, Maximilian the Optimist, that Juárez would spare you, and when you were imprisoned at the Teresitas Convent and you dictated to Blasio the schedule for every day that you would spend locked up in Lacroma, with everything planned from breakfast to billiards, drinking port, reading Dante and the papers, hot chocolate and cigarettes, all except a few minutes of love for me probably because you thought that I would live far away, locked away forever in an asylum; tell me why, when you still had energy, Maximilian the Humorist, you gave Latin names to the disgusting bedbugs at the Convent, as they sucked your blood every night, as they devoured you, as everyone in Mexico devoured you, taking advantage of your naïveté and your kindness, Maximilian the Innocent, Maximilian the Kind, of your altruism, Maximilian the Altruist—why were you devoured by Almonte; devoured by Father Agustín Fischer; devoured by Gutiérrez Estrada and Napoleon III; devoured by mosquitoes, dysentery, the clergy, treason; devoured by your own indolence, Maximilian the Lazy—you were devoured by the humidity in the lowlands, by the fire of the temperate lands, while I was left with only traces of you: your eye sockets filled with black hail, your skin blackened and scaly, a few blond shreds left on your skull; tell me why, when you knew that Márquez would never return to Querétaro to fulfill his promise to bring back his cavalry to surprise Escobedo from the rear; why, when you found out that there was a tree at La Cruz that was the only example of the species in all the world, an acacia with thorns shaped like perfect crosses that prefigured your martyrdom; why when our friend López, whom you selected for the Empress's Guard because you liked to surround yourself with handsome people (you thought that a beautiful face was always matched by a beautiful soul); why, when our blond, blue-eyed *compadre* surrendered the convent on the dawn of May 14, 1867; why, tell me, when you found out that the moment you left your room at La Cruz,

642

the Republicans went in to loot it; why when at the Teresitas Convent you made Dr. Basch see that one of your guards was amusing himself with a dummy dressed in a blue frockcoat, red trousers and a crown on his head, its face a sort of moveable mask under which there was a skull that foreshadowed your death and the mockery that the Mexicans would make of it; why—when they made you spend a night in the grave as you told Basch, because they locked you up in the crypt of the Capuchin Convent at Querétaro, which made you remember your trip to Palermo on the day that a Capuchin guided you to another crypt with a skull-trimmed door and inside you saw with horror a group of mummified bodies and half-naked skeletons, some with hair still on their heads lying in grotesque postures in the open niches against the walls, kneeling, squatting, standing, and skulls with ruffled nightcaps staring at you from bottomless eyes, smiling at you with fleshless lips, mummies dressed in lace nightgowns, in frockcoats, with hands extended, which portended both your trip to Palermo and that night in Querétaro, your final resting place because, in the end, when you arrived in Vienna they would keep you, as they did with the other emperors and princes of the Holy Roman Empire and the Austrian branch of the House of Habsburg, dead and embalmed forever and ever in the crypt inside the imperial chapel of the Capuchins, although you must know, my poor Max, that even in death your Austrian brothers denied you the title of Emperor that belonged to you in life, because in the Kapuzinergruft those who were emperors all received a mausoleum and you don't have one—they did not build for you, as for Empress Maria Teresa and her husband Francis of Lorraine, a funeral monument surrounded by the three Christian virtues melting into a sea of marble tears, so that the Faith you had in your great destiny since your childhood does not cry for you, nor does the Charity that you always had for your servants, your subjects, and your friends, nor indeed the Hope that never left you while you were alive in Mexico; but tell me why, Maximilian, when you knew you would be tried, when you were sentenced to die in front of the firing squad, and when you found out that Juárez had denied you a pardon and would keep refusing despite all the begging of all the kneeling amazons in the world, and all the crowned heads in the universe, why on that morning of your execution, when you dressed and put a dozen handkerchiefs under your shirt to absorb your blood so you wouldn't look pathetic, in a gesture similar to one made by your hero Charles I of England who, the morning of his beheading, wore many shirts to keep from trembling from the cold so that the people would not confuse his shaking with that of fear, why when you were before the firing squad and you requested that no more blood be shed in Mexico after yours and your two generals', tell me, why, Maximilian, after you shouted "Long Live Mexico!" a few seconds before the discharge, like a fool and a weakling, like a gullible, like an innocent, like a naïve, like an arrogant and lazy, like a daring and false man, like an imbecile, tell me, why didn't you award yourself the great Chain of the Supreme Order of the Grand Dummy?

·

They say I'm mad because I broke all the mirrors at Miramare and Bouchout. I cannot, I do not, dare see that face that once smiled at Little Napoleon; those eyes that one day lit up at the promises of Gutiérrez Estrada. I gazed at my mother adoringly with those eyes but I used those same eyes to observe and desire your nude body. I don't want to see them in a mirror again; I don't want them to see my lips. With these lips I kissed old ladies' feet on Maundy Thursday. With them I drank from baptismal fonts in all the churches in Venice and I received the Sacred Host at Saint Peter's tomb from Pius IX. With these same lips I cursed the Pope and the Church a thousand times. I've put a black cap on my head because I never again want to look at my hair in a mirror. I don't want to touch it. This is the same head of hair that my father caressed but also the one that Colonel Van der Smissen covered with kisses. I've put on black velvet earmuffs; with these ears I heard your promises of love, spoken with your lips, but also the insults of the Mexicans. I never want to look at them in a mirror again. I refuse to touch them. I don't even want them to hear my own voice. I've slipped on some black gloves. With these hands I embroidered slippers for Papa Leopold, but I never put a single flower on his grave with them. With these hands too I held Frayssinous's books and with them I stitched the Lamb of God on a cushion and I embroidered the Holy Eucharist on another, and the Chalice of the Last Supper on still another. But with these same hands I caressed your chest matted with blond hair, and I caressed the fluff on your crotch. I have covered my body with black rags—I can't bear the sight of those breasts that you and Van der Smissen suckled; I don't want to see the belly that carried General Weygand, the thighs that pressed your waist and that parted to welcome Van der Smissen's penis, to bear the fruit of my lust. I don't want to look at those feet that have bled on the long, endless road that I've walked since I left Europe; those feet singed, Max, by the burning sand of all the Mexican deserts and bloodied by the thorns of all the cacti and thistles. They say that I'm insane because I spend week after week in my bed, under the sheets, because I've ordered the windows draped in black velvet, and I have them dress me, bathe me, and feed me in the dark, to let me do my business in the dark. I can't look at the world and I don't want the world to look at me. When we said good-bye forever, Max, in the perfumed air of Ayotla, the peasant girls gave me a crown and a scepter made from live fire-flies on stickpins. We could use that crown and scepter to light up the greatest hall in the Tuileries, Maximilian, but they would not be enough to light up my solitude and shame.

·

The telephone was invented, Maximilian, and so I ordered a secret line from my bedchamber to the aides-de-camp's quarters. Another one from my bed-chamber to the Hall of Diplomats. Another one from the Hall of the Great Chamberlains to Napoleon III's office at Saint-Cloud and to Empress Eugénie's chapel at Fontainebleau. Another one from the National Palace in Mexico to the Vatican. One more from Chapultepec Castle to the Borda Gardens. Yet another one from my carriage to Benito Juárez's stagecoach. Oh, if you only knew, Maximilian, how amusing it is to talk on the telephone all the time. I curse Eugénie every morning and remind her that her great-grandfather was a Scottish wine merchant. I remind Napoleon III that he's been nicknamed the Great Harlequin. They say I'm mad, Maximilian, that I act like a child because I use an invisible telephone to talk to the dead and the living. A line was installed from my bed to the clouds so that I can talk to the birds and the rain. Another goes from my nightstand to the bottom of the Adriatic so that I can talk to the fish and the sailors who have drowned. I had one put in from the Gartenhaus at Miramare to Neuilly to ask Grandfather Louis Philippe to gather all the eucalyptus seed capsules he finds in the castle gardens for me. I phoned my father in Brussels to tell him that I'm sending him an album, bound in red velvet, where I pasted photographs of all types of Mexicans: the water vendor, the chair caner, the knife sharpener, the clothes peddler. I told him also that I ordered a bust of him and of my mother Marie Louise from the sculptor Gees. I'm going to put both sculptures at the foot of my bed so that they will be the first thing I see when I wake up. I called Grandmother Marie Amélie in Claremont to tell her that she was wrong, that we were not both murdered in Mexico—only you. To tell her that I'm alive, more alive than she and all the rest. People say that I'm mad because I sail on a barge in Bouchout's pond while I talk to you and I beg you not to come back, not to renounce your Empire. I tell you that the black swans have returned to Bruges and that I'm ready to go back to Mexico. I'm going to take the Mexican flag I've had all this time, folded away in lavender leaves, with me. They say I'm mad because I beg you to take care of yourself. I want to find you alive and so, I implore you, when you go to Tenerife, don't eat precious stones; when you return to La Scala, don't drink tea from China; don't eat raw clams, Maximilian, because someone wants to poison you: with the juice of a *coyol*, with avocados from Tecozautla, with the sparkling water from the springs at Tehuacán. They say I'm crazy because I talk on the phone with the Pope. Because I called President Lincoln to beg him to help us. Because I call Benito Juárez to remind him that he's an Indian, that at thirteen he spoke only the Zapotec language, that he played his flute amid bamboo shoots in the Enchanted Lagoon, that he was expelled from Oaxaca and later from Mexico, that he was an orphan, that he was called "the Monkey dressed as Napoleon," that he was a prisoner at San Juan de Ulúa, that he rolled tobacco in New Orleans, that he spent his entire life running and hopping from Mexico City to San Luis Potosí, to Zacatecas, Havana, Acapulco, Chihuahua, and Veracruz. They say I'm insane, that I act like a child because I know you're dead but still beg Juárez not to kill you. Then I beg him, if he does kill you, not to hand over your remains to Admiral Tegetthoff. Not to allow you to return to Europe in defeat, without your entrails and your titles. I beg Juárez every single day, I entreat him, I kneel before him, I kiss his dark, rough hands, I remind him that he was a physics teacher, that he was Governor of Oaxaca, that he's the President of the Republic, that he's a translator of Tacitus, that he studied algebra and philosophy. I beg him not to kill you, not to embalm you. I beg him in the name of God, the same God that he invoked when he triumphed over the Empire, not to send your remains to Vienna. I beg him in the name of *The Lives of Saints* from which he learned Spanish grammar, to throw your body into Veracruz bay from a Mexican ship, or to bury it in Mexico. I beg him in the name of that image of Christ he followed through the streets of Oaxaca intoning the Stations of the Cross to let me dig your grave with my own hands and teeth, to let me die with you, to kill me too if he wants, and to let both of us rot in peace, alone and forgotten forever in a common grave in Querétaro Cemetery. But Juárez refuses to speak to me. He sends a message with his secretary that he's busy writing the Constitution, that he went to San Luis, that he has to give a speech in the Chamber of Deputies, that he's taking a nap, that Margarita Juárez is knotting his tie, that he has to make up a famous phrase. He replies that he must put on his reserve army uniform to defend the Isthmus of Tehuantepec from Spanish invaders, that he is preparing his reelection campaign, that he has to write an attack against the Scottish Rite Masons, that he is taking his little granddaughter to the park. He tells me that he doesn't remember me, that he doesn't know who I am. He sends me a message that he's been dead for fifty years, that he's no longer a president, no longer a lawyer, that he's not an Indian anymore, nor anything else. He's only a monument in Mexico City's Alameda Park, and a statue in every town in the Republic. He is the name of hundreds of avenues and thousands of streets in thousands of villages, the name of a city, of a flower. He sends a message saying that he is a pile of dust in the Rotunda of Illustrious Men.

In any case, he won't get away from me. He promised that history would judge both of you so he will have to understand that you were all of those Maximilians—the Fearless, the Worthy, the Magnanimous, the Kind, the Deaf, the Merciless, the Inflexible— and I will remind him of this every single day. I will beg him in the memory of his sainted mother to remember that, if you were resentful and ridiculous, unbelieving, improvident, blind and forsaken, stubborn and ignorant, I will plead with him in the name of his children—Maximilian the Mediocre and the Adventurer, the Liar, the Enlightened, the Understanding, the Deluded, and the Proud—I'll tell him that you were all those, and more: the Brave, the Hypocritical Maximilian, the Philosopher and the Artist, the Heroic, the Naïve, the Sportsman. I will put flowers on his grave—the Detached, the Romantic, the Patient, the Grateful, the Attentive, the Refined Maximilian—I shall pray each night for your soul, provided that he makes it known to Mexico—Maximilian the Rememberer, the Generous, the Noble, the Wise, the Liberal, the Maecenas, the Sybarite, the Elegant—so that he won't forget and he'll forgive you, so that he will understand that, if you had every vice and virtue, and you were Maximilian the Just, the Ambitious, the Loser, the Despised, the Forgotten—I will build him an altar and light him a candle in your name, in the name of Maximilian the Humorist, Maximilian the Innocent, the Optimist, Maximilian the Altruist, the Indolent, the Fool, the Weakling, the Gullible, the Naïve, the Trusting, the Arrogant, the Lazy, the Deluded, the Rash, the

False, the Idiot Maximilian—so that he will understand that, if you were a little of everything many times but never only one thing, then you were like all human beings: forever the usurper and impostor, as those who don't love you say, or, as I do, because I love you so much, forever the victim and the martyr.

XXII
"HISTORY WILL BE OUR JUDGE"
1872–1927

1. "What Are We Going to Do with You, Benito?"

Tell us, Benito:

"Who would throw out little fruits?"

"Little green fruits, to the parishioners?"

"Who would do it during Mass?"

"So that people thought they were raining down from the Heavens."

"Or that they were popping out of hell."

"Who was doing it?"

"An angel?"

"Or was it the devil throwing them?"

"Or was it only Pablo throwing them?"

"Pablo Benito Juárez, who is the devil himself!"

"The devil himself, the very devil himself!"

He felt the pain again. His whole chest hurt as though it were a throbbing ulcer, as though his flesh were raw on the surface or just under the skin, red, burning, like a devil's.

The devil himself.

"And who, who was it that in the lagoon with the enchanted name . . . ?"

"Who, who would talk to the birds?"

Not an angel, ever. He had never been an angel for anyone. Not even for his parents, Marcelino and Brígida. Not for Margarita . . . oh, only the devil!

"Who? Benito Pablo?"

He never remembered the faces of Marcelino and Brígida who had left him an orphan at such an early age. He never even found out if Brígida had ever breastfed him. But thinking about the lagoon and the language of the birds was like a fresh and sweet breeze caressing his chest. Yes, yes, he, he, Pablo Benito Juárez, was the one who talked with the birds and the sheep and all God's creatures, he, the Indian who knew the language of the beasts when he was a little shepherd in Guelatao. I, the Indian, I, Pablo, he meant to say. I, Benito he tried to shout, but he realized that he couldn't talk, that no sound would pass through his lips.

He also discovered that he couldn't close his eyes, and if he knew they were open it was because there was a shadow in front of him, darker than all the other dark shadows that surrounded him. And he discovered that the shadow had weight, that it had a form, dimensions, that it was a shape hanging over him like a gigantic bat, a vampire sleeping upside-down, hanging from the ceiling by the claws in its wings, and he also knew what that shadow was.

"Isn't that so, Benito Pablo?"

And just as he couldn't stop seeing, he couldn't stop hearing and feeling. First he saw a light coming from above, white, very pale and diffuse, a light like that of dawn coming down like a fine powder, very slowly, as though filtered through the windows and rosettes of a dome, and he heard a metallic noise like chains, perhaps, and something that was . . . yes, something like the sound of a leak, as though it were raining and the drops were seeping through the beams of the roof, they were seeping and falling, falling and going *plip-plop* on a washbasin.

Or like someone had left a faucet open.

And he could pick out the smell of gardenias and formaldehyde: an offensive, almost unbearable smell.

"Isn't that so, Benito?"

A devil . . . oh, he had surely been a devil many times for many people, for so many people: a devil of a lawyer, a devil of a governor, a devil of a president. He smiled then, or tried to smile, when he thought too that he'd also been a poor devil on a number of occasions: like in San Juan de Ulúa, in the humid and hot-as-hell dungeon through whose walls seawater would ooze, salty, burning water, that fell drop by drop on his wounded chest: darts of salt, *ay* Margarita, like thorns of salt in his flesh that so . . . *ay*.

"It burns me so much . . ."

He tried, but nothing came out of his mouth, not a sound or a syllable—but, just invoking her name in his thoughts, it was like she, Margarita, had blown on his chest, and on his chest his white shirtfront, fresh and white, white and cold, Mr. President, appeared; or it was like a hooded man in white had run some iris leaves over him . . .

"Because, Benito, you were a shepherd and a studious and clean little boy . . ."

"Yes, yes, that I was," he wanted to say, to shout at the shadows, and he remembered his uncle and godfather, Salanueva, he remembered when he was a student at the Seminary, and how he burned the midnight oil when he was studying to be a priest; but, damn!, this boy doesn't want to be a priest, he wants to be a lawyer!

"A lawyer, Benito?"

A flash, a spark came from the shadow hanging from the ceiling, a minuscule glint, a wink of light. And he again heard the clanking of a chain; the shadow was moving and it appeared to be gyrating, turning in on itself. He also heard the dripping, the *plip-plop*, while the other light kept descending like a very fine and very slow-moving dust, very slow and very fine, diffuse, almost imperceptible, and it began to illuminate the curved lines of what had to be a dome. Benito knew what dome it was, and from the beginning he also knew that he was stretched out, lying face up, with his chest bared, on something that couldn't be a bed, not even a cot; judging from its hardness and coldness, it had to be a table, a table that must have been very wide and very long. He tried to raise his arm and point toward the shadow that hung before him, to sit up on the table and touch it, but he felt paralyzed.

"A lawyer, Benito?"

"A lawyer for whom? For the devil?"

"Yes, a lawyer for the host of the devil, for the atheist masons, for the heretics and blasphemers, for the reds and priest-eaters!"

"Oh, Benito Pablo, traitor of traitors!"

"He betrayed his godfather," the voices said.

"His godfather Salanueva who wanted him to be a priest."

"I, a traitor? Betrayed my godfather Salanueva?" the President tried to say, but only a weak murmur came from his lips. A murmur that could have turned into a scream when he imagined, when he thought he saw, a man with a black hood over his head touching his chest with a lighted torch, burning his skin.

Yes, a traitor because that boy was a little Judas—however you say little and Judas in his native Zapotecan language—sometimes because he dreamt while awake and sometimes because he dreamt while asleep—because he abandoned his sheep, and he ended up abandoning his people, abandoning his mountains, betraying his occupation and his enchanted lagoon, and his uncle Bernardino, who wanted him to be a little shepherd.

"Where did Benito go? Where could he have taken himself?"

To places where he wasn't wanted: first to the city of Oaxaca, and later to that heresiarch's nest, the Institute. Oh yes, that Pablo Benito or Benito Pablo, whatever his name was, was always sticking his nose in where nobody wanted him, always.

"Isn't that so, Benito?" said a shadow very close to his face, and the breath of the shadow's voice burned his neck, dripped down his side like burning lava, burned his ribs.

"Isn't it true, Benito, that you always stick your nose where nobody wants you?"

Benito in Oaxaca with a bow tie and white shirt front. Benito the physics teacher at the Institute, in black frockcoat and patent-leather shoes. Benito at the state government offices, in gold eyeglasses. Benito, at the presidential palace of the Republic with silver-handled cane. Benito, venerable brother of the York lodge, lodge of the killjoys . . . But, hadn't he been called? Hadn't he, perhaps, been called to all those places?

"Your people called you, Benito."

So said some voices, and he felt like a breeze was kissing, caressing his breast.

"No, it's not true, Benito. No one called you."

"You were called by your Indians from the Sierra de Ixtlán, who would greet you in the Zapotec language. Do you remember? '*Tzaquilzil, tata.*'"

"No, it's not true Benito—no one called you."

"You were called by the poor people of Loricha, and that landed you in jail. You were called by the peasants of Chihuahua. The citizens of San Luis. The Liberals and the Republicans. The people of Zacapoaxtla. The whole country called you. America called you."

"No, it's not true, Benito, it's a lie," said the other voices.

But no, it wasn't a lie and his Indians knew it, his friends knew it and even his enemies; the country knew it, America, history knew it. "Isn't that so, Margarita," he said or tried to say, and when he said or thought he said "Margarita," it was as though someone, as though a man—or was it an angel?—his head covered with a white hood and a *margarita*, a daisy, in his hand, the flower from which Margarita had gotten her name, were slowly stripping its petals over his chest, and its petals were covering the ulcer and healing it: the petals of cold, fresh snow, Margarita.

But no matter how much he thought of her, no matter how many times he would call her name, she would not come: Margarita had died. The poor woman had died from having so many children and from having so many children die. Of having followed the lawyer and the president here and there, there and here all her life. Yes, Margarita had preceded him, and he, Pablo Benito Juárez, was condemned to die alone.

And that was without a doubt what was happening to him: he was dying. The President of Mexico was dying for sure.

He was dying of angina pectoris.

But he was also dying from other causes: he was dying of those shadows, of those voices and what they were saying. Of their slanders and their lies. Of their truths. Of what they didn't say. In spite of it all being a dream.

And he didn't doubt for an instant it was all a dream, delirium, nightmare.

Because that chapel didn't exist anymore. Because the dome from which the chain holding the body of the Archduke Ferdinand Maximilian had hung had fallen down at least four years before, and nothing but rubble was left of the Chapel of San Andrés Hospital in Mexico City.

But the fact is that he, Benito Juárez, was in that chapel, lying on the table of the Tribunal of the Holy Inquisition, where, after being embalmed for the second time, the body of the Archduke had lain, and now he was taking the place of the Archduke—but with a difference: he, Pablo Benito Juárez was alive. Perhaps he was going to die soon, but he was still alive. He was breathing, though painfully, with a great effort, as though a great rock had been placed on his chest, but nevertheless he was breathing. He, Juárez, was alive, and the Archduke was dead.

Yes, dead, with his eyes open. With his black, glass eyes open.

Dead and naked, he was hanging upside down, his feet tied to the chain that came down from the center of the dome of the Chapel, his arms tied to his sides.

Here and there, from some incisions made by a scalpel in his dry, yellow skin there oozed in several streams a thick liquid of an indefinite color: olive green perhaps, gray or ashen, that dripped drop by drop into a washbasin on the floor.

The body of the Archduke was now illuminated by a ray of that fine and dusty light that seemed to come down from heaven or from nowhere in particular.

In the background, way in the back, a triangle of fire with small blue flames began to burn, and in its center blazed a five-pointed star.

Benito Juárez made another great, an enormous effort to summon the cooling kiss of snow on his chest, the glacial breath.

For this to happen he needed to hear a voice or voices from afar, from his adolescence and his youth in Oaxaca, saying what many others had also said when Pablo Benito Juárez was young and a lawyer, well-read and able to write in Latin and Castilian, neat and clean, serious, a believer and in love with the daughter of the patrons who had sheltered him, a barefoot Indian in the great capital city of the state.

"There goes Juárez, Juárez, the intelligent one."

Because that's what they would say, or:

"There's Benito, Benito the honest one."

Because they swore he was. And then the iris, the irises would turn into white butterflies that would set their open, cool, white, mentholated wings over his burning breast, the breast of an intelligent, honest man: his wounded breast, that of an honorable patriarch.

But it had to happen right away, immediately. Before the pain suffocated him. Before his blood—his own and that of others—choked him.

"Oh, Benito!"

"Oh, Benito!"

"What are we going to do with you, Benito, a traitor to yourself, a man who sold his country, a murderer? What can we do with you except send you to hell?"

"Except send you to hell?"

Some malicious tongue had concocted the story that when he visited the Chapel of San Andrés and saw the Archduke's body on the table, Benito Juárez had whispered: "Forgive me."

But it wasn't true. He would never have asked for forgiveness, not when the Archduke was lying on the table, and not even now that he was hanging from the dome.

For the simple reason that the Archduke was dead, and dead people neither hear, see, feel, nor forgive. He looked at the Archduke's eyes. They shone, yes, but with the sparkle of mineral matter, lifeless. The thick green and gray liquids dripped from his body, they ran down from his chest or neck to his face, from the groin toward the belly and chest, and they converged on his face, the cheeks; they ran down the forehead, to the hair. Then they fell, drop by drop, into the washbasin on the floor.

Then Benito remembered the letter he had written the Archduke, who received it on his arrival in Mexico.

"Sir, man is given to attacking the rights of others, to seizing their property, to making attempts on the lives of those who defend their nationality, to making their virtues seem a crime, and to making a virtue out of his own vices . . ."

I wonder if the Archduke read the entire letter? Yes, of course, he most certainly did . . .

"But there is one thing," the President had written, "that is beyond the reach of such perversity, and that is the terrible verdict of History. *History will be our judge.*"

History's terrible verdict—are you listening to me Mr. Archduke of Austria? Are you listening to me? History will judge us, Juárez wanted to say out loud, almost shout it—or he thought he wanted to say it, thought he wanted to shout it.

But he realized it wasn't worth the effort.

Whether what was hanging from its feet in front of him was really the naked, embalmed body of the Archduke Ferdinand Maximilian, or whether everything was a dream—what else could it be but a dream, just delirium?—and the body of the Archduke was on the other side of the ocean, in the crypt of the Capuchin Church, wasn't it all the same? In any case, wasn't the body hanging from the middle of the dome of the Church of San Andrés or resting in a temporary Habsburg vault in Austria nothing more than a sack of dry, yellow or darkish skin filled with lifeless bones, myrrh, sawdust, preserved viscera, and a pair of glass eyes?

What archduke was going to be interested in the terrible verdict of history if there weren't any archdukes left?

History could only be of interest to those who were alive, while they were alive, President Benito Juárez told himself, and he remembered when as a young man he was beginning to read the Encyclopedists and the authors of the Age of Enlightenment, one of Voltaire's phrases had caught his attention: "History is a joke," the Frenchman said, "that we the living play on the dead."

Part of the joke, the fantastic joke, was of course that the dead never knew what was being said about them—and, not only that, they never even knew what people were saying *they* had said in life.

What kind of jokes would future historians play on him, Pablo Benito Juárez?

What words that he'd never said and never even wanted to say would they put into his mouth when it had already been eaten by worms?

He contemplated the Archduke's glass eyes. Liquid kept running down his skin, darker and darker, thicker and ever more foul-smelling. At times, as though there were a breeze or a light earthquake, the body would swing, gently, imperceptibly, back and forth, and the drops would drip out of range of the washbasin.

If it weren't for this intense pain, Pablo Benito Juárez thought . . .

Yes, if it weren't for that intense pain in his chest, the President would have thought it wasn't him there in the Chapel of the Hospital of San Andrés at all, but another Juárez, another Pablo Benito Juárez García that a future historian or playwright was dreaming up.

They were inventing his judgment. They were inventing the judgment of history. They were laying him on the table of the Tribunal of the Holy Inquisition, defenseless, paralyzed, unable to move a finger or say a word.

In front of him they'd hung the embalmed cadaver—decomposing and then embalmed again—of the Austrian prince on whose behalf the ladies of San Luis and Querétaro, the European ambassadors, and the princesses on horseback, or on their knees, had all begged for his mercy.

Yes, in front of Juárez, the future historian or dramatist had placed the Austrian, already dead, without any possibility of resuscitating him, of restoring freshness to his skin, of restoring the light—or even a different, more transparent tint—to his eyes. They had placed Abel in front of him.

So he could be accused of killing his brother.

The triangle of blue flames, the blazing star, as in a theater—everything was planned, as in a theater where a Masonic rite, a judgment, was being staged: the judgment of Cain, the judgment of Abel's murderer.

His accusers, he knew it, were the men in black hoods who were holding sticks greased with tar in their hands that they would turn into torches at any minute. But maybe they weren't sticks, maybe they were bull's tails or whips soaked in turpentine—anything that would catch fire, anything that would burn his breast, anything to beat or whip him with, to cause sparks to fly, to scar him.

His defenders, then, were the men in white hoods holding irises in their hands, irises that could have been something else, other flowers: daisies, for instance, or maybe not flowers, maybe they were soft white feathers, feathers from a swan or from the wings of an angel—all to caress his breast, to give him some respite, to heal his blisters.

But more than the fire—more, much more painful than the fire—were the words he heard spoken against him, to denigrate him, to condemn him, to accuse him, to shame him, and, what was worse, to bury him in oblivion: words all invented by those men from the future who had been charged with playing a particularly nasty joke on him—that is, who'd been charged with telling his story.

He tried closing his eyes again. Then he thought, if this is a dream, perhaps what I have to do is *not* close them. Perhaps I should be keeping them open.

He concentrated. He wanted to close his eyes to the hell of the Chapel and open them to a tranquil afternoon, lying on his bed, and for an instant, but only for an instant, he saw his personal doctor's face very close to his. And the doctor was holding . . . a pitcher? A smoking cup?

But the doctor's face turned into the black mask of one of the hooded men, and the pitcher or the cup had turned into a flare or a torch, and what the doctor might have been trying to tell him at that moment—"Sorry, Don Benito . . ."—turned into the voice of a ghost.

"Oh, Benito Juárez, what are we going to do with you?"

If they didn't know what to do with Pablo Benito, neither did he.

But one morning, one humid morning when he had gone, alone, to the Etla Lagoon, the place where he had made a diving board for himself and his friends, he remembered his sister had told him that, before dying, that people drowning would remember and relive their entire lives in one minute. He didn't think he was really wallowing in the bed of a lagoon, or that he was struggling with foam and water filling his lungs and suffocating him, but the President was absolutely sure of one thing: he was drowning. He was drowning in the pain in his chest and the weight he felt there, drowning in anguish and remorse, in his memories of Margarita and his dead children, he was drowning in his pride and tenderness and he knew he was going to die soon, so that perhaps he would still be able to relive his entire life in a minute, so that perhaps, as he saw it, he could tell it to his accusers himself, as it had really happened, and to himself as well—but who were his accusers? Those ghostly voices? The white-hooded men? The black-hooded men? History, historians? But yes, maybe then he could tell them, tell them what the hell they could do with him, with their Benito . . .

Whether to place him on an altar and bless him:

"May the Nation and its children bless you Benito because you gave them

657

freedom, because you separated the Temporal and Spiritual powers, and you put an end to the Church's rule . . ."

And call him a hero:

"And you triumphed over the invaders and the foreign Prince and restored the Republic . . ."

And consecrate him:

"Thank you, Benito, Saint Benito, Saint Pablo Benito Juárez!"

Or bring him down from his niche and curse him: for attacking the most sacred beliefs of his people, for trying to make Mexico a country of heretics and Protestants. And call him a traitor: for trying to sell Mexico to the United States, for doing whatever the Yankees wanted, for taking refuge every chance he got under the stars and stripes.

There, in that short span of time, he had now learned the rules of his ordeal—perhaps a trial, perhaps a farce—and that the same exchange would be repeated again, at each and every accusation . . . and there were so many: Juárez giving Tehuantepec to the United States in the McLane-Ocampo Treaty; Juárez recognizing the humiliating terms of the Mont-Almonte Treaty; Juárez staining his hands with the blood of the Archduke, spilled on Las Campanas Hill, as well as with the blood of the Díaz insurgents who were executed by Sóstenes Rocha at La Ciudadela; Juárez here and Juárez there; Juárez the hypocrite who had hired the archbishop as tutor for his grandchild . . . Juárez, finally, the bad son, bad child of the nation, bad nephew to his uncle, bad godson to his godfather. And at each accusation a merciless burst of fire would sear his breast.

The three or five—he never knew how many there were—black-hooded men were ready, torches in hand, on one side of the stage.

And for each of the blessings, there would be a corresponding caress, the kiss of snow over his breast. The white-hooded men were also waiting with their white irises at the other side of the temple.

And in the middle, and far to the rear, the triangle with little blue flames and the star of yellow fire.

And in the center, in the foreground, the body of Archduke Ferdinand Maximilian of Habsburg, naked and hanging by his feet, and facing him, laid out, motionless on the table, his own body, the President's, or almost his body, almost the corpse, almost the immortal stone statue of the President of Mexico, Pablo Benito Juárez.

But what happened next, he never would have thought possible: he felt lazy. He felt very lazy, like when he was a boy and he had fallen asleep on the lagoon and the piece of weedbed he was resting on broke loose, that floating garden that almost carried him away forever . . . that's what he wanted now, yes, to fall asleep on that table, on that bed, in that tomb, whatever it was, and let death carry him away. Carry him away without his noticing it, very gently.

He, the President of Mexico, the Honorable Governor of Oaxaca, the Supreme Court magistrate, Juárez the attorney, always such an early riser and so diligent, so responsible and hardworking, so punctual, so demanding towards himself, felt lazy. Yes, just like that: lazy. He couldn't be bothered with all this, anymore. And he wanted everyone to know it.

That was the truth of it. Not that he couldn't talk, or move a finger, or close and open his eyes. He could still do all that, but he simply didn't want to do it. He didn't feel like it. He felt lazy, very lazy.

Because he knew that no matter what he said, no matter what he did, it would be others who would choose and decide what he had been all his life—and in death as well—the most beautiful things, the ugliest things; the most important, the most shameful. But not he himself; he had no more say in the matter.

The memory of an afternoon when he and Melchor Ocampo had carried Guillermo Prieto in their arms on the beaches of Manzanillo—the three of them covered by gusts of marine fluorescence—mixed with his memories of the walks on the wharfs in New Orleans, the sails of a ship, and the smoke of a Havana cigar. Later, it mixed with his memories of the day he arrived at the home of the Maza family in Oaxaca and he met the girl, Margarita, her skin so white. He didn't want to know anything else anymore, didn't want to remember anything . . . He didn't—nor would he—make any attempt to defend himself . . . Let history, yes, let history do whatever it wanted with him.

One of the black-hooded men walked up to him and put a torch to his chest:

"History will condemn you, Benito Juárez," he said.

And Benito Juárez felt a great pain.

Then it was one of the white-hooded men's turn, and he approached him with an iris in hand, and with the iris, he caressed Benito's breast:

"No, Benito, history will absolve you," he told him.

And Benito Juárez felt a great relief.

He looked the Archduke in the eyes. But the Archduke wasn't even an arch-duke anymore, nor, as everyone knew, were those his eyes. Benito realized then that time had gone mad, and that relief had not followed the iris nor had pain followed the fire on his breast. The pain had been the first and last thing, the only thing he'd felt during this delirium or dream that he was condemned to forget as soon as he opened his eyes, and all the other things besides pain that had and hadn't happened—everything and nothing—had lasted less than the second or the fractions of a second that elapsed between the instant in which he felt the first and only burning and the moment at which he opened his eyes, saw his doctor holding some kind of smoking pitcher, and realized that the doctor had just poured boiling water on his chest.

"What are you doing?" he asked. "Don't you see you're burning me?"

And just as soon as he said "burning," he realized he had forgotten the whole dream and that the only, now almost invisible, images that still lingered in the air in front of his eyes—a flame, the dome of a temple, and something hang-ing above him like a bat—were fading . . . as was that stink that had seemed to come from inside his own body, from his own organs . . . all this faded away in an instant and he knew that nothing he did could ever bring them back.

"Why are you burning me?"

The doctor excused himself to Don Benito and explained he had to resort to such a violent remedy—spilling boiling water on the Presidential chest—to revive a heart that had almost stopped beating, and that, perhaps, it might be necessary, he added, fanning Benito's chest, to apply the same treatment once again, begging his pardon, and of course with Don Benito's permission.

This was done and Don Benito's heart beat for a few more hours. But only for a few more hours.

Benito Pablo Juárez García, President of the United States of Mexico, died from angina pectoris, with a scalded chest, at eleven-thirty on the morning of the 18th day of July, 1872.

2. The Last of the Mexicans

Twenty-four years before the death of Empress Carlota at Bouchout Castle, the brothers Orville and Wilbur Wright launch the Age of Aviation.

And in the year she dies—1927—Charles Lindbergh crosses the Atlantic in his *Spirit of St. Louis*.

That same year, Al Jolson stars in history's first talking picture.

The film is titled *The Jazz Singer*. Jazz had already been born, and along with it, the fox-trot and the Charleston. The tango is a hit in Europe and Gardel becomes famous singing "*El día que me quieras*."

Meanwhile, while people danced the tango in Paris and James Joyce published his *Ulysses* and margarine was invented and Surrealism and Cubism and the Jehovah's Witnesses were being born, and Gustav Mahler wrote his *Symphony No. 9* and Chaplin was filming *The Gold Rush*, and Walt Disney was drawing Mickey Mouse and workers were being murdered in the streets of Chicago, while Alfred Dreyfus was being decorated with the medal of the Legion of Honor and Captain Boycott was rebelling against the accords of the Irish Agrarian League, and the Irish Free State was being born and Detroit was transforming itself into the automobile capital of the world, and the Nobel Prize, linotype, and aspirin were introduced, and while in the United States a man named Adams was creating an industrial empire based on the rubber of the gum tree that he had seen Santa Anna chew when the Mexican general was in exile on Staten Island, and the star Auriga was discovered in the skies, and the language Esperanto was invented on Earth . . . While all of that was happening and insane Carlota was still taking forever to die, all of the other characters in our tragedy, the principal and the secondary ones—and along with them all the friends Carlota had had at one time or another, everyone she knew and all her enemies—were dead and gone. All of them.

Napoleon III died a few months after Juárez, in January 1873, in the place he chose for his exile: Camden Place, Chislehurst, in the south of England. Thus he survived the two greatest humiliations he suffered in his life by a few years: the failure in Mexico and the Franco-Prussian War. This war, which ended the Second French Empire and culminated with the proclamation of the German Empire in the Hall of Mirrors of the Palace of Versailles, cost France Alsace and Lorraine, and along with these two provinces, the million citizens that inhabited them, and a great source of wealth, in its mines, vineyards, and textile mills.

Some historians say that the Mexican adventure decisively influenced France's defeat at the hands of the Germans. Moreover, others see the Second Commune as a direct consequence of the Franco-Prussian War. Still suffering the consequences of a long siege—during which it seems not all Parisians went hungry, for there are reports that zoo animals were killed for the tables of the rich, and that in first-class restaurants one could dine on kangaroo ribs and elephant filet—Paris became mired in the bloodiest civil war of the nineteenth century: a revolution that started with a carnival of blood on January 22, 1871, in front of the Hôtel de Ville, and would end a few months later, Sunday, May 28th, when one hundred and forty-seven executed Communards were buried in a common grave at Père Lachaise Cemetery, next to the wall that would go on to be named the *Mur des Fédérés*, the Communards' Wall, in the history of infamy.

Between fifteen and forty thousand people—we'll never know the precise number—lost their lives during the Second Commune. It's calculated that one-fourth of the victims were women. But there were also many children: the forces of Mac-Mahon and the illustrious Adolphe Thiers respected neither age nor sex when they charged the barricades with guns blazing or bayonets drawn. The bodies were thrown into the Seine, or into the sewers built by Baron Haussmann.

Paris burned for days on end, and along with Paris, the Palace of the Tuileries: whole sections were reduced to ashes. After the fire, part of the ruins were bought by Duke Pozzo di Borgo, a Corsican by birth, who used them in the construction of a palace looking out over the Gulf of Ajaccio, where the first Napoleon had been born.

A short time later, in the world of haute couture, a new color would become fashionable: ashes of Paris.

With the death of Napoleon III, his only son, Imperial Prince Louis Napoleon became the head of the Bonaparte dynasty, but those who wanted to restore it using the Prince would soon see their hopes evaporate. "Loulou will catch a Zulu!"—the English newspapers would say when Loulou, a cadet at the Military School of Woolwich in 1879, decided to participate as a volunteer with the British army in the war against the Zulus in South Africa.

The night of June 10th of the same year—as Robert Goffin tells us in *Charlotte l'Impératrice Fantôme*—a hurricane pounded the Camden Place Garden and a big tree was toppled there. That same day, Loulou, while on a reconnaissance mission commanded by a certain Captain Carey, fell in an ambush. According to subsequent reports, Carey and all the soldiers in his battalion that had had enough time to mount their horses and flee did so, abandoning the Imperial Prince, whose body—pierced by seventeen of the traditional spears of assegai wood used by the Zulus, and his face devoured by jackals—was found next to a river with a name that couldn't be more suitable: Blood River. Carey was declared innocent of the mishap and the English Parliament rejected the idea, proposed by Queen Victoria, of erecting a statue of the Prince in Westminster Abbey. Victoria had to settle for a sculpture of him in the Chapel of St. George in Windsor Castle.

Eugenia Ignacia Agustina de Guzmán, Palafox y Portocarrero, Countess of Teba and ex-Empress of the French, survived the death of her son—"I have the courage to tell you I'm alive, because pain doesn't kill," she wrote her mother—and she lived on, for many more years. A personal friend of Victoria, Eugénie never left England, except for brief periods to travel to Paris or to her summer residence at Cape Martin, which bore the Greek name for Corsica: Villa *Cyrnos*. She also traveled to Ceylon, and she traveled to Zululand to see the place where her son had fallen. But she suffered a great disappointment there, on account of Victoria: square-tiled flooring, and in the middle of it a cross that had been hurriedly erected on the orders of the Queen of England, so that Eugénie would find the memorial there on her arrival—instead of the hole or ditch, the stones, the grass, and the dust that the blood of the prince had soaked and that Eugénie would have liked to soak in her tears. Lastly, she traveled to Spain. She didn't want to die without seeing the skies of her native Castile once more. And it was under this sky that she did die, in Madrid, in the Palace of Liria, at ninety-five years of age, and more than forty years after Loulou's death. It was July 10, 1920. Her body was taken to England so it could rest in Farnborough next to the remains of her husband and her son.

But Carlota outlived her. Carlota outlived General Prim and Marshal Bazaine, both of whom would die in Madrid.

Prim died due to the bullet wounds—eight in total—that he received at the Calle de Alcalá from the blunderbusses of some never-identified men—assassins sent by the Duke of Montpensier, Carlota's uncle, who didn't become king of Spain, perhaps?

Achille François Bazaine was disgraced and declared a traitor to France after he surrendered at Metz, two months after the Battle of Sedan, at the end of a siege that lasted one hundred and fifty-four days, at the head of one hundred and seventy-three men of the Army of the Rhine. After the Marshal's surrender, the Prussians took possession of one thousand four hundred pieces of artillery and fifty-three French flags. When Bazaine was being held prisoner in Kassel, his wife Pepita Peña visited him on the eve of giving birth to their child. They say a relative of Pepita's brought a sack of dirt from Lorraine that was scattered around Pepita's bed so that she could say that Bazaine's son had been born on French soil. Judged by a military tribunal in the Trianon, presided over by another of Carlota's uncles, d'Aumale, Bazaine was condemned to die. His sentence was commuted to twenty years in prison on the Island of Santa Margarita, whence he would later escape, assisted by Pepita, who awaited him at the foot of the prison wall with a rope and a boat. Bazaine died in 1888.

Carlota also outlived all the Mexicans who supported or fought her during her ephemeral empire: Santa Anna, Márquez, Hidalgo, López, Díaz.

Antonio López de Santa Anna died in virtual poverty in Mexico City in June 1876.

Leonardo Márquez gave up the ghost in Havana in 1913.

Manuel Hidalgo y Esnaurrízar died in Paris in 1896.

Miguel López outlived his son's Imperial Godfather by twenty-four years and died in 1891 from the bite of a rabid dog.

General Porfirio Díaz, President of Mexico for thirty-five years and over-thrown by the Mexican Revolution, died in Paris in 1915.

And still Carlota remained alive, first in Miramare, then in Laeken and Terveuren and finally in Bouchout, alive and insane, while the world was entering a new century, and with the new century came hormones and the ultra microscope, four-dimensional geometry and the photoelectric cell, and Amundsen reached the South Pole and the *Titanic* sank and in Chicago the first skyscraper was built . . .

Because Carlota outlived not only Maximilian, Juárez, Napoleon, Eugénie and all the rest, but also a whole era, a whole concept of the history and destiny of mankind and of the idea that man had of himself and the universe. In 1927, it was already sixty years since Karl Marx had published the first volume of *Das Kapital*; thirty-two since the appearance of Freud's *Studies on Hysteria*, which would establish the basis for psychoanalysis, and twelve since the formulation of the General Theory of Relativity by Albert Einstein. Carlota then dies alone in a world that had little or nothing to do with that other world from whose lucidity and insanity she had escaped long before. The structure of the atom having already been established, and then the mechanism of its disintegration having been discovered in 1927, Carlota died at the dawning of the Atomic Age.

In the year Carlota died, 1927, there was no one left to weep for her out of all those servants, courtiers, and friends who had accompanied her to

Mexico, or had been around her in Mexico. They were all dead: the Count of Bombelles and Señora del Barrio, Tüdös the cook and Blasio the secretary, the Count of Orizaba, Doctor Basch and the Countess von Kollonitz, Father Agustin Fischer and Señora de Sánchez Navarro. Also dead were some of the ladies-in-waiting that were assigned to her, like Madame Moreau, who died in 1893, or Mademoiselle Marie Bartels, dead in 1909, or Mademoiselle de la Fontaine and Mademoiselle Anna Mockel, who both passed on in 1922.

Even the child prince, Agustín de Iturbide, whom Maximilian had the habit of placing on his tummy while he rocked in his hammock in Cuernavaca, had died an old man turned monk in the United States.

Colonel Van der Smissen had committed suicide.

Juan Nepomuceno Almonte had died in Paris.

In Paris the Communards had shot Jecker the banker dead.

It's a rather long list: Colonel Dupin, Monsignor Meglia, Archbishop Labastida y Dávalos, Richard and Paulina Metternich, Émile Ollivier, Saligny, Eloin and Schertzenlechner, Radonetz, Count Jadik and Marquis de Radepont, the singer Concha Méndez, Princess Salm-Salm, Queen Victoria, Lorencez and de la Gravière, Marshal Forey: they were all dead in 1927.

Prince Salm-Salm didn't get to see ultraviolet lamps because a French bullet ended his life in the Franco-Prussian War. Giovanni Maria Mastai-Ferretti, also known as Pius IX, creator of the dogma of papal infallibility, never climbed aboard a Rolls Royce because he died in 1878, and then the three popes who followed him also died before Carlota: Leo XIII, Pius X, and Benedict XV. Moreover, Garibaldi never flew in a helicopter because he died in 1882. Victor Hugo never composed a poem with a typewriter because he passed away in 1885. General Mariano Escobedo never shaved with a Gillette because he died in 1902, two years before it was invented. But the ultraviolet lamp and similarly the mechanical vacuum cleaner, the automobile and similarly mass production, the helicopter and the wireless telegraph, the typewriter and X-rays, the bicycle, the gramophone, and the telephone, the Pullman car and sulfonamides, the modern Olympics and vitamins, beauty contests and the Wimbledon tennis championships, the Brooklyn Bridge and television: all of these were invented, discovered, constructed in 1927, the year Carlota dies.

In the year Carlota dies, 1927, all the world leaders who would either decide the course of the twentieth century or else be swept away by it have already been born: from Churchill to Stalin, from John F. Kennedy to Fidel Castro. Hitler is no longer an employee of the Kunsthistorisches Museum of Vienna and has already published *Mein Kampf*. Mahatma Gandhi has begun his civil disobedience campaigns, and General Chiang Kai-Shek is preparing to take over Shanghai and Nanking. Kemal Atatürk, Patrice Lumumba, Ernesto "Che" Guevara, Francisco Franco, Charles de Gaulle, and Ben Gurion have already been born in 1927. And four years earlier, one of these leaders has already made Italy the first fascist country in history: his surname is Mussolini, and his father called him Benito because he was an admirer of Benito Juárez.

Meanwhile, other great figures of the century were born and ended their lives. That was, for example, the case with Rosa Luxemburg. Also with Lenin, who was born three years after Carlota lost her mind and died three years before the Empress. The same thing occurred in Mexico with Francisco Madero, Emiliano Zapata, and Pancho Villa, all three of them born after 1866, all three assassinated before 1927, victims of a revolution that devoured its own children, and soaked the fields and cities of Mexico with the blood of a million dead.

By 1927, twenty-three years after the inauguration of the Trans-Siberian Railroad, thirty after the discovery of the malaria bacillus, and fifty-eight after the publication of *Twenty Thousand Leagues Under the Sea*, Carlota's two brothers, the Count of Flanders and Leopold II of Belgium, had also died, but their royal house, that of Coburg, was one of the few European dynasties that outlived the Empress of Mexico. Leopold II, a monarch who was bathed every morning at six by his servants with bucketfuls of frozen seawater, loved greenhouses and loved being surrounded by palm trees and ferns, orchids and rhododendrons. But he also loved power, and besides doing everything in this power to transform Brussels into a miniature Paris, he decided to give Belgium an overseas colony as well. He thought about China, he thought about Japan, and he declared that European colonization was the only means by which to "civilize and moralize those lazy and corrupt nations of the Orient." But he also thought about Latin America and he made several attempts to establish Belgian settlements in Guatemala. Finally, he decided on Africa. He wanted, he said, to take the blessings and benefits of civilization to the Dark Continent. Leopold gathered all sorts of explorers, geographers, and investors at his court. He created the African International Association under the aegis of a flag displaying a gold star on a sky-blue field, and from the mouth of the Congo River in Western Africa, following the course of the river, he conquered a territory of two million three hundred and fifty square kilometers. Leopold named himself Sovereign of the Independent State of the Congo, and in order to finance the development of the new colony he tried all sorts of tricks, from pawning titles and decorations to dipping into his sister Carlota's inheritance. But Leopold did something else, too. When in 1866 his personal envoy to Mexico, Baron d'Huart, died at the hands of some Mexican guerilla fighters, in a letter to his brother Philippe—quoted by Mia Kerckvoorde in her book, *Charlotte la passion et la fatalité*—Leopold stated that the tragedy at Río Frío had filled him with horror, and that only in the heart of Africa, in the land of cannibals, could a parallel be found to such events. The man who wrote those words and who appears not to have paused for a moment to recognize that in any civilized European country, the attack of an army of resistance on an army of occupation—which the Belgian army was—would have been considered a normal act of war, this same man—determined to complete consolidating the conquest of the Congo and to accelerate the production of the most important raw material produced in the region, rubber—committed in the very heart of the Dark Continent a series of unspeakable atrocities against the natives. Entire villages were burnt to ashes by the Belgians in the Congo; they whipped and killed men and women of all ages, held chained children as hostages, and cut the hands off those workers who didn't respond fast enough to please their white masters. All the severed hands were placed in baskets and taken from town to town as a warning. Leopold II had several mistresses, and as he got older his lust became insatiable. It's said that he would travel to London to visit a special brothel full of girls below the age of puberty. One of his last mistresses—when he was already a septuagenarian—was a sixteen-year-old French prostitute—she was called "*la Reine du Congo*," ("the Queen of the Congo,")—with whom he performed all sorts of "sexual perversions" in a room full of mirrors.

However, the great fortune he amassed with the exploitation of the Congo didn't bring happiness to Leopold II, who never got over the loss of the crown Prince, the Duke of Brabant, who died of pneumonia a few days after falling into a pond. This was one of the occasions on which the so-called "Curse of the Habsburgs" struck the Coburgs of Belgium as well.

The curse also ruined the life of Leopold's older daughter, Louise, who under the king's orders was confined to an insane asylum. People would say, "Aunt

Carlota's insane, and now the niece Louise," and for a while everyone referred to them as the lunatics of the Royal House of Belgium. But it seems that Louise was never really insane. Her father had her locked up at Purkersdorf after she decided to abandon her husband, another prince of the Coburgs of Saxony, to run away to the Riviera with a certain Count of Mattacic. Louise escaped from the asylum and returned to Paris to end up ruined in the arms of her count.

Leopold's second daughter, and therefore Carlota's niece as well, Princess Stephanie, called the "Rose of Brabant," married the son of Franz Joseph and Maximilian's nephew, Prince Rudolf—one of the classic and better-known victims of the curse of the Habsburgs. On January 31, 1889, Rudolf, the only male son of Franz Joseph and Empress Elisabeth, was found shot dead at the Mayerling Hunting Lodge, near the village of the same name in lower Austria. Rudolf was twenty-nine years old. Next to him, also dead, and covered with roses, was his lover, seventeen-year-old Baroness Maria Vetsera. Exactly what happened that night at Mayerling will probably never be known. However, everything seems to indicate that Rudolf and Maria Vetsera made a suicidal love pact.

Maximilian's sister-in-law, Empress Elisabeth, the beautiful Sisi, outlived her son Rudolf by nine years. On September 10, 1898, a mason named Luccheni drove a stiletto into her chest. Elisabeth died a few minutes later. When Franz Joseph received the telegram from Geneva communicating the news of her death, it's said he murmured, "I've not been spared any pain in this life." Elisabeth's coffin was placed in the Capuchin Crypt in Vienna, between the catafalques of her son Rudolf and of her brother-in-law, Maximilian, the Emperor of Mexico.

Franz Joseph's reaction to the death of Archduke Franz Ferdinand and his wife Sophie Chotek, both murdered in Sarajevo on June 28, 1914, by Gavrilo Princip, was very different: "A higher power," he said, "has restored the order that I myself was not able to maintain." The truth is that Franz Joseph must have been quite pleased, since he could never tolerate the idea that his successor to the throne of Austria-Hungary would be that antique collector and grower of exotic roses, Archduke Franz Ferdinand, famous for having inherited the despotism and cruelty of his grandfather the King of Naples, called "Bomba" ("Bomb"). But, without a doubt, the crime of Sarajevo was the culmination of the curse of the Habsburgs, for it was the light that set off the powder keg of a conflict so enormous that it came to be known, and justifiably, as the First World War.

Franz Joseph of Austria didn't live to see the end of that war. He died in 1916 when he was eighty-six. His was history's longest reign, sixty-eight years. Victoria ruled for sixty-four in England, and though a monarch for seventy-two years, Louis XIV of France only exercised power during fifty-four, after Cardinal Mazarin's death. Like all, or almost like all, Holy Roman Emperors, Maximilian's brother operated under an ambiguous kind of morality during his reign, and he had several mistresses. The best-known of them all was the actress Katharina Schratt. Franz Joseph was also a sexual predator. When he was sixty years old, walking by himself in a garden close to a country house he had in Hietzig, he encountered a little girl, the daughter of a basket weaver. Franz Joseph raped her and from that encounter Hélène Nahowski, future wife of the composer Alban Berg, was born. Empress Elisabeth is also known to have had a daughter out of wedlock, a daughter who was born at the Castle of Sassetôt in Normandy: Caroline, who would be later known as the Countess Zanardi Landi. Caroline went to live in the United States, wrote a book titled *The Secret of an Empress*, and had a daughter who became famous as a Hollywood actress. It's probable that Caroline was the daughter of an English aristocrat, Bay Middleton, with whom Empress Elisabeth went hunting every year.

With the war, the Habsburg dynasty would also come to an end. The successor to the Austro-Hungarian throne, the popular Charles I, was forced to leave the country after the signing of the armistice, and he died in Madeira of tuberculosis in 1922. It was then, they say, that the hawks that had followed the Habsburgs from the Swiss village of Aargau to their imperial residences in Vienna, forever abandoned the Hofburg and the Palace of Schönbrunn, and with them the curse also took flight, and was gone.

In other words, five years before the death of Carlota in Bouchout, the end came for a dynasty that over the centuries had extended from Portugal to Transylvania and from Holland to Sicily and Spanish America, and in which the medieval concept of the Empire was combined with a German brand of humanism, as the historian Adam Wandruszka notes, as well as the politics and religious concepts of the Counter-Reformation and the baroque, the philosophy of Italian illuminism, the theories of the French physiocrats, Romanticism, and German classicism and the ethnic nationalism of Eastern Europe. The dynasty that, according to the historian A. J. P. Taylor, represented not a multinational but a supranational empire. Taylor says that the Habsburg monarchy constituted an attempt to find a "third solution" in Central Europe that would prevent its fall under Russian or German dominance, and that when the Habsburgs became satellites of the Germans, they betrayed their mission, and they themselves had signed their death warrants.

It's worth pointing out that when a curse hangs over a rich and powerful family, believers tend to see it as a sort of divine justice: a balance between God's generosity as well as His capacity to allow suffering. It's certainly true that power attracts the terrorist and madman, and wealth makes murderers out of those who want to inherit it. However, there are in the world, and always have been, millions of human beings living in poverty whose tragedies are ignored, because the weight of their suffering can't be encompassed. In the light of this greater and actual curse, the so-called "curse of the Habsburgs," falling as it did on the rich and powerful, can't really be taken seriously—except of course as raw material for a melodrama.

Along with the Bonapartes and Habsburgs, another three European dynasties came to their ends before Carlota's death: the Hohenzollerns, the Braganzas, and the Romanovs.

After the Berlin upheavals of 1918, the last Hohenzollern monarch abdicated and exiled himself to Holland. But by that time, the authority of Wilhelm II, the last King of Prussia and Emperor of Germany, had already been annulled by Hindenburg and Ludendorff.

Charles I of Portugal and his eldest son, Prince Louis Philip were assassinated in Lisbon in 1908. The reign of his other son, Manuel II, was brief and turbulent, and the revolutionary movement inspired by Carbonarists and Masons finally triumphed, and the Republic was proclaimed in 1910. The Braganza reign had ended in Brazil in 1889.

Finally, on March 15, 1917, the Czar of all the Russias, Nicholas II, abdicated. The Revolution started after the death of Rasputin, and Nicholas, his wife, and children were all assassinated on July 16th of that same year at Ekaterinburg. That was the end of the Romanovs.

Carlota thus outlived the October Revolution and the Mexican Revolution, and also many other revolutions and wars, big and small, and then the implacable race between Europe and the United States to get a piece of everything still left unclaimed on the planet, as dictated by their imperialist ideals. While she was alive, a madwoman in Bouchout, the Maori wars almost annihilated the entire native population of New Zealand, and the war in Paraguay ended with the death of the Paraguayan dictator who had asked Napoleon III's permission to become king of that South American country: Francisco Solano López. While Carlota grew old, alone and insane, locked up in her castle, the

Italians were defeated in Ethiopia by Sultan Menelek, and Lawrence of Arabia was rallying the desert tribes to triumph over the Turks; the War of the Pacific between Chile, Peru, and Bolivia erupted and ended; Italy annexed Tripoli and Cyrenaica, and France took possession of Madagascar and signed a secret treaty with Spain to split Morocco between them; Great Britain seized the diamond-mine region in Kimberley, South Africa; the United States took possession of Guam, the Philippines, Puerto Rico, and Hawaii; and the Anglo-Indian army invaded Afghanistan. While Carlota was alive and the Armenians were being massacred in Constantinople, the New Hebrides became an Anglo-French protectorate; Uganda, Nigeria, and Egypt were becoming British protectorates; and the Japanese destroyed the Russian fleet in the Korea Strait. And while Gabon was being annexed to the French Congo and France was integrating Annan, Tonkin, and Cochin China as the Union of Indochina, and adding the Ivory Coast to its colonies and Dahomey and Laos to its protectorates, and while Great Britain was seizing the Tonga Islands, subduing the Ashanti of the Gold Coast and beginning its control of the oil properties in the Persian Gulf, assuming a mandate over Palestine in the Middle East and, as a result of the Boer War, annexing the Transvaal and the Free State of Orange; and while Greece and Turkey were fighting for control of Crete, and six European nations were sending an expedition to China as punishment for the attacks by the Boxers, or brothers of the "Society of the Harmonious Fists," against some Western Christians in Peking; while all of this was happening, Carlota was still alive.

Of course, of all the wars Carlota outlived, the most important one was World War I. The war passed by her while she was locked up in Bouchout, just like the soldiers of the German army, because a sign was posted on the exterior of the castle saying: "This castle, which belongs to the Crown of Belgium, is the residence of her Majesty, the Empress of Mexico, sister-in-law of our dear ally the Emperor of Austria-Hungary. German soldiers must abstain from singing, or disturbing this home." Carlota's country suffered a great deal during that first violation of its "perpetual neutrality." Countless atrocities were committed during the German reign of terror in Belgium, among them the destruction by fire of entire towns, and the mass execution of citizens—including priests, women, and children. But Carlota's nephew, Albert I, never left Belgian territory: he ordered the flooding of the Yser River Valley in order to stop the German advance, and was left confined to a zone of barely twenty square miles next to the seashore. When they advised him to leave Belgium, he cited Benito Juárez as an example of a ruler who had never left his country, even after it was invaded by a foreign army.

And finally, finally, one day, Charlotte Amélie of Belgium also died. According to some authors, like Robert Goffin, her death was preceded by two ominous signs: a few days before, a gigantic tree fell over, dead, in the Garden of Bouchout—an omen identical to that of Camden Place—and, the day before, the statue of Marguerite de Bouchout also fell over, inexplicably, and its head broke off and rolled onto the flagstones. The next day, Wednesday, January 19, 1927, at seven in the morning, Charlotte, or Carlota, died. A mortuary chapel was installed in the Royal Chamber of Bouchout. Carlota's body, covered by a mound of roses, and the branches of Judas trees, rested on an oak bed topped by a lofty, sky-blue canopy. Carlota was buried on a snowy day. According to Praviel's account, Princes Leopold and Charles walked in the funeral procession; as did the Court's Grand Marshal, Count de Mérode; Baron Goffinet, grand master of the Empress's House; and the local burgomaster. In the church the Duchess of Vendôme, Princess Genevieve d'Orléans and Countess de Chaponay awaited the procession. As did Monsignor Van Roey, Archbishop of Mechlin. Very few of those Belgian boys who had fought in Mexico as volunteers could have been alive at this point, but the government managed to find six, all octogenarians, of course, who carried the coffin of the Empress of Mexico to the Chapel of Laeken on their shoulders, where it was destined to rest next to that of her mother, Queen Louise Marie.

•

As the saying goes, with the death of the dog, no more rabies—and with the death of the Empress of Mexico, the threat of her insanity was over, and the snow that fell on her sarcophagus and her sepulcher—it had also snowed sixty years earlier on Maximilian's coffin when his remains arrived in Vienna—covered the last page of a grotesque and somber personal melodrama.

But the last page of the story of the Emperors and Empire of Mexico, the one that would, ideally, contain that "Verdict of History" of which Benito Juárez wrote, would never be written—and not only because the insanity of History didn't end with Carlota's, but also because, rather than a true, impossible, and (in the final analysis) undesirable "Universal History," we only have many little histories, personal and under constant revision, according to the perspectives of the times and places in which they are "written."

Since Carlota's biographers don't tell us whether she ever stopped dreaming about Mexico and her Empire, we can assume that she never gave up her obsession, and that the dream only left her when she died. Seen now, at a distance, we might surmise that the Empire was never likely to be anything more than that: a dream. Carlos Pereyra says that the Mexican Empire was "stillborn," and that the first emperor of his century, as the Mexican historian calls Napoleon III, "placed a fetus in the prodigal hands of the Archduke." Octavio Paz, for his part, says that the idea of founding a Latin empire with a European prince at its head "that would set up a barrier to the expansion of the Yankee republic wasn't really such a bad idea in 1820, but it was anachronistic by 1860: the monarchic solution was no longer viable because monarchy was associated with the situation prior to [Mexican] Independence."

It's possible that it happened that way, and that Benito Juárez didn't intend to "open the door to *slogans*"—that is, facile Yankee imperialist philosophy— "when he closed it to Europe," as La Malinche, Hernán Cortés's Indian mistress, states in a play by another Mexican poet, Salvador Novo. It's possible, yes—and even probable—that *nothing* would have stopped the expansion of Yankee power over the rest of the American continent, and that at any rate, the purpose—if not false, at least secondary—claimed by Napoleon III when justifying France's Intervention, to stop what he called "the sinister Anglo-Saxon and Protestant influence in Latin America," would necessarily have had to go unfulfilled however the Intervention and Empire turned out. If Europe itself couldn't escape North American influence and domination, how could the perpetuation of Maximilian's Empire have stopped them in Mexico?

Even though the terrain for this kind of supposition is always slippery, it's not difficult to presume that had the Archduke stayed on the throne, he couldn't have endured the economic pressure of the Americans—even if the word "geopolitics" hadn't been coined yet, the reality was still very much in operation—nor could he have controlled the internal corruption that would absolutely have opened the doors to Yankee imperialism. The American ambassador in Paris, John Bigelow, knew it well, telling Seward: "My theory is that we're going to conquer Mexico, but not with the sword." It's easy to think that an heir to Maximilian's throne, an Iturbide perhaps, would have been overthrown just as Díaz was, by a revolution, and that nothing could really have stopped the advance of the United States.

Another possibility is that, as Justo Sierra points out, the French intervention united Mexicans and saved the country from anarchy and chaos . . . But only for a few years. It isn't difficult either to imagine that Maximilian, who wanted to be one of the most enlightened and least despotic of all the enlightened despots of Mexico, would've turned into a tyrant for other nations—Guatemala, for instance—as happened to his antecessor Joseph II, who was the one who solidified the Austrian dominion over Lombardy, and then, obligated by political and administrative circumstances, followed the destiny of Frederick the Great of Prussia, who, as John G. Gagliardo points out in *Enlightened Despotism*, ended up being the most absolutist of all the monarchs of his era.

Moreover, one can also assume that Juárez wouldn't really have minded opening up the door to those dreaded "*slogans.*" Nor to Protestantism, which he favored without reservations: "The Indians," he said on one occasion, "need a religion that obliges them to read and not spend money on candles for saints." These were curious times, when many of the Mexican liberals were Americanists, that is to say pro-Yankee, and many of the conservatives were anti-American. But the United States was not yet an empire—though the beast had already shown its claws and fangs—and its War of Independence and Constitution, the martyrdom of Lincoln, and the triumph of the abolitionists clouded other considerations and made people forget past insults. These pro-American feelings were shared outside of Mexico by persons such as Friedrich Engels—the industrialist who was financing Marx's studies in London. He declared his satisfaction on Mexico's defeat in 1847 and said that for the sake of its development, it was good for Mexico to fall under American tutelage. Marx as well, praising what he called the sentiments of independence and the worth of the individual, shared Engels's scorn for Mexico. Marx would say that the Mexican people have all the vices of the Spaniards—grandiloquence, boastfulness, and quixotism—but without the solidity of the Spanish people. However, the author of *Das Kapital* would add, the Spanish have never produced a genius such as Santa Anna. This wouldn't be the only time that the man who fought for the equality of all workers of the world expressed his disdain for a people or a race. For Marx, the Slavic peoples were nothing more than hordes who had remained backward, and whose only hope was to be led by a cultured people like the Germans.

One way or another, the offenses committed by the United States were to continue. One of the main actors in the drama of the Mexican Empire, José Manuel Hidalgo y Esnaurrízar, said, in his *Apuntes para escribir la Historia de los proyectos de Monarquía en México* (Notes towards writing the history of the monarchy projects in Mexico), that it wasn't the Monroe Doctrine that the United States should follow, but the advice of the "illustrious and prudent"

George Washington, who warned that nations should not take advantage of other countries' misfortunes. Hidalgo said, "Oh, if I could only write in the margin: Mexico, Cuba, Nicaragua, Panama . . ."

Hidalgo, of course, was alluding to past abuses committed by the United States against these nations, but at the same time his words were prophetic: between 1868, when he published his *Notes*, and 1927, the year of Carlota's death, the United States had intervened once again in those four countries, and in almost every case its intervention was less than justified, and had ne-farious consequences. Following the arrest of some Yankee sailors in Tampico in 1914, North American troops invaded Veracruz, where they remained for several months. Shortly before the nineteenth century came to an end, in 1898, the United States had declared war on Spain in order to "help" Cuban independence, and the price they exacted for their victory was: firstly, the political and economic control of the island, which became a de facto American protectorate in 1901; and, secondly, the acquisition of the already mentioned Spanish possessions of Puerto Rico, Guam, and the Philippines. The pretext was the explosion and sinking of the American warship *Maine* in Havana Bay, an act attributed to Spain. In time people came to the conclusion the Spaniards had nothing to do with the *Maine* incident, and that it is very probable that the Americans themselves, seeking a casus belli, had blown it up themselves. In 1925, the North Americans invaded Nicaragua and began an eight-year occupation—opposed by the guerrilla force led by General Augusto César Sandino—in an attempt to broaden their military control over the region and in view of a possible second interoceanic passageway. A few years earlier they had intervened in Colombia to provoke a rebellion leading to the excision of the Province of Panama, in order to carry out the same project in which Eugenia de Montijo's cousin, Ferdinand de Lesseps, had failed so miserably: the construction of the Panama Canal. Tocqueville's prediction that some day Russia and the United States would divide the world between themselves was thus being fulfilled inexorably during Carlota's lifetime. Most probably, as we've pointed out before, if Carlota hadn't lived insane for so many years in Bouchout, but sane in Chapultepec instead, things wouldn't really have turned out much differently.

With regard to the individual acts, the ethical and political responsibilities of Maximilian and Carlota, the impossibility of reaching a universal agreement as to the details of their story, which in turn prevents the formation of a "universal" judgment, has in no way deterred the proliferation of *personal* judgments, stemming from the contradictory versions of events as recorded by the participating individuals—and, as usually happens, these judgments haven't only been made by historians, but also by those novelists and playwrights who have yielded to the fascination of history.

The Mexican writer Rodolfo Usigli, infatuated with the tragedy of Maximilian and Carlota, says in his prologue to *Corona de Sombra*—a historical drama that he calls "anti-historical"—that if history were only as precise as poetry, he would never have turned away from it. Several decades later, the Argentinean writer Jorge Luis Borges declared that he was more interested in what was symbolically true than in what was historically exact. And twenty years after *Corona de Sombra* was written, the Hungarian writer György Lukács stated in his book, *The Historical Novel*, that it is a "modern prejudice to suppose that the historical authenticity of a fact will guarantee its poetic efficaciousness." If one understands what Usigli meant, shares Borges's preference, and agrees with Lukács, one can always—with talent—push history to the side, and, based on an event or on some historical characters, construct a self-sufficient novelistic or dramatic world. The allegory, the absurd, the farce are some of the possible modes available to an author for creating such a world: everything is permissible in literature, so long as you aren't pretending to adhere to history. But what happens when an author can't escape history? When an author can't consciously forget what has been learned? Or, better yet, when an author doesn't see fit to ignore the overwhelming mass of facts available on a subject—crucial in terms of their influence over the lives, the *deaths*, the destinies of the characters in his tragedy, a tragedy of his own? In other words, what happens—what can you do—when you don't want to avoid history, but do want to achieve poetry? Perhaps the solution is not to pose only one alternative, like Borges, or to elude history like Usigli, but to try and reconcile everything that might be true in history using the exactitude available to invention. In other words, instead of pushing history to the side, place it alongside invention, alongside allegory, and even mix it together with some wild fantasy. Not letting ourselves worry that historical authenticity alone, or whatever we feel that authenticity is, doesn't guarantee poetic efficaciousness, as Lukács warns us, our poetic reinvention would go hand in hand with history: a history, however, whose authenticity—as we must warn the reader—as I must warn the reader—cannot be guaranteed, except on the level of the symbolic.

In my opinion, Rodolfo Usigli couldn't avoid history. In his play, one clearly sees a long and conscientious investigation, the enormous abundance of data he must have collected in order to write *Corona de Sombra*, and that of course serves to structure and give life to the work. One can assume that it was the discovery of his initial ignorance and with it the ignorance of all the other so-called authorities on the subject—and then the slow, almost painful, incredulous, astonishing discovery of the innumerable lies, intrigues, betrayals, misconceptions, falsehoods, childish illusions, myths, and other chimera that may have contributed to the events leading to the double tragedy—the tragedy of Mexico and the tragedy of Maximilian and Carlota—that caused his anger, his distaste for the inexactitude of history; though what he claims, in the prologue to *Corona de Sombra*, is that it was the scarcity of works of the imagination dedicated to that great episode of the history of his country—aside from what he calls "the formal, historical efforts"—that most provoked his ire.

Usigli wrote *Corona de Sombra* in 1943. Before that date there are only half a dozen poems about Maximilian and Carlota, written by some Europeans—Carducci, an English poet, a German—and then as many more by Mexicans. Among the theatrical works there's an excellent one by the Austrian Franz Werfel, *Juárez and Maximilian*, which masterfully recreates some aspects of the tragedy—Maximilian, says the Mexican General Díaz in Werfel's drama, was "a born martyr." The rest are small works with very modest pretensions. Only a handful of novels exist, almost all very bad, affected, and falling far short of sublime. Among them, *El Cerro de las Campanas* by the Mexican Juan A. Mateos, and then Praviel's and Princess Bibesco's narratives. Also some novels by another Mexican, Victoriano Salado Alvarez. Nothing, or very little, else. And then *Corona de Sombra*—which Usigli wrote because, as he says in his prologue, "Maximilian's blood and Carlota's insanity deserve something more from Mexico."

And it would seem that this is so, that one's death and the other's insanity deserve, by their very magnificence, something more from Mexico, something more from those who write its history and its literature. If nothing else, of all the major players, they deserve to be considered the ones who had the most extenuating circumstances to explain their crimes, to make them sympathetic to us, to their chroniclers, in the private judgment that each author is forced to make about the characters in his tragedy.

In Carlota's defense, there's the plea of insanity. Sixty years would seem like a punishment, a purgatory, more than sufficient to make restitution for her ambitions and her arrogance. Also—poor Carlota—there is her appalling failure. And, in Maximilian's, there is his death, there are the drops of his blood that mixed with the soil at the Hill, and there are his last words, his *Long live Mexico!* When he faced his end, as he did, he transformed it by force of will into a noble and meaningful death, into a courageous death. In a word, into a very Mexican death.

But, "in the end it is history that tells us," the Mexican playwright also says in his prologue, "that only Mexico has the right to kill its dead, and its dead are always Mexican." And thus the problem is not that we killed Maximilian in Mexico, or that it was in Mexico, perhaps, that we made Carlota go insane; the problem is that we didn't bury either one of them in Mexico. In other words, neither Maximilian—"the last heroic European prince" and "his century's magnificent suicide," as Usigli calls him—nor Carlota—the Ophelia waiting for a Shakespeare to sing of her insanity and her tragedy, as Pierre de la Gorge said—neither one of them, neither he nor she were absorbed by this land fertilized equally by the remains of our heroes and our traitors—with the almost unnecessary caveat that not all of these were necessarily heroes or traitors all the time. Thus, for instance, much could be said about the patriotism of Miramón and Mejía, who appeared to have been convinced—or were at a given time—that the best thing for their country was *not* to be a republic, but a monarchy. Perhaps their sin was—as Octavio Paz has said—that their solution was anachronistic: numerous caudillos and Latin-American heroes had considered establishing empires and monarchies for their countries in the years before the Intervention. Not only the Priest Hidalgo and his followers who, as we have said, were hoping for the much sought-after Fernando VII; many Bolivians and Bolivarians advocated an empire in South America, Simón Bolívar himself was given the title of Emperor of Peru, and in 1815, Belgrano and Rivadavia offered the crown of Río de la Plata to a Bourbon prince, provided that the province would have a government independent from Spain.

But let's get back to Maximilian. A lucid witness to his time, the under-secretary of Maximilian's navy, Léonce Détroyat, in his book, *L'Intervention Française au Mexique*, says that Maximilian didn't understand that he would have been better off being the first of the foreigners in Mexico, but instead, by changing roles, he was transformed into "the last of the Mexicans." The last one yes, perhaps, but indeed a Mexican. Maximilian and Carlota "Mexicanized" themselves: one, until his death, as Usigli says, the other, I say, until her madness. And we have to accept them as such: granted, not Mexicans by birth, but Mexicans by death. By death and madness.

And perhaps it would be good for us to do just that—accept them—so they stop haunting us. The souls of the uninterred always cry out against their abandonment. The same way that Hernán Cortés's shadow still cries out and frightens us to this day. Giving them the place they deserve in our Pantheon, on the other hand, requires no justification of their behavior: neither their excessive ambitions nor the arrogant and imperialistic nature of our first and last European conquerors, adventurers, it's true, but no less Mexican for that—in the same way that the traitorousness in our traitors, and the dictatorialness in our dictators, doesn't detract from their Mexicanness. With the difference, again in Ferdinand Maximilian's favor, as Usigli also points out, that this Emperor was or wanted to be a democrat, a liberal, and a magnanimous monarch. In his own way, to be sure, but it was the only way he could do it. The reader may consult the juridical analysis of the Empire made by Martínez Báez, in which the relative enlightenment of the legislations adopted or proposed by Maximilian is discussed.

To continue, the desire to be a Mexican on the part of a prince who, like Maximilian, occupied the second place in the line of succession of the Austrian Empire, and therefore was destined to be the governor of at least one— and in the best case, *all*—of the towns under the Imperial rule, and that same desire on the part of a princess like Carlota, who was destined to be the wife of the prince or sovereign of a foreign people, does not necessarily imply hypocrisy, though that can't be discounted either: One mustn't forget that the divine right to govern nations, inculcated indelibly in the minds of many of these European princes, and then the political necessities imposed by the matrimonial alliances among the members of the royalty of the different European countries, caused many of those princes to grow up with the conviction that they had the capacity to govern and the duty to love any foreign people they happened to be placed over, and who, with luck, would accept them, and with even more luck, would also love them—as indeed happened in some, if not many, cases. Moreover, and as Edward Crankshaw points out, there was less arrogance in the attitude—when it was sincere—of those who believed themselves chosen by God to govern than there is and has been on the part of any candidate for a public office in a so-called democracy for whom there is no corresponding call from God, but just raw ambition, and the belief—born of vanity alone—that he can do things better than others.

Therefore, with a bit of concentration, we can accept the possibility that Maximilian and Carlota were to a certain extent honest in their wish to become Mexicans, and deluded enough—perhaps Maximilian more than she— to believe they had managed to do it.

And if they didn't manage to become Mexicans at the time, perhaps one day they will. Perhaps, if we help them a little. If we give those two events—Maximilian's execution and Carlota's madness—for him the end of his life, for her an endless death—if we give these events, what Usigli thought they deserved: more of the imagination of Mexico, and of Mexicans.

Oh, if only we could invent an insanity that was unending and magnificent for Carlota, a delirium expressed in both past and future tense, and then in every improbable or impossible tense to boot—to give her, to create in her name and for her sake, the Empire that was, the Empire that will be, the Empire that could have been, the Empire that is. If we only could enter the imagination of the madwoman of the house, of the castle, of Bouchout, and allow her, mad and unbound, mad and winged, to travel through the world and through history, through harsh truth and tender emotion, through eternity and dream, hate and falsehood, love and agony, free—yes free and omnipotent, though at the same time a prisoner, a butterfly stunned and blind, condemned, always revolving around an ungraspable reality that dazzles her and burns her and eludes her—poor imagination, poor Carlota—every minute of every day.

If only we could also invent a more poetic and imperial death for Maximilian. If only we had a bit of compassion for the Emperor and didn't have to allow him to die as he did, so forsaken, on a dusty hill overgrown with *nopal,* on a gray and barren hill full of rocks. If we killed him instead in the most beautiful, grandest plaza in Mexico . . . If only for a moment we would put ourselves in his place, and put ourselves in his shoes, and in his body, his mind, and then, with the awareness that we are a Prince and an Emperor and that we have never been lacking in humor or courage, or in genius or elegance, and that we have always loved order and ostentation, pomp and circumstance, spectacle; if only we could write in Maximilian's handwriting, as a warning, a memory, and an example for any future Emperor who might lose his life at the hands of his own subjects—or of those he believes to be his own subjects—and offers his blood for them: a *Ceremonial for the Execution of an Emperor . . .*

3. Ceremonial for the Execution of an Emperor

First and Only Chapter

First Section: On the Time and Place of the Execution.

The center of the Empire's Main Square shall be the place of the execution. The time: seven o'clock sharp.

Second Section: On Preparations and the Procedures Thereof.

On the day of the execution, the Emperor's valet shall wake him at five in the morning.

The valet shall leave the room so as to allow the Emperor to carry out his morning ablutions.

Later, the Emperor shall call the valet, who shall come to the Imperial Bedroom followed by three honorary valets.

They shall all wear black velvet dress coats and short pants, white silk stockings, and patent leather shoes.

The valets shall help the Emperor get dressed.

The Emperor shall wear the full-dress ceremonial uniform of Commander-in-Chief of the Mexican Imperial Army, as required for the Great Ceremonies of National Mourning.

The uniform shall be black with silver embroidery.

The Emperor shall also wear the Great Chain of the Mexican Eagle, and on his chest, crossing from his left shoulder to his right side, a sash with the Mexican imperial colors.

At five-thirty in the morning four chaplains of the Court shall come into the Imperial Bedroom to guard the Emperor on his way to the Imperial Chapel.

The chaplains shall be dressed in black sackcloth habits.

The Emperor shall walk to the Imperial Chapel preceded by two of the chaplains. The other two chaplains shall walk behind the Emperor.

Following these two chaplains, the representatives of the different parishes shall march in rows of two in the following order: Sagrario Metropolitano and San Miguel. Santa Catarina Mártir and Santa Veracruz. San José and Santa Ana. Soledad de Santa Cruz and San Pablo. Salto del Agua and Santa María. San Sebastián and Santa Cruz Acatlán. Santo Tomás la Palma and San Antonio de las Huertas.

They shall all wear black sackcloth habits and shall have lit candles.

The Emperor's Confessor shall wait for him at the Imperial Chapel and shall offer him holy water and give him a missal and a rosary. Then, he shall precede him to the altar.

The missal covers shall be in black lacquer with silver gilt. The edges shall be silver-plated.

The Hail Mary beads of the rosary shall be carved from obsidian.

The paternoster beads shall be made of silver.

The chaplains and the parish representatives shall remain outside of the Imperial Chapel.

The Emperor shall kneel down on the prie-dieu.

The cushions of the prie-dieu shall be made out of black velvet, with borders and fringes of silver thread with no embroidery.

The Emperor shall offer his confession.

During this confession the Confessor shall abstain from addressing the Emperor as Imperial Majesty, and shall address him by his first name.

After the absolution, the chaplains and the parish representatives shall come into the Imperial Chapel.

The Confessor shall celebrate the sacrifice of the Holy Mass that the Emperor will hear on his knees.

At the end of Mass the Confessor shall offer the Emperor communion and shall give him the Holy Viaticum.

Then the Emperor, preceded by his Confessor and followed by the chaplains and the parish representatives, shall walk through the rooms and halls of the Imperial Palace in order to bid farewell to the Court dignitaries and functionaries, as well as to the employees and servants of the Palace.

The ladies shall be in front.

The parish representatives shall continue holding lit candles.

The Palace Guard shall line up on both sides of the Emperor's path.

Their helmets shall have black plumes.

The Emperor's route shall be as follows: The Emperor's staircase. Gallery of the Palace Guard. Iturbide Gallery. Antechamber. Council Hall. Gallery of Paintings. Yucatán Hall. Emperor's Hall.

All lamps in the Imperial Palace shall be adorned with black crepe.

The Emperor shall limit himself to saying farewell with a slight nod. Court dignitaries and others present shall remain motionless. Upon reaching the

Emperor's Hall, the Emperor shall be presented with a decree for the liberation of a predetermined number of criminals under both civil and military jurisdiction. The Emperor shall sign these and other petitions standing up and then shall continue immediately to the Charles V Hall, where he shall be served breakfast.

The Emperor shall have the choice of two menus and two kinds of wine.

The Emperor shall be left alone. The Confessor, the chaplains, and the parish representatives shall remain at the door.

The silverware shall be made out of silver with the Imperial Monogram.

The tablecloth and napkin shall be of white silk with the Imperial Monogram embroidered damask style.

After breakfast, the Emperor shall finish his ablutions and shall prepare himself for his final meditations.

Meanwhile, the Grand Retinue shall be assembled, and be preceded by a squad from the Palace Guard, footmen, grooms, horse-breakers, and foot lackeys, precisely as indicated in Chapter Three, "On Entourage," *Section One*: "The Grand Retinue," in the *Protocol for the Honor Duties and Court Ceremonial*.

The Grand Retinue and the great dignitaries and Court officials shall gather in the Great Patio of the Imperial Palace and shall proceed to the Imperial Main Plaza to take their respective positions in accordance with a plan drawn by the Court draughtsman.

Their positions shall be similar to those of the grand receptions in the Emperor's Hall with modifications appropriate to the occasion.

Then, considering that during the execution the Emperor shall be at the center of the Plaza with his back to the Imperial Palace and to his right the Metropolitan Cathedral, the positions shall be as follows:

The Captain of the Palace Guard accompanied by a lieutenant of the same shall be to the right of the Emperor and a few steps back. At the same level and to the left of the Emperor there shall be another lieutenant of the Palace Guard.

All of these officers shall wear black crepe bands on their left arms and on the hilts of their swords.

The Grand Master of Ceremonies shall stand facing the place assigned to the Emperor, a short distance away, and a few steps before him shall stand the Prime Minister.

The Grand Master of Ceremonies shall wear a black crepe band crossing from his left shoulder to his right side. His cravat and gloves shall be white.

To the right of the Emperor and in successive order shall stand: I. The Imperial and Iturbide princes. II. The cardinals. III. The Members of the Order of the Mexican Eagle. IV. The Court's Grand Marshal. V. The Grand Chamberlain. VI. The Head Groom. VII. The Civil Quartermaster-General. VIII. The ladies-in-waiting and maids of honor.

To the left of the Emperor and in successive order: I. The Imperial and Iturbide princesses. II. The Order of the Grand Cross of San Carlos. III. The Chief Lady-in-Waiting. IV. The General Aide-de-Camp. V. The Head Almoner. VI. The Empress's Grand Chamberlain. VII. The ladies-in-waiting and maids of honor.

All of these Court dignitaries and officers shall wear clothing appropriate for National Mourning.

The ladies-in-waiting and the maids of honor shall wear black wool frocks and black jewelry.

Their faces shall be covered with black veils.

All attendees shall carry unlit candles.

To the right of the Emperor, with their backs to the Imperial Palace, shall stand: The Court Physician and his consultants. The head staff. The stablemen. The chamberlains. The Court Notary.

Also with their backs to the Imperial Palace and to the left of the Emperor: The honorary chaplains. The Court chaplains. The officers of Orders. The officers of the Palace Guard. The aides-de-camp.

The Court Physician shall have with him all the necessary instruments to certify the Emperor's death.

The Court Notary shall be accompanied by a secretary to whom he shall dictate the contents of the Emperor's Death Certificate.

In front of the Emperor, or facing the Imperial Palace, and to his right and in successive order, the following shall line up: The Prime Minister and the ministers. The Head of the State Council and the council members. The Chief Justice of the Supreme Court and its justices. The Mexican ambassadors. The Head of the Court of Accounts and Supplies and its ministers. The Grand Order of the Mexican Eagle. The Mexican plenipotentiary ministers. The Dean of the Diplomatic Corps. The members of the Diplomatic Corps. The Attorney General and advocates general of the Supreme Court. The Grand Order of Guadalupe. The Commander of the First Military Division and his officers. The Chief Justice of the Superior Court and the justices. The Archbishop and the clergy. The Director of the Academy and its academicians.

In front of the Emperor, also facing the Imperial Palace, to his left and in successive order shall be: The remaining awardees of Imperial medals and decorations. The Heads of the Criminal and Civil Courts of First Instance, with their personnel. The City Mayor and aldermen. The Departmental Prefect and the Department Council.

In the center and facing the Imperial Palace: The First Secretary of Ceremonies. The Second Secretary of Ceremonies. A few steps back: The Officer of the Palace Guard Services. The Service Chamberlain. The Service Aide-de-Camp. The Official of Service Orders.

The firing squad.

The Draughtsman and the Clerk of the Court, who shall be in charge of recording the details of the proceedings for history.

A few steps behind, facing the Imperial Palace, the ministry undersecretaries and their staffs and departments in the following order, from the Emperor's right to his left: Foreign Commerce. Navy. Justice. Public Instruction and Religion. Development. War. Treasury.

All civil officers of the State shall wear black suits and gloves, as well as black crepe in their hats. Their ties shall be white.

The soldiers in the firing squad shall wear black dress uniforms with white belts and sashes across their chests. Their gloves shall be white.

They shall all be of the same height.

If the Emperor chooses to be executed on horseback, the firing squad shall be made up of cavalry soldiers.

Their mounts shall be black and low to the ground.

The harnesses and the saddle shall also be black and plain.

Behind them and always facing the Imperial Palace: I. The representatives of all the dioceses and parishes of the nation. II. Delegates from all of the nation's convents. III. Teachers and students from the schools in order from the Emperor's right to his left: the Tecpan School, the Business College, the Imperial School of Agriculture, San Carlos Academy, the College of Medicine, the Imperial School of Mines, the school of San Juan de Letrán, the school of San Ildefonso, the Conciliar Seminary, the Military School. IV. Boys and girls of the Empress's Nursery. V. Residents of the Empress's Home for the Elderly. VI. Residents of the Empress's Home for the Poor. VII. The sick and the disabled from the San Carlos Hospital and other hospitals across the nation. VIII. Members of the Mexican nobility who are not in the service of the Court. IX. Representatives of Banking and Industry. X. Common people.

The ladies and gentlemen shall dress as indicated in the Regulations for National Mourning events.

The ladies shall cover their faces with a black veil.

The townswomen shall wear black wool dresses.

The townsmen shall wear white cotton shirts and trousers and black crepe bands on their hats and left arms.

The Imperial Palace staff and servants, including the Mistress of the Empress's Wardrobe, first and second maids, butlers and doormen, ushers and table inspectors, lackeys and night watchmen, as well as servants, the head chef and cooks, confectioners, and bakers, kitchen helpers, and others not listed, shall remain inside the building.

These employees and servants shall be allowed to watch the execution from the Imperial Palace windows and balconies, which shall only be opened after the Emperor leaves the building.

All windows and balconies of the Imperial Palace shall have unembroidered black drapes, trimmed with silver-threaded cords, tassels, and fringes.

The Imperial Balcony shall remain closed.

At six-forty in the morning the Confessor shall knock on the door of the Charles V Hall and ask the Emperor if he's ready. The Emperor shall answer affirmatively and he himself shall open the door of the hall.

The Emperor shall be escorted by the chaplains and the parish representatives, and preceded by the Confessor to the Main Patio of the Imperial Palace.

When the Emperor arrives to the Main Patio, the Chief Groom, who shall hold the bridle of the Emperor's mount, shall approach.

This horse shall be white with black leather saddle and black velvet harness and a black horse mantle embroidered in white silk.

Four aides-de-camp, on foot and hatless, shall follow the Emperor's horse, leading their respective horses by their bridles.

These horses shall be black and shall have black saddles and harnesses also, and black horse blankets discreetly embroidered with silver thread.

The horses shall each have large black plumes, and the tails cut in the English style and tied with black crepe.

The Emperor shall mount his horse. A valet de chambre shall approach him with his hat.

The Emperor's hat shall be of white felt with a black velvet band and a black leather headpiece ornamented with silver.

The aides-de-camp shall put on their hats, and mount after the Emperor.

The Emperor shall give the order to march.

The horseshoes of the Emperor's horse shall be made of silver.

Two aides-de-camp shall precede the Emperor. The two other aides-de-camp shall follow him.

All horses shall maintain a slow gait.

The Emperor's Confessor shall walk at his left.

Upon arriving at the Imperial Palace's main entrance, a white-clad girl from the Empress's Nursery shall hand the Emperor a bouquet of white violets.

Third Section: Procedures for the Execution.

While the Emperor approaches the site of the execution, there shall be absolute silence in the plaza.

The Grand Master of Ceremonies shall have ordered the placement of a red carpet at the place of the execution so that the Emperor's body does not touch the ground.

In case the Emperor decides to be executed on horseback, the carpet shall be removed but the four aides-de-camp accompanying the Emperor shall remain at an adequate distance in order to catch the body before it touches the ground.

In this case, if the Emperor does not fall off his mount when hit, his aides-de-camp shall take him in their arms and dismount him.

The Emperor shall place himself at the center of the plaza, facing the squad.

The aides-de-camp shall dismount. Four grooms shall lead their respective horses away by the bridle.

Should the Emperor choose to be executed standing up, the aide-de-camp to his left shall hold his horse by the bridle and help him dismount.

Should the Emperor choose to be executed on horseback, the aide-de-camp shall be at his right and shall limit himself to holding the horse by the bridle.

The Court Notary shall step forward and deliver to the Minister of Foreign Affairs an envelope sealed with black lacquer and the seal of the Empire.

This envelope shall contain the Emperor's death sentence.

The Minister of Foreign Affairs shall break the seal and hand the envelope to the Emperor's Crier who shall read it aloud. Having done this, the Crier shall hand the sentence to the Grand Master of Ceremonies who in turn shall hand it to the Court Notary.

The soldiers in the firing squad shall be given orders to take their positions.

The soldiers in the squad shall present arms.

The rifles shall be black with ivory butts and silver inlay.

All rifles shall be loaded with only one bullet, except one, that will contain a blank cartridge.

The bullets shall be of lead with silver tips.

The Emperor's Confessor shall proceed to the blessing of the rifles. After the blessing, the Grand Master of Ceremonies shall announce the Emperor's farewell address to the nation.

The Emperor shall give his farewell address to the nation. It shall end at six fifty-five in the morning.

Following this, the Emperor's Service Valet de Chambre and two Honorary Valets shall approach.

The Emperor shall hand his hat to his service valet. The first Honorary Valet shall hand him the Great Chain of the Mexican Eagle. The second Honorary Valet shall carry a sash with the imperial Mexican colors.

The valets shall leave without turning their backs to the Emperor.

The Court Treasurer shall give the Minister of Foreign Affairs a pouch with gold coins.

The coins shall be gold ounces minted in the Emperor's Royal Mint, and thus shall bear the Emperor's portrait on one side and the Mexican Imperial Eagle on the other.

The Emperor shall approach the soldiers in the squad and give each a coin.

The soldiers shall remove their right-hand gloves to receive the coins. They shall put them in their left coat pockets, and they shall each shake the out-stretched hand of the Emperor and give the military salute in turn.

The Emperor shall not remove his gloves.

If the Emperor has chosen to be executed on horseback, the soldiers in the firing squad shall dismount to carry out the described operation.

The Emperor shall remain on his mount.

Following this, the soldiers shall put their gloves back on, and if on horse-back, shall remount.

Next, the soldiers of the firing squad shall ask for the Emperor's forgiveness and he shall grant it.

Without turning his back on the squad, the Emperor shall return to the site of the execution.

The Confessor shall approach the Emperor to bless him.

The Emperor shall kneel for the blessing.

During the blessing the Confessor shall abstain from addressing the Emperor as His Imperial Majesty, and shall address him by his Christian names.

In the event the Emperor has chosen to be executed on horseback, the horse shall be made to bend its front legs for the duration of the blessing.

After the blessing the Emperor shall again face the firing squad.

The Grand Chancellor of the Orders of the Empire shall hand the Grand Master of Ceremonies a blindfold laid out on a black velvet cushion.

The blindfold shall be made of white silk, without embroidery and with simple white borders.

The Grand Master of Ceremonies shall take the blindfold, approach the Emperor and offer it to him.

If the Emperor accepts the blindfold, two valets shall come forward to assist him.

If the Emperor refuses the blindfold, the Grand Master of Ceremonies shall return it to the Grand Chancellor.

The firing squad's commanding officer shall ask permission from the Grand Master of Ceremonies to order his squad to ready arms.

When permission is given, the officer shall give the order.

Two valets shall approach the Emperor to unbutton his coat, and shall leave without turning their backs.

If the Emperor has chosen to be executed on horseback, he shall take off his gloves and he shall unbutton his own coat.

He then shall put his gloves back on.

In this case, an aide-de-camp shall walk to the left of the Emperor's mount. He shall kneel on one knee and hold down the animal's head by the bridle, to keep it from raising it.

When the clock in the belltower of the Metropolitan Cathedral peals the first stroke of seven in the morning, the Officer shall ask permission from the Grand Master of Ceremonies to give the order to aim the rifles.

As soon as permission is granted, the Officer shall give the order.

The Emperor shall pull his coat open and shall thrust his chest forward.

When the clock of the Metropolitan Cathedral peals the sixth stroke of seven in the morning, the Officer shall ask permission from the Grand Master of Ceremonies to give the order to fire.

At the last stroke of seven, the Officer shall give the order.

As the Emperor falls there shall be absolute silence and all of those attending the execution shall remain motionless.

After a few seconds, the Court Physician shall come forward to examine the Emperor. If the Emperor has died, the following section shall be ignored and the procedure shall continue with the fifth section.

Fourth Section: About Special Provisions for the Coup de Grâce.

If the Emperor is still alive, the Court Physician shall inform the Grand Master of Ceremonies, so that he in turn may communicate it to the Grand Chancellor of Orders of the Empire.

The Grand Chancellor shall then bring forth a bullet to be used for the coup de grâce on a black velvet cushion.

The bullet shall be of lead with a silver tip.

Meanwhile the spectators must observe absolute silence.

In the event that the Emperor has chosen to be executed on horseback, and his aides-de-camp are holding him, he shall remain in their arms throughout.

The Grand Chancellor of Orders of the Empire shall give the bullet for the coup de grâce to the Grand Master of Ceremonies.

The firing squad's Officer shall come forward to receive the bullet from the Grand Master of Ceremonies and shall load the weapon chosen for the coup de grâce.

To carry out this step, the Captain shall remove his right glove, and then put it back on.

The soldier chosen to fire the coup de grâce shall receive the weapon from the Captain's hands.

The Officer shall approach the Emperor, unsheathe his sword, and with its tip he shall point to the location of the Emperor's heart.

The soldier shall aim and await the order to fire.

If the Emperor has chosen to be executed on horseback, the firing squad Officer and the soldier chosen for the coup de grâce shall dismount in order to proceed as described above.

When the Grand Master of Ceremonies has granted permission, the Officer shall give the order to fire.

After a few seconds of absolute silence, the Court Physician accompanied by the Court Notary shall approach the Emperor's body in order to examine it.

Fifth Section: About the Pronouncement of the Emperor's Death and the Dissemination of the News.

If after examining the Emperor, the Court Physician pronounces him dead, he shall inform the Grand Chancellor and the Court Notary.

The Notary shall issue a death certificate and hand it over to the Grand Master of Ceremonies who shall in turn hand it over to the Court Crier.

The Court Crier shall read the certificate aloud.

The Court Grand Chamberlain shall give the Emperor's two aides-de-camp and two naval aides the flag with the colors and the coat of arms of the Mexican Empire.

The Emperor's army and naval aides shall cover his body with the Imperial Mexican Flag. On his body they shall place the Great Chain of the Mexican Eagle and a sash with the imperial colors.

At a signal from the Grand Master of Ceremonies and simultaneously:

A boy from the Empress's Nursery Home shall release a white dove with a ribbon of black velvet tied around its neck.

The onlookers shall light their candles.

Four messengers on horseback shall leave at a gallop toward the Empire's four cardinal points to spread the news of the Emperor's death.

Another two messengers, also on horseback, shall leave toward the Port of Veracruz to board the *Novara* and carry the news to the Emperor of Austria and to the Empress of Mexico.

The messengers shall wear black velvet coats and breeches, white stockings and patent-leather shoes.

Their horses shall be white and tails trimmed English style and tied with black crepe bows.

At the National Palace and at Chapultepec Castle, the footmen shall close all the windows and balconies and shall draw the drapes.

The same shall be done at Miramare Castle and the Abbey of Lacroma.

Simultaneously all flags in the nation shall fly at half-mast.

The same shall be done at Miramare Castle and the Abbey of Lacroma.

The masts of all these flags shall be covered with black velvet and shall be crowned with a black crepe.

A Requiem Mass shall be celebrated at the Metropolitan Cathedral and all other cathedrals in the country.

Simultaneously all the bells in the nation shall begin to toll in mourning.

The Imperial bells at Miramare and Lacroma shall do the same.

All of these bells shall be crowned with black crepe.

The clapper of the main bell at the Metropolitan Cathedral shall be made of silver.

XXIII
BOUCHOUT CASTLE
1927

Because I am a vivid and trembling memory, a flaming memory that feeds and burns itself up, that consumes itself to be reborn and spread its wings. I have eagle wings that I stole from a Mexican flag. I have angel wings that sprouted out as I dreamed of you last night, while I created you in my dreams. I'm nothing if I don't create my own memories. You will be a nobody, Maximilian, if my dreams don't invent you.

That is why, Maximilian, the day I die you will die with me. I am your love dressed as a sailor. I am your doppelganger hiding behind mirrors, your chest tattooed with codices, your penis wrapped in banana leaves. I am your tongue wrapped around Concepción Sedano's. Your beard tangled in the blooming thistles embroidered on my pillow, your lips that kiss the dust at Las Campanas Hill. Maximilian, I am your flesh smeared on the rock at the Cuesta China, your spit that flows through Los Remedios Aqueduct, your nails embedded in watermelon pulp. I am your bones playing a marimba, your blue eyes now encrusted in the Indian's face. I am your navel, Maximilian, hanging from the moon over Querétaro.

Did I ever tell you, Maximilian, that you created Mexico and the world for me? But that was also just a lie: I created you so that you would create those things. That's why no one can tell me—the person who nestled you into your mother's womb, who made you drink the crystals of dawn for your mother's milk, who gave you her breath and took you by the hand through the darkened hallways of Schönbrunn so that you could hear the Duke of Reichstadt's last breath along with the falcons flying overhead, the one who pointed with her index finger from the shores of Bahia at those kingfishers that pierced the seething surf like arrows—just imagine it—the person who sketched the shape of your hands in lilies and gave you a heart like a collection box for you to save my love in, the person who made the night lie on your body, made a swamp creep up to your armpits, your intestines turn into a river of golden flies—can they tell me that for you the bells of Dolores clothe their clamor in the rich resonance of water, and bullets their tails in fire, that the dahlia sings the ballad of June 19th in the rain at Orizaba for you, and the spurs of Amozoc with their silver spikes point toward the scaffold? Don't they know, Maximilian, Emperor of Mexico and King of the Universe, that I invented bells and fire, bullets and spurs, the rain that slid down in warm rivulets from Mexican skies to kiss your brow? Don't they realize that I invented the chameleon that ate the rainbow at Zempoala? I, Maximilian, the one who knew the jade phlegm that congealed in your throat, the almond-colored clots in your liver, tell me, are they going to describe my dreams to me? Don't they know that you painted your portrait in water and you sketched yourself in the landscape? Haven't they seen you alive at the bottom of Lake Xochimilco? Didn't they see you dead in the shade of a tamarind tree? Oh, Maximilian, thirst has colors unknown to the wind; hunger has a gleam unimagined by fire. I make your teeth from wind and fire, from dust and nothingness; I make a grape cluster out of your teeth and with your veins; I make a net of blue threads to catch you alive and sell you at the market. For you, to invent you, to throb in your amber aura, I wagered my life in a cockfight; I will bet my death on a flip of a coin. I am Carlota, Empress of Mexico and America. Today, Maximilian, I'm returning to Mexico with you. I will even repent again, though they'll say that I'm mad. But they don't realize that the real madwoman was Queen Isabella when she didn't change her shirt until Granada fell. Why do they call me mad just because I drink tequila from the stone fountain at El Arenal? It's just the opposite. Have them bring me a whole barrel. Am I crazy because I know that you try to find yourself among the scars of the waves, and that you hide yourself in unquiet ink? Am I mad because I like going to Evangelistas Plaza in Mexico City so they can use that same ink to write my life story? No, the truly insane ones were Juana the Mad who shit in her bed and Christian of Denmark who foamed at the mouth and ordered his friend Holck to whip him. Am I crazy only because I know that your breast holds a whole sun, the sun of Mexico?

Or am I crazy, or am I a whore—especially a whore—because the son I bear in my womb wasn't sired by the Emperor of Mexico? No, Maximilian. The real whores were your sister-in-law Sisi who had a daughter with a foxhunter and your mother who had a son with the King of Rome. His mother was a whore too since she gave him an army of bastard siblings with her one-eyed general, as I myself was given by my father Leopold with the whore von Eppinghoven. Another whore was Czar Paul I's mother, who conceived him with Count Saltykov. Inês Esteves, mother of the founder of the ducal dynasty of the Braganzas, Alfonso of Portugal, was also a whore because she conceived him with João I out of wedlock. Likewise a whore was Alfonso's grandmother, Theresa Lourenço, who had a bastard son, Pedro I. Then there was the whore Arabella Churchill, the mistress of Jacob I of England and the mother of his bastard child, the Duke of Berwick. Napoleon III's mother was a whore; she bore his half brother, the Duke of Morny, illegitimate son of the Count Flahault—himself the son of the whore, himself a bastard—with Prince Talleyrand. Both queens of Spain were whores as well, Maximilian: María Luisa who had Ferdinand VII's son with Godoy, and Isabella II who was able to give an heir to her subjects, Alfonso XII, because she opened her legs and her uterus for a North American dentist—and everyone, even that idiot Cousin Victoria, looked the other way. But I'm not a whore, Maximilian. I was never unfaithful. The son I'm expecting wasn't conceived by you, but, listen to me, neither was he sired by Colonel Van der Smissen, nor Léonce Détroyat, nor Colonel Feliciano Rodríguez. The son I'm about to have will not be Marshal Foch's chief aid, nor will he sell trout and turbot in London's East End. He will belong not to one father, but to everyone. They all impregnated me without my knowledge, as I dreamed with my eyes open. Marshal Achille Bazaine impregnated me with his baton and Napoleon with his sword. General Tomás Mejía got me pregnant with a long cactus covered with thorns. An angel with quetzal-feather wings got me pregnant with the hummingbird-feathered snake between his legs. I was made pregnant by the wind, by the vacuum, by fantasies and absences. I'm going to have a child, Maximilian, of peyote, a son of *cacomixtle*, a son of *tepeizcuinte*, a son of marijuana, a son of a bitch.

If they tell you that I'm no longer a Mexican because it's been years since I've lived in Mexico . . . if they tell you that the Mexico I dream of ceased to exist a long time ago, tell them, Maximilian, that it's a lie because Mexico is the Mexico that I make up. I gave Lake Chapala's waters their coolness. I invented Sonora silver. I gave the Anáhuac Valley's blue skies their particular kind of transparency. If they tell you, Maximilian, if they tell you that Mexico isn't the same, tell them it's a lie, because I'm the same as ever. Mexico and I are the same. I have spent sixty years in front of a mirror, motionless, while the world turned around me as it did that night—remember?—when you held me in your arms for the first time at Laeken Palace. Sixty years, Maximilian, and time has left me intact. I swear that I don't have a single gray hair, not a single wrinkle, I haven't lost a single tooth; I never go to sleep like Empress Popaea, wearing an egg-and-flour mask; I don't tint my hair with an infusion of berry leaves; I don't keep my skin fresh with lotions made from boar brains and wolf's blood as Sisi did, I swear to you, Maximilian, because every day that goes by I'm more and more beautiful. I swear to you that to keep my teeth white I don't rub them, as the Duchess of Kent suggested, with a powder made of deer antlers and rosemary ashes. I have no warts to remove with slime from ground snails, nor stubble to remove with the milky juice of the Christmas flowers that Joel Poinsett sent me in a huge pot. I swear, Maximilian, that my breath is still fresh and I don't scent it with betel and spearmint because I get younger every day. Go and tell that to Mexico. Tell them that I'm more beautiful than I was in all of Le Gray's daguerreotypes and in the portraits that Portaels painted of me in Brussels, and Winterhalter at the Tuileries. Go and tell them that they won't have to remind me of the colors of my palace guards' uniforms—I'm not blind. Tell them that they won't have to scream the imperial Mexican anthem into my ears—I'm not deaf, and I still remember all the words. Tell them not to dare take me to San Hipólito Cathedral in a wheelchair—I can still walk. Do you remember, Maximilian, the Charlotte you met when we went to the opera in Brussels? Do the Mexicans remember the Carlota they first saw when the *Novara* docked at Veracruz with its entourage of vultures? Do you remember, tell me, the Guardian Angel of Yucatán that looked at its face in the waters of a sacred well? Tell them, as I tell you, Maximilian, that they won't recognize me because I'm the most beautiful woman in the bounds of the Gulf Stream, the fairest in the Eastern Sierra Madre, in the dunes of Antón Lizardo, in the Revillagigedo Islands, in the plains of Tlaxcala, the most beautiful, Maximilian, of all Mexican women. Go and tell them all that. Tell them also that I shall return to Mexico so that it can see itself in my mirror.

Tell them to play the *jarabe tapatío* so that they can see me dance on top of Napoleon III's tomb. Tell them to bring me a guitar, a hat, and bandoliers because I'm going to fire off some rounds at the San Juan Fair. Tell them that I'm going to ski over Lake Chapala on my bicycle. That I'm going to fly on my winged bike over Sonora so that my Tarahumara Indians can wave at me from below. That I'm going swimming in Necaxa Falls. That today I'm going to the rodeo with Baron Neigre and Carmen Sylva, dressed in chaps and a leather jacket embroidered in Arizona silver. Tell them to bring me mariachis so that Juárez and his ministers can serenade me with "*Las Mañanitas*" and to listen to me sing along. Tell them that today I'm going out on the town in Mexico City with Princess Bibesco and Eugenia de Montijo to burn up Judas effigies, to eat sugar skulls, to whack piñatas, to sing litanies and *posadas* asking for shelter in Mexico, to clack ivory and bone rattles, to dance in Chalma, to kiss the hands of Our Lady of Remedies, to kiss the feet of Our Lord of Venom. Tell them to bring my *huipil*. Tell them to bring me a *rebozo de bolita* and *china poblana* skirts, with beads and sequins. Tell them to bring me my huaraches, and a serape from Saltillo to dress as a Mexican woman and astound the whole world. I'm going to wear a skirt made of raccoon tails and a Michoacán devil's mask, an iguana-skin blouse, a hat made of macaw feathers. I'm going to wear a necklace made of mockingbird tongues, Maximilian—that bird of four hundred voices—because I am all those voices, all those tongues. Because every day I invent history. I travel the world with the Cambrai-cloth wings that Santos-Dumont made for me; with the alabaster wings that Leonardo invented for me, with the tissue-paper wings that Marco Polo brought me. Nothing and no one can keep me locked up, Maximilian. They all think that they had me locked up for four months in Miramare, locked up for ten years in Terveuren, locked up for fifty years in Bouchout. They all think that I've always been locked up within myself because they don't know that I stitched together all the edicts, the letters, the blank pages you left scattered in your Chapultepec Castle office into a parachute to jump out of my window. They don't know that I didn't shear off my hair as Maria Theresa did when her husband, Francis of Lorraine died, or as Cosima did to put in Wagner's casket when he died so that he would go straight to hell. I didn't cut mine so that I could grow it for sixty years, long enough to make a braid and rappel down from my castle balcony. They don't know that when the messenger comes dressed as that magician Houdini he turns me into the Princess of Lilliput. That by day I hide in my doll house and at night I ride on the back of a bat that comes all the way from Bruges to take me to Dunkirk. From there I ride on the back of a flying fish all the way to Mexico.

Please tell them too that I am a Mexican because I know perfectly well where I left my heart. Tell them that you, on the contrary, don't know where you left yours. Tell them that your cousin Ludwig of Bavaria's heart is kept in the votive chapel at Altötting and that the hearts belonging to the Habsburg emperors and princes are kept in urns at the Loreto Chapel in the Hofburg, but that you, Maximilian, have no idea where your heart ended up. Tell me, what did the Indian do with the pieces of your heart after Dr. Licea quartered it? Did he put them in formaldehyde to leave them for his great-grandchildren? Did he sell them to a Texan collector? Did he feed them to an eagle? Did he use them as bait for sharks in Chetumal Bay? You, Maximilian, have no idea where your heart is, but tell all of the people who tell you that I'm not Mexican because I was born in Brussels, because I've lived longer outside of Mexico than I lived in it, dying, and because I am a Princess of the House of Orléans and Saxe-Coburg, tell them that I am indeed a Mexican because I left my heart in Puebla de los Angeles, where I dress in white to celebrate my birthday. That I left it on the way to Toluca where I went to meet you on horseback. That I left it in Cuajimalpa, in El Peñón, in the bedchamber at the National Palace where I was eaten up by bedbugs. And I left it, Maximilian, in Ayotla, on the day that I said good-bye to you, never to see you again, in the perfumed shade of flowering orange trees.

And if they tell you that my heart was too small for Mexico as your pine coffin was too small for your body, or the Borda Gardens were too big, and your horse Orispelo too small, and if they tell you that I'm mad from head to toe, that not only are my arms crazy because I plunge them up to the elbows in bogs and fountains, that my nose is crazy because it smells you in the cinnamon blossoms, that my mouth is crazy because it sounds out your name with the white scorpions that sucked on your brain, because it swears to you in the pages of books, that it damns you in the beads of rosaries, tell them it's not so, that I know perfectly well what I'm saying. Tell them that nothing is too big or too small for me because I'm wearing a dress today that I myself made to my own specifications. So, the Czarina Maria Feodorovna is coming to make me a gift of the three-strand diamond necklace she wore when she blessed the waters of the Neva, so that I won't return to Mexico? So Princess Metternich is coming to bribe me with the Sancy Diamond that Charles the Bold pinned to his hat on the day he died pierced by Swiss halberds in Burgundy, and that Paula took away to London wrapped in newspaper? So the Duke of Marlborough is coming to offer me the head of Sirius the Dog? So your mother Sophie is laying the Wittelsbach emeralds at my feet so that I won't go to Mexico and will stay here instead, locked up in Bouchout, knitting, cross-stitching landscapes, rotting alive? Well, Maximilian, you can tell the Czarina that she can throw her diamonds to the hogs in the Winter Palace sties. Tell her that I made a necklace out of the Usumacinta River instead. Tell Paula Metternich to return the Sancy Diamond to Charles the Bold at the frozen lake where they found his body—today I wear the city of Guadalajara as a hat. Tell the Duke of Marlborough to give Mambrú the Sirius Ruby next time he goes to Malplaquet. Tell your mother she can keep her Wittelsbach emeralds and the silver chest Napoleon gave to Josephine, and the sacred lance that Longinus used to pierce the side of Our Lord, and she can keep Maria Theresa's golden sleighs and Charlemagne's imperial crown. Tell her to keep all the relics and jewels of the House of Austria, as well as all her castles and palaces. Tell her, Maximilian, that I have Mexico. While you're at it, tell her that she's dead and I'm alive, that she won't be able to cry about her betrayal, to repent and to call you to Austria, to repent of having said that she preferred to see her son dead than to submit herself to that mass of Viennese students, later changing her mind, later confronting them, later showering them with hot chocolate and iced champagne from the Hofburg's balconies, as Lola Montez did with the students in Munich, instead of running to hide at Laxenburg. Tell her that she can keep Laxenburg. That she can keep her Hofburg and her Schönbrunn. Tell your mother, Maximilian, that I have the forests, the mountains and the deserts of Mexico as my castles. If Josephine finds the opal called the Fire of Troy, if she finds it and wants to give it to me, and if England wants to give me back the sapphire that George IV left his daughter Charlotte, my father's first wife, upon whose death the English Crown took the sapphire back from Belgium, and if Czarina Alix offers me the string of Fabergé pearls her husband Nicholas gave her, so long, they say, that it reached her knees, and if Queen Mary of England comes to give me the Hanover pearls, or Ferdinand I of Romania comes to give me the iron crown wrought from a cannon captured at the Battle of Plevna, or my niece María de las Mercedes, Queen of Spain, comes to bribe me with her crown of five thousand diamonds, or Pauline Bonaparte comes to offer all of her coral necklaces, or Eleanor of Provence offers her silver and sapphire peacocks, if Edward VII wants to give me the Cullinan Diamond, which he was given in exchange for the autonomy of the Transvaal, and if his wife, Queen Alix, wants to give me the string of pearls that fell apart during the opening of Parliament, tell them no, Maximilian. Horses can trample the pearls that rolled under their hooves outside Westminster Abbey. Alix can go to Moscow's Red Square to jump rope with her pearls. My great-grandmother Marie Antoinette can keep her diamond necklace and wear it on the day she is beheaded in the Place de la Concorde. Princess Lamballe can keep her ivory beads and wear them when they display her head on a spear. Catherine of Russia can take the diamond that she dropped into a beggar's soup bowl on the day of the foot washing. She can eat the stone along with the soup. Tell Cousin Queen Victoria of England, Empress of India, tell her, Maximilian, that she can stick the Kohinoor Diamond up her ass. Tell them all, Maximilian, that I have Mexico at my feet.

Tell them that it's in my hands because I dream it up anew every day, Maximilian. I make all of them up. I give them life and I take it away. I dress and undress them. I bury them and exhume them. I take away their souls and give them my breath. I take their laughter and give them my tears. I live and die for them. I am Napoleon III dressed as Madame Pompadour. I am Benito Juárez dressed as a matador. I am Juana the Mad who thinks she is Charlotte Corday. One of these days, Maximilian, while you're taking a chocolate bath in your *múcar* coral stone tub from Veracruz, I shall murder you, I shall plunge a dagger into your heart when you take a tequila bath in your coral tub; I shall take your life, Maximilian, when you take a rattlesnake-milk bath in your turquoise tub. And then I'm going to put my head into that tub because I'm dying of thirst. I want to get drunk on your blood and that hyacinth tea, on Hungarian wine and orange blossom nectar, on spearmint tea, and poison, pulque, tequila, cochineal juice, on your lymph, on champagne and burgundy, on agave juice and your saliva, on your love. I want to get drunk again on you, to drink you until your love and mine are one and I become you. Once again I will be the child from Schönbrunn who dreamed of being Robinson Crusoe. Once again I'll be the sailor who was dazzled by nude slaves in Smyrna. I will travel to Brazil to see the violet tanager. I will go to Florence to rock my heart on the banks of the Arno. I will travel to Mexico again to found a new Constantinople between the two Americas, as the old city of Byzantium rose between the confines of Europe and Asia. Do you know what, Maximilian? I'm leaving with Blasio for Cuernavaca and at night I'll visit Concepción Sedano and cover her with kisses and poinciana petals. I'm going with Miramón and Mejía, and again I'm going to Querétaro with Márquez and Salm-Salm to play whist and eat dog-meatballs. When they lead me to Las Campanas Hill to execute me, I won't ride a black buggy but sit on a silk swing that hangs from the necks of two black horses. The soldiers won't shoot me. Instead, it will be your own generals disguised as Judas who will fire blow guns loaded with poisoned streamers. I'll arrive in a giant mother-of-pearl baptismal font carried by the four popes that I've buried since I left Mexico. Mexican children dressed as angels will kill me by slinging arrows from their harps. This time it won't be you who parts the golden beard that cascaded down your chest, to make it easier to aim for your heart. It will be me who unbuttons my blouse and takes off my corset to show the Mexicans the breasts from which they will keep on sucking their milk. Then I'll lift up my skirts to show those Mexicans my black and curly whiskers. I'll show them the place whence I gave them all—and will keep on giving them—birth.

•

I am Mamá Carlota. The Mexicans decided that the woman who is everybody's aunt—Europe's, Albert the Belgian King's, Frederick III of Prussia's, his wife Victoria's, the Grand Duke of Hesse Ludwig IV's, his wife Alice's—and great aunt of Wilhelm II of Germany, of Constantine I of Greece, and of Haakon VII of Norway—they, the Mexicans decided that the great aunt of George V of England, of Nicholas II, Czar of all the Russias, and of Alfonso XIII of Spain—would be called Mamá Carlota. They, the Mexicans, made me their mother and I made them my children. I am Mamá Carlota, mother of all the Indians and all the mestizos, mother of all the whites and the dark-skinned, the blacks and the mixed races. I am Mamá Carlota, mother of Cuauhtémoc and Malinche, of Father Hidalgo and Benito Juárez, of Sor Juana and Emiliano Zapata. Because I am as Mexican—I've already told you, Maximilian—as all of them. I am neither French, nor Belgian, nor Italian. I am Mexican because my blood was changed in Mexico. Because there they tinted it with wood from Campeche. Because in Mexico they scented it with vanilla. I am mother to them all because, Maximilian, I am their history and I am mad. How can I not be mad? And it wasn't with a gourd full of *toloache* that they tried to drive me insane, nor was it with the water from the sacred pool, nor the *ololiuque* they gave me at La Viga Causeway on the afternoon I disguised myself to go to the market with Señora Sánchez Navarro to buy herbs to make me fertile. No, it was Mexico that they used to drive me mad, and they succeeded. It was Mexico's skies, her orchids, her colors, that drove me crazy. It was the light in her valleys that made me blind. It was the freshness of her air that made me ill. It was the fruit—the custard apples Colonel Feliciano Rodríguez gave me, the pineapples, the peaches from Ixmiquilpan—that poisoned my soul with their sweetness. Tell your mother, tell her, Maximilian, that today I'm leaving for Irapuato to eat strawberries with the Countess von Kollonitz even if they're toxic. Tell Napoleon and Eugénie that I'm leaving for San Luis to eat cactus pears with the Marchioness Calderón de la Barca, even if I prick my tongue and my hands. And tell your brother Franz Joseph that I'm off to Acapulco to eat mangoes with Baron von Humboldt, even though I'll die of indigestion.

Tell them also that I intend to marry you again, and for those who oppose your marrying me to take me to Mexico, tell them that I'm the one who's taking *you* and that I'll refuse to let you have the dowry of 100,000 florins people say my father gave you. Tell them that I'll refuse to give you a dowry like the one that Catalina of Braganza gave to Charles II of England: Tangiers and Bombay; or a dowry like the one Louis the Great of Hungary gave one of his daughters: the Kingdom of Poland; or the one that Maximilian the First gave Margaret: almost all of Burgundy; or that Philip II gave his daughter Isabella Clara Eugenia: the Low Countries. I'm going to give you something much bigger. I'm going to give you Mexico. I'm going to give you the Americas. I'll make you a gift of Orizaba Peak so that you can see Cortés coming from the summit. I'll give you the gift of Florida for you to find the fountain of eternal youth there with Ponce de León, and drink the waters so that you can stop growing older at thirty-five. I'll present you with the Amazon so that you can ply its waters with Orellana and the tyrant Aguirre. I'm going to give you Patagonia, Maximilian, so that you will see Ferdinand Magellan sail by. I will present you with the Galapagos Archipelago so that you can study the tortoises with Charles Darwin. I will present you with San Salvador Island so that on its shores you can see Christopher Columbus arrive. And I will present you with the mountains of Chihuahua so that you can cross them on horseback in the company of Ambrose Bierce and General Pancho Villa.

Quick, quick, my life is ebbing away and my words are waning. Dress my lackeys in their finest livery. Call the grand marshal of the court. Gather all the Fuggers and all the Rothschilds to bring the money that my brother Philippe hid from me to Miramare. Call the Archbishop and the Nuncio. Command all my ladies-in-waiting to report to the castle immediately. Light the *Novara's* furnaces. Call the grand master of ceremonies. Gather all the palace guards. Order the *Chasseurs* and the Zouaves to present arms. Call the Egyptian battalion and the Austrian volunteer corps. Prepare the open carriage and the six Isabelle-colored mules with zebra legs. Have the Empress's Dragoons and the rural guards report. Get my royal-purple cloak ready. Call together the aides-de-camp and the division generals and the commanding officers. Pack up the furniture at Miramare, the brocade draperies with the phrase "Equity in Justice," the Maria Theresa cabinets, the Henry II dining room chairs, Marie Antoinette's writing desk, the Tyrol-granite façade stones. Crate up the laurel trees in the garden, the magnolias, the Moorish kiosk. Quickly, because I'm returning to Mexico even if I'm dying, even if I get there dead—the messenger has told me, has promised me, that I will return to Mexico, alive or dead.

Tell the Mexicans to prepare my throne. Tell them to dig me a grave. Tell them to polish the silver dinnerware. Tell them to dig a hole in the foothills of Popocatépetl, in the Mapimí Dust Bowl, in Lake Xinantécatl. Tell them to sweep Santa Anita Causeway. To bring together all the crown jewels so that I can jump into a sacred pool wearing them around my neck. Tell them that I shall return, alive or dead. If alive, I will be crowned with a wreath made of bees and larks. If dead, I will come back like a Guanajuato mummy, wrapped in bloody tatters from your shroud. Alive, I will come barefoot so my Mexican Indians can kiss my feet. Dead, I will come in an open casket so that they can kiss my brow and toll the bells in mourning, and my dukes and marquesas will wear black crepe. Alive, I will come on my knees, chanting the rosary, with cactus needles piercing my breast to get Our Lady of Guadalupe's pardon. Dead, I will cross the ocean in a black-sailed ship escorted by white gulls. And on a black barge I will ride up the Pánuco and the Tamesí Rivers escorted by blue butterflies, and in a black gondola I will remain still, like you, amidst the Xochimilco water gardens, surrounded forever by all the flowers in the world. Alive, I will return to Mexico in the train that climbs the heights of Acultzingo and crosses Metlac Bridge and the Plains of Texcoco. From the windows of my imperial wagon I will wave to my people and throw them kisses and gold maximilian pieces. I will come back in an ivory carriage with Titian's angels on its doors and a rose garland entwined in its wheels that will cross the Avenue of the Empress from one end to the other, in the shade of the ash trees for my people to throw confetti and blessings as I go by. I shall return in a silk balloon propelled by the trade winds that will descend from the sky into the heart of the Valley of Mexico, among my people, so that the air will be filled with doves and bells will sound the alarm. But if my life deserts me, Maximilian, if I arrive in Mexico dead, I will be in a crystal coffin, turned to ashes to darken the snows of Mount Iztaccíhuatl, to poison the clear springs of Borda Gardens. And I will come in a pine box to be buried in Mexico, so that Mexico gives me back at least nine feet of my lost empire.

•

I am Marie Charlotte of Belgium, Empress of Mexico and of America. I am Marie Charlotte Amélie, descendant of Saint Louis, King of France, and of the great Empress Maria Theresa of Austria. I am Marie Charlotte Amélie Victoria, great-granddaughter of Philippe Égalité and wife of Ferdinand Maximilian of Habsburg, Emperor of Mexico and King of the Universe. I am Marie Charlotte Amélie Victoria Clementine, Regent of Anáhuac, Grand Duchess of the Valley of Mexico, Baroness of Cacahuamilpa. I am Marie Charlotte Amélie Victoria Clémentine Léopoldine, Vicereine of the Caribbean and the Falkland Islands, Governor of Darien and Paramaribo, Marchioness of the Río Grande, Landgravine of Paraguay, Czarina of Texas and California, Potentate of Uxmal, Countess of Valparaíso. The messenger arrived today, bringing along Cecil Rhodes, and with them both I went to go and create a kingdom in Africa. With the messenger and Lawrence of Arabia I went to fight the Turks in the Sahara. With him and Jules Verne I went around the world in eighty days. The messenger told me, Maximilian, that the League of Nations was created, that the Mona Lisa was stolen from the Louvre, that the Aswan Dam was inaugurated, that they took Cleopatra's obelisk to London from Alexandria, that the corrupt Bulgarian Czar, Alexander of Battenberg, was abducted and forced to abdicate by the Russian army, that Dumas, the Younger, Baudelaire, and Jules Goncourt all died of syphilis, that Count Chambord died without an heir to the throne he never occupied, and the illustrious fool, Czar Alexander III of Russia, died when the Imperial train derailed in the Crimea. He said that José Martí, Alexander Scriabin, Ferdinand de Lesseps, Gustave Eiffel, Gustave Klimt, and Sarah Bernhardt died. He said that the Ku Klux Klan was revived and that Coca Cola was invented in Atlanta, and that Mexico City shook the day Madero entered, and that an earthquake destroyed San Francisco, and a fire turned Chicago to ashes, and that Plutarco Elías Calles's men defeated Christ the King's soldiers in Colima. He also told me that Franz Wedekind wrote *The Awakening of Spring* for me, and Rubén Darío published his *Songs of Life and Hope*. He told me, he swore, that Rodin dedicated *The Kiss* and that Joyce dedicated Molly Bloom's monologue to me. He said Offenbach wrote *The Grand Duchess of Gérolstein* for me, and that, inspired by my thirst, my insanity, the fire that consumes my mouth and my womb, Ottorino Respighi composed *The Fountains of Rome*.

•

I am Marie Charlotte of Belgium, Empress of Mexico and America. The messenger arrived today. He brought me a bouquet of marigolds. He brought an amulet and the dog that followed Quetzalcóatl in his travels through Mictlán. He brought me a vase of black clay pottery from Oaxaca, a red feather cape from Belgium, and Emperor Moctezuma's headress and shield. He brought me a tile kitchen from Puebla; he brought me the Aztec calendar and a skull covered with black agates from the Appalachians, and he said it was the skull of Princess Pocahontas; and he brought me a skull covered with blue flies and he said it was the skull of Juana the Mad; and he brought me a skull covered with your kisses and he said it was the skull of Marie Charlotte of Belgium. Today the messenger came and told me cellophane was invented and with it I shall wrap all the rosebushes of Miramare to keep them alive until you arrive, and he told me that celluloid was invented and so you and I shall play ping-pong with a celluloid ball on the *Mauritania*'s deck. He told me the washing machine was invented, and so you and I shall wash your *charro* necktie and my shawls, the uniforms of the students in the Carlota School, and the bed-sheets of Chapultepec Castle in one; that neon gas was invented, and so I had a brilliant sign that reads "Long Live Mexico" placed on the tallest turret at Bouchout, so that Ludendorff's submarines can spot it with their periscopes all the way from Ostend.

I am Marie Charlotte Amélie Victoria Clémentine Léopoldine, Princess of Nothing and of the Void, Sovereign of Foam and of Dreams, Queen of the Chimera and Oblivion, Empress of Lies. The messenger arrived today to bring me news from the Empire and he said that Charles Lindbergh is crossing the Atlantic on a steel bird to take me back to Mexico.

London, 5 Longton Grove, 1976
Paris, Maison du Mexique, 1986

The translators gratefully acknowledge Prof. Leon Schwartz for his important contribution to the completion of this project. We thank our spouses, Mirta A. González and José A. Clark for their patience and understanding during this lengthy and difficult collaborative process. We recognize our late mentor John S. Brushwood of the University of Kansas for his knowledge and inspiration and thank the Dalkey Press personnel for their invaluable help in making the publication of this magnificent novel a reality.

SELECTED DALKEY ARCHIVE PAPERBACKS

PETROS ABATZOGLOU, *What Does Mrs. Freeman Want?*
MICHAL AJVAZ, *The Other City.*
PIERRE ALBERT-BIROT, *Grabinoulor.*
YUZ ALESHKOVSKY, *Kangaroo.*
FELIPE ALFAU, *Chromos.*
    Locos.
IVAN ÂNGELO, *The Celebration.*
    The Tower of Glass.
DAVID ANTIN, *Talking.*
ANTÓNIO LOBO ANTUNES, *Knowledge of Hell.*
ALAIN ARIAS-MISSON, *Theatre of Incest.*
JOHN ASHBERY AND JAMES SCHUYLER, *A Nest of Ninnies.*
DJUNA BARNES, *Ladies Almanack.*
    Ryder.
JOHN BARTH, *LETTERS.*
    Sabbatical.
DONALD BARTHELME, *The King.*
    Paradise.
SVETISLAV BASARA, *Chinese Letter.*
MARK BINELLI, *Sacco and Vanzetti Must Die!*
ANDREI BITOV, *Pushkin House.*
LOUIS PAUL BOON, *Chapel Road.*
    Summer in Termuren.
ROGER BOYLAN, *Killoyle.*
IGNÁCIO DE LOYOLA BRANDÃO, *Anonymous Celebrity.*
    Teeth under the Sun.
    Zero.
BONNIE BREMSER, *Troia: Mexican Memoirs.*
CHRISTINE BROOKE-ROSE, *Amalgamemnon.*
BRIGID BROPHY, *In Transit.*
MEREDITH BROSNAN, *Mr. Dynamite.*
GERALD L. BRUNS,
    Modern Poetry and the Idea of Language.
EVGENY BUNIMOVICH AND J. KATES, EDS.,
    Contemporary Russian Poetry: An Anthology.
GABRIELLE BURTON, *Heartbreak Hotel.*
MICHEL BUTOR, *Degrees.*
    Mobile.
    Portrait of the Artist as a Young Ape.
G. CABRERA INFANTE, *Infante's Inferno.*
    Three Trapped Tigers.
JULIETA CAMPOS, *The Fear of Losing Eurydice.*
ANNE CARSON, *Eros the Bittersweet.*
CAMILO JOSÉ CELA, *Christ versus Arizona.*
    The Family of Pascual Duarte.
    The Hive.
LOUIS-FERDINAND CÉLINE, *Castle to Castle.*
    Conversations with Professor Y.
    London Bridge.
    Normance.
    North.
    Rigadoon.
HUGO CHARTERIS, *The Tide Is Right.*
JEROME CHARYN, *The Tar Baby.*
MARC CHOLODENKO, *Mordechai Schamz.*
EMILY HOLMES COLEMAN, *The Shutter of Snow.*
ROBERT COOVER, *A Night at the Movies.*
STANLEY CRAWFORD, *Log of the S.S. The Mrs Unguentine.*
    Some Instructions to My Wife.
ROBERT CREELEY, *Collected Prose.*
RENÉ CREVEL, *Putting My Foot in It.*
RALPH CUSACK, *Cadenza.*
SUSAN DAITCH, *L.C.*
    Storytown.
NICHOLAS DELBANCO, *The Count of Concord.*
NIGEL DENNIS, *Cards of Identity.*
PETER DIMOCK,
    A Short Rhetoric for Leaving the Family.
ARIEL DORFMAN, *Konfidenz.*
COLEMAN DOWELL, *The Houses of Children.*
    Island People.
    Too Much Flesh and Jabez.
ARKADII DRAGOMOSHCHENKO, *Dust.*
RIKKI DUCORNET, *The Complete Butcher's Tales.*
    The Fountains of Neptune.
    The Jade Cabinet.
    The One Marvelous Thing.
    Phosphor in Dreamland.
    The Stain.
    The Word "Desire."
WILLIAM EASTLAKE, *The Bamboo Bed.*
    Castle Keep.
    Lyric of the Circle Heart.
JEAN ECHENOZ, *Chopin's Move.*
STANLEY ELKIN, *A Bad Man.*
    Boswell: A Modern Comedy.
    Criers and Kibitzers, Kibitzers and Criers.
    The Dick Gibson Show.
    The Franchiser.
    George Mills.
    The Living End.
    The MacGuffin.
    The Magic Kingdom.
    Mrs. Ted Bliss.
    The Rabbi of Lud.
    Van Gogh's Room at Arles.
ANNIE ERNAUX, *Cleaned Out.*
LAUREN FAIRBANKS, *Muzzle Thyself.*
    Sister Carrie.

JUAN FILLOY, *Op Oloop.*
LESLIE A. FIEDLER, *Love and Death in the American Novel.*
GUSTAVE FLAUBERT, *Bouvard and Pécuchet.*
KASS FLEISHER, *Talking out of School.*
FORD MADOX FORD, *The March of Literature.*
JON FOSSE, *Melancholy.*
MAX FRISCH, *I'm Not Stiller.*
    Man in the Holocene.
CARLOS FUENTES, *Christopher Unborn.*
    Distant Relations.
    Terra Nostra.
    Where the Air Is Clear.
JANICE GALLOWAY, *Foreign Parts.*
    The Trick Is to Keep Breathing.
WILLIAM H. GASS, *Cartesian Sonata and Other Novellas.*
    Finding a Form.
    A Temple of Texts.
    The Tunnel.
    Willie Masters' Lonesome Wife.
GÉRARD GAVARRY, *Hoppla! 1 2 3.*
ETIENNE GILSON, *The Arts of the Beautiful.*
    Forms and Substances in the Arts.
C. S. GISCOMBE, *Giscome Road.*
    Here.
    Prairie Style.
DOUGLAS GLOVER, *Bad News of the Heart.*
    The Enamoured Knight.
WITOLD GOMBROWICZ, *A Kind of Testament.*
KAREN ELIZABETH GORDON, *The Red Shoes.*
GEORGI GOSPODINOV, *Natural Novel.*
JUAN GOYTISOLO, *Count Julian.*
    Juan the Landless.
    Makbara.
    Marks of Identity.
PATRICK GRAINVILLE, *The Cave of Heaven.*
HENRY GREEN, *Back.*
    Blindness.
    Concluding.
    Doting.
    Nothing.
JIŘÍ GRUŠA, *The Questionnaire.*
GABRIEL GUDDING, *Rhode Island Notebook.*
JOHN HAWKES, *Whistlejacket.*
AIDAN HIGGINS, *A Bestiary.*
    Bornholm Night-Ferry.
    Flotsam and Jetsam.
    Langrishe, Go Down.
    Scenes from a Receding Past.
    Windy Arbours.
ALDOUS HUXLEY, *Antic Hay.*
    Crome Yellow.
    Point Counter Point.
    Those Barren Leaves.
    Time Must Have a Stop.
MIKHAIL IOSSEL AND JEFF PARKER, EDS., *Amerika:*
    Contemporary Russians View the United States.
GERT JONKE, *Geometric Regional Novel.*
    Homage to Czerny.
JACQUES JOUET, *Mountain R.*
    Savage.
HUGH KENNER, *The Counterfeiters.*
    Flaubert, Joyce and Beckett: The Stoic Comedians.
    Joyce's Voices.
DANILO KIŠ, *Garden, Ashes.*
    A Tomb for Boris Davidovich.
ANITA KONKKA, *A Fool's Paradise.*
GEORGE KONRÁD, *The City Builder.*
TADEUSZ KONWICKI, *A Minor Apocalypse.*
    The Polish Complex.
MENIS KOUMANDAREAS, *Koula.*
ELAINE KRAF, *The Princess of 72nd Street.*
JIM KRUSOE, *Iceland.*
EWA KURYLUK, *Century 21.*
ERIC LAURRENT, *Do Not Touch.*
VIOLETTE LEDUC, *La Bâtarde.*
DEBORAH LEVY, *Billy and Girl.*
    Pillow Talk in Europe and Other Places.
JOSÉ LEZAMA LIMA, *Paradiso.*
ROSA LIKSOM, *Dark Paradise.*
OSMAN LINS, *Avalovara.*
    The Queen of the Prisons of Greece.
ALF MAC LOCHLAINN, *The Corpus in the Library.*
    Out of Focus.
RON LOEWINSOHN, *Magnetic Field(s).*
BRIAN LYNCH, *The Winner of Sorrow.*
D. KEITH MANO, *Take Five.*
MICHELINE AHARONIAN MARCOM, *The Mirror in the Well.*
BEN MARCUS, *The Age of Wire and String.*
WALLACE MARKFIELD, *Teitlebaum's Window.*
    To an Early Grave.
DAVID MARKSON, *Reader's Block.*
    Springer's Progress.
    Wittgenstein's Mistress.
CAROLE MASO, *AVA.*
LADISLAV MATEJKA AND KRYSTYNA POMORSKA, EDS.,
    Readings in Russian Poetics: Formalist and Structuralist Views.

FOR A FULL LIST OF PUBLICATIONS, VISIT:
www.dalkeyarchive.com

SELECTED DALKEY ARCHIVE PAPERBACKS